QUEEN OF THIS REALM

QUEEN OF THIS
REALM

JEAN PLAIDY

A NOVEL

THREE RIVERS PRESS · NEW YORK

Copyright © 1984 by Jean Plaidy
Reader's Group Guide copyright © 2004 by Three Rivers Press, an imprint of the Crown Publishing Group, a division of Random House, Inc., New York.

Excerpt from *Loyal in Love* copyright © 1983 by Jean Plaidy

Published in the United States by Three Rivers Press, an imprint of the Crown Publishing Group, a division of Random House, Inc., New York.
www.crownpublishing.com

THREE RIVERS PRESS and the Tugboat design are registered trademarks of Random House, Inc.
Crown Reads colophon is a trademark of Random House, Inc.

Originally published in hardcover in the United States by G.P. Putnam's Sons, New York, in 1985.

Printed in the United States of America

Design by Karen Minster

Library of Congress Cataloging-in-Publication Data

Plaidy, Jean, 1906–1993.
Queen of this realm.
Includes bibliography.
1. Elizabeth I, Queen of England, 1533–1603—Fiction.   I. Title.
PR6015.13Q44   1985   823'.914   84-17896

ISBN 0-609-81020-0

10 9 8 7 6 5 4

First Three Rivers Press Paperback Edition

QUEEN OF THIS REALM

The Passing of a King

WHEN I LOOK BACK OVER THE FIRST TWENTY-FIVE YEARS of my life and consider the number of times I was in danger of losing it, I believe—as I have since that wonderful day when I rode into my capital city in a riding dress of purple velvet, beside me my Master of Horse, Robert Dudley, the most handsome man in England, and listened to the guns of the Tower greeting me, and saw the flowers strewn in my path—yes, I fervently believe that my destiny was to be a great queen. I swore to God then that nothing should ever stand in the way of my fulfilling it. And I have kept that vow.

I could rejoice in those early twenty-five years—and indeed all through my life have done so—because during them I learned many a bitter lesson and it has been my endeavor never to forget one of them. I was young, lacking experience in the ways of men and women; and over my defenseless head—as dangerously as it ever did over that of Damocles—hung the sword of destruction. One false step, one thoughtless word, even a smile or a frown and down would come that sword depriving me of my life.

I was not quite three years old when I had my first encounter with adversity and my fortunes changed drastically. I cannot say with truth that I remember a great deal about my mother though sometimes I fancy I do. In my mind I see the most brilliantly fascinating person I have ever known. I sense the soft touch of velvet and the rustle of silk, long perfumed dark hair and a wild sort of gaiety born of desperation. But there is one image of her which remains vividly in my mind and as long as I live I will never forget it. I am in a courtyard and my fascinating mother is holding me in her arms. At one of the windows there appears a glittering figure—large, imposing, red-bearded. It is the King and she is trying to say something to him through me. She is holding my hand and waving it at him, appealingly, desperately. For a brief second he regards us with exasperated indifference before he turns away. That actually happened. Later I discovered it took place three or four days before she was arrested and taken to the Tower. The memory of her desperation and his cruel indifference stays with me forever, and I vowed that no man should ever do to me what my father did to my mother.

Before that she had been a presence of power, and my governess Lady Bryan, who was a kinswoman of hers, was overwhelmingly anxious to please her as was Mr Shelton who was also a family connection. My mother looked after her own when she had the power to do so. But there came that bewildering sadness . . . the end of her visits . . . the days when I asked for her, and Lady Bryan turned away to hide her emotion.

My father was a more tangible presence. I thought he was the most powerful man in the world. He certainly was in England. I was fourteen when he died so I could say I knew him fairly well. He was one who inspired fear and yet affection with it, and despite all his cruelty and all his ruthlessness he never lost the love of his people. That was one way in which I intended to emulate him. I learned from my studies of our history that it is a foolish monarch who loses the esteem of the common people.

Lady Bryan told me that my father had once been very proud of me and used to stroll in the gardens at Hampton Court or Windsor—wherever the Court happened to be—holding me in his arms. I liked that picture—myself magnificently attired swinging high in the arms of a splendid king as his courtiers walked with him exclaiming at my perfections.

That ended with an executioner's sword which severed my mother's beautiful head from her willowy body.

What I do remember clearly is catching Lady Bryan by the skirts and demanding: "Where is my mother? Why does she never come now?"

And when she tried to run away to weep in silence, I refused to relinquish her and insisted she tell me. She took me onto her knee and said: "My Lady Princess, you have no mother now."

"Everybody has a mother," I said, for I was logical as soon as I was old enough to reason.

"Your mother has gone to Heaven," she said.

"When will she come back?"

"People do not come back from Heaven."

"She will come to see me."

Lady Bryan held me to her and wept so bitterly that she bewildered me.

Then I began to realize that something terrible had happened but it was a long time before I gave up hope of seeing my mother again.

I talked of her with Lady Bryan and made her tell me about my birth.

"It was in Greenwich Palace," she said, "a beautiful palace and one of the favorites of the King and Queen. You first saw the light of day in the Chamber of Virgins. It was given that name afterward, but before you arrived it was just a chamber the walls of which were lined with tapestry and this tapestry depicted the lives of the holy virgins."

"Did my mother want a boy?" I must have heard some whisper of a servant to put that into my head. It was important, I knew, for Lady Bryan turned pale, and for a moment or so did not answer.

Then she said: "She wanted a boy. The King wanted a boy. But as soon as you were born they knew that you were just what they wanted."

I was soon to discover how false that was, but I loved Lady Bryan for telling the lie. My mother's life had depended on her giving birth to a boy. If I had been a son, they would not have sent to France for that sword which cut off her head. She would have been an honored queen instead of a corpse lying in her grave in the Church of St Peter ad Vincula.

"The Queen said," went on Lady Bryan, "people will now with reason call this room the Chamber of Virgins, for a virgin is now born in it on the vigil of this auspicious day on which the Church commemorates the nativity of the Holy Virgin."

"Was that what she said?" I asked wonderingly.

"It was. You were born on the eve of the Virgin Mary's birth. Just think of that."

My dear governess did so much to comfort me, but even she could not keep the truth from me. I could not but know that I who had been the important Lady Princess was now of no consequence and few cared what became of me. My mother was dead, executed for treason against the King because she was accused of taking five lovers—one her own brother, my uncle George Boleyn. Her marriage to the King had been proved by Thomas Cromwell—the King's influential minister—to have been no marriage at all, and because of this I was branded illegitimate. And naturally bastards of the King were not of the same importance as his legitimate offspring.

I began to notice the change when my gowns and kirtles grew thin and threadbare and Lady Bryan spent long hours trying to patch them.

"I don't like this old dress," I grumbled. "Why cannot I have a new one?"

At which the good Lady Bryan turned away to hide her anger against somebody—certainly not me, for she took me in her arms and said I was her Lady Princess and always would be.

She was very angry with Mr Shelton, who had a high place in my household, because he insisted that I should sit at table in some ceremony and would give me wine and help me to highly seasoned dishes. I heard Lady Bryan quarreling with him. "It is unsuitable to let the child eat such foods," she said.

Mr Shelton replied: "This is no ordinary child. Remember she is the King's daughter."

"Oh, he still acknowledges her as that, does he?" Lady Bryan spoke angrily. "I am glad of that! Do you know, Mr Shelton, it is months since that child had new garments. I cannot go on patching forever."

"I repeat she is the King's daughter and we should never forget that. Who knows . . ."

"Just what is your implication, Mr Shelton?"

He did not reply. I kept my eyes and ears open and because I knew strange matters were being decided outside my nursery I began to realize that for some reason Mr Shelton was trying hard to win my good graces and wean my affection from Lady Bryan. He never denied me anything that he could and he was always most obsequious.

At first I thought what a nice man he was and then when I discovered that Lady Bryan restricted me and meted out her little punishments because she felt it was her duty to do so, I did not like Mr Shelton so much; and whatever disagreement there was between us I always turned back to Lady Bryan when I was in need of comfort.

Mr Shelton, like Lady Bryan, was related to my mother, and that was the reason why they were at Hunsdon in my household. Those two were in constant conflict. Once I heard Lady Bryan declare to him: "You want to keep my Lady in royal state as long as you can, do you not, Master Shelton? But I tell you this: it will avail you little. There has been a new Queen now ever since the death of Queen Anne, and she is with child, and if that child should prove to be a boy . . . what of our lady then?"

"But what if it is not a boy eh?" demanded Mr Shelton. "What if Queen Jane goes the way of Queen Anne."

"Hush," said Lady Bryan. "Such words are treason and should never be spoken. All I ask of you is not to indulge the child. Do you not understand that these highly seasoned foods are bad for her digestion? I believe you give her sweetmeats outside meals, and if you do not desist from such I shall be forced to make complaints where they could come to the ears of the King."

Mr Shelton was unimpressed and I learned later that she did write to Thomas Cromwell himself, telling him that I had neither gown nor kirtle, nor any manner of linen, and begging him to send something for me to wear. She also complained of Mr Shelton's insistence that I sit at table where spiced foods were served and suggested that I have plain wholesome food served in a way suitable for a child of my age.

I did get some new clothes but I think that may have been due to the intervention of my sister Mary. She was twenty years of age at that time, which seemed very old to me. She was pleasant-looking and very serious, spending a great deal of time on her knees. An example to me, said Lady Bryan, for I was far less dedicated to my religious studies than Mary had been as a child. (Lady Bryan had been her governess, too, so she could speak with conviction.) I was interested in so many things and asked too many questions, I was told. "There are matters which must be accepted without question," said Lady Bryan. "One's faith for one, loyalty to the King for another." Even at that stage I was beginning to have doubts of sustaining either.

Lady Mary's mother, Katharine of Aragon, had died a few months before my own, and my sister was stricken with grief because they had been especially devoted to each other. Before her mother's death Mary had not liked me at all. On the rare occasions when we had met, young as I was, I had sensed that my presence angered her. Now it was different. We had both lost our mothers; both had died outside the King's favor; we were both branded bastards. It was because of her uncertain position that Mary was not married, and it was strange for a King's daughter to reach the age of twenty without having a husband found for her. But now she was quite tender toward me and since I tried to please her we were becoming friends. When one has no mother and one's father is a king whom one rarely sees, it is very pleasant to have a sister. I hoped Mary felt this too.

I was very sad when Mary left Hunsdon but she was delighted to go, for Queen Jane had asked for her to go to Court. Much of this I learned later. Because of my extreme youth I must have been very much in the dark at this time. It was when Katharine Champernowne came to be my governess that I made my discoveries through her. Katharine—I was soon calling her Kat— was the most indiscreet and delightful person I had ever known and I grew to love her dearly.

It appeared that the King could deny his new wife nothing; fair where my mother was dark, docile where she was vivacious, Queen Jane was the greatest possible contrast to Queen Anne for whom out of the white heat of his passion had grown a burning hatred. Moreover Jane was almost immediately pregnant after her marriage, which took place, most shamefully, ten days after my mother's death by the sword.

Queen Jane, it seemed, asked the King if Mary could come to Court and be with her during her pregnancy.

"She shall come to thee, darling," Kat told me he said; and so gladly Mary went.

I missed her, but like everyone else I wanted to hear of the birth of the child.

When Lady Bryan took me to her own private chamber, I knew I was going to learn something important. She put her arms round me and drew me close to her.

"The Queen has given birth to a son," she said. "The King and the whole country are very happy."

I felt my face go hard as it did when I was angry. Lady Bryan had told me of it many times. "A bad habit," she said, "and one which can bring you no good." I tried to curb it but on this occasion it was difficult, for how could I prevent the resentment which rose in me when I heard another than my mother called the Queen? Moreover this new Jane had given birth to a boy—the son which I should have been.

"The bells are ringing all over the country," said Lady Bryan. "The King is so happy. This little boy will one day be King though, God willing, not for a very long time. His Grace the King has sent word to Mr Shelton and to me that you are to have the very special honor of carrying the chrisom at the christening. There! What do you think of that?"

I thought very well of it. At last I was going to Court.

How happy I was on that October day when I sailed along the river to Hampton Court, most sumptuously attired as befitted one who was to take part in such an important ceremony.

There lay the palace, majestically beautiful seen from the river. Small wonder that my father had said when it had belonged to Cardinal Wolsey that it was too fine a residence for a subject and had taken it for his own. I was enchanted by its enormous gatehouse, its privy gardens, its tennis courts and its fireplaces, each of them large enough to roast an ox. It was in settings such as this that I belonged.

I was delighted by the respect shown to me and I deluded myself into thinking that this might be the beginning of a change for me, and I wondered whether the pallid Queen who had replaced my mother was responsible for it.

Looking back it is not easy to say whether I remember the details of that ceremony or whether they were related to me afterward. I was only four years old but I do remember how happy I was—contented rather—to be among those powerful and important people. The King was not present in the chapel. He had remained with the Queen in her bedchamber for it was reported that she was very weak indeed. But several important people were there. The Duke of Suffolk, the Marquis of Exeter, the Earl of Arundel and Lord William Howard held the canopy over the baby who was carried by the Marchioness of Exeter. I heard that among the nobles was my grandfather Thomas Boleyn, Earl of Wiltshire, with a wax taper in his hand and a towel about his neck, playing his part in the ceremony. I did not see him and I was glad I did not, for it occurred to me later that it was somewhat contemptible of him to take part in such a ceremony since his own daughter had been murdered by the King in order that the mother of this child might replace her. At the time I was completely happy. I was part of all this splendor, and the gloriously appareled infant who was the reason for the ceremony was my brother.

Because of my youth and the length of the proceedings I was carried in the arms of Edward Seymour, brother of Queen Jane. This was my first encounter with the family who later on were to play an important part in my life. Their elevation through the King's marriage to their sister had been swift. A few days after the christening Edward Seymour was created Earl of Hertford.

My sister Mary, who was godmother to the little Prince, gave me an encouraging smile when Edward Seymour set me down at the font. I returned it gratefully and eagerly watched while the little boy was wrapped in the christening robe and his state proclaimed.

"God, in His almighty and infinite grace, grant long life to the right high, right excellent and noble Prince, Duke of Cornwall and Earl of Chester, most dear and entirely beloved son of our most dread and gracious lord, Henry VIII."

In spite of all the excitement I was feeling a little sleepy as the ceremony had lasted three hours and it was nearly midnight. My sister Mary must have seen this; as Lady Herbert picked up the train of my magnificent gown, Mary took my hand so that I did not stumble. I noticed how happy she looked. It was because she was at least back at Court and had the high honor of being godmother to this important Prince, our brother. I loved him already. He was the reason for my being here. His coming had so pleased my father that he was even ready to smile on my sister Mary and me who had committed the unpardonable error of being born girls.

Queen Jane lay in her bed, propped up by cushions, in a beautiful bed-gown, but her pallor and sunken eyes proclaimed how exhausted she was.

As we entered the bedchamber the trumpets sounded so loudly that I who must have been half asleep started with terror, which made Mary smile.

Our father was there. He looked splendid, glittering with jewels, and he seemed a head taller than other men. How genial he looked, a great benefi-cent god—very different from the man I had seen in the courtyard! My father, I thought, is the greatest man in the world. His eyes were very small and so was his mouth, but perhaps they seemed so because his face was so large; and as I looked at him I could not help thinking of my mother, and fascinated as I was, admiring him as I did, I was afraid of him.

The Prince was placed in his mother's arms and she gave him her bless-ing.

The ceremony was over and we went back to Hunsdon.

THERE WAS GREAT CHANGE in the next few years.

The King, having got his son, was more benign. He rejoiced in Edward even though he had cost Queen Jane her life, for, poor pale creature, she died about a week after that ceremony in her bedroom.

To me the event of great importance was the coming of Katharine Champernowne.

Lady Bryan had become Lady Mistress of my little brother's household because she was considered to have proved her abilities in bringing up my sister Mary and me; and of course this position in the household of the heir to the throne was a great honor. She was in the royal nurseries at Hampton Court for a while and afterward was removed temporarily to Ashridge and later to Hatfield. To my great joy, when I was there, I shared my brother's nursery and even though he was so young he showed an immediate fondness for me.

But the big change in my life was wrought by Katharine—my Kat as I called her. She must have been in her mid teens at that time and from the moment I saw her I knew I was going to love her dearly. She was well educated—otherwise she would not have been appointed as my governess—but certainly she bore her scholarship lightly; she was inclined to be frivolous, but it was her gaiety and warmheartedness which endeared her to me. She supplied something which up to that time I had sadly missed without realizing the lack.

So Kat came, dear indiscreet Kat, who told me so much that had been kept from me and to whom I should be grateful all the days of my life.

Life became interesting, less restricted than it had been under Lady Bryan's sterner rule. We moved frequently from house to house which was necessary for the sweetening of the place. The privies would smell foul after a while and the rushes seemed to harbor horrible insects which irritated even the dogs. So when a house became intolerable we went to another while the privies were emptied and the rushes removed and the abode generally sweetened.

Kat used to tell me all sorts of things which were happening in the outside world and this delighted me for there was nothing I disliked more than to be kept in ignorance.

For one thing I learned that my father, for all his professed grief at the loss of Queen Jane, was desperately trying to replace her.

"Heirs, heirs, heirs!" said Kat. "That is a king's great need. Though why he should feel so desperate now, I cannot see. He has the longed-for boy and then there is my Lady Mary to say nothing of my own sweet Elizabeth—daughters of the King, both of you, and he has never denied that despite the fact that he got rid of your mothers—one in the law courts, one on the block—but rid himself nevertheless."

That was how Kat talked—not so much when I was very young, but afterward when I was getting older. She was the most intriguing person I knew in those days, and if she had not been so indiscreet she could not have been so exciting.

When my father was on the point of marrying the Princess Anne of

Cleves, Kat was full of information. "Who knows," she declared, "this could mean a new way of life for you, my Princess."

"How so?" I asked.

"What if the new Queen wants to meet her stepdaughters? She is sure to be curious to see them."

I was not yet seven years old when that disastrous marriage took place and I was very different from the child who had taken part in her brother's christening at Hampton Court. I grew up very quickly and life was full of interest, especially when Edward and I were in the same household, which quite frequently happened. We shared tutors and we had a great deal in common for we both loved learning. I found no difficulty at all in mastering languages—nor did Edward; and I think even our tutors were a little astonished at the speed with which I gained a mastery over French, Latin and Italian. I could converse fluently in all three. Edward was determined to surprise our teachers too. He was amazingly precocious and at the age of four was quite a scholar. I loved to be with him, to treat him as a little brother, and he loved that too for he was lonely, surrounded as he was by so much ceremony. No one could ever forget that he was the heir to the throne and so very precious that if he as much as sneezed, those about him were thrown into a panic.

"They guess," said Kat to me, "that if aught befell my lord Prince, the heads of those whose duty it is to serve him would become somewhat insecure on their sturdy shoulders."

"You do talk wildly, Kat," I reproved her.

She fell onto her knees and half mocking, half serious, cried: "You would never betray your poor Kat, would you, mistress?"

It was strange that one as learned as Kat could also be so frivolous. But that was Kat and my life had become considerably more agreeable since she came to me.

We soon learned that my father deplored his marriage to Princess Anne of Cleves. She lacked the beauty of her predecessors, and after receiving Holbein's picture of her and the accounts of her perfections which had forestalled her arrival, he was bitterly disappointed. He found her quite repulsive.

She was my friend for many years and I often wondered why he had disliked her so much. She was wise and kind and by no means uncomely. I can only believe that he had a particular taste in women, however variable, and she did not fit any of his predilections, and so poor Anne of Cleves was discarded as two of my father's queens had been. She was lucky; she did not suffer as my mother or Mary's had; and according to Kat was as happy to be relieved of the King as he was of her. Their marriage was declared null and void. Thomas Cromwell who had arranged the match lost his head. He had once been my mother's enemy and helped those who cost her that lovely head and so I gained some satisfaction from that.

"Four wives so far," said Kat. "I wonder, my lady, who will be the fifth, do you?"

I said it would be interesting to wait and see.

"We shall not wait long I fancy. The King has his eyes on a relation of yours, young Katharine Howard. She is a young beauty, if ever there was one."

"You gossip too much."

"So it is Madam Princess today, is it? Very well, I will keep my news to myself."

But she did not of course. I would not let her. So I was well aware of my father's courtship of Katharine Howard. My father was infatuated by her, I heard. She was a lovely girl and she took an interest in me because not only was I her stepdaughter to be but she had been my mother's first cousin. I guessed she would do her best to restore me to my father's regard and I was right. She pleaded with the King that I should be allowed to go to Court, and as he could deny her nothing, gladly I went.

I had reached my seventh birthday then and although I had read a great deal and my tutors agreed that I was exceptionally talented for my age, I was a little childish in my knowledge of the world; and when I saw my mother's cousin in all her youthful beauty and vivacity with so much affection to give to anyone who asked it, I felt that all would be well. My father seemed to see no one but Katharine. I heard it said that only once before had he felt such unstinting passion, and that was for my mother Anne Boleyn in the days when she had had his favor.

The memory of my mother's fate was always somewhere in my mind and when I saw my father I often recalled that look he had given us in the courtyard and it sent a shiver through me; to see him happy with this young girl helped to soothe me. She was a Howard . . . a little like my mother, they said, and if she lacked her cousin's wiles, her vast sophistication, her wit and her lively mind, she made up for it with an infinite sweetness and good nature.

"Just fancy," she said, "I am your stepmother. And I hope you will let me be your friend."

Who would have expected a queen to talk thus to a girl who had been brought out of obscurity at her request?

The King smiled on me now because the Queen was fond of me. She talked round-eyed of my achievements and what my tutors had told her, opening her beautiful eyes wide and declaring that even to contemplate such learning was beyond her. At which the King said he was thankful for that, since she was perfect as she was—his rose without a thorn.

On the first night she dined in public with the King, she insisted that I be there as well. So there I was, opposite her, unable to take my eyes from her lovely laughing face, and watching the King touch her arm and her hand with such loving tenderness, calling her sweetheart in a voice which was soft and overflowing with love.

Kat said: "All will be different now. We shall have our rightful place. We shall be recognized as the King's daughter, which we are, of course. But our new Queen has a fancy for you, my Lady, and if she asks for your company, rest assured the King so dotes on her that she will have her way."

If only it could have stayed like that I believe it would have made a great difference to us all. The King would have been happier for undoubtedly he loved her and, as Kat pointed out, she was not under the same stress to produce a son as my poor mother had been. "Moreover," said Kat wisely, "the King is no longer in his first flush of youth. Don't whisper a word that I said so or it might cost me my head . . . but it is the truth and even kings cannot change it. No, His Grace the King has a delightful wife. Let us hope that he never wants another."

But it seemed inevitable that the rumors must start. Kat told me of them.

"Wicked and unscrupulous men are plotting to bring a case against the Queen," she said.

I could not understand but Kat explained that when the Queen was very young she was overflowing with affection. She was loving and giving . . . and that sort drew men to them like bees to the flowers and wasps to the honey. The Queen was so kind and tender to men that she found it hard to say no to them. When she was quite young it seemed she had said yes when she should have said no; and now those cruel people were looking back into her past to uncover some scandal.

"They think the Howards are getting too strong," said Kat. "My faith! A little while ago it was the Seymours . . . now it's the Howards. The most dangerous thing on Earth is to be married to the King. A woman is better on her own. It may be that our little Queen would have been happier as the wife of Tom Culpepper, who they say adores her—and she not indifferent to him—than as the Queen of England."

I did not see Katharine again. I heard terrible stories. They were accusing her of treason—that simple child whose only purpose was to be happy and make others so too. How could they? But even she, who had harmed no one, had her enemies. Thomas Cranmer questioned her about her past, accusing her of having entered into marriage with someone called Francis

Dereham and thus in marrying the King committing adultery. There were tales of her wanton behavior with other men and she was arrested.

Kat said that the King was most distressed and would not at first believe those accusations against her. I was glad of that and hoped he would forgive her, but I suppose he was angry at having been deceived in her, thinking that all her loving had been inspired by him alone, and to learn that others had enjoyed it would be galling to a man of his nature.

I was very moved. I was reminded more vividly than ever of my mother. I kept wondering what she, who had held off the King's demanding passion for so long before she had submitted to him, had thought in her lodgings in the Tower, knowing that she was going to die, falsely and maliciously accused. And now poor little Katharine. She must have known what her fate was going to be. It was history repeating itself.

She was distraught, hysterical and terribly afraid. She was so young to die; and she did not believe that the King would agree to her death. She believed that all would be well if she could only see him and explain what it had been like in her grandmother's household where she had been brought up with all those young and lively people about her, and how they had been amused by her flirtations, which had grown into something more, and had helped her evade the rules laid down by her grandmother, the Duchess of Norfolk. She must have felt that she could make the King understand that she was older and wiser now and that she truly loved him and wanted to be a good wife to him. He was in chapel one morning when she escaped from those who were guarding her chamber and tried to reach the King; she ran along the gallery screaming but they caught her before she could get to him, and dragged her away. I wondered what would have happened if she had been able to speak to him. Would her life have been spared? I like to think that it might have been.

That February day stands out clearly in my memory. I had been thinking of her constantly since I knew that the King had given the royal assent to her attainder. Only two days later she was taken to the scaffold.

The poor child faced death meekly, they said, almost as though she did not understand what it was all about.

They buried her close to my mother in the Church of St Peter ad Vincula.

I felt ill for several days after. I dreamed of her mangled corpse and I shivered with a terrible fear for the fate of women in the hands of cruel men.

THE FOLLOWING YEAR my father the King took yet another wife and the result of this was that I was brought right into the family circle and began to feel more important than I had since the death of my mother. It was the first time in my life that I felt I belonged to a family.

Katharine Parr had been married twice before and of course Kat knew a great deal about her.

"Not much of a life," she said. "First married to Lord Borough . . . old enough to be her grandfather some say. Well, at least he had the decency to die when she was seventeen, but what did they do but marry the poor girl to Lord Latimer who had already had two wives before. He only died this year, and there she is thirty years old and at last free . . . or so she thinks. I'll tell you something . . . she had hopes of Thomas Seymour . . . yes, our Prince's own bold uncle . . . a fine upstanding gentleman, they say, and poor Katharine Parr head over heels in love with him, which is easy enough to understand."

"It must have been his brother who carried me at Edward's christening," I said.

"Thomas is quite different from my lord Earl, they say. Stern . . . that's Hertford . . . seeking high office, never forgetting for a moment that he is the uncle of the heir to the throne. Perhaps Thomas doesn't either . . . What a handsome man he is! I saw him once . . ."

"And is Katharine Parr going to marry him?"

"Well, they say the King himself has his eye on her."

"It can't be. He's . . . old."

"Who says the King can't do as he pleases? Will it be a crown for the widow Parr? I'll warrant she'd rather have a plain gold ring from Thomas Seymour. There is a certain risk to a woman who becomes the wife of your royal father. There! Forget I said that."

"But it's true, Kat," I said soberly.

My father married Katharine Parr in July just over a year after that February day when Katharine Howard laid her pretty head on the block.

Katharine Parr proved to be different from my father's other wives. I think the most noticeable of her qualities was her motherliness. She was meant to be a mother and she deeply regretted that none of her marriages with old men had brought her children. She mothered the King, which was perhaps what he needed at his time of life. He was fifty-two years old now, his indulgences had been many and he was showing his age. I suppose the death of Katharine Howard had a particular effect on him. He had been happy with her for that short time; she might not have been so exciting as my mother, but her docility and overflowing affection had pleased him; he had not really wanted to be rid of her, but he could be ruthless when he believed himself to have been deceived. His rude health was failing him now;

his bulk was turning to fat and he had an ulcer on his leg which caused him great pain and made him very irritable. Katharine Parr knew how to dress it and he used to sit with his foot in her lap, which gave it some ease. She had had a great deal of practice in looking after ailing husbands, and she was very capable at it. The King was fond of her in a mild way, but that seemed to suit him nowadays.

It was that motherliness in her which brought her to beg a favor from the King. He had a family, she reminded him, and it was sad that they were not all together under one roof. Mary Tudor was a woman now; but the two younger ones, Elizabeth and Edward, should be together. She would be a mother to them and he should be a good father.

He gave way, and for the first time I found myself within a family. I was delighted. For one thing it brought me closer to Edward, who was not only my brother but the future King. I was at the time ten years old and every day growing more and more aware of what intrigues went on about me. I realized now that because of my position as the King's daughter the smallest event might be of the utmost importance to me.

The peaceful existence of those days was due to my stepmother's influence. Yet being young I quickly chose to forget how suddenly storms could blow up and it did not occur to me that anything could happen to disturb this newly found contentment. One of my chief pleasures was the company of my brother. He was somewhat pale and thin and not overfond of outdoor sports and pastimes, a fact which did not please my father; but he loved his books, and so did I. We used to run into the schoolroom even before lesson times and could not wait to get to work. We were different in some ways although we looked alike—both had the same white skin and reddish gold hair and bright eyes with a tawny look in them—alert eyes that darted everywhere and took in everything. Edward was perhaps more of a scholar than I was. He absorbed facts, stored them in his mind and never forgot them. He accepted what his books told him and never questioned anything whereas I hesitated over every problem. I was constantly asking the question why.

During this time, when Edward was about six or seven and I was four years older, we would converse together and I would express my doubts, which I was amused to see shocked him a little. Kat used to listen to us and say we were a pair of old wiseacres; and although we did not always agree we never quarreled. The love between us was great and growing. I think he was disturbed by so much responsibility weighing on his frail shoulders; he felt more insecure than I did and looked to me for companionship and even some protection.

Because of his importance he could not be taught by someone like Kat. To tell the truth I was getting a little beyond her myself. "You know more than I do," she said ruefully on several occasions. The Queen realized this and consulted my father with the result that the most learned tutors in the land were found for my brother, and because I shared his apartments I was fortunate enough to share his tutors as well. There was Dr Richard Cox, the Provost of Eton, who was a very erudite gentleman, and later on Sir John Cheke himself came from Cambridge. He brought with him Roger Ascham, who was very interested in my work and wrote letters of encouragement to me.

There were many at Court who marveled at this intense desire for knowledge which my brother and I possessed; they thought it unchildlike, but Kat said it had come about because my brother grew so tired out of doors, but he never did with his books; and as for me, it was the manner in which she had taught me which had encouraged my love of learning. "I never forced you," she said. "Roger Ascham once said to me, 'If you pour much drink at once into a goblet the most part will dash out and run over; if you pour it softly you may fill it even to the top and so Her Grace (meaning you, my Lady) I doubt not by little and little may be increased in learning that at greater length cannot be required.' I remembered that, and I always made learning fun, didn't I? You and I could make of it a game which we could play together . . . until now when you have become so wise as to outgrow me."

I said to her then: "And who is this wise man? Roger Ascham, did you say?"

That was before Sir John Cheke brought him to us and the first time I heard his name.

Kat said a little coyly that he was a friend of Mr Ashley, who was a gentleman friend of hers. "He is a connection of the Boleyns," she added proudly.

I did not think much about Mr Ashley then because I was so absorbed in what was going on. A new tutor had joined us. This was William Grindal, a scholar from Cambridge—so we continued to have the best tutors in the land.

Our stepmother managed to spend quite a lot of time with us. She was deeply religious and believed firmly that the new Reformed Faith was the only true one; she talked of this so eloquently to Edward and me that he was completely carried away. I was less inclined to accept theories than Edward, though I respected the deep and genuine faith of my stepmother and recognized the validity of many of her arguments.

There had been a great upheaval in religion since my father had broken with Rome in order to rid himself of Katharine of Aragon to marry my mother. It was a time when it was considered unwise to discuss these matters too frankly because it was so easy to say something which was not acceptable to one group or the other. However I could never resist an argument and I stated that I believed there was only one God and one Church, and all this argument over different doctrines was a waste of time.

"I believe in Christianity," I said, "and it does not seem important to me in what method one worships God as long as one does."

This aroused storms of disagreement from my brother and stepmother, and we continued to bring forward our points and tried to convince each other. It was the sort of discussion which I enjoyed.

Unfortunately my brother must have repeated something I had said to someone who in turn reported it to the King; my views clearly annoyed him and the result was that I was sent away from Court.

Kat and William Grindal came with my little retinue and we went back to Hunsdon. I was desolate. The days seemed dreary and I missed my brother. Lessons without him were not the same for that friendly rivalry was lacking. How foolish I had been to state freely what I thought! That was a very important lesson learned. Never say anything that might offend those who have power over you. I blamed myself, and my only consolation was in my books and gossip with Kat.

Happily the banishment did not last very long. My stepmother, who was still in high favor with the King—such a comforting nurse she was, no one could dress his leg quite as she could—begged that I should be allowed to return, pleading my youth and my lively mind, which she was sure I had inherited from my father. Edward joined his pleas to hers and complained that his studies were not nearly so interesting without me there. And the King at last gave his permission for me to return.

What a joyful reunion that was! Dear Edward! Dear Katharine Parr! I often thought of that in the years to come and I felt very sad about Katharine. However I was back.

My stepmother said: "Your tutors give such fine accounts of you that I think your father is somewhat proud of his daughter."

The thought of his being proud of me gave me the greatest pleasure—even more than the welcome I received from Katharine and my brother. That was strange, for my father showed little kindness to me. I used to dream sometimes that I was in the Church of St Peter ad Vincula and I saw the ghostly figures of my mother and Katharine Howard there. I thought often of his cold indifference all those years ago when I was in the courtyard. He was cruel and ruthless, yet he was the great King and his good opinion was more important to me than that of anyone else.

There were some changes in the household. Lady Jane Grey had joined it. She was related to us, her mother being the daughter of my father's sister, Mary, and Charles Brandon. She had two sisters, Katharine and Mary, but Jane was the clever one and no pains had been spared to give her a good education. Her tutor had been another Cambridge man, John Aylmer, and he had coached her thoroughly in Greek and Latin. She was about the same age as Edward and as clever as he was. He took to her from the start. She was too pallid for me . . . I mean in temperament . . . too good. She never showed any temper or malice—all very laudable, of course, but insipid, and I told Kat so.

"Do I detect a little jealousy?" asked Kat, and I felt quite angry with her.

"Why should *I* be jealous of such a mouse?" I demanded.

"Our little Prince likes her very much."

"Let him!" I retorted. "They are but children."

However it was impossible to dislike Jane for long. She was such a good girl and I did respect her cleverness.

But while we were at peace in our nursery danger was brewing round us. That it could involve our gentle stepmother seemed incredible. It was not that the King was passionately enamored of her as I had seen him with his previous Katharine, but that she was such a comfort to him. He looked so pleased with her when his leg was laid on her lap and she was so gentle and always eager to please him. And then suddenly disaster threatened just as it must have done in the case of my mother and Katharine Howard.

Her life was in danger.

It was then that I first became aware of Stephen Gardiner who was to be my enemy in the years to come. He was the Bishop of Winchester and a fanatical Roman Catholic. It was now becoming generally known that my stepmother was a firm believer in the Reformed Faith. Perhaps she was not as watchful as she should have been. Because she was on such good terms with the King and he seemed delighted with her, she must have been lulled into a sense of security. She was nurse, wife and good companion. He suffered a good deal from the pain of his ulcerated leg and it could not be expected that a man such as he was should make great efforts to control his temper. He would curse his attendants and threaten them with all sorts of dire punishments for no reason at all than that they had not been quick enough to answer a summons or were guilty of some minor carelessness. They all tried to avoid him when he was in such moods.

On this occasion he was in his bedchamber and Katharine was binding up his leg which was particularly painful. She had often beguiled him with her arguments about the Reformed Faith and he usually liked to listen and lead her into discussion. He was amused and used to say to her—so she told us—"Come, Kate, what of the Reformed Faith today? What shall we talk of?" So on this occasion she had plunged into argument hoping that he would forget the pain until the unguents did their work. But he was irritable and contradicted her. Thinking he wanted her to put the other side of the question she proceeded to do so, at which he cried out in a rage: "A good hearing it is when women become such clerks; and much to my comfort in mine old age to be taught by my wife!"

It was enough, and by ill fortune the scheming Gardiner was present. According to Katharine he hurried to commiserate with the King, and the others in the chamber fell silent for a terrible dread had fallen on them. When a man has disposed of two of his wives by decapitating them, uneasy thoughts must quickly enter the heads of others. They would wonder how long that necessary part of the body would be with them.

Poor Katharine! She was most dismayed. I could see that she wished more heartily than ever that she had married the man of her choice and was Thomas Seymour's wife instead of the King's.

She retired to her apartments overcome with dread, which made her ill, and I realized that it was not only her own fate which was causing her concern. Anne Askew, a friend of hers who was a firm believer in the Reformed Faith, had been recently arrested. All this beautiful and noble lady had done was to profess her belief that the Reformed Faith was the true one; she had been accused of corrupting others and introducing books into the royal household. Katharine had been overcome with grief contemplating what was happening to Anne in the Tower and had sent her comforts by way of her ladies of the bedchamber. She was prostrate with sorrow when she heard that Anne had been put to torture and that when Sir Anthony Knevet had ordered the jailer to modify his use of the rack, Chancellor Wriothesley and his accomplice Rich had thrown off their gowns and worked the terrible instrument themselves with the utmost vigor.

And the King had given his assent to all this.

The noble lady had been condemned to be burned alive, and when this terrible sentence had been carried out the Queen had taken to her bed. It was given out that she was sick; and if the King knew that it was because of what had happened to her noble friend, he had not said so then.

Thus when Katharine heard the King speak to her in such a way and was aware of the malicious intent of Stephen Gardiner, she was so terrified that she collapsed and had to be taken to her bed.

Kat knew what was going on and could not keep it from me. She dared not tell Edward for fear he spoke to the King, and poor Kat trembled for her own head if ever it was thought that she had interfered. But she trusted me so I knew what was going on and I prayed for my good sweet stepmother and I marveled that I could still find it in me to admire my father who with his words and frowns could inspire such terror in those who had given him nothing but love. So it had been with Katharine Howard. I did not know whether my mother had loved him but I had seen for myself that these two Katharines had done everything in their power to please him. Such devotion had not saved Katharine Howard's head. Would it save that of Katharine Parr?

How relieved and happy I was when my father and stepmother were friends again. I think he must have missed her nursing, for she was so ill that she could not leave her bed. Her physician Dr Wendy was sent for and he reported that her sickness was due to uneasiness of mind. She wept piteously and could not control the trembling of her limbs. My father must have regretted giving such a ready ear to the complaints of her enemies for they had gone so far as to plan her death and were already looking out for a new queen who would be favorable to the cause of Rome. They had forgotten that the King was old, and a good nurse was more appealing to him than the sensuous charms of women like my beautiful mother and sweet Katharine Howard.

Dr Wendy, the Queen's good friend, had told her that the King missed her and he believed that if she spoke humbly to him and expressed deep sorrow for any fault she might have committed, he would be ready to turn to her because he was certainly not happy with the estrangement.

I saw my stepmother after the King's visit to her bedchamber. The change in her was miraculous. She no longer wept and that fearful trembling had ceased. She told me that after the King had said a few kind words to her he had tried to lure her into an argument. But Katharine was clever and having been primed by Dr Wendy she made an acceptable reply. She was but a woman, she said, with the imperfections of her sex. Therefore in all serious matters she must refer herself to His Majesty's better judgment. "God has appointed you to be the supreme head of us all," she added piously, "and of you next to God shall I ever learn."

"It seems not so," said the King. "You have become a doctor, Kate, to instruct us and not to be instructed of us as oftentimes we have seen."

"Indeed," replied my stepmother, "if Your Majesty has so conceived, my meaning has been mistaken, for I have always held it preposterous for a woman to instruct her lord; and if I have ever presumed to differ with Your Highness on religion, it is partly to obtain information for my own comfort regarding certain nice points on which I stood in doubt, and sometimes because I perceived that in talking you were able to pass away the pain and weariness of your present infirmity, which encouraged me in this boldness in the hope of profiting withal by Your Majesty's learned discourse."

How clever she was, my kind stepmother! Those words were well worth remembering. What a clear estimation of his character she had, for he replied: "And is that so, sweetheart? Then we are perfect friends."

If only Katharine Howard had been able to reach him when she had made that frantic dash along the gallery to the chapel! Could she have changed him with her loveliness as wise Katharine Parr had with words? I asked myself then, great as my father was, so powerful that the fate of us all rested in his hands, was he not a little childlike? But was he seduced by Katharine's words or was he seeking a way out of a difficult situation which would placate his conscience? The fact was that he did not want to lose Katharine Parr. If he had wished so, nothing she could have said or done would have saved her.

The reconciliation was timely. The next day was that which had been arranged for her arrest, but now that the matter had been smoothed out between them, the King asked her to sit with him in the gardens. So she went, with her sister, Jane Grey and Lady Tyrwhit in attendance—so they were witnesses of the scene which followed.

While they were seated there, Wriothesley, the Lord Chancellor, came into the gardens with a body of guards to carry out the arrest to which before his visit to her bedchamber the King had previously agreed.

My father was furious when he saw them. Presumably he had not informed them of the change in his feelings or they would not have come.

He shouted at them in fury and told them they were beasts, fools and knaves and they had better get out of his sight or he would want to know how they dared invade the privacy he enjoyed with his Queen.

Much as I disliked Wriothesley, I felt a twinge of pity for him and so it seemed did the Queen who murmured that there must be some mistake.

My father became very sentimental, as he could on occasions when he was cruel. "Ah, poor soul," he said. "You do not know, Kate, how little he deserves grace at your hands. He has been a knave to you . . . as have others."

Ah my dear father, I thought. And what sort of a knave have you been to this good woman who has never been anything else but the most faithful and devoted wife to you? I would never marry, I assured myself. I would never give any man power over me.

The incident appeared to be over, but my father never felt kindly toward Wriothesley again, and as for Gardiner, he showed his acute displeasure toward him. Looking for excuses for his own part in the near betrayal of the Queen, he must have his scapegoats.

It had been a terribly anxious time and often when I sat with my stepmother and we did our needlework together I would look at her serene face and contemplate how near she had come to the fate which had overtaken my mother, Anne Boleyn, and Katharine Howard.

DURING THE NEXT YEAR or so I never felt quite the same again. I could not look at my stepmother without thinking how near she had come to losing her head. My father was getting old; he was often unable to stand; his body had become unwieldy and the ulcer in his leg had grown worse. There was an uneasiness everywhere. Edward was a boy and the country had a dread of kings who were minors. It always meant that power-seeking factions were formed. That was what was happening now, and the rival families were the Seymours and the Howards. Religion was the dominating factor in all our troubles and I supposed this was inevitable since my father had broken with Rome and the Reformed Religion had come into being. I watched it all intently and I thought how foolish they were to make such an issue of religion. My sister Mary was a devout Catholic still and my stepmother and Lady Jane were turning just as devoutly to the new faith. But what did it matter how one worshipped God? Wasn't it the same God? Young as I was I vowed no such folly should ever determine my actions for I had seen fanaticism wreak naught but harm. But then we had these two families—the Seymours upholding the new Reformed Faith and the Catholic Howards who continued to support Rome. The Seymours were more powerful because of their relationship to Prince Edward and it seemed likely that he would be King before long. The Howards had seen the daughters of their family, Anne and Katharine, wear the crown—now both headless in their graves—but Jane Seymour had been triumphant, at least her family had. She, poor thing that she was, had produced the heir of England for their benefit and died in her bed before she was able to savor glory . . . I could never forget that she had supplanted my mother, whose brilliance some still whispered about.

My thoughts were turned from these matters by complications in my own household. I had noticed a change in Kat. She had become prettier and a little absent-minded, and I knew that something, of which she had not told me, was happening.

I demanded to know the reason for the change in her, for I am afraid I was beginning to be a little imperious since I had been allowed to come to Court and share a schoolroom with my brother. Edward was so fond of me and made it clear that he wanted my company and people were becoming more and more anxious to please him. We were all thinking of him not so much as a prince but as a future king and the fact that I had a very special place in his affections had made me feel quite important.

So I said to Kat: "I insist on your telling me what makes you go about as though you are somewhere else."

"Well," said Kat, "I will tell you. You know Mr Ashley?"

"Know Mr Ashley!" I cried. "That gentleman comes up again and again in your conversation. It is not possible to be much in the company of Mistress Katharine Champernowne without knowing something of Mr Ashley."

"Then you will readily understand," retorted Kat. "He has asked me to marry him and I see no reason why I should not."

"Marry! You!" I must confess the first thought which came to me was, But what of me?

She knew my nature well and she immediately fell to her knees and buried her head in my skirts. "My lady, my dearest Princess, never will I leave you."

"Not for Mr Ashley?"

"I think Mr Ashley could become a member of your household. I am sure no objection would be raised against that."

I was dubious. Kat! Married! No longer entirely mine!

People did marry, of course, and Kat was young and comely. But I felt shaken. There was so much change in the air, and I did not want change though I knew it must come. There was too much tension in the air . . . throughout the Court, throughout the country. I felt it in the streets on those occasions I rode out for I was very sensitive to the mood of the people.

And now Kat was to be married.

Lovingly she assured me that nothing could ever make any difference in her devotion to me. I was her special charge, her Princess, close to her heart, never to be dislodged. She made me feel that she would even abandon Mr Ashley if marrying him meant losing me.

Fortunately she did not have to make such a choice. My good stepmother said that there was a simple solution. Let Mr Ashley join my household. "I feel Thomas Parry is not as efficient as he might be," she said, "and John Ashley is a very clever young man."

So our problem was solved and Kat became Kat Ashley. Parry stayed of course but John Ashley became a member of the household; I was very pleased because not only was he Kat's husband but there was a family connection between him and the Boleyns.

We were at Hatfield and I was delighted to be there because Edward was with me. We used to converse in Latin—a language we both loved. I had a secret with which I intended to surprise him. There was a woman in my household, Blanche Parry, a Welshwoman, who was very proud of the fact that she had rocked me in my cradle. She was very fluent in her native language and I suggested she should teach it to me. With my aptitude I was soon able to speak in Welsh with Blanche and I thought it would be rather amusing to let Edward know that I had acquired the Welsh language of which he and the erudite little Jane Grey were ignorant. After all we Tudors had Welsh blood in our veins and royal as we were, we had inherited through our ancestor Owen Tudor.

But before I did this there was disturbing news that my relatives Thomas Howard, Duke of Norfolk, and Henry Howard, his son, Earl of Surrey, had been thrown into the Tower.

Kat, as usual, knew all about it.

"How could Surrey be so stupid?" she demanded. "Do you know what he has done? He has assumed the right to wear the arms of Edward the Confessor. He says the concession was granted to his family by Richard II. Of course the College of Arms forbade this, but what does my Lord Surrey do but ignore them."

"And do you mean to say that for such an offense Surrey and his father are in the Tower?"

Kat came closer to me and whispered: "It's the Seymours. You wouldn't expect them to miss a chance like this, would you? He has played right into the Seymours' hands. Silly Surrey!"

"Kat," I said severely, "you forget yourself."

"So I do," she replied.

"You should not speak so flippantly of the Earl of Surrey. He is a very great gentleman."

"He must be if he can sport the royal arms."

"That was foolish of him."

"He might have known the Seymours were ready to pounce."

I was upset. I had felt quite a fondness for Henry Howard. He was a very handsome man but what made him more attractive in my eyes was that he wrote beautiful verses and people said he had me in mind when he wrote them. I always read them avidly and they gave me great pleasure so it was distressing to think of him in that cold dank prison. And his father with him—for the Duke of Norfolk could not be very young. He had once been my mother's chief adviser and although he had presided at her trial and arranged for her execution, he was still a blood relation—my own uncle.

"It is all Seymour now," said Kat. "My word, how they have come up in the world since their sister married the King. Edward the elder is a sharp one and he has the King's ear. As for Thomas . . ." Kat smiled knowingly. "Now there is a man. Do you know, I don't think there is another at Court to match him."

"Match him for what?" I asked.

"For grace . . . for charm . . . He is so good-looking . . . so tall, so com-

manding. He's much more of a man than his brother. They say there is a little rivalry between Thomas and Edward Seymour. Thomas has no wife—as
yet."

"Kat," I cried, "since you have discovered the glories of marriage you
think of nothing else. Have a care or Mr Ashley will be taking you to task."

She laughed but I could not join in her merry mood because I was thinking of poor Henry Howard in the Tower where my own mother had lodged
before her death.

I was quite fond of Hatfield then, although later I came to regard it as a
prison. There was an air of peace about the ivy-covered walls, and Edward
kept splendid state in the lofty banqueting hall. When we dined there I
always sat beside him and we would talk seriously together, for Edward, who
was as aware of the growing tension as I was and far more frightened of it,
was becoming very serious indeed.

I heard that the King was at Whitehall, the Duke of Norfolk and the
Earl of Surrey still in the Tower, and the Queen in constant attendance
upon the King who could not bear her out of his sight these days.

It was December when visitors came to Hatfield. Kat saw the party in
the distance and hastened to find me that she might be the first with the
news. We went up to one of the turrets to watch the riders approach.

I said: "I'll guess they are coming to tell us we are going to Court and I
must warn Edward of their approach."

"Yes, you two should go down to greet them," replied Kat.

We had a shock instead of a welcome. Our visitors were guards who had
come to escort us—not to Whitehall as we had thought—but Edward to
Hertford Castle and me to Enfield. We were to be separated! We protested
with horror at being parted but were assured that these were the King's
orders and must be obeyed without question.

How different was that Christmas from what I had anticipated! Poor
Edward had been so unhappy at our parting and, since he was younger, he
was less able to control his grief. I wrote a little note to tell him that I was as
unhappy as he was by our forced separation and I was thinking of him all
the time. He wrote such a tender letter back. I still have it.

*The change of place, dear sister, does not so much vex me as your departure
from me . . . It is a comfort to my regret that I hope shortly to see you again
if no accident intervenes . . ."*

Tragedy intervened. We saw each other, but only briefly.

In January I heard that the Earl of Surrey had been beheaded on Tower
Hill. This depressing knowledge did not help me to bear the separation from
my brother. Poor reckless Surrey! How prodigal people were of life . . . in

risking it and taking it. It seemed to me such a trivial matter to die for. Oh, but I knew it was more than arms on an escutcheon. It was the deadly rivalry for power between two leading families—the upstart Seymours and the ancient one of Howard. The Seymours were in the ascendant. Of course they were. The Seymour brothers were the uncles of the King to be.

To my great joy Edward was brought to Enfield.

It was the last day of January, cold and frosty, when Edward arrived in the company of Edward Seymour, Earl of Hertford, and Sir Anthony Browne. I was amazed to see these two together in apparent harmony because Sir Anthony was a firm adherent of the Catholic Faith, and Hertford, because of his powerful position in the country, was the man whom followers of the Reformed Faith looked upon to lead them.

As soon as they arrived I was summoned to the hall. Edward was standing there with Hertford on one side of him and Sir Anthony Browne on the other.

"Edward," I cried, forgetting ceremony. I ran to him and we embraced.

The two men stood silently watching us and neither of us cared whether they considered this a breach of etiquette. There are moments when such matters can be forgotten and affection given full rein.

It was Hertford who made the announcement.

"My lord and lady, I have grave news for you. Your father, our great and good King Henry the Eighth, has died in his Palace of Whitehall." Then he fell to his knees and taking Edward's hand cried: "God save the King."

Edward looked startled. Then he turned to me. I put my arms about him and we wept. We had lost our father. I was old enough to know that we were fast moving into danger. I was not yet fourteen years old but I felt that I had been learning how to wade carefully in treacherous waters. But Edward . . . poor little Edward . . . to be so young . . . and a king!

We were crying bitterly and my tears were more for my frail little brother than for the great and glorious, cruel and ruthless yet magnificent King who had just passed out of this life.

A Man of Much Wit and
Very Little Judgment

MY LIFE CHANGED FROM THAT TIME. ONE THOUGHT WAS uppermost in my mind. It bewildered me—but not for long. It was so dazzling, so truly wonderful, so remote—and yet it was possible. One day I could be Queen of England.

After having been known as the bastard daughter of the King, of no great significance, scorned and kept in mended garments, sent from place to place at the convenience of others, I had become of no small consequence. Henceforth people would treat me in a different manner. I began to see it immediately. I noticed the covert looks. Be careful, said their eyes. She could be Queen one day.

I was savoring what a glorious sensation power can be. I was being given just that faintest glimmer of that which my father had enjoyed since the days when he was eighteen years old and became the King. To rule a country—a great country—what a destiny! And it could be mine.

This new state had come about because of the conditions of my father's will. I was to receive three thousand pounds a year—riches for me—and a marriage portion of ten thousand pounds. True, I could only marry with the consent of the King—my little brother Edward now—and his Council. Edward would be easy enough to handle, but what of the Council? No matter. There was no question of marriage yet. But if any man tried to marry either my elder half sister Mary Tudor or myself without the consent of the Council, serious charges would be brought against him and my sister and me. That did not greatly concern me, for being not yet fourteen I had no mind to risk any lives for the sake of a romantic marriage.

The crown, of course, would go to Edward. If he died without heirs, it passed to Mary; and if Mary should die, then I was the next in line, although the Catholics believed that my father had never really been married to my mother and I was a bastard! As this will was made a year or so before my father's death, he had stated that before Mary or myself would come any heirs he should have through Katharine Parr—adding ominously "or any future queen."

I could not stop myself from summing up the situation, turning it this way and that. Edward was very young and frail. I wondered whether he would marry and could be expected to get healthy offspring. Mary? Well, Mary was thirty-one and unmarried. Would she find a husband? Most certainly. And if she bore a son, what hope had I?

So I warned myself again and again that I must not be overdazzled by even the remote prospect. I must rejoice that it was a possibility and prepare myself to play a waiting game.

My father was buried at Windsor and his heavy body had to be lowered into the grave by means of a vise worked by sixteen of the strongest men of the Yeomen of the Guard. The members of the King's household had stood around his grave, the Queen's old enemy Gardiner with the Lord Chamberlain and Lord Treasurer among them. In accordance with custom they broke their staves over their heads and threw them down into the coffin.

So passed the great King who had astonished the world by breaking with Rome and bringing about the biggest religious controversy ever known, who had had his will all his life, who had married six wives and murdered two of them—and God knows there might have been a third victim but for her adroitness and his failing health—all this and yet they mourned him. Was it because in spite of all his cruelty and his ruthlessness he showed great strength? Above all things, it seems, men admire strength. He was sentimental too and he had a conscience which would never let him rest. What strange contradictory characteristics were his! Yet, withal, men mourned his passing and turned regretful, fearful eyes to the new boy King.

There was a macabre story about something which had happened just before his burial. Kat told me this hesitatingly, pretending she could not tell and having to be forced to do so.

"People are whispering about it," she said. "I cannot say that it is true, but there are those who saw—"

"Come on, Kat," I said more imperiously than ever for was I not a potential heiress to a throne? "I command you to tell me."

Kat raised her eyes to the ceiling, a frequent gesture.

"And I dare not disobey my lady's command. On the way to Windsor the cortège broke its journey at Sion House and there the body rested in the chapel. It was at Sion House, remember, that poor Katharine Howard stayed when they were taking her to the Tower. Poor child, they say she was almost mad with fear, for did she not have the example of her cousin to remind her of what lay in store for her? Well, the coffin burst, for the King's body was too great for its fragile wood, and the King's blood was spilt on the chapel floor. Now this is the shocking part. Are you sure you want me to go on? Very well. A dog was seen to run forward and lick the blood clean and although they tried to draw him away he snarled and refused to budge until there was not a speck of blood on the floor."

"Kat, where did you hear such a tale?"

"My dear lady, it is being whispered throughout the land. You do not know of this because you were not then born but when the King was thinking of ridding himself of his first Queen, one Friar Peyto who cared nothing for what might befall him stood in his pulpit and declared that the King was as Ahab and that the dogs in like manner would lick his blood."

"What a terrible story!"

"'Tis terrible times we live in, sweet lady. The Lady of Aragon suffered greatly and was there any one of the King's wives who did not? Your own beautiful mother so desperate . . . And we saw the terror of the last Queen for ourselves, you and I."

"Kat, how dare you talk so about my great father!"

"Only because commanded to do so by one who may well herself be mistress of us all one day."

Kat was smiling at me, and because she was Kat and said such words I could forgive her anything.

I told her she was the most indiscreet person I knew and I hoped she did not chatter to others as she did to me. She was as excited as I was about my prospects and being less thoughtful and logical than I, she believed that I was almost on the throne.

"The little King is very sickly," she said. "He won't make old bones. And as for Mary, I sometimes think she does not enjoy good health. Whereas you, my precious one, are full of vigor. I said to John Ashley only the other day, 'Our girl is destined for greatness. I feel it in my bones.'"

"You are the most foolish creature I ever knew and I wonder that I love you. If any heard you express such sentiments, what do you think they would say of you? You would be accused of ill-wishing the King and you know I love Edward dearly."

"I don't think John Ashley wants to be rid of me yet," said Kat flippantly, "so he won't betray me. Nor will you, my lady, for I cannot see you ever reaching that stage when you would not want your Kat there to look after you—throne or not."

"Oh Kat, do have a care," I said, laughing.

She would take no heed. It was not long before she was talking about a marriage for me.

"Well, 'tis a merry state and one necessary to a woman."

"All women?" I asked.

"All women, my clever lady."

"I am not so sure. What of my mother? Do you think she thought what a blessed state it was when she was on her way to Tower Green? Did Katharine Howard think it so when she ran screaming through the gallery? And what of Katharine Parr when she was confined to her bed in mortal peril? Do you believe they thought it then?"

"You are talking of queens."

"Queens—or those who may be queens—must surely take special care before they embark on matrimony."

"Marriages are usually made for queens, dear lady."

"I have a fancy that I shall make my own, if indeed I ever decide to make one."

"I know one who would be very happy to take you."

"Who is that?"

She was conspiratorial and her voice had sunk to a whisper. She put her lips to my ear.

I flushed. I could not pretend that I had not noticed him and that I did not think him one of the most exciting men I had ever seen. He was tall, extremely good-looking and more than that had an air of gallantry and indefinable charm. There was only one man at Court who could fit that description: Thomas Seymour.

"Ah, my lady," went on the incorrigible Kat, "I see that you are inclined to look with favor on this very desirable gentleman."

"You see much which is not there, Kat Ashley," I reprimanded her. "And how do you know he might have plans regarding me?"

"Because I have eyes, my lady, and I have seen his own linger on you with much affection."

Was it so? And how did Thomas Seymour regard me? When he looked at me with that affection which Kat had perceived, did he see me wearing a crown? Was he, brother to that very Jane who had supplanted my mother, uncle to the frail King, looking out for his future?

"If he asked for your hand, Princess, would you take him?"

"You are impertinent, Kat Ashley," I said and I slapped her face.

She put her hand to her cheek. "And you, my lady, are hasty with your hands," she said.

I put my arms round her and kissed her. "I'm sorry I did that, but you can be very aggravating sometimes. I do not want to hear any more about Thomas Seymour."

"Do you not?" said Kat. "Shall we then discuss the weather or the new blue silk you have . . . or your embroidery?"

"You would be safer talking of such things."

She laughed and I laughed with her and she went on to tell me that Sir Thomas Seymour had been created Baron of Sudeley and made Lord High Admiral. "The late King left him two hundred pounds in his will and I verily believe, my lady, that had His Majesty lived there would have been the honor of marriage into the King's family for him. The King loved Thomas Seymour . . . and who would not love such a fine, witty and handsome gentleman?"

"I believe there are some who do not love him."

"Oh, that brother of his—the Duke of Somerset if you please now. He is the big man. He has the King in his charge. They say Thomas is a little jealous of his brother."

"*They* say, Kat? It seems to me that it is Kat Ashley who says this and that, and she is the very mistress of gossip throughout this land."

"And who profits from what I discover more than my lady?"

That was how we talked and there was hardly a day when Thomas Seymour's name was not mentioned between us.

I had to admit I was thinking a great deal of him. I had known for some time that he was interested in me . . . even before my father's death. He was my brother's favorite uncle. I believed that Edward was not very fond of the elder Seymour. Edward Seymour, Duke of Somerset to give him his newly acquired title, was a man of immense ambition and extreme ruthlessness. Now that my father was dead, he had become Protector of England and was in a position of complete authority. It was natural that Thomas, the younger brother and favorite uncle of the young King, could not happily accept a subordinate position.

However the Seymours were the important family in the country now. They had nothing to fear from the Howards. Surrey had been beheaded and the Duke, his father, was still in the Tower; his death warrant was to have been signed on the night before the King died, but the King being too weak to add his signature to the documents, the execution had been waived, though Norfolk continued a prisoner.

Almost immediately after that conversation with Kat, a letter arrived through her from Thomas Seymour. She brought it to me with an air of intrigue, and when I opened it and saw from whom it came, my hands trembled.

It was brief and to the point. The Admiral had long admired me. He was a little older than I but age was unimportant when love reigned. He admired my beauty more than that of any other and was asking me to give him my hand in marriage.

I was overcome with emotion. I had to admit I had been a little fascinated by the Admiral. He was the most attractive man at Court and, having been a person of little importance for so long, I was very susceptible to admiration. I was not beautiful enough to be sure of my attractions. I had youth, of course, and a fine clear skin, milk-white and fair; I had good reddish hair, the same color as my father's, and I resembled him in my appearance. He was a handsome man but what is handsome in a man is not necessarily attractive in a woman. I had lively tawny eyes to match my hair but my eyelashes were too fair; my nose was long rather than short, but I was thankful that I had not inherited my father's mouth, which was small and cruel and had been really the most expressive of his features. I wished I had inherited my mother's appearance with the attributes of my father—not all, of course—but the best, those qualities which had made him a good sovereign. I think I had to some extent, but how I wished I had my mother's ravishing and singular beauty! Perhaps because of a certain lack of assurance as far as my personal charms were concerned I always wanted to hear them proclaimed. So with Thomas Seymour's letter before me I tried to convince myself that I was loved for myself and that his affections had nothing to do with the fact that I was the King's daughter who might one day inherit a crown.

Kat was in a state of twittering excitement and tried to get me to reveal the contents of the letter. I would not, but she guessed. She went on and on talking of the good looks of the Admiral, how my father had singled him out for favor, and how she was sure that had the King lived he would have betrothed me to him by now.

I listened and thought about the Admiral. My brother Edward was very fond of him. He would certainly have the favor of the new King. But Edward was in leading strings and it was not the Admiral who was holding them but his brother. There were moments when I allowed myself to dream silly girlish dreams, when I thought how pleasant it would be to listen to the Admiral's compliments and allow myself to believe that I was the most desirable girl in England.

But there was another side to my nature—that shrewd observer who had never allowed any event of importance to be passed over. I hesitated while I brooded on what the future might bring and at last I came to my conclusions. I would not be fourteen until September. I had a great deal to learn and I was in a most unusual position.

I took up my pen and wrote to Thomas Seymour telling him that I had neither the years nor the inclination to think of marriage at this time, and I was surprised that anyone should mention the subject to me at a time when I was entirely taken up with mourning my father to whom I owed so much. I intended to devote at least two years to wearing black for him and mourning him; and even when I arrived at years of discretion, I wished to retain my liberty without entering into any matrimonial engagement.

When I had written it, I read it through once and hastily sealed it. Then it was dispatched.

I had moved with my household to the Dormer Palace of Chelsea which my father had built after he had possession of the Manor of Chelsea. It was a charming place with gardens running down to the river. I was looking forward to being there with my stepmother for we had always been good friends and I was delighted that the Council had decided that she should have charge of me.

I was feeling very excited. Ever present was the realization that I could have a glorious future and in the meantime I would have the attentions of the most handsome man at Court. It was a pleasant prospect. But my good sense insisted that it would be folly to agree to any engagement with Thomas Seymour. If the Council were against it—and I felt sure that Somerset would never agree to it—we should both be in trouble. The Admiral was a daring sailor and might be ready to risk that sort of trouble for the sake of a crown. I was not. I was vulnerable because I was so young but I had acquired one bit of wisdom inasmuch as I realized I was too young and inexperienced to put myself in a dangerous situation. Perhaps I was by nature cautious— the opposite I was sure of my dashing Admiral. But I had seen what folly women exposed themselves to for love.

Kat tried to persuade me to accept him with constant references to his charms. He was adventurous both at sea and in the ladies" boudoirs. "You'll have a very accomplished lover, my lady," she said, and although I told her that I most certainly would not have him and had written him to tell him so, she did not believe me. "My lord is not a man to take no for an answer," she declared. "We shall see . . ."

She talked and I listened—I must admit, with mounting excitement.

"He'll come courting, I know it," she said.

And I realized that although I was averse to marriage, to be courted seemed to me a rather pleasant and exciting pastime.

My stepmother was delighted to receive me.

I complimented her on her appearance for she looked younger than I had ever seen her look before and there was a brightness about her. She looked like a girl though she must be thirty-four or -five years old. Then I considered how she had lived as Queen of England, the butt of my father's irritations; I thought of her dressing that leg which must have been revolting at times, of the manner in which he used to put it on her lap and expect her to nurse it; I remembered most of all that hysterical fit of weeping in her bedchamber when she must have felt the axe poised ready to descend on her defenseless neck. No wonder she had become young again.

What an example of the joys of single blessedness! For the first time in her life she was free. She said how happy she was to have me with her. We would sit together over our embroidery and she would talk to me of the Reformed Faith just as she did when Edward, Jane Grey and I were in the royal household. It was not such dangerous talk now for the Reformed Party was in the ascendant. Sometimes she mentioned Edward and shook her head over him. He was so young for such responsibility.

I replied that Edward was not allowed to have much responsibility. There were those who told him exactly what to do.

"Meaning Edward Seymour," said my stepmother, her lips tightening a little.

"Who else?" I asked. "Who commands the King but his uncles and their family?"

"It is Lord Hertford—now the Duke of Somerset—who sets himself up as master of us all," she replied. "And his wife would do the same if she could. I never could abide Anne Stanhope—a greedy, ambitious woman, highly suitable for Somerset, I dare swear. Oh, it is my lord Somerset who is our King now. I have always thought that my lord Admiral should share the responsibility of looking after the King. I am sure he would prefer Thomas to Edward Seymour."

I agreed that he would.

My stepmother had grown pink with annoyance. She really did dislike the Duchess.

"Do you know," she went on, "I verily believe the elder Seymours plan to marry their daughter to the King."

"They would never do that," I said. "He should have someone royal."

"They say how interesting it would be to have another Jane Seymour as the Queen."

"Jane Seymour the first was not so fortunate," I cried. "She bore Edward but did not live to see him grow up."

"Edward is very fond of Jane Grey," said my stepmother tentatively. "She is such a clever, good girl."

"Oh yes," I replied with a touch of asperity, "she is a model of virtue." I was a little tired of hearing of the brilliant scholastic attainments of Jane Grey. I could challenge her in that field, of course, but I could not match her saintliness and it was that which irritated me. Jane Grey has no spirit, I used to say.

My stepmother understood and laughed at me. "Edward thinks so, I am sure," she said.

"I wish I could see him more often," I went on. "I wish he would come here and we could all be as we used to be."

"He is the King now, Elizabeth."

"Well, why should he not live with the Dowager Queen?"

"If he were a little younger . . ."

"Everyone is saying if only he were a little older! Poor Edward, I don't think he is half as happy as he was when we were all together."

And so we talked and very often I was tempted to tell her of Thomas Seymour's proposal and that I had seen fit to refuse him. But I never did. Something seemed to warn me to keep it to myself.

One evening Kat was seated at the window. It was dark and I was just on the point of retiring to bed. She stood up suddenly in a state of great excitement and cried: "My lady, I saw him!"

"Saw whom?" I demanded.

Her eyes were round with wonder as she whispered: "My Lord Admiral."

"At this hour! I don't believe it."

I was at the window. She went on whispering: "I thought he was going in at the main door, but he moved away—round to the side . . ."

"I believe you *dream* of the Admiral. Really, Kat, if Mr Ashley knew he could be jealous, and certainly very angry that his wife should talk in such an unseemly fashion of another man."

"Oh, he would know it is not for me that the Admiral comes into the Palace."

"And suppose it was the Admiral? For whom should he come sneaking into the Palace?"

"For one fair lady . . . my lady Elizabeth . . . whom one day I am going to call Her Majesty."

"Kat, you are mad. If you talk so, you will find yourself lodged in the Tower one fine day. Have you no sense? How could you have seen him at this hour?"

"I would know him anywhere."

"Let us wait and watch awhile. If he has come calling at this time of the evening, my stepmother will soon send him away. I'll swear it was one of the grooms you saw going round to the back of the Palace. You conjure up images of that man out of nothing."

"My lady, did you ever see a groom who looked like my Lord Admiral?"

"No."

"Then wait with me. He will come out in a moment. He will look longingly at your window. Perhaps he will climb the ivy. Shall we let him in, my lady?"

"Sometimes I wonder whether I am *your* governess not you mine. If it were known what a frivolous creature you are and the mischief in which you try to involve me, you would not stay a day longer in this household."

"I'll try to be sober, my lady, but with such as you, with such a gallant admirer . . . it is not easy."

We waited at the window for quite an hour but no one emerged.

I told Kat she had been carried away by her fancies.

→>-<←

CHE WEEKS BEGAN to pass quickly. Spring had come and it was beautiful at Chelsea. I used to ride with a party in the fields and gallop along by the river. People came out to see me ride past. They would smile and curtsy and some shouted: "God Bless the Princess." That was sweet music in my ears. The people's approval was very precious to me. I loved the sun on the river and the green fields. England! I thought. My country! To be Queen of England! I could ask no greater prize from life than that.

Once I met Thomas Seymour at Blandel's Bridge, which was also known as Bloody Bridge because it was the haunt of robbers who thought nothing of slitting a traveler's throat for the sake of his purse.

Thomas bowed low and gave me such a look that there could be no doubt of his feelings for me. I asked him if he was on his way to the Dormer Palace and he said that he was but since he had met me in the fields, might he be permitted to ride with me?

I knew this would be dangerous and if we were seen, which we almost certainly would be, it would give rise to gossip, and what if that reached the ears of the Council? So I haughtily refused permission. He bowed his head in submission and I whipped up my horse. I had thought he would pursue me. Surely that was what one would expect of a reckless admiral. But when I looked round he had disappeared.

I was tingling with excitement.

It was a few days later when my stepmother and I were seated over our needlework and she dismissed all her attendants so that we were alone together. She began to talk to me about her life in a strange sort of way, telling me things which I knew already.

"I am not an old woman," she said, "and until now I feel that I have never been young. I was little more than a child when I was given in marriage to Lord Borough of Gainsborough. He seemed very old to me. His children were older than I. I was his nurse until he died. You would think, would you not, that I would have been allowed a free choice. But I was given to Lord Latimer. He, too, was elderly, and I was a wife and stepmother all at once. It seemed to be my fate . . . until now. I suppose I seem old to you, Elizabeth. You are so young. Imagine, not yet fourteen years old! Oh, I think back to the days when I was fourteen. I had my dreams. And then my first marriage. I was terrified, Elizabeth. Can you imagine a girl little more than a child to be given to an old man? But my Lord Borough was kind to me . . . so was Lord Latimer. I had my stepchildren but none of my own. It was something I longed for—a child of my own. And when Lord Latimer died I was thirty years old and I told myself, I am free."

"Then you married my father."

She nodded and I wondered afresh why she should be telling me this which I knew so well. There was a reason I was sure. She was leading to something which she was finding rather hard to tell me. I listened patiently.

"I thought," she went on, "now I shall marry for love. There was one man, and I was not the only one who considered him the most attractive man at Court. There is really something rather magnificent about him. We would have been married. But the King chose me . . . and because of that Thomas had to leave Court."

"Thomas," I repeated.

She smiled tenderly. "Thomas Seymour and I were all but betrothed before my marriage to the King. But I became the Queen. Sometimes I dream of those years . . ." She shivered. "I have had dreams, Elizabeth."

"I understand."

"Nightmares when . . ."

"Please don't talk of it. It distresses you, my lady. I understand."

"You know I came within a day of death."

"Yes," I said quietly.

"Only those who have undergone such a trial could know what that means. Perhaps with some it is different. They can face the axe . . . and some worse. To do it for one's faith I suppose would be different. There was Anne Askew. You remember her."

"Yes. She was burned to death."

My stepmother covered her face with her hands. "She was a saint, Elizabeth. I am not made of the stuff martyrs are made of."

"Perhaps none of us knows what stuff we are made of until we are called on to face the supreme test."

"You are a wise child. That is why I talk to you. I want you to know before it becomes common knowledge. I want you to understand." She had lowered her hands and was looking at me. Now her emotions had completely changed. No longer was she looking back; she was looking forward, and the radiance had returned to her face. "I could not wait any longer," she went on. "I was afraid, Elizabeth, that happiness would once more be snatched from me. I had to seize it and . . . he said we must. We would marry and tell afterward."

"Marry! You cannot mean . . ."

She was laughing now. She looked lovely for she was a beautiful woman, particularly now that the little signs of age which had begun to appear when she was looking after my father and had lived in fear of losing her life seemed to have been wiped from her face. She looked almost like a girl.

"Yes," she said, "Thomas and I were married secretly."

"Thomas!"

"Thomas Seymour, Lord Sudeley. He always loved me . . . all the time I was married to the King. And I loved him, but of course we dared not show it. I was entirely faithful to the King. But as soon as I was free . . . Elizabeth, do you know, he asked me a week after the King's death."

A week after the King's death! It must have been when Thomas Seymour had my own letter refusing him!

I felt numbed by the shock.

Oh the wickedness, the perfidy of men!

IT WAS IMPOSSIBLE for them to keep their marriage secret and there was great indignation among the Council, none being more incensed than the bridegroom's brother, Somerset. The marriage was an insult to the late King, it was said. What right had the Queen to marry so soon? Did she hope to foist the son of Lord Sudeley on the country as an heir to the throne? That would be an act of treason.

However it was soon clear that my stepmother was not pregnant.

Thomas had been clever in getting the consent of the young King to his marriage. I could imagine that scene. My little brother, who was quite overwhelmed by his magnificent and charming uncle, would readily give his consent to anything he asked; and although the Council, headed by Somerset, was infuriated by the insolence of the Admiral and what they called the reckless behavior of the Dowager Queen, they could not inflict punishment for something to which the King himself had given his consent. However, they could make life as uncomfortable as possible for the newly married pair.

In the first place Queen Katharine's jewels were confiscated. They were the property of the Crown, said Somerset. Thomas would not accept that, and Katharine, who would follow him in all things, declared her intention of fighting to keep them. They were very valuable, and Thomas, I was beginning to understand—though perhaps in my heart I had always known it—was rather fond of possessions. The Duchess of Somerset—whom my stepmother called "that odious Anne Stanhope"—refused to carry the Queen's train at ceremonies, a duty she had performed when Katharine had become the Queen. She declared she would not accord the same homage to her husband's younger brother's wife.

This was the beginning of the great animosity between the brothers. At the root of this was Thomas's determination to marry the King to Jane Grey while the Somersets coveted the role of Queen of England for their daughter Jane.

There was strife then in the Seymour family itself. Thomas did not care. He was one of the most reckless men I ever knew in the whole of my life.

Now that the marriage was acknowledged it meant that Thomas Seymour joined our household. I guessed this would prove to be a matter of some embarrassment to me. How should I feel living under the same roof as a man who had asked me to marry him and within a few days had proposed to my stepmother?

"Only a blatant adventurer would have done such a thing," I said to Kat. "There is your fine gentleman!"

Kat was bitterly disappointed, but still she could see no wrong in the Admiral. I told her she was a very stupid woman and I gave her a slap or two during those few days after I had received the news. It relieved my feelings. She had talked of him constantly; she had made me think of him and see him as the handsome hero of romance.

I called him "The Buccaneer of the Bedchamber," which amused Kat.

I said: "After all he has done, after the way in which he has deceived my stepmother, you still talk about him as though he were a god."

"There is no one like him at Court," insisted Kat. "He is indeed a man."

I wanted to be alone to think about him, yet I wished I could get him out of my thoughts, but I could not dismiss him as easily as I wished. If he had not been so good-looking, so commanding, so light-hearted and amusing, I could have hated him. But if I showed my fury that would indicate that I cared enough to be angry. I must not show my feelings. What effect that would have on a man such as he was, I could well imagine. He believed himself to be so attractive that whatever he did he could never be anything but irresistible.

Kat told me that Thomas Parry wanted to talk to me. Sir Thomas Parry and Kat were the best of friends, I think largely because they were both inveterate gossips. John Ashley was quite different, far more sober than either of them, and much cleverer. I often wondered why he had fallen in love with Kat, but perhaps it was because she was so different from himself.

Tom Parry looked rather sly; his lips were pressed together as though the words were ready to tumble out and he was trying to restrain them in order to savor the full effect they would have on me.

I said impatiently: "Come on, Thomas, what is it?"

"My lady, this news . . . it has been a shock to us all."

A shock? Had it? I thought of the Admiral's nocturnal visits to the Palace. It must have been he whom Kat had seen skulking round to the back on that night. Forestalling his marriage, no doubt, the rogue.

"Come, Parry, you have not asked me to see you to tell me that."

"He took the Queen, my lady. But I think he would rather it were the Princess."

"What Princess?"

"My lady Elizabeth herself."

"Stop talking of me as though I am not here. What is it you have to say? Say it quickly and stop hedging."

"It was the day after the King's death, my lady. The Admiral came to me . . ." He hesitated.

"Came to you? For what purpose?"

"He wished for a detailed account of your possessions and felt I was the one to give it."

"I see," I said. "Why was I not told?"

"The Admiral made me swear secrecy, my lady."

"Oh, I see. You serve him, do you? I thought you were my servant."

"I am, my lady, with all my heart, but I thought it could only mean that he was seriously contemplating matrimony with you and that seemed a great and marvelous thing."

"And you think my possessions satisfied him then?"

"He seemed as satisfied with them as he is with your person."

"I suppose you and that gossip-monger Kat Ashley think I should feel honored to be so well endowed by my late father that I can attract the attention of the Admiral?"

"Kat Ashley and I agreed that he was as enamored of you as your possessions."

"Master Parry, have you ever wondered what it would be like to occupy a cell in the Tower?"

"My lady!"

"Look to it," I said. "You may discover one day. You should be more cautious and guard well your tongue. You are a simpleton, Tom Parry—and Kat Ashley with you."

I went out for I could bear no more. He had weighed up my possessions, considered them worthy of his attention and then proposed marriage. When I had refused he had immediately gone to the next on the list.

Was that not enough to infuriate any woman particularly when—it had better be confessed—she had quite a fancy for the handsome philandering rogue?

I could see that I had betrayed my feelings too much. I had not yet mastered the trick of hiding them. Parry had gone straight to Kat and I was sure he would tell her that I was angry because of the marriage and had secretly wanted Thomas Seymour for myself.

They were a pair of scandalmongers and I was often exasperated with them both. But they so obviously loved me, and I believe I was more important to them than anyone else; and for that reason I could never be annoyed with them for long. Sometimes I trembled for their lack of wisdom. How right I was soon became clear.

MY SISTER MARY wrote to me asking if I would like to leave the household of the Dowager Queen and Thomas Seymour for she was sure that to live with those who had conducted such a misalliance would be distasteful to me.

Mary was at Wanstead whither she had come from Norfolk. She was seventeen years older than I and therefore must be much wiser. She was, however, a very firm upholder of the Catholic Faith, and her desire to see it again established in England clouded her judgment and from time to time put her in considerable danger. I knew that she was horrified by the attitude of the Council toward religion for now they were mainly supporters of the Reformed Faith she considered anathema. Edward himself had always inclined strongly toward it, so I could see that I must on no account set myself beside her, for if there was later to be a choice of religion I must be free to take whichever course would help me best. I had long decided that preoccupation with the method of worshipping was not so important as faith itself and I did not intend to become involved in it or committed to any doctrine to my detriment.

I knew Mary well enough to understand that she would want the throne, not for her own aggrandizement, but for the opportunity of bringing England back to Rome. I could see great dangers for the realm in that determination, but I knew that devout Catholics—among them men like Gardiner—would agree wholeheartedly with Mary.

Thomas Seymour had written to my stepsister asking her to give her blessing on his marriage to Katharine Parr and Mary was very angry. He had written as though the marriage had not taken place, but she knew very well that the Queen was already his wife for she had her spies to keep her informed. She considered the marriage outrageous—in fact almost criminal because our father was so recently dead. How could Katharine have so quickly forgotten her husband? she would ask. *I* could understand Katharine's need. I had seen her terror under my father's rule and I knew of the irresistible—or almost—wiles of the Admiral. Perhaps I was more worldly than my sister even though she was seventeen years older. Perhaps I understood our stepmother's desire for marriage as Mary never could.

She had extended this invitation to me. I was so young, she wrote. It was wicked to submit me to such an embarrassing and unfortunate situation. I could come and stay with her for as long as I wished.

Life with Mary, my pious sister! I imagined it. Prayers! Morning, midday, afternoon and evening . . . and no doubt in between! "My dear sister, I am going to instruct you in the ways of truth . . ." I was fond of Mary in some ways. She had been remarkably kind to me despite my mother's displacement of her own. Oh, but I could not bear to be in her household. Whereas here I was at Chelsea with the stepmother to whom I was devoted, with my tutors, with this pleasant easy-going household . . . and the Admiral. If I were honest I must admit that I was looking forward to some encounters with that plausible and fascinating man.

But I must not offend Mary and I should have to pen my refusal very carefully. Mary could easily be Queen for I had heard secretly that the King's health was certainly not improving since he had come to the throne. Mary Queen . . . a Catholic country again! I must indeed tread very warily. But on one point I had made up my mind. I was not going to leave the exciting place Chelsea had become.

I wrote several drafts. Words were so important, and the wrong ones could wreak irretrievable damage. I began by deploring the marriage. It was as abhorrent to me as it was to her, but I did feel that my sudden departure from Chelsea might create a difficult situation. There was a powerful party guiding the King, and the Protector was a Seymour. My position was not very safe, nor, I reminded her, was hers. We had to walk very carefully in these dangerous times. Moreover our royal father had appointed Katharine Parr as my guardian and to leave her would be going against his expressed wish. I knew my good sister would understand my feelings and much as I should enjoy being with her, I felt that my place was in the household of my stepmother—in spite of this unfortunate marriage.

I was rather pleased with that. It was my first real lesson in diplomacy.

I was looking forward with great excitement to the future.

SOON AFTER MY fourteenth birthday the household moved to Hunsdon. I was really finding life very stimulating. Learning was always a great pleasure to me and I spent a lot of time with my books, but there was a certain time for frolicking; and it was really a most unusual household because Thomas Seymour was part of it.

I was amazed at first to find that I could forgive him for his mercenary actions and for going at once to my stepmother when I had refused him. After all, I reasoned, he *had* asked me first. That, said my wiser self, was because you had the hope of a crown. You are not without means either.

No. But Katharine was richer, and he still asked me first, retorted the foolish romantic part of me.

I felt impatient with myself. That was Kat Ashley's reasoning.

The truth was that Thomas was an adventurer, a lovable, charming man but an adventurer. He watched me closely and sought opportunities for being with me. When he could, he would come upon me alone. That was what he liked best. He would touch my hair and comment on its brightness; sometimes his hand strayed to my throat. He was always ready to seize opportunities and I knew that if ever I gave him one he would take it with both hands. He wooed me in a way with his eyes and his gestures; and even when my stepmother was present he would keep up a bantering conversation—in which she would join—and I wondered why she could not see what his intentions were. He flirted blatantly with me and then he would pretend that I was only a child and that was why he behaved as he did; and she seemed to take that for truth. Fourteen is not too young for a girl to take a lover. That was what he wanted, I knew. That was his intention all the time.

Kat noticed it and giggled about it. She made whispered conspiratorial comments when we were alone. I really do believe that if I had been agreeable she would have helped me make clandestine arrangements with him. Kat wanted excitement all the time and she never gave any heed to what the consequences might be. As for myself I must admit that I was enjoying these situations. It occurred to me that it could not have been better. I did not want to marry and place myself in danger and possibly jeopardize my chances of taking the crown. What I wanted was to have all the fun of courtship without coming to the usual climax. In fact I wanted to be in a constant state of being wooed, and never won.

And this was what life was offering me.

Thomas enjoyed it too, for marriage was quite out of the question. Wasn't he married already? Unable to get the Princess, he had taken the Queen. He was enamored of me. There was no doubt of that. I supposed there must be some fascination in seducing a royal virgin for a man who has become blasé in his amours. He was always teasing me and he would make Katharine join in and she seemed to think it was delightful that her husband should be so fond of me. I was like a daughter, she said. In fact she had always thought of herself as my mother rather than my stepmother.

And so we went on during the autumn days of that year which had begun with the death of my father.

Jane Grey had become part of our household. She joined me in the schoolroom. I was not really jealous of her scholastic attainments. Mine were more than enough for any tutor to marvel at and Jane was inclined to hide her light under a bushel while I let mine blaze forth like the midday sun. It was true. Jane was quiet and retiring, almost apologizing for her very existence; whereas I was growing more imperious every day, blossoming under Thomas Seymour's admiration.

I was a little annoyed when he showed too much attention to Jane. He never actually flirted with her. Thomas was too clever for that. Jane might not have understood his meaning but she would have been horrified if she did. It seemed to me that Thomas showed a different side of himself to us all. He was the loving and tender husband to Katharine; he was benignly avuncular with Jane; and to me he was the reckless adventurer who was ready to risk everything for a smile—and more if he could get it—from me.

I laughed at him. I was very contented. I had become wise enough to know that this was the best way of enjoying his company.

Kat knew exactly why he wanted Jane Grey under our roof.

"She is destined for our little King," she said. "Thomas will get his revenge on his brother who is putting forward his own daughter Jane. But it is our Thomas who has the King's ear and I'll swear King Edward will go the way Uncle Thomas wants him to."

"He is a very scheming man," I said severely.

"Bless him. Let him be. He's the most handsome gentleman at Court . . . or at any court, I might say. He is charming to all, and men like that should be forgiven their sins."

Such a state of affairs could not continue. I should have known that. The Admiral was growing more and more reckless and I was becoming more and more fascinated. It surprised me that, loving my stepmother as I did, I could have indulged, to the extent I did, in this covert if innocent relationship with her husband; but his admiration was so stimulating and our teasing meetings gave a spice to my days. Moreover there was Kat to giggle with. She made up fantastic and titillating stories about the Admiral and myself, and I would lie in my bed and listen to them while we laughed together. I knew that I was in a dangerous situation, but life would have lost its savor if that danger had been entirely removed.

I was growing out of childhood. Less than a year ago I had not thought of the possibility of wearing a crown; and in addition the most fascinating man at Court was enamored of me. I was after all only just fourteen, so I have the excuse of youth to offer.

We were approaching a climax. Perhaps it began on that day when I had my new dress. It was a black velvet which Kat said was a little old for my years. But I adored it. It made my white skin look whiter and it seemed to set my hair on fire by its very contrast. It was low-cut and I looked at least two years older in it. I longed to see Thomas's face when he beheld me in it. The dress was a kind of challenge. You can't pretend I'm a child anymore, it said.

I tried it on one afternoon and preened before Kat.

"You look like a queen already," was her comment. "My word, you're going to be a haughty one. We shall all have to look to our heads when the great day comes."

"Stop your nonsense, Kat," I commanded.

At which she fell onto her knees and in mocking fashion raised her eyes imploringly to my face. I burst out laughing. "Kat, you are the most foolish woman I ever knew."

"Fools are often loved more than the wise," she replied. "Perhaps that is why my mistress loves me. But I love her even more dearly and we all know she is the wisest creature in all Christendom."

"Get up, idiot," I said, "and tell me whether my skirt hangs correctly."

She scrambled to her feet and arranged the folds of my dress with loving care.

"You look wonderful," she whispered. "But not my little girl anymore. Why, see who has come into the garden. My lord and lady. He is looking at her most tenderly. See how she leans on his arm."

I looked with Kat. There they were walking together, looking loverlike, his arm through hers. He was saying something and she was smiling up at him. He looked as magnificent as ever.

"The peacock!" said Kat indulgently. "Look at his jewels! Those rubies must have cost a fortune. The dear Queen looks drab beside him, does she not? The peahen to his peacock." Her eyes sparkled with mischief. "Are you going down to show them your gown?"

That was just what I was planning to do. I turned to Kat and we laughed together.

"Let us see what the naughty man has to say of your gown," said Kat.

I did not need to be persuaded.

When he saw me approaching, the Admiral bowed ironically and my stepmother smiled at me.

"What has happened to the Lady Elizabeth?" said Thomas in a voice of wonder. "Do you see what she is wearing, Katharine? Do you allow your stepdaughter to dress up as a lady of mature years while she is yet a child?"

"Pray do not talk nonsense," I said. "I am past fourteen."

"Oh, is that so?" said Thomas, opening his eyes very wide. "I don't like the dress, do you, Katharine? Do you think it is a little er . . . revealing?"

Katharine said: "It is very becoming, Elizabeth. It does make you look older though. Thomas really likes it. He is only teasing."

Only teasing! He came close to me and would have laid his hands on me, but I eluded him and went to my stepmother. I was suddenly a little frightened. There was a purpose in his eyes which alarmed me. Their brilliance was disconcerting; he put out his tongue a little and licked his lips. His eyes seemed to burn right through me.

"I wanted to know how you liked my gown," I said, looking intently at my stepmother. "Kat, like you, thought it was becoming but a little too old for me."

"I suppose she is right, dear," agreed my stepmother. "But you have to grow up one day, don't you? Pray do not do so too quickly."

"It is no use pleading with the Lady Elizabeth," said Thomas. "She will have her own way, and if she says she will grow up quickly, she will endeavor to do so, unless . . ."

I regarded him coolly but my heart began to hammer against my bodice and I wondered if he noticed.

"Unless what, my lord?" I challenged.

He came close to me . . . There was a look of such intense desire in his gleaming eyes that I thought my stepmother must surely be aware of it. "Unless," he said, "we stop her."

I held my head high. I was enjoying this. I had rarely felt so excited and because my stepmother was present I felt safe.

"Pray do not attempt to do that," I said.

Then he did an extraordinary thing. He took the jeweled dagger from his belt and, holding it up, pointed it toward me.

"Thomas!" cried my stepmother in amazement.

"This child must be taught a lesson. What say you, Katharine. Shall we allow her to command us, eh?"

I moved close to my stepmother. He approached and picking up my voluminous skirt he slit it from hem to waist.

There was a silence which seemed to go on for a long time. My stepmother and I were too astonished to move. Then I heard him laugh and he went on cutting my skirt. Then his hands were on the bodice. If he had attempted to cut that, he might have cut me. I felt his hands tugging at it and then it was torn down the front and it fell away from my shoulders. I was exposed in my petticoats.

"Help me, Katharine," he said. "We will show this wayward daughter of ours. I am going to cut this gown into ribbons and nothing will stop me."

The Queen was laughing. She said: "Oh Thomas, you take your games too far."

"Come, Katharine, hold her," he commanded.

She put her arms about me holding me tightly and I allowed myself to stand still while he finished his work on the dress. An irresistible excitement possessed me.

"You . . . you . . ." I panted. "You have ruined my dress!"

"And shown you what I feel," he said. "*We* have done that, haven't we, Katharine?"

"You are such a boy, Thomas," she said.

"You have ruined my dress," I repeated in mock anger. "You will have to pay for a new one."

"Most willingly and I will make sure that it is of *my* liking."

I think my stepmother must have become aware of watching eyes from the window.

"Elizabeth," she said, "you are half naked. You had better go in at once. What will they think?"

"They will think that I am a man who will have his way," said Thomas, and I am ashamed to say that the ambiguity of his words was thrilling to me.

"Not with me," I said; then realizing that my stepmother was right and I could not remain in the gardens thus, I turned away and ran across the lawns into the Palace.

Kat was waiting for me, agog with excitement. She had, of course, seen it all.

SOON AFTER THAT INCIDENT my stepmother told me that she was expecting a child. She was so happy but I felt a great pity for her as well as the tenderness she always aroused in me. I could not help wondering whether she was aware of the manner of man she had married. She did not appear to be, and it struck me that she deliberately closed her eyes to his true character. What did she think of his flirtation with me? She called it "teasing" as though it was the kind of behavior which was natural between an indulgent parent and a stepdaughter of whom he was fond. How could she have been so blind?

That disgraceful scene in the garden was the beginning of the change in our relationship. It was almost as though he was telling me that he had finished with the preliminary stages, the foreplay, of his courtship of me. He was clever; he knew that I was aware of his intentions and he also knew that my feelings for him were far from indifferent.

We were in a highly dangerous situation. If he reached the climax toward which he was moving, he would do more than endanger his marriage, he could commit a crime against the State. I was no longer merely the bastard daughter of the King. Under the late King's will, I was in line to the throne if anything happened to Edward, and if Thomas carried out his intention, which was surely seduction, that could be treason and he could lose his head. Did he know this? Of course he did, but danger was the breath of life to him. He was reckless by nature, ambitious and confident. What was he thinking of, besides seducing me? I was not so simple as to believe his plans did not go beyond that. To marry me? To share a throne with me? But he had a wife. Wives could be removed. I sometimes wished I did not possess such a logical mind.

What amazed me about myself was that knowing this . . . being fully aware of the ruthless ambition of this man, I could still be fascinated by him and want him to go on pursuing me.

I used to lie in my bed sometimes and think of him under the same roof.

Kat Ashley slept in my bedroom. I was glad of that, for much as I enjoyed these amorous skirmishes with him, I did not share his desire to bring them to the usual conclusion. I would preserve my virginity until I was absolutely certain that to relinquish it would not impede my climb to power. Therefore I needed protection from assault, and if I could be sure of that, I was very happy to continue with the game.

One early morning I was awakened by the sound of stealthy footsteps and the door of my bedchamber was slowly opened. Thomas! I thought and looked for Kat who was not there. She must be with my other ladies as it was nearly time for me to rise. I thought of running to the adjoining chamber but it was too late.

The bedcurtains had parted and Thomas stood there in his nightgown and slippers. He was smiling down at me. I gasped and sitting up pulled the bedclothes up to my chin.

"My lord," I cried. "How dare you!"

"There is nothing I would not dare for the Lady Elizabeth," he said.

"Go away. My ladies will see you."

"They will see a fond stepfather coming in to say good-morning to his little stepdaughter."

"Surely it is customary to dress in a fitting fashion before doing so."

"Are you and I concerned with what is fitting, my adorable red-headed Elizabeth?"

"Go at once. I will not tolerate such . . ."

"Loving attention," he finished. "And how will you stop me? Don't you think you have played your reluctant game long enough?"

"I do not understand you, my lord."

"Then I will enlighten you." And with that he leaped onto my bed and grasped me in his arms. He kissed me full on the lips in a manner which bewildered me, and I felt I ought to scream for help and yet . . . I did not want to. On the other hand I was afraid because I had no intention of letting any man dominate me.

"Thomas!" The door had opened and my stepmother stood there.

Thomas was in complete command of the situation, and it occurred to me then that he must have had practice in extricating himself from similar predicaments.

He turned to smile at her. "Look at this child, Katharine. She is in an ill temper this morning and refused to say good-morning politely to her step-father. I looked in to say it and she glares at me and spits like a wild cat. What shall we do to punish her? Come, Katharine, help me."

With which he began to tickle me until I screamed for mercy, but I knew I was safe because of my stepmother's presence. He insisted that she join with him which she did and we were all laughing together until we were exhausted.

"Really, Thomas," said my stepmother. "You behave like a schoolboy."

He tried to look suitably boyish, and it was only when his eyes met mine that I saw the familiar gleam in them. It was the gleam of passion, not con-trition for his behavior.

How long could it go on? I asked myself. Why did my stepmother not see it? But perhaps she did and deceived herself. People were like that. They did refuse to see what they did not want to.

KAT SAID TO ME: "Mr Ashley is most disturbed."

"And why?" I asked.

"He says the Admiral's conduct toward you is unseemly."

"And what did you say to that?"

"I said he was a gallant gentleman and you were a very beautiful young lady and so . . . these things happen."

"And what then?"

"He had heard of the cutting of the gown."

"Which you told him doubtless, as you saw it. Do you think I did not know that you were watching from the window?"

"Well, that was mentioned and the romping in the bed chamber."

"My stepmother was there . . . she joined in the romp."

"Poor lady! But Mr Ashley says it is my duty to speak to the Admiral. I should put myself in the right, he says."

"What does he mean?"

"Mr Ashley is a very serious gentleman. He would always know what should be done."

"Well, are you going to speak to the Admiral?"

"I am afraid Mr Ashley insists that I do. But if you forbade me to . . ."

"I would not presume to come between a husband and his wife."

"Only when it is a handsome Admiral," said Kat; and got her face slapped for her insolence. But she was accustomed to my sudden onslaughts, and they were quickly forgotten.

I was very interested to hear what the Admiral would say to Kat and demanded she give an account of the interview.

"He looked so handsome," she said. "He was in purple velvet, and he has the most well-turned legs I ever saw on a man."

"We know full well what the Admiral looks like. It is his words I am interested in."

"He seemed surprised when I told him that people were whispering about what was happening between you and him, my lady. He said: 'How so? Is she not as a daughter to me?' I mentioned the rompings and he said, 'May not a man joke with his stepdaughter?' I told him that Mr Ashley was of the opinion that it was dangerous for the Princess Elizabeth to be involved in such scandals, and he said that the Princess was a child and had a fondness for childish games and jokes and he and the Queen were only indulging in these to amuse her. He said they wanted you to be happy in your home. That was why they lived simply at Chelsea. He and the Queen had no thought but for your good. He spoke so beautifully and he was so kind to me. He said if I heard any more ill-natured talk I should tell him who was responsible for it. He knew that I was his friend and that I would always speak well of him with you. It was just a display of fatherly affection, and I am sure Mr Ashley will be satisfied with his reply."

"Kat," I said, "I love you but there are times when I think you one of the most foolish women I ever knew."

She looked at me roguishly. "Go on with you," she said. "You will have your jokes."

IT WAS INEVITABLE that the time must come when even Thomas would not be able to go on deceiving his wife. One afternoon when the household was quiet, I had gone into one of the small chambers to read a book which William Grindal had given me to study.

I had not been there long when I heard the sound of stealthy footsteps outside the room. Experience had taught me to guess who was coming. He must have seen me enter the room and had come after me. I was faintly alarmed for we were in a rather isolated part of the palace, but that overwhelming excitement was taking possession of me. This time there was fear with it.

I stood up clutching the book against my bodice as he entered.

"Ha," he said. "I've caught you."

"My lord," I stammered, "please go. I have to read this book. It is a lesson for Mr Grindal."

"I have lessons to teach you which are more important than those within Mr Grindal's scope," he said, and with that he was beside me. "Caught!" he went on. "Do you know, we are alone now. Isn't it time we stopped this game of feigned reluctance?"

"It is not feigned," I said.

"We shall see."

He had seized me, and I was aware of the strength of the man and my own vulnerability. I wanted to fight him off and yet I did not. He had slipped my bodice from my shoulders.

"No, no!" I screamed, for something within me told me that this must go no farther. And yet on the other hand a part of me was hoping that it would.

I was saved by my stepmother, and was often in the years to come to thank God and my good fortune for her timely arrival, though at that moment I wanted to fade away in my shame.

She stood in the doorway, her dear good face creased with unhappiness. Her body was unwieldy now because she was about six months with child. She must have been suspicious of all that romping, the cut dress, the tickling, the boisterous games. Perhaps she could no longer go on pretending to herself and must at last accept her philandering husband for what he was. In any case she had caught him now . . . and me with him.

All my desire for the Admiral faded. I felt sick and wretched and overcome with shame. How could we have hurt her, she who had shown us nothing but loving kindness? She cried: "Thomas!" and there was a world of misery in her voice.

I stood before her, my face flaming red. He was silent. There was nothing he could answer now. I tried to pull my dress back over my shoulders.

She said: "Elizabeth, I think you had better leave us now."

I tried to look at her pleadingly, but she would not meet my gaze; she was looking at me with such utter sadness that I thought it would haunt me forever more.

"Go," she said to me, and the coldness in her voice made me want to weep.

I went to my room. I lay on my bed. Kat came to me and tried to question me. Angrily I dismissed her. I felt sick and ill. My head was aching violently. That was the beginning of the headaches which were to plague me for the next few years. I believe they were brought about by my extreme distress.

I lay there, hating the Admiral, but most of all hating myself.

IT WAS SOME HOURS before my stepmother sent for me. She was very composed but completely aloof.

"I think," she said, "that you should prepare to leave at once. You realize that you can no longer stay under this roof."

I hung my head. I could not bear to see the pain in her face.

"You will need to make ready for your departure. I wish you to be gone by the end of the week. I would speak with Mistress Ashley. You will go to Sir Anthony Cheshunt. You may be his guest until it is decided what residence is best for you."

"My lady, you have been so good to me."

She held up her hand to silence me. "I wish you to go as quickly and quietly as possible. I will speak to your governess. Pray ask Jane Grey to come to me now."

She was not like my dear stepmother. She was a remote stranger now. I could understand the misery she was enduring and it grieved me doubly to know that I was partly the cause of it.

I left her and sent Jane Grey to her. Then I conveyed the message to Kat and told her that the Queen wished to see her.

Kat came back to me, red-faced and in a mood of depression.

"What has happened to my lady?" she asked. "She has never spoken to me thus before. She accused me of not taking good care of you. She said I have allowed you to behave with levity and in a manner unbecoming to a princess and that I have neglected my duty. We are to leave immediately, as soon as we can be ready to depart. What does it mean?"

"You may well ask," I said angrily. "You know the Admiral has shown some fondness for me."

"Who does not know that? Coming into your bedchamber indeed! So that is it!"

"Yes," I said, "that is it. The Queen came into the little chamber and found me in his arms."

Kat's mouth fell open and she regarded me with horror.

"Don't stare at me like that!" I shouted. "You know . . . You encouraged him."

"Oh no, my lady. I—didn't want it to get to that!"

"Go away, Kat," I said, and as I turned my head I saw Thomas Parry standing in the room. Unable to curb his curiosity he had come to see why the Dowager Queen had sent for Kat.

"Go away, both of you!" I cried.

They went out and I put my hands to my throbbing head and wept.

I FELT BETTER at Cheshunt but I was wondering all the time what was happening at Sudeley Castle where my stepmother had gone to await the birth of her child. The Admiral was with her. I wondered what he had told her about that encounter with me, how he had explained the lover-like embrace? I had no doubt that he would have done his plausible best to talk himself out of a distressing situation; but somehow I did not believe that even he would be able to do it this time.

Being Katharine Parr she would not upbraid him publicly and would doubtless try to give the impression that all was well with them. She was not going to give Anne Stanhope the chance of rejoicing in her humiliation. There was something else too. In making advances to me, Thomas was not only committing a moral offense; in view of my position his actions could be a crime against the State. Katharine would be well aware of that. She loved him truly, I believed, and whatever sins he committed she would never place him . . . or me for that matter . . . in danger.

I tried to imagine what their lives would be like at Sudeley Castle. At least, I thought, if she is thoroughly disillusioned with her husband, she has the child, and I knew how desperately she had always wanted to have a child of her own. I prayed that she would have a successful confinement and that the child would bring her that joy which Thomas and I with our reckless behavior had snatched from her.

I began to feel a little easier. I was beginning to see what a lucky escape I had had, and lying in my bed night after night I warned myself that never again must I permit myself to indulge in such folly just for the sake of temporary sensations of pleasure. I made that vow to myself then.

The sad death of my tutor William Grindal took my mind off my stepmother for a time. I had been fond of him and he had been such a good mentor to me; but to my great joy Roger Ascham begged for the post and his request was granted. He was so delighted with me. He told me that my French and Italian were as good as my English; and that if I could not converse quite as well in Greek as I could in Latin, that too would come with practice. We read all of Cicero together and a great deal of Livy, and each morning we would spend some hours studying the Greek Testament and Sophocles. I could scarcely wait to get to my books, and it was as it had been when Edward, Jane Grey and I had vied with each other over our lessons. Moreover Master Ascham had a love of music which rivaled my own so this was an additional joy. I discovered to my gratification that he said he had never known such learning in a person of my age and that it was one of the greatest pleasures he could ever know to instruct me.

So, gradually, I began to think less of what was happening to the Queen and the Admiral. Lessons with Roger Ascham, and lighter moments with my beloved Kat, helped time begin to pass tolerably well.

August was turning toward September and I was again thinking of Katharine. This was the time when the child should be born.

"We must have news soon," I said to Kat.

I was right. A few days later we had a visitor at Cheshunt. It was a servant of the Admiral whom I remembered as Edward. I saw him coming and hurried down to the hall to hear what he had come to tell, and I knew at once from his melancholy countenance that it was not good.

"Oh Edward," I cried. "How is my lady? What of the child?"

"The Queen gave birth to a fair daughter," he said. "My lady Elizabeth, I have grievous news of the Queen."

"She is dead," I said slowly.

He nodded. "My lord is a sorrowful man."

"Oh Edward," I said, weeping, "not the good Queen my friend. How was it? I pray and trust she did not suffer."

"She suffered greatly, my lady. But the child is well. We thought that my lady's joy in the child would restore her quickly to health. But seven days later . . . that was the end."

I could not speak. I could only remember that the last time I had seen her, she had ordered me to leave her house. I was overcome with sorrow and remorse. Sorrow for my loss in her whom I had loved, remorse that I had given her cause for grief.

I bade the servants look after Edward and I went to my room. I pulled the curtains about my bed and lay down with a heavy heart.

SOON I HEARD the whole story from Kat. She had managed to prize it from Edward, the messenger. I was shaken with further remorse, and into my sorrow for the death of my stepmother there crept a certain uneasiness akin to fear.

"The Admiral was with her at the end," said Kat. "He was most tender and loving and did all he could to make the Queen comfortable. And when the child was born . . . a girl . . . and you know how he wanted a boy, and indeed astrologers had all told him that he would have a boy . . . he showed no anger and declared that though he had prayed for a boy, now that he had this girl she was exactly what he had wanted. The Queen was grievously ill, but it was thought that now she had her child she would get better quickly. But she did not. She wandered in her mind. Lady Tyrwhit was with her and she saw and heard it all. The Queen seemed to have lost her love for the Admiral and she cried out to Lady Tyrwhit, 'I am most unhappy because those whom I have loved love me not. They mock at me. They laugh at my love. They wait for my death so that they may be with others. The more good I do to them, the less good they do to me.'"

I shivered. "Did she really say that to Lady Tyrwhit?"

"She did indeed, my lady. There were witnesses. The Admiral was quite put out and said she wandered in her mind. He sat on the bed beside her but she shrank from him as though she feared he might do her some harm.

'I shall die,' said the Queen. 'I have no wish to live.' The Admiral talked of their child, but she turned away from him."

"I do not believe this, Kat," I said. "She loved him dearly."

"That was before . . ."

"Be silent, Kat."

"Yes, my lady," said Kat meekly.

After a while she went on: "My lady, should you not write a letter of condolence to my lord Admiral?"

"Do you think he needs condolence, Kat?"

"It is the custom and it would show correctness."

I could not shut out of my mind the thought of him as he had looked at me in the chamber. And his wife Katharine had seen that! What had those weeks been like while she waited for the birth of her child, the child of her faithless husband? Condolence? How much had he ever really cared for Katharine Parr?

"No," I said firmly. "I will write no letter of condolence because I do not think he needs it."

"I shall write to him then," she said and waited for me to forbid it; but I did not. Let her write or what she wished.

She did and I allowed the letter to be sent.

THE WEEKS PASSED. Rumor abounded and it chiefly concerned the Admiral and myself.

It was widely believed that now his wife was dead, the Admiral would marry me. I was not at all sure how I felt about that. If the Council gave their consent, perhaps there would be no reason why the marriage should not take place. Sometimes I was rather inclined to romanticize about that prospect. On the other hand, I drew back; I had no desire to be dominated by a man. I preferred those little skirmishes, those approaches and timely retreats. It seemed to me that while they persisted, it was the woman who was in control; it was she who said no. Once she had said yes, it would appear that she gave up her power and submitted. Look at my dear stepmother who had given her heart so freely. It was a battle between the sexes, and I was beginning to realize that I was of a nature which preferred conquest to being conquered.

And yet . . . the Admiral was a very exciting man.

If only I were a little older. Fifteen is really very young, and a knowledge of Greek and Latin does not help one to solve the problems which arise between a man and a woman.

Kat was excited.

"He keeps on the Queen's household," she whispered. "Perhaps he wishes to have that ready and waiting for his new bride."

"Methinks she would want to choose her own," I said curtly.

"Oh yes . . . in time, but just at first . . ."

"You talk as though a new marriage is imminent."

"Who shall say?" said Kat dreamily.

I knew that she and Parry gossiped constantly. Mr Ashley tried to curb his wife's chatter, but who could stop Kat? If I could not, no one could.

Parry even had the temerity to ask me whether, if the Council approved, I would marry the Admiral.

I hesitated for a second or two. I knew I must speak with caution even in my own household, so I said: "When the time comes to pass, I shall do as God shall put into my mind."

"The Admiral will surely ask for you, my lady," went on Parry. "I know that the matter is on his mind for he has spoken to me, as your cofferer, of your estate and possessions and the number of persons you keep in your household and of their cost to you."

"He seems to take a great account of these matters," I said coldly.

"He does indeed, my lady, and he is pleased that you are to have three thousand pounds a year as arranged in your father's estate. He asked so many questions about your lands and whether they were on lease or whether you had them for the term of your life that he must indeed be serious. I told him that these were matters beyond my knowledge."

I was silent. The Admiral is a rogue, I thought. But I had always known that. Had I not seen him with my stepmother? And I knew what his plans were for me.

I would be wise to have nothing to do with the man.

"There is one other matter, my lady," went on Parry. "The Admiral has asked me to suggest to you that you write a letter to his brother's wife. She has a great influence with her husband, and the Admiral thinks it would be an excellent idea if you sought her friendship. He has it in mind that you might be successful in persuading her—and through her, her husband—that you have a great eagerness for a marriage with the Admiral."

"I do not believe he said that, Parry," I said angrily.

"By my faith he did, Madam."

"Then," I retorted with indignation, "you may tell him that I will do no such thing."

I dismissed him, feeling very uneasy. I wondered how much he knew of what had happened. That Kat Ashley was very well informed I had no doubt, and of course she could never stop her tongue wagging.

➤➤◄◄

I SENT FOR HER.

"What have you told Parry?" I demanded. "Do you often speak of me?"

"My lady, he was in the household. He would have seen much for himself."

I gripped her arm so hard that she winced. "But you have tattled," I said. "You have told him, have you not, why we left the Queen's household so hurriedly?"

"Well, my lady, he asked so many questions . . ."

"And you told him! That was traitorous to me."

"My lady, he would never tell. I made him swear secrecy and he said that if he were torn asunder by wild horses, he would never tell a soul."

I dropped her arm, but my fear deepened. "There are times," I said, "when I am uneasy about the Admiral. And all to do with him."

"No need to be, my lady. He is a lovely gentleman. Parry and I agree that there is no other man in the world we would want for you."

I was very unsure. The handsome gentleman did not have the same charm for me when he was absent. Then I could see all manner of dangers arising from my association with him. And as he seemed as equally interested in my possessions as in myself, I had no doubt that these possessions included a possible crown of England. I knew I had to tread very warily.

DURING THE NEXT WEEKS I was to realize as I never had before how many awesome dangers lie in wait for those who have a claim, however slim, to the crown.

It was a cold day in January when I was at Hatfield that I heard Thomas Seymour had been arrested. I retired to my room; I could not stop shivering and my head was aching so violently that I had to lie down. Kat came to me and lay on the bed with me and we talked of the Admiral.

Kat said: "It is that brother of his. He was always jealous because the Admiral is so much more handsome and popular."

I answered: "Methinks the Admiral is not without envy of his brother either. But watch your tattle, Kat. It can be dangerous now . . . more so than ever."

I think even Kat realized that.

We learned what charges had been brought against him. Indeed he had played a very reckless game. I knew he had always wanted to get command of the King and to marry him to Jane Grey, who would be as meek as young Edward; they would have been perfect puppets in the hands of Thomas Seymour who longed to govern the realm.

But one does not govern a country with good looks, fair words and jaunty manners. One needs subtlety and judgment, and it seemed to me that Thomas had neither of these very necessary qualities.

He had made an enemy of his own brother who, as Protector of the Realm, was the most powerful man in the country. He had resented the fact that his brother Somerset should have power over the King simply because he was the elder uncle when he, Thomas, was the King's favorite.

We heard that he had sought to turn the King against Somerset. Edward had been kept short of money and Thomas had supplied him with some. Somerset had laid down a stern rule in Edward's household because he thought it necessary for the upbringing of this important boy. Thomas had visited him, condoled with him and, most foolishly and recklessly, had discussed with him the possibility of ridding themselves of Somerset—killing him, if necessary, it was reported—so that Edward could be a real king with Uncle Thomas beside him to help him rule.

Somerset had some time before quarreled with his brother over the marriage to Katharine Parr, and when Katharine died the matter of her jewels was revived. They belonged to the Crown, said Somerset; but Thomas would not relinquish them.

Thomas had believed—as he had shown in his domestic life—that his charm would always extricate him from difficult situations. He always kept several irons in the fire—to see which way to jump. He could control Edward—or he could marry me. Therefore he was quite ready to take on his powerful brother. He started to gather a group of friends who saw an advantage in overthrowing Somerset and setting up Thomas in his place. He boasted that he would create "the blackest parliament that ever was in England," words which were overheard and repeated to Somerset and the Council. He began to collect arms at Sudeley Castle. He had become involved with Sir William Sharington, who was the Vice Treasurer and Master of the Bristol Mint. Sharington was later found to have brought about a tremendous fraud by buying church plate and turning it into coins with two-thirds alloy, and in addition he had falsified the records of the Mint, which had enabled him to rob the Crown of some four thousand pounds. The Admiral had discovered this, but instead of bringing Sharington to justice, he had blackmailed him into continuing the fraud—and giving the greater part of the profit to Thomas to help raise an army of mercenaries.

Sharington, however, while feigning to accept these terms, went to Somerset and confessed what he had done and what the Admiral was forcing him to do. Sharington was pardoned. He had given the Protector what he needed—that evidence which would allow him to arrest his brother as a traitor.

So Thomas Seymour, my would-be lover, was in the Tower.

I thought about him a good deal, and there was a terrible misgiving in my heart. I was old enough to realize that because it was known that he wished to marry me, and because of my position in line to the throne, I could be drawn into this.

I HAD BEEN RIDING in the woods, my thoughts still with Thomas Seymour. I wondered whether the Protector would stand by and see his brother condemned to death. After all there was a blood tie between them. Did men, for ambition's sake, forget those early days when they had played together in the same nursery?

My brother Edward had told the Council that Thomas had indeed bribed him with money, and he admitted to the conversations they had had about the Lord Protector. I wondered at Edward. He was such a calm, serious boy, and I thought he had loved Thomas. How could he have betrayed him—and without a show of reluctance? I did not understand my brother. In the nursery days he had seemed so loyal. Yet it was true that Thomas had used and exploited him. It was long since I had been close to my brother. They had taken him away and made a king of him. A boy king vulnerable to the wiles of these shrewd Seymours as I was beginning to characterize them.

When I reached Hatfield House, a quietness seemed to prevail. The grooms took my horses and I went into the house. A strange man and woman came to greet me. The man bowed; the woman curtsied, while I looked askance from one to the other.

"My lady," said the man, "I must tell you that I am Sir Robert Tyrwhit, and this is my wife. We have been sent by the Lord Protector to have charge of your household."

"I . . . do not understand."

"There have been changes," he said.

"Changes! Without consulting me?"

"Yes, my lady."

"I shall want some explanations."

"Your servants John and Katharine Ashley with Thomas Parry have left Hatfield."

"Left! But they were here—"

"They left on our arrival."

"They left! Without my permission! This is my household. *I* give orders here."

"No, my lady. I have orders from the Protector and the Council. My lady will take the place of Mistress Ashley."

"Where is Kat Ashley?"

"My lady, she is on her way to the Tower of London for interrogation."

The hall seemed to swim around me. My head was pounding and I could feel one of my dreadful headaches coming on.

He went on: "Her husband and your cofferer Parry are with her. They are to be questioned too."

"But . . . for what reasons?"

I disliked the man Tyrwhit. He looked at me slyly. "You might know the answer to that question better than I do, my lady."

The man was insolent. How dared he be! And then I understood that he had reason for being so. I was, as I had feared I might be, under suspicion. His very presence meant that I was, in effect, under his guard even in my own house.

He turned to his wife. "Pray help the Princess to her chamber. This has been a shock to her."

Lady Tyrwhit came to me and laid a hand on my arm. I shook her off angrily.

"I will know more of this." I remembered that I was still the late King's daughter. "I shall demand an explanation."

"You will get it very soon, I have no doubt, my lady." There was a threat in his words and I felt limp with horror, and although I had had my misgivings I was taken by surprise.

One thought kept hammering through my aching head: Be calm. Be careful. You are in acute danger.

HOW WRETCHED I WAS without Kat! I dearly loved the frivolous creature and I was very anxious for her. And Parry . . . foolish Parry who couldn't even keep his household accounts in order, how would he fare under questioning, under torture even?

I hated Lady Tyrwhit, mostly because she wasn't Kat. I glared at her and refused to talk to her except when it was necessary. She was a patient woman and she showed no resentment. In fact she behaved rather like a jailer and even at such a time I recognized that hint of hesitation which all displayed when dealing with someone who had a claim to the throne. It suggests that they do not really believe one will ever reach that exalted position—but caution bids them play safe in case one should.

I do not remember how many days passed before Sir Robert Tyrwhit came to my bedchamber. He had sheaves of paper in his hand. These were, he explained, the confessions of Parry and Katharine Ashley.

I took them and read them. It was all there . . . the rompings, the tickling in bed, the cutting of the dress, the morning visits to my bedchamber in his nightgown with bare legs. They had told everything. Parry had said that wild horses could tear him asunder and he would not tell. How different was the true case.

I did not blame them. I just thought of them—and particularly of Kat—in some dark dungeon waiting with trepidation the hour of questioning, no doubt dreading in terror the terrible means that could be used to prize information from them. The thought of Kat on the rack was more than I could bear. I forgave them . . . readily . . . for telling all they knew.

I was ill and rather glad of it. I could shut myself away in my bedchamber and with good excuse, and only answer Lady Tyrwhit when absolutely necessary. I remembered that she had been lady-in-waiting to my stepmother and had been present at her death-bed when Katharine had accused the Admiral of wishing her ill and to be with others. And that meant me. I could understand then that vague attitude of triumph that I, who had caused her beloved mistress so much anguish, was now suffering myself.

Then I began to realize that there was some good in Lady Tyrwhit. She was better than her odious husband in any case.

The whole country was talking about Thomas Seymour. He had always caught people's attention because of his presence and good looks; and I had noticed that people like little better than to see those who are mighty brought low.

They talked more of his matrimonial ventures than his treason to the Crown. The affair of the Bristol Mint was not so interesting as what his life had been like with the Dowager Queen. It was proved that he had tried for me first—and to my horror and astonishment that he had also had his eyes on the Princess Mary and Lady Jane Grey, all not without some claim to the throne. Had he poisoned his wife? it was being asked. She had accused him on her death-bed of wanting to be rid of her. Had he not had his eyes on the Princess Elizabeth?

How do these matters become public knowledge? There are spies everywhere, as every royal daughter knows. The distressing nature of malicious gossip is that it is embellished as it passes along. It grows like a living evil, like a malevolent disease.

They were destroying my reputation. Seymour and I had been lovers, they said. I had had a child by him. One account had it that a midwife had testified that one dark night she had been taken to a house blindfold so that she would not know where she was going. She saw nothing in the house but candlelight, but she did know that she had delivered a fair young lady of a child. There was an even more horrible version. It claimed that the child had been taken away and destroyed.

I accepted the fact now that I had been entirely foolish in allowing the

Admiral to pay court to me when he was married to my stepmother; I had been duped. But the monstrous nature of these accusations infuriated me.

After much reflection, I rallied my courage. Though fearful, I wrote a carefully worded letter to the Lord Protector in which I told him that I trusted and believed in his good will toward me. I asked him directly to make a declaration that people should refrain from circulating falsehoods about me, for they must know that they were falsehoods, and I was sure they would wish to protect the King's sister from such calumny.

As a result of that letter, the Council replied that if I could point out these people who were spreading lies about me, they should be suitably punished.

It was at least some slight consolation.

I fretted for Kat. I wanted her with me. I missed her love and her gossip. I decided to plead with the Protector for her return. I could not bear to think of her a prisoner in the Tower.

"My Lord," I wrote,

"I have a request to make . . . peradventure you and the Council will think I favor her evil doing, for whom I shall speak, which is Katharine Ashley, that it would please Your Grace and the rest of the Council to be good unto her. Which thing I do, not favor her in any evil (for which I would be sorry to do), but for these considerations that follow, the which hope doth teach me in saying that I ought not to doubt but that Your Grace and the rest of the Council will think that I do it for other considerations. First, because that she hath been with me a long time, and many years, and hath taken great labor and pain in bringing me up in learning and honesty; and therefore I ought of very duty speak for her; for Saint Gregorie sayeth, 'that we are more bound to them that bringeth us up well than to our parents, for our parents do that which is natural for them that bringeth us into the world, but our bringers-up are a cause to make us live well in it.' The second is because I think that whatsoever she hath done in my Lord Admiral's matter, as concerning the marrying of me, she did it because, knowing him to be one of the Council, she thought he would not go about any such thing without he had the Council's consent thereunto; for I have heard her say many times that she would never have me marry in any place without Your Grace's and the Council's consent. The third cause is, because that it shall, and doth, make men think that I am not clear of the deed myself but that it is pardoned to me because of my youth, because that she I loved so well is in such a place . . .

"Also, if I may be so bold and not offending, I beseech Your Grace—and the rest of the Council to be good to Master Ashley, her husband, which because he is my kinsman I would be glad should do well.

"Your assured friend to my little power, Elizabeth."

I hoped my appeal would not fall on deaf ears. I did have some faith in Somerset. He lacked all the charm and good looks of his brother, but I believed him to be a just man and honest as far as men can be when the acquisition of power is the main object of their lives.

I felt numbed when a friend whispered to me that the Admiral was condemned to death. That spy Tyrwhit would be watching me closely. I must prepare myself to show no emotion when the news was brought to me of his execution.

It arrived on a blustery March day. I had steeled myself. When Tyrwhit came to me, he was not alone. He wanted evidence of the manner in which I received the news so that he could report with corroboration to his masters.

"My lady," he said, "this day Thomas Seymour laid his head upon the block."

They were watching me, all of them. I clasped my hands. They did not tremble.

I said clearly, for I had rehearsed the words: "This day died a man of much wit and very little judgment."

Calmly I took my leave of them and went into my chamber.

Through the Traitor's Gate

THREE YEARS HAD PASSED SINCE THE DEATH OF THOMAS Seymour, and I believed I had succeeded in living down the scandals which had been circulating about me at that time. I had become very ill. I do not think I realized until after the Admiral's death the strain I had endured. I had not exactly loved him—in fact I still find it difficult to analyze my feelings toward him—but death is so irrevocable and when it befalls someone whom one has known well it is a shock, particularly when one has been in fear of one's own life.

My youth, I was sure, had saved me and also the fact that I was considered of no great importance; but I knew that as my years increased, so would the danger with them.

Lady Tyrwhit was kind to me during the months following the Admiral's death and I grew fond of her, but no one could replace Kat. The Protector was, I think, a little concerned for my state of health and sent Dr Bill, a good physician, to look after me. Dr Bill realized that the cause of my debility was not entirely physical and he prescribed that my old governess, who had been released from the Tower but forbidden to return to me, should be brought back, for he was sure her presence would have a beneficial effect on my health.

To my great joy the Protector agreed, and what a glorious day that was when we were reunited. We just clung together weeping and assuring ourselves that it was really true.

Poor Kat, she had had a terrifying experience and she told me of her fears when she had been taken away. "The Tower, my lady . . . and we had betrayed you. Parry and I betrayed you . . ."

I hugged her and kissed her and told her she was a treacherous old idiot and I did not know why I loved her.

Then she said very seriously: "I would serve you with my life." And I knew she would, and I fervently hoped she would never come within the shadow of the rack again.

I had resumed my studies with Roger Ascham and they were a source of great joy to me. Edward and I wrote to each other and he was very annoyed because we were not allowed to be together. Edward was at this time thirteen and I was seventeen. After the Admiral's death I was kept very much in the background and hardly ever asserted myself; and when Edward suggested that I ask for a meeting I refrained from doing so, having learned a lesson. A seventeen-year-old girl would appear in a very different light from one of fourteen. I must never again become embroiled in what could be construed as treason. But when Edward asked for my portrait as he could not see me in person, that was one request with which I could comply.

Soon after Thomas's execution, dark clouds began to gather about the head of the Protector. The state of the country was not good; there was trouble with the Scots in the North and they had taken several castles on the Border; war was declared by the French; but the chief cause of friction was perhaps the religious conflicts within the realm. Moreover, through miscalculations, more land was being turned from arable into pasture which created hardship and resulted in the depreciation of the currency; there were risings in Oxfordshire, Buckinghamshire and Norfolk, and this last was developing into more than a revolt of the peasants. It was a rebellion, which was at length crushed successfully by John Dudley, Earl of Warwick, a man of immense ambition. His triumph in Norfolk was the start of his campaign against the Lord Protector. He obviously wanted to oust Somerset from his place and take it himself. I did not know John Dudley, but I did remember a son of his whom I had met during one of his visits to Court when I was about eight years old. We had danced together. He was about a year older than I, and something in our natures had attracted us to each other. I think we both had an unusually high opinion of ourselves, children though we were!

So when I heard that John Dudley was emerging as an enemy of Edward Seymour all I knew of him was that he was the son of the powerful Edmund Dudley who had been held responsible for the taxes imposed by my grandfather King Henry VII and whom my father had sacrificed to the block in order to placate the people soon after his accession. That . . . and he had a son named Robert.

Although I was far from the center of events, I had my own informants, careful though they were—so I was aware that two ambitious men were determined to rule the King, and through him the country. Each had his supporters, and I confess to thinking that Seymour, as the King's uncle, would prevail, for although Edward was but a boy, his word must be taken some account of, and he would always remember—even though he had rebelled against his sternness—that Edward Seymour was his uncle.

After his success against the Norfolk peasantry, John Dudley, Earl of Warwick, as he was by then, had brought two hundred captains to Seymour to demand more pay for the work they had done. When the Protector refused this, Warwick suggested that they gather together a body of men who were tired of the Protector's rule and overthrow him. Somerset, however, managed to raise ten thousand men and went to Windsor with the King. But the Council had had enough of Somerset by then. He was an able man, if ambitious, but he was stern and his manner brusque—the opposite of his brother's—and that had not endeared him to them.

Events turned against him, and it was not long before he too was judged a traitor and lodged in the Tower.

How thankful I was then to be away from Court. I did wonder what part my brother had played in this. Had he also resented those days when Somerset controlled his purse strings?

Warwick took over the role of Protector, but he could not bring himself to agree to Somerset's execution; nor could others. I supposed it crossed their minds that they could as easily be in Somerset's shoes.

So he was released, and when his eldest daughter Anne married Warwick's eldest son, Viscount Lisle, it seemed as though the two families had patched up their quarrel. Perhaps Somerset hoped to return to his former position; perhaps Warwick feared him; but it was not long before the King's uncle was once more in acute danger.

A death struggle was taking place between Edward Seymour and John Dudley. Each had his advocates but surely, as the King's uncle, Seymour must prevail even though Edward had never liked this uncle. Thomas had been his favorite and yet he had given evidence against him although he had always been so affectionate toward him. I did not altogether understand my young brother. There was something aloof and cool about him. He could not be swerved from an opinion, and he was quite fanatically religious, having more and more turned to the new reformed faith.

Events might have turned out more favorably for Edward Seymour if he had not fallen ill and had to take to his bed. That gave John Dudley his chance. He immediately gave himself a grander title than that of Earl of Warwick, and became the Duke of Northumberland; and his close friends were similarly raised to the peerage.

Then, one of his adherents, a certain Sir Thomas Palmer, who had served my father well and acquired a reputation for great courage along with a fair amount of property, decided that he had not prospered as he would have wished under the Seymour regime, and could look for advancement under that of John Dudley. One day he called on the Duke and asked if he might walk with him in his gardens. There he disclosed what he called the plot. He had evidence, he said, that Edward Seymour was planning to kill the newly created Duke of Northumberland. He was sure of this because he had been one of the conspirators. However, he had changed his mind and no longer wished to support Somerset and he was therefore throwing himself on Northumberland's mercy. The plot was to raise the country against Northumberland and bring about his downfall.

Shortly after that Edward Seymour was arrested and sent to the Tower.

For six weeks he remained there while evidence against him was collected and sifted. He was then accused of plotting to destroy the city of London, seize the Tower and the Isle of Wight and secure for himself and his heirs the crown of England.

I could scarcely believe that the man of whom we had all lived in awe for so long was now himself a prisoner.

Some months before this I had come out of my retirement. I thought the scandals had been forgotten by this time and I did not want to remain buried in the country forever. Perhaps I was safer there but after the period following the Admiral's execution I had felt so shut away that I was longing for some excitement however dangerous it might be.

My sister Mary arrived in London a day or so before I did and was given a warm welcome, but Mary was such a firm Catholic, holding so tenaciously to the old ways, that people did watch her rather warily; and when I rode in shortly afterward, there was no doubt of their pleasure in me.

I caught the whisper: "How like her father she is! It might be great Henry himself riding there! That is just how he must have looked in his young days."

I had his reddish hair and general coloring. I sat my horse well. I was upright, but whereas he had had great bulk, I was very slim. They cheered me. "Long live the Princess Elizabeth!" And I went on hearing those words echo long after I had left the streets. They were the sweetest music to me. I wanted more of their admiration after my long isolation. I responded with a rush of happiness. The truth was that I wanted to ride among them, to see their smiling faces and to hear and sense that they loved me.

Edward was delighted to see me, and made a great show of his affection, which made everyone marvel because with most people he was so aloof. He made me tell him what I was studying with Roger Ascham and we talked of Cicero and the Greek Testament with more excitement than I was sure Edward showed for the affairs of the country.

I told him about my household and the latest indiscretions of Kat Ashley, which made him smile. I had Parry back with me now, which was another great joy, but as I told Edward, now I was watchful of the household accounts myself.

We read to each other and chatted in Latin and were very happy together.

He said nothing about the trouble between Northumberland and Somerset and I was wise enough not to mention it, although I should have loved to know what his feelings were, considering it was his uncle who was in the Tower awaiting death. Perhaps he did not care, for he had been fond of Thomas and appeared quite indifferent when he went to the block.

I was very disturbed to receive a letter from Edward Seymour begging me to speak to the King on his behalf. He knew the King's love for me and he was sure I could influence him more than anyone else. If I would remind the King of their relationship and the love his uncle had always borne him . . .

I pondered that. I should have liked to show people the influence I had with Edward, but caution was at my elbow. Remember Thomas Seymour, it said. Whatever happens, do not become embroiled in their quarrels. If Northumberland knew that I had pleaded for his enemy, what would his feelings be toward me?

No, certainly I must take no part in their quarrel.

"Being so young a woman," I wrote to him, "I have no power to do anything in your behalf"; and I went on to explain that the King was surrounded by those who would resent my making such a request to him.

I was delighted to come out of my retirement and I was pleased that so many people were intent on paying respect to me. Whether this was due to the King's affection for me or whether many of them were looking ahead to the future when, if certain events took place, I might one day be Queen, I did not know; but it was very gratifying. The previous year Mary of Guise, who had married the King of Scotland, had come to Hampton Court. She had been granted safe conduct when she was returning to Scotland from France, whither she had been to visit her mother at Joinville, and storms had driven her into Portsmouth Harbour, so she had stopped at Hampton Court to pay a visit to the King. She was received with many honors and she and her ladies, although they were only in the country for a week or so, had a great influence on the fashions. The French costumes were copied, and hair was worn frizzed and curled just as the French ladies wore it.

This had the effect of making our ladies all look very much alike, so I decided to have none of it. I wore my own hair smooth and clung to the plainness of my ordinary garments. This meant that I attracted attention everywhere I went, and if the ladies of the Court thought I was out of step, the people in the streets liked it. I heard warm compliments everywhere— "Our little *English* Princess," they called me. And the approval of the people in the streets meant more to me than that of frivolous courtiers. It was also perhaps a sense that I was gaining of how to be entirely myself that I might always be marked for my individual view and never one to accept the mode of the moment, whether of dress or of more important matters.

In due course the inevitable happened. Edward Seymour lost his head on the block—three years after the death of his brother, the Admiral.

Our master was now John Dudley, Duke of Northumberland.

→>-<←

CLEARLY I REMEMBER that Christmas of 1552. The festivities were held at Greenwich and I was looking forward to spending much time with my brother.

As soon as I was in his presence I noticed that he looked rather more tired than usual, although he had never been robust. I inquired anxiously after his health and he told me he had a wretched cough which kept him awake at night.

I asked what his physicians thought about it. "They are always hanging round me," he told me.

There were the usual entertainments, which most seemed to enjoy, but I was aware of a certain preoccupation in the minds of those present, not least the Duke of Northumberland, and I guessed there was a good deal of concern for the King's condition.

I myself felt very uneasy wondering what would happen if Edward died. Mary—according to my father's will—should be Queen, but for so many years there had been such deep divisions among the people about religion. She was fanatical in her beliefs and declared that she would die for them, so if she became Queen it was certain that she would attempt to bring Catholicism back to the whole country as the one true faith. There were many who were violently against that—Edward himself for one—but if it came to it, he would not be here to have a say!

I could see great trouble if Edward should die. I must tread warily among those who continued to watch me. If Mary came to the throne and England became again a Catholic country, what next? Should we have the dread Inquisition introduced into the land? Mary's mother had been Katharine of Aragon of course, and she had brought up Mary close to Spanish as well as Roman influences. There would be many to stand against any purge of the new faith, my friends assured me. But I was determined to hold my own counsel in matters of faith. Fanaticism had no appeal to me.

Edward being so poorly, all these thoughts must enter the mind, and in view of my own position as one who had had a Protestant upbringing—even though I could be very flexible in the matter of religion—I knew I was passing into dangerous times.

I was alert, watchful—that was a memorable Christmas for me.

I do not know whether Edward felt death near, but during the months which followed he began to concern himself very deeply with the poor and needy. He talked to me about them and how it grieved him to contemplate their sufferings. He wanted to do something for them and no matter what opposition he encountered he intended to.

There was, as a matter of fact, no opposition to his proposals. Perhaps those about him felt they had to humor a dying boy.

The first thing he did was hand over the Palace of Bridewell to the corporation of London as a workhouse for poor and idle people, which meant that there could always be a roof over the heads of some who would otherwise be homeless, as long as they were prepared to comply with the rules of the institution. He had arranged that Christ's Hospital, the old Greyfriars' Monastery, should be turned into a school for poor scholars, and that St Thomas's Hospital should be used for the treatment of the poor who were sick.

These arrangements seemed to give him much pleasure and I told him that his goodness would be remembered for centuries to come and that contented him and I am sure made him feel that however ineffectual he was as a king, he had achieved something of value which would live after him.

I could have wept when I looked at his pale thin face; he had lost a great deal of weight during the months since Christmas. He said he felt tired always.

Once, when I was riding through London, I saw two men in the pillory and on asking what had been their offense, I was told that they had talked unwarily of the King's illness and said that he was being slowly poisoned.

I shivered, though I did not believe this calumny for a moment. But it did mean that the country was preparing itself for the death of the boy King, so I went down to Hatfield and decided to watch events from some little distance.

I had been made aware—by some who held concern for my future—of what was in Northumberland's mind. Lord Guildford Dudley was married to Lady Jane Grey. Guildford was Northumberland's fourth son, but the others were all married. Later I often thought how close Robert Dudley came to being in Guildford's shoes.

July had come and on the sixth of that month a terrible storm blew up— the worst in living memory. The sky darkened and the thunder rolled; and people gazed in terror at the sky, fearing such a storm could only be an expression of God's anger.

My brother Edward lay in his bed at Greenwich Palace. He must have known that he was near the end of his life, but he would not be afraid to die. In fact I believed he would welcome death. He was not suited to his role; he would never be a great king; he was as different from our father as it was possible to be. I thought of Mary who stood next in line. She had been kind to me always but I knew she would alienate the people, with her intense religious fervor, and there were many people in the country who were determined to remain Protestant. Oh, why had a perverse fate in the first place made me a girl and in the second set me so far from the throne! I had had the good sense to go to Hatfield realizing that it is necessary to remain at a safe distance from great events, until one has decided what is the best way to act. The time was not yet ripe for me.

It was on that same sixth day of July that a messenger arrived at Hatfield. I did not recognize his livery but he asked if he could speak to me alone. I immediately granted this permission, and when he told me he came from William Cecil, I was all attention.

Sir William Cecil had been Protector Somerset's secretary, and when his master fell, Cecil had been put into the Tower where he stayed for two months. It was clear, however, that he was a man of exceptional ability, and so he was released and became one of the Secretaries of State. He had effected some business for me once during the lifetime of Somerset, and I had a fancy that he had been rather impressed by me and felt a certain friendship for me. I understood that he secretly saw me as the hope of the future as far as the Protestants were concerned. He feared the accession of my half-sister Mary and the havoc it could bring and he had risked a great deal to send to me now.

The messenger told me that he was a very confidential servant of Sir William who had entrusted him with this errand. The Duke of Northumberland, he told me, had prevailed upon the ill young King to name Lady Jane Grey as his successor.

"That is impossible!" I cried. "My father stated clearly in his will that the Lady Mary, as his eldest daughter, was to follow Edward if he died without heirs."

"That is so, my lady, but the Duke of Northumberland has persuaded the King to change that. It is for this reason that Northumberland has married his son Guildford Dudley to the Lady Jane. They intend her to be Queen, and Guildford King."

"The country will never allow it."

"So thinks my master. But he has sent me hither, my lady, to warn you that you are in grave danger. As soon as the King dies, the Duke will request you and the Lady Mary to come to London. When you arrive you will be placed in the Tower—for your safety, he will say. My lady, my master has sent me to say that you must find some excuse for not obeying that summons."

"I see," I said. "Thank your master. I shall not forget his service to me. I intend to retire to my bed with a grievous sickness which will prevent my leaving here until I am well enough to do so."

"That is what my master thinks you should do, my lady."

As soon as he had gone I went to bed, and sure enough later that day Northumberland's messenger arrived. He begged to see me at once and was told that I was sick. I sent Kat down to see what he had to say.

She returned breathless. "The Duke of Northumberland sends hastily to you. The King is grievously sick and wishes to see you."

I thought to myself: Edward is already dead. Oh, William Cecil you are a very good friend to me.

Kat returned to tell the messenger that I was much too ill myself to leave my bed but as soon as I was well enough I should go to my brother.

That had to satisfy him for the time.

Kat came back to me a little reproachfully. "The King has been a good brother to you, my lady."

"Indeed he was."

"And what is this sudden sickness?"

"An attack of wisdom, Kat. Northumberland wants me in the Tower. He knows the people will not easily accept Jane Grey."

Kat was bewildered, but I told her what I knew, so that we could talk together.

A few days later, the news was released.

The King was dead, and before he had died, since both of his sisters were declared bastards, he had named Lady Jane Grey heir to the throne. For that reason the Duke of Northumberland, following the King's wishes, had proclaimed Lady Jane Queen of England.

Even though I had been expecting this, it was hard to believe it. How dared Northumberland! John Dudley was a bold man, I knew, but this was madness. He had made Jane his daughter-in-law with this in mind, of course, but the country would never accept this flouting of the natural laws of succession. I would be ready to swear that my sister Mary was already gathering forces to take the crown. But . . . which way would the battle go? So much depended on the people. Mary was the rightful heir but did the people want an ardent Catholic? Mary had right on her side, but Northumberland was a very powerful man.

The country was aghast. I heard that many believed that the great storm which had thundered while the King lay dying was an indication of God's wrath because the wishes of King Henry VIII had been set aside and his daughters disinherited for the sake of his sister's granddaughter.

Would the people accept the violation of the law?

But, to my outrage, the fact remained that Lady Jane Grey had been proclaimed Queen of England.

I WAS RIGHT when I had thought the country would never accept this flagrant violation of the rights of succession. Men flocked to Mary's banner and deserted that of Northumberland. Within a week or so the Duke and Jane Grey, Guildford Dudley with her, were in the Tower. My sister Mary

was proclaimed Queen of England. Poor Jane, she had never wanted to be
Queen; she had even had to be beaten into submission before she would
agree to marry Guildford Dudley, and I heard that she had fainted when
they had told her that she was the Queen. She was not yet seventeen and had
never been ambitious; she was merely the tool of power-seeking men. I was
very sorry for her. She had been ensconced in the White Tower, living with
the state of a queen awaiting her coronation, and straight from there was
taken to the House of the Lieutenant of the Tower, there to await the axe.
Guildford was sent to Beauchamp Tower with his brothers. I thought fleet-
ingly of Robert and supposed this would be the end of him. He must have
been fighting with his father when he was captured. I was sorry; he had been
an interesting boy and I had noticed him from the first. I remembered now
how something had been said about marriage and I had replied very firmly:
"I have no intention of marrying . . . ever . . ." which had made him laugh
and tell me I was only a girl and would change my mind later. Strange that
I should remember that. I supposed it was because he was now a prisoner in
the Tower destined for imminent death. The Tower, where my beautiful
mother had lost her head! I had felt this sadness at the time of Katharine
Howard's death, and I thought again now how close the axe was to us all.
And perhaps a little nearer to some than others!

I should have to be even more wary. I was only one step from the throne
now and Mary was not exactly a robust lady, nor was she very young. She
would have to be quick if she were going to produce an heir to the throne.
And if she did not . . . I could grow dizzy contemplating the prospect. But
none knew more than I that there were dangerous times to be lived through
first.

What should I do now? I needed William Cecil to advise me. My own
wits told me that I should do nothing until commanded to by the Queen. I
wondered what Mary's attitude to me would be. My great dread was that she
would try to make a Catholic of me. I must not accept that. I had guessed
the mood of the people and I knew they did not want Catholicism again in
this country, and from now on my actions were going to be those which
would best please the people. But I must needs disguise my religious con-
victions meanwhile. Such as they were.

Messengers from my sister arrived at Hatfield. It was her wish that I
should ride beside her when she made her triumphant entry into London.
Now was the time for me to recover from my illness and prepare for my
journey.

On the twenty-ninth of July I left Hatfield and attended by two thousand horsemen armed with spears and bows, I came to Somerset House,

QUEEN OF THIS REALM

which now belonged to me. With us came the members of my household, all very splendid in green coats faced with velvet, taffeta or satin. I was proud of them, for I did not want to show myself to the people of London as a pauper.

The next day I set out for Wanstead where my meeting with the Queen was to take place; but I did not take my armed band with me this time. My instinct told me that this would displease my sister and her advisers and very likely suggest to her that I wished to display a show of might. I wanted to convey to her that I was not only her affectionate sister but her loyal subject.

We met at Wanstead. Mary had disbanded her army and had merely a bodyguard and her attendants to show that there was no need for protection; she came as the acknowledged Queen. She greeted me with a show of affection and kissed me. The watching crowds cheered. I was aware all the time that I was the one they watched, the one they smiled at, and I knew that they cheered more for me than for my sister. I presented some of my ladies to her and she kissed them to show friendship.

Beside Mary I felt young and vital and I was convinced that everything I ever wanted would one day be mine. It was a wonderfully exhilarating feeling as we rode side by side. I was twenty, and at moments like this I always looked my best; I was taller than Mary and straighter; the bright color of my hair attracted attention and it was accentuated by the milky whiteness of my skin, whereas Mary was thirty-seven and she looked it. I could not help the glow of satisfaction which it gave me to consider the contrast we must make. When the people cheered I smiled at them and lifted my hand in acknowledgment. Mary gave no smiles. Perhaps she thought it was beneath the dignity of a queen to do so. I do not think she understood the people as I was beginning to do.

And so we rode to Aldgate and from there to the Tower of London.

As we entered the fortress I could not help wondering whether Jane Grey could see us from her prison window, or perhaps Robert Dudley. Would he remember the little girl who had danced with him at that Court function long ago? I was very different now; so must he be.

Then I forgot about the prisoners, for we were being received by the Lieutenant of the Tower and other officers and everyone was eager to show homage to the Queen.

Mary thanked them with grace and dignity, and to show that she meant to be a merciful Queen, several of the prisoners received their pardon. They were all Catholics. First there was the same Duke of Norfolk, who had been saved from execution by my father's timely death; the next was Stephen Gardiner, Bishop of Winchester, who had been a prisoner in the Tower for

some years. I had never liked him; he was a bigoted Catholic and one of
those who had tried to bring about the fall of Katharine Parr—and that was
something I would never forget. He had in the last reign offended Somerset
with his religious insistences and as a result found himself in the Tower.
When he fell on his knees before Mary she was very moved and bade him
rise and gave him his freedom. Whereupon he declared his greatest joy
would be to serve her with his life. My heart sank. He was an enemy of mine
and he would now, I was certain, receive a high place at Court.

There was another prisoner who attracted more attention than the others because of his tall bearing and handsome fair coloring. He looked what
he was—a descendant of the Plantagenets. It was because of this that he had
been a prisoner in the Tower since he was twelve years old, which was nearly
fifteen years before. Poor young man, his fault was that he was a great-great-
grandson of Edward IV.

As the sun shone on his fair hair he looked very attractive and even
younger than his twenty-seven years. My sister seemed very impressed by
him. His father had been executed at the time of Edward Courtenay's incar-
ceration, and when Mary told him that his title of Earl of Devonshire should
be restored to him with his estates he was overcome by gratitude. Mary
looked less stern as she regarded him and that was more becoming in her.

It was a triumphant entry and when we sat down at the banquet which
had been prepared for us, I was still at the Queen's side.

MY SISTER HAS BEEN condemned for her cruelty and by the end of her
reign for generations to come she was known as Bloody Mary. But she was
in many ways a kind woman. She was not really cruel; she avoided the shedding of blood unless she believed it was necessary to shed it. But she was
bound all the time by her fanatical belief in the Church of Rome, and like
most fanatics was not content that she herself believed this, but insisted as
well that everyone else must do the same. Those who were not Catholics
were in her opinion doomed to eternal damnation, and it seemed to her that
the only possible action she could take to save them was to help them reform
before death. If they persisted in ignoring the truth, then they were doomed
to eternal torment, and it could not matter much if they went to it earlier
than later. What were a few years in eternity?

I believe that there is a hint of madness in all fanaticism and I determined then that I should never become the victim of it. The only matter
which would arouse my unswerving devotion and effort would be the good
of my country, and if ever I was fortunate enough to rule, I would act in
whatever way I considered best for my realm.

There was a similarity of purpose in us: Mary's was to return England to

the Church of Rome; mine was to make my country great, and I would sway
with circumstances whenever it was necessary to make her so.

I could not help it, but during that ride through the streets of London
to the Tower I could almost feel the crown on my head. But I must remember Jane Grey—a queen in her state apartments one day, a prisoner the next.
I must remember Norfolk, Gardiner and Courtenay. A few days can bring
about disastrous changes in the life of those in high places. I was well aware
that the perils about me were increasing.

This was borne home to me by a visitor who had come to say goodbye
to me before he left. Sir William Cecil had shown himself to be my friend,
and I was in need of friends, so I received him with pleasure.

He had, of course, been totally opposed to the plan to make Lady Jane
Grey Queen.

"Northumberland made the decision and forced it on the judges and the
nobility," he declared. "I objected and only added my signature to the document under protest, making it clear that I signed as a witness only. I then
resigned my post as Secretary of State. Queen Mary is the rightful heir to the
throne. It is well that Northumberland was defeated, but I feel sorrow for
Lady Jane Grey."

"I do not believe the Queen will be harsh with her," I said. "She knows
that Jane was not at fault. She was forced to do it, as she was forced to marry
Northumberland's son."

"Let us hope the Queen will be merciful to the innocent. I have come to
warn you, my lady, of the dangers which beset you."

"I know they are there."

"Perhaps you do not know the full extent of them. You have a powerful
enemy in Gardiner."

"I know it well. I shall never forget how he tried to destroy Katharine
Parr."

"You must be wary of him, and there are two other men against whom
you should be on your guard."

I looked askance at him and he went on: "Simon Renaud, the Spanish
Ambassador, and Antoine de Noailles, Ambassador of France. They have
orders from their masters concerning affairs in this country. The Spaniards,
as you know, demand a return to Rome, and then a marriage would doubtless be arranged between Queen Mary and Philip, son of the Emperor
Charles. Then it would be inevitable that before long our country would be
ruled by Spain. Our people will not tolerate persecution and the setting up of
the Inquisition. They will revolt against it and look to the Protestant heiress."

I turned pale. I said: "Do you mean that there could be war in this country . . . war against the *Queen*?"

"That could well be. I feel certain that the people of England will never tolerate Spanish bigotry. Renaud knows this, but he will instill the Queen with his ideas and if this Spanish marriage takes place, we shall have Philip himself here to subdue our people. Renaud knows this; the Spaniards know it. That is why you have become an object of interest to them. I believe they may well plot against you."

"You fill me with fears, Master Cecil."

"I merely warn you, my lady. You must be on your guard. This Court is full of enemies . . . your enemies now. The last hope for England could rest with you."

I said: "I would serve my country with my life if need be."

"I believe that to be so. Renaud is not the only enemy. There is the French Ambassador to consider. The French would like to see a return to the Church of Rome, but their interest is more political. The little Queen of Scots is betrothed to the Dauphin of France and the King of France believes that it would be an excellent idea if Mary were Queen of England as well as Scotland. You see what I mean?"

"You mean that not only men like Gardiner are seeking to destroy me, but the Spanish and French ambassadors as well?"

"I mean, my lady, that having become aware of your mettle I know that you are one who will listen to advice—however menacing—and perhaps for that very reason give your full consideration to it."

"I know you speak with wisdom and out of concern for me. I thank you with all my heart, and if ever the time shall come . . . you will not be for-gotten."

He told me that my wisest plan would be to leave Court entirely, when I could do so without ostentation. "Do not attempt to go as if in fear. Invent a plausible excuse."

"I shall be ill."

"That is the best. Let them think you sickly. But I warn you, that will not prevent their schemes from taking shape."

"I know that since my father's death I have stepped from the shade of obscurity to the blaze of noon."

"True," he said. "Your actions will be observed and reported to the Courts of Spain and France . . . and to your sister. Tread warily, my lady Princess, for the hearts and hopes of our people will rest with you."

I thanked him again and he took my hand and knelt as though I were already Queen of England.

Soon after that he left Court and went to live quietly between his houses at Wimbledon and Burleigh.

→>-<←

CHE COURC MOVED to Whitehall and I was with it. Stephen Gardiner had been made Lord High Chancellor of the Realm and Edward Courtenay was always at the Queen's side. She treated him rather as though he were a young boy and there was a certain childishness about him which I supposed was due to having lived all those years shut away from the real world in a prison. He had never really grown up. I did not forget what William Cecil had said to me, and I was very wary in everything I did or said.

The great problem was religion. The people now regarded me as the Protestant hope. To them I represented a more tolerant way of life than they believed they would find under a return to Rome; and in view of the increasing stories we had heard of the repressions and torture of the Inquisition—and especially in Spain—the people did not relish a similar state of affairs in England.

If ever they should reject Mary and her Catholicism, they would look to me, so I knew that it was imperative for me not to accept the Catholic Faith. If ever I did, I should not be preferred to my sister—a young bigot would be just as bad as an old one, perhaps worse.

The first trouble came when there was a requiem mass for my brother. The idea of having mass for him was wrong in any case because it was the last thing he would have wanted. He had been almost as fanatical a supporter of the Reformed Faith as my sister was of the Catholic. I knew that whatever happened I must not attend.

Mary was very angry and I asked for an audience so that I could explain to her, but she refused to grant it.

I wondered how I could get away from Court, but to go now would seem like running away. I must face it, and as I had some faith in Mary's natural kindness of heart, which had been shown to me in the past, I was sure that if she would see me, if I could be alone with her, I could explain.

When Parliament was called, Gardiner's first act as Lord Chamberlain was to declare my father's marriage to Katharine of Aragon legal, which meant that Mary was legitimate and therefore that I was not.

I was sure that if Sir William Cecil were here he would say that in itself was not such a bad thing, as it implied that I had no right to the throne and that should, of course, make me less vulnerable to attack at the moment. However, I strongly resented it, but kept my resentment to myself.

In due course Mary said she would receive me, and when I went to her she allowed me to kiss her hand, which I did with the utmost respect, and I told her that it grieved me greatly that she was displeased with me.

"All you have to do to please me is to return to the true faith," she said.

"I find it hard, Your Majesty, to make myself believe. I can only believe what my mind allows me to."

"Belief will come. You must open your mind."

I almost said she was asking me to shut my mind as tightly as hers was shut, but of course I did not. It would naturally have angered her, when what I desperately needed was to placate her, to gain her forgiveness, her leniency, and yet deny what she was trying to press on me.

Could I go to Mass? Would it be easier? I thought of those shouting crowds. "Long Live the Princess Elizabeth!" There was an affinity between those people and myself. They saw me as their Queen-to-be just as I saw myself; it was what they wanted and what I wanted.

I must tread very carefully.

"As you love me . . ." I began.

"You are my sister," Mary interrupted me, "and as such I have regard for you, but I cannot love a heretic. That would go against God's Will."

Since when, I wondered, had God taught man to hate his fellow man?

I covered my face with my hands as though in great grief. "My sister," I said, "I shall never forget your kindness to me when I was small and alone. We were both outcasts then. We were together . . ."

"The mistake was in your upbringing. You had teachers who cared more for scholarship than for religious teaching."

I begged her to be patient with me.

"I have shown patience," she said. "But if you would please me, you must go to Mass. There you will in time understand the truth. You may go now. But remember this. You shall go to Mass. It is my command."

I was trembling when I left her. So I should have to go to Mass. The people would hear of it. They would say, "So she is not our Protestant Princess after all."

I knew I dared not disobey the Queen's command. Gardiner was only waiting for a chance to put me in the Tower. After all, what had been Edward Courtenay's fault? Only that he had been a Plantagenet. For that accident of birth he had spent fifteen years of his short life in prison.

So I went to Mass. As usual I took refuge in illness, but still I had to go. My ladies almost carried me into the chapel. I made it seem as though I were half fainting, and as we came into the chapel I caused them to stop and rub my stomach. "I am afflicted by grievous pains," I said.

That would be reported. It might tell the people that I had been most reluctant to go to Mass.

MARY SHELVED HER ANNOYANCE with me during the Coronation. Perhaps she knew that because of my popularity with the people I must be seen to play a prominent part in it.

It was the usual grand ceremony which the people loved and expected on such occasions and whatever king or queen was on the throne everyone was determined to have a good day's outing and enjoy the pageantry.

Three days before the event Mary left St James's for Whitehall and from there took a barge to the Tower accompanied by her ladies—and with me beside her.

It was thrilling to arrive at the Tower and hear the guns roar out their welcome and to see all the craft on the river with their streamers and musical instruments.

The next day we made our procession through the streets of London surrounded by a splendid array of Court officials and noblemen. I noticed my two archenemies among the party—Renaud and de Noailles. Mary was borne in a splendid litter drawn by six white horses and covered in cloth of silver. She wore a gown of blue velvet trimmed with ermine and on her head was a gold net caul covered in pearls and precious stones. She looked pale and I guessed that caul must be a great weight; and she did suffer from headaches. It was different with me; I too suffered from headaches but mine had the pleasant nature of never appearing on occasions which I could enjoy as I did this one.

I followed just behind my sister in a chariot covered with crimson velvet and with me rode my father's fourth wife—the only one now alive, Anne of Cleves, a very pleasant lady of whom I had always been fond. We were dressed in robes of cloth of silver with long hanging sleeves which fell back most becomingly when I waved to the crowds. The cheers for me were deafening, and I felt gleeful because they were greater than those for the Queen herself—although I knew this could be dangerous, for I would not be the only one who noticed this.

I loved the pageantry and all the time I was thinking: One day this will be for me.

I laughed heartily over the four giants who greeted us in Fenchurch Street and the angel perched on the arch in Gracechurch Street, who looked like a statue until she suddenly came to life and blew her trumpet. The people were already getting merry on the wine which ran in the Cornhill and Cheapside conduits as the Mayor escorted the Queen through Temple Bar to Whitehall.

On the morning of the Coronation itself we took to the barges and landed at Westminster stairs when we went to the Palace and prepared ourselves for the great occasion.

The procession from the Palace to the Abbey began at eleven o'clock. The Barons of the Cinque Ports held the canopy over the Queen and I walked immediately behind her, which was the place for the heir. She is thirty-seven years old, I kept telling myself. She will marry soon. She must.

But will she get an heir? She looked so pale and tired, but she would certainly do her best to get a Catholic heir. How much did she resent me in the place I now occupied?

I might be called a bastard, but my father's will had named me as the next in succession after her and they could not go against my father's will. They had seen what had happened to Northumberland when he had tried to do that.

Gardiner was performing the ceremony. She had chosen him although it was usually the duty of the Archbishop of Canterbury. Gardiner was going to be her chief adviser. And he was my bitter enemy. I did believe that if he could have removed me without causing too much bother he would have done so by now.

I listened to the words.

"Here present is Mary, rightful and undoubted inheritrix by the laws of God and man to the Crown and royal dignity of the realm of England, France and Ireland . . ."

It was true that she was the rightful and undoubted heir and one day— God willing—I should stand in her place.

When the ceremony was over, we returned with the whole train to Westminster Hall for the banquet, and I was happy to notice that all due respect was paid to me. The Queen had me seated beside her on the left hand and next to me sat Anne of Cleves. I was aware of all eyes on me and I forgot the warnings and the dangers as I dreamed of the future.

Edward Dymoke made the challenge, throwing down his gauntlet, which no one picked up, proclaiming to all that Mary was the true Queen and accepted as such by all the company.

I felt elated until, the ceremony over, we took to our barges for the short journey to Whitehall Stairs, and as the cold river breezes touched my face, I knew there were untold perils all about me.

KAT ASHLEY BROUGHT me rumors of what was being said at Court, and one such was that the Queen might marry Edward Courtenay.

"She is very fond of him," said Kat, "and she would be able to command him absolutely."

"Well," I replied. "Perhaps it would not be such a bad thing. He is after all a Plantagenet and so has royal blood."

But that proved to be merely a rumor, for soon after that it was announced that the Queen proposed to marry Philip of Spain.

How foolish it was of Mary to agree to this, but I supposed that Gardiner and Renaud, the Spanish Ambassador, persuaded her. One thing I was sure of: the French Ambassador would be most put out. The last thing he wanted was to see a strong alliance between Spain and England. What Mary had not considered was the reaction of the people. It very soon became apparent that there was growing uneasiness among those who followed the Reformed Faith, and even those English people who were not so concerned with religion did not care for foreigners or foreign rule. They had heard of the possibility of a marriage with Edward Courtenay and this was what they favored.

Mary was making herself unpopular, something no sovereign should do. Then I became really alarmed because there was a suggestion that *I* should marry Edward Courtenay. That terrified me. I wanted no hurried marriage, for the future was uncertain. I wanted to be free to do whatever was necessary when the time came.

I felt nothing would come of these suggestions because Gardiner would surely be against such a marriage. He could not want me to marry a man who could be said to have a faint claim to the throne through his Plantagenet ancestors.

Now that I had been proclaimed a bastard, which I must be if the marriage between my father and Mary's mother was valid, others took precedence over me, even though I was heiress presumptive to the throne. The Countess of Lennox, the daughter of Margaret Queen of Scotland, was one, and even the Duchess of Suffolk, whose daughter Jane Grey was still in the Tower, was another.

I found this hard to endure. I had more headaches. I began to look delicate and one day the Queen noticed this.

I told her I was feeling unwell and longed for the country air. She said nothing at the time but she must have consulted Gardiner on the advisability of sending me away from Court. I believe he was rather concerned that in spite of his efforts to denigrate me, I still had the favor of the people in the streets and whenever I appeared they made this apparent. Perhaps because of this he agreed that it might be a good idea to let me go, and the Queen sent for me to tell me of her decision.

I was greatly relieved. I fell on my knees and thanked her for her kindness.

"Dear Majesty," I said, "I beg of you do not believe any ill you may hear of me. If such a thing should happen, will you please do me the honor of receiving me so that you may hear the truth from my lips? For I am not only your sister but your servant."

She said she believed me and gave me a pearl necklace and a hood of rich sable fur as a token of her regard for me.

And feeling more easy in my mind than I had for some time, I rode down to Ashridge.

→>−<←

IN SPITE OF MY determination to live quietly in the country, out of harm's way, I was now passing into what some might say was the most dangerous period of my life. I knew there were strong feelings against Mary's proposed Spanish match; Sir William Cecil had made me aware of the antagonism of the powerful Spanish and French Ambassadors; what I did not know was that those who wished me well could prove my undoing.

Jane Grey was still in the Tower but I felt sure that in due course my sister intended to release her. I had heard that the Spanish Ambassador had urged her to sign the order for Jane's execution and that Mary refused, saying that the girl was in her present position through no fault of her own, for she was just turned sixteen years old and it was certain that she had never sought the greatness which had been thrust upon her. I was glad that Mary could still stand firm against Renaud, but I wondered how firm she would be when she married Philip, if it came to that.

I was sorry for Mary in a way. She suffered such ill health and from what I had seen she was ready to idolize Philip. Since her mother had died there could have been little love in her life, and Mary, like so many of those stern and forbidding people, craved love more than most of us. I had had to make do with the devotion of my servants, people like Kat Ashley; but I had had that, and I had always been sure of my ability to attract people to me. The cheers of the people in the streets filled me with wild exulting happiness; but that was different. I wanted no lover who would, as lovers do in time, seek to control me. I did not want love as Mary did. She had not yet seen Philip yet her eyes softened at the mention of him, her voice grew gentle and she glowed with a rare softness. Oh, if ever Philip came to England he would have an easy victory. He would so subjugate the Queen that he would become the country's unquestioned ruler—unquestioned by her, but not by the people. I had a feeling that they would never tolerate the yoke of Spain. They would look to others to release them from it. I shivered yet exulted at the thought.

Never, never again, must I go to Mass, however unwillingly.

It seemed that Mary was satisfied with shedding the blood of Northumberland—with which everyone would agree. He had been the instigator of the plot; he was the villain who had tried to change the succession. She blamed him and few others. The Dudley men were still in the Tower under sentence of death; even Guildford still lived. It was certainly wrong to brand Mary a cruel Queen.

She wanted peace, and she wanted Philip and an heir to the throne; but what she wanted more than anything was to bring England back to Rome. As I saw it that would be her tragedy and that of the nation, for she did not understand the English people well enough to realize that although they will appear acquiescing up to a point, although they will give the impression that they are too lazy to care much about serious matters, there will come a point when they take a stand, and then they will be formidable.

I knew this, but then I had made the people of England my special concern, and I always would, for I knew that finally they are the ones who make the decisions.

It was not long before there was a protest about the proposed marriage, and because of my position and in spite of the fact that I was hidden away in the country, I was made the center of it.

Whether Thomas Wyatt would have become involved if Edward Courtenay had not approached him, I doubt. Courtenay, who had been such a favorite of Mary's since as a prisoner in the Tower he had knelt before her on the Green and obtained his pardon, was naturally angry because she had turned from him and was planning to take Philip of Spain for her husband. Perhaps some latent ambition in Courtenay had been fired; perhaps he had set his mind on being King through Mary. He had not taken kindly to the idea of marriage with me. Nor had I. I considered him weak and I had no admiration for weak men. Moreover I saw in marriage a trap—not only to my personal freedom but to my future plans. When the time came . . . *if* the time came . . . I wanted to be free and uncluttered.

However, the plotters calculated that if Mary could be deposed and I set up as Queen with Courtenay as my husband (no foreigners were wanted) we should put an end to the Spanish threat and ensure a Protestant country.

Thus Sir Thomas Wyatt became leader of that insurrection which was to put me in acute peril.

He was the son of that other Thomas Wyatt, friend of my father, who had been in love with my mother. After a somewhat wild youth he had distinguished himself in military operations, and had supported Mary when Northumberland had tried to put Jane Grey on the throne; but the decision to marry Philip of Spain had disturbed and angered him. Yet he might have been like so many of his countrymen, resentful but inactive, had he not had a communication from Edward Courtenay suggesting that he should stand with him against the Spanish match.

Wyatt was a good soldier but an impulsive young man. Instead of weighing up the chances of success, he immediately declared his willingness to join in; and he was certain that he could arouse the whole of Kent to the cause.

Accordingly he invited all the noblemen of the neighborhood to Allington Castle, the Kentish home of the Wyatt family, to discuss plans. In the meantime Courtenay with the Earl of Suffolk and others tried to do the same. Their efforts met with no success and they were soon betrayed and arrested which left Wyatt as leader of the operation to which he had merely been called in to take a part.

It was too late for him to desist as he had always made his feelings clear and put himself in a very unsafe position, so he went to Maidstone, proclaimed his intentions there and, using the skill he had acquired in the army, soon had fifteen hundred men under his command while as many as five thousand had promised to join him. Cannon and ammunition were sent to him by sympathizers and when news of what was happening reached the Queen and her advisers in London, it was decided that action must be taken.

First a proclamation was made, offering free pardon to all those rebels who would go peacefully to their homes. This had the effect of depriving Wyatt of a great many of his followers. Some of those who had set out to join him had been intercepted and dispersed by the Queen's forces.

In a week or so the euphoria had faded and Wyatt's position looked desperate. It had not been his idea in the first place and I fancy he must have been regretting that he had ever been caught up in an enterprise which had little hope of succeeding. He tried to uphold the spirits of those who remained with him by telling them that help from France was on the way, which seemed plausible enough because the last thing the French wanted was a union between England and Spain.

At Ashridge I waited eagerly for the news. I knew, as did everyone else, that the object of the insurrection was to depose Mary and set me up in her place. My feelings were mixed. I did not want to come to the throne in this way. History had taught me that it is most unsafe for one monarch to depose another. I thought of Henry IV and my own grandfather Henry VII. Neither of these men had worn the crown with any sense of security. Always they had been on the lookout for those who would rise against them. When the crown came to me I wanted it to come naturally . . . by right of inheritance. I did not want to snatch it from my sister who many would continue to think was the rightful heir. Had my advice been sought I would never have agreed to Wyatt's making this effort.

But he had done so and I—however unwillingly—was involved.

Wyatt had a stroke of luck. The Queen sent a force to meet him, but she and her advisers had foolishly miscalculated Wyatt's strength. The force was not as strong as Wyatt's and when it reached Rochester and realized the size of the army ranged against it, the Queen's men lost heart. Some of them even joined Wyatt; the leaders fled; and soon Wyatt was marching on London at the head of four thousand men.

The government was in a panic. It needed time to raise an army and, to gain time, it offered to parley with Wyatt. Mary then showed herself to be a true Queen, and her father's daughter. She went to the Guildhall and there spoke to the people of London, telling them that they must rise and save the city from the rebels. She was the Queen and had no intention of parleying with traitors and she called on the citizens of London to come to the protection of their city.

In the midst of all this a messenger came to Ashridge.

Kat came bursting into my chamber, full of excitement. Her experiences in the Tower had subdued her a little, but there were times when she could not suppress her excitement at what was happening. She was so certain that I was going to be the savior of my country, and the sooner I was on the throne the better.

"My lady," she cried, "there is a gentleman below who would see you. He says it is of the utmost importance."

"What gentleman is this?" I asked, and I felt alarm beginning to stir in me. If it was someone connected with the rebellion, I wanted none of it.

"It is young Lord Russell, my lady. The Earl of Bedford's son."

"What does Bedford's son want here?"

"Better go and see, my lady," replied Kat, her eyes glistening.

I hesitated. Should I see him? Was it wise?

I went to him. He fell on his knees before me, a gesture which both delighted and alarmed me.

He said he had come with a message from Sir Thomas Wyatt. Sir Thomas begged me not to go near the metropolis . . . in fact to remove myself farther from it than I was at present.

I replied: "Why should I do this, my lord?"

"My lady, great events are afoot. Sir Thomas Wyatt is anxious that you should be kept out of danger."

"I have no part in Sir Thomas Wyatt's matters," I said.

He bowed and replied that he had merely come to deliver the message.

I was relieved when he went.

A few days later the Queen's messenger arrived.

I was very cautious now and I remained in my bedchamber whenever anyone came to Ashridge. Thus I did not emerge until I was sure who the visitors were, so I did not see the Queen's messenger until I was prepared for him.

Kat came to my room, her eyes wide, and even she was alarmed.

"He has come to escort you to London on orders of the Queen," she said.

I felt faint. I did not believe for one moment that Wyatt would succeed; moreover one of his fellow conspirators was Suffolk, the father of Jane Grey.

If the rebellion was a success, I would not be the one he would want to see Queen. Jane was a prisoner in the Tower and Suffolk's plan would surely be to release her and put her back on the throne.

I looked at Kat. I was already pulling off my gown.

"Come, help me to bed," I said.

She stared at me.

"Hurry!" I cried. "I am grievously sick and far too ill to go to London."

It was only when I was in my bed, with the sheets drawn up to my chin that the Queen's messenger was allowed to be sent to me, and when he came he was clearly dismayed to see me in my bed.

"You must tell me your business," I said faintly.

"My lady, the Queen's orders are that you must come to her in London without delay, where you will be most heartily welcome."

"Pray convey my thanks to Her Majesty and tell her how grieved I am to be laid so low that I cannot take advantage of her goodness."

"The Queen will be most displeased if I return without Your Grace."

"Tell her I rejoice in her goodness to me and how sad I am not to be able to take advantage of it."

He was very reluctant to go, and would not until I had written a letter to the Queen telling her that I was too ill to travel, but as soon as I was able I would come to her, and I begged Her Majesty's forbearance for a few days.

After the messenger had gone I was taken by a fit of trembling and I had no need to feign illness.

Kat was concerned. "You are really ill," she said. "Tell me, where is the pain?"

"It is in my head," I replied, "which has suddenly become very insecure on my shoulders."

News from London dribbled in. Many had rallied to Mary's banner and Wyatt had been proclaimed a traitor. The Tower and the bridges were fortified and a reward of land was offered to anyone who could capture Wyatt.

I did not write to the Queen myself, but commanded the officers of my household to do so, telling her that my indisposition was the sole reason why I did not hasten to London. They daily hoped for my improvement, but at the time there was no sign of it and they considered that in the circumstances it was their duty to let Her Majesty know of my state.

It was respite. But I knew it could not continue.

Poor foolish Wyatt! He had planned so fecklessly. He had thought he could march on St James's and capture the Queen. But there were traitors in his following who were only too ready to betray his plans for the sake of reward. Mary's Council decided to allow him to advance right into the city and then descended on him from all sides. When he came through Kensington to Hyde Park he was met by some of the Queen's men and after a skirmish his forces were considerably depleted and many, who had no heart for the fight, slunk away. He passed St James's without making an attempt to capture the Queen, for she was too well guarded, and passing Charing Cross and coming to the Strand and Fleet Street, he found his way was barred at Ludgate, and unable to make an assault on the gate, he retreated; but by this time his forces had so diminished that he must have realized the hopelessness of the enterprise.

He surrendered and was sent to the Tower.

I lay in my bed, realizing how much I wanted to live. My future, which had seemed so bright before me, was now filled with terror. There was one thing I dreaded above all else and that was to become a prisoner in the Tower of London. Death did not appall me half as much. Death came swiftly and brought an end to tribulations on Earth, but to become one of the prisoners of the Tower with death hanging over one uncertainly, on and on . . . day after day . . . year after year . . . never to be free . . . and in time forgotten—that was the most terrible fate of all. It had happened to so many, and especially to those who, like myself, were of royal blood.

I knew I was in greater danger than I had ever been when a party arrived at Ashridge led by Lord William Howard, Sir Edward Hastings and Sir Thomas Cornwallis, and to my intense dismay with them came two of the Queen's physicians, Dr Owen and Dr Wendy, whose purpose it was to decide whether I was fit to travel.

It was late at night when they arrived. Kat hastened to my bedchamber to inform me.

"Oh, Kat!" I cried. "What next? I thank God the hour is so late and I shall have the night in which to prepare my answers."

But almost immediately there was a knock at the door, and an usher entered to say that the lords and doctors would have speech with me.

"It is too late tonight," I said. "I will see them in the morning."

But they would not accept this. They were outside the door demanding admission in the Queen's name.

I was angry as they entered the room. I lay back in my bed gasping with fury. "Is the haste such that it might not have pleased you to come in the morning?" I demanded.

They did not answer but said they were sorry to see me in such a low state of health.

"And I am not glad to see you at this time of the night," I retorted.

I was relieved that my great-uncle Lord William Howard was a member of the party. Surely he must feel a tenderness for his own flesh and blood.

Dr Wendy came forward. He took my hand and looked at me intently.

He was a very clever doctor and I hoped he would not diagnose my illness as fear. On the other hand I remembered his treatment of Katharine Parr when she had been distraught as I was now. He had warned her how to act and had probably saved her life.

They did retire then, saying they would visit me in the morning when the doctors, on the Queen's orders, would decide whether I was fit to travel.

What a night that was! There was no sleep for me. Kat lay with me and we clung to each other. I wondered whether it was the last time we should be together.

In the morning I learned my fate.

Both doctors said that although I was suffering from acute disability and was certainly unfit to travel on horseback, there was no reason why I should not go by litter, and guessing this might be the case, the Queen had sent her royal litter for my use.

I knew then that there was no escape.

Just as we were setting out I heard that Lady Jane Grey and her husband Guildford Dudley had been sentenced to death. I supposed that was inevitable now and no doubt men such as Gardiner and Renaud were pointing out to the Queen the folly of showing mercy to dangerous men and women.

Nature came to my aid and I really was ill. There is nothing like anxiety of the mind to impair the body. It responds to the call of the mind—and this was certainly the case with me. During the journey I was half fainting most of the time, but when we came close to London I aroused myself. I was very eager that the people should keep their regard for me. I ordered that the curtains of the litter be drawn back so that they could see me; and there I sat under their scrutiny—pale but proud—and I tried not to show a trace of the fear I was feeling.

There were no cheers that day. How could they cheer one who was being taken to London, virtually a prisoner accused of treachery against the Queen? But all the same not a voice was raised against me, and I saw the compassion in their faces and knew that they wished me well.

Much good that would do me now. I was caught and it was going to be difficult to prove to Mary that I had taken no part in Wyatt's rebellion.

The very day that I entered London, Jane Grey laid her head on the block. Poor child, she had asked for nothing but the peace and contentment of her books and the companionship of those she loved. Now her innocent blood had been shed. Whose would be next? Was I not more menacing to the Queen than Jane was? I was not entirely without guile. I had dreams such as I was sure Jane had never had. Yet she had gone to the scaffold.

It was five o'clock in the afternoon when we came to Whitehall and

entered the palace through the gardens. At least it was not the Tower. If I
could see Mary, if I could explain my innocence, I believed I could convince
her. She would not want to shed my blood; she had been lenient to Jane
Grey; how much more so would she be toward her own sister?

The suspense was almost more than I could bear and I did not now have
to feign illness. I was, in fact, a prisoner; I had been allowed to keep with me
only six ladies, two gentlemen and four servants from my own household.
The others whom I had brought with me were sent away. Guards were stationed at the doors of my apartments in the palace and none of my household was allowed to leave.

There was one consolation. Mary was under the same roof. If only I
could see her! I *was* innocent. I longed to be Queen, it was true, but I had
no wish to replace her. I accepted her as the true Queen while she lived. I
must let her know this.

I begged the guards to take a message to her, and this they did. The reply
was that the Queen had no wish to see me.

It was not long before the questioning began. I was interrogated by Gardiner and Lords Arundel and Paget, and I quickly understood that they were
all determined on my destruction. They tried to force me to admit guilt. I
stood resolute, insisting that I had known nothing of the insurrection and I
had had no part in it.

"Do you admit that Lord Russell came to Ashridge and asked you, on
behalf of Sir Thomas Wyatt, to remove far from London?"

"I admit this was so, but I remained, for being innocent I saw no reason
for running away."

"You have had other communications with Sir Thomas Wyatt."

"I have had none."

"He has accused you and Courtenay with complicity in this plot which
was for you to marry Courtenay and take the throne."

"It is lies. Do you believe what a man says under torture?"

"He has mentioned your name and that of Courtenay who is lodged in
the Tower."

I felt sick with fear. If these men were lying about me what hope had I
of proving my innocence?

"Letters have been intercepted between Wyatt and the French Ambassador."

"To what effect?"

"That there is a plot to marry you and Courtenay and set you on the
throne."

"Why should the French Ambassador support such a plot?"

"Because the French are against the Spanish marriage."

"Do you imagine they would support me? They have a pretender to the throne of their own—Mary Stuart."

"There were letters."

"It is all lies."

Innocence is a powerful advocate and mine helped me to stand out against them. The fact that Wyatt had implicated me was damning. How could he? But how can one question what a man says under extreme torture?

At last the questions ceased and I was left alone.

The weary days passed. Mary would not see me. Each day I waited. Each day the fears increased.

It was difficult to get any news but I did hear that Wyatt and Courtenay were in the Tower under sentence of death and it seemed very possible that I should soon be in like case.

From the window I could see the white coats of the guards who were stationed round the palace lest there should be an attempt to free me. More guards were at my doors. They were determined to keep me closely watched.

Then one day what I had been dreading happened. The Earl of Sussex came to me with another member of the Council to tell me to prepare to leave.

"For what destination?" I asked fearfully.

Then came the answer which I had long feared. "You are to be lodged in the Tower, Your Grace."

"No!" I cried and covered my face with my hands.

Sussex said gently: "It is the orders of the Queen, my lady. The barge is waiting to conduct you there."

"I cannot go to that place," I said. "It is not for honest subjects of the Queen."

"My lady, these are my orders and I must obey them."

There was a kindliness about him. He did not wish me ill as Gardiner did.

I said: "I must see the Queen."

"The Queen will not see you, my lady."

"If I write to her would you take a letter to her?"

He hesitated. He knew that the Queen did not want to receive a plea from me, but he was a good man and I was young and I suppose appealing.

There was another thought which occurred to me. I was next in line to the succession. Events often took an unexpected turn. Perhaps he remembered that he could be dealing with his future Queen.

Whatever the reason, he softened and said that if I wished to write to the Queen, he would do his best to deliver the letter.

I sat down at once and reminded her of our last meeting when she had promised that if she heard anything against me, she would not condemn me without giving me a chance to defend myself, and it seemed that now I was condemned, for I was to be sent to the Tower, a place more suitable for a false traitor than for a true subject of the Queen. I did not deserve such a fate, and I prayed to God that I might die the most shameful death if I did. Therefore I was pleading with her to let me answer to her before I was sent to the Tower, and if that was too late, before I was condemned. I reminded her that I had heard that Thomas Seymour had said that if he had been allowed to see his brother, he would never have been condemned to death. I prayed that the evil persuasions to set one sister against another would be shown to her to be false as I knew them to be. I begged her to see me that I might assure her of my innocence.

It was the Saturday before Palm Sunday, and clearly they did not wish the people to see me conducted along the river on such a day. The plan had been to take me after dark so that I could not be seen and thus the people would not know I was being taken to the Tower until I was safely there.

However, in allowing me to write my letter over which I took some time, Sussex had made the mistake of missing the tide. There was consternation for this meant that the journey along the river could not be made until daylight. My spirits were lifted a little—a very little—because they should set such store by the people's not seeing me, which showed it was something of which the good citizens would not approve. My enemies knew of my popularity and even if they believed me guilty of trying to stop unity between England and Spain, they would not be so averse to that either.

It was decided that I should go during the time of morning service when there would be few people about. At least that gave me a few more hours of freedom from that terrifying place.

At nine o'clock on the Palm Sunday morning I was taken to the stairs. I had to walk through the gardens to the river and all the way I was praying that someone would come to my rescue.

I looked back at the palace. There were people watching but no one came forward to speak to me.

"I marvel," I said bitterly, "what the nobles mean by suffering me, a prince, to be led into captivity, the Lord knoweth wherefore, for myself I do not."

The barge sped quickly along the river. They were very nervous, those men. My words had sunk home. I was the heir to the throne and I was being hurried ignobly into captivity.

The tide had not yet risen high enough to allow us to shoot the bridge and the fall of water being so great at that point, there was danger to the boat. The boatmen declined to go forward. I was exultant. Were they telling me that they would not be party to this terrible action which was being taken against me?

My escorts however insisted that we proceed. The Queen had expressed displeasure that I had not been taken to the Tower on the previous night as had been arranged. There would be great trouble if there was further delay. She would be very suspicious, construing it as a reluctance on the part of her subjects to imprison her sister. The stern of the boat struck the piles at the side of the bridge and for a moment I thought we were all going to be thrown into the river. I did not greatly care. But the barge righted itself and we were on our way.

My dismay was great when we came to rest at the stairs of the Traitor's Gate. "Not here," I cried out. "I am no traitor."

"These are our orders, Your Grace" was the reply.

The rain had started. It was a blustery March day. Palm Sunday! It was a time for rejoicing although the following week the fickle people had cried, "Crucify him."

"My lady, you must alight here," I was told.

The water was splashing about the stairs. "How can I?" I asked. "Must I walk through the water?"

"My lady, you must."

So I stepped out and the water splashed over my shoes.

The Lieutenant of the Tower had come out to greet me and someone offered me a cloak which I declined. I said in a loud voice so that all could hear: "Here lands as true a subject, being prisoner, as ever landed at these stairs."

Several of the warders and servants of the Tower came out to see me, and I was deeply moved when many of them knelt down and cried out: "May God preserve Your Grace."

How that heartened me! Even as a poor prisoner I had not lost the power to draw out their affection. Some of them were weeping and I knew that this was because they did not expect me to leave this place alive.

Before me rose the gate—the Traitor's Gate—and I could not bring myself to pass through it. I sat down on the cold stones and stared ahead of me.

The Lieutenant of the Tower came to me and said gently: "Madam, you sit unwholesomely."

"It may be that I am better here than in a worse place," I answered.

One of my ushers burst into tears and seeing him thus weeping gave me strength.

"Come," I said, "you should be comforting me, especially as you know the truth, that I am innocent of charges brought against me, so that none has any cause to weep for me."

I stood up and allowed myself to be led to the room which had been prepared for me. It was on the first floor of the Bell Tower—a large vaulted chamber with three pointed windows and deep window-seats.

The door was bolted on us. I sat down wearily, damp, cold and desperate.

That which I had feared for so long had befallen me. I was a prisoner in the Tower of London.

WITHIN THOSE DARK stone walls there were many memories and chief of these must be of my mother. In such a way had she been brought to this grim fortress; the same despair had been hers. Her husband had been determined to destroy her; my sister felt the same about me. But did she? I could hardly believe that of Mary, and I could not help feeling that had I been able to speak to her, she would have listened to me. I remembered so vividly that terrible moment in the courtyard when my terrified mother had held me up to my glittering, all-powerful father. His cold indifference was what had made it so hard to bear. Was Mary indifferent to me? She was surrounded by men who wished to destroy me because they thought I was a threat to their ambitions. Mary believed that I was damned because I refused to accept her faith. She was not devoid of sisterly feelings, but she was a fanatic and fanatics let no human feelings stand in the way of what they believe to be right. Mary intended to bring England back to Rome and I stood in the way.

The days seemed endless; the nights even longer. Kat had not been allowed to come with me and how I missed her! But I had one or two good friends with me. Lovely Isabella Markham who had recently married Sir John Harrington was one, and Elizabeth Sand another. They did their best to make me comfortable.

Isabella said: "Did you notice how respectful the guards were, my lady? They remember you are the King's daughter. They will treat you well."

"Being the King's wife did not save my mother from death."

They were silent. They knew I only spoke of my mother in moments of extreme stress.

I put my hands to my throat and said: "When they send me out to Tower Green I shall ask for a sword to be sent from France. I will not have the axe."

They all fell to weeping and I had to comfort them.

The following day Gardiner came with nine Lords of the Council and when I saw my hated enemy I feared the worst. He had come to extract a confession from me to the effect that I had been involved in Wyatt's schemes, and began by accusing me of receiving letters from the traitor.

"I received no letters from Wyatt," I insisted.

"Letters from him to you have been intercepted," retorted Gardiner.

"Then perhaps that is why I received none."

"Wyatt has confessed to your involvement."

"Then Wyatt is a liar as well as a traitor."

I was always at my best in these verbal battles and in spite of my terrible fears I answered the questions lucidly, and Gardiner could not trap me.

One of the members of the Council, Henry Fitzalan, Earl of Arundel, looked uncomfortable while Gardiner was badgering me. Arundel was an ardent Catholic. He would see me as a danger to the plans for a Spanish marriage and the conversion to Rome, and I had thought he would be a deadly enemy; oddly enough I seemed to arouse some compassion in him. Perhaps in spite of my proud and fiery nature and my determination never to be subdued by any man, there was something essentially feminine about me. I had noticed it many times and this quality seemed to arouse a certain protective instinct in the opposite sex. Now here it was with Arundel. Because of the ever-present danger in which I stood, my awareness had intensified and I saw his attitude changing as Gardiner proceeded with the questions.

At length he held up his hand and looked at Gardiner with some distaste. "It is clear to me," he said, "that Her Grace speaks truth and for my part I am sorry to see her troubled on such vain matters."

Gardiner was very annoyed with Arundel, particularly as some other members of the Council were swaying toward the Earl, and Gardiner saw that he was losing sympathy—and with it authority.

They took their leave and when they did, Arundel went on his knees and kissed my hand. That gave me new courage. I had a certain power of which people were aware but I must not allow myself to be deceived by undue optimism and must try to look clearly into the hearts and minds of my enemies. How much of the deference these men showed me was due to my own personal abilities and how much to the fact that I was young and Mary was ill and aging? How many were asking themselves: This young woman who is being persecuted could be our Queen one day. What then? She will remember me this day.

But I had begun to regain a little of my spirits and with that came hope.

One day seemed to merge into another—so alike were they. When I awoke my first thoughts were, What will happen today? I used to dream that the people rose up and came to free me. They had always loved me better than Mary. They said I was my father's daughter, that I looked like him, that I had his spirit. Would any care enough? It was significant that my room was immediately below the great alarm bell. Had they put me there to remind me that at any attempt to escape that bell would ring out, warning my captors of my flight?

In my mind I died a thousand deaths during those weeks. I would wake in the morning and put my hands to my throat. My mother had said hysterically, when she knew what her fate was to be: "I have a little neck . . ." I wished I could stop thinking of her.

Such mental anguish must have its effect on the body. I became ill and had to keep to my bed. This alarmed my jailers and I was quick to sense their uneasiness.

The day for Wyatt's execution came and on the scaffold he made a brave speech in which he accepted full responsibility for his actions and wholeheartedly withdrew the accusations he had made against me and Courtenay under torture.

I was greatly relieved because now there was no true case against me. Gardiner, Renaud and all my enemies would have to be very careful before they sentenced me to death. It was like a reprieve.

News drifted in from the outside world. My servants talked with the guards and so I learned something of what was going on. Wyatt's body had been barbarously treated after the execution and parts of it were exhibited over the town, while his head was attached to a gallows at Hay Hill near Hyde Park.

When I heard that after Wyatt's confession Courtenay was released but exiled, my hopes rose. Surely they could not keep me prisoner now! Wyatt had confessed that he had wrongfully incriminated me and that I had nothing to do with his insurrection, so what reason had they for keeping me in the Tower?

A very big one, they might say. I was a menace to the plans for returning England to Rome, which the greater majority of the people did not want. I would not be the first person of royal blood who had been sent to a lifetime in the Tower for no other reason than that she or he possessed a claim to royalty.

But they were very much afraid. My health was causing anxiety. They wanted my death but they did not want to be accused of causing it.

A doctor was sent to me and it was suggested that I should take a little air and exercise. There was what they called a lead—a very narrow path— which the warders used when they wanted to get from one Tower to another. This path between the battlements went from a door in the Bell Tower to one in the Beauchamp Tower. I could have no hope of escaping from this narrow path and just in case an attempt was made, two guards were to walk in front of me and one behind.

Even such a small concession was welcome. It was pleasant to be able to escape from the stone walls to the fresh air even with such restraints.

I was quite friendly with my guards for that affinity with the common people was ever present in my nature and they were courteous to me—partly because no doubt they remembered that I would one day be their Queen.

We would pause on the path and look round and I would ask questions about the Tower of which they were very proud and knowledgeable.

We would walk right along the lead to the Beauchamp Tower.

"I'll swear there are prisoners in there who would long to walk along the lead as far as the Bell Tower," I said.

They agreed that this must be so and one added: "I know of one who more than most chafes against inactivity, my lady."

"Oh? And who might that be?" I asked.

"Lord Robert Dudley. He is there . . . poor gentleman . . . a most handsome nobleman of much grace. He is under sentence of death and knows not each day when he wakes whether it will be his last."

"I knew him once," I said. "He was at my father's Court with his father. We played together when we were children. The others I have forgotten but I remember Robert Dudley well. I am sorry he is in such state now, but his father rose against the Queen and has paid the price for treason, and Robert Dudley stood with his father."

"His brothers too, my lady. It is not long since Lord Guildford and my Lady Jane walked to their deaths."

"Poor Lady Jane! She was blameless. Her father forced her to it and she had no choice but to obey."

I fell silent after that. I should not be talking thus; but then I was always over-friendly with those below my rank. It was what made me so popular with the people.

When I returned from my walk on the lead, I could not stop thinking of Robert Dudley. His position was more unsafe than my own for he was actually under sentence of death.

I shivered, hoping that he would escape such a fate. Why should I care? Didn't he deserve it? He was one of those who had tried to put Jane Grey on the throne. But only because he had stood with his father. It was Northumberland who had raised the rebellion and made Jane Queen for little over a week at the cost of his own life and those of Jane and his son Guildford.

The Queen was justified in sending Robert Dudley to the Tower and sentencing him to death for that matter.

All the same he had made quite an impression on me as a child and he had an exceptional charm. I did not like to think of his handsome head being severed from his body.

SOME WEEKS LATER I was told by the guards that permission had been given for me to take a walk in the Tower Gardens. It is amazing what pleasure such small concessions can give when one has so little; and I well remember my walk in the gardens where the spring flowers were in bloom and the air seemed so fresh and balmy.

Moreover there were children playing in the gardens and I had always been interested in children. I had the same affinity with them as I had with ordinary people. I could speak to them as I could to the people, without royal reserve—which is very rare in persons of high rank.

There was one charming little boy. He must have been about five years old, perhaps younger. He smiled at me and said: "Good-day, Mistress."

I paused and asked his name.

"It is Martin, Mistress," he replied. "What is yours?"

"Elizabeth," I told him.

"Do you walk in these gardens often?" he asked.

"Whenever I can. Do you?"

He nodded. "We live over there."

"Martin!" Someone was calling him. I looked round and saw a young woman hurrying toward us. She dropped a curtsy and I smiled at her.

"I trust, my lady, the boy was not annoying you," she said.

"Far from it. We were enjoying our conversation, were we not, Martin?"

He stared at me, tongue-tied before the woman who I presumed was his mother.

She told me that her husband was Keeper of the Queen's Robes and that Martin was allowed to play in the gardens because they did not often have distinguished visitors to them.

I said: "I trust my presence here will not mean that Martin is kept away. I should be most distressed if that were so."

She took the child by his hand and bobbed a curtsy.

"You are very kind, my lady. Martin is a friendly boy and likes to talk."

"Then I hope there will be other meetings for us, Martin," I said.

I watched while she took him away. I felt warmed by the encounter.

After that I saw Martin often. He would smile when he saw me and run to me gleefully. Once he brought me some flowers and I was so delighted with this show of affection that he made a habit of it.

One day he said: "There is a gentleman in there." He pointed to the walls of the Beauchamp Tower. "I see him when I go with my father."

"What sort of gentleman?"

"A very nice gentleman."

"Does he talk to you?"

"Yes, he does."

"As I do?"

He nodded.

"What does he say?"

"He says there is a princess in the Tower. My lady, is it you?"

"Yes," I said. "And did you tell him that you had spoken with me?"

He nodded.

"And what did he say?"

He said: "Tell the Princess . . . tell the Princess . . ."

"Yes, yes."

He was concentrating hard trying to remember. He said: "Tell her . . ."

"Yes, yes, tell her what?"

He frowned and finally burst out: "That I am thinking of her and—"

"And what?"

"How . . . I can serve her."

"He really asked you to tell me that?"

He nodded vigorously.

"And you have not told anyone else . . . only me."

Again that nod. "The gentleman said . . ."

"Yes, yes."

"Only tell you . . . and no one else."

I stooped and kissed him. "Thank you, Martin. You are a very clever boy."

He looked pleased and when I went back to my prison I thought a great deal about Robert Dudley.

THE GLOOM SEEMED to be lifting. I felt alive again. It was ridiculous. I was still a prisoner in the Tower and my enemies were still plotting my downfall; but the thought that there was someone here—a young handsome man of about my own age—who was thinking of me, sending me messages, assuring me of his devotion, worked like a miracle with me. My health improved. The great occasions of my days were those interludes in the gardens. Another child had joined us. This was Susannah, the daughter of one of the warders. The children would walk with me and enliven me with their childish prattle and young Martin, with the dignity of his five years—I think Susannah could not have been more than three—conveyed messages between Robert Dudley and me. He was able to tell Lord Robert that his messages had heartened me and my thoughts were with him, even as his were with me.

It was an exciting game for the child, and his youth made him an excellent participator in the intrigue. I could have wished he had been a bit older though, then perhaps our messages could have been more productive; but I suppose if he had been I should not have been allowed this friendship with him.

There was little Robert Dudley could offer me other than comfort, nor I him. We were not such fools as to think about escape. That would be folly. Failure would surely cost me my head. What we did for each other was to establish a communion of friendship which I was to remember always, and often in later years my thoughts would go back to that garden and the messages of comfort which I received from the prisoner in the Beauchamp Tower. Robert's close presence gave me strength when I needed it and courage to endure what was waiting for me, as my responses did for him.

I do not know how long this would have gone on but for one unfortunate incident.

I used to tell the children stories of my life and they knew that I was a princess. I would describe the Court to them and the feasts which used to take place in the great banqueting halls. They listened avidly and it dawned on them that I must be living very differently as a prisoner in the Tower.

Their eyes would fill with tears when I told them that I had been brought here because the Queen was not pleased with me. I was flattered because they could not understand how anyone could be unkind to me.

One day Susannah found a bunch of keys in the gardens. They must have been dropped by one of the warders when he was hurrying from one tower to another . . . Keys opened doors, reasoned Susannah; and she had seen the guards escort me to and from the gardens. Her experiences of the Tower told her that people were locked up there, so she thought that if I had the keys I should be able to open doors and escape.

She brought the keys to me.

"They are for you, Mistress," she said. "Now you can open the doors and stop being a prisoner in the Tower."

Her innocent eyes were full of love for me and delight in her cleverness in giving me the means of freedom. I put my arms round her and kissed her and I said that I wished some of the mighty lords of the kingdom would have done as much for me.

Martin cried excitedly: "They will open the doors, Mistress." He looked sad suddenly. "You will go away." He brightened. "We shall come to see you."

I took the keys and said: "May God bless you, my children. But I do not think these keys will open the right doors. So you still have me with you."

They clapped their hands and just at that moment one of the guards came out.

"I must ask you, my lady," he said, "to give me those keys."

I explained that Susannah had found them in the gardens.

He took them from me. I guessed that one of the guards must have lost them and was feeling very anxious about them, and the fact that they had fallen into my hands gave him twinges of anxiety, for although the keys would have been no use to me, there was something symbolic about keys— as the children had thought.

There must have been great consternation among the guards. The lost keys had been found, but the children had brought them to me. Just suppose they had been the keys to my prison cell. They must have been filled with terror to contemplate the consequences if, through the carelessness of guards, I was to escape from the Tower.

The next day when I went down to the gardens the children were not there. I was very disappointed. Not only had I lost them but also the heartening messages from Robert Dudley.

Then a few days later I saw Martin. One of the gates had been locked and he was standing on the other side of it. He stretched out his arms and said: "Mistress, I am to bring you no more flowers."

Almost immediately his father appeared and taking him by the hand led him away.

I WAS MOVING fast into a very dangerous period and when I look back it seems as though Heaven was surely watching over me for I had at least one miraculous escape from death.

There was more and more opposition to the Spanish marriage and the near-certainty of having the Catholic Faith imposed on the nation. Already the use of English prayers and Protestant rites was prohibited, and the Protestant community, which was in the majority, was feeling restive. No one disputed Mary's right to the throne; on the other hand there was fierce opposition to her religious intolerance. Gardiner, aided by Renaud, the Spanish Ambassador, who since the proposed alliance with Spain had become one of the most important men in the Queen's Council, was agitating for my death. I was a great threat to the Queen and her projects, they pointed out, because I was the Protestant heiress to the throne. I realize now that Mary must have been distracted by the voices at her elbow. Her conscience would torment her if she agreed to my death; but she could not fail to see that I might stand in the way of her most cherished dream, and to a woman of Mary's unquestioning faith the life of one young woman was of small importance against the establishment of the Church of Rome in England.

Strangely enough the Catholic Earl of Arundel was against my death; so were Pembroke and Sussex. They were kindly men who could not agree to the murder of an innocent young woman, and my perilous situation aroused their sympathy. Then there was my kinsman Lord William Howard, Admiral of the Fleet. It was hardly likely that he would agree to the execution of a close relative who had been proved innocent of complicity in the Wyatt conspiracy. Moreover he held great authority, having the fleet at his command.

Therefore Mary had to go cautiously, and so anxious was she that she became ill. News filtered through to me that this was the case and I had, as a matter of fact, noticed a certain increase in the deference shown to me. I might judge the state of the Queen's health by this. My feelings were mixed. I had always had some affection for Mary. It was not overwhelming, I must admit. I thought her foolish to let religion rule her judgment, particularly a form which was not popular among the majority of her subjects. She was aloof—not a person who displayed much affection or encouraged others to—but she was my sister, and I had lived with her from time to time, and there was a family tie. Ever present, too, was the knowledge that her death could be my life—not the life of a prisoner, but that of a queen. I had had visions of people's storming the Tower, demanding my freedom and that of Lord Robert Dudley too. I could picture his kneeling to kiss my hand. I could hear the shouts of the people in the streets. The time was ripe now. I was no longer a child but a young woman capable of becoming the Queen of a great country. She is my sister, I kept telling myself. It was true and I was fond of her . . . in a way, as she was perhaps of me . . . but how can one help one's thoughts?

It was her ailing health which almost proved fatal to me.

One of my greatest pieces of good fortune was that Thomas Bridges, who had recently become Lord Chandos, the Lieutenant of the Tower, was a good and honest man, and one who was not afraid to do what he considered his duty. But for that I should never have walked out of the Tower alive.

He came to me in some distress to tell me that he had received a warrant for my immediate execution. Because the matter was presented with such urgency and there was no reason why the warrant should have been issued at this time, his suspicions were aroused. Had it been at the time when Wyatt was in the Tower and I was suspected with him, it would have been another matter; but my innocence had been established by Wyatt's confession on the scaffold. Moreover the Queen was confined to bed with a serious illness.

He read the warrant to me. I felt numb but I shed no tears. What I had dreaded had come to pass and I could not help wondering about my mother's anguish when she had been presented with such a warrant. Now it was my turn.

"When will this evil deed be done?" I asked.

"The order is that it shall be done without delay."

"So be it," I said. "My time has come. Those who shed my innocent blood will have to answer for their deeds to God."

Chandos looked like a stricken man. I knew that he hated this to happen while he was in charge of the Tower, but of course he would have to obey orders.

When he left me I felt extraordinarily calm. One of my women came in and I told her what Lord Chandos had said. Poor woman, she fell into such weeping that I had to comfort her.

"Do not weep for me," I said. "It is those who are left who are going to suffer. I have nothing with which to reproach myself. I have always been the Queen's faithful subject. My enemies have poisoned her mind against me and she will suffer deeply over this."

I waited. I was praying silently all the time—not so much for deliverance as to be given the strength to face with courage what lay before me.

Lord Chandos came to me again. He dismissed my women and spoke to me earnestly. "I do not intend to carry out this order and I wish you to know that without delay."

"You will not dare to go against the Queen's order."

"My lady, I believe this to be no order from the Queen, but from others."

"Please explain, Lord Chandos."

"When I received the document and knew what it was, I was overcome with grief and I thought you should be warned at once in order to make your peace with God, for I feared the executioner would not delay his visit. But when I examined the warrant closely, I saw that it did not contain the sovereign's signature which is usual in these cases."

"Not the Queen's signature! Then . . ."

"My lady, the Queen is very sick and has taken to her bed. It occurs to me that some may have taken advantage of this."

"Stephen Gardiner has done this," I said.

Lord Chandos did not speak but I guessed that he agreed with me. The Queen was ill and Gardiner was terrified that I might come to the throne, for he had clearly shown himself to be my enemy, so his plan had been to dispatch me speedily and when the Queen recovered—if she did—to present her with a *fait accompli*, and the country would be without its Protestant heiress.

"What shall you do, my lord?" I asked.

"I shall say that I refuse to carry out such an order except under the command of the Queen."

An immense relief swept over me because I believed fervently that she would not sign my death warrant until Gardiner, Renaud and the rest of my enemies could prove something against me. This would not be easy to do because I had committed no treason and I should take good care not to do so.

So Lord Chandos saved my life, for it was true that Mary had no knowledge of such a document and when she recovered and learned what had been done she was very disturbed. It must have occurred to her that one who would go so far as to send a death warrant, hoping that the absence of the royal signature would not be noticed, would stoop to any means to be rid of me. She, who was truly religious, did not want murder on her conscience.

I discovered later that her attitude toward me changed from that time, and she was most displeased if anyone spoke disparagingly of me. She referred to me again as her sister, and my portrait, which had been taken away and hidden, was restored to its place in the gallery beside her own.

She was very uneasy and clearly did not trust those about her. She must have been a most unhappy woman. I was in danger of imminent death but even at such a time I would not have wished to be in her shoes.

Chandos came to me. He was in a state of bewilderment.

He said: "The Queen is sending Sir Henry Bedingfeld to be in charge of the Tower and I think this is because of recent happenings."

I was overcome with horror. "But, my Lord Chandos . . . do you mean that Sir Henry Bedingfeld is coming here to guard *me*?"

"It would seem so, my lady. I wish you well. I am sorry I can no longer be of service to you."

"You have served me well, Lord Chandos, and that is something I shall never forget. Tell me . . . this Bedingfeld, what sort of man is he?"

"A stern Catholic, my lady, but I believe him to be a man of high principles."

"One who would be ready to commit murder for a cause?"

"I think not."

"Was it not his father who was the jailer of my father's first wife, Katharine of Aragon, when she was at Kimbolton?"

"The same, my lady."

"I do not think he showed great kindness to that lady."

"He obeyed the orders of the King and now I am sure his son will obey those of his Queen. He may be a stern custodian but I believe him to be a deeply religious man. I would say that under his care you may be restricted but your life will not be in jeopardy."

"It would be comforting to believe you, my lord, but much royal blood has been shed in this place and when men come in such a manner as this, it seems that there must be plans behind it."

"I must tell you, my lady, that Sir Henry Bedingfeld will not be the Lieutenant of the Tower. He will have for a while command over me, but his stay here will be temporary. He is coming here while it is decided where you shall be taken. I believe you are to be removed from the Tower."

"From one prison to another. Perhaps it will be easier to dispose of me in some remote castle. Where will they take me? Have they said?"

"Pomfret has been suggested."

"Oh, dear God preserve me! That was where they held my ancestor Richard II. Some believe that he was murdered there."

I was sick with fear. I had dreaded coming to the Tower, but I did not wish to be removed to some gloomy faraway castle remote from my few friends in London and haunted by the ghosts of murdered men and women. Robert Dudley was here, and although I could not see him, his presence comforted me.

Almost immediately Sir Henry Bedingfeld arrived. I disliked him immediately because I saw at once that he was one of those men who would not have the slightest compassion for my feminine helplessness. He was the stern supporter of my sister and he saw me as a menace to her safe holding of the throne. It was true that he was deeply religious and I at once sensed that he was sincerely so. This should have comforted me, but I disliked him and feared him; and he came with one hundred and forty armed men—to guard one poor prisoner! He seemed old to me—in fact he must have been about forty-three years of age! He had no graces, no charm, and I showed him clearly that I found his presence near me distasteful.

The Dangerous Days

IT WAS ON THE TWENTIETH OF MAY—TWO MONTHS AFTER my arrival at the Tower through the Traitor's Gate—that I left that formidable fortress.

I should have been delighted, but I could not rid myself of the terrible fear that I was leaving one prison for another which might be even more dangerous.

I felt a sudden wave of hope, though, when I heard that I was going to Richmond, for the Queen was there and I believed that if I could see her I could convince her of my loyalty to her and appeal to her sisterly feelings for me.

As we moved along the river I could not but exult in my freedom, brief though it might be. How beautifully green were the trees, and the fragrance of the wild flowers was particularly poignant to me because it seemed so long since I had smelt them. Rose-colored apple trees and white cherry were in bloom in the orchards close to the river and the hawthorn was weighed down with buds. I wanted to capture the colors and smells, for they meant freedom. And there was Richmond Palace which had been built by my grandfather on the site of old Shene. I alighted at the stairs and went through the gates into the palace.

As soon as I was in the apartment allotted to me, Sir Henry Bedingfeld came to inform me that the Queen had graciously agreed to see me. Haughtily I inclined my head. I hated the man and I wanted to demand how he dare address me as though I were some wayward schoolgirl. I supposed to men of his age I did seem young, but I was now twenty-one years old . . . old enough to be a queen.

I was ushered into my sister's presence and saw to my relief that we were to be alone. I should have been dismayed if that old villain Gardiner had been there.

The first thought which struck me was how old and ill she looked. The crown seemed to be a heavy burden for her to carry.

I knelt and she gave me a hand to kiss but there was no real warmth in her greeting.

"I trust your health is improved, sister," she said.

I thanked her for her concern and said that I was as well as I could hope to be after my sojourn in the Tower.

"Let us hope that you do not return there," she said enigmatically.

"I share Your Majesty's hope," I replied quietly.

"You come to me as a prisoner of the state," she went on. "It grieves me that it should be thus with my own sister. You are my father's daughter and that I do not forget. My ministers and I have discussed your future. There have been suspicions regarding your conduct and although the traitor Wyatt exonerated you from complicity in his plot when he was on the scaffold, there are certain matters which remain unclear."

"Your Majesty, I know full well that people have poisoned your mind against me, but I assure you, with all my heart, that I am your most loyal and faithful subject."

"I understand that you will not go to Mass."

"I was not brought up to go to Mass, Your Majesty. As our brother was not either."

"That was sad for England and has done untold harm," said my sister. "However we shall right that as best we can. You will not willingly accept the true faith and I tremble for you when the time comes to face your Maker."

I was silent.

She went on: "But you are young and unwise, so I have a husband for you. There are some about me who tell me that while you are in England you will cast envious eyes on my throne."

"Your Majesty has been misinformed."

"That is as may be. But you are, I sense, impatient for the throne. It will never be yours, sister. I shall shortly marry a great ruler and our son will be the next King of England. There is no place for you here. That is why I am offering you Philibert of Savoy, the Prince of Piedmont. He is agreeable to the match and you can have a happy life with him."

I was cold with horror. Go to Piedmont! Leave England! That would be to say goodbye to the throne forever. No! I would never do that. I would rather stay here where I was in perpetual danger. In that moment I realized how desperately I wanted the crown. There was something within me which told me it was my right, that it was my destiny. I was meant to be Queen of England and I must never agree to anything that would divert me from that purpose. I struggled for composure . . .

My sister was regarding me coldly.

"You do not seem overcome with joy, sister," she said. "You have not yet understood your good fortune. Philibert is a great Prince. Oh, I know you are a Princess, but a bastard Princess and known to be such now that it is acclaimed that our father was not truly married to your mother since his marriage to mine was valid."

I wanted to shout at her, to tell her that it was not long ago that we were both declared bastards. I did not care if I was. I only knew that I was the King's daughter and that I was meant to be a queen.

"Your Majesty," I said, choosing my words very carefully, "I have no desire for the married state."

"You are being foolish," she said testily.

"It is true, Your Majesty, that the thought of marriage sickens me. It is something in me which is not as others of my sex. I was born in the Chamber of Virgins under the sign of Virgo. Your Majesty, I beg you to understand that I cannot marry . . . that I would rather face anything than that."

"You are stubborn. I have no wish to force you into marriage, but I tell you this: It is a matter of marriage or captivity. You may choose which."

I was silent for a few moments, grappling with myself. But I knew what I had to say. It was my destiny. If I left England now, I should never attain the crown.

Then I said slowly: "I must then continue to be a prisoner who faces captivity without knowledge of the fault which has placed me in restraint."

She was impatient with me. She had been hoping to get me married and out of the country and out of her conscience.

But I was too wise for that.

I HEARD THAT I was to go to Woodstock, where I should be in the care of that same Sir Henry Bedingfeld. The servants who had so far accompanied me were to be dismissed. I said my farewells to them and wept bitterly.

"Pray for me," I said, "for I think I am to die soon."

They knew that I meant that when royal persons were sent away to remote country castles they were either left to be forgotten or removed; and since in my case I was an undoubted threat to the Queen, it seemed obvious what fate was intended for me.

I was so certain that I was being taken to my death that I had come to a point where I accepted my fate. I was overcome by melancholy because somewhere in the recesses of my mind had been the certain feeling that one day I should be Queen. Now it seemed I had deluded myself. Death seemed inevitable.

My attendants must have felt the same for many of them wept openly and some were so blinded by their tears that they could not serve me. I admonished them gently but their love for me was a great comfort.

One of my ushers went to Lord Tame, a gentleman of the Court, and demanded to know whether I was in danger that night and if there was a plot to kill me before I left Richmond or if it had been decided to do the deed elsewhere, at which Lord Tame cried out in anger: "Marry, God forbid that any should consider such vileness. If it were intended, I and my men would die defending her."

The good man came to tell me what Lord Tame had said. "I am sure he spoke in earnest, Your Grace," he said. "Whatever evil there is abroad, there is good too, and you will have many to protect you besides the members of your household."

Such incidents are great balm when one is in dire need of comfort.

The next day we started on our journey to Woodstock, and once again my spirits were lifted for as we rode into the country people came out to see me pass. The manner in which they ran to me was very touching. I saw their good wishes and affection in their eyes. "God bless the Princess!" they cried with such emotion that Bedingfeld was most displeased. He believed, and rightly I was sure, that a "God bless" for me meant a curse on the Queen.

In one village we passed through, the bells started to ring and when Bedingfeld asked what was the occasion for it, he was told: "It is for rejoicing that our Princess is no longer in the Tower."

He raged against them. They talked like traitors, he said. They had no right to sing the praises of one who so recently had been suspected of treachery and was not yet wholly proved innocent.

The bell-ringing was stopped. I think they were all terrified that they might be accused of treason.

In due course we came to Ricote in Oxfordshire and stayed at the mansion of Lord Williams of Tame, who came out to greet me with an air of great deference and said that his lady was giving orders in the kitchens and the best apartment had been prepared for me. He added that he was deeply honored because I, the Princess Elizabeth, daughter of great Harry, was to stay under his roof.

He made me feel that I was not a prisoner and I blessed him for that. He sat me in the place of honor in his great hall and I was royally served; he had even arranged an entertainment to divert me which grew very merry until the miserable Bedingfeld complained. It was not meet and fitting, he said, that such treatment should be shown to the Queen's prisoner.

Lord Williams looked stunned. He said he was merely entertaining the Princess Elizabeth in a manner such as his purse and humble house would allow him. He believed it must seem very poor in the eyes of royalty, but he trusted I would understand that it was the best he could do.

"My dear lord," I said gently, flashing a look of hatred at Bedingfeld, "there are some whose pleasure it is to humiliate me. You have cheered me mightily by giving me this wonderful welcome."

Lord Williams was pleased but I could see that Bedingfeld was angry. I hoped he would not report Lord Williams to the Council. But perhaps he would not. I grudgingly admitted to myself that he was a just man and only acted in accordance with what he believed to be right.

We left Ricote in the morning and in due course arrived at Woodstock.

Woodstock! How dreary it was! I had been as well off in the Tower. There were soldiers to guard me day and night. They paraded round the walls at night and every door and gateway was supplied with locks. I could not move without being spied on. I was never alone in the gardens. Everywhere I looked there were guards watching me. They must have been very much afraid that I would escape.

I look back on that period of my life and shudder. The days seemed never-ending and even my books could not entirely comfort me. It is true that I did not hate Sir Henry Bedingfeld as much as I had at first, for I did gradually come to realize that he was a good man, the sort I respected and would have been glad to have on my side. Of course he was a fanatical Catholic and he regarded me as a lost soul, a heretic; but I began to understand that the rigorous guard he placed on me was as much to ensure my safety as to prevent my escape.

This was brought home to me on the occasion when Sir Henry had to leave Woodstock for a few days. He put a trusted man in charge of the place, which meant in charge of me, and it was while he was away that an attempt was made on my life.

I felt certain that Gardiner was behind it. I suspected that man of every villainy. He was ambitious like many churchmen, and if ever I came to the throne he would know that he could never have a chance of reaching the power he sought. Therefore he had every reason for wanting me out of the way, and it would have been foolishly careless not to have suspected that he would have some plan for getting rid of me.

A man named Basset came to Woodstock with the story that he was from the Council and that he had an urgent message for the Princess Elizabeth which he had been instructed to deliver into her hands only.

Fortunately for me, Bedingfeld had left me in the charge of a man who proved worthy of his trust, so he and several of the guards accompanied Basset to my chamber. Basset said he came from the Queen and had a party of men waiting to escort me to her. The waiting party was interrogated while its leader was absent and a bigger parcel of ruffians it would be hard to find.

Basset was told that a messenger was being sent to Sir Henry Bedingfeld to tell him of their coming and as he was with the Queen they must wait at Woodstock until permission came from Sir Henry.

Basset said he would explain to his men and they would find quarters for the night. What they actually did was make off with all speed, knowing that they would be betrayed as soon as Bedingfeld heard of their arrival.

I often wondered what Basset and his men intended to do to me. It did not require much imagination!

My jailers became even more careful than they had been before. It was fortunate that they were. Otherwise I might have been burned in my bed, for my enemies had even managed to get their spies into the household.

This must have been the case because a fire broke out in the chamber immediately below mine, and I could easily have been burned in my bed with no means of escape, if it had not been discovered in time. It was clearly a fire which had been deliberately started.

To be the victim of those who wished to murder me put me in a state of continual tension.

Meanwhile events were moving fast, for Philip of Spain had arrived in England. I could well imagine all the pomp and ceremonies; and I did hear accounts of what was going on for there were messengers going constantly between the Court and Woodstock and the servants gossiped. I had always made a habit of talking to them and establishing an easy relationship with them so I was able to piece together scraps of news and fit them into a complete picture.

Philip had arrived at Southampton on the twentieth of July. The Queen was at Winchester for she had decided that the marriage should take place there; the ceremony would be conducted by the odious Gardiner, of course; she would not have Cranmer, the Archbishop of Canterbury, because she did not accept his religious views, which were of the Reformed Faith. Men like Cranmer must be feeling very uneasy now that Philip was actually here. The alliance could not bode well for him, nor for any who were not of the Catholic Faith.

Philip had been given a great welcome and to row him ashore the Queen had sent a barge lined with tapestry of the richest colors and seats of gold brocade. When he mounted the steps at Southampton he was met by a deputation sent by the Queen which included all the great noblemen in the land. Arundel immediately presented him with the Garter and a magnificent horse was provided for him. Philip himself was dressed very simply in black velvet making, so I heard, an austere contrast to all the glitter, and which gave him a special dignity. There were the usual eulogies which fall to royal brides and grooms, regarding his personal appearance, but secretly I heard that he was far from prepossessing with scanty sandy hair, a lack of eyebrows and lashes and watery little blue eyes—all this not helped by an expression of intense gloom.

My thoughts were with my sister. She had fallen in love before she saw him and, knowing Mary, I guessed that nothing would deter her from continuing in that blissful state once she had decided on it. He had sent her magnificent jewels worth fifty thousand ducats, I heard, and his Grand Chamberlain, Don Ruy Gomez da Silva, who carried them to the Queen, was as dignified as his master.

The weather was appalling—driving rain and wind, which was not to be expected as it was July, and, said those who were against the match, it was a bad omen. Philip however braved the elements and came in slow dignified Spanish fashion from Southampton to Winchester.

Apparently the meeting between the pair was entirely amicable. I imagine Mary did not see Philip so much as a man as an important part of her plan to bring England to Rome. As for him, how did he see Mary? He saw a crown, I was sure, and the domination of our country. I felt angry and frustrated. If there should be a child of this union my hopes were dashed forever. And apart from that I could not bear to see my dear people forced under a rule which they did not want. There would be no tolerance. I knew that people were persecuted with more violence in Spain than had ever been known in England. Would Philip and his Inquisition, with a pliant Mary, be able to subdue a proud people?

On the twenty-fifth of July, which was the festival of St James and therefore very appropriate, he being the patron saint of Spain, Mary was married to Philip.

I listened to the gossip. Both Mary and Philip were pleased with the marriage. Their first duty would be to get an heir and the prospect of that filled me with so much melancholy that only then did I realize the greatness of my hopes. Ever since my father's death I had lived with the idea that one day I could come to the throne, although at that time it had seemed most unlikely, with Edward and Mary to come before me, both of whom might have offspring.

When Edward had died and there had been merely Mary, my hopes had risen, for Mary had been aging then and had no husband. As the time passed my hopes grew to a dedication. Every observation I made taught me something. I followed events as far as I could. I weighed up what had happened and considered what might have happened. I loved my country passionately. I loved the people as neither Edward nor Mary ever had. I was fitted to rule as neither of them had been.

And now Mary was married; she loved her bridegroom and she was not too old to bear a child, and that child would stand between me and the throne.

Meanwhile I remained a prisoner. If they could prove something against me I should be led to the block as my mother had been, as Katharine Howard and poor innocent Jane Grey had been.

But so far they could prove nothing against me, and I was determined that they should never have a chance of doing that, so the impulse came to me to write down my determination somewhere where it could be read by people for years to come. I took the diamond ring from my finger and scratched on the windowpane:

> *Much suspected—of me.*
> *Nothing proved can be*
> *Quoth Elizabeth, prisoner.*

I WAS SUMMONED to Court for the Christmas festivities. Did this mean that I was no longer a prisoner? My excitement was intense. It might well be that my sister in her happy condition—for she said she was pregnant—no longer considered me a threat. I was sure her bridegroom was an astute man and he would quickly sense his lack of popularity in England. Perhaps he wished to please the people by recalling me. There must have been a reason—perhaps many. But the fact remained I was summoned to Hampton Court.

When one is a prisoner and life, though fraught with danger, is tedious, any little diversion is welcome even if it holds an element of even greater danger, which a trip to Court must surely hold for me.

So with growing excitement I prepared to leave for Hampton Court in the company of Sir Henry Bedingfeld. We spent the first night at Ricote where I renewed my pleasant friendship with Lord Williams and was so right royally treated that I felt I had left my prison behind me already. After two more days of travel we came to Hampton, and as my guards stayed with me I supposed that my status had not changed as I had hoped.

I had not been an hour in the apartments allotted to me when I had a call from the Council headed by Gardiner. Before they could speak I cried out that I was glad to see them and I hoped they would plead with the Queen and King to release me from my imprisonment.

"My advice to you," said Gardiner, "is to confess your faults and throw yourself on the Queen's mercy."

"As I have never offended against the Queen," I retorted, "either in thought, word or deed, rather than confess to a fault I have not committed I would lie in prison all my life."

"The Queen marvels at your boldness," said Gardiner. "Your refusal to confess suggests that Her Majesty has wrongfully imprisoned you. You must do other than plead your innocence if you are to be set at liberty."

"Then I will stay in prison with honesty," I cried. "I stand by everything I have said, and may God forgive you for what you have done to me."

I saw no use in trying to placate this man. Whatever I did or said he would be my enemy. I was not so much a person to him as an obstacle to his ambitions.

They left me. I knew that I had not behaved as they expected me to. They judged me wrongly. Having endured so much I was not prepared to barter my hopes of the crown—forlorn though they might seem now—for a brief concession. I was playing for high stakes, and if my death was the result, that was more acceptable to me than ignoble capitulation.

For a week I was left alone and I wondered what the motive could have been to take me from my prison in Woodstock merely to put me in another at Hampton Court.

But at last the summons came. The Queen wished to see me.

I faced her with some trepidation as I fell to my knees and she gave me her hand to kiss. She looked at me steadily and said: "I hear that you will confess to no fault."

"It is hard to confess to what is not, Your Majesty."

"You swear that you speak the truth?"

"I swear," I said.

"I pray God this may become manifest."

"If aught can be proved against me," I said stoutly, "I shall be prepared to accept with meekness any punishment Your Majesty may think fit to bestow upon me."

"So you say you have been wrongfully treated?"

"To say so is not possible in your presence."

"Because it would imply my injustice, you mean? So you do not tell me I am unjust, but I doubt not you report so to others."

"Your Majesty, I have never said that you were unjust," I replied coolly. "I have borne and must bear Your Majesty's displeasure, but I swear I have never been aught else than Your Majesty's loyal and true subject."

She looked at me somberly and murmured as though to herself: "God knoweth."

I suspected that she was inclined to believe me and that she was not happy with this rift between us. I had always been vaguely sorry for Mary. I had sensed in her that desire for affection. She had had it from her mother—the only person it turned out to be from whom she ever did have it; and she had seen that mother suffer humiliation, repudiation and imprisonment at our father's hand. No wonder she was warped, no wonder she was starved for affection. I had heard that she lavished it on Philip. And, dear God, I thought, she is with child by him!

She made me sit beside her and my spirits were lifted a little because I felt she was showing friendship toward me. She would while we were together thus but when in conclave with her advisers, my archenemies Gardiner and Renaud, she would allow the suspicions to creep back.

There was a certain unwieldiness about her body. So the child was already making its presence known.

While we were talking together I was aware of a certain movement at the curtains. I fancied that when I turned my head sharply someone had moved back. Could it be that we had a witness to this scene, someone listening to every word that was uttered, noting them to discuss afterward with the Queen? I must be doubly careful.

During that interview, which was growing more and more cordial, I kept an alert eye on the curtains behind which was the retiring chamber. Someone was there who could not resist taking a peep through the curtains. I could not believe it! I had caught a glimpse of black velvet. Philip! Who else could be in the retiring room? So Philip of Spain was eager for a few covert glances at his sister-in-law while he listened to what she said to his Queen.

ALTHOUGH I WAS still guarded I was not treated like a prisoner and as the Christmas festivities began I took my place at Court and was usually seated in a place of honor at the table. I had now been presented to Philip who showed excessive courtesy toward me. It was true that he was far from prepossessing; he had those sandy lashes like my own but mine were thick and my hair was abundant and shining while his was scanty. Moreover my skin was white while his complexion was mud color. He had a very high forehead which coupled with an alert expression gave him a look of cleverness and I was sure he was an extremely brilliant man. Anything he lacked in appearance he made up for in dignity and exquisite manners.

I caught his eyes on me calculatingly and I remembered that he had spied on me when I was with my sister. Meeting him exhilarated me, as clever people always did, and when I realized I had to be very wary of him, I was doubly stimulated.

It was wonderful to be back at Court and arouse the interest of important people. There were feasting and tournaments for we were not only celebrating the season but the wedding as well. I had been provided with some beautiful clothes and it was very pleasant to appear as a princess again instead of a prisoner.

I wished I could see Kat and I wondered what was happening to her. I did hear that Robert Dudley had been released from the Tower and I wondered whether I should see him at Court. But that could hardly be expected;

he might be free from imprisonment but he would hardly be received with honor since his father had succeeded in putting Jane Grey on the throne even if it was only for nine days. Robert Dudley, it seemed, was now in the army or in Norfolk, where some years before, he had been married. If he had not been, *he* would have been chosen as the husband for Jane Grey. When Northumberland saw the opportunity of putting Jane on the throne, Guildford had been the only remaining unmarried son at that time.

I was recovering from my melancholy and when I was dressed in my magnificent gown of white satin decorated with myriads of tiny pearls, I could not believe that I had ever been reconciled to death. This sojourn at Hampton Court had made me realize how much I loved life, how I loved my country and the English people, and that I would never give up hope, however distant, of ruling them one day.

In spite of all this euphoria I did not lose sight of the fact that I was in danger. The Queen looked very sickly. Could she reach a successful confinement? I asked myself, and I knew that others were asking it. Chief of them perhaps Philip himself. Why did he look at me with such speculation? Surely he did not think that if Mary died he could marry me . . . Elizabeth, the heretic! How could he? But heretics are acceptable when a throne goes with them, and I was sure Philip would have no doubts as to his ability to rule a woman as well as a country.

Not this one, my lord! I thought. But I liked him to regard me in that light for he must be comparing my physical aspect with that of Mary. She was getting so old; she was really pathetic; she followed him with her eyes; she loved him completely. It was folly to allow one's feelings to become involved and even greater folly to show them.

Yes, he was comparing my youth with her age, my liveliness with her languor, my challenge with her cloying devotion. I had made it my business to study people and I knew a great deal about Philip of Spain.

There were moments when he cast off his dignity. He might appear to be cold and restrained but I believed there were times when he could be less so. Ever a collector of what the people were saying, I discovered that he was not averse to a little dalliance. Some of the women were giggling about the repulse he had received from Magdalen Dacre, one of Mary's ladies of honor, when Philip had peeped through her window while she was dressing and tried to open the window and get to her. The window could only be opened a little way and she, seeing his arm protruding into her chamber, gave it a sharp rap which made him withdraw it hastily, showing him clearly that she had no intention of engaging in frivolous behavior with anyone, even the Prince of Spain.

Magdalen Dacre was certainly an exceptionally beautiful girl. Philip must have noticed her and perhaps he hoped to seduce her which he probably thought would be easy, he being who he was. One thing I did like about him was that after the rap and his humiliation, he did not attempt to take revenge and always treated her with extra special courtesy as though while desiring her he could yet respect her virtue.

Mary had hardly been seductive before her body had swollen, and it is not the custom of princes to deny themselves. It was reported—but it may well have been malicious gossip—that he liked to visit some of the more questionable haunts of London and that he had a fancy for little girls of the lower classes.

There was a rhyme about him which people sang constantly. It went something like this:

> "The baker's daughter in her russet gown
> Better than Queen Mary without her crown."

At the tournaments I was seated beside my sister and Philip was on the other side of her. I noticed how his eyes were often on me, assessing my physical attractions, I guessed; he already knew my political views. Mary did not notice. I supposed she had not heard the rhyme about the baker's daughter, and I was sure Magdalen Dacre would not mention the Prince's pursuit of her. Mary was innocent of guile. Perhaps that was why she could not please the people.

I guessed that the Spanish Ambassador was of less importance now than he had been. His main mission was accomplished with the marriage, but of course he would still be making sure that events went as Charles the Fifth and Philip ordered that they should. Then there was the French Ambassador, de Noailles, who must not be forgotten. His mission was to bring the English crown to Mary Queen of Scots. He was more my enemy now than Renaud.

Wherever I looked there was intrigue but I thrived on it. After the tedium of prison this was a stimulating life.

As the winter passed, the Queen grew larger and we all awaited her confinement with great expectancy. If it were a healthy boy or girl, that was the end of my hopes. It was the health of the child, not the sex, which would be decisive this time. A living child would mean that England was doomed to return to Rome with all the intolerance and persecution which were pursued in those countries under the domination of the dreaded Inquisition.

I felt I was justified in hoping that the child would not live, though naturally I never said a word of this to anyone.

Mary's skin seemed yellow in daylight; her body was becoming more and more clumsy. One of my ladies whispered to me: "There is a rumor that what the Queen is carrying is not a child."

"What do you mean?" I asked.

"That her swollen body has another cause."

"This must be nonsense."

"I can only tell you what is being said, Your Grace."

HOW SAD THOSE DAYS were for my poor sister! Much as they heralded good news for me I could not but be sorry for her. She had so set her heart on a child. She was so certain that she was pregnant; there had been all the signs. What a terrible blow! What almost unbearable humiliation! It was no child she carried. She was suffering from some hideous form of dropsy.

I think she nearly died of sorrow. She had so longed for that child and she had been so proud to be able to produce it. She needed a child so much and now all her hopes had gone.

She was desperately ill for a long time. People were very careful how they treated me and I enjoyed the deference. I think they were daily expecting news of her death. When I woke up in the morning my first thought was: Will it be today?

Philip was genial with me. I was sure he was a little in love with me, and I was always gratified when men fell in love with me, particularly those who could not ask me to marry them. I still regarded marriage as a state which must be avoided, for when I became Queen I wanted to be Queen in my own right with no one at my side. But it was pleasant to think that Philip admired me. Of course it was a different feeling from that which he had for the bakers' daughters—but there was a part of that too. Philip was not the cold, sexless man he might have been believed to be because of his black velvet, rather somber clothes and the exaggerated ceremony of his manner.

Philibert of Savoy had appeared at Court during the Christmas festivities and another attempt had been made to bring about a match between us. The Queen had been eager for it; she still wanted me safely out of the way; but Philip had not insisted that I marry Philibert, which he might so easily have done, and the reason was, I guessed, that he was looking ahead. If Mary died he would secure the crown of England for Spain by marrying me . . . heretic or not. I'll swear he thought he could soon subdue me on that point. No, no, Master Philip, I thought. Admire me, make your plans, imagine yourself my doting husband, if you will, but it is not to be, for I want no husband. When I am the Queen of England I shall be the Queen . . . absolute Queen with no husband beside me attempting to usurp my power.

After that illness, Mary had changed. She had given up hope of bearing a child, so Philip had discovered that he had duties in Spain and when he left Mary was heartbroken.

I think I owed something to Philip of Spain. I have said his attitude to me had been one of friendship, even something warmer, but at the same time he would have been ready to agree to my elimination if I had threatened his political schemes. However, instead of setting him against me, the fact that Mary was not going to bear a child had made him eager to preserve my life. I was sure he thought of marrying me. Mary Queen of Scots presented a problem. She had already staked her claim to the English throne. I suppose Philip thought it was better to have a heretic Queen for England—whom he might marry and convert—than that the French should become too powerful in England through Mary of Scotland.

So I had not only moved nearer to the throne but stepped out of imminent danger. Of course men like Gardiner and certainly the French Ambassador would seek to destroy me, but the Spanish Ambassador would not wish me to die if my continuing to live was important to Philip of Spain. So my danger was slightly less than it had been, since my powerful and influential enemies had decreased.

I was told that I might retire to Hatfield. I should not be entirely a prisoner but my movements would be under surveillance. Sir Henry Bedingfeld was to be relieved of his duties and Sir Thomas Pope was to be put in charge of my household. He would watch over me and prevent my entering into conspiracies with undesirable people. I had already met Sir Thomas Pope and found him a charming and honorable gentleman, and although I had become somewhat reconciled to Sir Henry I was not displeased at the change. When I arrived at Hatfield great joy awaited me for I found Kat Ashley there. "Come to serve Your Grace," she cried, and we flew into each other's arms.

IT WAS NOT only Kat who was awaiting me at Hatfield. Her husband was with her, Parry too; and to my great joy, my dear and respected tutor Roger Ascham also. Even if I were not entirely free, I could not be unhappy surrounded by such people.

Moreover Sir Thomas Pope was a very different person from Sir Henry Bedingfeld. He was a merry man as well as a kindly one and in order to show me how pleasant life was going to be at Hatfield he decided to give an entertainment in the great hall to amuse me. It was to be a masque and a pageant such as my father had loved. Even the minstrels wore disguises and every lady and gentleman was warned that they must make themselves so different from their usual selves that even their most intimate friends would find it difficult to recognize them. There was dancing and at the banquet we all unmasked and showed ourselves and there was much laughter and exclamations of amazement to the delight of all.

I could see that life was going to be very different here from what I had endured at Woodstock.

Unfortunately news of those particular revels reached the Queen and no doubt Gardiner or someone like that pointed out to her the danger that could arise from such entertainments. If people came in disguises why should not spies make their way into the company? Sir Thomas told me regretfully that he had had orders from the Queen that such revelries must cease.

I was still suspect and not to be trusted.

"There are other ways of amusing ourselves," he said. "However, disguises are forbidden."

It did not matter. I had my friends about me. It would be a great pleasure to talk in various languages with someone as interesting and erudite as Roger Ascham.

At this time there broke out in the country the very worst wave of persecution that was ever known and which I believe will never be forgotten as long as men live. With her marriage to Philip of Spain, Mary had in fact passed over the government of her realm to him; she had brought the country back to Rome, and although the Inquisition had not yet been set up in the country, its rules were being introduced.

I was glad to be shut away in the country. I was filled with shame for my sister. Her folly was beyond my understanding and she earned the hatred of many of her subjects and that adjective which was to be used often when her name was mentioned: Bloody Mary.

So this was what religious fanaticism did to a woman who was by nature humane. I swore I would have no part in it. Perhaps the Spaniards had endured it and would go on doing so. I did not think the English would.

I was sickened as were so many. How could she allow this to be done in her name?

There were two men who urged her to this cruel folly. Gardiner was naturally one and Edward Bonner, Bishop of London, was the other. I despised them both and I could not believe it when I first heard it. I discussed it with Kat in a highly emotional way and with Roger Ascham more calmly, but with none the less revulsion.

To burn men and women at the stake for their religious opinions was not only hideously cruel, it was quite stupid. How could she say: I worship in this way and therefore it is right, and because you do not agree you will be burned to death! I had heard their miserable arguments: The victims were destined to hell fire, so what did it matter if they began their life of torment a few years earlier? How I loathed those persecutors! How I despised them! Not only for their cruelty but for their folly. It was an affront to all reason.

So passed that dreadful year when the fires of Smithfield sobered all London and palls of smoke and the smell of burning flesh hung in the air even in the smallest towns. It was as though my father had never broken with Rome. But it was not quite as it had been. He had been ruthless, true; he had condemned men to death, but it was because they stood in the way of his personal wishes. That was wrong, of course; but this death and torture for a divergence of *belief* was something I could not understand.

There were few of us who did not go in fear of our lives. I myself dreamed of standing in a square while they bound my body to a stake. I had been alarmed at the thought of the axe. But that was merciful compared with the terrible slow death by fire.

Yet many were suffering it.

We went to Mass. I did, yes. I admit it. I accepted the Catholic Faith. At least I forced out the words they wished me to say, but I could never believe that the differences between one sect and another were of any importance. Was I a hypocrite? I do not know. If I was, I was a *sensible* hypocrite. I was certain now that I was going to rule my people and when I did I would put an end to this senseless persecution. I could be of greater use to my people alive than dead and when the time came they would surely forgive me for a few words mumbled in a chapel.

Mary was a sick woman. Her husband had left her and was very happy to do so. He had made a marriage and brought the countries together; they had brought England back to Rome and were now merrily burning her people who refused to accept the faith they would impose on them. Spain had done its work. Our country was as unhappy as theirs. And Mary was aging, ill, and still yearning to bear the child which she never could.

And beside her, those archvillains, tools of Spain and Rome—Gardiner and Bonner—catching their prey, questioning, torturing and condemning to the flames.

Great men died at the stake, men such as Nicholas Ridley who had been a Bishop of London, Hugh Latimer, Bishop of Winchester, and John Hooper, Bishop of Gloucester and Worcester. These men died with great bravery; they were the martyrs. The people watched them sullenly. How long can this last? I wondered.

There was much talk of the manner in which these men had died. Hugh Latimer's last words were repeated over and over again. He had been tied to a stake next to that to which Ridley was bound and he cried out in ringing tones: "Be of good comfort, Master Ridley, we shall this day light such a candle by God's grace in England, as I trust shall never be put out." Fine words from a man about to suffer a cruel death. They were truly martyrs.

Not long after the death of these two it was the turn of Thomas Cranmer to burn at the stake. He had recanted earlier to save himself. I did not blame him for that. In my opinion it was the sensible thing to do; but he had repented the act in the end and as the flames were lighted he held out his right hand. "This hand has written lies," he cried. "It has written them to save my life and therefore it should be the first part of my body to burn."

And later they heard him cry out: "This hand has offended!" and those watching saw him hold it in the flames unflinchingly.

"They will never be forgotten," I said to Kat. "My sister is mad. For a while some may accept this, but the people will hate her for it. Does she know nothing of the English?"

"The people wait patiently for you, my lady," said Kat earnestly. "They wait now . . . as they never did before."

And when I looked into her face I knew that she spoke the truth.

IT WAS NOT surprising that there should be discontent. The time was ripe to rid the country of the Queen and her cruel persecutions. I dreaded these rebellions. My name was always associated with them because if Mary were deposed, I was next in the line to the succession. I wished people would understand that there was no need for rebellion. Mary was more ill each day and all her actions were those of a woman sick in mind and body; her false pregnancies—she had had another of those—her fanatical religious mania and her persecution of what she called heretics, all were more than devotion to her faith; her obsession had turned to madness and showed clearly that she was nearing her end. I knew it. We should be patient and wait. It was much safer to let death carry her off than to raise a rebellion when there would surely always be some to take her side. They would never understand that the waiting game was the safe one.

The first of the plots was devised by Sir Henry Dudley, some remote connection of Robert Dudley, who was not himself, I was relieved to learn, involved in the plan of his reckless kinsman. The plot, however, appeared to have the backing of the King of France who was greatly disturbed by the alliance between his two enemies, England and Spain. Like all such conspirators they used my name as a basis on which to build their schemes, at the heart of which was to depose Mary and set me on the throne.

De Noailles had become very friendly with me since the Spanish marriage and took great pains to let me know that he would do anything to help me. His was a very dangerous friendship, I knew—and of course there was no true friendship in it; it was expediency. Two of the officers of my household named Peckham and Werne were involved in the plot and this disturbed me because it immediately increased the suspicions which would come my way whenever these plots were revealed.

The two men were arrested and what was so disconcerting was that Kat Ashley was taken off for questioning again with a very innocent young Italian, Baptiste Castiglione, who had been engaged to help me perfect my conversation in his language. Some of my ladies, too, were taken for questioning, and when I heard that they were in the Tower and that Kat was in the Fleet Prison I felt that it was going to start again—the terrible anxiety, the fear of what would happen from one day to the next, while my enemies closed in on me. I pictured Kat—dear indiscreet Kat—being forced to make all sorts of statements which would be damning against me, and I became very ill, as I had been during the trials in the past years. The strain was too much. My skin grew yellow with jaundice and I could not stand without feeling dizzy. There was nothing to be done but to take to my bed, and this in itself could be construed as some sort of guilt.

There was one matter for rejoicing. Gardiner had died—not violently as would have been fitting for a man who had caused so much misery, but of dropsy, quietly in his bed.

There was one enemy the less; but I doubted not that many more would spring up to take his place.

I kept to my bed while Kat's apartments were searched. Nothing concerned with the plot was found in her rooms but certain pamphlets which were called seditious—which meant Protestant—were found there and I was in a state of nervous prostration, seeing Kat brought to the stake and hearing her piteous cries as the fire touched her limbs.

I thought: I can bear no more of this. Nothing is worth it. I cannot subject my friends to perpetual terror.

There was another development. A young man appeared at a place called Yaxley and declared he was Edward Courtenay and my husband. It was such utter nonsense that I was not afraid of this one. The young man was a tall golden-haired giant with the Plantagenet looks. This was easily explained because my great-grandfather had been a man who had had countless mistresses of all sorts and conditions in every corner of the country, so there were a great many people who bore a resemblance to him.

I was sure I could not possibly have been arrested for complicity in such a plot as that but had Gardiner been alive he would have found some reason for implicating me.

I was receiving communications from de Noailles who had shown such friendship for me since my sister's marriage. His letters were urging me to take advantage of his King's invitation to visit the Court of France where I should be safe until the time came for me to mount the throne.

A few months before I should have scorned the invitation, seeing it for what it was. I knew that the aim of Henri Deux was to set his daughter-in-law Mary Stuart on the throne of England. I think I must have been very weak just then. I could not sleep. I became so ill with anxiety that I did not greatly care what happened to me.

When I look back I marvel at myself. But it is strange what illness can do to one, particularly the sort of mental anguish from which I was suffering since the fresh wave of insurrections and the fear aroused by wondering what evil could befall a country which sent good men to a horrible death because of their faith.

I wanted to get away. I felt I could endure no more and the thought of the elegant French court was inviting.

I sent a message to Lady Sussex who had always been a good friend, and I asked her to discover in secret more of this plan from the French Ambassador. I really believed—I must have been suffering from hallucinations—that I could remain at the French Court and come back at the appropriate time to claim the crown.

Then there happened one of those miracles which seem, looking back, like Divine intervention and made me certain of my destiny.

When Lady Sussex was able to meet the French Ambassador she found not de Noailles, whom she had been expecting and who had been the instigator of the plot to get me out of England, but another in his place. Because the Dudley rebellion had begun in France with the backing of the King, de Noailles's communications with me had been noted and some intercepted. Consequently, he had been dismissed abruptly and his brother, the Bishop of Acqs, had been sent to take his place.

I never did understand why the Bishop should seek to protect me. He was certainly not following in his brother's footsteps. Or it may even have been that the King of France did not wish me to leave the field of action, and it had been seen by him that the de Noailles policy of capturing me was not the best for France. Whatever it was, the Bishop told Lady Sussex that if I went to France now, I should never come back, and if I hoped to wear the crown I should be on the spot when the moment came to take it.

When Lady Sussex told me this I saw how foolish I had been. I went onto my knees and thanked God for His merciful act in saving me.

Whatever happened, I must stay. I had come through great dangers. The end must be in sight, and if I could manage to keep alive for a little longer I should be triumphant.

I wrote to my sister assuring her of my loyalty. It was true that the men Peckham and Werne were of my household, but I had known nothing of their schemes any more than I knew of this ridiculous man who turned out to be named Cleobury and who had called himself the Earl of Devonshire.

Kat and the other members of my household returned to Hatfield and as soon as I saw them I began to feel better; my old strength returned and I marveled afresh that I could have been so foolish as to have almost committed an act which would have been fatal to my future.

So there I was at Hatfield—almost a prisoner inasmuch as I could not leave without the Queen's permission, and everything I did was reported to her.

IN THE FEBRUARY of the following year Philip returned to England.

Reports came to us that my sister's health was much improved and my immediate thoughts were that there might yet be a child. Moreover I wondered what Philip's reaction would be to the attempted risings which were an indication of the rumblings of dissatisfaction throughout the land. He must have had a purpose in coming. I was sure it was not merely to be with Mary.

The result of his return was a cordial invitation for me to go to Court. Mary appeared to have accepted my protestations of innocence and I imagined—with some amusement—that I had been invited at the urgings of Philip.

When I rode into London through Smithfield and Old Bailey and Fleet Street to Somerset House the people cheered me. I had wondered what effect my submission to my sister's will in religion, which had now become the law of the country, would have on them; but I was sure the dear good people were wise enough to know that I did what I did to preserve my life so that when the time came I could be alive to serve them.

At every turn they showed their love for me and I managed to convey to them that I was aware of the immense debt of gratitude I owed them.

It was wonderful to be at Court, where I was received with honor as the Queen's sister and heiress to the throne. Chiefly I was gratified by Philip's attitude toward me. I saw plans in his eyes when they alighted on me. He was not insensible to my youth and charms, and with the crown and all that meant I must have seemed to him a glittering prize. I would never marry him, but there was no harm—indeed there was every necessity—in letting him imagine that I might.

Mary was very simple. She was delighted that Philip showed such regard for me. She thought he would be suspicious of one who had been a heretic. Nothing of the sort! I had the impression that he was just waiting for the death of his wife.

I was, therefore, a little taken aback when he once more introduced the subject of Philibert of Savoy. Then I began to wonder whether I had correctly assessed his motives. If I married . . . what then? Who would take the throne when Mary died? Was he planning to set himself up as King and sole ruler of England? It could not be. Even his Spanish arrogance must realize that that would never be allowed.

I was adamant. I would not marry. I clung to the virgin state, I declared. Marriage was entirely repulsive to me.

He sighed and said his friend Philibert was the best of men. I reminded him that Philibert had been making love to the Duchess of Lorraine, so it seemed to me that, friend of Philip's though he was, he was something of a philanderer and I would have no mind to take such a husband, even if I had not resigned myself to the single state.

He made no sign but I heard afterward that he told Mary she should insist on my marrying. She was the Queen and I was the subject. There again I was mystified as to his real intentions.

But that was Philip, as I was to discover later—much later—he was devious and as dangerous as a snake.

There was yet another insurrection. A certain Sir Thomas Stafford had been at the Court of France where he had received some favors from Henri Deux who, it was believed, had urged him to attempt rebellion in England. The French King was growing more and more alarmed at the friendship between England and Spain which since the marriage of Mary and Philip had become very close indeed, Mary being completely under the domination of the husband she adored.

Stafford landed on the coast of Yorkshire and took Scarborough Castle with ease. He tried to rally men to his banner by declaring that, in marrying Philip, Mary had passed over the country to Spain, and that the Spaniards were about to land and complete the enslavement. The Inquisition was preparing to land on our shores. This was, of course, the way in which to arouse the people, but Stafford was not clever enough. His mission was known before he arrived for there were many spies at the Court of France.

An army had been sent up to Yorkshire under the Earl of Westmorland, and in a short time Stafford's men, who were helpless against trained soldiers, were routed and Stafford himself captured, and very quickly sentenced to the barbarous death of hanging and quartering which took place in May at Tyburn.

Fortunately I was not implicated in this, although the aim of every plot was to depose Mary and I was naturally the one to step into her place.

Philip was restive as he always was in England. His heart was in Spain; moreover I think he wanted to get away from the cloying affections of Mary.

I knew that her sickly looks were repulsive to him, and whereas he might have stayed longer if she had not tried to force her affections on him, as it was he was very eager to escape.

Philip took advantage of the Queen's annoyance and that of her ministers in the interference of the French over Stafford to get further English help for Spain against the French; and having succeeded in this I fancy he felt that his visit was not altogether without results. He had not married me off, but he had succeeded in involving England in his conflict with the French.

I was sorry for Mary after he had gone. She was so pathetic, so ill, so lacking in feminine attractions; and in her heart she knew that he had no love for her at all. Strangely enough it was to me she turned in those months which followed. After all, whatever conflict there was between us, I was her sister, and she was a very lonely woman. She had no friends of whom she could be sure, and her only hope of close contact with her own was through me.

I knew this and I tried to be tender to her. I could not exactly love her. It was not easy to love Mary; and in those last days I could never be in her presence without thinking of those people whom she had sent to the stake in the name of religion. Indeed, if one rode out into the streets of London one could not but be aware of the pall of smoke which hung over Smithfield; and I was often sickened when I fancied I could detect the odor of burning flesh in the air. Yet she did not suffer any qualms about the terrible suffering which was being inflicted in her name.

She was such an unhappy woman—but perhaps she should have been. If only she had not suffered so in her youth and seen her beloved mother so humiliated; if she could have married when she was young and had children, she might have been different. She was never one to show her affection— except with Philip. She was more honest than I. I could act and imply friendship when it was wise to do so. I could go to Mass, but when the time came I was going to stand firm as the Protestant Queen. All this I could do; but Mary never could. She would never dissemble and would always stand by what she considered to be the truth.

We talked now and then together in a sisterly fashion. There was a possibility, she said, that she might yet have a child.

I said I hoped she would be blessed.

So I did, but not with a child. Sometimes I would wake in the night and start up thinking that my sister had been delivered of a beautiful boy. Then I would come back to reality and I knew in my heart that she would never bear a healthy child. I knew too that time was running out for her.

I hoped it would not be long. I wanted to be Queen while I still had my youthful freshness, which was important to me. I was paid many compliments but I did realize that the nearer one came to the throne the more glowing they would be. I liked to think of myself as beautiful but in my franker moments I knew that while I was pleasant to look at, I lacked that beauty which many Court ladies possessed. I had my bright hair and my eyes were large and tawny which made them rather striking, but my eyebrows and lashes were pale. I needed long dark lashes and well-defined brows to show off my eyes. I was tallish and straight and elegant in figure and my white skin and hands and tapering fingers were my greatest beauty. So I was fair enough and being royal, I could be called a beauty. But when I rode through the streets to be acclaimed as Queen I did not want to have lost my youthful freshness.

I spent my time between the Court and Hatfield, and during that time Hatfield was still something of a prison because I was guarded night and day and no one came and went without its being reported to the Queen.

Sir Thomas Pope was always trying to divert me and I was often allowed to hunt. When we journeyed from one place to another we went in search of the hart and Sir Thomas always made that something of a ceremony. I would have my retinue of ladies dressed in white satin seated on their palfreys and my yeomen all in green, and I of course would be splendidly clad and the privilege of cutting the throat of the captured animal always fell to me.

Gustavus Vasa, the King of Sweden, was asking for my hand for his son Eric and again I felt a mingling of excitement and determination to refuse, but it pleased me very much to be asked in marriage though I had every intention of refusing.

The relationship between my sister and myself had so improved that when I went to Richmond to visit her she sent a royal barge for me with an awning of green silk decorated with fresh flowers—a mark of her respect for me and my position as her heiress.

To be in her company might have been something of a strain but I was adept at guiding the conversation in the way I wished it to go, and because outwardly I accepted the Catholic Faith Mary was guileless enough to believe that I was converted. I had to avoid the subject of religion and the terrible events in Smithfield for if they were mentioned I feared I might show my repugnance.

I was delighted that she made no effort to persuade or even force me to marry. She knew of the offer from Eric of Sweden which I had rejected, but I had carefully said in my reply that I should not dream of marrying without the Queen's consent, which had pleased her, for Gustavus had approached me first, which was unusual in these matters. I insisted that I had no wish to marry.

"You will one day," she answered.

"As yet," I replied, "the virgin state is the one I wish for."

She smiled at me. "There are great blessings in marriage," she said wistfully.

Blessings! Had she found them with Philip? An indifferent husband, whose sole reason for marrying was the power and political advantage it would bring him, whose visits to her were clearly distasteful to him, an unpleasant duty which must be performed in the hope of getting an heir, slinking off incognito for an assignation with the baker's daughter. Marriage! Oh no, not for me! Mary might have kept her dignity intact if she had never married.

The more I thought of marriage—and when I did my thoughts were dominated by my mother—the less I desired it.

The safe subject with Mary was the child she believed she carried and I was making some garments with the most delicate embroidery—at which I was quite good—and Mary was delighted with them.

I shall never forget the sight of her as she sat holding the tiny shift in her hands and that look of bliss on her face as she contemplated the joy of having the child she hoped to bear. It was particularly poignant as I was sure—as was everyone else—that she would never have a child.

But she softened toward me, and I toward her, because I saw her then as she was, a lonely woman reaching for affection. She spoke of Philip tenderly—and it was not the Philip he was but the one she had gulled herself to believe he was. "A great man," she said, "and a great King. I am the luckiest woman on Earth to be his wife."

I could not bear it. I was not given to tears but I wanted to weep then.

She twisted the ring on her finger. It was black enamel and gold. She called it her betrothal ring.

"I look at it often," she said. "It reminds me of Philip when he is absent. Of course, it is inevitable that he must be absent. He has a great country to rule. I would that he could be beside me all the time. One day, sister, you will know the blessings of a good husband."

I could scarcely prevent myself from protesting. I wanted no husband, least of all a power-seeking cynic like Philip.

"This ring is so precious to me," she said. "I have vowed it shall never leave my finger while I live."

I took her hand and kissed it.

"I hope, sister, that it will remain there for a very long time," I said, which was not exactly true. Yet I pitied her.

Was it wrong to hope for Mary's death? Perhaps. But what had life to offer her but lost hopes, a heartless husband and a childless fate? Even more important, what had England to hope for under her rule? In any case one

QUEEN OF THIS REALM

cannot help one's thoughts and I knew that I was the one chosen to lead my country from disaster.

So friendly did she become toward me that she proposed to visit me at Hatfield. Sir Thomas Pope was thrown into a fever of anticipation and he and I discussed with great excitement how we would entertain the Queen. The cost would be enormous, but Sir Thomas was a very wealthy man and I was not poor so we determined to entertain the Queen in a royal manner. Sir Thomas had in his possession a set of superb tapestries representing the siege of Antioch and I proposed that we decorate the state chamber with these. He was very ready to do anything to please me and agreed immediately.

When they were hung we reviewed them with great pride and Sir Thomas said to me: "It may well be that when Her Majesty comes, she will urge you to marry."

"Sir Thomas," I replied firmly, "since I have become mature I have made up my mind that I do not wish to marry."

He smiled indulgently, for we were the best of friends. "Your Grace will change her mind when some suitable person comes to you with the Queen's consent."

"My dear Sir Thomas," I replied, "what I shall do hereafter I know not, but I assure you upon my truth and fidelity and as God be merciful unto me, I am not at this time otherwise minded than I have declared unto you. No, though I were offered the greatest prince in Europe."

He merely smiled at me. I was sure he thought my remarks were not to be taken too seriously.

"Come," I said, "let us talk of other matters. We should have a play to entertain Her Majesty."

So we went on with our arrangements. There was a play after supper which was performed by the choirboys of St Paul's which pleased the Queen. We had been careful not to arrange a boisterous entertainment but to concentrate entirely on the tastes of the Queen, which meant presenting music and singing. I accompanied one of the boys on the virginals. He had a pure and lovely voice which enchanted the Queen.

It was a very successful visit and I was glad that Mary and I were on better terms and she seemed no longer to suspect me of plotting to depose her. One only had to look at her poor yellow face and her swollen body—not with child as she so fondly hoped, but with disease—to realize that she could not live for many more months.

It was a disastrous year for her. The time had come when she had to accept that she was not pregnant and never had been. The protuberance which she had fondly hoped was a child was some growth within her. It seemed now that my accession was inevitable. She accepted it and so did Philip; and so did the people. With the coming of the new year, so disastrous for Mary, so thrilling for me, events were moving fast.

Appeals were coming from the town of Calais, the only town left to England of all the conquests of Edward III and Henry V. The French, enraged by England's alliance with Spain, had marched on Calais and on a bitterly cold January day we heard that the town had surrendered to the Duke of Guise.

Mary was frantic. Calais was not so very important; it was difficult to defend it; but it was the last possession on the coast of France and it had been held for generations as a symbol that the English still had one foot in France. And she had lost it because she had allowed Philip to persuade her to join him in war against the French.

I often wondered then if that poor unhappy woman ever thought what disaster the Spanish marriage had brought to her and her country. Oh, what a lesson! The people had been against it and one must always have the people on one's side. Yes, the people had hated the Spanish marriage; it had brought a religious intolerance to England, not known since the persecution of the Templars. Men and women were being burned at the stake. Who was ever going to forget Cranmer, Ridley, Latimer and Hooper? The marriage had failed to produce the only thing which would have made it worthwhile from Mary's point of view—and now the last disaster. The English had lost Calais.

Unreasonable in her grief, the Queen begged the Council to spare no effort to regain the town which she called the chief jewel of our realm. The Council pointed out to her the cost of such an operation and if the town were regained it would have to be held at even more expense, for it was obvious that, having captured it, the French would be determined to retain it—and in short, the town was not worth the effort of recapturing it.

Mary mourned deeply. She said that when she died they would find "Calais" written across her heart.

Meanwhile life at Hatfield was changing. There was a less rigorous guard on me. Sir Thomas Pope had always been my good friend so there was little change in his attitude toward me. It was different with others. Visitors came to Hatfield from Court and there was a clear indication in their manner toward me that they already regarded me as their Queen.

One of my best friends was Sir Nicholas Throckmorton, an ardent Protestant. In fact I detected a certain fanaticism in him which I did not share, for I did not like that stern unrelenting attitude from whichever side it came. It was dangerous, bred cruelty and intolerance and prevented one from changing one's mind when it would be wise to do so.

All the same I knew that Sir Nicholas would be a good friend to me because in spite of recent deviation for form's sake, I represented the Protestants. He had been suspect at the time of Wyatt's rebellion and had only narrowly escaped death then. He was well versed in political affairs and had a wide knowledge of what was happening at Court; and his visits to Hatfield were becoming more frequent. I knew from Sir Nicholas how rapidly the Queen's health was declining.

"There are rumors of her death," he said, "even while she lives."

"One must be careful not to be misled by rumor," I replied.

"Indeed that is so, Your Grace. The Queen is so sick and clearly on her death-bed. People are being put in the pillory because they are saying she is already dead."

"I shall need proof before I believe it. And the burnings?" I continued.

"They go on apace. It would seem as though the Queen believes that the more people who die in torment, the greater her glory in Heaven. As I left London a poor woman named Alice Driver was preparing for her death and the people had come out to watch her last minutes. She had already had her ears cut off and was calling Her Majesty Jezebel as they tied her to the stake."

I shivered. "The Queen knows of this . . . and death is close to her!"

"The Queen believes she does God's work, Your Grace."

"It is beyond my understanding, Master Throckmorton," I said.

"The people are looking to you, Your Grace. They say when your turn comes there will be an end to this misery."

"There shall be, Nicholas, my friend. There shall be. It would appear to be near now but we must step with caution. I have faced death too many times to want to challenge it. I have my enemies. It is not too late for them to turn against me . . . while the Queen lives."

"Which cannot be long, my lady."

"You speak carelessly. I will not claim the throne until I am certain that my sister is dead. There is a ring she wears day and night. She calls it her betrothal ring because it was given to her by Philip. I will not believe that she is dead, until I hold that ring in my hand."

"It shall be my duty, Your Grace, to bring it to you."

And so I waited at Hatfield and each day when I rose, I wondered: Is this the one?

THERE WERE SO many visitors to Hatfield, so many who wished me well. I often said to Kat: "How many of these men would be coming to me now if they thought I had little chance of mounting the throne? How many come for love of me? How many for hopes of what good will come to them?"

"It is hard for queens to tell the difference, my love," said Kat, wise for once.

"Perhaps one can never be sure and since one cannot it is well to make certain that one never has a chance of finding out . . . unless one wants to."

"Oh, you are a shrewd one," said Kat.

At least I was sure of her love. It had remained steadfast through all my adversities and so would it be to the end of our days.

We had one visitor at Hatfield who threw Kat into a flutter of excitement. In fact it had the same effect on me, though I was more discreet about it.

So many visitors to Hatfield—so what could be so special about one more? He was exceptionally tall—not too broad but broad enough to give an impression of masculine strength to his elegance. He had dark hair and eyes, with a fresh complexion and the most perfectly shaped features I had ever seen . . . not too finely chiseled, as Kat said afterward, but with that little touch of rough hew which was so becoming in a man. His clothes were rich, the colors not overbright but tastefully blended. He was the most handsome, the most graceful and the most attractive man I had ever seen—even including Thomas Seymour.

I never forgot that meeting; all through the years I have carried with me the memory of Robert Dudley as he was when he presented himself to me on that autumn morning.

I was told he begged an audience of me though I could never imagine Robert begging anything. He would ask it in a manner which suggested he was sure of success. Confidence was ever his way.

When they told me that Lord Robert Dudley was asking to see me, I was excited even before I saw him. I remembered the boy I had known at my father's Court; even then there must have been some quality in him which impressed me; then there had been the time when we had been in the Tower together and the fact of his nearby presence had given me courage and lightened the dark days. Now here he was at Hatfield asking an audience.

I went down and received him in the great hall.

When he saw me he fell onto his knees. He took my hand and kissed it and lifted his eyes to my face.

"Welcome to Hatfield, Lord Robert," I said.

"My gracious lady," he replied. "It is indeed good of you to see me."

"There is no need to remain on your knees," I told him.

He rose and then I saw how tall he was, while he looked at me as though in wonder and I felt a glow of pleasure, for his gaze was not only of respect for my rank but deep admiration for my person.

"Why have you come, Lord Robert?" I said to hide a certain confusion. "Is it for the same reason that many come to Hatfield now?"

"I have just returned from battle."

"Yes. I believe you did good service for your country. And now you are here . . . as many others are."

"I came to bring you gold," he said. "I have sold some of my estates so that I might have the money. I trust you will not need it, but if there should be trouble it would be well for you to be prepared."

"You bring me money, Lord Robert!"

"I have it here. My man will bring it to you. Your Grace, if it should be necessary to fight for what is yours by right, here is one who will stand beside you and cares so much for your cause that he has sold certain of his estates to raise money for any need or emergency which may arise."

"You are indeed a friend," I said, "and I thank you."

"There was a time when you and I were both prisoners in the Tower," he said, his eyes never leaving my face. "There was a young boy . . ."

"Little Martin," I replied. "He brought me your messages of cheer until they stopped him."

"Your Grace remembers! It is more than I dared hope. I never forgot, and I shall be with you should you need my help."

"Thank you, Lord Robert. I accept your offer and your friendship."

"I shall be watchful of Your Grace. There is much coming and going on the road to Hatfield. The Queen is very sick. If anything should go wrong, Hatfield could become a prison."

"If aught goes wrong? What mean you by that?"

"None knows more than Your Grace what a dangerous world we live in."

"Lord Robert, are you telling me there are plots against me?"

"I know of none. None would confide in me. I have always been Your Grace's most ardent supporter."

"Except," I said, a little sharply, "when you were among those who tried to put Lady Jane Grey on the throne."

"That was my father, and as he was my father I was forced to stand with him. It was no disloyalty to Your Grace. I am yours to command. My lands and goods are at your disposal. This I have brought with me is but a token. Whatever need you should have of me, I am yours . . . these arms, this heart . . . this man."

I was so touched I held out my hand, which he took and kissed fervently. He was a little too bold, perhaps, a little too intense, but I was honest enough to admit that I liked his fervor.

I said: "Thank you, Lord Robert. You may go now. I shall not forget this magnanimous offer. I may hold you to it, you know."

"I shall be here whenever you need me."

He bowed low and departed.

I went to my room. I did not want to speak to anyone for a while. I just wanted to think of him. I would remember every word he had said, every inflection of his voice, every expression which had touched his handsome face, the ardor in his eyes.

I should see him again soon and perhaps then I should be Queen.

MY SISTER KNEW that she was dying. I heard that she had received a letter from Philip in which he urged her to name me her heir. I did not see that that was important. I *was* her heir on the terms of my father's will. It was not for Mary to name me, or anyone else. But it did show that Philip realized I must follow her. He must have been extremely nervous about French aspirations through Mary Stuart and I still believed that in his heart he was hoping to marry me. I was certain that he was a little enamored of my person and because of his nature he would look forward to marriage with one who was young and attractive; moreover, in his arrogant way he would think he was quite capable of bending me to his will. How mistaken he was!

I was a little surprised when two members of Mary's Council arrived. I thought they might well have come to announce her death and I was wondering whether I should believe them. I had to watch for traps. I had said that I would not accept that my sister was dead until I held her gold and ebony ring in my hands, and I meant that.

But the councilors had not come to kneel to me as their Queen. They bowed with due deference and one of them said: "The Queen has sent us to Your Grace to tell you that it is her intention to bequeath the royal crown to you. In return for this favor there are three conditions with which you must comply. The first is that you will not change the Privy Council; the second that you will make no alteration in religion; and thirdly that you will discharge the Queen's debts and satisfy her creditors."

I felt anger rising within me, but I said calmly enough that I could satisfy her on the last of these matters with the utmost ease as she was asking nothing more than what was just. "As to the others," I went on, "there is no reason why I should thank the Queen for her intention to give me the crown for she has neither the power to bestow it upon me nor can I be deprived of it. It is my hereditary right. I respectfully point out that I should be allowed to choose my own councilors as she chose hers."

I could see they were really taken aback and I really believe they thought I should be overcome with gratitude because the Queen was giving her consent to what was mine by right. But now I had come to the dangerous clause: religion. It was always religion which caused the greatest trouble. The Queen was not yet dead and I still had to walk warily. I paused to consider my reply. Then I said: "As to religion, I promise this much, that I will not change it providing only that it can be proved by the word of God which shall be the only foundation and rule of my religion."

They looked bemused, as well they might. Experience had taught me that it is always wise to be obtuse when discussing religion, and if one could bring in God as one's advocate so much the better.

The Councilors went away. I fancied they were gravely considering my words and I felt that I was getting very near to the crown.

ᴄʜᴇ ɴᴇxᴛ ᴄᴀʟʟᴇʀ was the Count de Feria, the Ambassador from Philip himself. He was extremely affable, and I was inclined to be a little aloof, for I fancied I did not have to be so careful in manner toward him as I had been in the past. He and his master would immediately lose their importance when my sister was no longer there to sustain it and it pleased me to let these arrogant Spaniards know that England was slipping out of their clutches.

He began by conveying Philip's friendly feelings toward me.

"He has ever been kindly disposed toward Your Grace," he said. "You will remember that it was through his persuasion that you came to Court."

"I remember it well," I replied.

"Moreover, it was he who advised the Queen to make you her heir and you must feel gratitude toward him for this."

There was nothing which annoyed me more than to be told that my sister had had to be persuaded to give me that to which I had a right, and I felt my anger flaring up. I said coldly: "This was no matter of persuasion. I am the heir to the throne by right of birth. As my father's daughter, I am so named in his will. Therefore no matter what your master said to my sister, my right to the throne is my own, and I believe the people of England will see right done."

"I am sure you will be grateful for the continued friendship of my master."

"Friendship is always to be preferred to enmity and I shall remain friendly with all those who mean well to my country."

"Through his marriage my master became King of this country."

"He was the Queen's consort it is true, although he spent very little time with her."

"He had so many duties in Spain . . ."

"And now he will be even more engrossed in his duties," I said, referring to the death of the Emperor Charles which had occurred the previous month.

De Feria could not deny that. I was smiling, inwardly wondering what he would report to his master.

I went on: "As you know the King, your master, urged me more than once to marry Philibert of Savoy. Ah, if I had, where should I be now? Not here, most certainly. I should have been ill advised to have listened to him."

"My master believed at the time that it would have been an excellent match for you. He was eager for your good."

That was too much and I need not be subservient now.

I said sharply: "Your master has the good of his own country ever at heart, and that is all that can be expected of a ruler. My sister lost favor with her people when she married a foreigner and brought him to these shores."

De Feria was nonplussed. I wondered if he had been told to sound me out about marriage with Philip. If he had, he evidently decided that this was not the moment to raise the matter. Nor was it, with Philip's poor wife, my sister, not yet dead, certain though it was that her end was imminent.

He went away somewhat crestfallen and I felt I had handled the situation very well.

THE TENSION WAS MOUNTING. I wanted to be alone to think. Mary was dying. It could not be many days now. I went into the gardens and as I was there I heard the sound of horses' hoofs. A party of riders were close. I stood still, my heart beating fast. Then I saw them.

They were members of the Council and they could only be here on one mission.

They dismounted and came toward me. They fell to their knees.

"God save Queen Elizabeth!" they cried, and they took my hand and, in turn, kissed it and swore to serve me.

I listened to them and was exultant. This was the greatest moment of my life.

I was overcome with joy but perhaps because of the vicissitudes through which I had passed I felt strangely humble.

Often during my most dangerous moments I had made Kat read Psalm 118 with me and I knew it by heart.

"It is better to trust in the Lord than to put confidence in princes."

"Thou hast thrust sore at me that I might fall; but the Lord helped me."

Often I had repeated those words and they came once more into my mind and I cried aloud: "This is the Lord's doing; it is marvelous in our eyes."

EVERYONE WAS NOW converging on Hatfield, all eager to proclaim me Queen.

Nicholas Throckmorton arrived with the gold and ebony ring, and he

QUEEN OF THIS REALM

was a little put out because the Council had reached me first. I thanked him for his good service, which I promised I should not forget.

There was one other who came riding at full speed on a magnificent white horse.

I was delighted to see him and when he knelt down, kissed my hand and cried: "God save the Queen!" I almost wept with an emotion which I had to conceal.

"I would I had been the first to reach you," he said. "As soon as I heard the news, for which I was earnestly waiting, I took my fastest horse. I wished to be the first to call you Queen and offer my life in your service."

"I forget not that you came earlier," I said. "Rest assured, Lord Robert, that you will not be forgotten."

"My lady . . . so young . . . so fair . . . and a crown to carry!"

"Do not fear for me," I answered. "I have long been prepared."

"Fortune is smiling on England this day," he said.

"Perhaps too it will smile on Robert Dudley," I said. "I offer you the post of my Master of Horse. What say you?"

He was on his knees again. His eyes sparkled with pleasure and all the time they watched me. I was young . . . so was he. We were of an age.

"Master of the Queen's Horse," he said slowly. "There is nothing I could have wished for more . . . because it will bring me close to Your Majesty. I shall be beside you for as long as you need me."

Oh, glorious day! Dull November perhaps, but for me no day could have been brighter.

Truly it was marvelous in *our* eyes. At last I had my crown. I had the homage of my subjects, the love of my people—and the passionate admiration of Robert Dudley.

Vivat Regina

ALTHOUGH THIS WAS A TIME OF GREAT TRIUMPH FOR ME, I must not forget that it had come about through my sister's death and I thought it would be proper to show a little sorrow for her. I did not have to feign this entirely. I had often thought of Mary and the tragic failure of her life. I had looked on it as an outstanding example of how not to act. The people did not mourn her. How could they when they could smell the smoke from Smithfield? But that was in the past. This was the time for rejoicing. Young Elizabeth had taken the place of aging Mary, and the ties with Spain, that hated enemy, were broken. They looked forward to golden days and they must not be disappointed.

I had decided that I should remain a few days at Hatfield House out of respect for my sister. It was two days after her death before I was formally proclaimed Queen at the gates.

The next day I held my first Privy Council. Hatfield House had become a Court. People were gathering there all hoping for some place in my service. But I already knew whom I should employ. The trials through which I had passed had given me a good idea of whom I could trust and who had the ability to serve me as would be necessary. Therefore I was delighted to welcome William Cecil to Hatfield for I had never forgotten his help and was well aware of his astuteness. I had made up my mind that when I formed a government, he should be part of it.

At that first Council meeting I got some inkling of the state of the country, and it was decidedly depressing. We were sadly weakened; our exchequer pitiably lacking; food was dear; we were at war with France and Scotland, and the French had recaptured Calais so that we no longer had a foothold in France. But there was one thing I had always known and that was that wars brought no good to either side. Perhaps because I was a woman I had no desire to indulge in them. I had no glorious dreams of riding into battle; my victories should be those of diplomacy. I remember William Cecil's once saying that a country gains more in a year of peace than by ten years of war. I agreed with that sentiment, and I made up my mind that my country should not go to war unless it was absolutely necessary to do so.

The more I thought of it the more I knew that Cecil was the man for the most influential post in the government, and at the first meeting of the Council I announced that I had chosen him for my chief Secretary of State.

I did keep certain members of Mary's Council in office. The Earl of Arundel and Lord William Howard were two of them, and another was William Paulet, Marquess of Winchester, whom I made Lord Treasurer. Nicholas Bacon was Lord Keeper of the Great Seal, and Sir Francis Knollys, who was a second cousin by marriage, became Vice Chamberlain. He was a firm Protestant and had found it necessary to leave the country during Mary's reign, but I knew he was a good honest man, and I liked to favor my mother's relations, provided they had the ability.

I was satisfied that I had built up a strong government, and it suddenly occurred to me that none of the members I had chosen was young. Cecil, oddly enough, was the youngest, and he was thirty-eight. I was glad of this for I was a great believer in experience—a valuable asset which few people have the wit to appreciate. But being aware for so long that sooner or later I could become Queen, I had many times planned which men I would choose to serve me. It was exhilarating to be in the position to make those plans reality.

We were no longer going to be ruled by priests. I had a company of able and trustworthy men and I intended to turn my country from debt and bankruptcy into a great state when every man and woman in it should be proud to be English.

I had to give Kat a post to keep her close to me so I made her my first Lady of the Bedchamber and her delight in her new dignity greatly amused me.

"It will make no difference to me, queen or not," she told me. "You'll still be my Elizabeth and I shall say what I please."

"You will have to be careful, Kat," I warned her. "Only fools anger princes."

"Well, you have always said I was a fool, mistress."

I boxed her ears playfully. I made her husband Keeper of the Jewels and my dear Parry was Treasurer of the Household. I was not one to forget my old friends.

Even aged Blanche Parry, whose learning I had always valued and who had taught me to speak the Welsh language, was not forgotten. Indeed why should she be? She was very clever and erudite and quite worthy to hold the post of Keeper of the Royal Books at Windsor Castle, an honor which delighted her.

There was another side to my glorious position and that was one—such was my nature—which I awaited with eager anticipation: my ride through my capital city, my acclamation by the people, and my coronation which must take place as soon as possible for there is a belief among the people that a monarch is not a true one until she—or he—has been crowned.

An added delight to these preparations was that they would be supervised by my Master of Horse, and that gave me an excuse to have many consultations with the man in whose company I took such delight.

Robert Dudley was for me the ideal companion. He showed me in a hundred ways that he adored me . . . and not just as a queen. He had graceful manners so that while he was bold he always remembered who I was. For me it was the perfect relationship. I had always been susceptible to admiration; I greatly enjoyed compliments even when the wiser side of my nature told me they were not true; and in spite of the fact that the thought of marriage was repulsive to me, courtship I found exhilarating. And this was the relationship which was springing up between Robert Dudley and me. He admired me; his looks, his gestures, his words, implied that he was in love with me. He was particularly eligible because he was already married and for that reason I could dally with him to my heart's content.

A week after Mary's death I came to London. What a glorious day it was when I rode through my capital city, and how the people rejoiced! I was deeply moved by their trust in me. They looked to me to bring happiness and prosperity back to the country and I vowed I would do so. This was the end of the Smithfield fires. This was the beginning of the great era which I vowed would be known forever as Elizabethan. I swore to myself that I would never betray them. I loved these people with their honest faces and their shining belief in me. I would show them my love for them. I felt as Joan of Arc must have felt riding into Orleans. She had been sure she had God's blessing—and so was I.

How they cheered me! They came to me with nosegays—some very humble. I took them all and kissed them and that made them cheer more wildly. I gave them to one of my women to hold for me while I tenderly thanked the givers. My people must never think me too proud to speak to them whenever they wished to speak to me. I knew that the approval of these people was necessary to keep me in my place, and that was something I should never forget.

And riding beside me was that incomparable man. How he sat his horse! There was no man in England who could manage a horse as he could. He was rightly Master of Horse. Moreover his office meant that he was often beside me, which was what I wanted as much as he did.

As we came into Highgate we were met by a procession of Bishops; they dismounted and knelt in the road to kiss my hand and offer me allegiance. Bishop Bonner was among them—but when he would have taken my hand and kissed it, I turned away and stared over his head. The watchers noticed and a cheer went up, for he was one of the most hated men in the country, who had been responsible for sending many Protestants to the stake. I wanted the people to know that I spurned the friendship of such a man.

I knew that I looked splendid as I rode through the City. I was wearing a riding dress of rich purple velvet which was very becoming and I, being especially upright, looked well on a horse. Robert Dudley rode beside me and every now and then our eyes would meet and I was sure mine reflected the exultation in his.

London Wall had been hung with tapestry. The guns of the Tower boomed out and the real ceremonies began. Schoolchildren stopped our progress to recite verses praising me; choirs of children sang in similar vein. I stopped and spoke to them thanking them for their welcome. I wanted to impress on these people that although I was their Queen I was also their friend, and I did not hold myself so high that any should feel they could not approach me. I knew by the cheers and the murmurs of approval that I was taking the right course. It was one I intended to cling to as long as I was Queen.

It was a dramatic moment when I entered the Tower. We paused and there was a deep silence all about us. Many must be thinking, as I was, of that dismal Palm Sunday when I had been brought to this place through the Traitor's Gate. Then I came in great dejection; now I came in triumph.

I lifted my hand and my voice rang out over that silence. "Some," I said, "have fallen from being princes of this land to be prisoners in this place; I am raised from being prisoner in this place to be prince of this land. That dejection was a work of God's justice; this advancement is a work of His mercy; as they were to yield patience for the one, so must I bear myself to God thankful, and to men merciful, for the other."

After I had spoken there was a silence of a few seconds and then the cheers rang out.

Deeply moved I went into the Tower.

I asked to be taken to the Bell Tower and to that room which I had once occupied when I was a prisoner in this place.

Robert was beside me as I stood in that room and the past came back to me, and I felt again that despair, when I had listened with apprehension to the sound of a key in the lock and wondered if I was to be led out to the axe.

I was so overcome that I sank to my knees and once more thanked God for His deliverance.

"I was as Daniel in the lions' den," I cried. "And the Lord delivered me."

Robert knelt with me, and when he helped me to my feet he took my hand and kissed it.

"Come," I said, "I would walk on the lead as I used to."

He came with me. In places we had to walk in single file from the Bell to the door into the Beauchamp Tower.

"There were you, Lord Robert," I cried, "and I used to think of you when I walked along this narrow path and wonder what you were doing in your prison."

"I thought of you," he answered. "God knows, I thought of little else."

I believed him . . . because I wanted to.

We made our way back and stood for a few moments in my old prison in the Bell Tower and we looked steadily at each other.

"Everything that has happened has led to this," said Robert.

His eyes were wild with dreams and I thought: If he were a free man I might be tempted to marry him.

But he was not a free man and if he had been at the time of his brother Guildford's marriage, he would not be here now. He was older than Guildford. He would have been the one to marry Jane Grey. But fortune had smiled on him. He had to be thankful for his marriage, and in my more thoughtful moments, so was I.

During the seven days I resided at the Tower, there were many meetings of the Council. I had already shown my disapproval of the religious persecutions in my sister's reign by refusing my hand to Bonner. I longed to reassure my people. What I wanted was to be proclaimed Head of the Church as my father had been and thus diminish the power of the Church of Rome. But I saw at once that I must tread warily in this matter. There could not be a complete turnabout—particularly as when I had been in fear of my life I had outwardly followed the rules of the Catholic Church.

But this brought home to me the need for a quick coronation, because only when I had been appointed and acclaimed Queen could I feel I had a firm grip on the crown.

The day must be right. There must be no evil omens.

I had naturally talked over the matter with Kat and she said we should consult Dr Dee.

Dr John Dee was a mathematician and astrologer whose powers of seeing into the future were highly respected. Kat had often talked of him and she had been in correspondence with him when we had been at Woodstock. He was a Protestant and I believed one of my supporters, which meant, Kat pointed out, that I was going to have a long and prosperous reign for Dr Dee, who could see into the future, would not have been so eager to support me if this were not the case.

I told Kat she was too gullible but I did feel that luck played a great part in survival. At least it had in mine, and I wanted to be sure that I did not choose an unlucky day for the Coronation.

Kat, as a firm believer in fate, was an enthusiastic admirer of Dr Dee, and I did not need much persuasion to share her enthusiasm. It is all very well for those who have nothing to lose to laugh at soothsayers, but for a young woman in my position no possibility must be rejected. Therefore I agreed to see Dr Dee.

He was in his early thirties, a startling-looking man with rather wild eyes which seemed to be looking at something which others could not see, and this inspired belief in him. He had passed through dangerous times, having come within hours of losing his life. He had been suspected of uttering words which could be said to be against Queen Mary, and accused of conspiring to kill her either through magic or poison.

All the man had said was that her health was failing, and any who saw her must have known that. He had been in the Tower about the same time as I had and had shared a cell with a certain Barthlet Green who was one of those who had been burned at the stake for his religious opinions. The ever zealous Bonner therefore suspected Dr Dee of heresy, but the doctor was too clever for his questioners, and he came out of his ordeal a free man.

The fact that he had been imprisoned on suspicion of attempting to murder Mary meant that he was certain to be one of my supporters. I was all eagerness to consult him and, when the Earl of Pembroke presented him to me and Lord Robert recommended him, I was won over completely. He should have a place in my household, I said. It would be an excellent idea to have an astrologer on hand to advise on important occasions.

My Master of Horse would naturally be in charge of all ceremonies and that meant the Coronation; so Robert consulted with Dr Dee who, after spending some time in meditation, came up with the date of Sunday the fifteenth of January as the day best suited to this auspicious occasion.

"January the fifteenth let it be," I said; and preparations were set in motion.

ALL WAS GOING WELL, but I had a reminder that I must continue to act with caution. To do what I wanted to do, to make drastic changes, could bring me to trouble. The Catholic priesthood was strong and they had wielded great power over Mary, with Philip of Spain behind them assuring them of success in foisting their religion on the people. They had been about to set up the Inquisition in the country and had indeed returned England in many ways to Rome.

I was going to change that. No foreign power would rule my country; but caution was needed. They were too strong, these priests. They were sure of themselves and I had to show them who was their mistress—but calmly, gradually.

This was brought home to me at my sister's funeral when the sermon was preached by Dr White, Bishop of Winchester. It was fortunate that he spoke in Latin, which so few people could understand. But I understood perfectly, and I did not like what I heard.

He broke into eulogies of the late Queen. He reminded the people that she had had the pious humility to renounce the Crown's supremacy over the Church and bring it back to the domination of Rome where it belonged. St Paul, he said, had forbidden women to speak in church, and it was not fitting for the Church to have a dumb head.

I was growing more and more incensed every moment. How dared he talk thus, particularly when I was urging the Council to proclaim me Head of the Church! How dared he speak disparagingly of my sex when I intended to show the people that they would prosper under a woman as never before!

He then enlarged upon Mary's sufferings; how patiently she had borne her afflictions; how blessed was England to have been given even briefly the devotion of such a good religious woman.

I was watching the congregation. Were they too thinking of great men who had burned at the stake—as I was? Cranmer, Ridley and the rest. Surely they must.

My fury reached its height when he began to speak of me.

Queen Mary's sister was now on the throne. She was a lady of great worth also and they must needs obey her. Then he committed the final insult by referring to me as a "live dog" and Mary "a dead lion"; and implying that they must needs do with what they had, as I was alive and Mary dead.

This was too much. If the people understood what he was saying, harm could be done to me. Fortunately there were few as well versed in the Latin tongue as I, and although the congregation knew he was praising Mary they did not realize that he was denigrating me.

I must curb my anger, but such a man must not be free to speak again as he did. He had flung down the gauntlet. Very well.

As he left the pulpit, I rose and cried to my guards: "Arrest that man."

They hastened to do my bidding and the Bishop of Winchester and I faced each other. I thought he looked pleased and I guessed he was one of those men who court martyrdom. They were the dangerous ones—religious fanatics, sure of their place in Heaven and certain that those who did not agree entirely with them were destined for Hell—they were the men to be wary of.

"Your Majesty," he said as the guards seized him, "I must warn you that if you attempt to turn from Rome you will be excommunicated."

I retorted: "Take him to the Tower."

And they did so.

When I returned to the privacy of my apartments, I sent for Cecil. He had heard of the arrest of Dr White and knew that it was this matter which I wanted to discuss with him.

I told him everything the man had said. "By great good fortune in Latin," I told him. "But he cannot be allowed to preach against me in such a manner."

Cecil agreed but said: "We must go cautiously with regard to Winchester. Let him cool in prison. Your father would have had his head. I am sure you will see the virtue in greater caution."

I saw at once. Indeed Cecil was voicing my opinion and, as usual, we were in agreement.

But it was a lesson learned. I must act cautiously and especially in this matter of religion.

I TOOK A tentative step forward on the morning of Christmas Day. I was in the chapel where the service was being conducted in the way it had been during Mary's reign and the Bishop of Carlisle was at the altar about to officiate at High Mass when I rose and, with my ladies, left the chapel.

It was a carefully calculated action. What I had done would soon be known throughout the capital and the country no doubt, and I would wait to see what the people thought of it. If they were displeased, I could easily make excuses; I had felt unwell—or something such. Illness had stood me in good stead in the past, so why not now? If there was approval I should know how to act.

I was left in no doubt of the people's feelings. They were joyful. I then decided to take another step. Services in my chapel and all over the country should be conducted in English.

I was concerned with my coronation and I was determined to make it a day which all my subjects would remember with joy.

On the twelfth of January I went from the Palace of Westminster to the Tower, for an English monarch must set out from that fortress for the Coronation, and the previous day's journey is almost as ceremonious as the day of coronation itself.

I sailed in my state barge and all along the river were craft of every description with flowing banners of welcome and sweet music. The Lord Mayor's barge was fitted with artillery, which was fired off at intervals. There was wild cheering everywhere and nothing could have gratified me more. I landed at the Tower and, as always, I must think of that other landing at the Traitor's Gate.

On the afternoon of the next day I left the Tower in a chariot covered with crimson velvet, and when I entered the city the cheers were deafening. Everywhere people shouted: "God save Your Grace."

I called back to them: "God save you all. I thank you, dear people, with all my heart."

How they loved me! I don't think any other monarch had shown such regard for them. They came to me with their flowers and I took them all and thanked them with emotion, and I laid them tenderly in my chariot that they might see how I prized them.

One of the things which pleased me most during that ride was the tableau in Gracechurch Street which represented the royal line from which I had sprung. There was my grandmother, Elizabeth of York, stepping out of a gigantic white rose to take the hand of my grandfather, Henry VII, who was emerging from a red one; but my greatest pleasure was in the effigy of my mother, who was set up beside my father. It was the first time since her execution that any homage—or common decency—had been paid to her. From these two sprang another branch, and there was an effigy of myself seated on a golden throne surrounded by entwined red and white roses.

I clapped my hands, which might seem undignified in a queen, but I was not so much anxious to uphold royal dignity as to win the love of my people. I had the power, I discovered, and I developed this later, to be able to speak to them and be with them as one of themselves, which I think was the chief reason I kept their good will.

All along the route there were pageants and children to sing my praises. I remember still the glory of Cheapside on that day with the tapestries hanging down from the windows and my dear subjects assuring me of their loyalty. I hope I made them aware of my love for them and my determination to serve them well.

On the morning of my coronation, I left Whitehall whither I had come from the Tower and came to Westminster. I looked very regal in my ermine-trimmed crimson velvet. I was a little anxious because the bishops had refused to crown me. They knew that I was determined to make myself Head of the Church, like my father before me, which, as I saw it, was the only way of restoring tolerance and reason in religious matters to my realm. Because the See of Canterbury was vacant, it was the duty of Nicholas Heath, Archbishop of York, to perform the ceremony, but as Heath was aware of the changes I proposed to make, he refused to crown me. Tunstall, Bishop of Durham, pleaded that he was too old and ill for such an exacting occasion, and the task therefore fell on Owen Oglethorpe, Bishop of Carlisle.

Oglethorpe would have liked to refuse, I believed. First he pleaded that he did not possess the necessary robes for such a function, but someone found robes and that excuse was not good enough; and oddly enough it was Bonner who lent his. It was very disturbing to have this conflict within the clergy, but I knew it was what I had to expect. If it meant displeasing the Church to please the people, then I knew what I had to do.

And so I came to the altar and there was anointed—an operation which I did not greatly enjoy as the oil was greasy and smelt vilely—but its significance was great and therefore to be endured.

But how pleased I was to be dressed in my golden mantle while the Bishop put the crown on my head and when I sat in the chair of state and my subjects came and knelt to me to swear allegiance, I was very happy.

Then to the ceremonial banquet in Westminster Hall where I sat in state while Sir Edward Dymoke rode into the hall and made the traditional challenge under the eyes of the eight hundred guests at the long tables and the assembled serving men. I was sure no one present would ever forget that occasion; as for myself it was the one I had dreamed of all through the dangerous years. Now here I sat in my velvet and ermine robes with my crown on my head while two of the greatest noblemen in the land, Lord William Howard and the Earl of Sussex, stood beside me and served me with food and wine. I ate sparingly. I was not a great eater and I had rarely felt less like food. I was in a state of great exultation; I was filled with emotion and determination in equal part. I was making my vows as earnestly as any nun ever did, but instead of dedicating my life to the service of the Church, I was giving mine to my country.

It was not until the early hours of the morning that the feasting was over and I could retire to my bed.

Kat was waiting for me.

"You are exhausted, my love," she said. "Kat will put you to bed."

"Kat," I reminded her, "you will have to remember that I am your Queen."

"Tomorrow," she promised. "Tonight you are my tired little one."

I was very glad to be divested of my robes, too tired to talk, even to Kat.

I lay in my bed and thought about this significant day, and my hopes were all for the future.

CHERE WERE LONG CALKS with Cecil and constantly he impressed on me the need to marry.

He said: "The King of France has proclaimed Mary Stuart Queen of England and the Dauphin, King."

"Let him proclaim," I retorted. "Words will hurt no one. I have been anointed and crowned Queen. Do you think the people of England would accept Mary Stuart—half Scot, half French, the hated enemies of the country!"

"The people would have to accept what was forced on them. Let us make your position secure, and the best way you can achieve that is by marriage and the bearing of an heir."

"I have no wish for marriage," I said.

"It would be wise to take a husband and bear a child," insisted Cecil.

I did not intend to argue with him further. I would wait until the suitors appeared, which would not be long I was sure. In the meantime I would concern myself with the religious controversy because I knew my people expected me to restore the Reformed Faith and put an end to religious persecution.

I had made up my mind. I would be Head of the Church as my father had been; and there was no need for me to pretend any longer to accept orders from Rome.

Accordingly I wrote to the Princes of Germany, Sweden and Denmark—those lands in which the Protestant Faith had flourished—and I told them that I would like to make bonds of friendship with them since my views coincided with theirs. At the same time I ordered Sir Edward Carne whom my sister had sent to Rome as Ambassador to Pope Paul IV to announce my accession and coronation to His Holiness, asking him also to inform the Pope that I had no intention of using violence against my subjects on account of their religion.

As might have been expected, the Pope was most displeased at this information, but I was not in the least perturbed. If I was to break with Rome my people would not expect me to take orders from him, and his enmity would certainly not harm me in their eyes.

Carne replied that His Holiness was against liberty of conscience and that he could not understand the hereditary rights of one not born in wedlock, and that the nearest relation of Henry VII was, in his opinion, Mary Queen of Scotland and Dauphiness of France.

If, however, I chose to place the matter of the right of succession in his hands, he would consider it. I had no doubt that he would—or what his conclusions would be. Thank you very much, I thought. But I decline your generous offer!

What I did do was recall Carne, whereupon the Pope threatened the poor man with excommunication if he left Rome without Papal consent. Poor Carne was in a dilemma. He knew that I was breaking away from Rome and he was a stern Catholic—one of my sister's most trusted adherents. He chose to remain in Rome. I did not blame him. I had said that I did not intend to punish my subjects for worshipping as they pleased, and I meant it.

Even so the Pope was displeased—with me, of course—and he took his revenge on poor Carne and robbed him of his ambassadorial standing and made him governor of an English hospital in Rome.

I told Cecil that we should not insist on his release as at this stage it would be unwise to enter into further conflict with the Pope, and Cecil replied that I was already showing wisdom.

So I dismissed the matter. But I had made my course clear. I knew now the way I had to go.

Religion was only one problem. The overwhelming one in the minds of those about me was marriage. They were all determined that it should take place without delay. Marriage! The subject fascinated me and repelled me. It was not that I did not like men. Indeed I liked them very well. There were two sides to my nature. Oh, I know well that we all have many facets to our character, but to have two so diametrically opposed as those that warred in me made me perhaps unusual. I was shrewd; my wits were quick; I had amazed my teachers with my ability to profit from learning; I possessed those faculties which could make me an able ruler. That was one side. On the other, I was vain, inclined to coquetry; I desired admiration for my person; I craved compliments even though my wiser nature reminded me a thousand times that they were false; I longed for men to pine for love of me even though my wiser self reminded me that they feigned to do so because they were ambitious and lusted after those favors which only a queen could grant. From one side I deluded myself; from the other I saw all—including myself—with the utmost clarity.

Yes, there were two Elizabeths—the one clever and the other foolish; but the foolish one was not so foolish as not to see her folly; and the clever one was not clever enough to stop, or even want to stop, the frivolity of the other.

The foolish one was in love while the shrewd one looked on almost cynically, watching the other closely, knowing that she would never allow her to fall into the trap which could be set for her. The clever one said: "Remember Thomas Seymour." And the foolish one replied: "It was one of the most exciting times of our life. Seymour was a wonderful man, but no one is quite like Robert Dudley."

Both acknowledged that there never had been, nor ever could be, a man to compare with Robert Dudley. To ride with him—and his duties demanded that he be constantly at my side—to see the gleam of desire in his eyes when they fell on me, added the greatest pleasure to the thrilling days through which I was living. No matter how often my wise self pointed out that it was in great measure the glittering crown which set Robert's eyes sparkling, still I did not care, and even the cynical one sometimes said: "It might be both, the two of us *and* the crown."

The circumstances delighted me. Robert Dudley, the only man whom I would have considered marrying, already had a wife. It was a situation which appealed to both sides of my nature. Perpetual courtship.

Philip of Spain was courting me and his Ambassador, the Count de Feria, was constantly calling on me. The last man I would marry would be Philip of Spain, but I saw no reason for telling de Feria so. I was quite enjoying raising my brother-in-law's hopes. It amused me and it was necessary to keep the King of France guessing. The last thing he would want would be yet another alliance between England and Spain. It was also the last thing I wanted, but I must be diplomatic. So I pretended to consider Philip's proposal.

De Feria was most attentive. What fools these men are! Did they think I would forget their treatment of me in the past?

On one occasion he told me that his master was pleased that I had accepted the allegiance of the Catholic peers in spite of my—forgive him but he must say it—misguided attitude in some matters.

I replied breezily that I was of the nature of a lion, and lions did not descend to the destruction of mice.

He smiled uneasily. I really did enjoy my encounters with de Feria. He was having rather a bad time, and I thought that sooner or later Philip would become exasperated with him. Then I heard that through de Feria Philip was offering bribes to some of the Catholic peers, suggesting that they work for him and try to reestablish the Church as it had been in Mary's reign. The first thing Lord William Howard did—for he was one who had been sounded as a possible recipient of Philip's bounty—was to come to me. I advised him to tell de Feria that I gave my consent to his accepting the money.

I could imagine de Feria's face when Lord William Howard told him that. I could not resist teasing the Spaniard further and when he next came into my presence I said: "I hope, Count, that His Most Catholic Majesty will not object if I employ some of his servants he has here among my courtiers."

It was a clear indication that Philip's clumsy attempt to set spies about me was not going to succeed.

These conversations with de Feria always put me in the best of moods. The poor Spaniard had little humor. He was courtly, impeccable in dress and manners—all that one would expect of a Spanish Ambassador—but he was serious in the extreme, and he did not understand the frivolous side to my nature at all. If he glimpsed it, he would dismiss it as feminine vagary and most unsuitable in a sovereign. *I* found it most suitable and often it brought me an advantage as it did now, for instead of giving an outright no and breaking off negotiations, which would give great offense to Spain and delight France, I was reveling in my dalliance with Philip through his solemn Ambassador.

"Do you think a marriage between your master and me would be successful, Count?" I asked tentatively.

"I think it would be most felicitous to both Your Majesties and our two countries," was the answer.

"When my father went through a form of marriage with his brother's widow that gave rise to much controversy. It was said that it was no true marriage."

"That was because your father wished to repudiate Queen Katharine and marry your mother."

"Of that I am aware, but you do not deny that the circumstances gave rise to conflict. My father's conscience worried him greatly on that store."

"Your father had a most convenient conscience," he said sharply.

Poor de Feria. He was beginning to lose his temper.

"Let us not speak ill of the dead, Count. And a great King at that."

"I am sure Your Grace will want to face the truth. There need be no obstacle to a marriage. My master is assured the Pope will give a dispensation."

"The Pope? Oh, he is no friend of mine."

"That would soon be rectified, Your Majesty, if you were married to the King of Spain. My master would ask for the dispensation and you would have no need to fear the Pope once you were married to the King of Spain."

"I am sure that the Pope and your master are indeed good friends, but as I have no fear of the Pope, I do not need your master's protection from him."

He was exasperated but the foolish man did not believe that a woman could rule, and this was one of the attitudes which incensed me and made me determined to show these arrogant men how wrong they were. He went away crestfallen and I was sure anxious not to return to Spain to admit the failure of his mission.

IT WAS ONLY NATURAL that there should be other suitors. Nothing pleased me more. I pretended to consider each in turn. There was the Archduke Charles son of the Emperor Ferdinand, as well as Eric of Sweden.

When I sat with my Councilors, I said: "I do believe that the people would not wish me to take a foreign husband."

That remark had an immediate effect which amused me very much. In the quiet of my bedchamber, Kat and I would have our little gossip—rather undignified in a queen, but the frivolous side of me enjoyed the indulgence. I always delighted in gossip. In fact, even my sterner side admitted that it was not an entirely wasted pastime. From it I did discover what the common people were thinking. Kat was my intermediary and as she prattled with high and low whenever she had the opportunity, my sources of opinion were very wide indeed.

I knew that the people were elated by my treatment of Philip of Spain. I do believe that had I agreed to marry him, I might have lost a large measure of my popularity. They had had a taste of Spanish intolerance and the subjugation of a queen. They wanted no more of that. Moreover, I do believe that had there been an attempt to force it on them, they would have rejected it strongly.

My remark about not taking a foreign husband had set their tongues wagging. The Earl of Arundel was the first to offer himself. I suppose he thought he had a chance. I did not disillusion him. It was a great pleasure to be asked to marry and I always felt a special fondness for the men who wanted me as a wife. It was ambition that prompted them, of course, but it was reasonable to presume they had some admiration for my person. I was twenty-five years of age and if I was not exactly handsome I did have some good points—my coloring, my lithe figure, my white skin and my beautiful hands. I was attractive without my crown but with it I was irresistible.

I favored Arundel for a while, and Robert was very jealous—an added pleasure.

Once he said: "I curse myself for having made that ridiculous marriage."

"I have heard your Amy is a very pretty creature," I said.

He was silent, bemoaning his fate, for he was sure that had he been unmarried, there would have been no hesitation and I would gladly have taken him. There was a modicum of truth in that. It was why the wise side of me rejoiced in Robert's Amy tucked away in the country.

Then there was Sir William Pickering—a very handsome courtier though by no means young. He must have been about forty, but he was well preserved in spite of a life in which gallantry had played a big part. He was rich because his father had been given grants of land by mine. He was extremely charming, and I pretended to consider him. The courtiers then began to make bets as to whether I would marry Arundel or Pickering for they were quite convinced that I would take one of them since I would not have a foreigner. So with all this speculation raising the hopes of first one and then the other, and with Robert glowering jealously on the scene, I found I was enjoying the matrimonial maneuverings.

The Count de Feria was angry and demanded an answer. I did not want to spoil the fun so I hesitated and gave him a little encouragement. People were saying that I would never have taken either Arundel or Pickering. It would have to be a foreign prince. Eric of Sweden was the favorite for a while.

Kat and I used to laugh about it. "I know my Queen. You'll have none of them. At least that's what you say."

"Most emphatically I say it, but only within these four walls. Just for your ears, Kat. And remember, not a word outside. If you gossip about me, I'll have your head, that I will."

"Now don't you be too handy with people's heads," warned Kat. "You always said your sister made the mistake of killing off some of the best."

"And you would call yourself one of the best?"

"Without a doubt."

"As you always will be, Kat," I said seriously.

She was pleased and went on to tell me the latest gossip, which was that the Duchess of Suffolk had married her equerry and everyone was extremely shocked by the misalliance.

"Let her enjoy her equerry," I said. "Her marriage is not a matter of state."

"The silk woman was wanting to see you rather specially this afternoon."

"Oh, what matter of moment has Mistress Montague to lay before me? I will say this for her, she is the best silk woman we have ever had. What say you, Kat?"

"I am in agreement with Your Majesty, and these stockings she has brought look very fine."

"Stockings! Where are they? Why was I not shown them before?"

"Being so occupied with matters of state . . ." began Kat.

"Bring them to me at once, insolent creature."

She did. They had been knitted in silk. The first I had ever seen.

"Try them, Your Majesty," whispered Kat.

So, of course, I did. They clung to the legs and made them look so much more slender than the cloth ones.

"Tell Mistress Montague that I am delighted with her work."

"I have anticipated Your Majesty's commands and I have set her knitting others."

"Good Kat," I said.

"I knew I was safe," added Kat, "for if Your Majesty was misguided enough as to disapprove of the stockings, there would be others to take them with the utmost speed."

Kat returned to the discussion of my marriage and told me what they were saying in the streets. "They are glad you have sent the Spaniards pack-ing and would like an English marriage. Nothing would please them more than to see you married to one of our own. I have heard it said that it is a great pity Lord Robert already has a wife."

I smiled enigmatically. So they thought Robert would be suitable . . . if he had not a wife. That was interesting. Lord Robert, yes. He was the only one. But he had a wife—and as I have said I was not altogether displeased about that!

Cecil was very disturbed. Philip of Spain had become affianced to the sister of the King of France.

"Now," said Cecil, "we have the King of France and the King of Spain united by this marriage; and the King of France has already declared his daughter-in-law, Mary of Scotland, the true heir to the English throne. Our two most powerful enemies will now be allies."

"But I was right not to enter into a marriage with Spain. It turned the people against my sister."

Cecil agreed that this was so.

"And the marriage between France and Spain is the outcome of my refusal."

"True," agreed Cecil. "We are facing formidable enemies and the best thing for you to do is to marry with as much speed as possible. If you had a child, your position would be more secure."

"My dear Cecil," I said, "I have a band of great ministers in whom I trust. I have my people who love me. My subjects will be loyal to me, and if God will be my guide and help me, I have no fear of any enemies who should come against me."

"Your Grace has shown wisdom rare in one so young. The people are with you as they were with your father, and in a manner which both your sister and your brother failed to win from them. I know that you will have the wisdom and the courage to succeed, but still I tell you it would be well to marry and give the country an heir."

"My dear Cecil, you know I am giving the matter my consideration."

"I pray Your Grace will continue to do so and come to a quick decision."

"Marriage is a matter to which much thought should be given before embarking on it. It can be disastrous. I have been hearing of the misalliance of our own Duchess of Suffolk. I am amused that such a proud lady should marry her horsekeeper."

"Ladies in love often do not consider consequences. Indeed, Madam, what you say is true. The Duchess has entered into matrimony with her horsekeeper. She might say that Your Majesty wishes she could do the same."

I looked at him while the color rushed into my face.

I could think of no reply. So my feelings for Robert were as obvious as all that!

Cecil continued to regard me quizzically. I wanted to chide him for listening to gossip and for not showing due respect for his Queen.

But my wise self reminded the other that I wanted honesty from Cecil—and in any case whether I wanted it or not, I would get it, and if I objected, he would leave my service. He was that sort of man.

So I shrugged my shoulders and said nothing.

The Mystery of Cumnor Place

THERE WAS A GREAT DEAL OF GOSSIP ABOUT ROBERT AND me. We were always together and he made no attempt to hide his feelings; and I fear that I was revealing enough to show my regard for him. He had such outstanding good looks and presence that he was bound to attract attention. He was very jealous of Arundel and Pickering, and as Arundel and Pickering were jealous of each other they quarreled when they met. Cecil said it was unwise to set them against each other, but I could not resist it and would favor one more than the other in turn. But Robert always had more of everything than others so his jealousy was far in excess of that of Arundel and Pickering.

The frivolous side of me enjoyed the situation immensely while the more sober side looked on indulgently.

Robert was essentially a very proud man and I would not have felt so favorable toward him if he had not been. He was frustrated because of his marriage and certainly believed that if he had been free I would have married him . . . a matter of which I was not entirely sure myself. When he saw me spreading my smiles between Arundel and Pickering he pretended not to notice and when I spoke to him there was a distinct coolness in his voice. He was polite and perfectly proper so there was nothing for which I could reprove him. It was just those ardent glances of love and tenderness which I missed—and I was astonished to discover how affected I could be by his seeming indifference. It was assumed of course, but it did show that he was hurt.

Philip of Spain had turned from me. Would Robert? But Philip had never loved me—only my crown. I had convinced myself that it was different with Robert.

The situation was becoming intolerable. There were others present all the time and I could not speak to Robert as I wished to with people eavesdropping—as they always did on my conversations—and they were particularly eager to do so when I was talking with Robert.

So I wanted to speak to him privately and told Kat to bring him to my apartment. Kat was shocked.

"But, my love, you cannot do that," she said.

"Since when has Kat Ashley seen fit to instruct the Queen?" I asked.

"Oh, we are Her Majesty today, are we?"

"Today and always," I reminded her, "and don't forget it, unless . . ."

"Unless I want my head to part company with my body? But listen, my dearest, there are watchers, you know."

"I must speak to him," I said.

She nodded. "He is a lovely gentleman and I know Your Majesty's feeling for him and his for you. 'Tis a pity he has a wife living . . . somewhere in Oxfordshire I believe it to be."

"Never mind where it is," I said. "Bring him."

So he came.

When we were alone together I gave him my hand to kiss.

"Robert," I said, "you have been somewhat sullen of late, and I like not sullen men and women about me."

"I have had good cause," he said sharply.

"Indeed. In what way?"

"I think Your Majesty knows full well. Arundel and Pickering . . . My God, you could not so demean yourself."

"Pray do not take the Lord's name in vain in my presence, Lord Dudley."

"Madam, I will state my case." He took both my hands and drew me toward him. I was too astonished—and delighted—to protest. Gone was the deferential Master of Horse; here was the passionate lover determined not to be denied.

I said: "State your case then, sir."

"I love you, as you know I do. I have put myself at your service and you spurn me."

"Spurn you! Have I not made you my Master of Horse?"

"It is not good enough."

"You forget to whom you speak."

"I speak to my beautiful Elizabeth whom I love. Whether she be Queen or not is no matter to me."

"Show more respect for my crown, I beg you, Lord Robert."

"I cannot think of your crown, but only of my love for you."

Then he kissed me in a practiced manner which reminded me of Sir Thomas Seymour. There was a similarity between those two men. Perhaps that was why I was almost ready to submit to both of them. Almost. But I was stronger in my determination to resist now than I had been in my younger days. Robert was the most fascinating man I had ever known but I would not allow him to become my lover. The sexual act was a symbol of domination on the part of the male, I had always thought, and I had no intention of being dominated for one moment even by the most attractive man I had ever known.

I said: "Robert . . . dear Robin . . . you know my regard for you."

"I know it and I will kill Pickering or Arundel if they dare take liberties."

"Do you think I would allow any to take liberties with me . . . save one?"

"Elizabeth . . . my love . . . whom I have loved all my life . . . from the time when we were children and danced together. Do you remember? You noticed me then."

"I must always notice you, Robin. You are a very noticeable gentleman."

"You love me, I know. Do you think I am not aware of it? Even when we were in the Tower we thought of each other, did we not?"

"Yes, Robert, we did."

"And was I not prepared to lay whatever I had at your feet?"

"So you said."

"And you take up this coquettish stance with Arundel and Pickering."

"I am the Queen, Robert. I may do as I wish."

"It is more than I can endure."

"Why so? It is only if I agreed to marry either of them that you should feel these emotions."

"So you will not marry one of them!"

I reached up to touch his hair. It was a long way and I had to stand on tiptoe, for although I was not small in stature he was very tall.

"You know full well that I will not marry either of them."

"They are urging you."

"I am being urged all the time."

"Philip has become affianced to France. You have refused Eric of Sweden and the Archduke Charles."

"Indeed I have."

"Is it because you love someone else?"

"And if I do?"

"I must know."

"Are you by any chance referring to Lord Robert Dudley? And if you are how could he be a suitor for my hand? Have you forgotten that he has a wife tucked away somewhere in the country?"

"Life has been very cruel to me," he said.

"Rather has life been good to you. Just think if you had not made that marriage when you did, you would be a headless corpse, for almost certainly you would have been the one your ambitious father married to Lady Jane Grey."

He looked at me helplessly.

I said: "There is only one course open to you, my lord. You must be a good husband to Mistress Amy."

"Elizabeth!" He caught my hands and drew me toward him. "She is sick. I do not think she will live long."

My heart was beating very fast. "Is that true?" I said quietly.

"True. I swear it. It could well be that within a few months I could be . . . free."

I was shaken. When he kissed me I wanted him to go on doing so. I wanted him to talk of his devotion, his unrestrained passion. Always between us had been the figure of his wife—Amy, the girl in the country who made it safe for me to dally with Robert Dudley. But if she were no longer there . . .

It was a dazzling possibility. The frivolous side of my nature wanted him free. The serious side was not so sure.

He looked at me eagerly and I was enchanted to see his devotion to me and I smiled at him when he said: "If . . ." And I knew he believed that if he were a free man I would marry him.

WHEN ROBERT SAID that his wife was ill he had shaken me more than I would admit to myself. I had to know more about her and his matrimonial situation. I couldn't ask him, so I set Kat to discover. She already knew a good deal. Since he had become such a favorite of mine, there was a great deal of gossip about him.

His grandfather had been that Edmund Dudley, statesman and lawyer, who had found favor with my grandfather King Henry VII because of his clever ways with finance, and who had been beheaded by my father Henry VIII when he came to the throne as a sop to the people who blamed Edmund Dudley, with Empson, for the heavy taxes they had had to pay. Robert's father was, of course, John Dudley, Duke of Northumberland, who had tried to set Lady Jane Grey on the throne after she had married his son Guildford, and had died on the scaffold. What did Robert feel about having lost his grandfather, his father and his brother to the headsman? That grisly fact must have made him anxious at times, though he never showed it. Robert had an enduring faith in himself and he was determined to marry me. I saw that in his eyes and my desire wavered considerably. There were times when I thought of being married to Robert, and then I said to myself: If he were free, I believe I would. But that other side of me was always there warning me: You would never be completely Queen, if you set up a man beside you. He would become the King. He would oppose your wishes, enforce his will on you, try to subdue you to his desires with soft caresses and with blandishments. No, I must not marry . . . not even Robert. Yet if he were free . . . But he was not free.

Kat was indefatigable in her search for information. I picked it up from others, too. Robert Dudley was the most talked-of man in England at that time—far more so than Arundel or Pickering had ever been, although courtiers were still taking bets on those two. I had been unable to hide my feelings for Robert and of course they were much discussed throughout the Court.

What I learned was that Robert's father, the Earl of Warwick, as he had been then, had gone as General of the King's army to Norfolk to suppress a rebellion of the peasants there. This he had done very successfully, much to the joy of the landowners in that part of the country because the rising had concerned the enclosures of land. It was while he was there that John Dudley had been entertained by one of those landowners, Sir John Robsart who had a daughter, Amy; and although he had several stepchildren, for he had married a widow, Amy was the only child Robsart had fathered and was his sole heiress.

Heiress though she might be, she would not be considered a suitable match for a Dudley. John Dudley, although not at that time Duke of Northumberland and Protector of England, was a man of considerable importance. Robert was not much more than sixteen and he fell in love with Amy and she, naturally enough, with him.

Why John Dudley agreed to the marriage I cannot imagine, but he had several sons and Robert was the fifth; so he probably thought that the Robsarts were rich enough. Whatever the case, Robert was married. Amy was a quiet little country girl and I can imagine how quickly his infatuation for her began to fade, and when his father's power began to increase rapidly, he must have realized how hasty he had been.

With Edward Seymour beheaded, John Dudley assumed the title of Duke of Northumberland. His ambition was boundless. A crown for one of his sons. Poor Guildford! He was the only unmarried one left. Oh, how easily it could have been Robert! Often I thought of that and I have no doubt he did also.

Jane Grey's brief glory was over, Mary on the throne, Northumberland and Guildford beheaded and Robert in the Tower under sentence of death. Such a tragic sequence of events should have made Robert cautious but I saw little of caution in my bold admirer.

One of his sisters, Lady Mary Sidney, was now serving in my bedchamber. Robert had asked me to give her the post and of course I had agreed; and no sooner did I meet Mary than I liked her. They had great charm, those Dudleys. From Mary I learned a great deal about Robert. He was the most outstanding of all her brothers—alas all dead now except Ambrose. She did not like to talk of Guildford who had died so tragically. "Our father was too ambitious," she said sadly, "and ambition can lead men into deadly traps."

I agreed with her and in any case I did not want to talk of Guildford. My interest was all for Robert.

"No one could compare with Robert," she told me. "He excelled at all games; he could ride faster than any. I have never seen anyone manage a horse as he does."

"Very becoming in the Queen's horsemaster," I said.

She looked at me wistfully. "I believe Your Majesty has as great a regard for him as I have."

"Lord Robert is a fine man," I said, and closed the conversation. I did not want to betray my feelings too strongly. But need I have worried? Didn't everyone know how I felt about Robert?

The whole Court was saying that there would be no need to look very far for the Queen's husband if Lord Robert had not already a wife.

But while he had a wife, marriage was impossible and this all-absorbing game of courtship could go on.

There were times when I wanted to show him how much I understood his frustration. I took a great delight in pleasing him. I wanted him to outshine every other man at Court, which he did naturally, but I wanted him to be the richest and the most powerful . . . under me, of course. When the lovely old Dairy House at Kew was available, I bestowed it on him; I gave him monastery lands and a much coveted license to export wool. I also invested him with the Order of the Garter.

Cecil asked me if I was not showing too obvious favor to Lord Robert Dudley, and I told him sharply that I would bestow favors where I wished.

He lifted his shoulders in some exasperation and I believed he was assuring himself that once I had been persuaded to take the sensible course and marry, Robert Dudley would fade into the background. As if Robert would ever allow that—or that I would, for that matter.

I was in love, I suppose. I could not stop myself talking about him. I arranged jousts so that he could excel and I would tensely watch his performance, knowing that as many eyes were turned toward me as to the jousters.

I heard it said that the Tudors formed fierce attachments, and thus my father had been when he was enamored of my mother.

Cecil was growing more and more restive. He said there were dangerous rumors abroad concerning my relationship with Lord Robert.

"There will always be rumors about monarchs, Master Cecil," I said.

"Yes, Madam," was the reply, "but these would appear to have some foundation in truth."

"What do you imply?" I demanded.

"By Your Grace's conduct and that of Lord Robert it might seem that a stronger relationship exists between you than is fitting for you both."

"People are jealous of him, Cecil. When a man is gifted and handsome beyond all others, that is often the case."

"And when the Queen takes no pains to hide her feelings for him, Madam, what can one expect? I would implore Your Majesty to take care."

"Have no fear, my friend, I shall take care."

It was from Kat that I heard most of the new rumors. Perhaps others were afraid to tell me, and when Kat began to be worried I, too, felt twinges of uneasiness. Kat was a great lover and purveyor of gossip; yet even she realized that the rumors were going too far.

"My dear lady," she whispered, "I am afraid. They are saying dreadful things of you and Lord Robert."

"What?" I demanded.

She turned away and did not want to tell me but I pinched her arm until she squealed with pain. "Tell me," I insisted.

"I dursn't," she replied.

"Idiot!" I said. "Do you think I can't guess? They are saying he is my lover, are they not?"

She nodded.

"They will always say such things."

"It is the rumors, my lady, wicked rumors . . . lies. There was old Anne Dowe of Brentwood. She walks the roads and learns much, she said, and she is believed to be a wise woman."

"Well let us hear of this wisdom."

"She has said that you and Lord Robert play legerdemain together."

I burst out laughing. "And because an old tramp says these things, should I care?"

"You should care, my lady, for what old tramps say one day, merchants will say the next, and such tales spread like wildfire through the land. That is not all. Someone said that my Lord Robert gave you a very fine petticoat and she cried out in the company of several: 'It is not a petticoat only that my Lord Robert gives the Queen. It is a child.' There were loud protests. 'But the Queen has no child,' they said. And Mother Dowe answered: 'If she has no child yet, Lord Robert has put one in the making.'"

I felt the blood rush to my face. Although I was ready to accept Robert's passionate devotion and did not care who knew it existed, the thought of childbearing was repulsive to me. The very idea sickened me and it angered me that this was being said about me.

Kat who perhaps knew me better than any understood this.

She said gently: "You remember, my love, what they said of you and Thomas Seymour."

"Yes, wild stories of a midwife's being taken to a house in the dead of night . . . blindfold. What wicked lies people make up about me."

"You are the Queen, my love. You should remember it. They are now talking of you and Lord Robert as they did of you and Thomas Seymour."

"And he lost his head," I mused. "What has happened to this woman Dowe?"

"She was taken into prison by the Sheriff of Donberry."

"She shall be released," I said. "I will show the people in what contempt I hold such stories by not treating them seriously."

Kat nodded. "And by acting in a way not to give rise to such," she added.

At which I gave her a push which sent her sprawling. She picked herself up, ruefully shrugging her shoulders.

"It is all such nonsense," I said. "What opportunities would I have? I am watched night and day. Am I not surrounded by councilors . . . ladies of this and gentlemen of that? I have no chance of being other than I am—a chaste virgin. But, Kat Ashley, if ever I took it into my mind to change that state, I should be the one to decide, and no one in this realm would stop me."

Kat sank to her knees sobbing.

"Oh, my dear Majesty," she said, "take care, take care. Remember Thomas Seymour. I nearly died of fright then."

"Because they took you to the Tower and you betrayed me."

Her teeth were chattering. "Dearest, take care, take care. Men will be the death of you."

"No, Kat, I will be the death of them, but I shall be in command. It is different now. Get up, you idiot, and stop sniveling. There is no need to cry for me. Everything is changed. I am the Queen now. It is for me to say what shall be."

She got to her feet and fell into my arms still weeping. I laughed away her tears, but I did feel a twinge of uneasiness.

WE RODE OUT to the hunt, Robert beside me. I told him how I felt about the rumors.

He looked at me ardently and said: "It will not be much longer."

"There is too much talk. Robert, we must be more discreet. You must not be with me so much."

"Do you wish that?"

"No, certainly not."

"Then surely the Queen's wishes should be obeyed."

"We must be wise. The people will not like to think that you and I are lovers."

"Should they not know the truth?"

"I mean lovers in another sense."

He laughed. "Well, we are in thought if not in deed. Soon, I trust . . ."

I shook my head and galloped ahead but he was soon beside me.

"Elizabeth," he said excitedly, "it is only Amy who stands in our way and she is a very sick woman. She has a malignant growth. My dearest lady, be patient . . . just a little longer."

"I do not like this talk of death," I said. "It is not right for a man to talk so of his wife to another woman."

"It is right to speak the truth. Be patient a little longer."

"Poor girl," I said. "Does she hear rumors of her husband's falseness in that house . . . what is it?"

"Cumnor Place. She has always felt uneasy about our marriage . . . knowing that she lacks the social gifts to share in such a union."

"You have a great opinion of yourselves, you Dudleys."

"Not quite as great as the Tudors."

"Indeed not, and how could it be so? But I do not wish to hear of your Amy. I grieve for the poor lonely soul whose husband rarely deigns to visit her."

"I cannot live without the warmth of the sun."

"I am the sun, am I? Well, Robert. I'm glad you enjoy the warmth in which you bask. But I think you should be a little kinder to your lawful wedded wife. You neglect her most shamefully. If you do not make a good husband to one, could you to another?"

This brought about one of those declarations of undying devotion and praise of my beauty and wit to which I so much liked to listen.

People were noticing us so I rode on and joined other members of the party.

I was in a strange mood that day. I was almost inclined to believe that I could have married Robert. I argued with myself that although the idea of marriage was not completely enticing, there was one man and one only with whom I would embark on it.

It was unfortunate—or so it turned out later—that I was in this mood when the Spanish Ambassador de Quadra approached me.

He was a very solemn gentleman and like all ambassadors more or less a spy for his master. Since the betrothal of Philip of Spain and Elisabeth of France our relations with Spain had been more difficult than ever. While Philip had been hoping for a marriage with me, the Ambassadors had been very affable. Now they were less so, but still urging their candidate—in this case the Archduke Charles.

I was in a frivolous mood and when de Quadra threw out his hints, I couldn't help bringing Robert's name into the conversation for it always amused me to see their panic when they contemplated a union between me and Robert. The fact that he had a wife made them feel safer about it—as it did me, but on this occasion I threw aside caution.

De Quadra remarked that Lord Robert had seemed somewhat unhappy during the hunt.

"He fears to lose Your Majesty's especial favor on the occasion of your marriage."

"Lord Robert doubtless thinks of his wife. She is dead or nearly so."

He looked at me in astonishment and immediately I realized I had been indiscreet.

"Pray, my lord," I said, "say nothing of this."

He bowed his head, but I knew he would write at once to Philip and tell him what I had said.

Cecil came to me that very day. He wanted to talk about the rumors regarding Robert and me.

"They are dangerous and I have to confess to Your Majesty a certain indiscretion."

"You indiscreet! I cannot believe that."

"De Quadra talked slyly, I thought, of Lord Robert's wife."

"Why should he speak of her?"

"There are rumors that Lord Robert would like to be rid of her in order to marry you."

"No doubt he would," I said. "Any ambitious man would look to exchange a country girl for a queen."

"He said there was a rumor that Lord Robert was planning to kill her himself and that it was being circulated that the lady was suffering from an incurable illness, to which I replied that I thought the lady was well and taking good care not to be poisoned."

"That does not seem to me to be so very indiscreet."

"I was sorry immediately I said it, but I had to confess to you. I wish that you would marry. Once you did and produced an heir, we should have an end to these damaging rumors."

"I will think seriously of the matter," I promised him, and I assured him that we were all indiscreet at moments and he had been honorable enough to tell me what had taken place. I did not tell him what I had said to the Ambassador.

A few days later the news broke.

On the previous Sunday, a day after I had told the Spanish Ambassador that Lady Dudley was dead or soon would be, she was indeed dead. She had been found at the bottom of a staircase in Cumnor Place with her neck broken.

→>-<←

I WAS NUMBED by the shock as the enormity of what had happened was brought forcibly home to me. The frivolous side of my nature retreated in shame and the sterner side took over. I had played my games too realistically. I was the first to know that in doing so I had placed myself in acute danger. When I thought of how carefully I had lived through those days when I had emerged from the Tower, how I had considered each step before I took it, I could not believe that I could have become so careless and foolish as to be involved in the death in suspicious circumstances of an unwanted wife.

I summoned Robert immediately. I must see him—and then send him away at once. It must not appear that I was in any way implicated. How could I say that? I *was* implicated. Mother Dowe and thousands of others were whispering scandal about me. What had I said to the Spanish Ambassador only the day before Amy Dudley died? What had Cecil said?

I knew that this scandal would go on reverberating round the world.

Robert must leave Court at once and I should have to put him under restraint. I must dissociate myself with all speed from this matter. It must be shown that however great a favorite a man was, if the charge of murder was brought against him, he must face it.

I arranged with Kat that he should come to me in secret, and when he entered the room he would have taken me into his arms, but I stood back, aloof, now the Queen.

Yet I knew that I loved him as I never had, nor ever would, love another person. Whatever he had done, I must still love him. I would always make excuses for him. Whatever he had done, he had done for my sake.

But more than Robert, I loved my royalty. I had to protect my future and my crown and at the moment my adored and adoring Robert was a threat to it.

"What happened at Cumnor Place?" I asked as coolly as I could.

"She fell from the top of a staircase and broke her neck. It was an accident."

"At such a time?"

"There is no knowing when accidents will happen."

"Who will believe it?" I asked.

"It matters not. You are the Queen. You will tell the people what they must believe."

I shook my head. "That is beyond my power. The people will believe what they think to be the truth, and there have been rumors about us, Robert."

He was a little impatient, even arrogant. Perhaps he saw himself already as King. Oh no, Robert, I thought. You shall not be King . . . not even you.

This has shown me clearly which way I must go. But I did not say that to him. I wanted to know whether he had indeed murdered his wife.

"Robert," I said, "did you . . . ?"

"I was nowhere near the place," he replied.

But a man like Robert would not need to be. Such distasteful tasks were carried out by servants. It was dangerous to employ servants to do such deeds. Servants, in certain circumstances, could be made to talk.

Oh, what a web I was caught up in. I should have known better. Had I not stepped into danger through Thomas Seymour? And now Robert. I should have learned my lesson.

"The people will never accept that she died by accident at such a time."

"Does that matter?"

Oh Robert, I thought, you have a lot to learn of the people and me.

"I must be beyond reproach in such matters," I said. "There must be no suspicion attached to me."

"I will defend you."

"Your main concern will be to defend yourself," I said sharply. "You are the one who will stand on trial for this."

"On trial?"

"Oh, we do not know what the outcome will be, but we must be prepared."

"You are the Queen."

"A queen might not survive through such a storm as this could raise."

"Your father killed two of his wives and was still loved by the people."

"The circumstances are different. They were accused of treason and the axeman killed them. This is the removal of a woman who, many will say, stood in your way."

"Never fear. We shall come through this and then . . . there is no obstacle."

He would have embraced me but I held him off. He did not see the change in me, but it had come. Never again would I risk my throne for the sake of a man. In future I should think first of the Queen.

"Lord Robert Dudley," I said, "I am placing you under arrest."

He stared at me incredulously.

"Yes, Robert," I said. "There will be many questions to be answered and until they are satisfactorily dealt with, you cannot remain at Court. You must see that. Go to your house at Kew. Stay there. You will be confined to that house on the Queen's orders."

He nodded slowly. "Yes," he said, "I see that, as always, you are right. I will go to Kew. I will stay there and I know that we can arrange this matter satisfactorily and when it is settled . . ."

No, Robert, I thought, it can never be now, for whatever the verdict you are able to bring about, suspicion will always be there and never must a finger be pointed at the Queen with the suggestion that she had a hand in the murder of her lover's wife.

First it must be seen that he was under house arrest.

So he left with the guards and I knew that in spite of my previous frivolity, I was now acting like a queen.

IN MOMENTS OF DANGER William Cecil showed himself as the cool, wise counselor he was. He was deeply disturbed by the death of Lady Dudley.

He talked to me very gravely and I was glad that he approved of my action in confining Robert to Kew.

He discussed at length the danger in which I had been placed.

"There will have to be an inquiry and the servants at Cumnor Place will all have to give evidence. Whether they will be in favor of Lord Robert who can say? But doubtless Lord Robert will know how to act."

"Do you mean he will be able to force his servants to say what he expects them to?"

"They are his servants. It is his affair. Your Majesty, your crown could be at stake. A verdict of accidental death must be brought in."

"Will the people believe it?"

"There will always be some who do not. But that is inevitable. If a jury brings in a verdict of accidental death that will have to be publicly accepted. There are certain to be those who will believe Lord Robert guilty of murder . . . and Your Majesty with him."

"That is impossible. I knew nothing of the woman."

"The people believe that you wish to marry Lord Robert and Lady Amy was in the way."

"I am innocent," I said. "I know nothing of her death. Is the end of one countrywoman so very important?"

"Of the utmost importance. The people will accept political killings— even those such as occurred in your sister's reign. There is usually an excuse for them which people understand . . . or some do. No one will tolerate the murder of a wife by her husband in order that he may marry another woman. We must at all costs stop a charge of murder. Anything is better than that, because if it were proved to be murder, Your Majesty would be implicated. You must face the fact that your hold on the crown is not as firm as we should like it to be. Until now the people have shown their love for you in no small way, but a scandal of such magnitude could alter that. There is Mary Queen of Scots across the water, with the French King—and now possibly with Spanish help—ready to put her on the throne. And even nearer home there is the Lady Katharine Grey whose sister was queen for nine days, and she, too, is the great-granddaughter of your grandfather Henry VII. Your Majesty must walk warily."

"I know it well, and I know too, good Master Cecil, that I can rely on your wisdom."

He nodded. "It is well that Lord Robert has been sent away from Court. We must ridicule all suggestions of murder. The verdict shall be accidental death; and Lord Robert must remain at Kew until we have the right verdict. In the meantime I will call on him there, which will show the people that I regard him as my good friend who cannot be anything but innocent, and show that his stay at Kew is by no means an arrest but merely undertaken in view of the delicacy of the situation. It will show that he himself feels it better to remain there until his name is completely cleared of this absurd suspicion."

"I thank you, Cecil. We shall come through this, and then we shall tread with especial care."

I LIVED IN a state of nervous tension awaiting the verdict of the coroner's jury. I knew that the country was aghast and that there was strong suspicion of Robert which included me. My enemies, of course, were making the most of the scandal. Sir Nicholas Throckmorton, who was now my Ambassador in France, wrote to Cecil to tell him that the Queen of Scots had laughed aloud when she heard the story and said for all to hear: "So the Queen of England is going to marry her horsemaster who has killed his wife to make room for her."

How dared she! The foolish pampered creature! I disliked her intensely, not only because she claimed my throne and was unquestionably legitimate but because the people at the Court of France were constantly singing of her exceptional beauty and grace, which, I told myself spitefully, was no doubt because now that Henri Deux had died so suddenly, she and her little François were Queen and King of France.

Our ambassadors reported from every country that it was the general opinion that Robert had murdered his wife in order to marry me. They sent strong advice that there should be no marriage with Robert.

They need not have worried. I, too, had made up my mind about that.

Robert, determined that at the coroner's court there should be a verdict of accidental death, had taken the precaution of sending a distant kinsman, Thomas Blount, down to Cumnor Place to brief the servants so that they should be aware of what their master expected of them. He knew Thomas Blount would do his utmost for, being a poor relation, he had everything to win through Robert. If Robert were to fail, he would fail with him. Such men make good servants.

Blount evidently did his work well and everyone who had been in the house on that fatal day was primed in what he or she must say. Most of them had been away from the house when the accident happened because the annual fair had come to the neighborhood and they had all wanted to attend it.

Lady Dudley had stayed behind. I thought of her in that house alone. Had she had any premonition? She could not have been ignorant of the rumors. They abounded. How would a lonely woman feel when her husband was paying court to another woman and there had been rumors that he was plotting her death?

Why had she allowed them all to go to the fair, leaving her alone in the house? That seemed to point to suicide. But would a woman who wished to kill herself choose such a method? How could she be certain of death? The same applied to murder—unless of course the victim was killed by some other means and thrown down the staircase to make it appear she had fallen down and, doing so, died.

There must be some explanation. I wished that I knew it. Or did I? Did I really want to know what had happened in that quiet house on that day when almost everybody had gone to the fair and Amy Robsart was alone?

I waited patiently for the jury's verdict. I guessed it would be what we wanted. How could it be otherwise? Accident? Suicide? Either would do, but accident was better. Murder it must never be called.

It was—as I had known it would be—a foregone conclusion. The jury would not want to offend a man as powerful as Robert was—nor did they wish to displease me. So there was only one verdict.

Amy Robsart's maid, Mistress Pinto, who had been with her for many years and who was devoted to her, did hint at her mistress's suffering. The theory of a growth in the breast was brought up. It could have been suicide. Suicide or accident, it did not greatly matter.

So the verdict was accidental death. Cecil was relieved; Robert was overjoyed; but I was sober. I did not think the matter could be so neatly dealt with as that.

ROBERT RETURNED TO COURT. No one dared mention the matter of Lady Dudley's death in his presence or mine, but that did not prevent its being frequently spoken of and I doubt whether many believed the coroner's verdict. Robert was watched even more attentively than before. He had acquired a new reputation—one which set men making sure they did not offend him. Clearly they thought he was a man who had the ability to remove those who stood in his way. I tried to behave as though nothing had happened. I wanted to give the impression that Robert was just a good subject who had rather special gifts and that was why I favored him.

He was constantly at my side and I talked to him of matters of State. He had a good grasp of these and he always looked at them with an eye to the advantage of the crown. During that time Robert was so certain that he would soon be sharing it that he could not stop himself behaving like a king.

I was tender toward him. I was sorry for all the suspicion which had been directed at him. If he were indeed innocent that would be galling for there is nothing so maddening as to be accused of something one has not done. And if he had murdered his wife . . . well then, he had done that for me. And I had led him on, tempting him perhaps too far.

I could not help my feelings, but I was more alive when I was in his company than that of anyone else. If he were absent, then I found the company dull. I liked his dark looks, his magnificent vital presence; I liked his arrogance; I liked his persistence and his ability to withdraw himself with an air of unconcern from an intolerable situation such as the one which had recently threatened to destroy him.

I was no less in love with Robert Dudley after his wife's death than I had been before.

Constantly he urged marriage.

"How could we," I demanded, "while there are rumors in the air?"

"If you do not marry me people will say it is because you do not believe in my innocence."

"But if I do, might they not believe in my guilt?" I went on: "Robin, this matter has caused grievous harm to us both."

"Nonsense," he replied, for there were times when he seemed to forget that I was the Queen, and I did not always reprove him. In fact I liked his insolence. It was all part of that overwhelming masculinity which so appealed to the feminine side of my nature. "It has done us great good. It has cleared the way for us."

At such times I thought: Yes, he is guilty. He arranged for that poor woman to fall down the staircase.

I could easily believe that, and yet it made no difference.

Cecil continued to be concerned about my unmarried state.

Time was passing, he said. I must produce an heir. Was I going to put off marriage until it was too late for me to bear children?

"I have many years before me yet, I would remind you," I retorted.

"Madam," he replied, "the people look for it."

I prevaricated and Cecil was too shrewd not to know what I was doing.

"I would agree to marriage with Robert Dudley, Madam," he said, "for I truly believe that in your fondness for him you would quickly conceive."

I was amazed.

"The scandal concerning his late wife is too recent," I said.

"I know. I know. Perhaps a secret marriage. Once the heir was born, the people would be ready to love you again."

"They will love me," I said firmly. "Give me time."

"Marriage is the answer and if it must be Robert Dudley, then so be it."

Perhaps he had thought such a suggestion would make me wild with joy. It did not.

I said: "Not yet. Not yet. I will decide in my own time."

I think I had already decided. Much as I loved Robert I knew his nature. He yearned to be King and once I married him he would be. He was too sure of himself. One would think he was there already. No! I wanted no man to stand beside me. I would be sovereign, and I alone.

Moreover, I had to win back the people's trust, and I would never do that if I married Robert Dudley.

When I came to think of it, the death of Robert's wife was the greatest lesson I was ever likely to learn and if I did not take advantage of that, I deserved to lose my crown.

The Earl of Leicester

THE LADIES OF MY BEDCHAMBER WERE A CHARMING AND handsome company of women. I should not have chosen them if they had not been. I was very susceptible to beauty in both men and women. I liked to have good-looking people around me. I had sufficient personal attraction myself not to be jealous of a pretty woman, and as I was surrounded by an aura of royalty, I must outshine them all.

The three who pleased me best were Mary Sidney, Jane Seymour and Lettice Knollys—and all for different reasons.

Mary Sidney was a dear affectionate creature, and as she was Robert's sister that made a special bond between us. Mary loved all her family but there was no doubt who was her special favorite. She was able to tell me little anecdotes from his childhood and we would laugh together over his boldness like two doting parents. Mary was such a faithful creature and I liked Henry Sidney, her husband, whom I had known since his boyhood. When my brother Edward had come to the throne, he had been made one of the principal gentlemen of the Privy Chamber. He had obviously been seen as a rising star since Northumberland had chosen him to marry his daughter Mary. It was a happy marriage, Mary being such a gentle, loving girl who, I suppose, would have made a success of most relationships. She certainly had become one of my dearest companions.

Lady Jane Seymour was another gentle girl. I took to her because she was Thomas Seymour's niece and I was sorry for her because both her father and uncle had gone to the block. I felt sympathy for the children who had been thus deprived of a parent—perhaps because I had myself. Jane was a very delicate girl and I was always scolding her about not taking more care of her health. In one matter she did not altogether please me and that was in her friendship with Lady Katharine Grey. Katharine gave herself airs. The silly little creature thought she had more right to the throne than I had, and it had been brought back to me—not by Jane Seymour I hasten to say—that she had said she should have been declared next in succession. I supposed there were some few who would agree that she should. But then there were some who talked of Mary of Scotland, not only as the next Queen but the rightful one. I was always on my guard against successors to the throne, for I imagined they were always casting covetous eyes on the present occupier. Moreover, clever people had a habit of paying court to such, and if too much favor was shown to them it might well be that they would wish to speed up the inheritance.

No! I did not like successors to the throne—unless of course one should be the natural heir of my body, which was very unlikely in my present mood or, I was inclined to think, my mood hereafter. Even some sons had tried to replace their fathers. Successors were a breed to be avoided rather than cultivated and I decided to keep a watchful eye on Katharine Grey. And the one thing which prevented my complete confidence in Jane Seymour was her close friendship with Katharine Grey.

The third of my favorite ladies was Lettice Knollys. She was quite different from the other two. There was nothing gentle about Lettice. She was a fiery creature. Her father, Sir Francis Knollys, had married the daughter of Mary Boleyn who was my aunt, so there was a family connection between me and Lettice. I always liked to advance the Boleyn side of my family when possible for, on the death of my mother, life had been hard for them. Thus Lettice would have been of interest to me even if she had not been an outstandingly attractive girl; and if she had not been one of the most beautiful girls at Court, she would have been noticed for her wit and vivacity. I liked her immediately but I realized that it might be necessary to curb those high spirits and a certain tendency which I discovered of trying to outshine everyone . . . including me.

She danced well and dancing was one of my special accomplishments. I never tired of it. I loved to glide across the floor and I knew that I looked my best when dancing because of my tallish willowy figure. I often chose to dance with Robert, who also performed well. Very often when we took the floor others would fall away as though to suggest it would be sacrilege to dance while Robert and I cavorted together. The applause would always ring out when the music stopped, and I would smile at the appreciation on the faces of the courtiers knowing that part of their eulogies were directed to the crown; but nevertheless I was an expert performer.

And this girl Lettice Knollys danced as well as I did. None would say she did, of course, but they knew it; and she often called attention to herself when I was dancing and it irritated me faintly; but whatever her charms and accomplishments she had no crown to augment them.

She was inclined to be a little familiar too—presuming on the fact that we were some sort of cousins. I often found the need to rebuke her and sometimes gave her a sharp rap across the knuckles for her clumsiness when she helped to dress me, and I knew that when she hung her head and assumed a humble attitude, she was quite aware that the rebuke had been incurred not for clumsiness but for her own attractions.

QUEEN OF THIS REALM

Sometimes I wondered why I did not dismiss her. But she was so pretty in a very striking way. I think she had my mother's eyes for they were dark and heavily lashed but whereas my mother had been dark-haired, Lettice's hair was honey-colored. It was abundant and curly. She must have been very like her grandmother, Mary Boleyn, my mother's sister who had been my father's mistress before he married my mother Anne. I heard that Mary had been one of those yielding women who are irresistible to men. I always supposed this was because the men knew there need not be long delays in reaching their desires. Mary was said to be one of those who could not say no, and those are the ones who are naturally irresistible to men, being a constant reminder to them of their own irresistibility.

We were in June. Robert's wife had died last September, but the rumors persisted. I tried to show my indifference to them and had long since ordered the freedom of Mother Dowe who had set the rumors about that I had borne a child or was about to have one. I wanted to show that such foolish gossip was not worth punishing anyone for and that I cared little for my detractors—much as my grandfather Henry VII had done with such good effect in the case of Perkin Warbeck. I was often glad that I had made such a close study of history. It was full of lessons for the living.

Robert was still hoping for marriage and I was still prevaricating. I would not give him a direct no. Nor would I accept any other suitor.

"Time is passing. We are growing older," pleaded Robert.

"We are still young and because of what happened, there must be a gap of time between then and any steps we take."

Robert grew sullen, hectoring, which made me laugh. I was constantly reminding him that I was the Queen and that he should not forget it. Poor Robert, how his fingers itched to grasp the crown!

There are men like that. They yearn for power. I could have told him that great tribulations come with a crown as so many of my ancestors had discovered to their cost. It would make no difference. Men like Robert stretched out their eager hands for it. They would do anything for it. They would fight for it, kill . . .

Mary Sidney was a strong advocate for her brother. "The burdens of state are too much for a woman to carry alone," she said.

"It depends on the woman," I told her, my eyes flashing so that she knew better than to pursue the subject.

She changed it. "Robert is planning a Midsummer's Day water party."

"I have heard nothing of it," I replied sharply.

"He wanted it to be a surprise for you."

"He is always planning for me," I said tenderly.

"Your Majesty, he has told me that he thinks of naught but your pleasure."

"There is no one like him," I said.

Mary beamed with pleasure. "I loved all my brothers," she went on, "but we all agreed there was no one like Robert. He shone among the rest of us from the time he was two."

"How I should have loved to see him when he was two!"

"He was very sure of himself even then, so they tell me," said Mary. "They always said he should have been the eldest. He looked after the family. The death of my father and brother . . ."

"I forbid you to speak of such things. I know Robert looks out for those he loves."

"And he loves none as he loves Your Majesty."

"I believe that to be true. I call him My Eyes, because he is always looking out for what is good for me."

"It is so comforting for a woman to have a man to care for her . . . even if she is a queen."

I gave her a slap across the hand—playful but there was a touch of irritation in it. "There are some women, Mary Sidney," I said, "who are capable of managing their own affairs, even if it be ruling a kingdom."

"I know that full well. Your Majesty is an example of such."

"Well, tell me about the Midsummer party."

It turned out to be an interesting occasion. It was a glorious day as was fitting for Midsummer and the sun shone on the pageant Robert had devised. He was an expert with such arrangements. He had several boats, all decorated with roses and other summer flowers, and it seemed as though the whole Court had turned out to witness the pageant.

There was stirring music coming from one of the barges and children's voices singing the sweetest songs, all in praise of me.

I was sumptuously gowned in white damask with a greenish pattern on it. Green was becoming to my coloring and brought out the red in my hair. My puffed slashed sleeves fell back to show my hands which were adorned with jewels. My hair was carefully dressed with a few false pieces to give it body and I always looked well with it piled high because of my high forehead. I tried to look as much like my father as possible. People still talked of him affectionately; moreover it reminded them that I was his undoubted daughter and the true inheritor of the throne.

Robert was magnificent as always in blue satin. The sleeves of his jerkin were slit from wrist to shoulder to show the doublet beneath which was decorated with pearls and embroidery. His breeches—a fashion borrowed from the French—were full at the top and narrowed at the knee, slashed and puffed looking like latticed windows with bars across which sparkled with jewels. He had the most perfectly shaped legs I have ever seen and had no need for garters. His stockings, with gold and silver thread woven into them, fitted perfectly. In his hat was a curling blue feather.

I listened for the cheers of the people. They were not quite so whole-hearted as they had been before the scandal but they were affectionate enough for me. Less so perhaps when Robert appeared with me, and I knew that I must still act with the utmost caution.

Lettice Knollys was in the same satin-padded, flower-decorated barge as I was and although she was much less elaborately dressed, she managed to look strikingly handsome. I felt a sudden qualm because I caught Robert watching her. She herself was gazing at the shore, but a certain smile played about her lips which could have implied something. What?

He is looking at that woman, I thought. And what was it I saw in his eyes. Lust! How dared he, when I was there.

Then I thought: Robert is a man. I would not have him otherwise. I have held myself aloof. Must I be surprised if he sometimes turns his eyes on other women? I blamed her. Was she playing some game with my Robert?

I would have to watch Madam Lettice. Robert too, perhaps.

I was faintly uneasy. I did not want the situation to change. Marry Robert I could not. I saw that clearly. What if I told him definitely that there could never be marriage between us? He was a free man now—no longer shackled to his little country wife.

Nothing stands still. Life changes. Was Robert growing restive? That was a matter of some concern, especially with a minx like Lettice Knollys close by.

Robert was beside me and I said to him curtly: "So you are admiring the view?"

Whether he knew I had been aware of his interest in Lettice or not, I was not sure. But he immediately turned to me. "I cannot see anything but Your Majesty when you are near."

"It did appear that you found other objects of interest."

"I was lost in thought," he said glibly, "wondering what I could devise for your pleasure."

The Spanish Ambassador de Quadra was standing near.

"I trust my lord," said Robert, "that you do not find our little entertain-ment too boring."

"On the contrary," said de Quadra, in his rather halting English, "I found it most interesting."

He was looking from me to Robert speculatively.

"Did you hear the people cheering the Queen?" asked Robert.

"I did. They love her well."

"We all love the Queen," went on Robert. "It is our bounden duty to do so, but there are some of us who love her with such intensity that we think of nothing else night and day."

"And you are one of these, Lord Robert?"

He looked at me fervently and I forgot momentarily what I had thought to be his interest in Lettice Knollys.

"I, more than all the Queen's subjects, love her with an undying love. In fact, my lord, you are a Bishop. Why should you not marry us here and now?"

I looked sharply at the Spanish Ambassador. He did not seem in the least surprised at such a request and looked at Robert almost as though there was some secret pact between them.

I said: "I doubt the Bishop would have enough English to carry him through the ceremony."

De Quadra was watching me steadily and his next words amazed me. "If you will rid yourself of William Cecil and the band of heretics who surround you, I would willingly perform the ceremony."

He bowed and turned away.

I said to Robert: "Why did he say that? It is almost as though he had considered the request before."

"Oh," replied Robert, "you know these Spaniards. It would have been a delightful way of marrying, don't you think? On a barge . . . on Midsummer's Day, unexpectedly . . ."

I felt uneasy. I said rather sharply: "It is not the way in which the people expect their Queen to marry."

I called Lettice to my side. I wanted to know whether I had imagined what I thought I had seen. She came demurely. Robert scarcely spoke to her. The poor girl must have felt completely snubbed. She did not appear to mind though and Walter Devereux joined us. He was Viscount Hereford, just about Lettice's age—quite a presentable young man but rather dull as I supposed every young man must be when compared with Robert. He seemed quite taken with Lettice and she was turning those startlingly beautiful eyes of hers on him in such a way that was inviting, promising—just as I had imagined she had looked at Robert a short while ago. It was her way with any man—not to be taken seriously.

What I was really thinking about was the strange words of the Spanish Ambassador.

They remained in my mind during the whole of that magnificent pageant.

MARY SIDNEY WAS NOT the sort of girl who could keep a secret and I very quickly discovered that something was on her mind. She was preoccupied, anxious and uncertain. I reproved her several times for her clumsiness; she did not even seem to hear me, which was strange because generally she was so sensitive and could be upset for hours after a reprimand.

I contrived to be alone with her after my toilette had been completed and I said: "Mary, you had better tell me what is on your mind."

She looked startled and then fell on her knees and buried her face in my gown.

"You should be careful," I said tartly. "Those aglets on the skirt can be very sharp if they catch your skin. I am always complaining about them."

She lifted her face to mine and there was no mistaking her woebegone expression.

I said: "Take the stool. Now confess."

"It is because we all love Your Majesty so dearly . . ."

"Yes, yes," I interrupted impatiently. "That is the opening when people are going to admit to have done me some wrong. Get on with it."

"We have done you no wrong, Your Majesty. Indeed not. There is not one of us who would not die for you."

"So many have offered me their lives," I retorted, "that the offer does lose its impact after a while—particularly as these offers are frequently given lightly, so that to offer a life to a queen has become almost a figure of speech. Don't try my patience further, Mary. Admit. Confess, whatever it is."

"Robert loves you dearly. You are his life. If you could have seen his pride, his joy when you referred to him as your Eyes . . . He cannot live in this suspense, Your Majesty."

"And what does he propose to do about that?"

"It was a plan."

"Do you mean a plot?"

"I mean that Henry and I and Robert thought . . . if we could get the help of Spain to your marriage, you would agree to it."

"And how do you think you could get the consent of Spain?"

"Your Majesty, Philip is no longer your suitor, but there is one thing that Spain desires above all else—perhaps more than an alliance through marriage. That England returns to Rome."

"What!" I cried, almost jumping out of my chair.

"Well, we thought—Henry, Robert and I—that if Spain had the promise that England should be returned to Rome in exchange for their support in the marriage . . ."

"Indeed!" I cried. "And I suppose *King* Robert would have arranged this after the marriage?"

Mary was silent. I sat very still. You are not yet King, Lord Robert, I thought. And this is what you would propose! Consent to the marriage and *you* will return England to Rome!

How right I had been! He thought himself already King. What had de Quadra said: "Dismiss Cecil." The cleverest and most unbiased counselor the Queen ever had! And all because he was what the Spaniards would call a heretic!

I began to laugh.

Mary looked at me wonderingly.

"Your Majesty is not angry?" she said pleadingly. "It is only because Robert loves you so much . . . because he is so impatient."

"And because he is so ambitious, eh? Because already he feels the crown on his head?"

"I should not have told you."

"It was your duty to tell me."

"I was very worried to be involved in such a plan without your knowledge."

"And so you should be. But you did well to tell me, and know this, and tell your fellow conspirators this, that whatever they think to plot without my knowledge, they will never succeed in it. There is one ruler of this realm and I am that ruler."

"Yes, Your Majesty."

"Bring me my looking-glass," I said.

She did and I studied my face. Not beautiful . . . as Lettice Knollys was, but attractive with that white skin and tawny hair and large tawny eyes which had a faraway look, yet penetrating, because they were a trifle short-sighted. I touched my hair with my beautiful white hands. No one had hands quite like mine—not even Lettice Knollys.

I said, "Get your combs. I need my hair a little higher. Hurry, and take care that you do not pull."

While Mary arranged my hair I was thinking: Sell my country to Rome! My dear Robert, you may be handsome, charming, much sought after by the women of my Court, but I am the Queen. I am the one who makes decisions. That is something you will have to learn.

No man shall govern me; and I shall govern my country.

CO MY DISTRESS Lady Jane Seymour died. She had been ailing for some time and had never been a strong girl. I had been quite fond of her and to please her family I ordered that she should have a state funeral in Westminster Abbey.

I missed her very much. Jane had been one of those good girls who never complained and was always willing to do what was asked of her.

I had always believed that I should show myself to my people, and I liked to move about the country so that those who lived in remote places could feel they had some contact with me.

Since the Amy Robsart scandal I felt more than ever the need to keep my people's good will and so I was traveling often. When we made these progresses through the country, the Court went with us. We stayed at the various big houses on the route and although my rich subjects found entertaining us very costly, they regarded it as a great honor and would even be piqued if their houses were not visited.

On this particular occasion we were in Ipswich and among my retinue was Robert, of course. As my Master of Horse he must always be with us and he would ride beside me which was all in keeping with the position he held and was one of the reasons why we had both thought it perfect for him.

I had not reprimanded him about his secret plot with the Spanish Ambassador, but I continued to hold him off, and he remained in a state of frustration which was sufficient punishment, I thought; since he was as ardently devoted as ever, I was quite satisfied with the state of affairs.

With us also was Lady Katharine Grey who had seemed very preoccupied of late. After Mary Sidney's confession, I wondered what Katharine was about. She was pale and there were rings about her eyes which I had not noticed before. She looked as though she was sickening for something. I was not greatly disturbed because she was after all a rival of whom I must always be conscious and my nature was not of a kind to endear me to such people.

It was while we were in Ipswich that Lord Robert surprised me while I was at my toilette.

It was early morning and he looked so disturbed that I dismissed my women and granted him an audience. I was looking quite attractive with my hair loose and in my petticoats, though when he appeared I immediately requested that a wrap be put about my shoulders.

When they had gone Robert seized my hand and kissed it.

"My dearest," he said, "I had to come to tell you this without delay for I fear someone else should bring news of what happened last night and misconstrue . . ."

"Tell me quickly," I cried. "I am all interest."

"Last night Lady Katharine Grey came to my bedchamber."

I felt myself go cold with fury but he went on quickly: "Oh, not on my invitation. She came to plead with me for help. I dispatched her with all speed, but I feared someone might have seen her either enter or leave my bedchamber and have come to you with some garbled story."

"You had better tell me what happened."

"She was not five minutes in my chamber. She was frantic with anxiety. That is why she came."

"What is her problem? Does she want you to help her take the throne from me, or would she offer my country to Rome as a bait for their help?"

He flushed a little. Then he said: "She is pregnant and in a dire state."

"Pregnant! She has no husband. I have never been asked to give my consent to a marriage."

"She has a husband."

"Who is he?"

"Lord Hertford."

"He is in France."

"Exactly so, and she does not hear from him. She swears she is married, but she has no proof of this until Hertford returns. Meanwhile she wants help."

I was angry. She had no right to marry without my consent. She was next in line to the succession and she was pregnant, which would call attention to my barren state.

"Help?" I said. "How dare she? To marry without my consent and that of the Council! It is feckless in the extreme. She should go to the Tower. Do you believe there was a marriage? Hertford is not in the country. There must have been witnesses."

"I dismissed her quickly from my chamber and know nothing but what I have told you, and that, I thought, should be imparted to you without delay."

"Indeed yes," I said.

He looked at me pleadingly. "How delightful you look so simply attired. I am not sure that you are not even more beautiful like this. I think you are. You do not need the adornments so necessary to other women. Simple, natural, beautiful, the Queen among women . . . in her natural state . . ."

He would have embraced me but I held him off.

"My women are close by," I said. "We want no more gossip."

"Then let us marry and put an end to it."

I sighed. "I fear that would be the start of it."

"My dearest, you would have nothing to fear with me beside you. I would protect you."

"Oh never fear, Robert, I will protect myself well enough."

"Then . . ."

"Now get out, dear Robert. I shall call my women to finish dressing me. I must see Katharine Grey at once."

SHE STOOD BEFORE ME—a poor frightened girl. I could almost feel sorry for her.

"You had better repeat that tale which Lord Robert has brought to me concerning you," I said.

She fell on her knees and I went on: "You are very humble today, my lady. That is unusual. Tell me everything."

"Your Majesty, Lord Hertford and I fell in love when I was at the Seymours' place where I went with Jane. Jane was very anxious for us to marry and helped us."

I nodded grimly. "So Hertford had to be pressed into it, did he?"

She did not answer.

"Well," I said, "so you married. What witnesses have you? Where is the priest? Girls dally with men, I know, and then are amazed at the consequences."

"Madam," she said with some dignity, remembering doubtless that she had a claim to the throne. "Lord Hertford and I are married."

"Well, then you should have no difficulty in proving it. Where is the priest who married you . . . without my consent I would like to add. I shall have a few words to say to that gentleman."

"I do not know his name, Your Majesty. I do not know where he is now. It was a secret ceremony in my lord's lodging."

"But you must have had a witness."

"It was Jane."

"Jane is dead," I said. "So there is no witness and no priest. But there is a husband, so you tell us."

"I do indeed," she said quickly.

"Do you realize that you have committed treason? Do you know of the law?"

"I know it, Your Majesty."

"You shall be taken this day to the Tower of London and there you will be held. Hertford shall be sent for and we shall hear his side of the story."

"It will be the same as mine, Your Majesty."

"Let us hope so. Go to your apartment and prepare to leave."

She bowed and retired, looking relieved. She had been in a state of acute anxiety and was clearly glad to give up her secret even though it meant that she had become a prisoner in the Tower.

ONE OF MY RIVALS was safely in the Tower but I felt very uneasy about her. There was bound to be talk and fresh urgings for me to marry when she showed that she could produce offspring; and if it were a boy I should be doubly bothered.

There were also rumblings in the direction of that other—and to my mind more dangerous—rival. Mary Queen of France and Scotland was in somewhat desperate straits and that at least gave me some pleasure. The spoilt darling of the French Court was so no longer. The King of France had died at the joust when a splinter had entered his eye and his son François, husband of my rival, had come to the throne to occupy it for a very short time. Poor boy, he had always been a weakling and it was said that his mother, Catherine de' Medici, who had a reputation throughout Europe for being one of the most scheming women alive, had, according to certain rumors, hastened his death in order to make way for another son who was completely under her control. François, it seemed, like most men, had come under the spell of the fascinating Mary and doubtless would listen to her rather than to his mother. Catherine, however, was one of those who did not find young Mary so enchanting and she was making it clear to her that there was no place for her in France, so there was nothing Mary could do but return to Scotland.

I could imagine how different those dour Scottish nobles would be from the gallant French courtiers and poets who had circulated round Mary. I had seen some of them and I was quite amused to think of her returning to them. On the other hand, I felt apprehensive to have her so close, just across the border, such a dangerous claimant to my throne.

What was particularly galling was that she had had the temerity to emblazon the arms of England on those of Scotland and France, and to style herself Queen of England.

I had to remember that although the country as a whole was against a Catholic monarch, there were a number of ardent Catholics in the land, and if I were to displease them it would not need much to raise protests against me, and there was this woman—supposed to be so fascinating and younger than I—waiting on the other side of the Border.

I knew that I was not unduly disturbed because Cecil was uneasy too.

We had made peace with the French, and there was in existence the Treaty of Edinburgh which set out that those French who had come to Scotland to help the Scots against us must retire; and another clause was that a fine should be paid by Mary for blazoning the arms of England with those of Scotland and France.

This treaty was not yet ratified. Therefore when Mary sent emissaries asking for a safe passage to Scotland, I was incensed. How dared she imagine that I would welcome her presence so close to England when the treaty was unsigned and she was blatantly laying claim to my throne?

When she was made aware of my reaction she pleaded that she had been under the command of her father-in-law, King Henri Deux, and her husband, King François; and therefore had no alternative than to call herself the Queen of England. My reply to that was that when the treaty was signed, she should have safe passage. Her excuse then was that she could not sign the treaty until she had consulted with her Scottish subjects, and this she could not do until she reached Edinburgh.

It was clear to me that she had no intention of signing the treaty, and therefore I refused her safe passage.

However, when she was in our waters, a fog arose and she managed to elude the English ships which were searching for her and thus she reached Scotland safely. I was disappointed. I should have liked to detain her in England as my guest. I had thought a great deal about her and not only did I want to know what she was doing but I was also curious to see what she really looked like and if she were as beautiful as she was said to be. Some of the poems those Frenchmen had written about her were too eulogistic even for royalty.

I received a request from her uncle, a member of the famous Guise family whose brothers were the great Duke and that Cardinal of Lorraine who had played such a big part in Mary's life—some said quite a sinister part. This plea for an invitation was from the younger brother but it was one which I found most intriguing. Besides being the Grand Prior of France, he was the commander of the French Navy and I was very eager to meet a member of that family which had played such a large part in shaping the history of France and had at times been more important rulers than the kings.

I was not disappointed. The Grand Prior was a fascinating man. There was little of the churchman about him. He was handsome, possessed of grace and charm, with impeccable manners and just the right touch of foreignness to intrigue me. He was the type of man I had always found extremely attractive.

I made him talk about his niece Mary whom he had known well. Her mother had been his sister and the Guises had taken charge of her when as a child she had first arrived in France. He said she was charming and beautiful and—perhaps because of his beautiful manners—he managed to convey that I was equally so.

I was determined to entertain him royally to show that we in England could treat our visitors with perfect hospitality even when not so long before we had been enemies.

I decided on a banquet to be followed by a ballet.

I had the banqueting hall hung with tapestries representing the parable of the virgins of the Evangelists, and with the Grand Prior seated beside me I explained to him that I had been born in the Chamber of Virgins under the sign of the Virgin which brought out gallant remarks about my not being allowed to remain in the single state for long. To which I replied that the choice lay with me.

His eyes sparkled with Gallic passion and he implied that he would greatly love to be the one who made me change my mind.

I laughed with him. I enjoyed this kind of conversation. Robert glowered a little, but he knew there was nothing to fear from this Frenchman. All the same he was becoming more and more possessive and hated to see anyone take up too much of my attention. He was also growing too bold and because I had granted him favors and shown my regard for him sometimes he behaved as a jealous husband might, and although there were occasions when I was amused at this, at others I was not. I suppose it depended on my mood.

The ballet was a great success. It was performed by my maids of honor representing the ten virgins—the foolish and the wise. They carried silver lamps, beautifully engraved, some carrying oil, some empty.

There was spontaneous applause. I glanced sideways at my handsome Frenchman and could be sure that he was enchanted by the sight, so perhaps it was as elegant as he was accustomed to seeing at the French Court.

The ladies set down their lamps and danced most gracefully. They came to the Prior and his entourage and invited them to dance, which they did.

I was ready to dance because I had arranged as part of the procedure that they should beg me to do so and that I should at first refuse and then give way because I wished to honor the Prior.

Later he complimented me on my dancing, my beauty and the elegance of my Court.

I turned to him smiling and said: "You are so gallant, Monsieur, that I love you, but I hate that brother Guise of yours who took Calais from me."

"Alas," he said, "that is war. But on this enchanted night let us not talk of unhappy things. I have seen you dance, and I could never be happy again if I did not have the honor of dancing with you."

I could dance through the night without the slightest fatigue, so I was delighted; and they all watched while I and the Grand Prior of France danced together.

In due course I said goodbye to the charming Prior and he left for France. I could imagine what questions the Queen-Mother, Catherine de' Medici, would ask of him but I was sure he had been impressed by the manner of his reception, and I did believe that he really had admired me a little.

My thoughts were constantly on Mary of Scotland and they brought me little comfort. Cecil shared my apprehension.

I said to him: "It is not a comforting thought to know that she is just across the Border and does not need to cross the seas to come to England."

Cecil said: "I know Your Majesty's great desire is for a peaceful reign, and that you agree with me that the best way to keep peace is to prepare for war. I have been meaning to discuss with you, when the time was ripe, the extension of the Navy. We should build more ships. It gives work to our people and work makes prosperity. It is better to spend money on such things than on war . . . and then should the need arise to defend ourselves we are prepared."

I smiled at him. "Dear good Master Cecil, I thank God for giving you to me."

He was moved and I felt better than I had since Mary Stuart had come to Scotland.

I LISTENED TO the young man who sat some little distance from me playing his lute. He had a delicate touch and the music moved me deeply. He was a handsome young man—very tall and elegant; his hair curled prettily about his head, but there was a petulant touch about his mouth. In spite of his handsome looks he was quite unlike men such as Robert Dudley, the kind I so much admired, for there was something almost effeminate about young Lord Darnley.

As I listened I wondered whether that petulance I had noticed was envy. Did the foolish boy really think he should be sitting in my place? It was amazing what notions crept into the mind of those who had a modicum of royal blood.

Of course he was of the male sex and that, in his eyes, set him above any woman however capable, however much closer she was to the throne. The assumption that women were somehow inferior to men always made me burn with indignation. I would show them one day that my sex was no handicap to my power and my ability.

But perhaps my young lute player's dissatisfaction had been inspired by his mother. There was a woman to watch. I was certain that she was up to tricks and had been ever since I came to the throne.

This boy was the second but eldest surviving son of Matthew Stewart, Earl of Lennox, and Margaret Douglas—and Lady Margaret was the daughter of my father's sister, Margaret Tudor. My father and his sister Margaret had never been on good terms, and he had been delighted when she married into Scotland; but Margaret Tudor had all the fire and determination of her race and she had had a very colorful life on the other side of the Border. This

Lady Margaret, Countess of Lennox, was the child of her mother's second marriage to Archibald Douglas, Earl of Angus, and she had always been an enemy of mine. She had been a great friend of my sister Mary and I believed she had even had the temerity to fancy she might follow Mary in my place. I discovered that she was responsible for certain activities at the time of the Wyatt Rebellion and had done her best to have me implicated in that affair.

When I came to the throne I extended the hand of friendship to her as I did to so many who had shown a certain animosity to me during my sister's reign for I hoped to win them over; but there are some who cannot be won and for a woman of Lady Lennox's nature together with her strong Catholic leanings and a drop of royal blood, there would always be resentment of me, and she had never overcome the covetous aspirations she had had toward my throne.

She was intriguing in Yorkshire so I brought her and her family to London where the Earl of Lennox was lodged in the Tower and the Countess and Lord Darnley were kept in restraint in the house of Sir Richard Sackville at Shene while inquiries were made concerning their activities.

From Shene the Countess wrote me most appealing letters assuring me of her desire for friendship and it had occurred to me that it would be better to have the family under my eyes at Court rather than intriguing somewhere in the country.

In due course I granted the Earl's request that he might go to Scotland, so he left his lodgings in the Tower and departed. I did not think either the Countess or the Earl were very clever and I was sure that their son would never win the people's approval—so I was not unduly worried about them. If it had not been for their royal connections, I would have dismissed them as nonentities.

However, Lord Darnley certainly knew how to play the lute and any good musician was welcome at my Court.

As I sat listening to him the Scottish Ambassador, Sir James Melville, was at my side and I could see that he too was moved by the music.

When Darnley stopped playing I applauded and the young man came and bowed to me. He had graceful manners and really was a very pretty boy.

I watched the rather dour Melville studying him as Darnley moved off and joined some of the ladies who were inclined to pet him.

I said to Melville: "Our pretty boy has a masterly touch with the lute."

"Very accomplished," agreed Melville.

"I believe his mother has ambitions for him."

"What mother is not ambitious for her son?"

"She is trying to regain her estates in Scotland."

"That is to be expected."

Ah, I thought, Master Melville is taken with the pretty boy and his forceful mother. I shall have to watch this.

"I was happy that Your Grace had permitted the Earl to visit Edinburgh," went on Melville.

"He is going to plead with the Queen of Scots for the restoration of his estates. Let us hope he will be successful."

"Then I doubt not the Countess and Lord Darnley will join him there."

I was a little puzzled because I was growing more and more certain that Sir James was working toward some end and it had suddenly occurred to me that it might involve the Lennox family.

I discussed it with Cecil who was always aware of intrigue wherever it sprang up.

"It would seem to me," said that wise man, "that the Countess might like to see her son married to the Queen of Scotland."

"Impossible!" I cried.

"Why so? The Queen is a widow. She is very young and will certainly marry." He looked at me sternly. "She owes it to her people to get an heir."

I did not answer that and he went on: "Why should it not be Henry Stewart Lord Darnley? He has royal blood; his grandmother was the daughter of a king. And if at the moment he lacks ambition, most certainly his parents do not. His mother is anxious for a crown . . . of some sort. She once had pretensions to yours, remember. It seems most natural to me that, failing the crown of England, she should set her son trying for that of Scotland."

"Darnley King of Scotland! I would never agree to that."

"Once he was in Scotland your consent would not be necessary. Moreover, consider it. What think you of Lord Darnley?"

"Very little. A frivolous, petulant, spoilt boy."

"That is exactly my opinion. Would it not be better for the Queen of Scots to marry a petulant spoilt boy than a strong man?"

I looked at Cecil and once again I thanked God for him.

"I see," I said slowly.

"We must certainly wait and see what comes of this matter. We will oppose it in public but in private . . . let us consider that for England it would not be such a bad thing."

WE WERE AT Hampton Court and the weather was cold for October. I had not been well for some days and had had a touch of fever. One of my pleasures was to take a bath which many of my ladies thought was bad for my health, but I found that to immerse my body in warm water, and lie there until it was cleansed of its impurities, refreshed me. Since I had become Queen, courtiers had become much cleaner for the simple reason that I had a very sensitive nose and could not bear anything evil-smelling close to me. All at my Court must wash and change their clothes regularly so that there was no unpleasant smell about them when they came into my presence. Consequently the production of soap had greatly increased. When I traveled my bath would be taken with other household goods so that whenever I felt the need I could enjoy complete immersion.

Kat said it was folly when I was not feeling well and she was sure I had some fever, but I told her to be silent; but perhaps she was right for I caught a chill and the next day I had to take to my bed.

When Lord Hunsdon heard that I was unwell, he begged to be allowed to come to see me. I was rather fond of him and he was my first cousin, being the son of my mother's sister Mary. When I came to the throne he had been plain Henry Carey. I gave him a knighthood at once and later created him Baron Hunsdon. I always tried to help the Boleyns and he was one to be proud of because he excelled at the jousts, and not long ago he and Robert had led the lists against all comers in a tournament we had had at Greenwich. I had been so delighted that my cousin and the most important of all men should so excel together.

So I allowed Lord Hunsdon to be brought to me.

When he saw me he fell on his knees by the bed in some alarm and begged me to allow him to summon a doctor in whom he had great trust because he himself had benefited from his skill. So I gave my permission for Dr Burcot to come to see me, and when he came I was furious that I had done so, for the man looked at me, touched my brow, felt the fever and said: "Your Majesty, you have the smallpox."

The smallpox! The dreaded disease which could be fatal and almost always was! And even if one survived there was a chance of one's being disfigured for life. The thought of my white skin—in which I took such pride—being hideously pitted was more than I could bear.

"I have not got the pox!" I cried. "I will not have the pox! Take this man away. He is a knave. A charlatan. He knows not what he talks of."

Dr Burcot bowed and retired and I lay back on my bed exhausted with rage and fever.

I lived in fear and each morning I searched my body for the dreaded sign. No spots appeared, but I felt no better. My fever increased. I knew now that they all expected I was on my death-bed and the Privy Council was called together to take a vital decision on the succession. Some naturally thought that Katharine Grey should succeed me; others thought that the choice should fall on Henry Hastings, Earl of Huntingdon, who was a Plantagenet through his descent on his mother's side from Edward IV's brother the Duke of Clarence. He was a strong Protestant and for that reason was sure of favor in many circles. The great fear was that Spain would take action and an attempt would be made to set Mary Stuart on the throne.

I was only vaguely aware of this as I lay in my bed and suddenly I opened my eyes and saw the members of my Council about my bed.

I struggled back to consciousness. This could mean one thing. I was dying.

My first thought was of Robert Dudley, which showed that I truly loved him. I thought: What will become of him? It was his great wish to rule the country and there was no doubt that he had great ability.

I said: "My lords, my end is near. That is why you stand there regarding me so solemnly."

And when they did not answer, I was sure that it was true.

"I beg of you to name Lord Robert Dudley Protector of the Realm," I went on. "This is my wish. Be good to my cousin, Lord Hunsdon, who has served me well. Scandal has been talked of me but I swear before God that although I love Lord Robert Dudley and always have, nothing improper has ever passed between us."

The Council was overcome with emotion and promised me that my wishes should be carried out.

I thanked them and closed my eyes.

But my cousin Hunsdon had great faith in the doctor whom I had dismissed and sent a messenger to him asking him to come back and help me.

Dr Burcot was a German and he made it clear that he took commands from no Englishman or -woman.

"She insulted me!" he cried. "She called me knave. If she would not listen to my advice when I might have saved her, I decline to offer it again."

The messenger, who believed that I was dying and perhaps for love of me—but more likely because he wanted to keep his master in high favor—took Dr Burcot's coat and boots and told him that if he did not come at once to my bedside he would run him through the heart—and he produced his dagger to prove it.

The doctor was either impressed by such fervor or afraid the man would carry out his threat—in any case he put on his boots and coat and came with all speed to my bedside.

I think I must have been very near death when he arrived. He grumbled that he was almost too late but there might yet be a chance. "The spots must come out," he said. "And I have to force them out."

Then he did a most extraordinary thing. He told them to put a mattress by the fire and had my body wrapped in a piece of scarlet cloth. I was then carried to the mattress and laid there, where I was given something to drink which was sweet and soothing. I drank deeply for he made me take as much as I could; and when I had drunk I saw the red blotches beginning to appear on my hands and arms.

"What means this?" I cried.

"I told Your Majesty that you had the pox," said the doctor. "You called me a knave. Well, now you will see."

"The pox!" I cried in horror. "I would rather die."

"Nonsense," said the doctor whose respect for my rank was nonexistent. "It is better to have the pox outside your body than inside where it can kill you."

I was overcome with grief though the fever had left me and I could only think that the smallpox marked people permanently. All my pretensions to beauty would be gone. I could not bear that. I realized then what a vain woman I was—vain about trivialities. Almost as much as a great ruler, I wanted to be a desirable woman.

I began to feel better. The terrible fever which had put me in a stupor was passing, but the fearful spots were rapidly covering my face, my arms, in fact every part of my body.

Mary Sidney came to me and said she would be with me day and night and that if I would restrain from scratching the spots there was no reason why I should not emerge with my skin as beautiful as it had ever been.

I never forgot what I owed to Mary Sidney. I knew that she was a good and loyal creature but I had thought her devotion might have been due to a desire to protect her brother's fortunes. Kat would have been with me but she was aging now and not well enough to stand the strain of nursing. But it was comforting at such a time to have someone near me who was so close to Robert.

Mary fed me, washed me, sat with me and watched over me.

I loved her dearly for what she had done for me. And after a while my spots began to fade but I would not leave my apartments until they were completely gone.

Then one day Mary did not come to me. I was desolate when they told me that what we had feared might happen had come to pass. She was suffering from the smallpox.

It did not take long for my skin to heal. I think I was very healthy. I had not overeaten as many of my subjects did—including Robert—and I had always kept my body especially clean. It may be that this helped me. In any case very soon I had completely recovered. For several days I wanted to keep looking at myself. Not a spot! Not a blemish! My skin was as dazzlingly white as it had ever been.

I knew that I owed this to the irascible Dr Burcot and I chided myself for dismissing him so vehemently on the first occasion. If I had not done so, I might have been more quickly cured and to show my gratitude I gave him a grant of land and a pair of golden spurs which had belonged to my grandfather King Henry VII. He thanked me for them in his gruff way, but I believed he was immensely gratified that I had emerged unscathed.

I wanted all those who had shown their love for me to know how grateful I was, but there was one I could never repay.

I cannot get out of my mind the day Mary Sidney came to me. She was cured of the pox and when she came in heavily veiled and knelt at my feet, terrible fears beset me.

"Oh Mary," I murmured. "So you . . ."

She lifted the veil and I saw her ravaged face. I could not speak. I was so overcome with emotion. My pretty Mary, to look so hideous, and it had happened because of her devotion to me.

"Oh Mary, Mary!" I cried and we wept together.

"Everything shall be done," I told her.

But she shook her head sadly. "Nothing can be done," she said sadly.

"And Henry?" I asked.

"He said it was just as it ever was between us . . . but I saw his face and he could not bear to look at me."

"My dear, dear Mary, you shall always be at my side."

She shook her head. "There is only one thing I want to do and that is hide myself away."

"You shall have apartments here . . . your own apartments. You shall receive only those whom you wish to and, Mary, I shall come to see you every day when I am here . . . We shall talk together . . . and, dear Mary, I shall never forget."

We clung to each other—but there was really no comfort I could offer her. I felt her misery acutely for she had incurred it for my sake and it could so easily have happened to me.

AFTER MY RECOVERY Lettice Knollys came to Court now and then. Although I was a little wary of her because of what I fancied I had seen pass between her and Robert, I was glad to see her. She had a lively wit and now that she was a mother, her beauty seemed to have deepened.

I used to talk to her a good deal and although there were occasions when she irritated me with too frank a comment, I could always give her a slap or a nip which silenced her and reminded her who was the mistress.

I missed poor Mary Sidney sadly, but I had given her very luxurious apartments and, although she rarely emerged from them, I hope she was not too unhappy. Whenever I was in the neighborhood I visited her each day and I would tell her everything that was happening, and we did spend some very happy times together.

I was furious when the Archduke Charles offered himself to Mary Stuart, and as usual I did not restrain my comment. Cecil reproved me, pointing out that although I did not want the man myself I wanted no one else to have him, which I suppose was true.

I wondered if Mary Stuart would take him. I knew the Lennoxes were now openly trying to put forward young Darnley.

Another of my suitors married. This was Eric of Sweden, and it was such a romantic tale that I could not help being affected by it. Apparently he had seen a girl selling nuts outside his palace when he rode in and out, and had become so enchanted by her surpassing beauty that he had fallen violently in love with her and married her.

"How romantic!" I sighed. "Do you know, I think he would have made rather a charming husband. Better," I added, "than that rake of Austria who offers his hand here and there to whoever he thinks might take it."

I was greatly interested in Mary Stuart. Would she take the Archduke Charles? What of Don Carlos, son of Philip? They said he was half mad, but would that matter if he were the heir to Spain?

I found myself obsessed by the woman. Was she really as beautiful as people said she was? I wondered how she was faring in those grim Scottish palaces—Holyrood House and Edinburgh Castle. How she must be missing France and those gallant poets. There would not be much poetry in Scotland, gallantry either.

I was always questioning the Scottish Ambassador about her. I would command him to sit beside me and try to make him talk of his mistress.

"I constantly hear of her beauty," I said. "Do you find her very fair?"

"Aye," he replied.

"All men are said to admire her. Do you, Master Melville?"

"She is my mistress and I could do nothing else."

"As your mistress you must serve her and such an upright gentleman as you would admire a hideous hag, I doubt not, if she were your Queen."

"The Queen of Scotland is not a hideous hag."

"Tell me of her clothes. They say she is more French than Scottish, and has brought much of France into Scotland."

"I know little of fashions, Your Majesty."

"How does she wear her hair? I am told that mine is of a striking color. What is Queen Mary's hair like? Do you think it is of a more attractive color than mine?"

I could not help laughing at the dour young man and I liked to tease him while I was gleaning information about her whom I was beginning to think of as my tiresome rival.

Melville said: "Your Majesty must ask others. I know nothing of such matters."

"Well, you would not notice your mistress's hair because it is so like that of other ladies, I doubt not. It is only when the hair is of an unusual color and particularly beautiful that people are aware of it. Now answer me this: Who is the more beautiful, the Queen of England or the Queen of Scotland?"

"The Queen of England is the fairest in England and the Queen of Scotland in Scotland."

"That is no answer," I cried.

"Your Majesty is pleased to plague this poor Ambassador."

"My skin is lighter, is it not? My hair fairer?"

"That is true, Your Majesty, but . . ."

"But what, man?"

"The Queen of Scotland is very beautiful."

"That is often said, but how much of her beauty does she owe to royalty?"

"The usual amount, Madam."

Poor man, he did not like this conversation. It must seem very frivolous to a man of his nature. On the other hand he did not want to say anything which when reported to his mistress might displease her. But I was relentless in my desire to know more of this paragon of beauty.

"Who is the taller, she or I?" I demanded.

"She is," he answered promptly.

"Then she is too tall," I snapped, "for I am told that I am neither too high nor too low. Does she hunt? Does she read? Does she love music?"

"She does all these, Madam, and is very fond of music."

"What instruments does she play?"

"The lute and the virginals."

"Does she play them well?"

"Reasonably well for a queen."

I said no more then but I was determined that he should admit that there was one thing at least in which I triumphed over that perfect mistress of his.

One day I arranged to play the virginals behind a curtain and instructed some of my ladies to bring Sir James Melville into the room so that he might hear the music and not know who was playing.

He had sat entranced during the performance, they told me, and when it was over he had declared that it was brilliant. When my ladies asked him if he knew who the performer was, he said he did not know, only that he was a fine musician.

"It is the Queen," they said, and drew back the curtains to disclose me, sitting there.

"Ah, Sir James," I said, "now you have heard my music. Does your mistress play as well on the virginals?"

He had to admit that he had rarely heard such a performance from any, and he believed that very few could rival me.

"Not even the talented Queen of Scotland?" I demanded with much incredulity.

"No one, Madam. You are indeed a musician."

That mollified me a little.

Then I danced for him and he had to admit that the Queen of Scots could not leap as high as I could, nor did she dance with such verve.

One day I said to him: "Your Queen is a lady of such talent and overwhelming beauty that I know of only one man worthy of her. You must go to her, Sir James, and tell her that I will offer her the finest man in my kingdom for only she is worthy of him and he of her."

He was looking at me as though I mocked him.

But I went on: "Oh yes, Sir James, I mean it. I shall rob my Court of its brightest jewel that it may adorn that of this most worthy lady. I offer her as the husband she needs, my dearest friend, Lord Robert Dudley."

CHE NEWS SPREAD around the Court like wildfire. I wondered what effect it would have on Robert and was quite prepared when he came bursting into my apartments with a face of thunder.

I said to the few ladies who were with me: "I see Sir Robert has forgotten again that he is in the presence of the Queen. Pray leave us so that I may deal with him as he deserves."

They hastily retired and I had no doubt that they would not go too far out of earshot. They all loved to add to the gossip about Robert.

"Well, my lord, what is the meaning of this most unseemly conduct?" I demanded.

He cried: "I have heard this monstrous rumor. It cannot be true. I demand an immediate explanation."

"Robin," I replied, "there are times when you try me sorely. Perhaps out of my regard for you I have allowed you certain friendly intimacies. You take advantage of them."

"I demand to know if you are aware of what is being said."

"I am the one who makes demands, you should remember."

He stamped his foot. His face was flushed, his eyes flashing with rage. "They are saying that I am to be sent to Scotland."

"To marry the most beautiful of queens . . . according to her Ambassador. Robert, surely you should be dancing with joy at your good fortune."

"You know of this. It is your doing."

I lowered my head so that he should not see that I was smiling. He came to me and took me by the shoulders. I could call the guards to arrest him, I reminded him.

He held me against him and shook me.

I said mockingly: "Robin is in a rage."

"How can you be so heartless?"

"Does a crown mean nothing to you?"

"That one does not," he said.

"And a beautiful Queen to go with it."

"There is only one Queen for me. You cannot be serious."

"I am serious," I said.

He looked at me in bewilderment and I felt I could not tease him anymore, but I did . . . just a little.

"You have led me to believe . . ." he began.

"*I* have led you to believe! Everything you believe, my lord, is in your own mind. How many times have I told you that I will not marry? I will remain a virgin. How many times have I told you that?"

"But you do not mean it."

"Robin, you want a crown. There is one waiting for you in Scotland."

"No!"

"And the fairest of queens . . ."

"The fairest of queens is here, standing before me now."

"I am not sure that Master Melville would agree with you on that."

"A barbarian from a barbarous land!"

"Perhaps you are right and it would be unkind to condemn my elegant Robert to that land. Perhaps I had better keep him here. I confess my Court would be a dull place without him."

He seized my hand and kissed it.

"I am tired of hearing of the perfections of that woman," I cried petulantly. "Do you think there are some in this land who would rally to her if she came against me?"

"I would soon rout the lot of them," he boasted. "There is only one Queen for this country and with God's help she will reign over us for years to come."

He was regaining his assurance. In his heart he must have known I would never let him go.

Again he kissed my hands. He would have kissed more if I had allowed it; but I held him off and he was faintly unsure.

"She will be angry when she hears of my proposal concerning you, Robert. She has said some cruel things about you, called you my horse master who killed his wife in order to make room for me. I hear that she has not a good word to say for me either, and what have I done save take my rightful inheritance, for which she craved? Perhaps she will accept you . . . and you, Robert, what will you do? You will refuse her. You will let Master Melville and his Scots know that you prefer the hope of a crown with me to a safe one with her."

"I like this not," he said.

"I like it well," I answered.

"You do it to plague me as you ever have done."

"Perhaps you would be better treated in the Court of Scotland."

"Don't talk of it," he said. "There is one place I want to be . . . here, beside you. Elizabeth, my Queen, have done with this nonsense. Let us marry. It is what everyone wants you to do. Even Cecil would agree to our marriage."

I said: "Not yet. And, Robert, there is something I have to say to you. Plain Lord Robert could not be acceptable to the Queen of Scots. Her husband must be an earl at least . . . so I thought this an excellent way of honoring you, and I have decided to create you Earl of Leicester and Baron of Denbigh, a title which, till now, has been used only by royalty. There will be estates to go with your titles. There is the Castle of Kenilworth and Astel Grove . . ."

He was staring at me with wonder. I knew Robert well. He was rather acquisitive and although he was becoming one of the richest men in the land, he could not have too much.

"I see," I went on, "that you are well pleased. On your knees, you ungrateful dog, for thinking I would cast you off when all the time I am planning for your pleasure."

CREATING ROBERT EARL of Leicester was the brilliant ceremony I intended it to be. I had dressed with even more than my usual attention to that important and absorbing matter and I sparkled as I walked to my place in the Presence Chamber with young Lord Darnley going before me, as nearest Prince of the Blood, carrying the sword of state. Surrounding me were several noblemen among them Sir James Melville and Lord Hunsdon who was carrying the velvet ermine-lined mantle which I should put on Robert when the moment came.

Robert followed in surcoat and hood. I was seated as he came forward and knelt before me and Lord William Howard gave me the parchment containing the letters of patent. Then Sir William Cecil read from it in a voice which could be heard throughout the chamber and Lord Hunsdon brought me the peer's robe which I put about Robert's shoulders. As I bent over him and saw the dark hair curling about his neck, I could not resist allowing my fingers to touch it and I tickled him to show how fond I was of him and that my pretending to give him to Mary of Scotland was just a joke so that I could bestow this title upon him.

I saw James Melville watching me, trying to hide his shocked expression, and I was greatly amused. I could not wait to ask him what he thought of my new Earl of Leicester and Baron of Denbigh.

"He is a worthy subject," replied Melville, "and is a happy man to have such a good prince who can discern and reward his good service."

"Yet," I replied, pointing to Darnley, "you like better yonder long lad."

He knew what I was referring to and he said: "No woman of spirit would make choice of a man who was more of a woman than a man, for he is beardless and lady-faced."

Sly Melville! He did not know how much I had learned of his intrigues with Darnley's mother to get Darnley to Scotland and married to Mary.

He was a wily one, this Melville; but I liked him for his loyalty to his mistress and the manner in which he had always sought to defend her even over the matter of her beauty and her achievements.

I was so proud of Robert as the second part of the ceremony took place. He looked so magnificent in his robes and it gave me the greatest pleasure to place the white sash over his right shoulder and present him with the sword and fix his cap and coronet. And there he was, standing before me in all his glory, my Robert, now the mighty Earl of Leicester.

His eyes glittered as he looked at me and I was overwhelmed by my love for him. I could see from the triumph in his eyes that he believed that this was a preliminary to marriage . . . our marriage. And in that moment I almost felt that I could have acquiesced. Almost . . . but not quite.

The trumpets sounded and we went to dine in the Council Chamber. It was a glorious and triumphant occasion.

Afterward some of the guests came to my bedchamber where the glow of candles flickered over the rooms giving a pleasant intimacy. I had rarely seen Robert so happy. This honor would mean that people regarded him with even greater awe than ever. It was four years since his wife had been found dead at the bottom of a staircase. Had people forgotten? I had an idea they never would. But at least they could not now believe that I had been implicated in the murder, for why, if I had agreed to Amy's removal that I might marry Robert, had I not married him now that he was free? Sometimes it seemed clear to me that I must never marry him for if I did—whatever the lapse of time—I should be suspected.

I was glad to see that William Cecil and Robert were talking together in the utmost amity. They had always been suspicious of each other but Cecil was so obsessed with the idea that I must marry and get a child that he was almost inclined to smile on Robert as a means of achieving that end.

Sometimes I wished that I had not the ability to see quite so clearly, for to see many sides to a question makes one uncertain. I liked Robert's company more than that of any other person; I was happy when he was near me and dissatisfied when he was not. Is that loving? Yet on the other hand I saw him just too clearly for comfort; he was avaricious, arrogant, determined to dominate all who came near him, ruthless in the extreme . . . yes, even enough to commit murder if the need were dire enough. All this I knew, yet I loved him. I should never be sure how Amy Robsart died, whether it was accident, suicide or murder . . . never wholly sure, and if it were really true that he killed her, should I not be very wary of a man who could act so to a woman whom he must have loved at one time? Then again it might have been that I was fascinated by Robert because I *was* unsure of him. I would not want a dull man like my cousin Lettice's Walter Devereux. There was a man who could be relied upon to do his duty to his country and his family. Yet such a man would tire me so much that I would not want him near me for long. I wondered how Lettice fared with him. She seemed happy enough; but she was sly. One would never know what Lettice was up to. It would not surprise me if she were deceiving poor Walter Devereux. But my feelings for Robert? Well, I loved him, I suppose—and I loved him as he was—ruthless and mysterious.

Melville was beside me and he asked me what I thought of his Queen's letter regarding the proposed match with the Earl of Leicester.

I replied: "She angrily refused him. I will employ lawyers to seek out who should be next in succession to me. I would wish it were your Queen more than any other, Sir James. My father had a wish to unite England and Scotland and would have declared his sister Margaret's son, James V of Scotland, next in line of succession after his daughter Mary; but at that time I was not yet born and there was my brother Edward to come. So it would seem that when I should die your Queen could likely come to the throne of England."

"There may be heirs of Your Majesty's body."

"Nay, I do not think that likely, Sir James. I was never of a mind to marry unless I was compelled by my sister's harsh behavior toward me to do so. But as you know I stood out against it and my victory brought me freedom. I have promised myself that I shall remain a virgin."

"Madam," he answered with his Scots canniness, "you need not tell me that. I know your stately stomach. Ye think gin ye were married ye would be but Queen of England, but now ye are King and Queen baith. Ye would not suffer a commander."

I smiled at him. He understood me well.

"Come," I said, "I will show you some of my treasures. I have them here to hand." I opened my desk in which I kept miniatures of those of my friends whom I loved best. I had carefully wrapped them and written their names on them so that I could select them and study them at will. On one of these I had written "My Lord's Picture". I unwrapped it and showed it to Melville. It was a very good likeness of Robert.

I said: "If the Queen of Scots saw it she would not hesitate to take him. What think you, Sir James?"

"Allow me to take it to her."

I almost snatched the picture from his hands. "I have only this one of him. If he goes to Scotland she would have the original."

I certainly was not going to give up Robert's picture. I feared that if the Scottish Queen saw how handsome he was, she might decide to take him in spite of his lack of royal blood.

No, Robert's picture was certainly not going to Scotland.

When I was alone in my bedchamber and my ladies concerned themselves with the intricate operation of preparing me for my bed, unlacing me, helping me out of my whalebone hips and petticoats, letting down my hair, placing the false pieces in their tray, I was feeling contented.

I knew which way I was going.

THERE WAS FURTHER trouble with the Grey family. It had been said that Jane Grey was remarkable for her wisdom. Perhaps—but it had not prevented her from going to the block before she was seventeen. They had no instinct for survival, those foolish Grey girls.

All the same they were a menace. Katharine was still under restraint. But she had given birth to two sons. The first was understandable, for she had achieved that in secret, but when her husband had been in the Tower with her they had contrived to meet and a second son was the result. Now a possible heiress to the throne who had two sons was in a fairly strong position, especially when the reigning Queen had declared her desire for virginity and was now past thirty. A plague on Katharine Grey! I thought; but it was entirely due to the plague's coming to London that she had been removed from the Tower and while her husband Lord Hertford was sent to his mother with the eldest child, she with the younger went to her uncle in Essex.

Of the three Grey girls Jane did seem the only one to have had any sense, for although she had lost her head it was through no fault of hers. The other two, Katharine and Mary, seemed quite feckless. I had not anticipated trouble from Mary. She was a poor creature, almost a dwarf. I suppose few men had looked her way—royal-blooded though she was—until one day she formed an acquaintance with a man who held a post at Westminster Palace. He was in fact distantly—very distantly—connected with the Knollys family and I supposed that was why he had been given the post of Sergeant Porter at the water gate. The foolish pair decided to marry secretly and this they did.

The match was most unsuitable in every way. Dwarf as Mary was, she, being royal, committed an offense by marrying without the consent of the Sovereign and the Council. Perhaps the silly creature thought it did not matter in her case. But the incongruity of the match was that Thomas Keys, the bridegroom, was unusually tall and the pair must have looked ridiculous together.

What if there should be a child of the marriage? It might be quite a presentable child for if she was minute he was large enough and the child could be somewhere in between which would make it normal, and through Mary it would have royal blood and a claim to the throne.

There was only one thing to do and that was separate the pair, so Thomas Keys was sent to the Fleet prison and little Mary to the Duchess of Suffolk, who was her step-grandmother. If she were not already pregnant that would prevent further complications.

Cecil discussed the matter with me in private.

I said to him: "We have the two Grey sisters under restraint, and so should sleep more quietly in our beds."

He looked at me shrewdly. I think he was beginning to respect me more than he ever had. He had deplored the frivolous side of my nature and that I could understand, for sometimes I deplored it myself, but I think he was beginning to see that there were times when I could use it to advantage.

I went on: "Mary of Scotland will always be the one to be feared most, and she is so taken with Lord Darnley that she is besotted by him."

"She intends to marry him. It will strengthen her claim, for he has a slight one himself."

"What do you think of Darnley?"

"Dissolute and weak."

"And do you think he will be a help to our lady of Scotland?"

Cecil shook his head.

"She has declared her intention of marrying him," I said. "The little boy is puffed up with pride and already sees himself as the King of Scotland which . . ." I added slyly . . . "is what happens with ambitious men when queens lift them from their humble status."

Cecil smiled. He was beginning to realize that I would never share my throne with any.

"Well, Master Cecil," I went on, "here we have the Grey girls in restraint where they can do little harm even if they had the wit to do so. Oh, I know they would be merely the figureheads of ambitious men as poor Jane was, but we have them safely under lock and key. And Mary of Scotland is to marry her Darnley. May she have quick joy of him for I'll warrant it will not last long."

Cecil nodded and I went on: "Should I not have reason for rejoicing?"

"Your Majesty is right," he said. "We should rejoice."

And we did even more when the news came to us that Mary had indeed married Darnley and he was proclaimed King of Scotland.

"I am confining the Countess of Lennox to the Tower for daring to bring the marriage about—another troublemaker out of the way. We shall deplore the marriage in public, Master Cecil, and only while we are alone congratulate ourselves that it has taken place."

"It can bode no good for Scotland," said Cecil. "And what is bad for Scotland must needs be good for England."

A TERRIBLE TRAGEDY occurred about this time.

I knew that Kat had been ailing for some time. I insisted that she remain in her bed and pass on her duties to others which she did most reluctantly, until she became too ill to be able to do anything else.

When it was borne home to me that she was not going to recover, I was overcome with grief and whenever I could escape from my state duties I was at her bedside. She loved to hold my hand and talk of the past. Sometimes her mind wandered and I believe she thought she was back in the Dower Palace at Chelsea where Sir Thomas Seymour had pursued me.

"You were a wayward girl," she said. "You led him on. Oh, it was dangerous . . . and so exciting. Do you remember when he cut your dress to pieces in the garden? Do you remember when he came barefoot to your bedroom?"

I said I remembered.

"And the terrible time they took me . . . and Parry, remember? The Tower . . . I never knew such fear . . . and I betrayed you, I betrayed my darling . . ."

Then I would go down on my knees and try to soothe her.

She had never betrayed me, I told her. She had only told what had happened and they had forced her to do that. She was my very dear Kat and one of the happiest days of my life had been when she had come back from the Tower.

So we talked and each day she grew more wan, her voice more faint, and she could not remember very clearly those events from the past. She merged Thomas Seymour with Robert Dudley. "Such men," she said. "The most handsome men in the world . . . both of them. We both loved them, didn't we, my precious."

I hid my tears from her but when I was in my bedchamber I wept for my dearest friend.

It was a very sad day when she died. I shut myself away and would see no one. There was nothing I could do but grieve.

THE POSSIBILITY OF A marriage for me still excited the minds of all those about me. I think Cecil had realized that I was speaking the truth when I told him I would never marry, but being the politician he was he was as interested as I was to receive offers from heads of state with whom he was eager to make alliances.

Catherine de' Medici was offering her son, now Charles IX, and as he was about sixteen years of age and I was past thirty we should have made a somewhat incongruous pair. Moreover I believed he was a little mad, but the crown of France, as Cecil pointed out, was not to be lightly turned aside. I replied that as Queen of England I should be expected to live here and as he was King of France he must be in France; I reminded him of the unsatisfactory state of affairs between Philip of Spain and my sister Mary. It was one of those points which people like to argue over and which are always so useful in making negotiations hang out over a long time. I always looked for them because although I was determined not to marry abroad—or anywhere—I found discussing the possibilities too fascinating to cast on one side. Then it was suggested that as the King of France would certainly have to stay in France why should I not take his brother the Duc d'Anjou. The age difference would be even greater, I said. But talks went on.

Then I made a discovery which infuriated me. I had suspected for some time that my cousin Lettice Knollys was interested in Robert and he in her. I had dismissed this because she was married to Devereux, and although for a girl of her nature that might not be an obstacle to a passionate friendship with another man, I did not think that Robert would jeopardize his future so certainly as to have a relationship with someone so close to me. That there were women in Robert's life I accepted. He was a normal man and I would not have had him otherwise. His wife was dead—not that he had spent much time with her—and I expected that he would have light affairs outside the Court, and I imagined that when he indulged in them he would be thinking with regret how different these women were from the prize he coveted.

I had often watched Lettice. She really was a very beautiful woman. That she was restless, I guessed, for it was clear that Walter Devereux would not satisfy her and I had given him a post which kept him in Ireland for most of the time. He was an excellent administrator but a dullard in company I could well believe.

I should have sent her away from Court before it happened because my instinct told me that any man on whom Lettice set her fancy would not escape very lightly, and that in many ways she would call the tune. In a manner of speaking she was not unlike myself. Perhaps that was why I felt I understood her so well.

I intercepted those glances; I noticed how embarrassed some of my ladies were when I referred to Lettice and Robert, so I was sure.

I felt like summoning them both to my presence and banging their heads together, and then dismissing them from Court. No! I would not give them a chance to be together. They should be clapped into the Tower.

This was folly. I must curb my temper. If I said I would marry Robert he would drop Lettice tomorrow like a piece of hot pie that burned his fingers. But that was too big a price to pay even to discountenance them.

I asked Lettice about her husband and whether she missed him. She made vague answers and I found myself accusing her of clumsiness, taking great pleasure in nipping her arms till she cried out in pain. Sometimes I slapped her with real venom, and because she received these marks of my displeasure with a veiled smile, almost of derision, I wondered whether she suspected I knew.

Robert did not appear to notice any change in my demeanor but then he was not as subtle as Lettice.

I had always liked handsome people around me, particularly men, and I let myself believe that they all meant the charming things they said to me. They all behaved as though they were in love with me—indeed that was one of the passports to my favor, and some of them did it remarkably well.

I had my favorites from time to time and I liked them to work well for me as well as admire me. Cecil was an exception. I did not want compliments from him; he would never have known how to pay them in any case. What I asked from him was all he was prepared to give—devoted service and the truth. Robert was unique. Whatever should come between us I knew could not be lasting. My love for him was a steady flame, yet something which appeared to be in danger of being doused, but I knew never would.

Two of my favorite young men at this time were Christopher Hatton and Thomas Heneage. Both were extremely handsome, with impeccable

Court manners; they knew how to dress immaculately and behave in the manner necessary to gain my favor. Hatton was one of the best dancers I had ever seen, and he and I dancing together were a spectacle to make watchers spellbound. He was clever too.

Thomas Heneage was older but none the less charming. I had appointed him a Gentleman of the Bedchamber soon after my accession and he had a seat in Parliament as member for Stamford.

Robert had already shown some jealousy of these two for he could never bear to see me show favor to anyone else and till now it had always been clear that however others pleased me there was one who remained firm in my affections.

However, I was very angry with Robert over Lettice and I was determined to show him that my fancy was not so deeply set on him that I could not feel affection for others.

The opportunity came on Twelfth Night when the great event of the evening was the ceremony of the King of the Bean. It was a variation of a game which had been played for centuries when some little device is used to name the one who will be honored for the evening and whom, until midnight, all must obey.

In this version, the Bean was placed on a silver platter and carried in with great ceremony by one of the pages who knelt before me and presented it to me. Then I would take the Bean and bestow it on the man of my choice who would then be nominated. The first thing the King of the Bean demanded—and it was a rule that all must obey that night—was to kiss the Queen's hand.

I always pretended to ponder and regard the gentleman before me earnestly as though assessing his right to the honor of the Bean, but I invariably bestowed it on the one who seemed to me to outshine all others. That, of course, always had to be Robert.

On this night, seated about me were several of my favorite young men and among them Robert, Heneage and Christopher Hatton.

Robert did not know the extent of my annoyance with him for he was smiling preparing to accept the Bean.

However, just as he was moving forward to kneel before me and be ready to take it, I cried out in ringing tones: "I name Sir Thomas Heneage King of the Bean."

I was almost sorry to see the change in Robert's face. He turned quite pale and his lips tightened while he looked as though he could not believe his ears. Much as I wanted to punish him for his philanderings, I felt sorry for him and I was sure that anything that had happened was the fault of that woman, Lettice Knollys.

Sir Thomas however was overcome with delight and was kneeling before me looking up at me with that brand of adoration which was so pleasing when it came from an attractive man.

"Come, Thomas," I said, "make your demands."

He looked at me almost wonderingly, and when I held out my hand for him to kiss, all the time I was watching Robert's glowering looks.

The evening progressed. Robert disappeared for a while and I noticed Lettice Knollys did too. I did not ask where they were but I noticed the time they were away and I was growing more and more angry. I had to restrain myself from sending someone to find them and bring them back to me; but that of course would be folly. It was almost as though Robert did not care that I had passed him over for Heneage. Oh, but he did! I had seen his face when I gave the Bean to Sir Thomas.

I danced a great deal that night, first with Heneage and then with Hatton. The floor cleared while Hatton and I performed and everyone applauded wholeheartedly. Sir Thomas forbade any to use the floor while we danced for he said everyone would want to see the most perfect, lively yet elegant performance of the Queen. I saw Robert come back to the ballroom. Lettice was not with him but they would not be so foolish as to return together but I was sure they had been with each other. I noticed, too, the furtive glances which were cast at Robert. He must have been aware of them, too. People were whispering about him, asking themselves if this was the end of his favor with me and whether I was thinking of setting either Heneage or Hatton up in his place. It must have been galling for Robert and I almost called him to me to comfort him and to show these crowing courtiers that they were quite wrong. My anger with him would pass as soon as he gave up sighing for my cousin Lettice and turned his attention entirely on me. But this was part of his punishment and I must not weaken toward him.

Sir Thomas announced that there was to be a game of Question and Answer, one which was played frequently at Court revels and as he was the King of the Bean, Heneage would say how it was to be played on this night. He would select the questions and then say who was to ask them of whom. I guessed, of course, that Robert would be selected for Heneage was as jealous of Robert as Robert was of him, and having seen Robert suffer the humiliation of not being selected to take the Bean, he would be only too ready to submit him to further discomfort.

"I command my Lord Leicester to ask a question of the Queen," declared Heneage.

Robert calmly waited while Heneage said slowly: "The question is, Which is more difficult to erase from the mind, an evil opinion created by an informer or jealousy?"

I smiled at Robert as he turned to me and repeated Heneage's words.

I thought: You are indeed jealous, my dear Robert, and I suppose so am I. How foolish we are to cause each other pain.

And I replied: "My Lord Leicester, they are both hard to be rid of, but jealousy would seem to be the harder."

Applause rang out as though I had said something profoundly wise, but Robert had flushed and he did not meet my eye.

It had not been a very amusing evening for me. I missed him for he disappeared again. He was indeed piqued. I was very sorry but I did not intend to allow him to carry on his philandering at my Court.

WHEN I HEARD that Robert was going to fight a duel I was filled with apprehension. It was exciting to know that they were fighting for my favor but terrifying to contemplate that Robert might receive some injury or—a prospect which appalled me—be killed.

It appeared that on the morning after the night of the Bean, Robert had sent a messenger to Heneage telling him that he was going to call and he would be bringing a stick with him for he had to administer a lesson. There could be only one response to that and Heneage made it. The Earl of Leicester would be very welcome and Sir Thomas Heneage would be waiting for him with a sword.

This was ridiculous.

I sent for Heneage. There was a hushed atmosphere in the royal apartments. I knew my ladies were whispering together just out of sight; their eyes would be sparkling with anticipation as they speculated on the outcome. They were all certain that Robert was falling out of favor, the idiots—as if he ever would! As for Heneage, he was a good-looking man and I did not want him hurt either.

Lettice was there. I should send her off. It would be simple to dismiss her and pack her off to her husband's house. But in a way that would be to admit defeat and to imply that I could not beat her on equal terms.

However, my first task was to stop this absurd duel.

Heneage knelt before me all eagerness. I really believe he thought he had increased my regard for him. Perhaps he was planning to kill Robert and hand me his head on a charger. The fool! If he harmed Robert—however slightly—I would never forgive him.

"So, Master Heneage," I said, "you have decided to fight duels, have you, when you know I forbid such folly?"

"Your Majesty," he began, raising his bewildered eyes to mine, "I . . . I but sought to teach a lesson . . ."

"So you have become a tutor, have you, my merry man. You would teach the Earl of Leicester good manners, would you, disregarding your Sovereign's wishes and strutting about waving your sword!"

"Your Majesty, the Earl of Leicester began this by threatening me . . ."

I pupped with my lips which they all knew was my way of expressing contempt. I kept him on his knees while I made it very clear that I would have no dueling in my realm.

"If you think to win my favor with your buccaneer's ways you are mistaken. I will not have brawling . . . and screaming of abuse. Though . . . if you must fight, fight with words."

"Your Majesty . . ." There was a certain protest in his voice. I suddenly had a picture of Robert lying mortally wounded on a stretch of grass with a triumphant Heneage standing over him and I could not bear it. I brought up my hand and gave Heneage a stinging blow about the head.

I watched the red blood flow into his face; he put up his hand and I was rather sorry for him. After all this had all come about through their feelings for me and if it was ambition which prompted them rather than love, I could not blame them for that.

"There, Master Heneage, you may go, and next time prate not so freely of using your sword against another of my subjects, wreaking damage on him . . . and yourself."

He went out shamefacedly and feeling sorry for him I called out: "I like to see you too well at my Court, Master Heneage. Remember that."

The smile came back to his face. He bowed as he retired; and I did not think he would dare challenge Robert again.

Then I sent for Robert.

If he had come humbly I think I should have forgiven him and then asked him outright about his affair with Lettice, banished her from Court and taken him back; but he was truculent. In a way I would not have had him pleading, and although part of me wanted him to, I was glad there was nothing mealy-mouthed about Robert. He flattered me; perhaps he professed to love me more than he did; but if part of that love was for the crown, there was still a large measure for me alone.

He was sullen, aloof, proud, telling me quite clearly that although I was the Queen he considered himself my equal—and that was something I would not endure.

I said: "So you think fit to flout my rules and brawl with Heneage?"

"I cannot submit to insults from such men."

"Such men? What mean you? Heneage is a worthy member of my Court."

"If Your Majesty thinks so . . ."

"I do think so. I tell you I think so."

He lifted his shoulders almost contemptuously and I thought: This is what comes of showing too much favor to one man. This arrogant Robert needs a lesson and by God's Blood he shall have it.

"I have wished you well," I cried and my voice grew louder as I continued: "But my favor is not so locked up in you that others may not have a share of it. I have other servants besides my Lord Leicester. I would have you remember, Master Dudley, that there is one mistress here and no master. I have raised up some, but they can as surely be lowered, and so they shall be if they assume an arrogant impudence because once they enjoyed my favor."

Robert was stunned. I admit now that I was a little, too. I was angry and deeply hurt, to see him standing there so far apart from me, his face as handsome in anger as it ever was. I almost put my arms about him and promised him that I would marry him after all.

But the sterner side of me said no. Have you not seen what happens to a man when a little power passes into his hands? What did Melville say of you: You will brook no commander. Remember it, for Melville is right.

So I stood there and for a few moments we stared coldly at each other in silence.

Then he spoke quietly and said: "Your Majesty, I ask your permission to retire from Court."

"You have it," I said, "and the sooner the better."

He was gone, leaving me angry, deeply wounded and desperately unhappy.

HOW DULL THE COURT was without him! I was fractious and ill-tempered. When I sat through the long process of preparing myself for the evening's revelries, I was constantly shouting at my ladies until they were reduced to such nervousness that they were even more clumsy than they would otherwise have been; and this added to my irritability. All the intricate processes of getting into bone and buckram, the tight lacing, the whalebone hips, the petticoats, the glittering picadillie ruffs, the gorgeous gowns of velvets and brocades glittering with pearls and precious stones . . . they all seemed pointless because Robert would not be there to see me. Lettice was still waiting on me, and I did have the satisfaction of knowing that, in any case, he was not with her.

I heard that he had gone to Kenilworth which had come into his possession with the title, and that he was making it into one of the most magnificent castles in the country.

I wondered if he missed the Court and me.

They were saying: This is the end of Leicester. His day is over. Well, he had a good running. Who will take his place?

Idiots! I thought. As if anyone could take his place!

One of Robert's chief enemies was Thomas Howard, Duke of Norfolk. I had favored Howard when I came to the throne because of his connection with my mother's family; moreover I needed his support because he was one of the leading peers in the country; but I never liked him. I thought he was arrogant and stupid with it.

Many of them were jealous of the favor I showed to Robert, of course, and Norfolk particularly so since the incident at the tennis court some little time before which I had forgotten.

I had been watching Robert play with Norfolk. My father had excelled at the game and loved to play it before spectators for he always won (it was the rule of the Court that no one should beat him). Therefore he had liked a goodly company of lookers-on, especially beautiful women.

In this particular game Robert was winning for he was very skilled in all games and although, like my father, he hated to be beaten, in Robert's case he had to win by skill.

This he was doing and Norfolk was becoming more and more disconcerted especially as when Robert made a good stroke I clapped my hands and my ladies naturally did the same.

During a pause in the game with Robert well in ascendance, he came to my side. I smiled at him lovingly and he returned my smile.

"You are too hot, Robin," I chided him. "You will take a chill."

At which he took my mockinder—a sort of handkerchief—from my girdle and mopped his brow with it. I must admit that I was a little taken aback by such an act of familiarity in public, but it pleased me in a way, even though I knew that it was such gestures which gave substance to the gossip that we were lovers.

Norfolk had seen it and he cried out: "You impudent dog! You insult the Queen!"

He approached Robert brandishing his racquet and I thought there would be a fight in my presence. I was too startled to cry out and before I could do anything to put an end to the scene, Robert had seized Norfolk's hand which held the racquet, twisting it so that the Duke yelled in pain and the racquet dropped to the ground.

I could blame Norfolk absolutely for he had started the brawl. I shouted then: "How dare you, Norfolk! How dare you behave in such a way before me! Look to it, or it may not be only your temper which is lost."

Norfolk was immediately subdued. He wanted to explain but I silenced him and he asked leave to retire.

"That I willingly give," I cried. "And pray do not return until I send for you." Then I turned to Robert and I said: "Methinks, my lord Norfolk does

not like to be beaten at tennis. Not only does he lose the game but his temper with it. And you, my lord Leicester, are somewhat overcome by the heat.
Pray be seated and cool yourself."

I indicated that he should sit beside me and as he did so, I took the
mockinder and replaced it in my girdle.

So now that Robert appeared to be in decline Norfolk would be jubilant
and with the help of Sussex and Arundel he thought he could destroy Robert
forever.

I was sure that they were behind the diabolical plan, when rumors
started to circulate once more concerning the death of Amy Robsart.

It appeared that John Appleyard, Amy's half-brother, had stated that he
had received large sums of money from Robert at the time of Amy's death
for his services in suppressing certain facts and now his conscience
demanded that he make those facts known.

I could imagine them all—Norfolk, Sussex and Arundel—rubbing their
hands together with glee. Leicester is out of favor. Let us kick him while he
is down. Let us destroy the gentleman once and for all.

Robert might survive my disfavor and occupy himself away from Court,
but if he were found guilty of murder, what then?

Old scandals did not easily die. Skeletons remained to confront the
unwary. But they had forgotten that if Robert could not afford to have the
circumstances of Amy Robsart's death brought into prominence, nor could I.

I thought of him surrounded by the splendors of Kenilworth. Was he as
lonely as I, as wretched without me as I was without him?

I knew what I would do. I would recall him to Court. I would show my
favor to him. I would let him know that when he was in danger there was
one who would not forget him.

I sent for him.

He came back with all speed. I shall never forget the moment when he
came into my chamber. He knelt at my feet and I touched his head—that
dark curling hair which I loved so much.

I said: "Rob, the Court has been dull without you."

"Elizabeth," he said. "My beautiful Elizabeth."

Then he was kissing my hands and I felt near to weeping.

"You are an evil man to displease me," I cried emotionally. "Never . . .
never do it again."

He stood up and would have embraced me but I stepped back. Too
much emotion might betray me into taking steps which I would regret later.

I said: "I want to discuss that knave Appleyard with you."

So we talked and it was as it used to be. He told me how lonely he had

been, how pointless life was and he had not much cared when Appleyard
had brought his monstrous accusations against him.

"The rogue shall be made to eat his words," I said. "I doubt not that now
you are back with me Norfolk and the rest will be less anxious to bay at your
heels."

"May God bless Your Majesty now and forever."

"Oh Robin," I said quietly, "it pleases me to have you back."

I ORDERED THAT John Appleyard be arrested and examined by the
Privy Council and I commanded Cecil to interrogate him first; and then the
other members of the Council should do so. This included Norfolk and Sussex. But I had no fear of them. My favor had drawn their teeth, and as Cecil
realized the need to discredit Appleyard, for accusations against Robert
could incriminate me, I could rely on the matter's being brought to a satisfactory conclusion.

I was right to act as I did. Appleyard confessed that he had received
money from Robert, but as he was his brother-in-law there seemed nothing
significant in this. He had, he admitted, asked Robert for money and Robert
had considered his demands as blackmail to which he would not submit,
and had cut off all communications with him. That had been the state of
affairs when he had been approached by two men who offered him money
to reopen the scandal. He was ashamed to say that he had agreed to do this.

He was a frightened man and I was grateful to Cecil for proving that this
had only come to light because Appleyard knew that Robert was out of favor
at Court. We did not know who the men were who had approached him,
but I was ready to swear that Norfolk had had a hand in it.

Appleyard was all contrition; he pointed out that he did not believe his
half-sister had been murdered and that all he would say—even when
bribed—was that he believed, because of the Earl of Leicester's standing at
Court, the matter had not been sifted properly. He had merely asked for a
reopening of the investigation.

The minutes of the inquest were presented to him but it was discovered
that the man could not read and they had to be read to him.

Here was a man who could not read, who had first taken money from
Robert—although it had been given out of generosity to a brother-in-law—
and who had accepted bribes from the men who would not come into the
open, but wanted to bring a case against the Earl of Leicester which they
thought at this time might succeed.

The whole case clearly had its roots in malice.

Cecil and I agreed that no revenge should be taken on Appleyard. We wanted no martyrs. All we wanted was no more talk about a matter which was best forgotten. So Appleyard was discharged with a warning that he should take more care in future.

Robert was back in higher favor than ever. I did not think he would lightly displease me again, and I was very happy to have him beside me.

As a precaution I summoned Lettice's father, who was the Treasurer of the Royal Household, and I told him that I did not like wives and mothers to be separated from their families for too long, and I thought it would be better if his daughter returned to her husband.

Her husband was in Ireland, he told me.

But I frowned and said her children would be missing her.

It was good enough. He knew that it was my wish that Lettice should retire from Court.

So she went and that, I thought, will be the end of Robert's little flutter with that woman which had caused me such unnecessary trouble.

The Ridolfi Plot

EVENTS IN SCOTLAND NOW BEGAN TO ASTOUND US. IT seemed that Mary could not be anywhere without raising a storm; she must always be at the center of great events. I had been amused to discover that she had quickly realized the nature of the man she had so romantically married. Lord Darnley was dissolute, unfaithful and a heavy drinker, and as soon as she had fondly but foolishly proclaimed him King of Scotland he made no attempt to hide his true nature. His behavior was despicable. He became involved in street brawls, picked quarrels with all those who dared contradict him and took every advantage of Mary's devotion to him. That devotion very naturally soon began to fade and she must have seen him in a very different light—seen what to me had been obvious from the start—the weakness of those sensuous lips, the blankness behind the pretty eyes. What a fool Mary was! She made me realize more than ever that I had been wise "to suffer no commander," as her Ambassador had put it.

In one thing she had succeeded. She had quickly become pregnant. Cecil brought me the news with something like reproach in his eyes, but I reminded him that Mary had been foolish to marry Darnley when she might have had the Earl of Leicester. To which Cecil replied: "Your Majesty knows that Leicester would never have been allowed to leave your Court. You cannot let him stay in Kenilworth long without recalling him."

"Robert would never have gone," I said with a smile, "so we waste time, Master Cecil, in discussing what can never be now. So . . . she is with child. That will please the people of Scotland, doubtless. But it is another little claimant to our throne."

"The Queen of Scots appears to be distressed by her husband's drunken frolics and his numerous infidelities. Doubtless the child will console her."

There were rumors about her Italian secretary, David Rizzio, an excellent musician of whom she was said to be inordinately fond. I could imagine that this Italian was a charming relief from the dissolute Darnley; and Mary was noted for gathering about her poets and musicians. I supposed she was trying to bring something of the French Court into that of Scotland. The contrast must be very depressing for her.

There had already been some scandal about a young French poet, Pierre de Chastelard, who had escorted her when she had first arrived in Scotland and returned to France to be sent back by Catherine de' Medici, probably to spy for her, as that wily woman would not have sent a charming young man merely for the purpose of diverting her daughter-in-law.

We had heard that Chastelard and David le Chante, as she called Rizzio, were constantly in her company. Chastelard was said to be the Queen's lover and had even been discovered hiding in her bedchamber, though I have to say that it was Mary and her ladies who found him there and raised the alarm; but as I said he could not have been hopefully hiding there unless he had had some encouragement.

The sequel of that little escapade was that Chastelard was obliged to place his head on the block in the marketplace of St Andrew's where he died bravely, poor young man, quoting Ronsard's *Hymn to Death* as he did so.

"Je te salue, heureuse et profitable Mort . . "

It was brave to die with such words on one's lips. Poor young songster, his death had not enhanced his mistress's reputation.

But there were even more dramatic events to follow. I often wondered whether Rizzio was in truth Mary's lover. That she had a weakness where men were concerned seemed clear, for she had smothered Darnley with affection before they married. I think she must have been a deeply sensuous woman and as Darnley clearly no longer pleased her, it might have been that she turned to the Italian for more than music.

So he was doomed. I heard many versions of that terrible night's happenings and in my mind I can see it clearly. Saturday night in Holyrood House. Outside the March winds buffeting the castle walls and the Queen in her sixth month of pregnancy. She was not feeling well enough to meet a great many people so she was taking supper quietly in a small room with a few of her intimates, her bastard brother and sister, Robert Stuart and Lady Jane, Countess of Argyle, among them. Her father, James V, although he had only one legitimate daughter had been very energetic outside his marriage bed. The doctor had advised Mary not to overtax her strength but to live quietly and eat red meat which explains why it was being served in Lent. The Laird of Creech, her Master of the Household, was there with her equerry and doctor. I asked for these details as I wanted to set the scene in my mind. And there was of course that other who was rarely absent from the Queen's side—David Rizzio. He was in a rich damask gown trimmed with fur, satin doublet and russet velvet hose, with a fine ruby at his neck. This was mentioned because they were all gifts from the Queen; and those who wished to vilify her noted these matters.

David was playing, singing and entertaining the company with his especial gifts as he had done so many times before. Suddenly this peaceful scene was disturbed by the appearance of Darnley who came in by way of the door to the private staircase. He had clearly been drinking too much, and went straight to the Queen and slumped down beside her. I could imagine the quick change in the atmosphere. Darnley was often noisily quarrelsome, so the company would have waited uneasily for his voice to be raised in a quarrel with the Queen.

But it did not happen like that this time, for almost immediately through the door of the private staircase came a man in armor. He looked like a ghost they said, or some harbinger of evil, which indeed he was. It was Lord Ruthven who, although he was on his sick-bed and near to death, stood there looking as though he had just risen from the grave.

What a vividly macabre scene that must have been. When it was related to me I shivered at the horror of it. In those few seconds the company must have thought they were looking at Ruthven's ghost. Then from behind him came others—men whose names had often passed between Cecil and myself when we discussed what our policy would be with the troublesome Scots—Morton, Kerr, Lindsay.

Ruthven, speaking in a deep voice, told David to come outside, for there were those who wished to speak to him.

The poor little Italian musician knew it was his blood they were after, and like a frightened child he turned shuddering to the Queen, who had grown pale and looked as though she would faint; he clung to her skirts crying: "No! No!"

What could that avail him? How had she felt, I wondered when she saw them drag him from her and plunge their daggers into that poor quivering body?

It would have seemed in that moment that they were not only going to kill Rizzio but herself also. Poor woman, heavily pregnant amongst those barbarous men!

They said she cried out: "Davie, Davie . . . They are killing you. They are killing us both. Is this the way to treat your Queen?"

But that crude man Kerr took her by the arms and forced her to be quiet or he would as he said inelegantly: "Cut her into collops."

Apparently she fainted then which I should think was the best thing she could have done in the circumstances.

I loathed the Scots more than ever. Mary was foolish and I had no doubt they resented having a woman as their Queen—the crude ungallant loathsome creatures! How dared they behave so to royalty!

When she came to consciousness she was alone with Darnley and, realizing what had happened, upbraided him, calling him murderer . . . murderer of Rizzio and possibly of her unborn child. He accused her of familiarity with Rizzio and preferring the musician's company to his own. The last, I should have thought from what I knew, was to be expected.

They took her to her apartments where she was more or less a prisoner and sent for a midwife because it seemed she would give birth prematurely. Darnley was with her during the night and because of this her chamber was left unguarded. What fools they were! They trusted Darnley. He was a very weak man and Mary must have had some sway, for she persuaded him to creep out of the palace and fly with her, and together they rode through the night to Dunbar Castle where one of the nobles, Lord Bothwell, and some of his followers were waiting for her.

That terrible night was over and she was free from Rizzio's murderers. But in what an unhappy state she was! Poor Mary, much as I liked to see her discomfited after her arrogant claims to my throne, still I was sorry for her. And I was all eagerness to hear further news from Scotland.

WE WERE AT Greenwich that June. It was one of my favorite palaces—I suppose because I had been born in it. The fields always seemed greener there than anywhere else, the trees more luxuriant. The Romans had called it Grenovicum and the Saxons Grenawic—so it was the Green Town to them too. There had been a palace there in the reign of my ancestor Edward III but it was not until later in the reign of Henry VI that the castle was embellished and added to. Now it was a most delightful spot.

The Court was in a merry mood and festivities were planned for the evenings—often al fresco as it was June and the weather was fine.

The evening was wearing on. We had partaken of supper; the musicians were playing and the dancing had begun. Robert and I were dancing together when I perceived Sir James Melville making his way toward me.

I knew that he had news of Scotland and I immediately stopped dancing. He came to me and whispered in my ear: "The Queen of Scotland has given birth to a boy."

My emotions were so strong that I could not restrain them. So . . . after all those fearful scenes, after witnessing the murder of her favorite, after riding through the night to Dunbar, she had successfully produced a son. I had been certain that she would fail in that.

All I could think of now was that she had succeeded and her success seemed an indication of my failure.

Two of my ladies, Magdalene Dacres and Jane Dormer, hastened to my side. Robert was looking at me in dismay.

"What ails Your Majesty?" asked Robert.

I said: "The Queen of Scots is lighter of a fair son and I am but a barren stock."

Robert took my hand and pressed it firmly, warning me not to show my chagrin. And of course he was right.

I assumed an air of great pleasure and I declared to the company that we must rejoice in my sister of Scotland's wonderful recovery from the ills which had beset her.

And I was thinking: A son! It would strengthen her claim. That miserable matter of the succession would be raised again and I should be harried either to marry and get a child or name my successor.

Later I saw Cecil who advised me to assume an air of pleasure and to hide any disquiet I might be feeling at the birth of an heir to the Scottish throne which he understood and shared.

I received Melville formally and after expressing great pleasure at the news, I asked, with some concern, after the health of the Queen.

"I have been feeling unwell these last fifteen days," I told him, "but this news has made me feel well again."

Perhaps that was too fulsome, and Melville was too shrewd not to understand that my joy was feigned; but in these matters it is what one says which is repeated; one's thoughts remain one's own, and there can only be conjecture as to what they are.

He replied in the same vein of diplomatic falsehood: "My Queen knows that of all her friends you will be the most glad of her news. She told me to tell you that her son was dearly bought with peril of her life and that she has been so sorely handled in the meantime that she wished she had never married."

I nodded solemnly. "The Queen has suffered cruelly and come through bravely, but so great must be her joy in this fair son that I am sure in her heart she can regret nothing that has brought him to her."

"The Queen of Scots dearly wishes that she could see you at the christening of this boy."

"What a joy that would be, and how I wish that my affairs might permit it! I shall send honorable ladies and gentlemen to represent me."

It was a very amicable meeting and nothing I had said could possibly offend Mary.

Accordingly I sent the Earl of Bedford to represent me at the christening, taking with him a splendid gift from me. It was a font made all of gold and worth one thousand pounds.

"It may well be that by this time the young Prince has overgrown it," I said jocularly. "If so, the Queen can keep it for the next."

I appointed the Countess of Argyle, Mary's half-sister, to be my proxy, and ordered my Ambassador up there to make sure that it was known that I did not accept Lord Darnley as King of Scotland.

This so incensed Darnley that in a fit of petulance he declined to attend the baptism of his own son. I doubt anyone mourned that.

The little boy was christened Charles James but for some reason the Charles was dropped and he was always known as James—I suppose this must have been because there was a line of King Jameses in Scotland.

So Mary had her son and my Council was growing more and more restive because I had no child and it seemed likely that I never would have. The birth of little James had certainly stirred them to further action, for when next the Parliament met all parties counseled me either to marry immediately or name my successor.

These were the two subjects which I disliked most. I did not want to marry. I had made that clear enough; I would not be dominated—or put myself in a position to be—by any man. And to name one's successor was always a dangerous step to take, because in one's lifetime people started to look to that successor; there would be comparisons, and what is to come often seems more desirable than what is. Unless it is one's own child, there is certain to be trouble. So I stood out against the Parliament.

"You attend to your duties," I told them, "and I will attend to mine."

But they would not be silenced. They said that it was a grave matter and many of them recalled the time when I had suffered from the smallpox and had indeed been near to death and in what confusion the country had been thrown.

"I have no intention of allowing my grave to be dug while I am still alive," I said, "nor of being bullied by hare-brained politicians who are unfit to decide these matters."

However they would not give in and declared that if I would not marry, I must name my successor, and that only a weak princess and faint-hearted woman would fail to do so.

I was furious, but I knew this was what the people wanted, and there was one thing which I always understood: a monarch only reigns through the good will of the people. I was in a quandary, but I knew most certainly that to marry would curtail my power and to name my successor could give rise to plots against me.

They continued adamant and as I needed an extra subsidy they declared that this would only be given me if I named my successor.

Cecil understood my reasoning and I think, in his heart, agreed with me. I looked to him for help and, calling together five counselors with him, I told them that my only wish was to serve my subjects and to keep them living in prosperity and peace. As for the subsidy, half of what had been asked would suffice, for I believed that money in my subjects' pockets was as good as that in the exchequer.

I was able to persuade them that I must have this money and that it was a matter apart from the succession; and when they agreed that I should have the money without committing myself I was overjoyed and saw that by choosing my words carefully I had won a victory. But I was put out by the plain speaking of the Parliament. They would never have dared talk to my father in that way. I modeled myself on him for he had ruled with a strong hand, but in spite of his ruthlessness he had retained a hold on his subjects' affections to the end of his life.

I dismissed Parliament with a speech telling them I did not like their dissimulation when I myself was all plainness. Indeed, they might have chosen a more learned prince to rule over them but one more careful of their welfare they could not have; and I bade them beware of trying my patience again as they had recently done.

There were other troubles besides the intransigence of the Parliament.

Robert and Sussex had been enemies for a long time. In fact, almost every head of a great family was Robert's enemy. Of course he was becoming one of the richest men in the country and had made Kenilworth the finest castle. Moreover, he still believed—and so did others—that in due course I would marry him and his power would be complete.

But while I still refused to give him a share of the crown he coveted, there would still be those who would attempt to overthrow him.

The feud between Sussex and Robert became so intense that neither of them could go out without an armed guard escorting him. I threatened them and I lived in terror that something would happen to Robert. He laughed at my fears. It was Sussex I should be worried about, he said. I knew there was nothing I could do except stop their open animosity.

Meanwhile I traveled frequently. I liked to show myself to the people and they liked it too. They wanted to think of the Queen as a warm-hearted human woman, not a remote figurehead as my sister had been. When I traveled they would come from their houses to speak to me and bring me flowers and tokens of their regard and when they brought them to me I always chatted with them to show my pleasure in their gifts, asked after their health and made much of the children whom they brought to me. This was no falseness, for I loved my people; I loved children; and I took as much trouble over studying what they wanted of me as I did over state matters. They were in any case a state affair, and even more vital than those I discussed with my Council.

Recently Robert had been elected Chancellor of the University of Oxford and as I had promised to visit the University, the fact that Robert would arrange my reception and be there to greet me made me doubly anxious to go.

Robert met me at Walvicote with a deputation from the colleges. They looked very splendid in their scarlet gowns and hoods. There was one incident which made Robert smile and that was when Dr Humphreys greeted me. He was a stern puritan and like all such people of extreme views was of the impression that he was right and anyone who did not agree with him entirely was wrong. I hated extremes from both sides and I did not think they made a happy country, so I let him know what I thought, for I was never one to hold back the mild reproach—unless of course it would be detrimental to me. So I said to him: "Mr Doctor, your loose gown becomes you well. I wonder your notions are so narrow." He was taken aback, but I smiled at him with friendliness, though I hoped he would consider what I had said.

It was particularly delightful to meet the young scholars who knelt and cried: *"Vivat Regina!"* to which I replied: *Gratius ego;* and when I addressed them it was in Greek. Knowing my love of plays they performed one for me . . . half of it on one night, the second half on the other, so long was it.

There was a tragedy on the first night when a wall and part of a staircase on one of the buildings collapsed and three people were killed. However, the play was performed, and it was very pleasant to watch particularly in the second half when some of the cast had to imitate the cry of hounds in full pursuit of a fox and the young spectators became so excited that they jumped up and down and called out that the fox had been caught.

This amused me very much and set us all laughing.

I was equally amused on the next day at St Mary's Church whither I had gone to hear the preaching of a Dr Westphaling. The good man went on speaking for so long and all—including myself—were extremely bored with his discourse, so I sent a message up to him to curtail it without delay. To my fury he ignored my request and went on and on. As I myself was to speak afterward I was getting really angry for I did not want to have a sleepy audience.

So long did the man continue that there was no time for me to speak that evening and I sent for Dr Westphaling. The man came to me somewhat shamefaced and I demanded to know why he had continued to tire us all when I had sent him a command to stop.

He replied with much humility, I must admit, that having learned his speech off by heart, he could not stop for fear of losing the place and he thought that if he cut out the middle he would never be able to find the end.

This so amused me that I couldn't help laughing, so even the tedious Dr Westphaling added something to our enjoyment.

The next day I addressed the company in Latin and when I saw Cecil standing there, for they all must stand when I addressed them, I stopped my discourse and commanded a stool be brought for him. "I know your leg gives you pain, Master Cecil," I said, "and I will not have you stand in discomfort."

Cecil was grateful and the whole company was impressed by my thoughtfulness; and I hoped that Dr Westphaling saw that I was quite able to stop my discourse and still not lose the thread.

It was a very successful visit to Oxford as everything arranged by Robert would be. He loved devising and planning and caring for me; and I was more anxious than ever that someone might do him an injury.

I said he was good at arranging matters, but there was one thing he tried to arrange with a certain Dr Dee and failed. We laughed at it together—but that was later. There was always laughter when Robert was near; even his arrogance and impertinence amused me, as he did when he tried to wriggle out of his difficulties and he could charm me even when he displeased me.

I had always been intrigued by magic, and the wizard Dr Dee interested me. Many people said that he was a quack and I knew his predictions were not always correct, but they were sometimes, and I believed that the future was arranged for us although we were free to avert disaster and gain advantages. When I look back over my life and see the many dangers through which I have passed, to only a few of them could I attribute good fortune. I saw that cautious planning had saved me on many occasions.

But it was exciting to try to see into the future and Dr Dee was a good friend of mine. If I hinted to him that I wished someone to act in a certain way he would often be able to bring it about. He could suggest to them that some danger was looming, some good coming to them if they did this and that. Yes, he was a good friend and a handy man to have around; and if one did not entirely believe in him, it was advisable to make a show of doing so for how could I be sure when I would want him to delude someone into thinking that he or she should take the doctor's advice.

When I was traveling in the area of Mortlake I called on him for he had a residence in that part. He had buried his wife only that morning and I thought my visit might cheer him. I would not let him entertain me as he must be mourning his wife, but I took a look into his interesting library where he had many volumes, globes and strange-looking objects. Among these was the magic mirror into which one could look and sometimes, if the time was right, see something of the future.

Robert looked over my shoulder as I gazed into the mirror so that his face was reflected there. I laughed aloud and then I saw Robert exchange looks with Dr Dee and I guessed he had tried to arrange with the doctor to show me his picture when I looked in the mirror.

Dr Dee said I should have eternal youth and boundless wealth as soon as he had discovered the elixir of life which he was on the point of doing.

It was all very interesting and though I did not believe half of it, it amused me in a way and comforted me too. Perhaps like most people I believed what I wanted to believe—which can be a wonderful antidote to the sorrows of life. On the other hand if one would be wise, one must know when one is doing it and perhaps allow oneself the indulgence as long as one recognizes it for what it is. The great secret of success in life, I was coming to believe, was self-awareness; and I was fortunate in having those two selves—the wise and the frivolous—and to know when one must give way to the other.

I fancied this was something which my sister of Scotland was lacking.

That was very soon to be proved true.

IT WAS HARD to believe that we were hearing the truth. Surely even Mary could not be so stupid.

Rumor was rife, and wild rumor at that. Bothwell was Mary's lover. There was even a tale of his having raped her in the Exchequer House in Edinburgh. I thought about that a great deal imagining her horror—or was it delight?—to be so subdued by the man who, according to all accounts, was something of a brigand and in complete contrast, I should imagine, to young ineffectual Darnley.

There followed the story of that mysterious night in Kirk o' Field when Darnley had been murdered. I could scarcely wait for the news. My messengers from Scotland were ordered to bring me any news immediately. I wanted to piece together the evidence. I desperately desired to know everything that was happening. I could not help being reminded of the death of Amy Robsart. She had been an unwanted wife; Darnley was an unwanted husband; and a bold lover was seeking to take possession of a wife and a crown.

Oh Mary, I thought, you are in acute danger. Do you realize that? I did, when something similar happened to me.

There was a difference. This was *proved* murder. Nobody could say that of Amy's death.

There had been an explosion which had clearly been intended to kill Darnley but when the premises had been searched the bodies of Darnley and his servant were found in the garden in their nightgowns. They were untouched by the explosion yet . . . mysteriously dead.

There could only be one explanation. The two men had been murdered and the explosion arranged to hide the crime.

This it had failed to do. Villainy was exposed.

And who wanted to be rid of Darnley? Who but the Queen and her lover Bothwell?

More news came.

Bothwell riding through the streets of Edinburgh, brandishing his sword, calling on any who accused him to come out and he would tackle them single-handed. He must have been a magnificent man for all his crudity and villainy.

He was tried for murder, but of course it had been arranged that he should not be found guilty, and the verdict should be: "James, Earl of Bothwell, is acquitted of any art or part in the slaughter of the King."

And there he was riding through the streets of Edinburgh once more shouting to the people of Edinburgh to come out and tackle him if any thought it was not a true and just verdict.

Who could have doubted that it was unjust, but who would have the courage to come out and say so?

You are in mortal danger now, Mary, I thought. Did she ever think of me and wonder what my feelings had been when Robert's wife was found dead at the bottom of a staircase? If she did not, she was a fool. She should remember how I had acted and see that her only chance was to be as aloof, calm and wise as I, now very forcibly, realized I had been. But when had Mary ever been calm or wise or strong?

She threw away her hopes, her life, her crown most likely when she married James Bothwell.

It was not even as though he had been free. He was married to a virtuous lady and it was necessary for him to obtain a divorce before he could marry Mary.

How could Mary have been so foolish! But then her life had been so comfortable during her youth she had never faced death as I had . . . many times. She had never had to learn how to dissimulate, to act with the utmost caution, to cajole, to pretend, to survive. She had had none of those lessons for which I now thanked God, much as I had suffered when I was learning them.

But Bothwell naturally had his divorce and she married him; and the whole world—the world of adulterers, poisoners and ruthless schemers—held up its hands in horror at the actions of this poor, simple and too loving woman.

Her family, the Guises, were horrified and scarcely owned her; Catherine de' Medici declared in public that she was too shocked to give expression to her thoughts although, of course, had she done so truthfully she would have told of her delight in the fall of the girl whom she had hated and driven from France; Philip of Spain was contemptuously silent. I alone felt pity, perhaps because something not dissimilar could have happened to me.

And this was the woman, this poor weak foolish woman, who would be Queen of England!

Little James was taken from her and given into the care of the Earl and

Countess of Marr; and the Queen must ride beside Bothwell to stand against those who came to depose her.

There was the disaster of Carberry Hill, and I wondered how much she grieved to fight against her own subjects.

I could picture her, though nothing so humiliating had ever happened to me. Whatever I had suffered, I had always had the sympathy of the people. I do believe that if I had lost that I should have lost heart. But Mary deserved their scorn. Had she regretted her submission to Bothwell, her abandoning of her self-respect: her placing herself under the domination of such a man, as she rode into Edinburgh with the mob screaming abuse at her? "Burn the whore!" they had shouted. "Death to the murderess!"

I could imagine her dirty and disheveled. Was that beauty, of which the poets had sung, apparent then?

So they had kept her in the Provost's House while through the night the mob screamed outside. I could see their cruel faces in the red glow of the torches and Mary there cringing, mourning the glory she had lost.

And so she became their prisoner. Lochleven first, where she charmed the suceptible young Douglas sufficiently for him to help her escape.

She had some loyal subjects—enough to enable her to go into battle at Langside against her enemies, to be followed by what seemed inevitable defeat. Mary was put to flight once more and knowing that at that time Scotland was no place for her unless she wanted to go back into captivity, she made her decision which, characteristically, was an unwise one . . . though I had no reason to complain of this!

I wondered how she reasoned as she waited there with the few friends left to her, to gaze no doubt across the Solway Firth to England and out to France.

Her family were now displeased with her; she knew that the Queen Mother of France was her enemy. Should she go to France? There was another choice. England! Foolish woman, did she think I would forget that she had emblazoned the arms of England on her shield? Did she think I would ever forget that she had called herself Queen of England?

She knew nothing of the world, nothing of people. Certainly she did not understand such as I was. She had listened too long to the poets, and she believed that her beauty had given her a right to act in a manner which would not be acceptable from others. She had never learned the art of survival as I had.

I was in a state of great excitement when I received word from the Earl of Northumberland that Mary had arrived in England. She had landed at the little village of Workington where Sir Henry Curwen had given her shelter at Workington Hall until the Earl decided that she would be more comfortable at Cockermouth in the home of a certain Henry Fletcher, a rich merchant of the district. Northumberland was not in residence in his own castle. He thought Mary could stay with the Fletchers until he received instructions from me as to what should be done with her.

There was a letter from Mary for me in which she referred to me as her dear sister and begged for my help.

"I entreat you to send for me as soon as possible," she wrote, "for I am in a pitiable condition, not only for a queen but for a gentlewoman, having nothing in the world but what I had on my person when I escaped . . ."

That must have been very distressing for the fastidious lady who had enchanted everyone with her exquisite gowns.

". . . I hope to be able to declare my misfortunes to you if it pleases you to have compassion and permit me to come to you . . ."

Oh, I thought, it is compassion you want now! Very different from a crown.

". . . I will pray to God to give you a long and happy life and to myself patience and that consolation I await from you.

"Your faithful and affectionate good sister and cousin and escaped prisoner, Mary."

I showed the letter to Cecil. He was noncommittal but as excited as I was.

I said: "The Ladies Grey are under restraint; the Countess of Lennox is in the Tower; and now Mary of Scotland is in England."

"God has delivered her into Your Majesty's hands," said Cecil slowly.

"Nay," I replied, "not God, but Mary herself. What now?"

"She is no longer the prisoner of the Scots."

"No," I said slowly. "She is mine."

He nodded slowly. Then he said: "She begs to see you."

I shook my head. "I shall not see her . . . yet. I will let it be known that while she is treated with the honor due to a queen, I cannot receive her until she is cleared of murder. Her actions, if we heard truthfully—and we know of her marriage to Bothwell when Darnley was scarcely cold—have been such that no virtuous lady can receive her, least of all a queen . . . and a virgin. I have my reputation to consider."

He smiled at me sardonically. Was he thinking, as I was, and as so many people would be thinking, of the mysterious death of Amy Robsart in which some rumors had it I had been involved? She must be comparing the similarity of the cases.

I did not want to see her, to listen to her pleas. I did not want a beautiful and fascinating rival at my Court.

Cecil agreed with me that a message should be sent to the North and for the time being she should be lodged in Carlisle Castle where she must be treated with the dignity due her rank.

This was a miracle. The greatest of my enemies had been delivered into my hands.

THERE ARE PEOPLE who must always be at the center of dramatic events. Mary of Scotland was one of them. It was unfortunate for her that a casket containing letters had been left behind in Edinburgh by Bothwell when he escaped to Borthwick. These were said to be the correspondence between Mary and Bothwell. I believed that some of them were forgeries, but like most good forgeries they could not be entirely false. It seemed certain that some of the letters had been written by Mary and if they were all true she was condemned, not only as being Bothwell's mistress before her marriage to him, but an accomplice in the murder of Darnley.

Her reputation was in shreds; but she still managed to charm her jailers. It was becoming more and more clear to me that I must not bring her to my Court. There she would no doubt practice her wiles and there were quite a number of Catholics only waiting for opportunities. She would always be a danger and must remain under supervision so that I knew at any given moment where she was.

She had been moved from several castles and there had been one or two attempts to free her. She seemed to have a way of bemusing her jailers; I did not forget how she had worked on George Douglas when she was sent to Lochleven until he was successful in maneuvering her out of the fortress.

The Catholic peers came up with a solution. Why should she not marry an Englishman with my consent, and then as I would not consider giving the country an heir, I could name her as my successor which would ensure peace with Scotland.

The Duke of Norfolk was suggested. I had never liked Norfolk. I remembered his feud with Robert and I knew that they were bitter enemies. Moreover, although he professed to be a Protestant, I believed he leaned toward the Catholic Faith, and it would not have surprised me if he had been one in private.

If I would marry and provide the heir all this plotting would stop, I knew; but it was too big a price to pay. Besides, Mary of Scotland was a good example of what men could do to a ruler. Robert had been the only one who had tempted me—but no, not even for Robert.

He seemed to be changing his tactics toward Norfolk, and I gathered, although he said little on this matter to me, that he was inclined to agree with those peers who would like to see Norfolk married to Mary. I knew my Robert well. Was he looking ahead to his future? Was he asking himself what his position would be if I were to die? All human beings were at the mercy of God, and people in high places were often at men's mercy too! Was his sudden friendship with Norfolk a sign that he was thinking of him as a future ruler of England? Favorites of past rulers were often not very popular with the reigning ones. Robert would have a good example of that in his own family for his grandfather had been one of the most highly prized of my grandfather's ministers, but when my father came to the throne he lost his head—more or less for that reason. Yes, Robert in some ways was a very cautious man. I was getting older. Soon it would not be possible for me to bear a child—and I was unmarried in any case. Perhaps Robert in his heart knew that I never would be wed and he was making certain provisions for the future.

I sent for Norfolk. I looked him straight in the eyes and said: "My lord, you have become a gallant. I see that you are in love. There is no more romantic sight than a man in love, be it with a woman or with a crown."

Norfolk looked shaken.

"Your Majesty," he began, "I know not what . . ."

"You know not what?" I interrupted. "My lord Norfolk, for such a lover as yourself there must be one thought uppermost in your mind and that is your inamorata—the Queen of Scotland. I know, Norfolk, that you plan to change your title of Duke for that of King."

I was amused to see the terror in his face. I believe he thought that I had guards waiting to arrest him.

"Nay, Your Majesty," he said, "I would not seek to marry such a woman . . . one who is known to be an adulteress . . . and some say murderess. I want to sleep on a safe pillow."

"A crown might be worth taking a risk for, Sir Norfolk, eh?"

Norfolk had always prided himself on his rank as the leading peer. I had heard that the family had hinted that they were more royal than the Tudors. He said rather haughtily: "Your Majesty, I count myself as much a prince in my bowling alley in Norfolk as she is in the heart of Scotland. Moreover how could I marry one who pretends a title to the present possession of Your Majesty's crown? If I were to do so, Your Majesty might charge me with seeking the crown of England."

"Remember it, Norfolk," I said grimly. "I might well do that."

When he left me I was sure he was well aware of my sentiments regarding the plan to marry him to Mary. She was a menace. Although I had been exultant when fate had delivered her into my hands I was realizing that she was more disturbing to my peace of mind in England than she had been when she was on her throne in Scotland.

What infuriated me was that she seemed to have the power to win people to her side. Bereft as she was, her throne lost, relying on my bounty, her reputation become very shady, still she attracted men to her cause. It must have been some essential femininity in her which aroused their protective instincts. I was sure I lacked that quality. I gave the impression that I was able to look after myself—which I was—but why it should be an asset not to possess this gift, I could not see. And yet I could. Men wanted to dominate. It was the very essence of their sex; and there were some women who sought to be dominated and this quality was that which attracted men so strongly. Mary had it to excess. As for myself, I did not possess it at all. My object was to prevent domination. Men professed to love me; they talked of my beauty, my many excellencies; but in my secret heart I knew that it was the crown which dazzled them, not the charms of Elizabeth. They loved me through fear of what might become of them if they didn't; they loved what good I could bring them in power, honors and wealth. But they loved Mary for herself. Perhaps this was one of the reasons why the thought of her so infuriated me, and not because of her pathetic claims to my throne.

Even men like Sir Francis Knollys were not immune to her charms. Sir Francis—my own kinsman and father of the saucy Lettice—had been uneasy with her and in time sorry for her. I trusted Knollys and it seemed to me that he was one of the best men I could have chosen as her jailer, yet I knew she pleaded with him to take her to me and that he pitied her when he gave her the answer he had been ordered to which was that I could not receive her for the sake of my own reputation until she was clear of the charge of murder. Knollys had begged to be released from the duty. But not yet, I thought, not yet.

He was a strict Protestant and when he took her to Bolton he tried to convert her to his views, and although I continued to trust him I began to feel that it might be unwise to leave one man too long in her company, and I had her transferred to Tutbury where the Earl of Shrewsbury could look after her. Not that I felt Shrewsbury would be aloof from her charms but he did have a very forceful wife who had already been much married and I guessed that she would know how to deal with Mary and be quite unmoved by that excessive femininity. I had the excuse for recalling Knollys when his wife died.

This was a great blow to me. Katharine Knollys had been born Carey and her mother had been Mary Boleyn, sister to my mother, so there was a strong blood connection. Katharine was a charming, gentle woman. I had often wondered how she came to have a girl like Lettice.

The whole Court knew how grieved I was by the death of my cousin, and I had her buried in St Edmund's Chapel at my expense. So I took the chance to recall Sir Francis and leave the troublesome Mary in the hands of Shrewsbury.

Robert was constantly in my company, as devoted and adoring as ever. He was persistent in his efforts to make me agree to a marriage, and I liked persistence in men. One would have thought that as the time passed and we were growing older, he would give up hope, but he did not appear to do so. I think his eyes strayed often to other women. I did not mind that as long as I did not know about them. I was prepared for him to have his light love affairs, providing they remained light, and that any engagements he might have with others could be dropped at a moment's notice when I beckoned.

I did notice that the two Howard girls were pursuing him. It amused me—two sisters fighting over one man—and my man at that. I thought Douglass Howard was the more likely to attract him. She was Lady Sheffield now but her marriage could not be very satisfactory as she cast such longing eyes on Robert—though I supposed no warm-natured woman of Lady Sheffield's type could fail to be affected by Robert's superb masculinity.

Douglass must have been rather like Mary Boleyn, the type who found it hard to say no to an attractive man, because they were not only of a giving nature but had fleshly desires of their own. I knew these women. One of my stepmothers had been like that. Katharine Howard. Another Howard. Was it something in the Howard breed? I must ask my Lord Norfolk!

Robert gave no sign in my presence that he even noticed Douglass Sheffield but he was a little piqued because I had given Christopher Hatton part of Bishop Ely's garden—a piece of fertile land between Holborn Hill and Ely Place. I reminded him that I had given him so much more and that all I asked in return was his love and devotion.

"You have that," he told me soberly, "and it does not need gifts or favors of any sort to maintain it."

There was a great tenderness between us at this time. I noticed a little white in his dark hair and that endeared him to me. Oh, it was true love I felt for Robert.

In spite of Norfolk's protestations to me I knew that his scheme to marry Mary was still being considered and that there were certain people whom I had thought to be my friends, who supported it. I was afraid of trouble in the North and I did not trust the Catholic peers, therefore I thought I had better put an end to the plotting.

One day when at table I told Norfolk that I wished him to sit beside me. He was a little nervous and I guessed this was because the idea of that marriage was still very strongly on his mind and he was wondering how much I knew.

I could not resist taking his ear between my fingers and nipping it so hard that he winced and referring back to his previous remark I said: "Methinks you should take heed of your pillow, Norfolk."

Everyone who heard that knew I was aware of the plotting and that I did not like it. Norfolk was very subdued, and a few days later I heard that he had left Court.

He wrote to me from Kenninghall assuring me that he had no intention of doing anything which should not have my favor.

It struck me that this plot had gone further than I had thought and I suspected that Norfolk might be a guilty man, so I ordered him to return to Court without delay. He pleaded illness and I could not prevent myself smiling as I thought of the days of my own danger when illness had been a frequent plea on my lips. I sent word to him that he must consider himself a prisoner, and within a short time he was in the Tower while inquiries were being made concerning the proposed marriage.

Then I had disquieting news which drove all thought of everything else out of my mind. Robert was ill . . . gravely ill . . . and begging me to come to him.

As if I would refuse! He was at Tichfield and there I must go with all speed. This I prepared to do, chiding my attendants for their tardiness. I was filled with a terrible foreboding as we set out on the road. I thought of him constantly . . . Robert over the years . . . Robert a young boy—arrogant even then—taking my hand in the dance. I was not the Queen then, only a princess, branded a bastard by some, and we had been on equal terms . . . almost. And then . . . that awareness of him in the Tower . . . and his of me . . . and his coming to me before my accession throwing his gold at my feet. Robert must not die. I could not imagine my life without him.

I went at once to his bedchamber. He was lying in his bed, pale and wan.

"Robert, my love," I cried.

"Dear one," he whispered, and his eyes lit up with joy. "So you came to me . . ."

"As if I would not, you foolish man! Certainly I would be with you and my first command to you now is to come forth from that sick-bed and get back the good health you have always had."

"I shall die happy now," he said, "because you are with me. I feared so much to go without seeing you."

"Be silent, Robert. I will not have such talk."

He appeared to be finding breathing difficult. "Dearest Majesty, I must talk to you . . . before . . . it is . . . too late."

"Save your breath," I commanded, for in truth it frightened me to hear his harsh breathing.

"I . . . must talk," he insisted. "There is a plot afoot. I . . . I am not guilt-less. I believed it would be good for England . . . and that is for you, my loved one . . . if Norfolk married Mary. I lived in perpetual fear that your life was in danger while the succession is unsettled and that woman lives."

"Have done with the succession!" I cried. "And stop talking. Save your breath. You need it."

"Nay . . . I cannot. I am in great fear that Your Majesty may be in dan-ger. Norfolk plots . . . in secret with the Queen of Scots. Many of your lords are concerned in this. I have been myself. They meant no treason. They plan to restore Mary to Scotland where, with an English husband, she could be a good friend to England . . . and to satisfy France and Spain . . . you name her your successor . . ."

"I understand," I said.

"Dearest Majesty, before I go . . . I must have your forgiveness. Your safety is my only concern. Your forgiveness . . . I beg you . . . for the part I played in this. It was no treason against Your Majesty, I swear . . . though some may try to make it seem so."

He lay back gasping on his pillow and my whole being shuddered with my anguish. I had never before fully realized how much he meant to me and how empty and dark my life would be without him. Hatton, Heneage, all the pretty men who danced round me . . . what were they compared with Robert?

"My dearest," I said. "It is forgiven. I understand."

"Then I can die in peace."

"You know I shall not allow that."

He smiled at me wanly. "One does not speak of death to you. You like it not. You are impatient of death. You are immortal."

"You are right and I will not have this talk. I shall stay and command you to recover."

"Already Your Majesty's presence has worked like the elixir of life."

"My lord Leicester, I shall have you out of that bed and dancing a high measure with me ere long. I insist on that."

"And surely even the angels will not dare disobey you," he said.

I kept my word and stayed there with him. His recovery was miraculous and he declared it was my presence which always had the effect of making him feel more alive than he ever could in my absence.

I did wonder how seriously ill he had been. He had certainly not been in his usual blooming health, but I pondered during those days whether his affliction was like one of those which had affected me so frequently before I came to the throne. Was it one of the illnesses of self-preservation? How deeply had Robert been involved with Norfolk? I did not believe for one

moment that he would seek to set Mary on the throne. No! I knew my
Robert. He had worked with Norfolk for the marriage with his eyes on the
future. He believed, as so many did, that when I died Mary would come to
the throne, and in that event he would not want to be completely out of
favor.

In any case, whatever his motive, for a short time I had lived through the
terrible prospect of losing him. Now he was rapidly improving; we played
games together and I took the utmost joy in scoring against him, for I knew
that my success was due to superior skill and not to royal privilege.

After that time of terrible anxiety the days of Robert's convalescence
were sweet indeed. He had no doubt now of my love for him. I could see
new hope springing up in his mind. Dear Robert, he would go on thinking
of our marriage however old he became.

Well, that was how I liked it to be.

Meanwhile Norfolk stayed in the Tower.

THERE WAS ONE MAN at Court who had served me well and to whom
I owed a great deal. He was not one of my favorite men for he was not in
the least handsome and lacked the dancing talent of men like Hatton and
the courtly grace of Heneage—but he was a man to be reckoned with, clever,
subtle and faithful. I refer to Sir Francis Walsingham. He was not an old
man being about three years older than I. He was very dark—not with the
bold and handsome darkness of Robert, but with a Moorish swarthiness. I
grew to appreciate his good works and became quite affectionate toward him
and gave him the nickname of The Moor. I had a habit of bestowing such
sobriquets on those around me and it was looked on as a mark of my favor
to receive one.

He was a stern Protestant and I had always felt that my enemies would
most likely be found among the Catholic hierarchy. He was rich and a
diplomat, a student of law, which I think was a great asset to him for he had
studied for five years in various foreign countries. He was alert and quick to
scent treachery. Indeed as I had often proved, a good man to serve me, and
when I look back over my life I often think that one of my greatest gifts was
an ability to choose the right men. The butterflies of my Court were in a separate category; they delighted and charmed me; but I never forgot for one
moment that my strength lay in men like Cecil. Walsingham was such
another.

I was deeply shaken when there was an attempted rising in the North by
the Earls of Northumberland and Westmorland, the aim of which was to
release Mary Stuart and bring back Catholicism to England.

I knew that Northumberland—a rather foolish man—had been

annoyed because I had not entrusted Mary to him. How could he think I would be so foolish! He was a well-known Catholic and thought of himself—as all the Percys did—as lord of the North. What was disquieting was that Walsingham had discovered that the Spanish had promised aid to Northumberland and Westmorland if they could bring sufficient numbers to rise against me. The Pope too was behind the rising.

And when I thought that even Robert had joined in the scheme to marry Norfolk to Mary without my knowing, I felt very uneasy.

The plot was well advanced. The Duke of Alva had promised to send over an army of Spaniards. The Marquis of Catena had arrived in England ostensibly to conduct an embassy but in fact to lead the army when it arrived. Pius V had given his blessing to the enterprise.

Fortunately the Earl of Sussex, when paying a friendly call on Northumberland, became suspicious. He came immediately to Cecil and me and told us that he feared a revolt against the crown was being planned.

Cecil advised me to summon Northumberland to London and when I had a letter from him pleading illness, all my suspicions were aroused and I sent guards to him with orders to arrest him if he offered any excuse for not accompanying them. However, Northumberland was just a little too quick for them; he managed to escape and join Westmorland and the two Earls put up their standards, declaring their intentions to bring Mary out of captivity and restore the Catholic Faith to England. It was alarming to discover that a force of seventeen hundred horse and four thousand foot were ready to join them. They were able to march to Durham where they set up the Mass in the Minster. Then they passed through the North celebrating the Mass wherever they went.

Sussex advanced on the North and soon put the rebels to flight and when defeat became obvious those who had enthusiastically marched to set up the Mass decided that they would be safer in their homes.

Westmorland escaped to the Low Countries and after evading his captors for some time, the Earl of Northumberland ended up on the scaffold at York declaring to the end his belief in the Catholic Faith. His head was stuck on Micklegate—a warning to all traitors.

I had to show the people that although I loved dearly those who were true to me and I wished to please them and do their will, I would not tolerate traitors and when I found them I could be as ruthless as my father had been.

Six hundred men had been caught and were soon lifeless corpses hanging on gibbets—a grisly warning to any who thought they could lightly challenge the rights of the Queen.

The North was plunged into mourning.

"This is Mary Stuart's doing," I said. "When she came into our realm, that was the end of the peaceful days."

"And so it will be while she remains in it," retorted Cecil.

I nodded. But how could I be rid of her? There was no evidence that she had been involved in this plot. Plotters used the names of those who were close to the throne, as I knew to my cost. How often had mine been used as the reason for rebellion!

No! Mary was not personally to blame for this—although but for her it would never have taken place.

SIR FRANCIS WALSINGHAM came to me on a matter of great urgency. He had uncovered a conspiracy, and it was his belief that immediate action should be taken.

"It is a plot against Your Majesty's own person," he declared.

"You had better explain," I told him.

"I have been watchful of a certain Roberto Ridolfi—a banker from Florence who has, on more than one occasion, been acting suspiciously," replied Walsingham. "I had reason to believe that he had been supplying money to the Northern rebels at the time of the rising. I took him into my house for questioning. However, nothing was revealed and I no longer had an excuse for detaining him. I let him believe that he was free from suspicion, for then I thought he would go about his business without taking any special care. At the same time I had him watched."

I nodded. I felt a great affection for men such as my swarthy Moor.

"It came to my knowledge that this man was in touch with Leslie, Bishop of Ross, whom I knew was an agent for Mary of Scotland. Norfolk is involved."

"Norfolk! That knave!"

"I have intercepted letters, Your Majesty, and I can tell you precisely what was planned. Mary was to marry Norfolk who will become a Catholic and together they were to set up the Catholic Church in England."

"In England!" I cried. "And what of the Queen of England? Is she supposed to stand aside and say, Do as you will, Your Majesties?"

Walsingham hesitated. Then he said: "Your Majesty, it has been suggested that you will be . . . assassinated and Mary will take your place. The Pope agrees to help as does Philip of Spain. The plan is that as soon as they have killed Your Majesty, Alva arrives with an army to subdue any rising against them. The letters were entrusted to a certain Charles Baillie whom I have arrested, and I trust I have Your Majesty's approval for doing so. I have put him on the rack and have had a full confession from him."

"You did not tell us what was happening, Walsingham."

"Your Majesty, I knew I was on a trail. I trusted no one and wanted to keep the matter to myself until I had something to show you, for I did not want to come to you until I had the evidence to lay before you. I have letters written in Norfolk's hand. He has signed two documents. One that he is a Catholic and the other pledging himself to stand at the head of an army which Philip promises to send when the moment is ripe."

"The perfidy of the rogue!" I said. "Why did I spare him before?"

"He was not implicated then, Your Majesty, as he is now."

"He is indeed now."

"As are Ridolfi and the Queen of Scots."

I nodded. "I thank you for your good services. They shall not be forgotten."

"It is my joy to serve Your Majesty."

"I will send for Cecil," I said. "I shall acquaint him with what you have said. And stay with us. I would like him to hear all from you and see your evidence."

It was damning.

There was nothing which could save Norfolk now.

SCENTING DANGER, RIDOLFI had returned to Italy where I heard later that the Pope had received him warmly and given him honors. He was out of our reach, but Norfolk was not . . . nor was Mary.

Mary had been proved an enemy once more. There were letters in her handwriting. She clearly accepted Norfolk as her husband-to-be and she knew on what terms help was coming from Philip of Spain and the Duke of Alva. She was as guilty as Norfolk.

There were some who said: "Here is your chance. Destroy this woman now and she will be out of your way forever."

I thought of it—indeed I had sleepless nights thinking of it. She was guilty. She had schemed to overthrow me and if necessary take my life to do so. She had plotted to murder me, or at least she had connived at it . . . just as she had in the case of Lord Darnley.

I had every reason to send her to the block, to condemn her to the death she had agreed should be imposed on me.

Oddly enough, I could not do it. I hated her. I wanted her out of the way. She was a menace and yet I could not give orders to kill her. She was a queen for one thing. One queen cannot kill another. There must be some respect for royalty.

Strangely enough, I was not sure that I wanted her out of the way. She maddened me but I liked to hear about her. I suppose I was more interested in her than in any other woman. I was foolish. How should I ever know when she was planning to kill me? Yet I could not bring myself to sign that death warrant.

The guard should be tightened about her. There should be no more smuggling in of traitors' letters.

She was my prisoner and she could never be anything else while I lived.

Sometimes I marvel at my leniency toward that woman. Sometimes I thought she fascinated me as certainly as she had all those fine gentlemen who fell victim to her charms.

I had no such qualms about Norfolk.

On a hot June day he went out to Tower Hill where the executioner was waiting for him with his axe.

Massacre

SHOCKED BY THE LENGTHS TO WHICH SPAIN, WITH THE help of Pope Pius, was ready to go for my destruction, I knew that I must seek some alliance with France . . . at least the pretense of one, and when Catherine de' Medici suggested a marriage between her son the Duc d'Anjou and myself I pretended to consider it.

Catherine was the most powerful figure in France at that time. Her son Charles IX was at best unbalanced, many said he was mad, and he was entirely in her hands. It was believed in some quarters that she had hastened his elder brother François—Mary's first husband—to his death so that she could rule through her weak-minded son. I do not know what happened in the case of François, but she certainly was the power behind the throne in France. And she longed to see one of her sons King of England.

I discussed the proposal at great length with Cecil, who was now Lord Burghley. I thought it was time I showed my appreciation and had made him a baron. It was no more than he deserved.

Anjou was nineteen. I was at this time thirty-seven, so I could reasonably demur about the differences in our ages. He was a Catholic, of course, and the English did not care much for Catholic consorts. One only had to refer back to the last reign and remember the abhorrence in which the country had held Philip of Spain.

But there was little I enjoyed more than these marriage projects, although I knew in my heart that I was going to refuse them all. I had not said no to the only man for whom I might have forsaken my freedom to turn to some arrogant sprig even if he did come from a royal house. I had no need of royalty. I had that from my father and my glorious ancestors; but I did like the world to know that although I continued in the virgin state it was from my own choice and I had had, and was still having, ample chances of changing it.

Those tête-à-têtes with La Mothe Fenelon, who was the French Ambassador at that time, always stimulated me and I loved to hear about the perfections of the Duc d'Anjou and his burning desire to become my husband.

I had plenty of spies at the French Court—Walsingham saw to that—and they brought back the true state of affairs there, so I knew that Anjou was at this time carrying on a passionate love affair with the Princesse de Clèves; and his only desire for marriage with me was to gain possession of my throne.

I remember well those conversations I had with La Mothe Fenelon. He would look at me with assumed admiration and tell me how worthy the Duc d'Anjou was to be my husband.

"The only person who *is* worthy of the alliance," he said.

"Oh," I replied lightly, "I know he is highly esteemed at the Court of France for his excellent qualities. He is worthy of the highest destiny the world can bestow on him. But is it not true, my dear friend, that his thoughts are lodged on a fairer object? I am an old woman, who but for the need to get an heir should not speak of a husband. Often I have been sought, but by those who would wish to wed a kingdom rather than a woman. The great are married without seeing each other, so the choice cannot lie with their persons."

Poor La Mothe Fenelon! He was faintly embarrassed but could not show it, of course. He knew that I was prevaricating and probably found it humiliating to have to work so hard to try to make me accept his Prince.

"And there is the King himself," I went on. "He is now a married man. I trust he knows great joy in his marriage."

La Mothe assured me that he did.

"Then let us hope that he does not indulge in the gallantries of his forebears. If he takes after his father and grandfather perhaps he will not be such a faithful husband."

He was taken aback and I was sure he did not know whether I was favorable to the match or not. That was how I wished it to be.

One day I gave my leg an unpleasant knock against the bedpost and cut it open. The wound would not heal and I was quite lame for a while. I had to sit with my leg on a stool for it was quite painful to move about freely. Every little thing that happens to a royal personage is reported, often embellished, and to such an extent that it is magnified sometimes for good but mostly evil; and as in his last years my father had suffered from a festering in his leg, it was immediately assumed that I was afflicted with the same ailment.

The news, naturally, was taken to the French Court and I heard reports of Anjou's reactions to it. It was clear to me that he had no wish for marriage and it was only his mother's persistence which made him agree to negotiations.

Although I did not want him, I did not care that he should be against the match and only agreed to it because of his mother's persistence, and I was very disconcerted when Walsingham's spies reported to me a rather alarming conversation which had been overheard between Anjou and one other.

"Monsieur," said the other, "you would do well to marry the old creature who has had for the last years an evil in her leg which will not heal. Let
them send her a potion from France destined to cure all ills, and let it be of
such nature that you will be a widower in the course of a few months, after
which might you not marry the Queen of Scotland and become the undis-
puted ruler of the two kingdoms?"

That threw me into a rage. How dared they talk of me so—and plot my
death!

Never, Monsieur d'Anjou! I thought. You will never get the better
of me.

But I was even more enraged when I discovered that the wily Queen
Mother was putting out feelers for a marriage between Anjou and the Queen
of Scots.

Burghley soothed me, and so did Robert. He looked at me reproachfully, dumbly asking why I would not take the only man whom I could trust
and who had loved me over the years.

I wanted to shout at him: "You fool, Robert, do you think I am going
to marry any of those French fops! While we are negotiating we are keeping
the friendship of France. Spain is against me. The Pope is against me. Scotland is as troublesome as ever, and I have the Queen of that country in my
hands. I need friends, Robert; and while I am negotiating to marry a Prince
of France, the French at least must be my allies."

Then the Emperor Maximilian, no doubt disturbed at the thought of a
French marriage, offered his son Rodolph as a prospective husband. He was
even younger than Anjou.

Catherine de' Medici was greatly disturbed by the thought of a marriage
with Maximilian's son and she cajoled and threatened Anjou, and even
asked Walsingham to talk to him and make him see the advantages of a
match with England.

I was amused. The more suitors the better. Then another appeared. This
was Henri of Navarre—a rather crude but adventurous young man; and it
was diverting to consider them all striving to win the prize—which was the
crown of England.

It was a moment of great triumph when, at one of our banquets, I called
for dancing and taking Christopher Hatton as my partner, I performed with
him for the amusement of the Court. I leaped as high as I ever had and
pirouetted many times. The applause rang out as I sat down and beckoned
La Mothe to sit beside me.

"You can tell Monsieur d'Anjou that I danced higher than any in my
Court and the reports of my sore leg are greatly exaggerated. It is as clean and

white now as it ever was, and there are years of life in the old creature yet. Pray tell those chemists who thought to prepare a dose for me that they will have to produce something very clever if they will have a French prince marry Mary Queen of Scots and take my kingdom and hers into French keeping."

Poor La Mothe! He was quite taken aback. He ought to have known what an excellent spy service I had through the good work of my swarthy Moor.

I thought the farce with Anjou had gone on long enough. It had served its purpose in keeping the attitude of the French open, so I sent word that if Anjou came to England he must change his religion. This gave him a graceful way out, and his reply was that he feared he could not do that.

I was amused when his indefatigable mother, refusing to accept defeat, offered Anjou's brother, the Duc d'Alençon.

This seemed a good joke and I could not help laughing when the proposition was put before me; and Burghley, with Leicester, joined in my amusement.

In the first place Alençon was even younger than his brother. Twenty-two years separated us; he was very small and no one could call him handsome. He had indulged overmuch in fleshly pleasures which had aged him prematurely; his skin was pitted with smallpox; and his ill-shaped nose was so large that it hung down over his mouth. He must have been a most repulsive object. The amusing side to this was that he had been christened Hercule; and anyone less like the great hero there could not have been.

Yet I did not give even him a definite refusal. I planned to have a little diversion with the hideous Prince.

All this coming and going of ambassadors suing for my hand did not prevent my round of engagements. At Greenwich I performed the Maundy ceremony, washing the feet of thirty-nine poor women. I have to admit that one of my yeomen of the laundry washed the women's feet first and, when they were clean, I came with my maids of honor who carried basins filled with herb-scented water, so I was presented with feet that had already been cleaned. Dirt and evil smells sickened me, and all knew of my passion for cleanliness so this seemed an acceptable way of performing the ceremony. Each of the chosen women received a gown, shoes and a wooden platter on which was half a salmon, ling and six herrings, in addition to a purse containing twenty shillings with which they seemed highly satisfied.

In August of that year I went on one of my pilgrimages through the countryside to show myself to the people, which was what they wanted. I always made sure that they had a good view of me and I paused on the way to chat with them, and thank them personally for the little presents they brought me, and however humble these were I always made them feel they were just what I needed. These journeys gave me as much pleasure as they gave the people, for always I was aware of that which was more important to me than anything else—the approbation of my subjects.

I was particularly happy on this occasion because Robert was beside me and we spent a short time at Warwick Castle, the home of his brother Ambrose, a charming man who had served his country well. He had been in the Tower with Robert when I had been there for he was arrested with his brothers for complicity in the plot to set Lady Jane Grey on the throne. I liked him well. He was something of an invalid due to a poisoned bullet which had struck him when he was defending Le Havre. I was especially fond of all Robert's family and I had never forgotten what I owed to his sister who had so valiantly nursed me during my attack of smallpox which she had caught, to be left disfigured.

I was received magnificently at Warwick Castle. There were the usual pageants and songs of praise for my beauty and wisdom. I could almost guess what the next line would be when they quoted their verses, but I liked them none the less for that; and it was delightful to see the pleasure these simple country people took in pleasing me and how conscious they were of the honor of coming face to face with their sovereign.

I would never slight any of them, though I must admit there were occasions when I found it hard not to give way to a yawn. One of these occurred in Warwick where they had arranged a civic ceremony for me, and the speech made by the Recorder went on and on, repeated in parrot fashion, at the end of which he begged me to take a small present from the town. The bailiff then came to my coach and gave me a purse in which was twenty pounds. I took it graciously and told them that I was loath to take anything from them, because I knew that many of them had given what they could ill afford; but I accepted it with hearty thanks and that I should never forget the honor done to me by my good people of Warwick. I then gave him my hand to kiss, which he did in some confusion.

Ambrose whispered to me that the Recorder, a certain Mr Aglionby, had been overcome with terror at the thought of having to address me, and had learned his speech by heart, so perhaps that was the reason why it had been rather more than usually dull.

Fearing that the good Mr Aglionby might have noticed my boredom, I sent for him at once, for it was always my aim that no one should be allowed to think anything but the best of me, which after all was the purpose of these tiring and often uncomfortable pilgrimages I took among my subjects.

He came and I held out my hand.

"Come hither, little Recorder," I said. "I hear that you thought you would be afraid to look at me and to speak boldly. I now tell you that you were not so afraid of me as I was of you; and I now thank you for putting me in mind of my duty."

The little man was almost in tears—tears of gratitude and admiration. I knew that he would be my ardent supporter for the rest of his life.

And so into the castle.

That would have been a very pleasant trip for me but for a somewhat unsavory piece of gossip which came to my ears during it.

I had noticed Douglass Sheffield at once, for that instinct I had for picking out women who would appeal to Robert had singled her out to me. I remembered I had heard something about Douglass's and her sister's being enamored of Robert. I had not taken much notice at the time because I imagined many women at Court were enamored of Robert—and I liked to think of their being so.

The gossip came through some of my women whom I heard discussing it. They would never have dared tell me outright but when I heard one say to another: "Do you think the Earl of Leicester really did it?" I pricked up my ears and burst in on them, demanding to know what Leicester had been accused of doing.

It was only my anger which prized the story from them. They were loath to tell me, saying every few minutes that it was only gossip, and I knew how slanderous that could be toward the best of people.

Yes, I did know, and I understood that a man in Robert's position had many enemies. But could this story be true? I knew that Douglass Sheffield and her sister had been enamored of him. Had others seen that—and when Douglass's husband died rather mysteriously, had they fabricated the story to discountenance Robert?

It might well be—but on the other hand it might not.

The gossips said that Robert had had a love affair with Douglass Sheffield. This was possible. He was a man and certainly he had no sexual satisfaction from me. I had often thought that he must seek that elsewhere, and if he did so all well and good . . . as long as I did not know about it, and it was done discreetly and out of sight. That was one condition which I was sure Robert understood.

Apparently this affair with Douglass Sheffield had gone farther. He had, it was said, written a letter to her which he had asked her to destroy as soon as she had read it, but, foolish woman that she was, she had failed to do this. In this letter he had stated that he would marry her when her husband died, and he had added that damning sentence "and that may not be very long."

It was like the casket letters all over again. What fools people were to put these dangerous thoughts on paper! What greater fools not to destroy them when they had been read!

She had kept the letter under her pillow to read it many times during the days and nights; and then the little idiot had dropped it; she hunted everywhere and could not find it. Of course she could not, for it had already been found by her sister-in-law who promptly took it to Douglass's husband.

And what did Lord Sheffield do on reading that letter? He decided to go to London to arrange for a divorce from the wife who, with her lover he believed, was seeking to murder him. Then came the damning part. Lord Sheffield died before he could show the letter to his lawyers and his death was due to dysentery—often the result of poison.

Why should Lord Sheffield have died so suddenly when he was about to disclose the relationship between Robert and his wife?

Well, it made a good subject for gossip. The alarming part was that Sheffield *was* dead. I could not believe though that Robert had planned to marry Douglass. He would know how furious I should be to receive such news, and he would never risk my anger for the sake of that silly little woman. On the other hand, could he have written such a letter? Yes, possibly in the hope of seducing the woman if she were holding out against him; and then when he was about to be exposed could he have arranged Sheffield's death?

I did not know. There was so much I did not know about Robert. Was that why he was so fascinating?

How often I had asked myself: How did Amy Robsart die? Was it an accident? Did she commit suicide? Or was she hastened to her death—and if so who would want that more than Robert? He would wish Lord Sheffield dead if he were going to create a scandal which would come to my ears.

I could never be sure.

It was a disturbing end to the otherwise pleasant visit to Warwick.

CHAT AUGUST WE had news of one of the greatest catastrophes the world has ever known. It set Christian men and women all over the world shivering and turning in disgust from the King and Queen Mother of France, at whose instigation it must have taken place.

I refer to the massacre on St Bartholomew's Eve when many of the leading Huguenots of France were gathered together in Paris for the marriage of Marguerite, daughter of Catherine de' Medici, and my one-time suitor Henri of Navarre. He miraculously escaped, but few of his faith did.

The horror of it, the cruelty of it, the folly of it, were hard to believe.

I could not stop thinking of that terrible night when the tocsins rang out announcing the massacre was about to begin and when the Catholics went into the streets bent on murdering those of their fellow countrymen who did not wish to worship God in the same way that they did.

Charles the King, we knew, was mad; but surely that wily serpent, his mother, knew better than this! Why had she roused the city of Paris to this frenzy? Could she not see that generations to come would revile her?

People at Court spoke of nothing else and they spoke in whispers—not with the usual excitement which one sees on people's faces when ill news is told of others. No! There was no one who was not bitterly shocked and dismayed by what had happened.

The French were regarded as monsters; I could not bring myself to receive La Mothe Fenelon, though that cultivated and fastidious gentleman was in no way to blame and I was sure fully realized the folly of this wanton cruelty and the odium in which it would place his country.

I saw him eventually and decided the meeting should take place at Woodstock, but to stress my horror at what had taken place I ordered that all my courtiers should be dressed in black.

There was a deep silence when La Mothe entered the chamber and, taking a few steps toward him, I said: "I regret that I have kept you waiting for an audience, my lord. Pray tell me is it possible that this terrible news we have had is true?"

"Your Majesty, I come to lament with you over this sad accident. My King deeply regrets that for the sake of his life and that of his family it was necessary to put down traitorous plots of men who had conspired against him. What has happened has been as painful to the King of France as though one of his arms had to be cut off to save the rest of his body."

"I do not understand, my lord. You must explain to me why it was necessary to murder thousands of Huguenots in cold blood."

I was sorry for La Mothe. It is always a difficult task for ambassadors to try to find excuses for their masters. He flustered through his explanations, stressing the perfidy of the great Admiral de Coligny, who, we all knew, was one of the most saintly men living.

"If the Admiral was indeed guilty of treason could he not have been tried and brought to justice?" I asked. "Was it necessary to kill so many?"

"It was a grim accident. Orders were misinterpreted . . ."

I took pity on him. One should not blame ambassadors for their kings' misdemeanors.

The Council came to hear his explanations.

"Accidents! Mistakes!" they cried. "St Bartholomew's Eve will be remembered in the centuries to come as one of the greatest blots on the history of France."

Burghley said: "It is the greatest crime since the Crucifixion."

AFTER THE MASSACRE there was a strong determination among those about me to be rid of Mary Stuart.

The chief instigator of this was, oddly enough, Burghley. He was by no means a bloodthirsty man, but he was an ardent Protestant and it was such as he who had been particularly horrified by what had happened. I think in his heart he was terrified that if anything happened to me, Mary Stuart would take the throne and he dreaded to think to what terror the country could be brought under a rule of the Catholics. I could understand that. It was not so long ago that we had smelt the burning flesh in Smithfield.

I was the one who hesitated. I could not forget that she was my kinswoman—and, of course, she was royal. I was very like my grandfather who did not want to shed blood wantonly. He would kill though if he thought his throne was threatened. I had believed I would do the same; but somehow I could not condemn Mary Stuart to the scaffold.

Burghley pointed out that I had ample reason for doing so. Had she not written to Norfolk? Did she not join in the plan to kill me and set herself up in my place?

I knew this, but somehow I could not believe that Mary had really agreed willingly to my assassination. Why not? Had she not agreed to Darnley's?

It was Robert who came up with the idea that we should let others remove Mary for us. It was a devious plot and perhaps characteristic of Robert. It occurred to me that he was good at such plotting. Had he plotted thus for the removal of Amy Robsart and Lord Sheffield? I reproached myself for these thoughts. Now he was only thinking of my good as he assured me he did night and day. My welfare was his chief concern.

Burghley was so sure that as long as Mary Stuart lived, there would be a threat of conflict in the country that he supported Robert's rather bizarre scheme. The plan was that I should free Mary ostensibly on condition that she return to Scotland. There she would be in the hands of those two rogues, James Douglas, Earl of Morton, who had been one of Rizzio's murderers, and John Erskine, Earl of Marr, who had become Regent after the murders of Moray and Lennox—both of whom were as eager to see the end of her as I was. These two were to bring her to trial and find her guilty and her execution was to be immediate and to take place not more than four hours after she had been passed into their hands.

A secret mission then ensued and a certain Henry Killigrew, an ambassador who had already proved his worth, was sent to Scotland to try to come to some agreement with these two villainous gentlemen who, it seemed, were quite ready to betray their Queen, provided they could see enough advantage to themselves in doing do.

Burghley had said that it was Killigrew's task to make them see those advantages and to find out what their terms for carrying out this task would be.

The bargaining was sordid and I hated the whole business; and it was only the earnest warnings of both Burghley and Robert that made me go on with it.

It may have been that Marr had no great fear of Mary, seeing himself safe in a Protestant Scotland. John Knox the preacher—the type of man I loathed, a religious fanatic, cruel and intolerant—who hated Mary with a fierce fanaticism, was delighted to join in the plot to kill her.

Eventually Marr had been ready to make an agreement but he died before it could be put into action. It was rather strange—almost as though the saints to whom Mary prayed so frequently really were coming to her aid, for Morton was much harder to deal with and he would not give way. First he demanded a pension which should be as much as it had cost me to keep Mary as my prisoner in the castles of England. I was shocked. I hated to see money wasted for I believed that prosperity came through frugality. I spent money on my dresses—and I will admit I had a goodly array of them—but I always assured myself that they were necessary to the dignity of royalty. I kept good state at my Court; there was rich food and wine served at my table. Not that I ate with any gusto. I had the smallest of appetites, and I always drank my wine diluted with water. I respected money without hoarding it. I think I must have inherited that from my grandfather. People called him a miser but his ways had made a prosperous country, whereas my father's extravagance had left the exchequer sadly depleted. I had taken it upon myself to pay all the latter's debts, and they were heavy, but I did not want anyone to go without the money which was rightly his or hers. I also paid those debts left by my brother Edward. The people knew what I had done—particularly the people of London—and they honored me for it. My father had thought that the privilege of serving the Court was enough for them. *I* thought they should be paid as well.

I had achieved prosperity—as my grandfather had—by care and a lack of extravagance, except in those particulars which I considered necessary to preserve my image in my people's eyes. They knew this and one of the French emissaries had said that the people of London treated me with something like idolatry.

So now I balked at the thought of paying out so much money to that villain Morton across the Border. And his demands grew greater. He must have guessed how earnestly Burghley wanted the conclusion of this affair and for it to be carried out without leaving a stain on my character. Let Mary be brought to the block by her ungallant knights, he said. Then no one in

England could be blamed and we could leave the matter to the barbarity of the Scots.

Then Morton came up with a condition which made the entire plot useless. He insisted that the execution could only take place if three thousand English soldiers under the command of the Earls of Bedford, Essex and Huntingdon were present.

When this ultimatum was delivered to us we knew that it was the end of the venture. The whole idea had been to execute her leaving me free from blame. Morton knew this. Was that why he suggested the presence of my soldiers?

"We are wasting our time," I said. "Morton knows he has asked the impossible."

Burghley nodded grimly. "God sent Your Majesty strength to preserve God's cause, your own life and the lives of millions of your subjects, all of which are manifestly in danger." He added: "God be merciful to us all."

I had to comfort Burghley. I shrugged danger aside and in my secret heart I was glad we had not been able to find those who would be ready to murder Mary Stuart.

IN SPITE OF the loathing the French Catholics aroused at this time not only in England but throughout the world, and the sure knowledge that my marriage with Alençon would be against the wishes of the people, I did keep up negotiations with Catherine de' Medici in secret.

She was an extremely clever and most devious woman and I never underestimated her for one moment. It surprised me that she should be so eager to see one of her sons take the crown of England that she still persevered in her efforts with the utmost zeal. Surely such a woman could see through my schemes. Perhaps she did. Perhaps she thought that I was as cynical as she was and cared nothing for the murdered Huguenots, not only in Paris but throughout the whole of France, for once started it seemed that the Catholics would not forgo their blood-letting.

However, La Mothe Fenelon presented himself with messages from the Queen Mother.

"Her Majesty wishes Your Majesty to know that the cure is succeeding with Monsieur le Duc and his skin is improving every day."

He was referring to Dr Penna who had claimed he had an elixir which could in time eradicate from the skin all traces of smallpox. His services had immediately been acquired by Catherine de' Medici who must have believed that her son's appearance was one of the impediments to the marriage.

"That is indeed good news," I said. "If it is really effective I must have the man here to see what he can do for Lady Sidney."

La Mothe was pleased. He believed that in spite of everything I was really considering the marriage. It was amazing that he could believe that when I had hesitated before the massacre, I would now agree.

We discussed the disaster of the smallpox which seemed more prevalent than it had a short while ago.

"I suppose our little Prince must count himself lucky to have come through with his life," I said.

"Indeed, Your Majesty, and in the case of such a charming Prince, that small disability is forgotten when one is in his presence."

"I suppose there are other parts of his visage to take the mind off the skin," I said tartly. I was really all eagerness to see that little Prince with his debauched eyes and a nose which some said was split in two giving him a most grotesque appearance.

Perhaps I should have been a little more sympathetic for to be attacked by the smallpox is a terrible experience; and then when, a few days later, I began to feel unwell I remembered my words to La Mothe Fenelon, especially when in a short while the spots began to appear on my face and I knew that once again I had fallen a victim to the dreaded disease.

Robert came and insisted on entering my chamber. He threw himself onto his knees and declared his undying devotion. I smiled at him and said: "Robert, go from here. I would not have your handsome face wrecked by the smallpox."

"I am here to serve you," he said masterfully, "and here I remain." And for once I did not remind him that I was the Queen who must be obeyed.

The Council was in a state of panic and I guessed they were all worried about the succession—the Protestants declaring that they would never have Mary; and while all the world was watchful, Spain and France were ready to pounce.

Strangely enough I did not feel ill this time. They say that if one has had a disease once one becomes immune. One catches the disease, but it passes over lightly; and this was what it did in my case.

Before long I was well enough to rise and when I studied my face I could not find a single blemish.

Another fortunate escape!

La Mothe Fenelon came to me and I joked: "It may well be that when Monsieur le Duc comes he will be a little disappointed. Perhaps he would like to see me with just a few blemishes so that he could find me in a state not entirely dissimilar to his own."

"Nay, Your Majesty," he replied. "Monsieur will rejoice in the preservation of your unsurpassed beauty. Moreover Penna's medicines are having such an effect on the Duc that when you see him you will find the rumors of his disfigurement greatly exaggerated."

"That will give me the utmost pleasure," I replied, and I added that perhaps the Duc would like to pay a visit to the English Court. I was amused to see that La Mothe was evasive about this and I guessed it was due to the fact that he feared that if I saw the ugly little creature before a proxy marriage there would never be one in actual fact.

Shortly after he came to announce the birth of a daughter to the King of France. La Mothe was having a very uncomfortable time in England for he could not defend the action of his masters, try as he might, loyal creature that he was; and there was shock throughout the country when the news broke that two supporters of Admiral de Coligny had been executed in the Place de Grève, and that the King, Catherine de' Medici and other members of the royal family had witnessed the execution which had taken place precisely as the Queen was giving birth to a child.

I was determined to let La Mothe know that I disapproved heartily of the callous behavior of his King and the Queen Mother. It would help me with my bargaining and dealing with the wily Catherine de' Medici, and I must not miss one advantage.

"His Majesty could not have wished more for the safe delivery of his child than I do," I said with diplomatic exaggeration. I went on to say with even more hypocrisy that I could have wished the Queen might have given birth to a dauphin, but I was sure he was very happy with the Princess. I regretted, of course, I added, that her royal father had polluted the day by so sad a spectacle and that he had gone to see it in the Place de Grève.

La Mothe Fenelon, struggling to retain his loyalty to a cause which he must have found abhorrent, agreed that it was a day in which happiness was mingled with evil. "My master was forced to witness the executions to follow the example of his great ancestors on such occasions," he replied.

I nodded gravely and added that the state of affairs in France did cause me some concern; and I was very distressed to see action taken against people who practiced my religion.

La Mothe bowed his head and said that out of his great friendship for me, his King would be happy if I would act as godmother to the newly born infant.

I accepted graciously as there could be no possibility of my going myself and I should have to send someone in my place which was usual in such circumstances.

I then discussed with Cecil who could be sent. The obvious choice was Lady Lennox, but I was certainly not going to send her. Who knew what plots she would become embroiled in with the serpentine Queen Mother of France? She was the grandmother of the little Prince James of Scotland and schemes were undoubtedly going round and round in that head of hers, concerning the little Prince and his mother.

We decided that our best emissary on this occasion was William Somerset, the Earl of Worcester. He was a Catholic but a man whom we could trust. So off he went with the font of gold which was my gift as the godmother of the child.

I was seeing Robert almost every day. He was sure that, after the massacre, I could not marry into the House of France. One day his hopes would be high, and he would see himself beside me on the throne; on another he would seem to understand that there could never be a marriage . . . either with him or with any other. I was past my fortieth birthday. What would be the point in marrying now? I could have Robert at my side whenever I wished. I was in complete command. Why should I want to change that? Of course I never would. But I did like the process of wooing; I loved to see hopes rise, and sometimes I even deceived myself into thinking that I might give way. Courtship was to me one of the most exciting games to play. It kept alive the myth that I was beautiful and desirable beyond any living woman. It was a pleasant dream to live in and while those about me played the parts with such zeal they gave reality to the dream.

I was amused by Robert's jealousy; and I did have a tendency to favor young and handsome men because I liked good-looking people. I could not bear deformity; consequently a young man who was personable, could dance well and converse with grace always attracted my attention, and as I liked to have such people about me, I gave them posts which would keep them there.

Naturally, there was no one like my Master of Horse, but I liked to keep even him guessing whether or not he might be ousted from my favor by some newcomer.

Christopher Hatton remained in favor; so did Heneage. There was one young man who was really very attractive; he danced beautifully and his conversation was witty. He was not a clever man like Cecil or Walsingham, my Moor, who was now in Paris getting restive there, wanting to come home to his family. But for the moment I could not allow that. Too much was going on in France and I needed my master diplomat to make sure my affairs were well looked after. But those two and others were my Clever Men. Edward de Vere, Earl of Oxford, was in the charming favorites category.

I had noticed Edward de Vere since he was twelve years old. That was when his father died and young Edward had become the Earl of Oxford. Because of his youth, a guardian had been found for him, and he had been put under the wardship of William Cecil; and as now and then I visited my chief minister, I saw the boy from time to time. Exceptionally handsome with a somewhat forceful personality, he caught my attention, and I expressed an interest in him from the first. He was a lively boy, wayward and reckless, and there was certain to be trouble where he was. When he was about seventeen he was involved in the death of one of the servants of the Cecil household—an undercook, I think. The man had offended him in some way and Oxford had hot-headedly run him through with his sword. The man had died and a great deal of manipulation was needed to extricate Oxford from serious trouble. Even noble earls were not permitted to murder the humblest servants. However, the jury was induced to bring in a verdict that the undercook had "run into the point of the Earl's sword"—thus making the verdict accidental death.

I daresay this was not good for my lord's character for he believed that he could act in whatsoever manner he wished and escape punishment.

A few days later he appeared at a special joust and so distinguished himself that I forgave him. He looked so handsome, so noble, as he faced his opponent; and he was romantically charming when he came to bow to me. He will think twice before he attacks his servants again, I tried to delude myself into believing.

The next event was his marriage to Cecil's daughter Anne. I suppose it was natural. They had been brought up in the same household and had grown very familiar with each other. I remarked to Cecil that it was the best basis for a happy marriage. I think Cecil was a little dubious, knowing the nature of the Earl, but I had no doubt that he was pleased to see his daughter marry into such a noble household.

Oxford was one of those young men who would always call attention to himself wherever he was and it was usually in the most outrageous manner. If only he had been content with his excellence at the joust and being a graceful addition to any social gathering! But he wanted to swagger on the stage at all times. He wanted all attention focused on him.

When Norfolk had been in the Tower, he had devised some hare-brained scheme for rescuing him, Norfolk being distantly connected with him through a Lady Anne Howard who had married into the de Vere family. Naturally it had come to nothing and Oxford quarreled violently with his father-in-law, Cecil, because of this.

There was one thing which worried me. When he had been foiled and the attempted rescue of Norfolk shown as the immature plot it was, Oxford was so incensed that he swore revenge on Cecil.

Cecil told me this and shrugged his shoulders.

"He is a willful boy," he said. "I know not what will become of him."

"I like not those threats of vengeance on you," I said.

"He is nothing but a foolish boy," Cecil assured me.

And I was inclined to agree.

"He now wants to be taken into the Navy," said Cecil.

"That shall not be," I replied firmly. I had two reasons. One, he was too reckless and I was becoming more and more proud of my growing Navy; and the other was that I enjoyed his company at Court.

"I persuaded him that as he enjoys Your Majesty's favor he would probably do better to remain at Court."

I nodded my approval.

But it was asking too much of a nature like Oxford's to live in peace with those around him. Very soon after that he was in conflict with another young man whom I admired.

This was Philip Sidney who had many talents to recommend him apart from the fact that he was the son of my dear Mary Sidney, whose nursing during my smallpox attack had cost her her good looks. I visited her frequently in her secluded apartments at Hampton Court, and I constantly let her know that I did not forget what she had done for my sake. So the fact that she was Philip's mother would alone have made me take a special interest in the boy. Moreover, he was Robert's nephew. Robert was very good to him in many ways, and Philip I believe looked on Robert as a kind of god. That pleased me. He was a very good-looking young man, somewhat serious, highly cultivated, and he wrote verse with a flow which I found most remarkable. Mary had shown me some of his writings with great pride—so he was a young man in whom I took a particular interest.

Oxford knew of my regard for him and was jealous of it; but his real enmity, I imagined, was directed against Robert, so he struck at him through young Sidney. Even such a rash young man as Oxford would scarcely dare challenge Robert himself.

The incident took place on one of the tennis courts where Sidney was enjoying a game with a friend. Oxford came along and, deciding he wished to play, ordered Sidney and his friend to leave the court free for him.

Sidney naturally retorted: "Why should I? You must wait until the game is finished."

"Don't be insolent, you puppy," cried Oxford; at which Philip Sidney was incensed and there on the spot challenged Oxford to a duel.

Fortunately I was informed of this proposition and I was furiously angry. Dueling was against the law, and in any case I did not want any of my people killed in senseless quarrels—particularly two young men who graced my Court and pleased me with their presence.

I sent for Philip Sidney and demanded to know what he meant by challenging the Earl of Oxford to a duel. He replied that Oxford had insulted him and his father by calling him a puppy and so implying that his father was a dog.

"Such folly!" I cried. "And over the use of a tennis court, I understand. That there should be such fools in my kingdom, I can scarcely believe. So you, my young coxcomb, would shed blood, would you, because of the rash words of another?"

"I would bear no insult, Your Majesty."

"Oh, would you not?" I said. "Would you rather bear your Sovereign's wrath? You should know, little boy, that if you are to stay at my Court, you must show proper respect to noblemen. You have dared challenge a noble earl!"

"Your Majesty, may I respectfully point out that the rights of men come before the rights of noblemen. Your noble father supported the rights of the common man against the aristocracy when he believed it was just to do so."

"You give a good account of yourself," I said. "Remember this: I could send you to the Tower for challenging a noble earl, but there are members of your family who are very dear to me. Do not take advantage of this. There shall be no duel. Understand that. Now you may go. I shall be lenient with you this time—but remember."

When he left me I was smiling. He really was a very charming fellow. He was not quite twenty years of age. Oxford was about four years older and I was certain Oxford had picked the quarrel with him because he was Robert's favorite nephew. These jealous men! I thought indulgently. But I was a little alarmed, for Philip Sidney had aroused Oxford's enmity and I believed the latter might be very irresponsible. I should hate anything to happen to increase Mary Sidney's anxieties for I knew how she doted on her son.

I suggested to Robert that such a cultivated young man should have the opportunity of foreign travel, and he agreed that he should go to Venice, where he could study Italian literature, astronomy and music.

I felt happier when young Sidney was safely out of the country.

Catherine de' Medici was working indefatigably to bring about my marriage to Alençon, and her special envoys were urging me persistently. They told me that the young Duc was madly in love with me. I pretended to be gratified. I was sure they thought me a vain and simpering woman, which was what I wanted them to believe, for the longer these negotiations went on, the better. How little they knew me!

I was fully aware that Catherine was eager for the marriage to take place *before* I saw her son, which confirmed all the stories I had heard of his unprepossessing appearance. Finally, however, she seemed to give way, and word was sent to me that King Charles would come to the coast of France with his brother whom he would send over to Dover that I might meet him.

This alarmed me a little. Perhaps the Duc was not so unprepossessing after all. What would the people say if they thought I was seriously considering marrying a prince whose brother was responsible for that terrible massacre on St Bartholomew's Eve?

Since I had sought the meeting, it was not easy to evade it, but I did so by adopting one of my coy maidenly attitudes. I replied that it was too decisive a step to be undertaken at this stage and not in keeping with my virgin state.

I could imagine Catherine's fury against me, but that lady should have realized by now that she was dealing with one as devious as herself!

I was saved from having to make a clear decision by events in France. Charles was a dying man; he had never really recovered from that awful night of slaughter and had been ailing ever since. He had always been a weakling physically as well as mentally, and it was obvious that he had not long to live.

His brother, the Duc d'Anjou, next in line to the succession, had become King of Poland, so he was far away. That must have given my little Alençon ideas. He was an ambitious gentleman, I will say that for him. He was always ready to take advantage of a situation. Of course, there was now great bitterness throughout France between Huguenots and Catholics, and Alençon decided that with his eldest brother in sight of death and his brother Anjou away in Poland, he had a good chance of coming to the throne himself.

He schemed with two noblemen, Mole and Coconnas, to seize the throne on the death of the King and consolidate himself there before the return of Anjou from Poland.

It was hardly likely that he would be able to succeed, for Catherine de' Medici was watchful on behalf of Anjou, who, it was said, was the only person she had ever loved; and very soon my little Prince's schemes were discovered by his mother. I heard that some sources in France suggested that I was involved in the plot. That was entirely untrue.

However, Alençon did not hesitate to betray his allies when the plot was discovered and they went to the scaffold.

In the midst of this Charles died. Anjou was proclaimed Henri III while Alençon took the title of Anjou as the new King's younger brother.

Denied the crown of France, Alençon—now Anjou—again turned his eyes back to England. I was amused for the situation was becoming really intriguing. I remembered that the new King had at one time been a suitor of mine and I wondered if he might renew the courtship now that he was King of France.

There was a certain irritation at home. I had suffered so much from the pretensions of Mary Stuart that I was especially sensitive about the actions of those claiming to have royal blood. Therefore I was much disconcerted when I heard of the marriage between Elizabeth Cavendish and Charles Lennox. These two young people had the most scheming mothers in the country. Charles was the son of the Countess of Lennox, Darnley's mother; she had already shown her ambition through her eldest son. And now she had married the younger, Charles, to the daughter of the Countess of Shrewsbury. I knew that lady very well. She was called Bess of Hardwick, being the daughter of John Hardwick in Derbyshire. She had only been married to Shrewsbury for a short time, but she had quickly shown that foolish man who was the master of the household. She had had three husbands—all wealthy—and had seen each of them out of this life after they had left her with their worldly goods. Bess had made sure of that.

Perhaps it had been wrong to put Mary Stuart into the charge of the Shrewsburys, but I had felt that Bess of Hardwick would make sure that a firm hand was kept on Mary and prevent her from trying her wiles on Shrewsbury, which was what I imagine she did with some of her jailers. None of them seemed entirely immune.

However what had resulted instead was a match—aided and abetted by Mary Stuart I gathered—and now Charles Stuart was married to Bess of Hardwick's daughter, and these ambitious ladies were already looking forward to offspring who would have a claim to the throne.

I flew into a rage when I heard this and Cecil had a hard task restraining me. "They have been intriguing at Sheffield Castle," I cried. "Imagine them! The three witches! Getting their heads together . . . Mary Stuart urging them on, reminding them of the Stuart pretensions to the throne. I shall throw the three witches and the happy married pair into the Tower."

"Your Majesty could hardly imprison Mary Stuart for approving of the match."

For a few minutes I would not listen to Cecil and, knowing me, he let me rage on.

"To bring the Queen of Scots to the Tower would be dangerous," he continued eventually. "There might be an attempt to rescue her on the way there; and the cause would scarcely be considered just. She would become a martyr and you well know the people's feelings for such."

Of course he was right.

But those women had arranged this marriage without my permission.

"Ah, there we have a point," said Cecil. "Charles, being of royal Stuart blood, should have asked permission before marrying, and failing to do this has broken the law."

That was good enough. Very soon I had those two energetic countesses in the Tower.

But all this was very disturbing, bringing home to me again the uneasiness of royalty, particularly that of a House which many must still believe had come to the throne not through the straight line of succession. There had been three generations of sovereign Tudors by now, but can one ever be completely safe? Even my father had had to make sure that those who might lay claim by blood to the throne were put out of the way.

That set me brooding on Mary Stuart. There would never be real peace in my life while she lived.

A further cause for annoyance was that, on his way home from Poland to France, Henri III had met and fallen in love with Louise of Lorraine whom he insisted on marrying. What was particularly galling was that La Mothe, I discovered later, had been instructed to keep the news from me as long as possible. I always felt piqued when a one-time suitor married. I wanted them to be like Robert and go on sighing for the impossible forever.

I pretended that my anger was because Henri had married a member of the House of Guise, which had always been my enemy and with whom Mary Stuart had close connections, her mother being one of them.

Then I heard that Catherine de' Medici and her Court had been amused by the action of dwarfs who had been dressed up to look like my father and myself and the Earl of Leicester. I could imagine what ribaldry had been intended; and I saw no reason for not giving expression to my indignation. I let La Mothe know of it, pointing out to him that if the courtiers of France wished to make fun of any they might first start in their own Court.

However, Catherine was still anxious to preserve good relations. She must still have hopes for the newly created Duc d'Anjou, for she sent placating letters. I was assured that the dwarfs who had taken part in the masquerade were all very pretty and the scene had much charm and had been carried out with the impeccable taste due to persons of distinction. If any offense had been taken, it must have been because of my Ambassador's imperfect knowledge of the French language.

I did not believe it, and I continued to show my displeasure.

All the same, negotiations for a marriage with my little French Prince were not broken off.

Kenilworth

ROBERT HAD LAVISHED A GREAT DEAL OF TIME AND MONEY on the Castle of Kenilworth, which had come to him with his title, and he often talked about the place, telling me how much he longed to entertain me there.

Why should I not visit his beloved mansion? I asked myself. I was constantly taking tours through the country. I liked the people to see me and I wished to be assured of their regard.

So in the summer I set out with my entourage. We made a rather impressive cavalcade passing through the countryside for we took not only trunks of clothes but household furnishings as well. I liked my bath to be taken along, for some of the houses were very primitive, and I am sure many of the inhabitants of them never dreamt of taking a bath. They had to be careful of their personal cleanliness when I was around though. I made sure of that. I liked them to know well in advance that I was coming so that they could look to the sweetening of their houses, for there was little I loathed as much as evil-smelling places and verminous rushes.

I was in good spirits when we set out, thinking of Robert whose company I should soon be enjoying, and imagining the lavish spectacles he would be devising for my pleasure.

Before we reached Itchingworth we were met by a party of riders, and I was delighted when I saw who rode at the head of them. I recognized him from a distance. No one sat a horse quite like Robert; no one had his air of distinction and mystery; it was a particularly delightful encounter because I had not been expecting it, imagining that Robert would have so much to prepare at Kenilworth that he would need to be on hand, waiting to greet me when I arrived.

"Why," I cried out as he rode up, dismounted and knelt in that wonderfully courtly fashion which none could practice as he did, "if it is not my Lord Leicester! We did not expect you here, my lord."

"My impatience to see Your Majesty was so great that I could wait no longer."

"And you were sure of your welcome, I'll be bound."

He was standing up now, so tall, so distinguished, my heart leaped with pleasure at the sight of him, as it always did after an absence.

"All is well at Kenilworth?" I asked.

"As well as it can be without Your Majesty's presence, but that I trust will soon be remedied; and then Kenilworth will be the happiest house in the world."

Such charming things he said! He was the constant wooer and that was how I wanted it to remain.

"Have I Your Majesty's permission to ride beside you?"

"You would incur Her Majesty's displeasure if you rode anywhere else, Master of Horse."

Then we laughed and talked and, as we rode into Itchingworth, I noticed there were two women in the party whose names had been linked with Robert's; one was Douglass Sheffield, the other was Lettice Knollys.

They were both exceptionally beautiful women and obviously of very differing temperaments. Douglass was a soft and clinging creature while the handsome Lettice, as I have said before, could take good care of herself.

I have no doubt that there were many women who could boast of encounters with Robert. Why not? As long as they were unimportant and Robert did not become heavily involved, I was not averse to his having a brief flirtation with such women. I knew very well that they were all substitutes and, he being a lusty man, they were necessary to him; any one of them would be dropped at a word from me. As long as that state was preserved I did not object.

I dismissed both women from my mind and gave myself up to the chase which was most enjoyable.

After Itchingworth we went to Grafton, which was one of my houses. The weather was very hot and, as we stepped into the cool hall, Robert said the first thing that I required was a drink of cool ale.

"As you do yourself, my lord, I'll swear," I said.

He admitted this was so and he called to the servants to bring ale which they did, but when I put it to my lips I spat it out.

I was furious. Why, in my own house, did they have such stuff? They knew I drank only the mildest ale, and this strong variety was not to my liking; and yet they had dared bring it to me.

Robert tried a flagon and when he had sipped, grimaced.

"It is as strong as malmsey," he cried. "I feel heady already." Then he roared out to the servants that light ale must be brought at once.

There was pandemonium throughout the house. Where was the ale the Queen preferred? Apparently they had none in the house at all. They had known I was coming yet had neglected to provision it, and here I was tired and hot and unable to quench my raging thirst in my own home!

"Bring something!" I shouted.

"I dare not let Your Majesty take the water," said Robert. "For all we know it could be contaminated. Leave it to me."

What a wonderful organizer he was! What a man of action! In a few moments he had sent his servants out in all directions telling them that they must return with light ale suitable for the Queen to drink.

I was astonished at the speed with which these men came, bringing with them just the ale which suited me.

"Robert," I said, "you are wonderful. Is there anything you cannot do?"

"Anything you ask me I will do for you," he replied. "There is one thing I would you would do for me."

"Dear Robert," I said, "who knows? One day perhaps all you desire will come to you."

A gleam of excitement shone in his eyes. I believe he was hoping for a great deal from the visit to Kenilworth. That was what I found so enchanting about Robert. He never lost hope.

And so we came to Kenilworth. What a magnificent sight! The massive Keep which formed the citadel of the castle was of great antiquity and was called Caesar's Tower. There was a beautiful lake on the southwest side, over which Robert had had a bridge built. I was very happy as I rode forward with Robert at my side. I noticed in the strong sunlight that there were streaks of silver in his thick dark hair now—which somehow endeared him to me— but there was a look of such boyish enthusiasm on his face that I could not help smiling.

I knew this was going to be the highlight of my trip—in fact, I believed, the zenith of all my wanderings—and not only because I loved to see the wonders of architecture and enjoyed the lavish entertainments my subjects devised for me, but most of all because it was Robert's achievement; he was proud of it but he could only be contented if I shared that pride.

I said: "Robert, this is to be compared with any royal palace I ever saw."

I was reminded then of my father—as I often was—for when he had seen the splendors of Hampton Court, he had commented that it was too grand a house for a subject, and had soon taken it from Cardinal Wolsey and made it his. I did not want Kenilworth. I was content for Robert to have it; there was pleasure enough for me in remembering that it had come to him through my bounty.

"It is only Your Majesty's presence in it that can make it that," he said now. "You transform it. It is royal because you honor it. Without you it is nothing to me but a pile of stones and empty baubles."

That was not quite true. I knew he loved it and was often here. But it was pleasant to see the love in his eyes for me . . . as well as for Kenilworth.

As we rode toward the Keep ten beautiful girls, all clad in white silk, appeared; they came toward us and one of them stepped forward and raised a hand. We pulled up, and coming to stand before me, she began to recite a

poem which described the happiness my presence brought to Kenilworth
this day, and the Sybil went on to proclaim that my coming to Kenilworth
was symbolic of my coming to the throne, and she went on to prophesy a
time of peace and prosperity for England under the great Elizabeth.

I said: "What a delightful girl, what a pleasant voice and what comforting verses."

Immensely gratified, the sybils retired gracefully and I rode on with
Robert until we came to a tiltyard, where a very big man, tall and square, a
giant indeed, stepped out to bar my way, brandishing a club in one hand and
carrying a bunch of keys in the other. He looked ferocious and quite terrifying and for a few seconds I wondered what was happening; but glancing
sideways at Robert, I saw the smile about his lips.

The giant demanded what was the cause of all the noise and who it was
who dared to come riding into his master's stronghold which it was his
bounden duty to protect. Then as he approached me, he looked as though
he had been blinded; he put his hands up to his face and fell to his knees.

"Rise, Sir Giant," I said. "You seem less fierce than you did a moment
ago. What has happened to change you?"

"My Gracious Liege," he cried in a parrot voice which suggested to me
that he had the greatest difficulty in memorizing his lines, "I have been
blinded by your glory. I have spoken rashly not knowing for a few moments
what joy had come to my master's house. Clemency, Your Gracious
Majesty, to your humble servant who, if you will forgive his initial mistake
and take his club and keys of the Castle, only then can he hold up his head
again and win back his master's regard for this terrible mistake."

"Rise and give me the keys," I said. "I take them most willingly, and I
congratulate your master on having such an excellent servant who is ready
to defend him and his castle from all intruders."

The giant rose and handed me the keys, looking very relieved because his
little act was over.

As the gates were flung open, six trumpeters who were stationed on top
of the wall, dressed in long garments of white silk, lifted their silver trumpets, and there was a glorious fanfare as we rode under the gateway into
Kenilworth.

There were more trumpeters on the walls of another tiltyard through
which we went on the way to the inner gate. Passing through this we came
to a pool on which floated a figure representing the Lady of the Lake; about
her were nymphs holding blazing torches. As I stopped to admire, the Lady
of the Lake began her peroration which was even more full of praise than
that of the Sybil. Everything was so beautiful and original; and I was all
attention wondering what was coming next.

The bridge across the lake was about twenty feet wide, Robert told me afterward, and seventy feet long; and he had had it constructed purely for my pleasure. I dismounted and walked across beside Robert, and as I did so I was met by young men and women each representing a god of mythology, all with offerings for me. There was Sylvanus, the god of the woods, who presented me with birds—bitterns and curlews, live in cages; from Ceres I had sheaves of corn, and wine from Bacchus, fish from Neptune and musical instruments from Apollo. It was an enchanting pageant.

As we came into the inner court Robert drew my attention to the clock in Caesar's Tower. It was one of the most beautiful clocks I ever saw, the face being a delicate shade of blue and the hands of gold.

I said: "But look! It has stopped."

"All clocks have stopped at Kenilworth," said Robert. "It means that while Your Majesty honors the Castle with your presence, time stands still."

He looked fondly at me and I thought: Would it be possible? Only with him. Never with another. And yet, would he be quite so tender, quite so caring, toward a wife—Queen though she was—as he was toward the one he was trying to persuade to marry him?

Marriage grew stale. Courtship never.

Even here at Kenilworth, I knew that I must be perpetually wooed but never won.

WHAT HALCYON DAYS!

Whenever I traveled my subjects took great pains to give diverting entertainments in their houses, but there had never been anything like this. Robert had thought of everything for my pleasure.

"Even the Queen must remember this forever," he said. "I want to make these days at Kenilworth some of the most memorable you have ever spent. I want no sadness to touch you, no irritation, however slight. Here is Your Majesty at this castle with your Master of Horse, whose great task and great joy in life is to serve you. I have thought of all that you love most to see and hear and do, and that is what I have planned. There shall be no moment of dullness. While Your Majesty is under this roof, every moment must be a joy, or I have failed."

"No one could ever arrange these matters as you can, Robert, but here you have surpassed yourself."

We hunted a great deal for he knew how I loved the sport, and he was always beside me. There were tournaments and tilting in the days and excellent feasting in the evenings when we would be entertained by tumblers, singers and musicians. There were colorful firework displays; and of course we danced every night. I danced chiefly with Robert. Although, of course, others implored the honor of partnering me, I never enjoyed dancing with anyone as I did with him—although men like Heneage and certainly Hatton danced more gracefully than he did. But I did not want too excellent a performance from Robert. He possessed all the masculine attractions to the full, and dancing perfection was not what I expected from Robert, although such as Hatton had won my regard for the performances they gave on the dance floor.

I liked my men to show their different talents—and they did so admirably; but although I had always known that none could rank with me so high as Robert did, I realized during the days at Kenilworth how very much I cared for him and how much a part of my life he was. During the years of my glory he had never been far from my side; he was closer to me than anyone else ever could be.

Sometimes when I watched him with others I felt twinges of anger. I saw him dancing once with Lettice Knollys while Douglass Sheffield, sitting on one of the benches, followed their movements with yearning eyes. I felt annoyed—not so much with Douglass as with the saucy Lettice.

When I was being helped to bed I noticed her there among my women, and I said to her: "It is time Devereux came back from Ireland, or you went to join him there."

"Oh, Your Majesty, I doubt I should be the slightest use to him there," she said blithely. "He is completely absorbed in the tasks Your Majesty has set him."

"A wife should be with her husband. Long separations are unwise."

She said nothing but I fancied she was smirking a little, and when she was helping to unlace me, I gave her a sharp nip on the arm and said she was clumsy. I added that she must be absentminded thinking of her family at Chartley.

She was never dismayed. She presumed too much on the Boleyn connection which made us some sort of cousins.

There is a smugness about her, I thought, and I believed that at one time she must have been rather friendly with Robert.

I would watch them. I was not having any immorality at my Court. Lettice was now a married woman, and if she did not remember it, I should.

When the women left me, I dismissed Lettice from my thoughts. I was wondering what delights Robert had prepared for the next day.

IT WAS SO HOT that July and because of this we did not go out hunting until the late afternoon and we would return in the twilight. Robert always had some new pageant to greet me and the days contained such a surfeit of entertainment that but for their brilliance and originality, they might have palled. I could never be sure what was being devised for my delight, and when I heard that the cost of all this exceeded one thousand pounds a day, I wondered at Robert's extravagance. When I mentioned this to him, he looked at me reproachfully and asked how he could count the cost when he was catering for the pleasure of his Queen.

It was all very wonderful, but life had taught me that it is not natural to enjoy such unalloyed pleasure, and perhaps I began to look round for a little canker in the richness. I found that my suspicions would not let me get those women out of my mind: Douglass Sheffield and Lettice Knollys. Douglass I felt I understood; I could sum up her nature: soft and yielding, demanding affection which she should have got from Sheffield; and then there was something unsavory about Sheffield's death. Robert had feared that his promises to her might be brought to my ears. It was disturbing to wonder whether he would murder on my account. That thought brought back echoes from the past.

However, the lady who caused me the most disquiet was Lettice. There was something so sly about her; she was harboring secrets. I had noticed the way in which she and Robert deliberately avoided looking at each other. That was not natural. Lettice was one of those women at whom men looked a good deal and Robert's studied indifference was too marked.

So there were these suspicions to ruffle the soft beauty of the paradise Robert had devised for me and, though I forgot those qualms for long stretches at a time, and I threw myself wholeheartedly into the entertainments, they remained.

Perhaps some of the most amusing moments occurred when the carefully organized pageants did not proceed as intended. I shall never forget the water scene which had been arranged to welcome me back to the castle after the hunt. It was on the lake, which always looked its best at night. Lighted by torches, the scene had a look of fairyland, and as I rode in I was greeted by the mermaid who was accompanied by a huge dolphin on whose back rode a masked man dressed to represent Orion.

As I approached the lake Orion started to recite his verses; the theme was that which I had heard many times since coming to Kenilworth. I was the greatest Queen in the whole world. I had been sent by God's Grace to rule England. All was well while I was on the throne and Kenilworth was blessed because I had deigned to stay within its walls. The trouble was that Orion could not manage his words. Like everyone else he must have been instructed to learn them by heart, for to have read them would have robbed them of their spontaneity; and it was in any case unlikely that these people would have been able to read.

However, Orion was having more difficulty than most and having stumbled his way through the first lines, he lost the thread and began again. I could see that Robert was getting very restive, but I was smiling pleasantly knowing that the humble man was doing his best.

He had come to a stop and clearly he had forgotten the rest of his speech. He tore off his mask so that his hot face, purple with exertion, was exposed, and he cried out: "I am no Orion. I am but honest Harry Goldingham, Your Majesty's most loyal subject."

There was just a brief silence. Harry Goldingham had suddenly realized that he had ruined the pageant and was looking fearfully at Robert, glowering beside me.

"But," I cried, "my loyal subject Harry Goldingham you have made me laugh, and I do declare that I like your performance as well as anyone's."

Harry Goldingham leaped from his dolphin and came to kneel at my feet. I gave him my hand and he kissed it fervently. I had made a friend for life, and it was incidents such as this and my natural instinct for dealing with them which won the love of my people.

I made it clear to Robert that I did not want Harry Goldingham reprimanded. I said: "I have enjoyed his efforts. There is a good man and a loyal one."

So that passed off very well and I said afterward that it was one of the highlights of my stay at Kenilworth.

People from the surrounding countryside were allowed to come in and see the performances, but I think most of them came to see me. I was always gracious to them, being aware always of the need to hold my people's approval, and that it was more necessary to me than anything else.

Some of the performances of these country folk could be a little wearisome, but I never showed that I was in the least bored nor that I compared their rustic antics with the sophisticated players who entertained me at Court.

I sat through *Hock Tuesday* which was played by certain men of Coventry and was founded on the massacre of the Danes in the year 1002. The insolence and cruelty of the Danes and the bravery of Hunna, commander-in-chief of Ethelred's army, was stressed. There were realistic encounters between Danes and English knights, which ended in the Danes being beaten and held captive by the English women. This I took as a compliment to my sex.

Afterward I expressed my delight in the play and my fears that the Danes might be victorious in swordplay.

"Oh no, Your Majesty," roared the English knights, "us 'ud never have let that be."

I said that I should have known the English must triumph.

I gave gifts of money to the players, which pleased them well, and to make it a very special occasion I bestowed knighthoods on five members of the nobility—among them Burghley's eldest son, Thomas Cecil.

There was one other play for my pleasure. This was entitled *A Country Bridal* and, compared with *Hock Tuesday*, it was a polished production.

It was the story of a country marriage which for some reason was considered to be a matter for ridicule. The bridegroom was by no means handsome and was clad in an old tawny worsted jacket, a straw hat, and had a pair of harvesting gloves on his hands as he came limping onto the scene. The morris dancers followed him with Mad Marian, a jester, and the bridesmaids—none of them below thirty years of age. A boy came next carrying the bride cup; and last of all, the bride, who was nearer forty than thirty, and made up to look as ugly as possible in a tousled wig and an ill-fitting smock.

The morris dancers danced and the pair were married and staggered off together to the wild excitement of the crowd who had been allowed into the grounds to see the performance.

How they loved it! And yet their eyes were more often on me than on the players; they were clearly gratified to see me laughing.

I did wonder why Robert allowed this piece to be performed. The bride, who was well past her prime, might have been meant to be a lesson to me. Was Robert trying to tell me that we were both getting old and if ever we were going to marry we should do so now? Subtlety was not one of Robert's gifts. However, so much did the people enjoy the play that I refused to consider that there might be some ulterior motive in its selection.

The next day there was an incident concerning Lady Sheffield.

I had been watching the ban dogs. There were thirteen of them and they were very wild, having been locked away and kept short of food to make them fierce. Before the dogs appeared the bear had been trundled into the arena. He looked vicious and very formidable. I was so close as to see his little pink eyes leering round him, scenting danger, ready for the attack.

Then the dogs were let out. The battle was fierce and bloody. I sat there watching, entranced. Sometimes I thought the bear would win . . . but no, the dogs were triumphing, but at what cost to them! The people shouted and cheered the dogs. There was a deafening noise and a constant yelping as the dogs, panting and bloody, went in again and again to the attack.

When the battle was over with no victor, for although one or two of the dogs survived they would never fight again, I was sitting in the shade with some of my ladies round me when a young boy ran up and stood beside me. With the innocence of children he placed his hands on my knees and gazed up at me wonderingly. He was a particularly handsome child, and I was always drawn to children.

"Why do you gaze at me, little boy?" I asked.

He replied: "You are the beautiful Queen."

I patted his head. "So you find me beautiful, do you?" I could never resist compliments. "Is it because I am the Queen, or would you find me beautiful if I were not?"

The child was puzzled, but he delighted me even more by nodding vigorously which I accepted as Yes.

"You know I am the Queen," I said. "But I do not know who you are. Tell me your name."

"Robert," he said.

"Robert!" I echoed. "That is a very favorite name of mine."

He smiled up at me, and I said: "Who brought you to Kenilworth?"

"It was my mama," he answered.

"And who is your mama?"

He looked at me in some amazement and said: "She is my mama."

I smiled and patted his dark head about which the hair curled prettily.

I turned to one of my women. "Whose child is this, do you know?"

"His mother is Lady Sheffield," was the answer.

"Indeed," I said. I was remembering the Sheffield scandal. How long ago was it that I had heard the story about Robert's letter to her, followed by Sheffield's death? Those were uneasy thoughts. How old was the child? Not more than three years I would say. Then was it possible that he had been born after Sheffield's death?

Then . . . who was the father?

I kept the boy with me, but the conversation of a child of three can be somewhat inconsequential and though some of his answers were clear enough, one must wonder how much was fantasy.

"Would you like us to remove the child, Your Majesty?" asked one of the women.

"No, no, let him stay awhile. Will you find the Earl of Leicester and tell him that I would see him."

It was not long before Robert was speeding across the grass.

The little boy gave a cry of joy and ran to him, falling against him and clutching his legs. Robert picked him up in his arms and the boy was laughing. Of course Robert had that charm which would attract even children, but it did seem to me that the boy and he were not strangers.

Robert said something to the child and looked about him. A woman came up and took the boy, who rather reluctantly allowed her to lead him away.

Robert came to me smiling and urbane, but was he just a little uneasy?

He took my hand and kissed it. "I trust Your Majesty continues to enjoy our presentation."

"Extremely so, Robert. You excel in everything. The entertainment has never been surpassed. What a charming boy!"

"Yes. A pleasant child."

"An exceptionally handsome one."

"Did Your Majesty think so?"

"Did you not? He seemed to know you."

"Oh yes, I have seen him before."

"Whose son is he?"

"Lady Sheffield's."

"An old friend of yours."

"I have so many friends."

"Not too many of those who have been involved in scandal, I hope."

"Rumor? Scandal? Who can escape it?"

"Not some of us, Robert, I fear. So she is a guest of yours here at Kenilworth—this Lady Sheffield?"

"Yes—one of the Howards, Your Majesty will remember."

"Wasn't there some mystery about her late husband's death?"

"Sheffield? Oh . . . not really. He died rather suddenly . . . dysentery, I think. It carried him off as it does so many. What thought Your Majesty of the bear?"

"A most unpleasant creature who deserved his fate."

"If he has amused Your Majesty for a short while, he has served his purpose."

"The little boy diverted me. I thought him a most delightful child."

Robert was uneasy, eager to divert me in order to stop my insistence on talking of the child. I took a shot in the dark.

"He reminds me of someone."

The shaft went home. Robert was very disturbed now.

"He seemed to be fond of you, Robert," I went on.

"Oh, children's fondness is not to be relied on."

"I suppose you seem very magnificent in that little one's eyes. He looked at you with something like adoration."

"If only I could arouse such feelings in one other! Do you remember the boy who brought you flowers and carried words of hope from you to me when we were in the Tower together?"

"I remember it well. How different life is for us now! We should be grateful for what God has given us, Robert, and not hanker for more."

"A man cannot help his dreams, Elizabeth."

I said: "Remember that there is always hope."

I saw the light leap into his eyes. I saw the fierce longing. He took my hand and kissed it and his eyes lifted to mine were full of adoration. This was how I liked to see Robert. That was how I wanted him always to be. Mine. The man who loved me throughout his life, whose love never swerved, he was always there, waiting, hoping that the word would be given which would make me his wife. Only Robert could fill that role for me; and he did it to perfection. I wanted it to remain thus and I was determined that it should; and no matter what he did outside that relationship I would accept—as long as it did not interfere with his devotion first to me.

All the same I was going to watch Lady Sheffield while I was here at Kenilworth.

I WAS, HOWEVER, not deeply concerned about Douglass Sheffield. It was Lettice Knollys whom I could not get out of my thoughts. That the woman was up to some mischief I had no doubt; and some instinct told me it was with Robert.

The Essexes' home was Chartley—not so very far from Kenilworth— and I had a desire to see what her family was like. She had four children, I knew, for when she had waited on me I had made her talk of them; and having an excellent memory for such details about the people who interested me, I remembered that there were two girls and two boys.

The day after the bear-baiting when I had seen the little boy, I went along to pay my daily visit to Mary Sidney. Although she preferred to stay at her home at Penshurst, Robert had prevailed upon her to come to Kenilworth. I would never command her to do what she did not want but I did add my pleas to Robert's and on this occasion she had agreed. Robert had arranged that she should have her separate apartments in the castle and she did not join in any of the festivities. As for myself I could never be grateful enough to her for ruining her beauty for my sake. She was a selfless woman, and always had been; and now lived chiefly for her family.

During our conversation on that day I asked her if she knew Chartley well.

"Not well," she said. "I have visited it. It is a pleasant spot and the beautiful estate is set in the midst of some of the best scenery in Staffordshire."

"It's Walter Devereux's place, I believe," I said.

"Yes. It has been in the Devereux family since the days of Henry VI. Then Agnes de Ferrers, a daughter of the Earl of Derby, married into the Devereux family and took Chartley with her."

"It is not very far from here. I thought we might stay there for a few days on our way back from Kenilworth."

"The Earl of Essex is in Ireland, Your Majesty."

"Yes, but the Countess is not. She is here at Kenilworth."

"Your Majesty would not mind staying there in the absence of the Earl?"

"My dear Mary, I know my cousin Lettice, and I am sure she would be capable of doing the honors."

"If that is what Your Majesty wishes . . ."

I nodded. "Your Philip seems in good spirits here at Kenilworth."

"He is always happy to be with his Uncle Robert."

I smiled tenderly. "It is heartwarming to see the affection between those two."

"Robert looks upon him as a son. It is a pity . . ."

I looked up sharply. Gentle as I was with Mary, I would not have her reproach me.

"It may well be that Robert has a son . . . or even a daughter . . . somewhere."

Mary was startled. "Your Majesty!"

"Oh, I daresay Robert has his adventures."

"Your Majesty knows well that Robert cares for one . . . and one only." Dear Mary! So loyal!

I sighed and said: "Your Philip is less sensitive now, I trust. We don't want him going about challenging noble earls to duels."

"Your Majesty will understand that Oxford provoked him."

"I know, I know. Mary, send for the Countess of Essex and tell her that I wish to call at Chartley when I leave here. Tell her that your brother has suggested that our party stay at Chartley and that she is to leave at once."

"Has he?"

No. But he will when I have spoken to him. She will need to make sure that the place is sweetened for our stay. Let her believe that the suggestion came from Robert. I will tell him and he will see you and work out the arrangements. Your Philip can accompany Lady Essex and help her since her husband is away. But I want Lady Essex to leave for Chartley tomorrow."

Mary Sidney was surprised; but she was accustomed to my sudden and often unpredictable commands, and she knew better than to question them.

I kissed her tenderly and left her.

Now Lettice, I thought, your pleasant days at Kenilworth are cut short. I very much look forward to seeing you in the midst of your family at Chartley.

I WAS RIDING beside Robert at the head of the cavalcade and we were a mile or so from Chartley when we encountered Lettice, who had come with a party to greet us.

She looked very fresh and beautiful in a coat of mulberry velvet, a hat sporting a magnificent feather perched rather jauntily on her head. She was certainly a very fine-looking woman. I watched Robert furtively as she approached.

I could not find fault with her manners. She was effusive in her welcome, at the same time stressing the fact that I would find Chartley a somewhat humble residence after Kenilworth and my own royal palaces.

I said: "We have chosen to come, cousin, and I believe you have a way of concealing your possessions."

I saw the wary look come into her eyes and I decided once more that she was a rather devious young woman.

I bade her ride on my left side; Robert was on my right; and so we came to Chartley. It was a charming little castle with a circular keep and two round towers; and as we rode through the park Lettice pointed out the cows which were smaller than normal and of a sand-white color with ears, muzzle and hoof tipped with black.

"They have been here at Chartley for generations," Lettice told me, "and they are always that sand-white color. Well . . . not always. There are occasions when a black one is born, but very rarely. Then there is consternation at Chartley because it is supposed to mean the death of the head of the house is imminent."

"I trust there will be no black cows born to your herd, cousin," I said. "You must be anxious for your husband."

"He is doing Your Majesty's work in Ireland and for that I applaud him," she said demurely.

"You must miss him sadly."

"Alas, Madam."

"But you are a mother of four, I understand."

"That is so."

"I look forward to meeting the children. They must be a joy to you."

She admitted that they were.

Robert was silent during this conversation, but I could feel a tension in the air and should have liked to know the real meaning of it. With Douglass Sheffield I could feel sure, but in the case of Lettice it was different.

Philip Sidney was at Chartley to greet us. What a charming boy! But he did not quite qualify as one of my special men. I could not imagine that he could ever give me the blatant flattery which Oxford, Hatton, Heneage and the rest practiced with such outrageous ease. He had the good looks and the learning, but perhaps he was too learned—and he could never be anything but scrupulously honest, and that was no quality to make a good courtier. Although I respected it, it was not always comforting, and the older I grew, the more I welcomed such reassurance. My hair was growing thinner and must be padded out with false pieces; my face demanded more attention than it had in the past; my skin was still very clear, smooth and pale but must have very special attention. More than ever I needed people around me to tell me I was beautiful, because in my heart I knew I was not . . . especially when compared with people like the Countess of Essex, an undeniable beauty, and she had something else besides—a sensuality, an air of promise which I had noticed in some women, and which had an immediate appeal to the opposite sex, presumably, I reasoned, because it was obvious that there would be no delaying tactics, no unnecessary preliminaries before the goal was reached. No, Philip Sidney was not, nor ever could be, one of those handsome men I kept fluttering around me, whose duty it was to keep me assured that I was the most beautiful and desirable woman on Earth.

The Essex children were presented to me.

There was Penelope—another such as her mother; she must have been about fourteen but already sexually aware; then there was Dorothy, a charming girl, and after her Robert and Walter.

Young Robert attracted me immediately. Perhaps it was simply because he was another Robert and I had such a fondness for the name. I guessed he was about eight years old, and later his mother told me that he would be nine in November. He was alert; he was bold too; he came to me and touched the aglets on my gown to see if they came off. He raised his eyes to me and smiled rather mischievously, I thought; he told me that his dog had puppies and he would show them to me if I liked.

His mother reminded him that he must show more respect because I was the Queen. At which he took my hand and kissed it in a most courtly manner and raising his saucy eyes to mine, he said: "I like queens."

Of course he won my heart. Many children did. I often thought that I should have liked children of my own if it were not for the undignified manner of getting them.

Penelope interested me too. She was going to be like her mother—very wayward, difficult to control. She had already formed a friendship with Philip Sidney, and there seemed to be quite an understanding between them.

I talked about them to Robert afterward. Perhaps a match could be arranged for them. "How would you like a member of your family to marry into that of Devereux?" I asked.

"It is a good family. I suppose it would depend on what Henry and Mary thought."

"Oh come, Robert, they would be prepared to take the advice of their powerful brother."

"I fancy Philip would have his own way."

"Yes, indeed. One must be wary of those quiet ones. They have wills of their own, I believe, and I have a fancy that if your handsome nephew wanted to marry Penelope Devereux, he would do so."

"They are very young."

"The girl, yes. Philip . . . not so young. How old is your nephew?"

"He must be twenty . . . twenty-one . . ."

"Ready for marriage, and Madam Penelope is fourteen . . . but a ripe fourteen, would you say?"

"I know little of that."

I gave him a tap on the hand. "Now, Robert, all know that you are wise in these matters."

"My attentions are so centered on one that I see little of others."

It was the remark I wanted to hear, but while I listened and was gratified, my suspicions remained.

"I am very sorry for Lady Essex," I said maliciously. "She must be a very lonely woman."

"She appears to be happy in her family."

"But the head of that family is missing. A woman such as Lady Essex needs to have a man beside her. Devereux is in Ireland. Perhaps he should be brought back or she join him there."

"There are her children."

"Children . . . and without a husband! If he stayed in Ireland that can be a problem. But if he were brought back . . . He does not appear to be making much of a success in Ireland. I have a fancy that Devereux is a man who would never make a success of anything . . . saving marriage, of course. Would you say he had made a success of that?"

Robert was clearly uneasy. He must be wondering if I had been listening to gossip.

However, he did seem quite indifferent to Lady Essex and devoted himself to the children. Robert was the sort of man they adored. It was that essential masculinity, that aura of power, that magnificence. His confident way with horses was endearing, for what child does not love horses? I found him once in the stables with young Robert Devereux, talking of horses, showing him tricks, giving him instructions in the art of *manège* which he himself had mastered from the French. He was telling young Robert how, after the massacre of St Bartholomew's Eve, he had tried to fill his stables with grooms from households where the owners had been massacred.

"But," he was saying, "these gentlemen have so high an opinion of themselves and demanded such fees for their services that I decided I could do better . . . and I could instruct my own Englishmen to do as good a job as they did."

"Of course you could," agreed young Robert. "Philip says you can do everything better than anyone else."

"Philip is a loyal nephew."

"And the French are wicked. Philip was there when the killing started. He told us about it. He was in the Ambassador's house and he heard the bells ringing and saw the people running into the streets. He said that night was a blot on the history of France which will never be forgotten. He said we must always respect the religious views of others."

"Philip is a good and noble gentleman," said my Robert with feeling.

They were then aware of me and the elder Robert came swiftly to my side and kissed my hand while the young one looked on.

"When I am grown up," he said, "perhaps I shall be your Master of Horse."

Little did I know then what an important part that boy would play in my life. I shall always remember him as the bright young boy he was during my stay at Chartley. I think I began to love him from that moment, which was surprising considering whose son he was.

But in that moment he was merely young Robert Devereux, one of the most enchanting children I had ever met.

I HAD CO ADMIC that the Countess of Essex had entertained us very graciously at Chartley. It was particularly laudable considering that she had the whole burden of the visit. There had been pleasant festivities in the great hall in the evenings, good hunting during the day; and the food was adequate, the ale of the desired quality, and above all the place sweet-smelling. The Countess had given instructions that the rushes be swept out every day. So many people failed to do that and I imagined their noses had become so accustomed to evil smells that they did not notice them. Dorothy Devereux told me that her mother had ordered that wormwood seed be mingled with the rushes for fleas could not live in wormwood.

"My mother knows full well that Your Majesty is the cleanest lady in the land, and she was determined that no flea should sup your royal blood at Chartley."

That amused me. They were bright, these Devereux children. They took after their mother, I supposed—and certainly not after Walter. Walter was a fool. There was no gainsaying it. It was a mistake to have sent him to Ireland. Cecil had said there was no hope of succeeding in Ireland. It was like trying to fill a bottomless pit. However much was poured into it, it would disappear. The reason was that the Irish were a people given to quarreling, so that if they were met on any point that would simply raise another. It was the quarrel itself which they sought—not the solution; so if one trouble was solved they lost no time in finding another.

I was beginning to believe that Cecil was right and governing Ireland was a thankless task; that was why it was best to send such as Devereux out there. The place abounded with traitors and dull as he was, Devereux could be trusted. He had, however, made some terrible mistakes. He had invited some of the chieftains to a banquet on one occasion and in the middle of the feast soldiers had entered the hall, seized the chiefs and murdered their attendants. There was no justification for this and Devereux's excuse had been that he had broken the faction which was working against him and made them all afraid of him.

There was no alternative after that incident but to recall him from Ireland.

He came to see me, full of excuses. I gave him credit for his loyalty; on the other hand he was no brilliant statesman. I was certain that Lettice must find him dull company.

Let her contend with his dullness. She had married him and he was the father of those four enchanting children.

I said to him: "There has been no happy result from the Irish question, but I daresay that is no easy matter to settle. You need a rest. I'll swear you are longing to be with your beautiful wife and children. I was at Chartley recently and I found the place delightful. Make sure there are no black cows born on your land, Lord Essex."

He was gratified by my interest and I could not help comparing him with Robert who was present at the meeting. How splendid he looked in that dark red velvet, a color becoming to his handsome dark looks! I liked the new Italian-style doublet with the long peak in front. It was set with rubies, and there was a white feather in his red velvet hat, and his loose traveling coat was of the same rich-colored material. What a fine figure of a man! And how insignificant Walter Devereux looked beside him!

Walter thanked me and said he would be glad to return to his family for a while, until I found some task for him which he trusted would be ere long as his one wish was to serve me.

I laughed to think of Lettice receiving him. I was sure she would be somewhat nonplussed. There were a great many rumors about her and a love affair she was having with a certain nobleman. Nobody mentioned the name of the nobleman in my presence, so I knew it was Robert.

I shrugged my shoulders. As long as he and Madame Lettice realized that he could be with her only when I did not wish him to be with me, I would accept what was going on. In fact I would enjoy showing Lettice that Robert was only at her service if I did not need him.

I became more and more certain of this when one of Robert's men brought up the suggestion that Essex should be sent back to Ireland.

I was amused. Get him out of the way again, I supposed. Leave the coast clear for Lettice and Robert.

Cecil, however, thought it might be a good idea for Essex to go back. He was loyal; he was not very bright, of course, but if he were given clear instructions he would not be a man to go against them.

As a result it was decided that Essex should indeed return with increased authority and to stress this he was given the title of Earl Marshal of Ireland.

He left in July. That was a year after our visit to Kenilworth. By September he was dead. He had died of a virulent attack of dysentery.

I felt a quivering of alarm. Dysentery was a disease suffered by many, which often proved fatal. Whenever it occurred there were suggestions of poisoning. Thus the sudden death of a man of thirty-five, who had been in excellent health when he left England, coupled with the recent scandals about his wife, gave rise to fresh rumors.

It was reported that a black cow had been born on the Chartley estate. Whether it was true or not I did not know; but there was a great deal of speculation.

Henry Sidney came to me and said that in view of the suddenness of Essex's death there should be an autopsy. I agreed but I must say I was terrified of what might be found and whom it might involve. Robert had been on the perimeter of too many mysteries: Amy Robsart, Lord Sheffield and now Walter Devereux.

I heard that Walter had died bravely, although he had suffered intense pain. He had written to me in his extreme agony and begged me to favor his eldest son. He also wrote along the same lines to Cecil.

I was very relieved when the post-mortem revealed that there was no trace of poison in him. I wished that I could stop thinking that there were some poisons which left no trace, and that Robert's own physician, Dr Julio, was an Italian who had a masterly knowledge as to the effects certain concoctions could have on the body.

However, the case was closed. Walter Devereux was dead and that little boy, Robert, who had made such an impression on me at Chartley, had become the Earl of Essex.

The Clandestine Marriage

MY POOR BURGHLEY RAN INTO A LITTLE FAMILY TROUBLE at this time. He had been rather flattered, I think, when Edward de Vere had married his daughter. It had seemed such a grand match. But Edward de Vere was a young man of very uncertain temperament and that he had too high an opinion of himself I had always known. He had been a favorite of mine—not the highest rank, but quite near it, for he was very handsome and such a good dancer; and he amused me. I had been delighted for him to marry Burghley's daughter, for I never ceased to be grateful and to appreciate the worth of my dear Spirit.

I sometimes believed, as I have mentioned before, that Oxford married Anne Cecil because he thought it would help to free his first cousin Norfolk, who was under sentence of death for his part in the Ridolfi plot, and when he did not succeed he was furious and vowed vengeance on Burghley.

Anne Cecil was giving birth while Oxford was abroad and out of revenge on Burghley, Oxford questioned his own paternity which was a great blow, not only to Anne, who was quite innocent, poor girl—but to my virtuous and strict-living Protestant Spirit.

Anne was heartbroken, Burghley was bewildered and he came to me at once to tell me the whole story. I tried to comfort him. Oxford was a wild and unpredictable young man, I told him.

When Oxford came back from his foreign travels, he presented himself to me. He had brought me some wonderful presents and these were all permeated with a delicious scent. There were elegant leather gloves which I found most acceptable and I said he must discover the name of the perfume, the like of which I had never smelt before, for I would have more of it. This he vowed to do and he was so charming in his manners that I could not believe he was really circulating lies about Burghley's daughter.

When I mentioned to him my displeasure in this he turned white with anger and told me that he would not take his wife back, nor would he own the child she had borne. I replied that to my knowledge Anne Cecil was a virtuous girl and I did not care for my good Burghley to be so disturbed as he was over this matter, and I insisted that Oxford should immediately reveal what evidence he had for making these accusations.

He replied that he would not blazon it forth until it pleased him to do so. As for the trouble the matter was causing Burghley, he preferred his own content to that of others.

I said: "I know that well." And I tried to dismiss the matter from my mind.

I disliked trouble between those who were dear to me and although Oxford did not have the place in my affections that Burghley did, I was sorry that there should be this trouble.

Anne Cecil had gone back to her father and Burghley found a great deal of pleasure in his grandchild.

Anne did after a little while go back to Oxford, and there were three more children. I used to hear of them from Burghley who took the little ones into his household, Oxford having no talent for parenthood but Burghley being a family man. I liked to hear him tell me anecdotes of his grandchildren and at least some joy had come to him through his daughter's marriage to the unreliable Oxford.

The days were passing so quickly that I was scarcely aware of their going. Another week, another month, and there I was a year older. From the time I rose to the time I retired I did not seem to have a moment alone. My life was a round of ceremony. Even getting dressed I was surrounded by women, and there was the ordeal of lacing and getting into those whalebone busks which accentuated the smallness of my waist. There was the ruff to be chosen, and not even my wardrobe women could tell how many dresses I had. I must look magnificent before I faced my courtiers and only twice in the whole of my life as the Queen was I seen by a man before I was fully dressed. The first time was on a May morning at Hampton Court where I happened to be looking out of my window because it was such a beautiful morning. I was in my nightcap and loose gown and young Geoffrey Talbot, Shrewsbury's son, happened to be walking below my window and looked straight up at me.

I stepped back in embarrassment and immediately took up a hand mirror. I was forty-five and well preserved; courtiers swore they believed I had the secret of eternal youth and looked like a girl of eighteen; they lied of course but I do believe I looked ten years younger than I was. My skin was as white as it had ever been and as smooth—it should be. It was well looked after. My eyes had lost none of their brightness, and because I was a little short-sighted they had a soft look, although when I was talking to people I would study them so intently that I appeared to be looking straight into their minds, which disconcerted them a little. However I was not pleased to be seen by young Talbot who bowed low and hurried away. I did not feel I could allow the matter to pass and when I next saw him—it was before dinner of the same day—I gave him a fillip across the forehead and I told the company that he had seen me before I was fully dressed that morning and I was ashamed to have been so seen. Of course Talbot said that he had been so blinded by my beauty that I had disappeared before he had had time to recover himself. All the same, I was put out wondering what he had really thought.

The only other time was quite disastrous. But more of that later.

There was no lack of devotion from my courtiers in spite of the fact that I was fast moving out of the stage when I could expect compliments, but perhaps because of it they were more fulsome and more frequent than ever. I loved my men—and I think some of them had a genuine affection for me. I was sure Hatton and Heneage did; and as for Robert there was a special relationship between us which nothing could alter. Men like Oxford never cared for anyone but themselves; and such as Philip Sidney were too inherently honest to be able to play the part of an admirer. I respected Philip for it but while I liked to have him at the Court—in any case I owed it to his mother and he was a favorite of his Uncle Robert's—he could never be in my immediate circle. Hatton was my Old Mutton or Bellwether. He was also My Lids. Robert was of course My Eyes—the most precious thing I had, and I always said he was continually looking out for my good. Burghley was in a different category; he was My Spirit; and Francis Walsingham, because of his dark looks, was affectionately known as My Moor.

Lettice Knollys was back at Court. I liked to keep an eye on her. I commented that she must be mourning her husband and feeling his loss sadly.

"Oh yes, Your Majesty," she said, lowering her eyes.

I thought: Sly creature! Is she up to some mischief, and with whom? Her attitude of mourning was not very sincere. She did not look like a sorrowing widow to me.

I said: "You must have been deeply saddened when you heard of Walter's death. It was so sudden . . . so unexpected. Poor Essex! He was not an old man, and he had so much to live for. I am glad it was discovered that his death was a natural one. That must have been a trying time for you. To lose a husband through God's will is disastrous enough, but if it should be by man's foul play that would be very hard to bear."

"Walter was a quiet man, Your Majesty. He had no real enemies."

"And not one to wish him out of the way?"

She lifted those beautiful dark eyes to my face with the utmost candor. "Oh no, Your Majesty."

She was one of two women whom I found it hard to get out of my mind. The other was Mary, Queen of Scotland. I imagined, although I had never seen Mary, that she had a quality similar to that of Lettice. It was an overriding attraction which I think most men found irresistible. They are of a wanton nature, I thought angrily, both of them! They want men as much as men want them. It is not superior beauty or skill . . . except perhaps in lewd conduct. But it is there in Lettice Knollys as it must be in Mary of Scots.

And in view of the rumors which had reached me about Lettice and Robert, I was particularly suspicious of her. What was happening between Lettice and Robert would be kept from me by those around me and the fact that some hints had filtered through told me there must be a great deal of it.

New Year came—always an enjoyable time of giving and receiving. My courtiers, of course, brought me the richest gifts—jewelery and garments, but I also had more humble presents from my household servants. For instance from Mistress Twist, the Court laundress, I had three handkerchiefs of black Spanish work edged with gold—all worked by her; and in addition she brought me four tooth cloths of rough holland wrought with black silk and edged with fine netting delicately worked with many colored silks. From Mrs Montague, my silk woman, I had a pair of sleeves decorated with roses and buds in black silk.

Philip Sidney brought me a cambric smock decorated with black silk work and edged with bone lace of gold and silver; it was covered with real gold spangles—a most delightful and acceptable gift. From my physicians I had pots of ginger and other preserves, and one of the cooks made a march-pane in the shape of St George and the dragon.

I had given Robert a doublet of white satin fastened with clasps of diamonds in which he looked very splendid. My favorite gift was of course his, not only because it was the most magnificent but because he had given it. That year it was a magnificent necklace of diamonds, opals and rubies. I wore it constantly.

Lettice brought me two wigs—one black and one red to match my own hair.

When I tried on the black one she stood back looking at me, her hands clasped together, all prepared to make the flattering comment.

I said to her: "I hear disturbing news about Lady Sheffield. I wonder what is the cause of her ailment. Do you know?"

"No, Your Majesty." The beautiful eyes were wide and her face a study of innocence. "I doubt not the doctors will have an answer."

"It is one of those mysterious illnesses which affect some," I went on. "They tell me that her hair is falling out and her nails dropping off."

Lettice shivered.

"No one can say what the cause of that is. And you know how ready people are to talk when others are beset by these illnesses. They begin to look around for reasons."

"Reasons, Your Majesty?"

"Well, it is possible that our meek little Douglass is being a nuisance to someone."

"She seemed a very mild gentle creature when I met her. Our encounter was brief certainly."

"I remember rumors about her at Kenilworth. Rumors about her . . . and one other."

In spite of her attempt at calm she was shaken. My suspicions that an affair was still simmering between her and Robert were heightened.

"I hope that Lady Sheffield recovers," I said. "There was that delightful little boy she had. He reminded me in a way of your young Robert. Another Robert, you see. What a popular name that is! And what of your son, eh? My Lord Essex now. I must give him his full title I suppose."

"He is well, Your Majesty, and with my Lord Burghley now."

"Yes. Burghley reports that he is a clever little fellow."

"He is certainly bright, Your Majesty. I am proud of him."

"And so you should be. You are young yet, Lettice, and a comely woman. I doubt your father before long will find a husband for you."

She was silent, her eyes downcast, but I did notice that the color had deepened in her cheeks.

"And how does this wig become me?"

I could see it hardened my face and added a few years to it. When one grows older one's hair must never be darker than it was in one's youth. Lettice had an eye for color; she was one of the most elegant ladies of the Court. She saw what I saw and I was amused by the tact of her comment. She said the black was too coarse for my fine skin. She added: "The golden red is ideal."

She was right. I made her get Robert's necklace and put it on me.

"Is it not beautiful, cousin," I said. "It is a gift from my lord Leicester. He always chooses so carefully for me."

She scratched me a little and I turned and nipped her on the arm. I had a feeling that the scratch was not accidental.

Lettice had an undoubted effect on me. I should have sent her away, and yet on the other hand I did enjoy tormenting myself with speculations as to a liaison between her and Robert.

As for Robert himself he was the same as ever—my devoted if unfulfilled lover, ever hopeful and able, at times, to hide a certain exasperation, knowing, of course, that negotiations for a French marriage were still going on and, I believed, casting lustful eyes on Lettice.

Sometimes I could be amused but at others I was quite angry; and in one of these moods I decided to play a trick on Robert just as I had when I had offered him to Mary of Scotland.

Princess Cecilia of Sweden was the sister of Eric who, at one time, had been one of my suitors. It had been said then that Robert had been bribed with the promise of marriage to Princess Cecilia if he could persuade me to take Eric. Those who put forward that suggestion clearly did not know Robert. It was hardly likely that he would consider Cecilia a fair exchange for me—for at that time he was certain that he was going to persuade me into marriage. Nothing came of that project and Eric went back to Sweden to meet his nut girl and Cecilia married the Margrave of Baden.

However Princess Cecilia visited England later and I was quite taken with her. She had very long straight fair hair which she could sit on when she wore it loose. She was at the time of her visit heavily pregnant and in fact actually gave birth here. Consequently I was godmother to the child.

She and the Margrave were a simple pair, and because I had made much of them on their arrival they had stayed too long, imagining that they could live at the expense of the country. They amassed vast debts and since they had no means of paying them, the Margrave was seized by his creditors and thrust into jail. When this was brought to my notice, I immediately paid his debts and he was released, but as he and his fair-headed bride were departing, her creditors arrived and seized her goods in payment of what she owed. So they departed penniless and it is easily understood why they were not very happy with their stay in England.

Cecilia was now a widow and as there had been a suggestion once that she might marry Robert, why not again? They were both free.

I would make my wishes known to Robert and send a message to Sweden without delay.

Robert was nonplussed.

He looked at me angrily and said: "Is this what you wish?"

To which I replied that he was very dear to me and as I knew he had aspirations to royalty, I thought he might acquire it through marriage with a princess.

White-faced, he strode from my apartment quite forgetful of the ceremony due to the Queen.

I could not resist teasing Lettice for if he married the Princess that would put an end to his frolicking with her.

I said to her: "It may well be that 'ere long we shall lose the shining star of our Court."

She hesitated and I saw an enigmatical expression flit across her face.

"I mean of course the Earl of Leicester," I went on.

"Lose him, Your Majesty?"

"Yes. There are plans for him to go to Sweden. You may have heard of the Princess Cecilia. There was a question of marriage between them long ago. She was held forth as a bait for him if he would further my marriage with her brother Eric."

She stood with bowed head, waiting.

"Knowing how he longs for royalty I thought this would be a splendid chance for him."

"Your Majesty is very kind to the Earl. I am sure he will be grateful."

"Grateful!" I shouted at her, and I picked up a hairbrush and threw it at her. "Grateful for sending him away! He is furious, poor man! He hates anything that takes him away from my side. When he is the husband of the Princess, I can scarcely keep him here, can I?"

"No, Your Majesty," she said quietly, picking up the hairbrush which she had managed to avoid and laying it on the table.

"I tell you this, my Lady Essex," I went on. "Robert Dudley is only a truly happy man when he is with me. The great desire of his life has been to marry me, and he is the only man I ever wished to marry. I do believe that if I had not vowed to remain a virgin, I might have done so."

She was silent and I dismissed her. She annoyed me standing there for I was certain now that Robert was not indifferent to her. I had to admit though that the manner in which she had received the news was very creditable.

The Princess Cecilia haughtily rejected the idea of marriage with Robert, as I had known all along she would.

Robert left for Buxton; he was suffering from the gout, he said; but I did wonder whether he merely wanted to get away from Court for a while. It was humiliating for him—first that I should suggest his marrying Cecilia, and then her refusing him.

I was sorry as I always was when Robert went away and if I thought he really was ill, I should be very worried indeed. But I did feel it was necessary to teach him a lesson now and then.

When he came back he was in high favor again as he always was after these little upsets between us. I wanted him to know that whatever happened that affection which had now grown over the years was too strong to be broken.

I was entertained by him at his house at Wanstead—a lovely manor house which he had bought some years before from Lord Rich. Robert had brought his special talents to bear in the house and had greatly improved it. It had a great hall with a ceiling painted to represent morning, noon and night and in which were statues representing Poetry, Music, Painting and Architecture. Exquisitely colored tapestries covered the walls and the gardens were beautiful with fountains and pieces of sculpture; and to make it more attractive it was surrounded by a forest in which deer abounded.

He had called one of the rooms the Queen's Chamber and this he had personally designed especially for me. The walls of this room were covered in some kind of tinsel material which shimmered in the sun's light and that of candles; and the bed curtains were of the same iridescent material. Knowing that this would appeal to me even more than the splendor of the furnishings, he had installed a little room adjoining the bedroom which he called a hot-house, because it was always of a higher temperature than the rest of the house, and in this was a bath, so that when I visited him I had no need to take my bath with me. There were no rushes on Robert's floors. He had carpets everywhere. He certainly knew how to make sure of comfort, and in his houses his first thought, it seemed to me, was how he could accommodate me when I visited him.

When Robert returned from Buxton I felt I had to be especially attentive to him. It *had* been rather unkind to offer him to the Princess Cecilia.

"Robert," I said, "don't be sullen. It ill becomes you. You know I only offered you because I knew she wouldn't take you. You don't imagine for one instant that I should have allowed you to leave me!"

He retorted that he would have refused to go even if the Princess had accepted him.

"Nonsense," I said. "You know you have always craved for a crown."

"Not a crown . . . only one woman."

"Dear Robert," I said. "You must take more care of your health. Why do you get this gout? Because you stuff like a pig. Look at me. How slender I am! Why do you think that is so? It is because I am not always concerned with what I am putting into my mouth. Eat sparingly and you will cease to suffer from gout, and if you will not of your own accord, I shall see that you do."

He liked to be scolded thus; and we were especially fond of each other for a while.

In spite of this frivolous side to my nature, it must not be thought that I was not deeply concerned with matters of state. I never forgot for one moment that I was the Queen of a great country. Even while I was dancing and acting in a most flirtatious manner with my men, I was having serious conferences with Cecil, Bacon and Walsingham on intricate matters of state. Robert, of course, often joined in these and believed himself to be something of a statesman, but he would never be a Burghley. I imagined that the difference was that Robert, being the man he was, must always think first of the advantage to himself. Burghley thought first of his country. I was the same. I loved my country. It came first. I saw my role clearly, and often when I appeared to be at my most flirtatiously frivolous I was most concerned.

Burghley and I were constantly considering the position of the Netherlands which gave us some anxiety. The struggle of that heroic nation with Spain was just beginning, for it was the aim of Philip to turn that essentially

Protestant country into a Catholic province. Burghley—stern Protestant that he was—believed that England should support the Netherlands heartily in their struggles against Spain, and the rest of the Council was with him in this.

Burghley was very lucid on the point. Our policy must be to weaken the power of France and Spain and to make sure that the Catholics in England took no comfort from them. We should help those who were fighting for liberty of conscience. "In the Netherlands they are struggling against the Pope and the tyranny of the Inquisition, which Philip is striving to set up in their land," he maintained.

I hated war, and I was determined not to put my country at risk by making it. War was costly and, I insisted, it brought no good to any . . . even the victors. I had no desire for conquest. I had my country, which meant everything to me. It was enough. All I asked was to keep that country at peace and prosperous, and I did not believe it was possible to have one without the other. It was England for me . . . and England only. I had not even the same feeling for Wales—the home of my ancestors—and certainly not for Scotland. It was the green and pleasant country around my capital city that I loved so dearly, and even when I went to the remote parts of England I did not feel they were quite the same to me.

Burghley earnestly pointed out the importance of the Netherlands, and although I saw the need to curb the power of Spain, I did not want to go to war on behalf of any country but my own. If any tried to invade England, then that would be the time to rise up, and none would be more fierce than I in the defense of my country; but the Netherlands was far away and the Netherlanders must sort out their own difficulties.

"There is one point which perhaps Your Majesty might like to consider," said Burghley. "If we stand aside, the French might not."

I saw the point of this but I reminded Burghley that while there was a possibility of an alliance between France and ourselves the French would not want to offend us.

"The negotiations for a marriage go on and on, and nothing comes of them," said Burghley.

"This much has come of them," I reminded him. "They have not broken down."

"True," he agreed, "and the Queen Mother suggests sending one of her ablest diplomats to plead her son's cause with you. To woo you on his behalf, she says."

That appealed to me. I should enjoy being wooed by some elegant Frenchman.

"Let him come," I said. "What keeps him?"

"Your Majesty, it will be necessary to treat the gentleman with some degree of seriousness."

"But indeed I shall. I have always regarded these marriage propositions with serious intent."

"Serious intent to refuse them," said Burghley grimly.

"My lord . . ."

He shook his head. "It would be a great help to Your Majesty if there were one to stand beside you and share your burdens."

"Are you suggesting, dear Spirit, that I am not capable of carrying them alone?"

"Never," he said. "But it would be helpful to you and perhaps . . ."

"Perhaps I am not too old to bear an heir? Come, Burghley, you deceive yourself."

"I would see Your Grace married to the man of your choice. And none of us has any doubt who that would be."

"Leicester!" I cried. "I tell you this: It would be unlike myself and unmindful of my royal majesty to prefer a servant whom I myself have raised up before the greatest princes in Christendom."

I had spoken lightly but I had raised my voice and there were others in the apartment, though not close to us. I heard the shocked silence, and I knew that there would be many to report to Robert what I had said. He would guess I was only teasing. Or would he? It was only a short time ago that I had offered him to Cecilia of Sweden.

"Come, Burghley," I said, "let us offer a warm welcome to this Frenchman who comes to woo me."

JEHAN DE SIMIER, the charming Frenchman who had come to woo me on behalf of his master, arrived in England and I was greatly looking forward to the exercise. Burghley, who knew me well, again warned me that I should have to take the utmost care. The situation with the Netherlands was tricky, and Walsingham agreed with him that it would go hard with us if either the French or the Spanish gained control there.

"The French will do nothing there while I dally with their little Duc through his proxy," I said. "This marriage is of the utmost importance to the Queen Mother. Did you know that one of her soothsayers told her that all her sons would wear crowns? It has come true with one exception. My little Anjou. You see how earnest she is in her endeavors to marry me to him. She would not dream of destroying the hopes of that prophecy's coming true . . . even for the sake of the Netherlands."

"Unless you propose to marry, Your Majesty must walk with extreme care."

"Dear Spirit, you must know that when I appear to step with little consequence I am picking my way with utmost care."

He bowed his head. He believed me.

I gave myself up to entertaining Monsieur de Simier, and what a joy that was! "I declare," I said to him, "I am fast falling deeper in love with the Duc d'Anjou through his proxy."

How graceful he was! How witty! He had all the social virtues and I had to admit that the French certainly shone in society. Simier could dance with grace; he had a deep knowledge of music; he was exquisite in his dress—less flamboyant than our gentlemen but somehow managing to outshine them in elegance without dazzling the observer only with the glitter of multicolored jewels. The compliments he paid were discreet and yet somehow tender and passionate and more provocative in intent than any I had received before. In fact Simier behaved like a lover—and the best sort of lover from my point of view; for this was a courtship which could go on as long as he was in the country, and I had no fear of an attempt to hurry me into a climax which might be detrimental to my dignity.

I could not have enough of Simier's company; in fact so successful was his visit that most of those around me thought that I intended entering into matrimony at last.

There were intimate discussions between the doctors and some of the members of my bedchamber as to whether I should still be able to bear a child and give the country the longed-for heir. The verdict was that this was distinctly possible. I was forty-five years of age but extraordinarily well preserved. I had all my teeth; my skin was white and clear; my face was unlined, and if my hair was not quite as bright and plentiful as it had once been, that was easily remedied. My ladies had some effective lotions and there were always false pieces and wigs to fall back on.

They were right. I was in the condition of a woman ten years younger than myself and although it was getting rather late for marriage, the verdict was that if I did not delay too long there might very well be a satisfactory outcome.

This was one of the most enjoyable periods I remember. I was being courted with charm, skill and a display of absolute adoration by one who clearly had been chosen for his abilities to represent his master. My own men showed clearly their regard for me and made it obvious that they were only in favor of the marriage because they believed it would be best for me; but the faces of those most near to me were melancholy during those days.

I asked Hatton what ailed him and he said he dared not tell me, at which I insisted.

Then he said: "Since Your Majesty commands, I will tell you it is because of this marriage."

"Oh, so old Bellwether does not like the French."

"I know," he said, "that this marriage would do good to the country." Then he raised his eyes to me with the most soulful expression and added: "I have to agree with the Council that it should take place, but when it does I shall suffer most dreadfully. Your Majesty fishes for men's souls and has so sweet a bait that none can escape your network."

I gave him a playful push. "It will make no difference to you, my dear Mutton," I said. "You will remain my friend as you ever were."

It was the same with Heneage. He raised his eyes to mine and said: "I know this marriage must be but it is hard for one who loves Your Majesty— even as the French Prince will, and the greatness of his kingly birth makes him fit to have Your Majesty it is true, but the love of this humble servant is no less great than that of the highest prince."

I replied with deep feeling that nothing would induce me to part with my dear friends, and no matter if I married the greatest prince in Christendom I should never do that.

John Aylmer, Bishop of London, may not have been able to express his devotion in such a flowery manner but he did so in a practical way. There was a great deal of talk at this time about plots devised by the Catholics, the aim being to depose me and set Mary of Scotland on the throne. In fact several waxen images of me had been found in the house of a Catholic priest in Islington. Such matters were promptly dealt with but they did give rise to concern and I began to be plagued by a nagging toothache, which grew so bad that I was unable to sleep at night and so anxious did my ministers become—they were always thrown into a panic at any disability on my part—that they called a conference of the physicians, one of whom mentioned a certain Anthony Fenatus who had a reputation for making fantastic cures.

"What if the man is a Catholic?" said Burghley.

"What if he is one of Philip's spies?" asked Robert.

"He might be a sorcerer," suggested Heneage.

Thus it was decided that Fenatus should not actually see me but should write a prescription which one of our men would make up.

Fenatus replied that he had no skill to produce an effective cure and if a tooth was hollow the only way to stop the pain was to withdraw it. However, if Her Majesty did not wish to submit to the chirurgical instruments,

the tooth could be stopped with wax which would loosen it, but care must
be taken that the wax touched no other tooth; then juice of the plant known
as fenugreek, which was to be found in Suffolk, should be applied. This
might loosen the tooth still more and make it easy to withdraw, for, he
repeated, the only safe way to be rid of the pain was to be rid of the tooth.

The method was tried without success. The tooth remained firm and
unbearably painful. My Council met and discussed the tooth as though it
were the gravest matter of state, which I supposed it was for the pain was
undermining my health.

Burghley implored me to have it withdrawn, but I was adamant. I could
not endure the pain of it.

Then it was that John Aylmer showed his love for me in a very special
way. He said: "Your Majesty, to draw a tooth is not as painful an operation
as Your Majesty thinks. The pain is sharp and short and to be preferred to
this enduring agony. I am an old man with few teeth to spare but Your
Majesty shall see a practical experiment on me for I would willingly give my
life in your service, so what is a mere tooth?"

Whereupon he called the surgeon and in a very short time one of his
teeth was pulled out. He uttered not a cry, but sat still holding a kerchief to
his mouth with a look of triumph on his dear good face.

After that I had no alternative but to submit to the operation and in a
very short time it was performed. Aylmer was right—a short sharp pain was
infinitely preferable to that continuous nagging agony.

Such devotion filled me with gratitude and I would never forget John
Aylmer's action and whenever I saw him afterward I asked him how many
teeth he had left and he would tell me with a smile and add that every one
of them was at my service.

I was fortunate in the men I had chosen to surround me. Years afterward, looking back, I often thought that one of my greatest gifts was an ability to sift the wheat from the tares. I had the greatest men in England serving
me, which was tantamount to serving their country, and I have never forgotten—and as I grew older this became more clear to me—what I owed to
these good and clever creatures.

Robert during this time was inclined to be sullen. His hatred of Simier
made me laugh. He said that the man was a poseur, a twittering Frenchman,
a man whose chief concern was the cut of his coat.

I replied: "Dear Robert, you dress rather splendidly yourself."

"I trust I do not mince and prance like your little French favorite."

I pretended to be annoyed with him and said that I intended to keep my
charming friend at my side, not only out of courtesy to one who came on

such an errand but because I happened to like his company and found it more amusing than that of some others.

I expected Robert to be overcome with remorse and seek a way of regaining my favor; but he was not and did not; instead he asked for permission to leave Court and this I peremptorily gave.

Rumors concerning the evil powers practiced by the French emissary persisted and it was believed that they came from the jealous Leicester; but the people in the streets were saying that I was being wooed by sorcery and that the Queen Mother of France was noted for dabbling in the black arts.

Realizing that such rumors were having an adverse effect on his courtship and guessing from where they emanated, Simier decided to have his revenge.

He came to me one day, his eyes sparkling with excitement which at first I thought was pleasure in seeing me. He took my hand and kissed it in that particularly fervent manner of his which so pleased me and said that his master was growing more and more impatient.

"When I write to him and tell him of your perfections, he is all eagerness to taste your sweetness. He cannot understand why you are so cruel as to keep yourself from him. Your Majesty, I beg you to say the word which will make him the happiest man on Earth."

I began the usual protest. I was an old woman. Our religions were different. My people did not care for a foreign marriage.

He lifted his hand and said: "May I ask Your Majesty one question. Is it because your affections are given elsewhere?"

I pretended to be astonished. "There are no other negotiations for marriage at this time."

"I mean one near to you . . . one of your own subjects. I refer, Your Majesty, to the Earl of Leicester. It is said that you are so enamored of him that he will always stand between you and any marriage that you might make."

"The Earl of Leicester has been my very good friend for many years."

"Yet he keeps secrets from Your Majesty."

"Secrets? What secrets?"

"Such as his marriage."

"Marriage!" I cried, taken off my guard.

"For some months, Your Majesty, the Earl of Leicester has been the husband of that lady who was previously the Countess of Essex."

"This cannot be true."

"It is a matter which is well known to most. Only Your Majesty appears to have been kept in the dark."

I cannot describe my feelings. That he should have dared! That he

should have deceived me so! Robert . . . to marry that woman! It was her
fault of course. She had captured him . . . worked her magic on him. The
she-wolf! How I hated her!

Simier was all concern.

"I should have broken the news more gently," he said. "I thought you
must be aware of it . . . as so many are. It is distressing to hear news of a subject's perfidy. Pray give me leave to retire and send your ladies to you."

I did not attempt to stop him. When he had gone and my ladies were
with me, I cried: "Send Burghley to me . . . Sussex . . . Walsingham . . . I
would have word with them without delay."

One of my ladies put a chair for me to sit in. She would have given me
a concoction to smell for she feared I was going to faint, but I pushed her
angrily away.

Sussex came with Burghley.

I cried: "Did you know that Leicester is married? He has married that
she-wolf whom I took into my care."

They said they knew.

"Everyone knew . . . except the Queen!" I cried. "By God's Precious
Soul, how can I ever trust those around me again?"

"My lady . . . Your gracious Majesty . . ." said Sussex, "the news was
kept from you out of concern for you."

"Concern for me! When those two scoundrels conspire against me!"

Sussex said gently: "It cannot be said that they conspired against Your
Majesty. They decided to marry, and they have a perfect right to do so. They
are not royal persons who need the consent of the Sovereign."

"They deceived me! They deceived the Queen! Let Leicester be sent to
the Tower at once."

Sussex looked at me earnestly and shook his head.

"Do you hear me!" I cried.

He said: "I hear Your Majesty, and I must tell you that you cannot send
Leicester to the Tower because he takes an action which he has a perfect
right to do."

I glared at Sussex. "You would tell me, my lord, what I must and must
not do?"

He looked at me steadily. "If I thought it was for the good of Your
Majesty, I would risk displeasing you."

There had always been something noble about Sussex. He prided himself on doing what he considered right. I could see that Burghley was gently
shaking his head; warning me that I must curb my anger. I must not let people see how deeply Robert's defection had wounded me.

Sussex was saying: "Your Majesty must consider the effect such an action would have on the people. If they saw how great was your anger, they would believe those evil rumors which were once circulated about you and Leicester. I tell you this because I am prepared to risk your wrath in my zeal to serve you well."

"And you, Burghley?" I said.

"Sussex is right, Your Majesty. You cannot condemn a man for entering into an honorable marriage if he is in a position to do so."

"They have deceived me all these months. When I was at Wanstead . . . even then . . ."

Both men regarded me solemnly.

"I will never have her at Court," I said. "I never want to see her evil face again. As for him . . . let him not think that he has escaped my anger. He is dismissed from Court. Let him go to Mireflore Tower in Greenwich Park and stay there."

Sussex sighed with relief.

The first shock was over.

I WANTED TO SHUT myself away, to grieve in private. I had never known torment of this intensity. I could not stop images coming into my mind. I saw them together . . . that woman and my Robert. And how long had they been deceiving me, laughing at me? How dared they! I would never forgive them . . . either of them . . . certainly not her. She should be banished forever. I was already beginning to long for Robert's company, to think how dull the Court would be without him. It would be amusing to command him to return to Court and let his she-wolf wait for him to come back to her, which I would make sure he had little chance of doing.

I called on his sister Mary. She was disturbed to see me in such a state. I could see her lips quivering behind the veil she wore.

I said: "The rogue . . . to deceive me so . . . to marry that woman. Devereux died . . . conveniently, did he not? And after all I have done for him . . . What would he have been without me?"

"Sir Robert Dudley," said Mary quietly, "member of an illustrious family."

"Many members of which managed to find their way to the block . . . through their own pride!" I cried tersely.

"My grandfather went to the block to appease the people who blamed him for the taxes imposed on them by your grandfather."

"Rogues!" I shouted. "The entire family. I should be thankful that I found out in time."

She said: "If Your Majesty will give me leave to retire . . . You will understand I cannot remain to hear my family insulted."

"You talk of insults. That brother of yours . . . he has taken everything and given nothing."

"He would have given his life for Your Majesty."

"Oh, Saint Robert! Lustful Robert who cannot keep his hands from a harlot!"

"Your Majesty is beside herself . . ."

"I would I were beside them. I would send them to the Tower . . . both of them . . . and imprison them in different towers. I would imprison them in spite of Sussex."

"Your Majesty is too wise to do any such thing."

"Wise!" I cried. "To trust those who have betrayed me!"

Mary was weeping silently and I found it hard to look at her, for even in such a moment I remembered all that she had suffered for my sake.

I turned away and went to my apartments where I shut myself in . . . alone with my grief.

The next day I heard that Mary had left Court. I wondered whether she had gone to him. They were a devoted family—those Dudleys; and they all looked on Robert as a god. They thought there was no one like him and so—God help me—did I.

Within a few days my anger against him relented. It was not his fault, I continually told myself. It was that she-wolf. She had special powers of sorcery, and what man could stand out against that? He had been seduced by that wicked woman.

I sent word that he might leave Mireflore for Wanstead if he wished. So he went and I suppose she joined him there. I heard that Mary Sidney was with them. No doubt they were discussing the fall of the Dudleys. Let them. Let them think he had ruined his chances at Court forever.

I took his picture out of the little box in which I kept it. How handsome he was. How well the artist had caught that look of distinction which no other man I had ever seen had possessed. I wept a little over that portrait. I kissed it and put it carefully away.

Then I plunged into an even more intense flirtation with Simier whom I affectionately called My Monkey.

I WAS ASSUMING a gaiety I did not feel to show my indifference to Leicester's marriage. Rumor reached me that Robert was furious with Simier for telling me of it as he had. Of course I should have had to know in time. I supposed Robert had been trying to formulate some brilliant scheme for breaking the news to me and making his excuses.

One day when I was on my barge not far from Greenwich, Simier came to join me there. We were laughing as we sailed along the river and the musicians were playing sweet music to the accompaniment of a boy singer. Whenever I passed along the river my people came out to wave to me and I never failed to show my pleasure and my gratitude that they had come to greet me. There were plenty of other craft all round for it was a pleasant day.

"The cheers, little Monkey," I said to Simier, who was standing beside me, "are for me and not for you."

He smiled and he said that he doubted the people saw him; all else would be blotted out by my dazzling presence.

"They see you," I said. "There is no doubt of that, but perhaps some of them are not very happy to see you. My people are not enamored of foreign marriages. I remember their feelings when my sister married into Spain."

"Ah, but your bridegroom will come from France, which is quite different from Spain. The Spaniards are so solemn, are they not? You would not say that of the representatives of France, would you, Your Grace?"

"Not of my dear little Monkey, most certainly."

Then suddenly in the midst of this banter the shot rang out. It had been discharged from a boat nearby. One of the bargemen fell fainting to the ground not six feet from where I stood.

There was shouting and screaming. The noise was great. Simier had turned very pale and was looking at me in horror.

"Your Majesty is unharmed," he said. "Thank God."

"It was meant for me . . ." I murmured.

"No, Your Majesty, I think not. I believe it was meant for me."

I tore off my scarf and gave it to one of the bargemen. "Bind up that poor man's wounds at once," I said, "and have him attended to."

Several people were round him and it was discovered that he had been shot in both arms.

They said afterward how calm I was. I could be calm in such moments. How different from the virago who had screamed for vengeance when she heard of Robert Dudley's duplicity!

The man who had fired the shot was shouting his innocence. He had meant no harm, he insisted. The gun had gone off by accident.

We returned to Greenwich and there I was prevailed upon to rest.

I knew Simier thought that Robert had made an attempt on his life, but I did not believe that Robert would have placed me in the slightest danger. He was too fond of me. I was sure of that. If he had married her, it was because he had decided that I would never have him and, wanton slut that she was, she had appealed to his senses. I could always pick out that sort of woman. And Robert was weak in that regard; he was, after all, a man. It would have been different if I could have taken him. Robert was not really to blame.

When they brought the man to trial he turned out to be a certain Thomas Appletree who swore with conviction that he had never been part of any plot and insisted that his firearm had gone off accidentally. He said he was in no way to blame for what had happened and if he had harmed his beloved Queen he would have turned the weapon on himself.

I intervened and said he should be pardoned for I believed in his innocence; and I asked his master to retain his services.

"Your Majesty is gracious and merciful," said Sussex. "There is a doubt and you have given this man the benefit of it."

"My lord Sussex," I replied, "I would not believe anything against my subjects which loving parents would not believe of their children."

This remark was repeated. Thomas Appletree, I knew, would be my devoted subject for the rest of his life, and the people loved me more than ever after the shooting on the barge.

Simier, however, continued to believe that it was a plot arranged by Leicester in revenge for his having told me of the clandestine marriage.

NEWS WAS BROUGHT to me that Robert was very ill at Wanstead.

"Serve him right!" I said. "He deserves to be ill. He is suffering from a surfeit of conscience, and I hope it plagues him for a very long time."

But that night I could not sleep. I pictured him, pale and haggard, on his sick-bed calling for me, begging my forgiveness, longing for me to speak a few gentle words to him. What if he did not recover? What if he were on his death-bed?

The next morning I decided that I was going to see for myself how ill Robert was. I sent a message to that effect to Wanstead which would warn the she-wolf to make herself scarce if she happened to be with him.

Wanstead was not far out of London and an easy journey. As soon as I reached the house I went straight to his apartments.

He looked very pale and wan lying there. I went to his bedside and seating myself, took his hands in mine.

"Robert!" I cried in dismay. "You are really ill."

I had half believed that he was shamming and had invented this to win my sympathy. I had put up some very good shows of delicacy myself in the past and it was not surprising that I should suspect others of doing the same.

He opened his eyes and smiled at me faintly. He was murmuring something and to catch it I had to bend over him. "My gracious lady . . . you came . . . to see me."

I was so worried that I spoke very sharply. "Of course I came. You knew I would. In spite of your folly . . . still I came."

I touched his forehead. It was not hot. Thank God, I thought, there is no fever.

I said shortly: "I shall stay here until you are better."

He smiled and shook his head with the melancholy expression of one who knows his end is near.

I was still a little unsure and I was really hoping that it was a pretense for I knew I could not bear for him to pass out of my life. It would be so empty without him and if he were shamming I was only glad that he had gone to such lengths to bring me back to him. I forgave him. Then I kept reminding myself that men were weak creatures and that the she-wolf was a sorceress.

"Now, Robin," I said, "you have been overeating, I doubt not, and drinking too much and indulging too freely generally in the so-called pleasures of the flesh. That is changed now. I shall look after you and my orders will be obeyed."

He smiled fondly and happily, I thought.

"Why, you already look better," I said.

"Of course I do. That is your healing presence."

I stayed with him for three days at Wanstead while I tended him myself and at the end of that time he was well again—apart from touches of the gout.

I spoke to him very seriously: "Robert," I said, "you are a fool."

He looked sheepish. "I know it well," he answered ruefully.

"You do not take care of yourself. You eat like a pig. Your complexion is growing very ruddy and you are too fat. I remember you so well when you came to Hatfield . . ."

"Ah, I remember too. I had sold my lands to provide the money you might need."

"And I made you my Master of Horse. You were not heavy then, Robert."

"We all must grow old . . . save you."

"I also, Robert—although I fight against it. It is a losing battle and time will win in the end. But I shall put up a good fight in the meantime and so must you, Robin . . . so must you."

"What should I do without you?" he asked.

"Very well," I answered tartly, "with your new wife. Very well indeed until the she-wolf shows her fangs."

He looked at me sadly.

"How could you, Robin? How could you so deceive me?"

"You gave me no hope. You showed your preference so clearly for the Frenchman."

"Robert . . . you fool! You know why, don't you?"

"I wanted a son. I could not go on . . . hoping. I had realized after all these years that my hopes would never come to anything."

"We belong together," I said, "you and I. Nothing can alter that . . . nothing . . . no one can come between us. Whatever happens, you know that."

He nodded.

"We have been through much together," I went on. "We are part of England. Your life and mine are interwoven. So will it ever be . . ."

"I know. That is why I could not bear that you should spurn me."

"You should have thought what my feelings would be before you took this disastrous step."

"You would not have me. You had wounded me deeply with that simpering Frenchman."

"You know why. You are a fool . . . a jealous fool."

"I admit it."

"I command you now to get well. You shall . . . in time . . . come back to Court."

"My dearest Majesty . . ."

I felt my face harden. "You . . ." I said firmly. "You . . . alone. I never want to look again into the face of that she-wolf."

So in a very short time there was reconciliation between us. I had accepted the fact that he was married; but I promised myself that Lettice Knollys should be denied the Court for as long as I ruled over it.

POLITICAL EVENTS WERE taking a serious turn. We could not afford to keep Anjou dangling indefinitely. The Treaty of Nerac had been signed, which meant that there was an end to the religious wars that had kept France busy for so long, and therefore the French were now free to take action elsewhere. We must be careful not to offend them. Our eyes were still on the Netherlands; moreover, the King of Portugal had died without issue and Spain was on the point of taking over its close neighbor, which would make it more powerful than ever.

"We must in no way alienate the French at this time," said Burghley. "We cannot go on putting off the marriage. Your Majesty must make a decision and if you have no intention of marrying, it would be better to go no farther in this."

"And incur the wrath of the Queen Mother and the whole of France as well as my little Anjou! Would that be wise?"

"Wiser than doing it later. So unless Your Majesty has decided that you will indeed marry, perhaps we should be considering how best to break off negotiations."

"This matter may be left in my hands. Let us make ready to welcome the Duc d'Anjou."

They were all convinced that I intended to marry my little French Prince. Simier was delighted with his success and word was sent at once to the Duc and the Queen Mother that I was all impatience to see my lover.

I was expecting the worst. The reports I had heard of him were not encouraging. I knew that he was disfigured by the smallpox for I had corresponded with his mother concerning remedial lotions. I knew that he was small and ugly. At Court they were asking themselves how I, who had always been so impressed by good looks, could tolerate such a creature.

When I saw him I was rather touched. It was true that he was one of the ugliest men I had ever seen. He was of exceptionally low stature and I admired tall men; his skin was hideously pockmarked—the elixirs, in spite of his mother's protestations, had been ineffective—and in addition to ruining his skin, the disease had worked its mischief on his nose so that it appeared to be split in the middle, and as it had from his birth been long, it hung down over his mouth. He reminded me of nothing so much as a little frog.

To compensate this he had the most beautiful manners I had ever known; he bowed gracefully and appeared to shrug aside his unprepossessing appearance as though he were unaware of it, and that made one forget it for long periods of time. His conversation was brilliant, for he was quite erudite, and to my astonishment I found myself enjoying his company. I was sure we looked incongruous together—he, so much smaller than I, looking up at me with that sophisticated adoration at which the French are so accomplished, and which made the compliments of my own men seem rather gauche.

So having been prepared for his ugliness I was not entirely displeased with my French Prince. I quickly christened him Little Frog, a term which amused him; and I had a brooch made in the shape of a frog. It glittered with diamonds and precious stones and I allowed him to pin it on me; and every time we met he would look for it and smile with satisfaction to see it prominently displayed.

My ministers were often in a state of exasperation. I dallied with the young Prince. I kept him at my side. I showed my pleasure in his company. Perhaps shrewd Burghley guessed that I was still smarting from Robert's behavior. However I prepared myself to enjoy the attentions of my little Frog Prince.

I never for one moment lost sight of the danger of the situation or that to offend the French could be disastrous for England. We had our spies in Spain and I was well aware what a deadly enemy Philip was. He had connived at plots to murder me; indeed he had given his full support to them. If he moved into the Netherlands, he would have no difficulty in bringing his armies across the Low Countries and from there it was an easy step to England. I had concentrated on the building of my Navy but I knew that it could not stand up against the might of Spain. Burghley had no need to point out to me that it was imperative that we did not affront France. If it were not for the fact that they hoped to see the Duc d'Anjou King of England, they might even attempt to land in Scotland, gather together disgruntled Catholics and march to free Mary of Scotland.

Dangers beset me on all sides and so much depended on how long I could go on playing the game of courtship with the Frog Prince, thereby holding the French at bay and giving the Spaniards qualms at the prospect of a strong alliance between France and England.

Even those ministers who respected my shrewdness and knew that I was as capable as anyone alive of playing a devious game, wondered how I could go on holding off my little Frog.

Fortunately this visit was to be a brief one of twelve days. Later he would come again, of course, and then there would be no excuse for delay—but I should have to find one.

My behavior with him—our tender gestures, our lovesick looks—those of mine no less than his—had convinced many people that there was going to be a marriage. Burghley, Bacon and such men in my close counsels knew that I was not going to marry, but the rest of the country believed I would. It was necessary that they should, for no indication must reach the French Court—and their spies in England were numerous—that my intentions were otherwise.

My subjects showed their great aversion to the match; and this was one of the rare occasions when I was angry with them. They seemed to think that I had been bemused by this ugly little Frenchman and that our union would be ridiculous since I was old enough to be his mother. As if I did not know that! They seemed to be of the opinion that I was a silly old woman who sought to be loved by a young man. And all the time I was pretending to consider marriage to save plunging them and my realm into war. Oh, I am not pretending that I did not relish the flattery, the extravagant manifestations of the great passion I inspired; I will not even say that I did not sometimes let myself believe in them. I had to, to play my part convincingly; and I did it for England. I never had intended to marry any man—not even

Robert; and that decision stood firm. At the same time I dared not let our enemies guess that I was engaged in a piece of diplomacy.

I was, therefore, very angry when a pamphlet was brought to my notice. This had been written by a certain John Stubbs, a Protestant and puritan, a learned young man who had graduated from Cambridge. His intense fear and hatred of the Catholics was apparent, but I knew that he was expressing the views of others—perhaps more influential than himself—and the fact that I was being so misunderstood and could do nothing to correct the people's views of me infuriated me.

The title of the pamphlet was *The Discoverie of a Gaping Gulf whereinto England is like to be swallowed by another French Marriage if the Lord forbid not the Banes by letting Her Majestie see the sin and punishment thereof.*

There was nothing disloyal to me in the pamphlet; indeed Stubbs's character emerged as most loyal; he had merely allowed his hatred of Catholicism and the French to overcome his common sense. He saw in the proposed marriage the very foundations of our country being destroyed and to quote him "Our dear Queen Elizabeth led blindfold as a poor lamb to the slaughter."

To hear myself described as a poor lamb led to the slaughter was more than I could bear. When I thought of how, since my accession, I had kept my country out of war, how I had served my people with unswerving devotion—and then to be thought of as a poor lovesick fool, for foolish a woman must be in her mid-forties to imagine a young man in love with her, splendid as she may be and ugly as he was—I was very angry.

I read more of the pamphlet which went on to say that I was too old for childbearing and to stress the state of health which prevailed in the Valois line. It was God's punishment on their flesh and bones for the lives of debauchery they had led. He finished by praying to Heaven to give me honorable and long sovereignty over my people with no ruling commander—especially the French Monsieur.

I could not accuse him of disloyalty to me, but his references to my age and the implication that I had been deluded, as some foolish girl might be, by the blandishments of a practiced libertine, set my anger simmering.

Stubbs, his printer and his publisher were brought to trial for publishing a seditious libel. They were found guilty and sentenced to that punishment which my sister had introduced when there was so much written about her marriage to Philip of Spain. It was that the guilty man's right hand should be struck off.

It was a cruel sentence and I deplored it; yet I could not control my wrath.

The printer was pardoned. He had merely printed what he had been given to print. It was different with the writer and the publisher.

I shall never forget that November day. It fills me with shame even now, and I knew as soon as it happened that I should have stopped it; I should have done so if it had not been for the ridicule I fancied the man had heaped upon me while I was striving all the time to do what was best for my country. Alas, my fury was not calmed in sufficient time.

So those two men—Stubbs and Page the publisher—were brought out from the Tower wherein they had been kept, to a scaffold which had been set up before the Palace of Westminster. There was a vast crowd to see the sentence carried out. I was sure that everyone in that crowd must have expected a last-minute message to stop the barbarity which was about to be performed on two good men.

But it did not come. First Page's hand and then that of Stubbs were struck off with a cleaver driven through the wrist with a beetle; and the wound seared with a hot iron. Page cried out: "I have left there the hand of a true Englishman"; and Stubbs said: "God save Queen Elizabeth." Then both men fell fainting to the ground.

When the news of how bravely they had met their punishment was brought to me, I was overcome with remorse for I knew that it should never have happened. I could have lost my subjects' esteem even more than I was in danger of doing through the proposed marriage. They might think me foolish to be bemused by an ugly little Prince, but they would still love me; they would feel very differently about an act of cruelty.

When I was furious with myself it was one of my less pleasant traits to try to blame someone else. I sent for Walsingham and asked him why he had not discovered that the pamphlet was about to be published. Did he have a secret service or not? How could he have failed to suppress it?

Walsingham was not a man to mince his words—unlike most around me. I think he was too sure of my need of him—as was Burghley. He more or less implied that he had known the pamphlet was about to be produced and he agreed with the sentiments expressed in it.

I was angry with him and told him maliciously that he should prepare to leave for France because he should be one of those whose duty it was to bring about negotiations for the marriage.

The next criticism came from none other than Philip Sidney. I could scarcely believe the young jackanapes had had the temerity to write to me in such terms. But he was a bold young man—quiet, serious and clever, and he was, after all, Robert's nephew. He wrote:

"How the hearts of your people will be galled, if not alienated, when they shall see you take a husband, a Frenchman and a papist in whom the very

common people know this, that he is the son of the Jezebel of our age—that
his brother made oblation of his own sister's marriage, the easier to massacre
our brothers in religion . . ."

I knew how strongly Philip Sidney felt about the massacre which had occurred on the Eve of St Bartholomew for he had been in Paris at the time. He was a Protestant and must have lived in terror during that terrible time, English though he was and therefore aloof from the quarrels of Frenchmen.

"As long as he is Monsieur in might and a papist in profession, he neither can
nor will greatly shield you, and if he grow to be a king, his defense will be
like that of Ajax's shield which rather weighed down than defended those
that bore it."

Wearily I tossed the letter aside. I wondered if Robert had seen it. Robert was against the marriage, of course. He would see his power greatly diminished if I took a husband. But you, my sweet Robin, I thought sadly, though back in favor will never be quite so close to me again now that you have taken that she-wolf to wife.

What should I do to Philip Sidney? I could not cut off his right hand.

The impertinent young fellow should be sent abroad for a while. I did not want to see him for some time. Perhaps in due course he would realize— as all my subjects might—that I was flirting so outrageously with the Frog Prince to prevent their being plunged into war.

WHEN I HEARD that Robert had a son my feelings were mixed. At first I rejoiced, for I knew that it was what he had longed for. What man does not want to see himself reproduced? Robert was no exception. I heard that there was great rejoicing at Leicester House and that a special cradle had been made for the child and it was draped with the most costly crimson velvet. It would be very splendid as everything was in Leicester House—and in every residence of Robert's.

I remembered when he had acquired Leicester House. It was about ten years before. The house was situated on the Strand and the gardens which ran down to the river were very beautiful. Many a time Robert and I had strolled among the flower beds to where the water lapped the privy steps and we had watched the craft sail along the river.

Then I imagined *her* there—the she-wolf—proud with the son she had produced. How like her to get a son! And so soon after the marriage! I could picture her smug, triumphant face with those magnificent eyes demanding admiration. And when I thought of her I was so angry that all my pleasure in Robert's triumph disappeared. *I* should have been the mother of his child.

I could have been . . . but at what cost! My independence! My sovereignty! They were my life. I could never have given them up—not even for the satisfaction Lettice was enjoying now.

And where was he? Was he in attendance on the Queen? Indeed not! He was preening himself as the proud father at Leicester House.

The Countess of Leicester indeed! I heard she gave herself airs. She had her own little court at Leicester House . . . at Wanstead . . . at Denbigh . . . at Kenilworth . . . wherever they happened to be. And how had he acquired his wealth and fine houses? Through his Queen. *I* had given him everything . . . and here I was alone . . . childless while that she-wolf sat in triumphant state.

Thinking of that newly born child my thoughts returned to another. It was at Kenilworth that I had seen that child who bore a remarkable resemblance to Robert.

Douglass Sheffield! What was that story? He had married Douglass, so Douglass was reported to have said. Robert, of course, denied that there had been a marriage. But there was the child.

Just suppose there had been a marriage. Then Madam Lettice would not in truth be Leicester's wife and the little boy of whom they were so proud in his crimson velvet cradle would be a bastard.

The thought soothed me. I sent for Sussex.

When he arrived I said I was a little anxious about Lady Sheffield. I had heard that she was suffering from a mysterious illness. What did he know of her?

Sussex replied: "Your Majesty need have no anxiety about the lady now. She was ill—mysteriously ill, indeed some thought that she might have been poisoned—but she has recovered miraculously and is now Lady Stafford. She married Sir Edward Stafford and they appear to be living very happily together."

"I am glad that she recovered, but was she not said to have made a previous marriage?"

Sussex knew very well that I was aware of the scandals concerning Lady Stafford. Naturally I would be, as they concerned Robert.

"Life has worked out very satisfactorily for her now," began Sussex.

"That may be, but if she were in fact previously married and her husband is still living, she cannot be married to Stafford."

Sussex looked perplexed and I went on: "I want you to look into this matter."

He was still bewildered. "Your Majesty will remember that the lady claimed to have been married to the Earl of Leicester."

"I do remember it," I said, "and if this is indeed true, my Lord Leicester must return to his true wedded wife."

"But Leicester—"

"He has gone through a form of marriage with the Countess of Essex, yes; but if he was really wed to Douglass Sheffield, the marriage to Lady Essex is no marriage at all, and if it can be proved that he was married to Lady Sheffield, he shall return to her." My calm deserted me and I shouted: "They shall live together or . . . he can rot in the Tower."

Sussex regarded me with dismay. I had betrayed myself, but I did not care. All I wanted was revenge on Lettice Knollys.

I INSISTED THAT there must be an inquiry. Lady Stafford must be questioned and I would be present at the examination. Sussex was against it. He was one of the very few men in my Court who dared go against me and he had exasperated me many times. I had raged against him, called him an idiot, told him he ought to be banished from Court. All of which he had taken with resignation; but when I called him traitor, he protested with righteous indignation and seemed not to care how he offended me. He was a man who would state his opinions no matter what such frankness brought down on his head; and I must respect him for that. He knew I would never banish him from Court. Honest men were rare and if Sussex lacked the brilliance of Burghley and Bacon and the charm of Robert, Hatton, Heneage and the rest, he was an honest man. I had not a more faithful servant at my Court.

So now Sussex did not hesitate to tell me that he thought I was wrong to raise this matter of Leicester's possible marriage to Lady Stafford.

"The Earl is married; Lady Stafford is married; and Your Majesty would do well to let be."

"I am the best judge of that, my lord," I said sharply.

"I think, Your Majesty, in the circumstances . . ."

I silenced him. He was alluding, of course to my well-known attachment to Robert. He deplored it, and as it happened he disliked Robert more than any man at Court. Robert's devious methods were abhorrent to him; yet at one time he had been ready to agree to a marriage between us because he thought I was so enamored of Robert that my happiness lay in such a marriage. I am sure that he was also of the opinion that any marriage was better than none and that with two so passionately devoted to each other as Robert and I were, a union was sure to be fruitful.

"So, Master Sussex," I said, "you are against this inquiry because Lady Stafford is a connection of your wife. Is that not so? Your good lady wants no scandal in the family!"

Sussex hesitated. There was an element of truth in that, he admitted; but his real objection was my involvement in the affair.

How involved was I in this?

"People will say that it is your anger against Leicester which prompts you rather than your desire to sift the truth—which can do little good now."

"Little good! Do you think of your wife's precious cousin . . . or whatever she is . . . do you think her reputation is of no account? I tell you this, my lord Sussex: There shall be no immorality at my Court."

He knew then that I would have what I wanted, and accordingly Lady Stafford was summoned and I listened while Sussex questioned her. He had succeeded in making me accept a secret inquiry, saying that if Lady Stafford proved that there had been a true marriage between herself and the Earl of Leicester then the matter could be taken to court. Of course he was right.

What a timid creature this Lady Stafford was! I wondered what Robert could have seen in her. When I thought of myself . . . and Lettice . . . strong women . . . women of personality . . . whatever could he have seen in this . . . mouse!

She looked half crazed and was certainly very frightened. She said that she was married to Sir Edward Stafford and it was a very happy marriage.

"But is it a marriage," asked Sussex, "if you are already married to the Earl of Leicester?"

"That was no true marriage."

"There was a time when you were pleading that it was," Sussex reminded her. "What has happened to change your mind?"

"I was mistaken . . ."

"It seems a strange mistake to make," I couldn't resist interjecting. "Do you mean to say you did not know whether you were married or not?"

She turned to me and fell to her knees, wringing her hands while the tears coursed down her cheeks. "Your Majesty," she said, "I thought I was married then . . . but now I . . . am not sure. There were those to say there was no marriage. I thought . . ."

I looked in exasperation at Sussex who began his relentless questions. Her meeting with Leicester, the sudden flaring of passion between them . . . he was irresistible . . . she had been a faithful wife until then . . . the letter he had written . . .

"What was in the letter?" demanded Sussex.

"That he would marry me when my husband died."

"But your husband was well, was he not?"

She nodded wretchedly.

"Then why did he talk of his death?"

"He . . . he said it would not be long before we could be legally married."

I was tapping my feet impatiently. I did not want a case of murder to be brought against Robert. I only wanted to separate him from the she-wolf.

"Where is this letter?" I demanded.

"I—I do not know . . ."

She told what I knew already. Foolish little creature! She had lost the letter; it was found by her sister-in-law and taken to her husband who left her and went to London threatening to divorce her, but before he could do so, he died.

"And when you were free, you married the Earl of Leicester."

"I . . . I think so . . ."

"Have you any proof?"

"I—I trusted him. He said we were married. It seemed like a marriage. Perhaps . . ."

"You must have some documents. There would have to be papers."

"I—I don't know. I have no papers. Oh please, my lord, Your Majesty, let me go . . . I have a good husband who cares for me. I want nothing of my lord Leicester. It was no marriage. I have no papers . . ."

She began sobbing wildly.

Sussex looked at me and said: "I think nothing can be gained by pursuing this inquiry, Your Majesty."

I was shaking with emotion, but I saw that he was right.

Lady Stafford covered her face and went on crying. "I know nothing . . . nothing," she murmured. "I can only say I trusted him. He said all was well. I don't know . . . I don't know any more . . ."

"The woman is hysterical," I said. "Go back to Sir Edward Stafford, Lady Stafford."

She was taken away.

Sussex stood before me. Much as he hated Leicester I think he was rather pleased by the outcome. His chivalry had been touched by the sight of that poor woman in distress.

I went back to my apartments. I was filled with a cold anger and the hatred I bore Lettice Knollys was greater than ever. She had won again.

But I will be even with her yet, I promised myself. She shall not hold Robert. His place is at Court with me, and that is somewhere you shall never come, my lady!

Father Parson's Green Coat

TWO YEARS HAD PASSED SINCE LEICESTER'S MARRIAGE.
I saw to it that he was constantly at Court, keeping my promise to myself
that I would exclude Lettice and separate the married pair as much as possible. This was not difficult, for when I commanded he must come; and as I
would not receive her, she must perforce absent herself. When I visited his
houses I gave notice that I was coming so that she could remove herself
before I arrived. I liked to imagine her chagrin, which must have been great.
I heard that she lived most splendidly, glorifying even Leicester's houses; she
lived like a queen, it was said. That gave me grim amusement. A queen in
exile, I thought.

I could not forget her. Whenever I saw Leicester I was reminded of her.
He was as devoted to me as ever, but sometimes I wondered when he was at
my side whether he would rather have been with Lettice.

Although he behaved as though his adoration of me had not diminished,
he could no longer talk of marriage; but he never gave the slightest hint that
he did not continue to regard me as the most desirable of women.

One New Year's Day his present to me was fifteen large gold buttons
and three dozen smaller ones to match, all embellished with rubies and diamonds in the form of lovers' knots; and enchanting as they were in themselves, there was no mistaking the sentiment they expressed.

I could not help asking him whether his wife had assisted him in choosing them. He answered gravely that the choice had been entirely his.

I thought angrily: Oh Robert, I know there had to be women, but why
could they not have been light love affairs such as you have had in countless
numbers? Why did there have to be this one . . . and with that woman?

But I did not mention her often and I kept him beside me.

In the autumn of that year I met a wonderful man whose exploits filled
me with pride and admiration. This was Francis Drake, a young man from
Devon. When I say young, he was about forty years of age, and it is significant that I was beginning to think of such as young.

He was the greatest sailor in the country . . . in the world, I would venture to say, and he had performed a magnificent feat in sailing round the
world.

Three years earlier I had learned of his intention to navigate the globe
and bring back treasure from far places. It was a plan which appealed to me.

I had always liked adventurous men, and had long realized that the strength of my country must lie in its Navy. We were an island; we needed special protection; so I had promoted the building of ships, and I wanted men such as Francis Drake to sail in them.

I could see that he was an adventurer—a man of daring with bold ideas and one who would not hesitate to carry them out. When the project had been suggested I had consulted Dr Dee, who had written a book called *The Perfect Art of Navigation*. It was clever as well as prophetic, and on his advice and that of Christopher Hatton, who was very much in favor of the scheme, I invested in it.

Hatton took it upon himself to manage these affairs and he himself invested heavily in the venture. This voyage of discovery appealed to me in more ways than one. The Spaniards were already probing the unknown world and I saw my country as a rival to Spain. If we could outwit the Spaniards so much the better, and if we encountered their treasure ships on the high seas, who was to stop us plundering them? Drake was the man to lead such an expedition. So with the financial investment he received, he fitted out his ship, the *Pelican*, for the voyage and chose those who would go with him. Before setting out he changed the name of the *Pelican* to the *Golden Hind* in honor of one of Hatton's heraldic beasts, for Hatton had made the voyage possible, not only financially but by helping Drake smooth over any political opposition there might have been. It was necessary to keep my good Burghley ignorant of the trip for he would certainly have raised all sorts of objections about the legality of maritime law. I suppose I was something of a buccaneer myself and that was why men such as Francis Drake appealed to me.

When Drake returned Hatton was beside himself with glee. The success of the enterprise had been beyond our most ambitious expectations. All those who had invested in the venture would share the profits, which were a four thousand seven hundred percent return on the original outlay. The hold of the *Golden Hind* was filled with precious stones and valuable articles, many of them taken from ships on their way to Spain. This was more than treasure. Drake had inflicted great damage on the grandeur of Spanish prestige. No Spanish ship had been able to cripple the *Golden Hind* and it and its crew had returned to port safely after three years of voyaging, and with enough treasure to make all its crew rich men.

The bullion was to be conveyed to a stronghold in the Tower. The Spanish Ambassador was furious. Christopher Hatton rejoiced and I said my old Bellwether had led me to a fortune. Robert and Walsingham both received four thousand pounds by royal warrant. Burghley and Sussex were the only two who refused to accept any of the spoils. Burghley had been offered ten golden bars and Sussex a service of gold plate. They both declined, declaring that they could not bring themselves to accept stolen goods.

I might have been annoyed with them, but I respected my men. I needed the upright ones like them as well as adventurers like Francis Drake. They all had their parts to play. I wanted all manner of able men in my service.

To show them that I had no qualms myself, I had a crown made from the diamonds and emeralds. There were five of these last which were of great size, quite three inches in length, and they made a wonderful frontage for the ornament. I wore it with great pride at the New Year's Day revelries and jocularly called Burghley's attention to my "booty."

The *Golden Hind* was laid up at Deptford and Drake begged the honor of entertaining me on board. This was an invitation which I could not refuse after such service as Drake had rendered to the nation, so I went there and on the deck of the *Golden Hind* this brave man was knighted and I allowed him to conduct me to the banquet. I was surprised to find that he was such a small man—I had expected a giant—but he was full of energy. He was handsome enough with large clear brown eyes and brown hair, much bearded and with a cheerful expression. He was clearly delighted with his success—and he had every reason to be—and it was pleasant to see how he reveled in the honor which he had won.

I sat beside him at the dinner, which was lavish. The sight of so much food nauseated me a little, but I made a pretense of eating and those who knew my tastes made sure when they could that I was served very little.

I talked with some of the men who told me about their adventures sailing with Drake. They obviously admired him and I was not surprised for there was a power in him, the quality of a true leader. I learned that he took artists with him to paint the coasts in their true colors, and how even in times of hardship he had been served at table with ceremony and that music was played to him while he ate. He was what a leader must be—strict and just and never asking his men to take risks which he would not take himself.

As a memento of the occasion he gave me a silver casket and an ornament made of diamonds in the shape of a frog—a nice compliment to my suitor.

I liked Sir Francis Drake. This was a man I needed, for the treacherous Spaniards could never be trusted to keep the peace.

MY FEARS OF SPAIN did not diminish after the return of Drake—rather naturally they increased. I knew that the Spaniards were my greatest enemy, considered to be invincible on the high seas. I knew that Philip was a fanatic as far as religion was concerned, and I had always felt that fanaticism in religion could bring about the downfall of a monarch. I had long since made up my mind that it should never be so in my case. I could never see why there should be these schisms, these differences. Surely it was enough to be a Christian, which simply meant following the teachings of Christ.

But there were few men or women who would agree with me. Religion was something they took very seriously.

Never far from my thoughts was the Queen of Scots who was still in England. I could never quite make up my mind whether she would have been more of a danger to me free than she was as my prisoner. While she lived there would always be plots about her. She was the Catholic figure-head. I had been constantly warned by men of such differing motives as Robert and Burghley that she should go. I had had my chance at the time of the Ridolfi plot, when the best of excuses had been given to me for bringing about her end. Yet I had shrunk from signing her death warrant.

None could know more than I the dangers I faced. My people were largely Protestant. They were Protestants by nature. They lacked that single-minded religious fervor which seemed to go hand in hand with Catholicism; they were tolerant by nature; they were always prepared to let things stay as they were, feeling, I am sure, that changing them might bring about unpleasantness. I understood them perfectly for after all I was one of them. Perhaps that was why we fitted each other so well.

But I must not forget that there were those who rebelled against the new order. We were a Protestant country not because I was a Protestant. I would have been ready to be a Catholic if that was what my people demanded of their monarch. The rites and ceremonies of the Church affected me little. My need was to give the people what they wanted.

My enemies were the Catholics and there was the Catholic Queen whom they were plotting to put on my throne. Before they could do so they must remove me—and consequently they plotted my assassination. The Pope had given help—financial and spiritual—to my enemies; there was constant plotting in various parts of the country and the Spaniards were just waiting for their opportunity. The French, too, had their schemes—shelved temporarily because of the courtship being conducted sporadically between myself and their little Duc d'Anjou.

And how important it was to keep that going! And how long could I manage it? For the answers to those questions I must wait and see.

In the meantime I must beware of Catholics.

New laws were made forbidding the Mass, and any caught partaking in it would be fined two hundred marks and be condemned to a year's imprisonment. Any who tried to draw my subjects from the country's religion—and this was aimed mostly at priests—were considered to be guilty of high treason.

I knew there were secret gatherings in various country houses. I knew that they kept their priests hidden in order that they could continue to conduct the Mass. In many of the old houses nooks and crannies had been turned into priests' holes into which the priests could scuttle at a moment's notice to prevent their arrest. What else did they talk of when they met in secret? I could not believe that it was only religion.

I would have been happier without these rules for I had always wanted my people to worship in a manner best suited to their needs and beliefs. The present position had been forced on me. Because of the implacable hatred of Philip of Spain, I felt it necessary to keep a watchful eye on Catholic households, and if any were caught breaking the religious laws they must be brought to trial.

Thus it was that Edmund Campion came to be arrested.

How fervently I wished in the years to come that it had never been necessary to do to him what was done. If only such men would keep to their learning, in which we all agreed they excelled. Why must they concern themselves with religion? Why could they not accept the laws of the land and do what they must in secret?

They had a certain nobility, those men, I granted them that. But they were fools; though it is true that in becoming martyrs they did more for their faith than they ever did by preaching.

Campion was a great scholar. I remembered him from when I had visited Oxford, for he had made a beautiful speech in Latin which had delighted me. I had asked about him and when he had been presented to me we conversed, he responding most gracefully and with the utmost charm. He went to Ireland where he wrote a book about that country; but it was there that he became so fervently Catholic and religion was the most important factor in his life. He had entered the Order of the Jesuits some eight years before and since then he had been in England as a missionary, whose great purpose was to turn people to his faith.

He was a celebrated man, a man much admired for his scholarship and nobility. Such men are dangerous.

He had, of course, been touring the country, staying in Catholic houses, hiding himself away in priests' holes when Walsingham's men of my secret service came prowling round.

He was caught eventually in the house of a gentleman at Lyford in Berkshire, betrayed by a man named George Eliot who had been a steward in one of the houses he had visited. Campion was taken with two other priests and lodged in the Tower.

Walsingham was sure that there were plots brewing all over the country and that the object of these was to kill me and set Mary Stuart on the throne.

He suspected every Catholic priest of being a traitor. I knew this was not the case and I believed that many of these men were concerned only with religion, but they could in truth be spies and I did see the need to scent them out.

Walsingham's method, when a priest was caught, was to draw from him the names of the houses he had visited, the intention being to keep a watch on those houses for possible plotters. The priests were often reluctant to betray their friends and in some cases they had to be cruelly persuaded. Campion was one of these. I was sorry to hear this.

"He has been racked," said Walsingham, "but even in the extremity of his pain would admit nothing."

I did not want to hear of this man's being tortured. I could not forget his young, innocent face when he had made his Latin oration to me. He was a brilliant scholar and I hated to think of such a man's being destroyed. Surely it would have been possible to reason with him, to point out the folly of setting such store in a few differences in the same religion. He might ask the same of me, but the answer was, of course, that I served my people. The majority of them wanted a Protestant monarch, so they had one. They had had enough of Catholicism during my sister's reign, and even though it was necessary now and then to arrest and torture men like Campion, who were fundamentally good, we were not inflicting on our people the horrors which were being endured under the dreaded Inquisition.

I would fight with everything I had to keep that fanatical institution out of my country; and that was why, if it was necessary to inflict torture on those Catholics whose aim was to introduce Spanish methods into this country, we must do so. It was nothing compared with what the Catholics were doing to those whom they called heretics.

I told Walsingham that I should like to see Campion and speak to him myself.

Walsingham was taken aback and said he would be afraid for my safety if such a man were admitted to my presence.

"Afraid of Edmund Campion! My dear Moor, that man would not hurt a fly."

"He is a fanatical Catholic, and Your Majesty knows that the Catholics plot to set the Queen of Scots on your throne."

"I do not think Edmund Campion will harm me."

I was so insistent that it was arranged that Campion be brought from the Tower that I might see him.

Robert was greatly alarmed at the prospect. "The man may have a concealed weapon," he insisted.

"He has come straight from the Tower, Robert. He has been grievously racked. I doubt he can walk without pain and difficulty."

Robert said: "I cannot allow it."

"And I cannot allow my subjects to forbid it, Robert," I replied.

He was on his knees, taking my hand and kissing it.

"How can you torment me so? How can I rest while you are in danger?"

"Nonsense!" I retorted. "And you can rest very well in the arms of your she-wolf. You have more to fear in that woman than I have in Edmund Campion!"

He begged at length to be allowed to be present at the meeting and that it should take place at Leicester House. I agreed, for that meant Lettice would have to move out and that always pleased me.

So Robert, the Earl of Bedford and two secretaries were present when Edmund Campion was brought to me.

I was horrified to see that once handsome young man; he now looked haggard and he found walking difficult. Poor man, they had treated him roughly on the rack. I felt angry with his tormentors and exasperated with him. He might have been leading a very pleasant life at Oxford.

I told him this and that it displeased me to see him in such state, to which he replied that he did what God told him to.

"Oh," I said sharply, "you are on intimate terms with Him then?"

He said that he conferred with God.

"You appear to think that none of the rest of us do."

"Oh no, Your Majesty," he said. "I trust all will pray to God and come to the truth."

"Then I will pray for you, Edmund Campion," I retorted. "I will pray that you cease this folly. I would rather see you as I saw you once before in Oxford using the talents God has given you than here like this."

"God has spoken to me," he said. "I do His work."

"And fine trouble that has brought you!"

"It is of no matter, Madam. What happens to my body is but passing pain. I look to eternal bliss."

"Which is reserved for those who worship in the way you choose for them, I suppose."

"I believe in the Catholic Faith," he said.

I could see that it was useless to try to reason with him. I felt impatient with him and yet he saddened me. I wanted to show those present that he was a good man, an innocent man; all he wanted was to worship in a certain way. If only the stupid man would do it quietly in his home! Why did he have to go round the country hiding in priests' holes, behaving like a criminal?

I said to him: "Do you acknowledge me as your Queen?"

He answered fervently: "Not only for my Queen but my lawful Queen."

I had known it. He was no traitor.

"Do you believe that the Pope could excommunicate me lawfully?"

He hesitated. He did not want to admit that he considered the Pope to stand above me in the Church for that indeed was against the law.

He said cautiously: "It is not for me to decide in a controversy between Your Majesty and the Pope."

I did not want to implicate him further because I feared he might go so far that there would be no hope of saving him.

If only it had been possible to save him I would have done so, but he would not help me to it. He was determined to be a martyr.

Shortly after he was arraigned with seven others at Westminster Hall. He was a brave and a brilliant man and he answered his judges with wit and distinction; but he was in a pitiable state and I heard that he was unable to hold up his hand when pleading in the required manner because he had been so brutally racked. The wretched George Eliot, who had been responsible for his capture, was the main witness against him and his evidence was proved to be unreliable. But Walsingham, stern Protestant that he was, was determined to allow no possible spies for Philip of Spain, no adherents of Mary of Scotland, to slip through his net. He wanted a verdict of guilty and he got it.

When Lord Chief Justice Wray asked the prisoners if they had anything to say as to why they did not deserve death, Campion replied: "It is not our death that we fear. We know that we are not lords of our own lives and therefore for want of an answer would not be guilty of our own deaths. The only thing we have to say now is that if our religion does make us traitors then we are worthy to be condemned; but otherwise we are, and have been, true subjects of the Queen. In condemning us you condemn all your ancestors—all ancient priests, bishops and kings—all that once were the glory of England. What have we taught, however you may qualify it with the odious name of treason, that they did not teach? God lives. Posterity will live. Their judgment is not so liable to corruption as those who are now going to sentence us to death."

Such talk could not fail to impress and inspire . . . and perhaps alarm . . . and people grow vicious when frightened.

I was deeply disturbed—as I so often was by the need to inflict death . . . I had not forgotten my mother's fate. I thought that Campion should not have been condemned, though I knew that, as a practical matter, Walsingham was right. I was in acute danger. The blow could come from the least expected quarter. I had to put my safety in the hands of my good and careful Moor; and he would allow no one the chance of harming me if he could help it.

I was glad that Edmund Campion escaped the final painful humiliation. They cut him up after his death, not before. What a concession!

I prayed for him that night. I asked forgiveness of God for my part in his death, and I took some comfort to know that he had left that poor tortured body of his behind him forever.

I knew that he was a good man, and I could not forget his bright and clever face as it had been when he had welcomed me to Oxford.

I COULD NOT keep Anjou dangling forever, much as I should like to gain more time. The situation in the Netherlands was even more delicate. That poor country had constantly asked me for aid against the Spanish and I had hesitated to give it, fearing it might involve my people in conflict. The French, however, had become very alarmed at the prospect of Spain's obtaining dominance there. On the other hand, they were a Catholic country and we were menaced by the Catholics of Europe who might join together to attack England. Fortunately there was a bitter rivalry among themselves.

My little Prince had always been a trouble to his family. His mother had no great love for him, nor had his brother; and it must have seemed a good idea to send him to the Netherlands to help the people against the Spaniards, since the last thing France wanted was to see a triumphant Spain. Anjou had flirted with the Protestant Faith, though he was no more stable in that direction than he had been in others. Therefore, why should he not go to the Netherlands independently of France—but secretly aided by them—and wage war on Spain?

This seemed to me an excellent idea. It was fighting my war for me and it was a state of affairs which I wanted to continue for as long as possible— as long as he was fighting independently of France, for to contemplate French domination of the Netherlands was even more alarming than that of Spain as they were closer to us and could invade more easily.

It was a very complicated and intricate situation and it needed the most skillful diplomacy. I must keep Anjou fighting in the Netherlands and he must be on my side . . . not that of the French. The French doubtless saw the marriage as bringing England back to Catholicism and obviously thought that when Anjou was victorious, they would join up with him and his victory would be that of the French.

I had no doubt that the wily Catherine de' Medici believed that she could rid herself of her troublesome son and win the Netherlands for France at the same time; and I had to keep her believing that that was what she was going to achieve.

But she was becoming impatient. Walsingham reported that the King of

France and his mother were exasperated by my delaying tactics with regard to the marriage; they were behaving in a very cool manner toward the English envoys and himself. Not content with complaining to my Council, he had the temerity to write lecturing me.

I smiled to think of what my father's reactions would have been to such a letter. Walsingham's head would have been in acute danger. But I understood. I respected my Moor. He was a man of courage and immense ability so I meant to keep his head where it could best serve me, even though it meant suppressing my irritation. There was logic in his reasoning and it did bring home to me the fact that I could not play this game much longer.

It was galling to see that my devious diplomacy was not always appreciated by my most able ministers. I had to play the part of a vain, coquettish woman—not so difficult for in some ways I was one—but they did forget that I was also an astute politician. When they came to look back over the past three years, they would see what advantage I had brought to my country by holding off the French while I could build up our defenses. I had plans, too, which might amaze them, for my little Anjou was a weathercock in his politics and I believed that he would sway toward whichever side could bring him a touch of glory. Poor little Frog, so unprepossessing, with a brother a King occupying a throne which he had hoped to get for himself, and with a mother who dominated her children and decided the policy of France. They would see how my plans for him worked out . . . if they would only be patient. But I must play the game my way and I could not yet explain to my Moor, or even to my Spirit. There must be no hint that matters were otherwise than they appeared to be, and if I was to play my part with conviction, I had to believe in the role I was playing.

It was agreed that Anjou should come to England again and this time there should be a definite decision.

Walsingham returned. "You knave," I said to him. "In the beginning you were against the marriage . . . none more so. Now you see it as inevitable . . . as part of an alliance with France. You are like a weathercock, Master Moor."

He was disconcerted but unrepentant. Men such as he do what they think right and no one—king or queen—is going to divert them.

I gave him a sharp slap on the arm and said: "You will see." But he knew that though I was displeased with him, I recognized him as a devoted servant, and his allegiance was even stronger because he respected me, though he believed, like the rest, that I had gone too far in this matter of the marriage. It was going to be difficult to extricate myself. I alone had to do that, and I was not quite ready yet. I had still to keep the French anxious and the Spaniards guessing.

When Anjou came, fresh from his victory after the relief of Cambrai, we welcomed him as the future consort of the Queen should be received, and so we set out to entertain him royally. We erected what we called a temporary banqueting hall in Whitehall which cost the amazing sum of one thousand, seven hundred and forty-four pounds, nineteen shillings, and we went to the further expense of putting the guests in luxurious lodgings in the area. I gave a splendid dinner party and so did Leicester and Burghley. The language presented some difficulty and Burghley produced some clever young interpreters, so that there should be no misunderstanding of what was being said and it should be clear that we wished to honor our guests. Among those clever young men was one who had come into prominence lately: young Francis Bacon, son of Nicholas and nephew of Burghley, who had already brought him to my notice.

We did everything we could to make this a splendid occasion. I wanted no one to guess just yet that I intended to break off the negotiations. All the finest furnishings were brought to Whitehall—pictures, carpets, plate, everything; and we had great entertainments such as jousting and bear-baiting as well as the banquets.

I had lulled the fears of the French and added to those in my subjects' minds. That could not be helped. There would have to be an understanding soon.

Anjou returned to France, triumphant, with plans to come to England in October—six months later—when all the documents would be ready and all that would be needed was his signature and mine.

There were rumors from the Continent. The French were growing restive. The Spaniards were secretly jeering. Delay, they said. Constant delay. The Queen of England does not intend to make this marriage.

Burghley told me that the Spaniards were gambling on it—one hundred to one against.

It could not go on. My ministers were very anxious. They had almost made up their minds that there would be a marriage. I was touched to realize that one of their main anxieties was that I might attempt to bear a child and endanger my life. There was no doubt that they wanted me to remain their Queen.

When October came, Anjou arrived at Rye. My clever Walsingham— the eternal spy—had arranged that prostitutes should be supplied for the French to make them happy. Not only did these women make the French happy, but Walsingham and Burghley also, because they came away with details of secret documents which gave us an idea of the French attitude. Thus we learned that if there was no marriage this time, there would be an end to the negotiations.

There was no doubt in the minds of my ministers that I had brought myself to an impasse and it seemed to them that there was no way out but through marriage.

I was as determined as ever to remain unmarried but I would not admit this . . . yet.

When Anjou and I met we greeted each other with great affection. He fell to his knees and regarded me, his grotesque face alight with adoration.

I stooped and kissed him, telling him that I had longed for this meeting. Robert was standing by and I noticed with pleasure that he looked very angry.

"Let us walk in the gallery," I said to Anjou. "I want to hear of your journey and to tell you of my joy in seeing you."

Anjou and I walked a few paces ahead with Robert and Walsingham behind when Mauvissière the French Ambassador came in unannounced. He made his way straight to me and said that he had orders from the King of France that he must without delay have a statement from me as to whether or not I intended to marry the Duc d'Anjou.

Here was a difficulty. What could I say? It was a matter of yes or no; and I was not yet ready for a no.

So I replied in the only way possible. I said: "You may write and tell this to the King: The Duc shall be my husband."

Then I turned to my little Prince and kissed him on the mouth, and taking a ring from my finger I put it on his.

Anjou was overcome with joy. He immediately took a ring from *his* finger and put it on mine.

We had plighted our troth.

"Come with me," I said, and I led him from the gallery to a chamber in which many of my courtiers were gathered. I told them in a voice which was audible throughout the room what had taken place.

The news spread rapidly. There was to be a marriage.

ROBERT BURST INTO my chamber. I had never seen him so upset.

"What are you doing here?" I demanded. "How dare you come in thus unannounced?"

He said: "I have just witnessed that scene in the gallery."

"Scene? My Lord Leicester, I don't understand you!"

This was how I liked Robert—all fire and jealousy. He could not be regretting a crown now since he was no longer free to marry. This was pure jealousy . . . for me.

"That . . . that *frog* . . ." he stammered.

I laughed and said: "Robert, you look as though you will explode. I like not that purple tinge in your face. To tell the truth it worries me. You will have an apoplectic fit one day, and none to blame but yourself. You eat too much . . . you drink too much. How often have I told you!"

He took me by the shoulders. Why did I allow such liberties? I suppose if one allows them in one direction one must in another. There had never been, nor ever could be, any relationship in my life like that I shared with Robert. I was happy now because he was jealous, because for a time at least he had forgotten Lettice.

He cried: "I demand to know. Are you that man's mistress?"

I laughed at him and he shook me. I was too astounded to answer for a few moments. Then I remembered my dignity.

"My lord Leicester," I said, "you take great liberties with me. Perhaps I have favored you too much and you have grown to believe you possess powers . . . even over me. You are mistaken, my lord. I could send you to the Tower in five minutes. Take your hands from me at once."

He obeyed and stood looking at me, the anger still in his face.

"Are you that man's mistress?" he repeated, almost pleadingly.

"My lord Leicester," I said with great dignity, "I am the mistress of you all."

He looked so distressed. He could not bear to think that I had given to another that which I had always denied him. He could always soften me. It was only when he was absent that I could be really angry with him.

"Robert," I said, "I have promised myself that I shall go to my grave a virgin. I still intend to do that."

He took my hand and kissed it then and I touched the dark curling hairs at the back of his neck as he did so.

I said gently: "You may go now."

I COULD SEE now that the farce was at an end. The French had ceased to help Anjou in the Netherlands, so the situation was changing. I would have to come out in the open. A few days after the scene in the gallery, I arose and declared to my ladies that I had had a sleepless night, which was true, for I was deeply anxious as to how I was going to plan the next scene.

When the Duc came to me, I said that I thought I could not endure another night like that through which I had just passed. I had been torn by my emotions and I was going to make the biggest sacrifice a woman had ever made. "I shall give up the thought of marriage for the sake of my people," I added.

He was dumbfounded and did not know what to say for a few moments. I could understand his confusion. I went on to say that I knew that if I married I would not live more than a few months. My people needed me and for their sakes I would not marry.

It was all such nonsense. No wonder he was bewildered, but when he realized that I meant what I said, he burst into tears and cried out that he would rather we were both dead than not married.

"My dear little Frog," I replied, "you must not threaten a poor old woman in her kingdom."

He said: "I meant no harm to your blessed person but I would rather be cut in pieces than not marry you and so be laughed at by the world."

So that was it. He feared ridicule.

"Alas, alas," I consoled him. "My heart is yours, little Frog, and now it is broken. But I am a queen and must do my duty."

"But it has gone too far. Your people know. They accept . . ."

"I know, little one. Leave this to me. My dear little Prince, how can I let you go?"

Perhaps I went too far for the purple color flooded his angry face. Never had he looked more grotesque; and now there was real misery on his ugly little face; he looked like a poor little frog who has been turned out of a very pleasant pond.

Tears welled up in his eyes and fell down his pitted cheeks. I took a kerchief from my waist and mopped his eyes.

"There! You are a great commander, remember. You will know great glory. I am sure of it."

In a fit of temper he took off the ring which I had given him and threw it onto the ground.

"English women are like their weather," he said bitterly. "They are all smiles one day and rain the next."

Poor little man. He was indeed put out.

I must be careful, though. I still had to think of a French alliance with Spain.

I continued to wipe his eyes, for the tears were still running down his cheeks. Tears of rage, I noted. Poor little Anjou, his mother would say, once again he has failed.

I said: "Perhaps this is not final . . ."

Hope leaped into his eyes. Could I really keep him dangling a little longer? If I could do that and keep him fighting in the Netherlands, the French and Spaniards would not form an alliance. Was it possible?

He looked a little hopeful. He was clutching at hope, anything rather than to appear to the world as the rejected one.

It would offer him small comfort to know that I had never intended to take him. I had played my part so successfully that I had deluded him into thinking that I would.

"We will talk later," I said.

Then he left me, his tears dried and a new hope in his heart.

BURGHLEY, WALSINGHAM AND THE rest were amazed at what I had done. Robert was secretly amused, and not surprised, I think. Perhaps he had known me better than the others.

"I have given him hope," I said.

"He will never believe that again."

"Perhaps not. But we have to help the little man to regain his self-respect. Let me see the settlements you have drawn up."

I took them and said: "There is one clause which must be added. The French must return Calais."

"They will never do that!" cried Hatton aghast.

"Assuredly they will not. That is why I shall demand it. Only the return of Calais will induce me to go on with the marriage."

"They would never let us back on their territory even for marriage."

"Exactly so. That is why we make this a necessary condition. We have kept Anjou in the Netherlands; we have delayed an agreement between France and Spain; and we have gained important time. Our ships are being built in our dockyards. The prospect of that French marriage has served us well. I should have liked to go on with negotiations a little longer, which would have served us even better. But the end is in sight. However, let us be grateful for the help it has given us."

They were astounded, but I saw the respect in their faces.

Burghley said solemnly: "The people of this country will know one day that their greatest ruler was Elizabeth."

"In the meantime," I said, "I shall be very happy with their affection. I believe there is rejoicing in the streets now because the news has leaked out that I have refused the French marriage. No, I do not wish my little Frog Prince to suffer too deep a humiliation. I was in fact quite fond of the little fellow. He was amusing and some of you would do well to learn from his gracious manners. So I am going to offer him money to continue the struggle in the Netherlands. They need help against the Spaniards. They have asked us for it again and again. Well, we will help them through Anjou, and my little Prince can fight our battles for us."

They were further surprised but I could see the excitement in their faces.

"It will have to be decided how much we can give him. It will have to be substantial. As you know, I am not in favor of Englishmen fighting wars—but I fully approve of others doing it for them."

I was delighted by the admiration I saw in their eyes . . . admiration and pride . . . in me, their Queen.

I looked at Robert, and he was smiling at me.

IT WAS LESS difficult than I had imagined it to be to placate my little Frog.

"Why," I said, "you have shown us all what a brilliant commander you are."

I looked at him sharply. Was that too blatant? He had often shown that that was the last thing he had proved himself to be. He swallowed it. He was thinking of his one success at Cambrai.

"My dear little Frog," I went on, "you are going to prove yourself even more. You will subdue the Spaniards in the Netherlands and come back to us a hero."

He was already seeing himself fêted, riding through the streets of London—a conquering hero. And finally, I should marry him after all and he would be able to laugh in the faces of both his brother and his mother. King of England! I was sure he could feel the crown already on his head.

"I have talked over this matter with my Council and it has been agreed that you shall have sixty thousand pounds—half within fifteen days of leaving and the other half fifty days after that."

He seemed delighted, and we smiled and chatted together, resuming our old relationship.

He lingered though and as I was eager for him to go, and realized that he lacked the funds to start, I arranged that he should be given £10,000 at once.

"Now there is nothing to hold you back," I said. "And I am going to send you an escort, at the head of which shall be the finest man in my kingdom."

They all knew who that was.

"And I myself shall accompany you to Canterbury," I added.

And so departed my little Duc. I rode between him and Robert on the way to Canterbury. Robert looked magnificent. He always did on such occasions. He loved the pomp and glitter. What a king he would have made!

The people came out to cheer as we went along. I smiled and waved. They were expressing their delight in the departure of my suitor.

I wondered if there would be another. Regretfully I doubted it. The game of courtship had always fascinated me. I enjoyed every minute because always at the end there was escape. It was the journey which was appealing, never the arrival. I wondered whether Robert and Lettice were as delighted with each other as they had been in the beginning. He must have thought a great deal of her to marry her and risk my wrath.

I smiled secretly. He would not be seeing her for a little while. She would know that he was riding beside me to Canterbury because I had selected him for the task of escorting Anjou. How she must be longing to come to Court! Go on longing, Lettice, I thought, I will never give you that satisfaction.

The time had come to say farewell and I embraced Anjou with a show of tenderness.

I said: "I would give a million pounds to have my little Frog swimming in the Thames."

To which he replied that he would come back with honors, and when he did there should be a marriage.

I sent for Robert.

"Now, my lord," I said, "you must take good care not to offend me as you have done of late."

He looked bewildered and asked in what way he had offended me.

"By not taking care of yourself. I watched you at dinner. You could scarcely get rid of the food in your mouth before you were shoveling in the next mouthful. You eat like a pig. You drink too much. Robert Dudley, I will not have it."

"My sweet lady . . ." he began.

"There will be no sweetness from me if you do not take better care of yourself. And I tell you this, if I hear of any disorder attacking you, I shall blame you for it."

His eyes looked yearningly at me in a manner which I knew so well and I said gently: "Robin, take care."

The cavalcade rode on to Dover, and when I heard that the Duc d'Anjou had set sail I went to my apartments and laughed aloud.

Hearing my laughter, two of my women came in and I seized them both and danced round the chamber with them.

I had to rejoice. I had come out of a dangerous situation very well indeed.

BUT I WAS NOT really satisfied until Robert was safely back.

Burghley came to tell me that he had seen him.

"And how looked he?" I said.

"In good health and high spirits, Your Majesty."

"I am glad."

"He said he left Anjou like an old hulk run ashore high and dry stuck in a sandbank."

"And he thought that amusing, did he?"

"He thought the Duc was rather ridiculous."

I said coldly: "My Lord Leicester gives himself airs and is pleased to laugh at his betters. He is a traitor like all his horrible family."

Burghley did not comment. He knew that whatever I said of Robert was said in affection; and no one would be allowed to criticize him in my hearing no matter what *I* said about him.

I went on: "This has been a costly matter, eh . . . this ridding ourselves of this suitor of mine?"

"Your Majesty," said Burghley, "we have paid a good price, but when we consider, I think we shall decide that what we paid was cheap for what we have gained."

I smiled and nodded and I thought: I will send for Robert and hear his version of the journey; and the prospect of seeing Robert always put me in a good mood.

IT NOW SEEMED clear to both Robert and me that whatever happened the bonds which held us together would never be broken; they might slacken or become frayed; but the relationship between us was different from any either of us had with another person. It was deep affection, I was sure; it had always been passionate and romantic, and all the more lasting because it had never reached what people called fulfillment. How many people fall madly in love and find their passion fading when their senses become satiated? Our affection had been kept constantly in flower because we had never allowed it to wither through excess. Was he as devoted to Lettice as he had been when he married her? I was sure he could not be; when I sent for him he came with such alacrity.

He had offended me never so much as he had by his marriage. With anyone else it would have been the end. Not with Robert. There could only be one ending to my love for him and that was Death.

Robert believed entirely in himself. Since I had shown that my affection for him was unimpaired, he had become more egotistical, more self-seeking, even more ambitious. If he had not been so, I doubted whether I should have admired him as I did. Robert never gave up. He had failed to marry me and in desperation had at last turned to Lettice. He had wanted his son to be heir to the throne, but he had had to make do with Lettice's child instead of mine. But he still had plans, and when I heard what those plans were I was almost as overcome with rage as I had been when I heard of his marriage.

Sussex told me of them. Trust Sussex. He never failed to bring me notice of anything concerning Robert which he thought would weaken my regard for him. He need not have bothered. I knew my Robert better than anyone else did.

Sussex said: "I trust my lord Leicester has consulted Your Majesty regarding the arrangements for the marriages in his family."

"Arrangements," I gasped. "What arrangements?"

"Those of his son and his stepdaughter."

"That baby! And his stepdaughter. Wasn't she married a little while ago to Lord Rich?"

"That was Penelope, the elder daughter, Your Majesty."

"A saucy wench, that one. She has something of her mother in her. A wanton brood . . . all of them. She was after young Philip Sidney at one time. He wrote some verses for her. Then she married Rich and young Sidney turned to Walsingham's girl. What marriages do you speak of?"

"There is another daughter—Dorothy. And Leicester is sending out feelers to Scotland to James, for he fancies a match between his stepdaughter Dorothy and Mary of Scotland's son."

I was dumbfounded. Dorothy Devereux! That she-wolf's cub to be Queen of Scotland! Aye, and if some would have it, Queen of England! What was Robert thinking of? He must be mad to think I would ever agree to that!

"I thought Your Majesty should know of my lord Leicester's ambitions. Moreover he suggests Arabella Stuart for his son."

"I find this impossible to believe," I said. "I always knew my lord Leicester had pretensions to grandeur. Send for him without delay."

Robert came, all eagerness. The rascal could not know that I had heard of his latest schemes, or perhaps he thought I was so besotted with him that I would agree to them. I admitted to myself that I must have given him grounds for believing that. After my initial rage, I had accepted his marriage and the only consequence of that was the banishment of Lettice Knollys from Court. Yes, I could see that Robert believed he could act in whatever way he fancied and still keep my affection. He had a lesson to learn.

When he saw my face he paused for I was glowering at him.

"So, my lord Leicester," I said, "you are making plans to advance your wife's family."

He was a little taken aback. How long, I wondered, had he been working in the dark to bring about these marriages behind my back? That made the whole project even worse. It was deceitful. He was a wicked man, my Robert.

"I . . . er . . . thought there was no harm . . . Of course my son is but a baby yet . . ."

"Royal princes are often betrothed in their cradles and grand alliances are made for them," I cried. "It is a pretty pass when plans are made for royal marriages and kept in secret from the only one who could give permission for them to take place. You have too high an opinion of yourself, Robert Dudley. You and that she-wolf give yourselves too many airs. How dare you seek to set your son on the throne!"

"Your Majesty, I never thought for one moment—"

"You never thought for one moment! You would marry your son to Arabella Stuart. I can see how your mind works, my lord. Arabella Stuart, daughter of Charles Stuart, whose brother Darnley married Mary of Scotland. Arabella's father is the grandson of my father's sister. Royal connections, eh? Claims to the throne. And born English too. The English like an English Queen, do they not? Just in case James Stuart does not reach the throne, Arabella might. Two chances . . . Dorothy Devereux for James—your stepdaughter, no less—and your son for Arabella. What reasoning, Robert! Two lines to success. But first of all the old lady has to die . . . or to be put out. What are your plans for that, master plotter?"

Robert had turned pale.

"How can you talk so? You know that if aught happened to you, my very desire for living would be at an end."

"I should not let that trouble you, Robert Dudley. You would have your she-wolf to comfort you . . . and her cubs all bringing you close to the throne."

He said: "It was merely an idea. When one has responsibilities to others, one has to seek the best for them."

"Oh yes, indeed. I tell you this: I will see that no such glory comes to your wife . . . through her cubs. You will regret the day you married her. Her daughter is like her . . . leading Philip Sidney on to write poems about her and then to marry Rich . . . I suppose because he lived up to his name."

"She married Rich most reluctantly," said Robert.

"Oh? Had she her eyes on James of Scotland?"

"You misjudge her."

"Poof! I am glad Philip Sidney is having Walsingham's girl and not marrying into that breed. That must be a comfort for your sister. And as for your plans, they are at an end. Do you understand?"

"They had not gone very far. Just an idea . . ."

"Robert Dudley, I advise you to curb your ideas. They could carry you into trouble."

He did not speak and as always when he was downcast I was sorry for him.

I had already made up my mind that the suggestions for these grand marriages had come from her not him. After all, they were for the glorification of her children.

I dismissed him, pretending to be angry with him, but after a few days he was back; and it was as though that incident had never happened.

I SUFFERED A sad loss that year. I had a great affection for my men, and although it was a different kind of love I had for some than for others, my feelings went deep. Sussex was a man I had admired; he was not exactly in the courtier class; there had never been any frivolous flirtation with him, but I had respected him. He lacked the brilliance of men like Burghley and Bacon, nor had he the astuteness of Walsingham; he lacked the charm of Robert, Hatton and Heneage and such. But he was a good man—a man of high principles. Many were the differences I had had with him, but I respected him for that. He had been ill for some time and I hated illness. It frightened me. They all knew this and did not speak of it in my presence— except in the case of Robert, who used it to extricate himself from difficult situations. That was different. Real illness was a depressing subject and because those about me knew how I felt regarding it, they behaved as though it did not exist.

I had seen Sussex laboring to get his breath and trying to pretend this was not so. I had insisted on one occasion that he go to the baths at Buxton, and he had gone. He had hated leaving Court, partly because he believed that, without anyone to curb him, Leicester would be more powerful than ever.

He loathed Leicester and greatly deplored my devotion to him. Like most upright and somewhat self-righteous men, Sussex imagined that others were worse than they were. He saw himself as an honest man, a man who would put his life at risk rather than act against his principles. While I respected such attitudes I often distrusted the men who held them. They grew into fanatics, and I had found that those who set themselves up as of impregnable virtue could often be much more cruel than those who suffered from ordinary human frailties. I knew Robert was ambitious, greedy, self-seeking, devious, ruthless and perhaps even capable of murder. But he was still the most exciting and attractive man I had ever known.

Understanding them all, seeing clearly into their minds and not being of a very upright nature myself—except perhaps where my country was concerned—I could forgive men their foibles and love them none the less for them. I was as good a statesman as any of my men, but in addition I possessed a certain insight which was entirely feminine. It was not merely intuition—but that might have been part of it; it was an immense interest in people, which most men lack. They are too absorbed in themselves to bother much with other people's motives. Women want to know what is going on; they are insatiably curious. This gives my sex that extra knowledge of how people's minds work; it helps us to assess how they will act in certain circumstances. I had this quality in excess; I was entirely female; but at the same time I could grapple with state matters as skillfully as my most able councilors. Since I could bring to problems my feminine flexibility and did not mind a little not-always-honest juggling, I was more fitted to rule my country than any of my men would have been, clever though they were. I owed this to the fact that I picked my advisers with skill; I understood them; I accepted their foibles; and I gave them my loyalty, which is the best way of getting that most essential gift in exchange.

Another fact was that I loved them all. They were my men and my children. They knew this and because in every man there is a desire for a mother figure . . . I was that too. I scolded them as though they were my wayward children, and they loved me for it. Even to those who looked upon me as a mistress—by which I mean a lover—I was a mother too. I looked to their health and when any one of them was ill that gave me great concern, which was what I felt for dear old Sussex at this time. He was fifty-seven years old—not so much older than I, seven years to be precise. A sobering thought.

Then came the day when I was asked to visit him at his home in Bermondsey. I went at once and was deeply grieved to see how ill he was.

I took his hand and he tried to kiss mine but I would not let him exert himself. "No, my dear friend, I forbid it. You must rest. Save your breath. That is your Queen's command."

"My lady," he said, "my joy in life has been to serve you."

"I know it well," I told him. "I want you to do something more for me. I want you to get up from this sick-bed and come back to Court."

He shook his head. "I shall never rise from this bed, Your Majesty."

"You are too young to die."

"I have grown old in your service."

"Come, Thomas Radcliffe, we both grow old. But I am not so old yet that I can dispense with your services."

"I have long felt death close to me, Your Majesty," he said, "and my greatest regret in leaving this life is that I may no longer serve you. I shall leave the Court to others . . ."

I shook my head. He looked so mournful that I knew he was thinking of Leicester who he thought had an evil influence over me; and yet when I had been incensed by Robert's marriage and had declared my intention of sending him to the Tower, it had been Sussex who had restrained me and pointed out that I could not do so. There had been a chance to take revenge on his enemy then, but he had not done so because it would have been wrong and harmful to me and because he was ever a just man above all.

I wept for him. "I cannot afford to lose my good men," I said. "I love them dearly. My lord, you have been very dear to me."

I took a tender farewell of him and said that I should send every day—or come myself—until he was well, for he was constantly in my thoughts.

Hatton was with him at the end. He reported to me what he had said.

It was: "I am passing into another world and must leave you. Beware of the gipsy. He will betray you. You know not the beast as I do."

By the gipsy he meant Robert, who had been given that name by some because of his dark hair and dark flashing eyes.

Poor Sussex! Even in death he could not forget his jealousy of the man I loved beyond them all.

A few days later he died.

I WAS VERY AMUSED to hear that Dorothy Devereux had astounded them all by snapping her fingers at their grandiose plans for her and had run off with John Perrot's son, Thomas. The young pair had fallen in love. It was an unusual story that we had from the vicar of Broxbourne in whose church they had been clandestinely married. He said that two men had asked for the keys to the door of his church, which he had refused. They had then departed, but feeling that there was something unusual in the request, the vicar had gone along to investigate, to find that the door of the church had been forced open and inside a young couple were being married.

"Why," I said, "this Dorothy Devereux has spirit. I will say that for her. And she has taken Tom Perrot and saved herself from her stepfather's proposed match with the heir of Scotland!"

I laughed with my women. Sir John Perrot, father of the bridegroom, was said to be a very close relation of mine. Whether he was or not remains a mystery, but I had to admit that I never saw a man who looked more like my father. Sir John was reputed to be his illegitimate son by Mary Berkley, who married a certain Thomas Perrot. Sir John was an enormous man; his build was exactly that of my father; he had a somewhat quarrelsome nature and was constantly involved in brawls. My father had encouraged him, and my half-brother Edward had made him a knight and helped him through financial troubles. And it was the son of this man whom Dorothy had married.

I could imagine Lettice's wrath for I was certain she was the one who had goaded Robert to his outrageous plans.

That was a year of death.

The first blow was the news that my dear little Frog had passed away. I had always known that he was no commander of men. He was a courtier, simply that. It had been a cruel joke to give this poor little man the name of Hercule—though he had been called François later. Not even of medium height, disfigured by the pox; it was as though Nature had regarded him as a joke, a travesty of a man. However education and upbringing had given him social grace but that somehow had made the contrast between manners and appearance more grotesque.

I had treated him badly, played on his vanity, allowed him to believe that I had thought him attractive . . . all in the name of politics . . . and my own desire to be admired, of course.

And now the little man had died—not in battle, but in his bed. He had lived a life of debauchery, I knew, which somehow seemed more to be deplored because he was so ugly and could only have found partners to share in his frolics because of his wealth and royalty.

I went into mourning for him and wept a little. Perhaps some of my men thought I was acting but I did feel a genuine grief.

Then there occurred another death—one which was to shatter the whole continent of Europe. William of Orange was murdered.

This was a great blow to the Protestant world. He was one of their most respected leaders—an upright, noble gentleman who had given his life to the protection of the weak against the strong. In his youth he had been a Catholic and had discovered through Henri Deux of France, that France and Spain were formulating a plot to destroy the Protestants in the two countries. The massacre which had taken place on the eve of St Bartholomew's Day had been only a step toward this. When William heard that the Duke of Alva was raising an army to come against Holland and that his object was to exterminate what he called heretics and set up the Inquisition in that country, he became a Protestant and steeled himself for the almost impossible task of fighting Philip of Spain. He was determined to sacrifice everything he had— including his life—to preserve the welfare and liberty of his people.

But there was no holding back the Spaniards and Alva arrived with ten thousand troops and established what he called The Council of Troubles and which the Netherlanders called The Council of Butchers. In a short time he had put twenty thousand innocent townsfolk to death.

William escaped to Germany where he attempted to build up an army, while his people were submitted to a tyrannous Spanish rule.

It had been believed that William could never regain his land. The Spaniards were there in strength; the bloody Inquisition was established and the most cruel deaths were being suffered by people who had committed no fault beyond—if that can be called a fault, which I called a virtue—refusing to accept the Catholic Faith.

Then a great event occurred—one of which the Dutch were justly proud. Many Dutchmen having been driven from their land had taken to the sea and formed themselves into a company of pirates who robbed the Spanish ships coming into Holland. They were known as the Beggars of the Sea. They captured the town of Briel which they fortified and declared they were holding for "Father William."

It was a turning point because it showed the Spaniards that they had not won the complete victory which they believed they had, and it enabled William to return to Holland. William the Silent—as they called him, for he was a man of few words—was in control again, proclaimed ruler of the land.

They were a valiant people, those Dutch, and they were heartened by the Huguenots of France who, disgusted by the massacre of St Bartholomew's Eve, came to Holland to help in the fight. William was seeking allies. That was when he had turned his eyes to us.

I wanted to help him; but I had a great aversion to involving my subjects in wars—however righteous. It was for this reason that I had been so pleased to send Anjou to Holland. It was not only to be rid of him but to assist a worthy cause.

Philip must have hated William the Silent, the man whose name was a magic talisman among his followers. He was a perfect leader; his people were devoted to him; he shone with his desire to make any sacrifices which would bring about their liberty.

Philip knew such men were dangerous, and desperately he wanted him out of the way. There had been many attempts on William's life—none of which had come to anything. His people believed that God preserved him to be their savior.

And so it seemed until that dismal day in July of the year 1584 when, in his city of Delft, he was shot dead by a certain Balthasar Gerrards. The irony was that Gerrards had begged from William himself, asking for alms for a poor Calvinist, and William had responded to his appeal. With the money his ruler had given him Gerrards bought a pistol and shot the great man dead.

Gerrards was immediately arrested and tortured. He confessed that he was Philip's spy and was executed most barbarously for the Dutch knew that he had dealt them the most cruel blow possible, and they wanted revenge. But revenge could not bring back William the Silent.

When we heard the news Burghley immediately called a meeting of the Council.

The position was grave, he said. The death of William meant that the responsibility for saving the Dutch from Spain now rested with England.

I was loath to accept this. I could see a long-drawn-out war fought on Dutch soil if it was true—I would never allow it to be the soil of England. I could see men dying and money wasted . . . and little success with it. If William had not been able to drive out the Spaniards, how could we?

"He was very successful in the circumstances," said Burghley. "If he had had more resources, who knew what he might have done?"

We had equipped Anjou to fight the Spaniards, I pointed out, and the Dutch owed us money which they had not repaid. They were hardworking people and were not poor. It was merely that the state of the country made it difficult for the government to impose taxes.

They agreed that what I had said was true but pointed out to me the danger of Spain's taking over complete control of the Netherlands, which would bring them uncomfortably near to us. We must never forget that the most dangerous enemy we had was Philip of Spain.

Could we not work out something in conjunction with the French? They would not want to see Spain victorious.

Our relations with them were not very friendly. They were still smarting from the humiliation suffered by the Duc d'Anjou and were probably realizing now that I had never intended to marry him and had merely dallied to gain more time to see what happened in the Netherlands.

There would be new uneasiness in France because the scene had changed there with the death of Anjou. Henri Trois had no son and the nearest heir was Henri of Navarre, himself a Huguenot.

I was disturbed when I heard that in desperation Holland had offered the sovereignty of the Netherlands to Henri Trois provided he would give them military help. This threw us into a panic for the idea of a French-dominated Netherlands was almost as alarming as a Spanish one. However Henri declined, for which we were grateful, but the situation was fraught with danger.

I was glad some of my counselors agreed that it would be unwise to meddle. Walsingham was one of them. We could not hope to succeed, he said; and our best plan was to make sure that our own country was well defended. We should push ahead with more rapid building of ships and make England impregnable.

I agreed wholeheartedly with this. Henri Trois was as unhealthy as his brother, I pointed out. They were a diseased race, those Valois. If he were to die everything would change in France, for Huguenot Henri of Navarre would come to the throne.

Walsingham's men brought alarming news. The Duc de Guise had formed an alliance with Philip of Spain. It was their avowed purpose that, when Henri Trois died, they would prevent Henri of Navarre from taking the throne and would purge France of its Huguenots so forcefully that in a short time they would have an all-Catholic country. They would extend their methods until the whole of Europe became Catholic.

Faced with such a problem, I did what I always did. I prevaricated.

I needed time, I said, to work out what was the best thing to be done.

+>-<+

ᏟᎻᎪᏆ ᎩᎬᎪᏒ ᏆᎻᎬᏒᎬ was yet another death. Poor Robert, he was very sad. He had been so proud of the boy. I was sorry I had castigated him so sharply for trying to make an alliance for the child with Arabella Stuart.

I always made excuses for Robert. After all, I asked myself, what father worthy of the name would not want the best for his child?

He came to me and told me that he had received news of his son's illness and asked leave to retire from Court. I gave it at once and sent him off, saying that I would pray for the swift recovery of the little boy.

I believe they were both at young Robert's bedside when he died. I even felt a little sorry for Lettice. She was, after all, a mother. But she had other children—four of them; whereas poor Robert had only one—unless one could count Douglass Sheffield's boy.

My thoughts were with him during that time, and it occurred to me that in spite of all his scheming he had failed to get what he wanted most. He had wanted to share my crown and I had denied him that, and the older we grew the more I realized my wisdom in doing so. He had tried to make grand marriages for his son and stepdaughter and I had foiled him in that, too. But I had made him the most powerful man in the country, and the richest. Not that he would ever feel himself to be rich! Whatever Robert had, he would spend more. Robert loved extravagances and it must cost him all he had—and more—to run those magnificent places of his where everything had to be of the best.

He was more full of faults than any man I knew.

But I wept for him now.

The little one was buried in the Beauchamp Chapel at Warwick.

I sent for Robert and when he came to me I dismissed all the others.

"I think you might want to share your grief with me alone," I said, at which he sat on a stool at my feet and leaning his head against my knees wept silently. I caressed his curling hair and wept with him.

I said: "Talk if you wish, Robin, but if you would rather remain silent, do so."

But he wanted to talk. He told me of the mental perfections of his son; physically he had always been frail. It surprised me that Robert with his magnificent physique could produce a fragile child—but nature is like that. He told me of the anxiety he had suffered because the little fellow had been subject to fits and when they were over he had been very weak indeed.

"Robert, we must bear our trials," I said. "You have much to be thankful for. This is a cruel tragedy but it will grow less as time passes."

He thanked me for my sympathy, which he said was the best thing in the world to him, and I replied that he should know by now that I would always stand by him when life used him ill.

He nodded and kissed my hand and there was great accord between us. We knew again that our love for each other was a very precious thing and that it would last until one of us died and left the other desolate.

"His mother is prostrate with grief," he said.

"It is natural that a mother should be," I answered.

"She is so unhappy at your anger with her. If you could allow her to come to Court, it would help to cheer her."

My softness dropped from me.

"No," I said coldly and firmly. "There is no place for that woman at my Court."

He was silent and so was I. The intimacy was over. He had ruined it by introducing a snake into our Eden.

BURGHLEY BROUGHT ME the pamphlet which he thought I ought to see.

I had had a pleasant evening, although it had been arranged to mourn and honor our lost friends, the Duc d'Anjou and William of Orange. I had dressed with the utmost care in black velvet decorated with silver thread and pearls. Over this I wore a shawl of silver mesh; it was as fine as a spider's web and had meant many hours of work by my good needlewomen to bring it to its perfection. My ruff was twinkling with gold and silver stars. I knew that I was looking my best.

I was still pondering as to what my action should be regarding the Netherlands problem. There were so many varying opinions in the Council and Burghley's view was that the Dutch, having failed to get Henri Trois to accept their crown in return for his aid, might offer it to me.

I was thinking of the magnitude of this when Burghley came to me and asked if I had seen the scurrilous pamphlet which was being circulated throughout the Court.

I said I had not and to what did it refer?

He said that it was entitled *The Copye of a Letter wryten by a Master of Arts at Cambridge* and was concerned with the misdeeds of a certain nobleman.

"Leicester?" I asked.

Burghley nodded.

"There are always those who will malign Leicester," I said. "He has aroused so much envy. Who is making mischief now?"

"The author of the pamphlet is a little elusive, but it is said to be written by a Jesuit priest named Robert Parson."

"I have heard his name. He is one of those who burn to restore the Catholic faith in England, I believe, and is ready to do so by any means however foul . . . like most of his brethren. England would be a happier place without his kind. Well, where is this pamphlet?"

"If Your Majesty wishes to see it I will fetch it, but I warn you it does not make pleasant reading."

"By which I infer I am mentioned in it."

He was silent.

"Bring it to me at once," I said.

And so it came into my hands, the most wicked and scurrilous document I ever beheld. It was so absurd that I felt it must be worthless. On the other hand there were parts of it which might have had their roots in truth. Jesuit Parson had not been clever enough; if he had been content with recording the more plausible incidents he might have succeeded in his purpose, which was to destroy not only Leicester's reputation but mine as well. But as is often the case with such fanatical fury, he had gone too far.

Venom leaped out from those pages. Heaven knew, Robert's record was not so pure that it needed such ferocious blackening. I was faintly amused in spite of my anger—and yes, alarmed—to see how Parson had betrayed his passionate envy. Not very clever for a man who claimed to have dedicated himself to God.

He referred to Robert as The Bear and as soon as I read the opening sentences I was prepared for what followed.

"You know the Bear's love, which is for his paunch . . ." It was ridiculous. Robert might indulge somewhat excessively in what is called good living, but he had many greater loves—for power, for glory, for possessions; and he had loved his dead son and Lettice—and I was sure myself.

"He is noble in only two descents and both of them stained with the block . . ."

That was so, but was it Robert's fault that his grandfather had died to placate the people who had blamed him for the taxes imposed by my grandfather? His father had come to the block through ambition, but was Robert to blame for that? My own mother had died on the block and so had many innocent people. The Jesuit was a fool.

"He was fleshed in conspiracy against the royal blood of King Henry's children in his tender years," he continued.

It was true that he was at Court when a child, but he had stood for me as long as I had known him and had sold his lands in case I should need money to hold my throne.

I was reluctant to read on because I knew that this man Parson would be no respecter of royalty. I was right. After an account of how Leicester had advanced his own family, he turned to his relationship with me. All the gossip, all the slander had been revived. The children who had been killed at birth or smuggled into secrecy . . . it was all there. I felt myself growing more and more enraged as I read.

He was a murderer, wrote Parson, not only of his wife, who stood in his way, but of others. He began with the death of Amy Robsart whom, he insisted, Leicester had ordered his servants to dispose of that he might be free to marry the Queen.

Previously he had said that Leicester exerted an evil spell over me which forced me to submit to his lusts. Surely all reasonable people would ask why, since he had murdered Amy in order to marry me, he did not use that sorcery to bring about the marriage.

The death of Lord Sheffield was described in detail. He had been murdered at Leicester's command because he had threatened to divorce his wife naming Leicester as her lover. So an artificial catarrh had stopped his breath. Lord Essex had been killed through a clever Italian recipe after he had learned that Lettice was with child by Leicester. The child was afterward destroyed. Lady Sheffield was being poisoned, and the evidence was that her nails were dropping off and her hair falling out, when her life was saved by her marriage to Sir Edward Stafford. And all knew that there had been an inquiry about that as there had been about the death of Amy Robsart. But Leicester's minions were afraid of him and they saw to it that the truth was not brought out into the open.

What a fool the Jesuit was! These crimes he had laid at Robert's door, while they could not be substantiated had their roots in fact—distorted fact maybe, but there was some reason for plausibility. But he was not content with that. Endowing me with children was absurd, as my movements were followed all the time and it would not have been possible for me to become pregnant without many being aware of it. So that made a nonsense of that particular scandal.

He had to invent absurd crimes and one of the most foolish concerned the death of the Cardinal de Chatillon. It was well known that Catherine de' Medici had wanted him out of the way and that she was a skillful poisoner. Why lay his death at Robert's door? There was no reasoning behind it. Parson's feeble answer was that the Cardinal had threatened to reveal how Leicester had obstructed my marriage with the Duc d'Anjou so the earl's spy poisoners had been sent to dispatch him.

I was horrified and fascinated. Not only was this a libel against Robert but many others as well. Myself for one. If that Jesuit was caught, this was going to cost him dear. John Dee, the astrologer, was implicated, so was Dr Julio, Robert's favorite physician, who, it was said, had brought the art of poisoning with him from Italy. He was named as one of those who had assisted Robert in bringing about the deaths of his victims.

According to Father Parson, Robert was well versed in the black arts, was lustful, greedy, a power-seeking murderer. The devil himself could not have been more evil.

As I read I was inclined to laugh at the absurdities. On the other hand I could see how dangerous this could be in the hands of my enemies. Robert and I were too close for me not to be linked with his villainies.

Old scandals would be revived. People would remember how Amy Robsart died. If I had married Robert, that would have been the end of my reign for the people would have turned against me in the same way that they had turned against Mary Stuart when she married Bothwell, Darnley's murderer. Oh, what a fool she had been! I wondered if she thought as often of me as I did of her. It was inevitable, I supposed, for constantly she was trying to escape from the prisons into which I put her.

Did she ever think how similar our lives had been at that point when I had been so attracted by Robert, and the wife who stood in our way had died? I had seen that as the end of all possibilities for marriage with Robert—only by not marrying him could I completely exonerate myself. For if I refused to marry him when he was free, how could I have connived at the removal of his wife? How different Mary had been. She had married Bothwell almost before Darnley was cold. Foolish, headstrong Mary. And wise Elizabeth.

Now I needed all my wisdom to decide what was to be done about this libelous pamphlet. Ridicule was always a good weapon—perhaps the best if it could be effectively used.

All the same I could not have that pamphlet circulating freely through the country.

I made an Order of Council to forbid the circulation of what had come to be known as *Father Parson's Green Coat* or *Leicester's Commonwealth,* and I gave my assurances that to my knowledge the contents of this scurrilous document were false.

Young Philip Sidney—he was now Sir Philip for I had bestowed a knighthood on him—composed a defense of his uncle very beautifully and movingly written in which he said that he was on his father's side of ancient, well-esteemed and well-matched gentry, but his chief honor was to be a Dudley. Dear Philip Sidney! I was always fond of him, partly because of his devotion to his uncle. He was such a good and clever young man, and surely he could not have been so devoted to one who was unworthy. It did me good to see the affection between him and Robert.

However, nobody wanted to read Philip Sidney's defense of his uncle. It was not lurid like the *Commonwealth* and people are much more interested in evil than in righteousness.

Even my order was not fully carried out. There would always be those who were ready to earn money by smuggling forbidden literature into the country. This was done and I imagined there was hardly a man or woman in the kingdom who did not know of *Father Parson's Green Coat.*

It was disconcerting too that it should be published abroad. Immediately there was a French edition—*La Vie Abominable, Ruses, Meurtres etc de my Lord de Leicester.* And how unfortunate it was that my English Ambassador should happen to be Sir Edward Stafford who had married Douglass Sheffield.

He was in a dilemma. He wrote to Walsingham and Burghley, calling attention to the translation, asking whether he could allow such a document, which was an insult to his Queen and one of her leading ministers, to go unnoticed; on the other hand to call attention to it was distressing to his wife who was mentioned in it. She had been prostrate with melancholy when the first edition had appeared, and now this one was sending her "out of her head" and he feared she was in danger of death.

When these letters were brought to me I could sympathize with poor Douglass Sheffield. I myself was slandered in the document and like Douglass could be said to be accused of complicity in murder. I was strong though, and she, poor soul, was a weakling. How she must regret the day she set eyes on Robert Dudley and allowed her feelings for him to get the better of virtue.

But what were we to do? That was the question.

Burghley said he thought that Stafford in his letter had provided the answer: The matter, he said, should be left alone, as a thing we make no account of rather than to speak against it, to make think "that a galled horse when he is touched will wince".

I nodded.

"Yes," I said, "Stafford is right. If we ignore this it seems we treat it with the indifference it deserves. To raise our voices in protest and anger would appear that we have taken this seriously and it might seem that we have something to hide."

"Let us treat it as the ramblings of a fanatic."

So it was.

But that was not the end of *Father Parson's Green Coat.* It was to be subversively printed and reprinted and it appeared throughout the kingdom for years to come. But Robert was strong enough to live down his reputation; and perhaps he was even more feared than ever, and people were more inclined to think seriously before offending him.

Robert snapped his fingers at the scandal and went on pursuing his brilliant career.

THE SITUATION IN the Netherlands was coming toward a climax. Burghley had hinted that we should have to make a painful decision soon.

As had been predicted, the sovereignty of the Netherlands had been offered to me and the Dutch delegates came to England imploring my help. They thought the offer of the crown would decide me; they did not understand that I was committed to peace and that my whole being cried out against war. Had it not been for the eternal menace of Spain I would not for a moment have considered interfering. But I knew my ministers were right when they said we could not allow Spain to have complete control over a country so near to our shores.

So it was decided that we would assist the Dutch with money and yes . . . with men; and we must be paid for this to the last farthing when the war was over. Until that happy event we must have solid pledges in the shape of a town in each province.

We agreed to send four hundred horse, four thousand foot and seven hundred garrison troops. Later we added to that number for it was clear that more would be needed; and I promised a further six hundred cavalry and a thousand foot.

Because I wanted to please Robert and Burghley I made Philip Sidney governor of Flushing and Burghley's eldest son, Thomas Cecil, that of Brill.

They were always seeking honors for those whom they were trying to bring to my notice. Even Burghley, who was not a power-seeker, was guilty of this, and I fancied he kept back those brilliant Bacon boys for fear they should outstrip his own son—not Thomas, the elder, but his little hunchbacked Robert who had already been brought to my notice and whom I recognized as a clever little fellow—probably doubly so because his disability had made him want to shine through his brains since he could not through his personal appearance.

The great decision was, who should command the expedition? I knew Robert wanted to, but I hesitated to give it to him only because I hated to have him leave Court, and the possibility of his being in danger terrified me.

But the general opinion was that the command should go to him.

Father Parson's Green Coat was still very much in people's minds and it would be well for him to absent himself for a while.

Both Burghley and Walsingham remarked that he was a great figure in England and the fact that we sent him would make people understand how important the matter was to us; moreover, Robert, who wanted the glory of the expedition, had the means to use a great deal of his own money in promoting himself; and although he was not a general himself, he would have able commanders with him.

So it was decided that Robert should go to the Netherlands.

I SUMMONED HIM to Court and kept him with me before he left. There was so much business to discuss, I said. Even the night before he set out I made sure that he did not return to Leicester House where no doubt Lettice was waiting to say a fond farewell.

So I was with Robert till the time he set off for Harwich where a fleet of fifty sail was waiting to take him on the first stage of his journey.

I heard of the wonderful reception he was given on his arrival at Rotterdam, where the banks were lined with men holding cressets high in the air, and the cheers, ran the report, were deafening.

Poor people, they must have been very frightened; and who could wonder with those fanatical Spaniards noted for their cruelty ready to subdue them. And how Robert must have loved such a welcome! In his heart he had always wanted to be a king.

I felt quite ill after he had gone. I should not have allowed it. What if he should be killed in battle? Of course, he had looked so splendid, sitting at the head of his cavalcade, and when I had voiced my fears, he had said, with characteristic charm, that he wished he had a thousand lives that he might place them at my service.

But I worried and that brought on my headaches and I wished fervently that we had never become involved in the Netherlands controversy. I would never have done so but for my fear of the Spaniards who were growing more and more powerful every day. I thanked God for our fine seamen like Sir Francis Drake who robbed and pillaged their ships whenever possible. I wished there were more like him and we could drive the Spaniards off the seas. Why could not they live in peace in their country and leave me to mine? Why did they have to have this fanatical desire to impose their power and their religion on those who did not want it?

But so it was, and because of this, fine men like Robert Dudley had to go to war.

My feelings took a sharp turn when the news was brought to me that almost immediately after his arrival Robert, regarded as the savior of the Netherlands, was offered the Governor-Generalship of the United Provinces—the honor of sovereignty which first Henri Trois had refused and then I had. And Robert had dared accept without consulting me! My fury drove away my anxiety. Why had I worried about Robert? He had not gone there to fight but to make himself a king!

I sent for Thomas Heneage. I cried: "What think you of this news? My lord Leicester has taken the honor which I refused. I suppose he is now setting himself up as King of the Netherlands."

Heneage was secretly pleased, of course, as they all were when I was angry with Robert, yet he was afraid to condemn him for they knew I was capable of turning on them if they attacked him.

"I shall write to him at once," I said, "and put a stop to all this nonsense. You shall take my letter to him and let him know the full weight of my displeasure."

Then I sat down and wrote to him in the heat of my anger:

"We could never have imagined had we not seen it fall out in experience, that a man raised up by ourself, and extraordinarily favored by us above any subject of this land, would have, in so contemptible a sort, broken our commandment in a cause which so greatly touches our honor . . .

"Our express pleasure and commandment is that, all delays and excuses laid apart, do you presently, upon the duty of your allegiance, obey and fulfill whatsoever the bearer shall direct you to do in our name: whereof fail you not or you will answer the contrary at your uttermost peril . . ."

Oh, I would have him humiliated! He had accepted the honor. Now he could publicly renounce it. I would have the whole of the Netherlands know that he was my servant and no one should forget it.

Such was my rage against Robert. But I suppose those about me, who knew me well, were aware that it would quickly subside and I would soon be feeling anxious for his dignity as well as his health.

Burghley advised caution. Let us discuss the matter. Let us not make hasty decisions.

I was already beginning to waver. I could imagine his joy when he accepted the great honor. Dear Robert, he would have done so with such charm and dignity. I wished I had been there to see him. Then I remembered what he had done. He had taken matters into his own hands. Moreover, how could he be Governor General of the United Provinces? His place was not in the Netherlands but in England at my side.

Then I heard news which infuriated me even more. Lettice was preparing to join him and she was proceeding in the state of a queen! She was assembling her wardrobe and in the city of London the merchants were busily making their way to Leicester House taking the finest materials for her approval—suitable for the wife of a man who was one step from a throne. She had ordered several coaches to be built and on these would be the arms of the Netherlands combined with those of Leicester.

Madam Lettice could only travel in the style of a queen!

I really gave vent to my feelings then. I swore by God that Madam Lettice was going to unpack her fine possessions with all speed. There was to be no triumphant royal trip for her.

"She is not going to join her King in the Netherlands," I said grimly. "She might join him in the Tower, for he has lost his crown and will soon be returning to England in disgrace."

So Lettice was commanded to stop her preparations. She could send the merchants back to their shops with their splendid materials; she could unpack her jewels. It was going to be very different from what she had imagined.

Heneage should leave at once for the Netherlands. He should tell Leicester that he must inform his dear subjects that his Queen, without whom he had no power whatsoever, had decided that he had acted rashly, foolishly and against her wishes in accepting what she would not allow him to take. And he must hand it back forthwith.

I had been getting over my anger with Robert but the thought of Lettice preparing to make a royal procession had sent it flaring up again.

Burghley was for keeping Heneage back for a while; so was Heneage himself. I know Burghley would have liked to see Robert humiliated, but he never allowed personal feelings to interfere with politics. That was what made him my most valuable servant.

He now pointed out the danger of publicly humiliating the man I had sent as my representative. Certainly Leicester must give up the Governor-Generalship; this country could not take on such a responsibility; but he must be allowed to do so in a manner which would create the least fuss. Some excuse must be found. Leicester must be extricated from a position in which a momentary aberration on his part had placed him. It should be widely understood that England had no wish to take on the responsibility of the Netherlands. It was a different matter to give them military aid. As it was, we were not at war with Spain—although we were in fact fighting in the Netherlands. The position was delicate. This action of Leicester's had exacerbated it to some extent; but we must not make it more difficult.

I saw the point of this and of course I would never have hurt Robert with a public humiliation. It would be enough to berate him in private.

WHAT A DISASTER that campaign was! I should never have allowed myself to be persuaded to go to war—for that was what it was. Hadn't I always known that no one profited from war! It was too costly in lives and property; and the idea of wasting money on ammunition when it could be put to better use infuriated me.

Robert was not really a soldier; he was a courtier. Of course he reveled in the spectacles, all the feasting and adulation. But the Dutch did not want him there for that. They wanted the Spaniards driven out of their land.

I had agreed that Robert should continue in his office until some plan could be made to qualify his title. Perhaps my great desire after my first flush of anger, was to let all know that there had been no collusion on my part. My feelings for Robert were universally known and there would most certainly be suspicions that I had maneuvered this great honor for him. I had made it very clear that I had not, and now I was ready to allow the Council to find some way out of it.

Robert was not meant for such a task. We should never have sent him. He despised the Dutch for their homely manners and referred to them in their hearing as churls and tinkers. His great desire now was to come home.

Moreover, as I have said, he was not a soldier and was no true match for the Spaniards. It is true he relieved the town of Grave and then seemed to be of the opinion that this decided the entire campaign and he could rest from fighting. But it was not long before Parma had recaptured Grave and Robert was quarreling with his captains, blaming everyone for failure except himself.

I could imagine how he missed Court.

Then something very sad took place. Philip Sidney had accompanied his uncle to the Netherlands to take up his command at Flushing. I could imagine Robert's discussions with Sidney about my annoyance over the Governor-Generalship; and young Philip would of course believe that his uncle could do no wrong. What a beautiful relationship there was between those two! Now I wished more than ever that I had never embarked on this adventure; it was bringing misery to everyone. If I had my way I would have entrenched myself in England—building my ships, fortifying my land for the day when the Spaniards attempted to conquer us. Burghley was sure that they would come, and I was beginning to believe that he was right.

Oh yes, that would have been better than this futile fighting abroad.

Philip Sidney must have been feeling very sad because he had recently lost both his father and mother. Their deaths had saddened me, particularly that of Mary Sidney whose devotion I would always remember. How I hated people to die! It was bad enough when they died in their beds but when they were hastened prematurely to their graves indulging in stupid warfare it was almost unendurable.

It happened at Zutphen. Philip had left his tent early in the morning and unhappily for him had met Sir William Pelham who had forgotten to put on his leg armor. Philip foolishly offered his and declared that he did not need that sort of equipment. How wrong the foolish boy was! During the ensuing battle he was wounded in the left thigh.

There was a saintliness about Philip Sidney—in spite of the fact that he had written those love poems to Penelope Rich, another man's wife. She was the she-wolf's cub so perhaps she had some special powers, inherited from her mother, to turn men to her.

Philip Sidney had certainly been devoted to Penelope in spite of his having a good wife in Walsingham's girl, Frances.

The story was that parched with thirst he called for a drink and as he was about to take it he saw a dying man looking longingly at the water. He was reputed to have said: "Take it. Thy need is greater than mine."

People who die young are always regarded as saints. Too good for this life! people say. So it was inevitable that they should have said that of Philip Sidney.

Robert had him taken to his barge and he was carried down the river to Arnheim. Frances Walsingham—who was such a good wife to Philip and did not deserve to endure the devotion he showed to Penelope Rich, spiritual though it was supposed to be—went out to nurse him, although she was pregnant.

But Philip Sidney died, in spite of all the care that was lavished on him.

I was sure Robert would be deeply grieved.

Everything had gone wrong for him since the day he had left with his magnificent equipage for the Netherlands.

He should never have gone. I should never have been inveigled into supporting the Dutch. I should have obeyed my own instincts which were for peace.

I hated war more than ever. My suspicions that there was no profit in it were confirmed. But Spain! It was always Spain. But what we were doing in the Netherlands would not deter Spain.

In the midst of all this that which came to be known as the Babington Plot emerged. And Mary Stuart became an even greater preoccupation than the Netherlands.

Fotheringhay

OFTEN WHEN I LOOK BACK OVER MY LIFE AGAIN AND AGAIN
I acknowledge the debt I owe to my ministers. Mine seemed to have been a
period which nurtured great men. I venture to think I may have influenced
this in some way. Although they respected my intellect they could never forget that I was a woman and that very fact brought out in them a protective
instinct. These men would have served a king well but with a difference. I was
a woman and for that reason I had a little more power than a man would have
had. They were always conscious of my femininity—my fierce loves and
hates, a certain predictable unpredictability—which sounds a contradiction,
but which is not really so. They knew how my temper would rise; they knew
it could quickly subside; they knew that while I ranted and raged I never lost
sight of what was best for Elizabeth—and that meant for England. They
served me with an extra devotion. They were all, in a certain measure, in love
with me, and I do not say that in any frivolous or coquettish way. It was not
a sexual love—or perhaps I should say lustful. It was a deep abiding affection.

Even my pretty men—Hatton, Heneage, Robert—were statesmen;
there were my adventurers like Drake and Raleigh, and they were not adventurers only. But perhaps the most important of all were my serious ministers, headed by Burghley and Walsingham. I believe my reign would have
been different without those two. They enjoyed special privileges, both of
them; I allowed them to criticize my actions for I knew that they could serve
me best through complete frankness—and indeed neither Burghley nor
Walsingham would have served me otherwise. They were both men of
absolute honesty; and they helped me to shape my destiny.

Sir Francis Walsingham was a stern Protestant—a small man of slim figure who almost always dressed in plain black garments. He lived for his
work, which was to protect me and England and to bring about peace and
prosperity. No one loved his country more than Walsingham, and it was a
passion he and I shared.

He was outspoken and would not alter his opinions because he thought
they were unpopular. That was what I liked about him. Even at the height
of our disagreements, when I would rage at him, he refused to change.

I could have sent him to the Tower, I could have threatened him with
death and Walsingham would have said: "Your Majesty must do with me as
you wish, but I know you are wrong in this."

As if I would harm a hair of his dark head! I loved the man for his integrity, his obsession with his work, and his complete dedication to my safety. He was my beloved Moor and it was always with the utmost pleasure that I looked upon that dark-skinned face with the brilliant all-seeing dark eyes.

Walsingham had a special place among my advisers. For a number of years now he had been building up a very efficient spy organization. It was a task ideally suited to him for he was a man who liked to work in secret; and at the very heart of his plans was the necessity to keep me on the throne and safeguard the future of a Protestant England.

He had agents all over Europe as well as in our own taverns and such places in England; and he had a constant finger on the pulse of feeling everywhere. Nothing was too unimportant for his attention; and although he received the considerable sum of four thousand pounds a year, this was not enough for his needs and he used a great deal of his own fortune to augment the cost.

His great obsession was to prevent the return of Catholicism to England. He saw acute danger from two people: Philip of Spain and Mary of Scotland. His spy service was especially active in Spain. He had agents in Madrid, Corunna and San Lucar taking in Cadiz and Seville; and also in Lisbon. He was watching Philip's preparations in his shipyards and he reported that Spain was building an impressive armada. He had several agents in France—another country which had always to be watched. He also had them in Germany and the Low Countries. Consequently I always knew what was going on long before I received official news; I realized how important this was.

But I believed he considered Mary of Scotland, the rheumatic-racked prisoner in the drafty castles of England, a greater menace even than the great King brooding in his gloomy Escorial.

Once he said to me: "As long as that devilish woman lives, Your Majesty cannot feel safe in the possession of your crown, nor can your faithful servants be assured of their lives."

I had chided him. He exaggerated, I said. I knew Mary had aspirations to a crown and that one possibly mine, but she was a wretched creature more often ill than in good health, and she was my prisoner.

He would not have it. He assured me that Philip was looking very seriously to Mary of Scotland as a figurehead for the Catholic army.

"Hasn't he always?" I asked.

"Not as seriously as of late. Conflict with Spain may come, Your Majesty. It is in Philip's mind. Why should he have his shipyards working at full speed? It is coming, and Mary of Scotland should not be here to make a rallying point for the Catholics in this country."

What Walsingham wanted was Mary's death. He was not a bloodthirsty man. His desire was purely a matter of plain reasoning. She was a menace and some means should be found for disposing of her.

He was a little reproachful for he had given me good grounds—legitimate ones—for bringing her to the block. What other monarch would have allowed her to live after the Ridolfi Plot which had resulted in the execution of Norfolk? I had had adequate reasons for destroying her and yet I had let her go free. Why? demanded Walsingham.

Did he not know that I had an aversion to shedding blood? I know men had died in my reign and I had done nothing to stop the executions. I had allowed a good and honest man like John Stubbs to lose his right hand; Edmund Campion had been barbarously killed. Mary was different. Mary was a queen and a kinswoman. I had never set eyes on her and yet she had played a dominating part in my life. I would be haunted by remorse forever if I signed her death warrant. I knew she was a menace to me; I knew that she was trying to plot my death. Why then could I not agree to hers when those about me, who had my well-being so much at heart, were urging me that it was the only wise action to take—the only safe one?

I knew that Walsingham was working hard to put before me the proofs of Mary's duplicity and intentions to murder me, and to present them in such a manner that I could no longer reasonably delay signing her death warrant.

A few years before, Walsingham had uncovered a plot which was being formulated in Paris. This was no Ridolfi affair—it was far more serious. Powerful forces were involved in it, including the Pope, Philip of Spain and the Guises as well as some leading Catholics in England—among these that pernicious little Jesuit Father Parson who had produced *Leicester's Commonwealth*.

Only Walsingham's superb spy system revealed what was going on and enabled him to arrest a Catholic gentleman named Francis Throckmorton. Walsingham had had him taken to the Tower where he was put to the rack and under torture confessed that he was involved in a plot with the Guises to invade England and set Mary on the throne.

Mary was concerned in these plots and had actually written to and received letters from the conspirators.

There was no reason, Walsingham pointed out, why she should not be brought to trial for treason. It would be an easy matter to prove that she was guilty and the penalty for treason was death.

Still I could not bring myself to it, and although Throckmorton was executed, Mary lived on.

I could understand Walsingham's exasperation and his determination to

QUEEN OF THIS REALM

bring matters to such a pass that it would be difficult for me in all good sense to turn away from what must be the inevitable conclusion.

I wondered what Mary looked like now. She must be forty-four years of age—younger than I was. There were reports of her illnesses. She suffered cruelly from rheumatism, which was not surprising for some of those castles were not only cold but damp. She would not have had the aids to preserve her good looks which I had had, and although according to the poets she had started life rather specially endowed, I could imagine she was far from the sparkling beauty she had once been.

Still, she had that indefinable sexual allure which apparently had been hers since girlhood. There had been violent quarrels with the Shrewsburys when she had been in their care. I supposed there would always be trouble where a woman like Bess Hardwick was concerned, but Bess had accused Mary and her husband of being lovers, a charge which Shrewsbury had stoutly denied, and I must say, knowing Shrewsbury, I could hardly believe to be true. The Shrewsburys had parted, but I think that was owing more to a quarrel about property than Mary. Shrewsbury seemed greatly relieved to be free both of his wife and the Queen. He mentioned in a letter to the Spanish Ambassador (and Walsingham reported this to me for he made a point of seeing all diplomatic correspondence that went out of the country) that he was overjoyed to be rid of those two devils, his wife and the Queen of Scots, which did not sound to me like the words of a passionate lover.

However, wherever Mary was there was trouble with men, so Shrewsbury was recalled. I sent Sir Ralph Sadler to take charge of her. He was over seventy and would be a stern jailer, so it would be amusing to see if rheumatic-racked, forty-four-year-old Mary Stuart could work her charms on him.

Although I did not know what was happening at the time, I learnt it in detail afterward and I realized that Walsingham could not be expected, after the Throckmorton affair, to allow matters to lie dormant. He was determined for the sake of my safety and the future of England to bring Mary Stuart to the scaffold. In a way I suppose he set up his own plot and this time he was going to make it absolutely foolproof.

He had working for him an able spy called Gilbert Gifford. Gifford was particularly useful because he was a Catholic and had been trained for the priesthood and could move with ease among Catholic communities, sure of their trust.

Walsingham set Gifford to work on a certain Thomas Morgan, a Welsh Catholic who had been involved in the Ridolfi conspiracy. For some reason he had been allowed to escape and had settled in Paris. He was taken into the employ of the Archbishop of Glasgow, who was Mary's Ambassador in

Paris. From there he wrote to Mary in cipher and arranged for her letters to be sent to the Pope and to smuggle them to Catholics in England.

When Walsingham brought me news of his activities I agreed with him that it would be advisable to arrest this man and bring him to England where he could be dealt with, but it was not easy.

It was at this time that William Parry was in touch with Morgan. William Parry was a Catholic member of Parliament for Queensborough in Kent. He had always put forward the case for tolerance toward Catholics and I was at heart in agreement with this. I wanted tolerance for any form of worship, but at the same time the burning zeal of the Catholics could bring disaster to a country, particularly if they introduced that Inquisition which had caused as much misery as anything in the world.

When Parliament passed a bill against Jesuits, seminary priests and such like disobedient persons, Parry rose in the House and denounced it as "a measure savouring of treason, full of danger and despair to the English subjects."

The House was amazed at such rebellion and Parry was arrested. I ordered him to be released for I did not care for men to be imprisoned for their religious opinions, and as long as they did not try to make trouble—which Parry had not—I was in favor of their having their liberty.

Walsingham's men discovered only six weeks after his release that Parry was plotting to murder me when I was riding in the park. He was arrested and executed but before he died he implicated Thomas Morgan in the plot to murder me, so I immediately asked the French to send Morgan to England. This they refused to do; but they did send him to the Bastille in deference to my wishes. But it was evidently not a very rigorous imprisonment and Morgan was allowed to receive visitors. This fact gave Walsingham an idea, and very soon Gifford was paying a friendly call on Morgan, for, as Walsingham said, since all our efforts to get this man extradited had failed, we could turn this to an advantage.

He had already intercepted letters between Morgan and the Queen of Scots, so clearly the French were not serious in their imprisonment of Morgan. Walsingham thought they might be preserving him to use against us, and Gifford as a trusted Catholic could carry letters between Mary and Morgan. Morgan rather naturally fell into the trap so cleverly prepared for him and had absolute faith in Gifford.

This was typical of Walsingham's work. Gifford had been primed and instructed continuously and he played his part well. He returned to England and was soon in touch with all the Catholic factions. He was entertained by them in their country houses; he learned their secrets, all of which were passed on to Walsingham.

Then he went to Chartley where Mary was at the time.

I had memories of Chartley. It was where I had gone after that splendid entertainment at Kenilworth. It had been the she-wolf's home at the time when she was married to Essex. Now of course she had the grander homes of Wanstead, Leicester House and Kenilworth. I ground my teeth with rage when I thought of her enjoying all that splendor.

But back to Gifford. Poor Sir Ralph Sadler had complained so bitterly of his health and his desire to be released from the task of guarding the Queen of Scots that I had at last relented and sent Sir Amyas Paulet in his place. Sir Amyas was a stern Protestant—a puritan in fact. He had been my Ambassador in Paris and Mary was most put out that such a man should be put in charge of her for, while in Paris, he had behaved in a most unfriendly manner toward her agents.

Indeed he had! I thought. He was working for me, the Queen of England, and not for the Queen of Scots! I wrote back to Mary and told her that Sir Amyas had done his duty well while he was in Paris and I was sure that he would to her.

But I knew she was far from pleased to be in the charge of such a stern man and one on whom, I commented to Hatton, she might turn her aging charms in vain.

It was interesting to see the letters which passed backward and forward, all of which Gifford brought to Walsingham; and I was amused that Mary was using her well-known powers of fascination on poor old Amyas, and to hear through her that Paulet was a man who thought little of anything but his own self-righteousness and was quite unprepared to accept bribes and to allow concessions in the hope of good things to come.

Gifford had had many talks with Mary. She told him that she feared Amyas Paulet might be suspicious of the letters she was sending and she did wonder whether he had means of intercepting them as it appeared—to her spies in England—that a great deal was known of secret matters. She would hesitate therefore to write anything of any great importance unless she was assured that it would reach its destination.

Then Walsingham had an idea. Let Mary believe that the letters were being smuggled out of the castle without Paulet's being able to get his hands on them; then she would be completely frank in what she wrote.

It seemed an excellent idea and Gifford went into the matter with a local Catholic brewer who professed himself willing to help. Full barrels of beer were delivered regularly to the castle and empty ones were taken away. Why should they not have a box in which Mary's letters could be placed and the box secreted in the empty barrel? This could be taken out of the castle without any suspicion. The answers could be sent in full barrels.

It was thus that we learned the full details of the Babington Plot.

First we heard of John Savage. He was a most ardent Catholic who had joined the Duke of Parma to fight for Catholicism in the Low Countries and believed that the only way to bring the Catholic Faith back to England was through my assassination. This was the ultimate goal. When he was in London he got into touch with John Ballard, a Jesuit, who was a member of a band of young men led by Anthony Babington which was plotting to bring about my death and those of my leading statesmen, as well as a rising of Catholics in England. This was to result in the release of Mary and to place her on the throne of England.

Ballard was in touch with people on the continent who were ready to support the rising once I was out of the way and Mary at the head of an army. Philip of Spain and the Pope would help; and certainly the French would, for the Guises wanted to see their kinswoman Queen of England.

There were two sets of conspirators—one under Savage and the other led by Anthony Babington. Gifford carefully brought the two together so that we had only one plot to deal with.

All through the June of that year they met in secret places—sometimes in taverns, sometimes in Giles's Field; and often in Babington's house in Barbican for Babington was a young man of some means who could afford to entertain his friends.

When he was young he had been in Sheffield Castle at the same time as Mary had been imprisoned there and he had acted as her page. As was to be expected, she charmed him and he must have made up his mind then that he was going to do everything he could to bring her out of prison and to my throne.

Foolish young man!

He proved himself to be even more foolish. It is a pity that the young can make such misguided mistakes and then have to pay for them in such deadly manner.

Walsingham was beside himself with glee—but that is not the way to describe it. He could never really be gleeful; but he was going about with an air of immense satisfaction. He told me that he would soon have something very important to report to me.

He now had letters which had come to him—by way of the brewer's barrels—in which Babington mentioned plans for killing me. He had the encouragement of Spain and the promise of help from them. My assassination and that of my most important ministers was now clearly stated as the first objective, and two who must most certainly be eliminated were Burghley and Walsingham. Their deaths—with of course that of myself—would be the signal for the Catholics to rise.

Walsingham went on playing the game, while he kept the conspirators under strict surveillance. There were thirteen of them including Savage and Ballard. They thought they were fourteen for they imagined that Gifford was one of them.

Walsingham made it clear to me that Mary Stuart was as deeply involved in this plot as she possibly could be, and when it was exposed—as it would be at the right moment—there could really be no escape for her this time.

Ballard was arrested first. He was committed to the Tower and racked. Walsingham wanted a confession from him, which he got, but the man would not betray any of the others. Not that it mattered. Walsingham knew them all and was ready to bring them in when he considered the time to be ripe.

His great aim was to implicate Mary and he wanted a complete search made of her apartments, so it was arranged that Paulet should tell her that he was a little concerned for her health and she was to leave Chartley for Tixall, the home of Sir Walter Ashton, who would be delighted to entertain her and there she might enjoy a little hunting. She knew that she would be well guarded at Tixall but she must have welcomed the change which would be good for her health.

While she was absent a thorough search was made of all her possessions at Chartley. Documents were found and many letters which would have incriminated her completely if Walsingham had not had enough evidence from the correspondence he had seen—but of course that was sufficient to send her to the scaffold.

Meanwhile Babington had become suspicious that they were being watched. Ballard had disappeared. He had a strong feeling that the plot might have been discovered and he applied to Walsingham for a passport to France where he wanted to go in order to spy on the Queen's enemies, he said. He stated that he knew these existed and that as he was a good Catholic, he would have an entry into Catholic strongholds.

Walsingham was intrigued by such a request. He wondered then if Gifford was suspected since here was Babington offering himself for the same role in which Gifford had been employed.

He did not reply immediately. He was a great believer in devious methods and he suggested to some of his servants that they try to strike up an acquaintance with Babington, invite him to dine, ply him with drink and see if they could get him to betray anything.

One of them subsequently made friends with Babington in a tavern and the invitation was given.

But here Walsingham's plan went a little awry. Babington did not get drunk though some of his hosts did, and it must have occurred to Babington that his application for a passport and this invitation to dine were connected in some way. He took the opportunity of being in Walsingham's house to explore his private sanctum and, looking through the papers on the great man's desk, he saw his own name on one of them and something written beside it which he could not understand.

But it was enough. He was on his guard. Walsingham knew something and as there were very dangerous things to know, Babington decided to flee. He slipped out of Walsingham's house and went to that of a Catholic friend in Harrow where he changed his complexion by staining it with walnut juice, cut his hair and decided to lie low with his friend until the hunt—if hunt there was—was over.

His capture was not long delayed. Walsingham had too detailed an account of his friends to be at much disadvantage; and very soon, with the rest of the conspirators, Babington was in the Tower.

There could be no other verdict than guilty. Walsingham had so much evidence against them; and right at the heart of the conspiracy to assassinate me and my ministers and to bring the armies from Spain and set up the Catholic Faith under a new Queen, was Mary Stuart herself.

Walsingham was triumphant.

"There can be no way out for her this time," I said, when her fellow conspirators were all sentenced to the traitor's death of hanging, drawing and quartering.

Crowds assembled in a field at the upper end of Holborn where the execution was to take place and first Ballard was subjected to the most horrible of deaths while Babington looked on. When Ballard had uttered his last cry of agony and his mutilated body was still, it was the turn of Babington.

He suffered horribly and when the news was brought to me I felt ill and I immediately said that the rest of the conspirators should not be cut until after death. They should merely suffer hanging.

I was glad I had done that. I did not want my people looking on such horror and remembering that the order of death came from me.

So Walsingham brought to an end the Babington Plot, which he had set in motion in a desperate attempt to bring Mary of Scotland to the scaffold.

Mary remained. She was as guilty as Babington himself. What should be done with her?

"She must never again be given the opportunity to threaten Your Majesty," said Burghley.

"We might not be so fortunate next time," pointed out Walsingham. "She could succeed. Your Majesty must see that the situation is too grave to be lightly set aside."

I did see it. But I deplored what they were urging me to do.

Five days after Babington and Ballard died so cruelly in the Holborn field, Mary of Scotland was lodged at Fotheringhay.

I WISHED THAT I could have gone to Fotheringhay to be present at her trial. But I could not do that. As we had never met in all the years she had been in England, it was hardly the time for it now. I told both Walsingham and Burghley who were present that I wanted a detailed account of all that was said, and this was promised me.

The trial was held in the great chamber at Fotheringhay Castle. Walsingham had arranged that a throne should be set on a dais. This was for me, and although I should not be sitting in it, its presence meant that those who conducted the trial did so on authority from me.

A chair covered in red velvet had been put out for the prisoner but when she came in she went straight to the throne thinking it had been provided for her. When it was explained to her that the throne was for the Queen of England, she said: "I am the Queen by right of birth and so it should be my place."

What a foolish woman she was! She would put her judges against her before the trial started.

"How did she look?" I asked Burghley.

He said: "She looked like a queen."

"Beautiful?" I insisted.

"I suppose one would say that."

Maddening man! How could she have looked beautiful?

She was forty-four and suffering acutely from rheumatism. She had spent—was it twenty years?—in cold damp castles.

"How was she dressed?" I demanded.

He could answer that. "In black velvet."

"And on her head?"

"Oh . . . a white headdress . . . rather like a shell."

I knew it. I had seen a drawing of it.

The charges against her were read out. She had been involved in a plot to assassinate the Queen of England and to destroy her realm, to take her crown and bring the Catholic Faith to these shores. What had she to say?

Mary had replied haughtily that she had come to England to ask my aid, and not as a prisoner. She was a queen and answered to none but God. "I will say," she added, "that I am not guilty of that of which I am accused."

The facts were then laid before her—the whole story of the planning of the Babington Plot. She denied that she had been involved, but was told that her letters, which had been placed in a box in beer barrels, had been intercepted and she was proved guilty.

Burghley then reminded her that she was also guilty of carrying the arms of England on her shield and calling herself the Queen of England, to which she replied that she had had no choice in that, for her father-in-law Henri Deux of France had commanded it and she had no alternative but to obey him.

"But," said Burghley, "you continued to state your claim to the throne after you left France."

"I have no intention of denying my rights," she retorted.

How tiresome she was! How reckless! But then she always had been. If she had been as wise after the murder of Darnley as I was after the death of Amy Robsart she might still be on the throne of Scotland and not fighting for her life in the hall of Fotheringhay Castle.

She was allowed to state her case and defend herself. From what I heard I think she was a very tired and disillusioned woman. I think she was not prepared to fight very hard for her life. She said sadly that she had been humiliated, treated as a prisoner ever since she arrived in England; and she longed to be free. She declared that she had had no part in the plot to murder me. It was true that she was a Catholic and her religion meant more to her than anything else on Earth. She may have written to foreign princes. She was a sick and weary woman. All she longed for was to be free and live in peace. She insisted that she had never desired my death.

The court broke up with Walsingham's declaration that he would bring the findings to me. She was guilty but it was for me to pass sentence.

This was what I dreaded. I wanted her dead but I did not want to have any part in her removal.

But the court at Fotheringhay had proved her guilty. The letters were as damning as they could be. She deserved to die, and yet . . .

When the court had adjourned at Fotheringhay it was announced that it should meet again in the Star Chamber at Westminster and there sentence should be passed. It was the 25th of October and I remember that day every year when it comes round. The day Mary Stuart was sentenced to death.

They were all urging me. Walsingham was triumphant. We could remove one of the greatest menaces to our throne for it had been clearly proved that this woman had plotted against my life, which was treason. She had been in touch with foreign courts; she wanted to bring about the ruin of the Protestant Church and set up the Catholic in its place. What greater treason could there be! The execution should take place without delay. It was unwise to dally. It would be better for the Queen of Scots herself if we acted promptly for she must know she was guilty and what the inevitable consequences must be.

I knew they were right. I knew that for the sake of my safety and that of my country she must die—and yet, I should be the one, in the generations to come, who would be accused of killing her.

If only she would die! If only I did not have to put my name to that death warrant!

I hesitated but they would give me no peace. Even Robert wrote from the Netherlands. He was thinking of me all the time, he wrote. He knew what a quandary I found myself in. Did he not understand my innermost feelings? But Mary of Scotland was a threat to me and to every Englishman who did not hold the Catholic Faith. I must sign that death warrant.

"Your Majesty must sign it," insisted Walsingham, Burghley, Bacon . . . all of them.

And still I hesitated.

My secretary William Davison came to me and told me that he was being entreated by Amyas Paulet to beg me to sign the death warrant without delay. It was difficult for him to carry on in such a state of tension. Every day they were expecting the order to arrive, each day the Queen of Scots prepared herself, and still the days passed and there was no decision.

"Davison," I said, "I am loath to sign this warrant for reasons you know well. I should have thought there might be some means of saving me from this unpleasant duty."

Davison looked taken aback. I felt impatient with him. He was not one of my favorite men. He lacked the grace of the charmers, and although he was able, he did not have the cold clear brain of the clever ones.

It was irritating to have to explain. Burghley would have caught my meaning at once.

"We have heard much of the sufferings of the Queen of Scots. She is not a young woman. Paulet is in charge up there. Could he not be persuaded to help us out of this delicate matter?"

Davison stammered: "You mean . . . remove the Queen . . . by . . . by secret methods . . ."

"I believe I have made myself clear," I said. "Write to Paulet . . . very discreetly. I am sure he will see the wisdom of this."

But I had reckoned without Paulet's self-righteousness. His miserable conscience came between him and his duty.

He was almost indignant. He could not perform an act which God and the law forbade.

"God forbid," he wrote, "that I should make so foul a shipwreck of my conscience or leave so great a blot to my poor posterity, to shed blood without law or warrant."

I knew I could not delay indefinitely. I had to stop trying to placate outsiders. I should have no criticism from the people who really mattered—my own Protestant subjects, who wanted the death of Mary Stuart as much as I did.

So I signed the death warrant and at eight o'clock on that February morning Mary Stuart entered the hall at Fotheringhay Castle and went to the block.

As soon as I knew she was dead I was thrown into a panic of remorse.

I had signed her death warrant. In generations to come I should be known as the one responsible for the death of Mary Stuart. It was no use trying to placate my conscience, to tell myself that *she* had planned *my* death. I could not forget that I had signed the paper without which she would have been alive. I could not ease my mind except by pretending that I had not meant it. I looked about me for someone to blame. I sent for Davison but I was told that he was suffering from an attack of palsy and was not at Court.

I knew that he was subject to these attacks and I had no doubt that this matter of the death warrant had brought on this one. I worked myself into a passion of dislike against this man, and when Christopher Hatton came to me, I burst out that I was distressed because of the death of my kinswoman.

Hatton was too much of a courtier to express surprise. He had been one of those—as indeed had every one of my councilors—who had urged me to sign the death warrant. He must have been a little taken aback but being Hatton of the graceful manners he waited for me to say what was in my mind.

"That fool Davison . . . He knew I did not wish him to send the warrant to Paulet . . . yet he did so . . ."

Hatton looked grave. I could see the words forming in his mind: Then why did you sign it? But he did not say them, of course. Wise, tactful Hatton!

"He hurried it off," I declared, "although I had told him to hold it back until he had permission to release it."

That was not strictly true. I had told myself that it was what I wanted and that Davison had known it. Had he? He was not a mind-reader. He had not the subtlety of Burghley and Walsingham.

"The Queen of Scots has been executed and it is Davison's fault. I want him in the Tower."

Hatton said: "He is a sick man. It may be that he has misconstrued Your Majesty's orders, but . . ."

"I want him in the Tower," I insisted.

Hatton knew better than to argue with me.

Looking back, I am ashamed. It is a great weakness to take a certain action and then try to defend it by blaming others. As always, I had done what my common sense urged me to do. It was just that I felt so deeply

about this woman. I had been so envious of her; she had had so much . . .
and yet so little. The Tudor claim to the throne was not built on a very
strong foundation. There were many who said that Queen Katharine had
never been married to Owen Tudor; there were many who would say that
my father had never truly been married to my mother and that I was a bastard. These matters rankled. The Stuart claim was legitimate, based on royalty. Then there was that legendary beauty of hers which attracted all men.
I had my admirers, but I had always known in the secret places of my mind
that the glitter of a crown and absolute power can be an irresistible magnet.
Yes, I had envied her in so many ways . . . and pitied her. I often thought of
what her childhood and girlhood had been at the elegant Court of France
and compared it with mine when I had lived through those formative years
under the shadow of the axe; hers so cushioned; mine so harsh; and then
myself on the throne triumphant and Mary an uneasy Queen and a captive
for twenty years. I had no reason to envy her and yet I could not altogether
erase that feeling from my mind. I had thought of her so much and the fact
that I should never see her somehow added to the mystic bond between us.

She had been such a fool. In fact it seemed to me that she had rarely
shown any wisdom at all. She had plunged headlong into disaster; she had
had lovers but what had any of them brought her but misery—except perhaps little François who had adored her, but that was in the early days when
she was the darling of the French Court.

It was true that she had obsessed me in life and now she was doing so in
death and in such a manner that to give myself some ease of mind I was
accusing a sick and innocent man of something he had never committed. He
had never swerved from his duty, yet here I was raging against him, insisting that the poor palsy-stricken creature be taken to the Tower.

Burghley was horrified. He came to me and said it would be well to
release Davison without delay.

"Davison has failed in his duty," I insisted.

"Your Majesty signed the death warrant, which was the right and proper
action to take. Davison merely delivered it to Paulet."

"He knew that I did not wish it to be delivered."

"Did Your Majesty tell him this?"

"It was understood, and since when has my Lord Burghley become the
Queen's judge?"

He was silent but very disturbed.

"I beg Your Majesty to release Davison," he said quietly.

I could not do it. I derived some comfort from blaming my secretary and
I needed comfort. I could not sleep at night. I dreamed of her headless body.
I saw her eyes fixed on me accusingly.

Davison in the Tower offered me some comfort and I clung to that.

He was charged with misprision and contempt, and tried in the Star Chamber. He said that I had signed the death warrant and told him that I could not be troubled anymore with it, which he had taken to mean that I did not want it set before me a second time. He said that there was nothing else he could say and that he had acted sincerely and honestly.

They fined him ten thousand marks and sent him back to the Tower to await my pleasure.

One thing he did not do—which he might have—was to disclose the fact that I had made him write to Paulet suggesting that the Queen of Scots might be quietly removed. I had behaved badly to that man; but while I could convince myself that I had never meant the execution of Mary to be carried out, I could placate my conscience. Like most people who have done some person an injury, I disliked that person more than I had before I wronged him. I built up the case against him in my mind. It was weak; and I hated weakness in myself more than in others. But this was a matter so disturbing to me that I had to ease my conscience even with untruths.

Davison was my scapegoat; but he stopped my nightmares about Mary Queen of Scots. In my fantasy I exonerated myself from having played the chief part in her execution. It helped me considerably.

The Great Victory and the Great Tragedy

ROBERT WAS HOME—A FACT WHICH GAVE ME THE GREAT-est pleasure, and the joy of seeing him far outweighed any rancor I felt for his behavior. It was always like that with Robert. I could be madly angry with him but when he stood before me bowing low, raising his face to mine, I thought how foolish I had been to let him go. We were not so young . . . either of us . . . that we could afford to waste time. I was not going to let him stray far away again.

So he was back in high favor. The Netherlands venture had been a ter-rible disaster. I had always known that wars brought little profit. I had been against going in; it seemed no easy task to defeat the Spaniards even in the Netherlands where they were far from their homeland.

There were disturbing reports coming from Walsingham about the preparations for war. Whom could they plan to strike against but England? And this was confirmed by the fact that they were assembling a mighty armada to come against us.

I was pleased to have in my service such men as Sir Francis Drake—buc-caneers of the sea who were really already at war with the Spaniards, inter-cepting their ships, taking their treasure and showing them that although they might have a great armada, the English were natural men of the sea and were a match for them. Drake had brought home great treasure and for that I was grateful. I was in need of money; the Netherlands had swallowed up vast sums—a waste of money I called it—and I was in sad financial straits; but even so I was not so poor as Philip, which was a comforting thought.

Drake had returned from one of his expeditions with quantities of booty—all taken from the Spaniards—and on the way home he had called in at Cadiz and as he said "singed the beard of the King of Spain." This meant that he had gone in among the ships in the harbor and sunk or burned thirty-three of them and brought away four of them laden with pro-visions.

He had also brought back news that Spain was fast preparing to attack England and that the conflict would take place at sea. Philip must be stopped now and forever. He believed that our ships, which might lack the grandeur of the Spanish galleons, would be a match for them when the time came for them to test their strength.

Younger men were coming to Court to seek their fortunes. The old favorites remained—Robert, Hatton, Heneage—and I loved them all. The fact that they were getting old did not make me love them less. When Walsingham fell ill and Burghley had a fall from his horse, I was really anxious and I visited them and scolded them for not taking greater care of their health. I was a mother to them and they looked to me for comfort. I never failed them as I knew they would never fail me. It was a very special relationship I shared with my men; it was only those who had never broken through into the magic circle—like Davison—who did not enjoy it.

There were two newcomers—two of the most exciting young men I had ever known. One was Robert Devereux and the other Walter Raleigh.

Robert had brought his stepson to Court and clearly wanted me to receive him well. I don't know why I took an instant liking to him—for he was the son of my great enemy, that she-wolf, whom I had never ceased to hate and who had been banished from my Court since her marriage to Robert.

But there was something disarming about Robert Devereux—Earl of Essex since the age of nine when his father had died rather mysteriously in Ireland, poisoned as the chronicler of *Leicester's Commonwealth* put it.

He had been seventeen when Robert had first presented him to me, and I remembered him as the charming boy I had noticed when I had visited Chartley after that memorable time at Kenilworth.

He was most attractive. I thought, grudgingly, that he had inherited his good looks from his mother. He certainly had her auburn hair and dark eyes. He had an unusual way of walking, taking great strides, holding his head a little forward and stooping slightly. There were many beautiful young men in my life but this one was outstanding. He appealed to me immediately not unlike the manner in which Robert had. There had been only two for whom I had felt this romantic feeling until this time. One was Thomas Seymour and the other, of course, Robert. Robert was of my own age, and now that we were old both of us knew that nothing could change between us. No one else could ever mean to me what he did; but I did feel this flutter of romantic feeling for Essex, which was extremely odd because he was Leicester's stepson and the son of the woman I hated more than any other. Perhaps these facts were a fillip to my emotions regarding Essex. I was unsure, but that they existed I knew full well.

My impulse would have been to reject him because obviously *she* would be hoping for his success at Court; but he immediately caught my attention as he had all those years ago at Chartley.

He was very raw—and I saw at once that he had no political sense. He was the sort of man who spoke before he considered the effect his words might have—so he lacked the first quality of a courtier. It was once said of him in my hearing: "He is no good pupil of my Lord Leicester, who is wont to put all his passion in his pocket."

I suppose that was true of Robert. No one knew better than he did how to dissimulate. One could never be absolutely sure with Robert. Perhaps that was what made him so fascinating. Essex left no one in doubt. I often thought this in him might bring about his downfall.

And then there was that other—that dark handsome brilliant man—Walter Raleigh. He was about thirty when he first caught my attention, and he had come to Court to do exactly that, hoping to make his fortune. He was the kind of man who must be noticed sooner or later. He was tall, well-built and outstandingly handsome. He had thick black hair and the ruddy complexion of a countryman; but what was most noticeable about him was his amazing vitality; he seemed to have twice as much energy as most men.

He came to my attention one day when I was out walking surrounded by a group of the ladies and gentlemen of the Court. We had come to a road which was muddy and we stood for a few moments contemplating how best to get across without picking up too much mud. Then Raleigh came forward. He was wearing a beautiful plush coat, which was obviously new, and with a flourish he took it from his shoulders and spread it over the muddy patch for me to walk on.

I always accepted these extravagant gestures gracefully, though I knew that in his heart the young man would count cheap the cost of a coat, however fine, if it brought him royal favor.

But I had noticed him and I asked about him and learned that he was one Walter Raleigh from Devonshire, the county which had brought me my most excellent Francis Drake; and I decided that I would know more of this enterprising young man.

I learned that he had been in trouble. That was inevitable, I assumed, with a man of his spirit. He was quick-tempered, but not reckless with it as Essex was. I thought Raleigh was a man who would weigh well his actions. He was far cleverer than my charming Essex. He was witty, his badinage amusing and his conversation sparkling. Much more than Essex he had the qualifications to make him a success at Court. He had quarreled with Thomas Perrot and that had resulted in a brawl which had brought them to the Fleet Prison for a few days. Then he had had a fight with a man named Wingfield over a game of tennis, which had meant a brief spell in the Marshalsea. He had certainly had some questionable adventures but he had won distinction at sea.

During his early days at Court he had been befriended by Leicester, who also liked his spirit, and he had fallen in with the Earl of Oxford whom, though one of my favorites, I did recognize as a rather disreputable young man for he had behaved abominably to Burghley's daughter and was a real scoundrel. Raleigh and he soon fell out, however, and became enemies.

There was great jealousy between them, but that often happened between my men. Our relationship was such that it engendered jealousy. They really behaved like petulant lovers sometimes. I did not complain. My nature being what it was, I enjoyed it and perhaps encouraged it.

I enjoyed Raleigh's company very much. He was one who set great store on climbing to fame. I did not mind that. A man who will rise must climb.

One day he wrote on a window with a diamond the words:

"Fain would I climb, yet fear I to fall."

And I replied with a diamond I was wearing:

"If thy heart fails thee, climb not at all."

He turned to me, his eyes shining, and I loved him in that moment, for he had the qualities which I admired most in men.

I said: "You will climb, Walter Raleigh. And I do not think you will fall . . . far."

At which he bowed low and said that he would climb to heaven or descend to hell in my service.

Soon after that I gave him a knighthood; he deserved the distinction and was very proud of it. And how watchful he was—and others too—of the favors I bestowed! Essex did not ask for honors; if anything was given to him he took it without question; but he never seemed overgrateful. Raleigh asked audaciously.

Once I said to him: "I wonder when you will stop being a beggar, Raleigh."

And he replied: "When Your Majesty stops being a benefactress."

He laughed and I could not help joining in with him. The exchange was typical of our relationship.

Burghley had brought along his son Robert hoping for advancement from me. I recognized Robert Cecil immediately as one of the clever ones. There was little of the courtier about him. He was very small and suffered from a slight curvature of the spine, which was accentuated by the shape of the coats men were wearing at this time; his neck was slightly twisted too and he had a splay foot; and among so many handsome men he looked like a little elf. I christened him that immediately. So his unprepossessing appearance had brought him to my notice just as Raleigh's gesture with the cloak had done—although, of course, I could not fail to notice Burghley's son. It was rather touching to see the dear old man's devotion to the boy. I loved him for it and determined to do what I could for the Little Elf, which would be easy for I recognized at once that sharp mind behind the pale face, and I believed that Robert Cecil would have done well at my Court without his father's influence.

Then there were the Bacon boys—Anthony and Francis. Francis was a clever boy but inclined to be tutorial, a characteristic which did not appeal greatly to me. Burghley kept them in the background because he did not want them to spoil Robert Cecil's chances; and I knew that if any important post became vacant, Burghley would want it for his son.

Francis, however, wrote a paper entitled *Letter of Advice to Queen Elizabeth,* which in itself was an insolence. It contained his views of the political situation, but they were quite ably expressed and I congratulated him on it. He had at this time become a member of Parliament for Taunton and a bencher at Gray's Inn, so he was entitled to plead in the courts at Westminster.

But of all the interesting young men at Court at this time the favorites were Walter Raleigh and Robert Devereux, Earl of Essex.

As the year progressed there was one thought in everyone's mind, and that was the growing menace of Spain. Everyone was asking: For what reason was Spain building the greatest armada that had ever been seen? There could be only one answer: To attack us.

Philip and I were natural enemies. It was strange to think that once he had been attracted by me when he had been married to my sister. I supposed he had never forgiven me for not leaping at the chance to marry him. If I had done that he would not have found it necessary to spend so much on the building of his armada. He would have taken England, installed the Inquisition and made my country part of Spain. As if I would ever have allowed that! As if I would ever sell my country to Philip of Spain . . . as my sister had done.

Enmity was growing fast between our two nations. We were rivals for sea power. He had fine ships and adventurers to sail them and they had traveled on voyages of discovery round the world; but there had been the English pirates, like Drake and Hawkins, to waylay their ships and rob them of their riches.

I don't think he ever forgave Drake for taking the *San Felipe*—the greatest prize of all—the King's own East Indiaman. Her cargo had been the richest haul even Drake had ever captured—bullion, precious stones, spices, ambergris, fine silks and velvets, materials of all kinds, gold and jewelery, all fell into the hands of Drake.

Moreover the name of Drake was spoken with awe and reverence by the Spaniards. They called him El Draque—the Dragon. They said he was the greatest seaman ever to rove the seas and he was not entirely human. He had the devil in him and that was why it was impossible to beat Sir Francis Drake.

I often thought of Philip—that gloomy fanatic—spending hours on his knees in his Escorial Palace. Did he remember me? He had cast somewhat lascivious eyes on me and there had been hints that he was not averse to frolicking with women. There was that rhyme I remembered from long ago . . . something about the baker's daughter's being more fun than Mary.

Men were very hypocritical and it would not surprise me if, when they knelt in prayer or scourged themselves with whips and tormented themselves with hair shirts, they were indulging in erotic fantasies.

There was a rumor at this time that a young man calling himself Arthur Dudley was treated with some respect at the Court of Madrid. He proclaimed himself to be my son, Leicester being his father. He said that he had been born at Hampton Court and a servant of Kat Ashley had been ordered to bring him up as his own child. He was about twenty-seven years old—a swaggering, swearing braggart, by all accounts. Philip must have known that he was an imposter, but I suppose he thought it politic to discredit me as much as possible, so he pretended to believe the young man and keep him at his Court at the cost of six crowns a day. No doubt he thought the money was well spent.

I could laugh at the absurdity of the tale, but it did bring home the fact that with every month the situation between us and Spain grew more dangerous, and I knew—as did those about me—that the day of reckoning could not be far off.

Walsingham's spies were busy. The armada was complete and ready to sail. There was a story being circulated in Madrid that two men had confessed to a Jesuit priest that they had seen a vision. The confessions were separate and the penitents did not know each other but each had had the same vision. They had seen a mighty sea battle in which the Spanish armada was engaged with another armada. The battle waged fiercely and neither side was winning until angels with great wings descended on the decks of the Spanish ships singing that they had come to protect the defenders of the Faith against the infidels.

"I'll wager our seamen against the angels any day," I said, and those about me laughed.

I knew that we could no longer delay. We had to be ready. I felt that this was the time to which all my reign had been leading. The outcome of this battle would decide whether England was to be free and I was to continue to reign over my beloved country.

I could not believe that I could lose. No, not all the might of Spain could make me believe that. I had my men, and what men they were! I do believe that no monarch had ever had—or ever would have—such men as I had. They were going to save England for me. I knew they would.

I made Robert Lieutenant-General of the troops to show everyone that in spite of what had happened in the Netherlands, I still had the utmost faith in him. Most of the fighting I knew would be done at sea for this was a conflict for sea power—and religion. My men would be fighting to keep out the intolerance of men such as Philip; they would be fighting against the thumbscrews and the terrible instruments of torture which were the weapons of the Inquisition; they were fighting for freedom, for their Queen and their country, and for the right to go on living as they wanted to. It was a great incentive. I doubted the Spaniards would have such a one to fight for.

I had appointed Lord Howard of Effingham to command the fleet, assisted by Drake, Frobisher and Hawkins—the finest seamen in the world. And we had a navy too—not as grand as that of Spain, but does one need grandeur in war? It is men who make ships what they are.

I had the men and it was part of my special talent to have the right men in the places where they could serve me best. I believed that we would defeat the Spaniards even though I was fully aware of their might. They had the largest armada in the world; they were practiced seamen; but the largest did not mean the best and I would stake Englishmen against Spaniards at any time.

Philip was putting up an absurd claim to the throne of England with himself as the legitimate heir through the House of Lancaster because John of Gaunt's daughters had married into Portugal and Castile. I was always uneasy when people laid claim to the throne; my own claim was not founded on such a rock-like foundation that I could lightly dismiss them. It proved to be rather a rash act on the part of Philip for it alienated the Scots who were certainly not going to help Philip come to the throne when in their opinion their own James, son of Mary Stuart, was the true heir.

The Pope had put himself beside Philip. His aim was to destroy me and he was trying to raise the whole of Papal Europe against me. There was a suggestion from some members of the Council that we should massacre all the leading Catholics in the country to avoid an uprising—a kind of repeat performance of the Massacre of Saint Bartholomew's Eve in Paris.

I rejected that immediately. I hoped I had brought a certain tolerance to the country. I know that open Catholic worship was forbidden, but in all other ways those Catholics were good subjects. I was right in this, for many of them proved of considerable value in our stand against the invader.

Rumors were rife and there was a mood of tension throughout the country. I believed that the sooner the battle began, the more relieved we should all feel, but I was horrified when I heard whispers that I had sent an agent to Rome to come to terms with the Pope, for that I would never do. I was head of the Church of England and I would have no foreigner take my place.

I ordered the Bishop of London to anathematize the Pope from the pulpit at St Paul's.

Ships! That was what we needed. Thanks to our foresight over the years we had a considerable navy, but Drake had said that we needed more ships and he was right.

I asked my people for ships and how heartening it was when the City of London, being asked for five thousand men and fifteen ships, immediately offered ten thousand men and thirty ships. That was the spirit of the people when we went out to face the armada.

The Spaniards were boastful. They said there would be one battle at sea and one on land and England would be theirs. I did not boast. I had a feeling that it was dangerous to do so, tempting the fates; but I was supremely confident. Walsingham's men were indefatigable in secret places and I was elated when I heard of the death of the Marquis de Santa Cruz, the Spanish admiral in charge of operations against England, for he was also one of the ablest seamen living. But for him the attack would have been launched earlier, but he, having been greatly impressed by the daring and reputation of El Draque, advised caution. He wanted his armada to be invincible and he needed time to assure himself that it was so.

Philip had upbraided him for sloth, which deeply wounded Santa Cruz, for his zeal was as keen as that of his master, but he was a wiser man. Then suddenly he became ill—no doubt through acute anxiety—and died. It was a great loss to Spain but a benefit to us.

I wanted to say: God is on our side. But I did not. I would not be boastful before victory was won and, whatever good fortune came our way in the end, no one was more conscious than I of the bitter battle which lay ahead.

Philip showed then that he was out of touch with reality when he appointed the Duke of Medina Sidonia as commander of his armada, not because of his skill and experience—he had little of either—but because he belonged to one of the noblest houses in Spain.

It was true that I had chosen Howard of Effingham, scion of one of our noblest families, but he was an able man who had been brought up in a naval tradition. His father, Lord William, and his grandfather Thomas, Duke of Norfolk, had held the post of Lord High Admiral with distinction; and my Vice Admiral was the bold Sir Francis, whose very name struck terror into the Spaniards.

I believed I was better served than Philip, and my men were defending their country which always gives an added zeal and often triumphs over the lust for conquest.

Not only were we preparing our navy but our land defenses also. Vulnerable places like Gravesend were fortified, and we put out barges to block the mouths of rivers to prevent a hostile fleet getting through. All over the country we were preparing for invasion should the gallant sailors fail to hold back the enemy at sea. It was a great joy to me to see the spirit of the people and to know that they were with me.

I was Commander-in-Chief of my army and under me was Robert as Lieutenant-General of the two armies—Lord Hunsdon in command of the second. Robert wrote to me from Tilbury—a letter which I have always preserved for it seemed to me to have been written not only by a soldier but by a lover. In it he set down his views as to how we should proceed if the Spaniards succeeded in setting foot on English soil, but through it all came his great concern for me. After setting out details of how we should march if we had to without much warning, he wrote of me.

"Now for your person, being the most dainty and sacred thing we have in this world to care for, much more for advice to be given in the direction of it, a man must tremble when he thinks of it, specially finding Your Majesty to have that princely courage to transport yourself to your utmost confines of your realm to meet your enemies and to defend your subjects. I cannot, most dear Queen, consent to that, for upon your well doing consists all and some, for your whole kingdom; and, therefore, preserve that above all. Yet will I not that so princely and so rare a magnanimity should not appear to your people and the world as it is. And thus far, if it may please Your Majesty, you may do; withdraw yourself to your home at Havering and your army, being about London, as at Stratford, East Ham, Hackney and those villages thereabout, shall be not only a defense but a ready supply to those counties in Essex and Kent if need be. In the meantime, Your Majesty, to comfort this army and people of both these counties, may, if it please you, spend two or three days to see both the camps and the forts. Tilbury is not fourteen miles at the most from Havering Bower . . .

"Lastly for myself, most gracious lady, you know what will most comfort a faithful servant; for there is nothing in the world I take that joy in, that I do in your good favor . . ."

I read and reread that letter. I kissed it; I folded it and put it away.

And I prepared to leave for Tilbury.

SO I INSPECTED MY troops at Tilbury. Beside me rode Robert, as fine and handsome a figure as ever was, and before me the Earl of Ormond, carrying the sword of state, while a page followed holding my plumed helmet. I was bare-headed and wore a polished steel corselet and a voluminous farthingale. When they saw me my troops broke into prolonged cheering and I was so moved that I was near to tears. I knew that since my accession I had enjoyed a love from my people rarely experienced by a monarch. I had worked hard to preserve it and to appear well in their eyes. They forgave me my faults and remembered my virtues—and that, of course, is the meaning of true love.

They waited for me to address them, which I did in loud ringing tones.

"My loving people, we have been persuaded by some that are careful of our safety to take heed how we commit ourselves to armed multitudes for fear of treachery; but I do assure you, I do not desire to live to distrust my faithful and loving people. Let tyrants fear; I have always so behaved myself that under God I have placed my chiefest strength and safeguard in the loyal hearts and good will of my subjects; and therefore I have come amongst you as you see at this time, not for my recreation and disport, but being resolved in the midst and heat of the battle to live or die amongst you all—to lay down for my God and for my kingdoms, and for my people, my honor and my blood even in the dust. I know I have the body of a weak, feeble woman; but I have the heart and stomach of a king—and of a King of England too—and think foul scorn that Parma of Spain or any Prince of Europe should dare invade the borders of my realm; to which rather than any dishonor should grow by me, I will myself take up arms—I myself will be your general, judge and rewarder of every one of your virtues in the field. I know already for your forwardness, you have deserved rewards and crowns, and we do assure you on the word of a prince, that they shall be duly paid to you. For the meantime my Lieutenant-General shall be in my stead, than whom never prince commanded a more noble and worthy subject; not doubting by your obedience to my General, by your concord in the camp, and your valor in the field, we shall shortly have a famous victory over the enemies of my God, of my kingdoms, and of my people."

The cheers rang out. I had never felt so proud, so determined to do well by them. My love for them was as great as theirs for me.

One man shouted: "Is it possible that any Englishman can abandon such a glorious cause or refuse to lay down his life in defense of this heroic Princess?"

That was the mood of the people. And it was the mood to bring about victory.

The events of that time are engraved on my heart forever so that I shall never forget them; nor, I venture to think, will the world. They will be talked of whenever men talk of England and will stand forever as a monument to us and an example to all other nations forevermore. Freedom is worth fighting for; it is worth paying a high price for, because to die for freedom is to leave this life in a blaze of glory which destroys our weaknesses of the past and makes us at one with the heroes.

It was a fine Friday afternoon of the nineteenth of July of that year 1588

QUEEN OF THIS REALM 371

when Captain Fleming's pinnacle arrived in haste in Plymouth Harbour with the news that the Spanish armada had been sighted off the Lizard. The whole town was agog—except its Admiral, Sir Francis Drake, who was playing a game of bowls on the Hoe.

Perhaps I was a little impatient when I first heard the story of how he had refused to abandon the game, declaring in his nonchalant way that there was plenty of time to finish the game and beat the Spaniards.

But I knew that was Drake's way. It was that in him which inspired his men with respect and the enemy with terror. Whatever his feelings, he was going to behave as though it were impossible that there could be anything but victory over the enemy.

On Saturday, the churches all over the land were full of people praying for victory. It was a solemn country on that morning, for there was not a man or a woman in England who did not know what it would mean to them if the Spaniards were victorious. Their prayers were earnest; their thoughts were with our sailors. Oh God, we prayed, never, never let the invader touch our shores.

And if they came we must be ready. But they would first have to win the battle at sea.

I had always felt that the savage sea was our ally. It had stood between us and danger many times. It was the reason why no foreign army had ever trodden our shores—except the Norman conquerors, some might say; but we *were* the Normans partly; we were a mixed race of Angles, Saxons, Jutes, Romans, Normans . . . It was the blood of all these people who made up an Englishman, so I could say with truth that no invading army had ever conquered *us*. And never should!

I prayed for the men in my ships. I said all the names over and over again: *Achates, Aid, Antelope, Ark* . . . all through the alphabet to *Vanguard, White Bear* and *White Lion*.

"Pray God preserve my men. Give my ships the victory they need so desperately. Take care of my great men. My Howard, my Hawkins, my Frobisher and my incomparable Drake. Give them the wit they need to make good judgment and the strength to carry it out."

I smiled at myself. Here am I giving instructions to God, treating him as a favored subject.

"Please God," I prayed. "Thy will be done, but let it be shown in favor of my great men."

There were the skirmishes, the days when I arose from nights of little sleep and asked for the news. Nothing decided. We had inflicted damage on their ships. They were finding it not so easy as they had thought to. They were failing in their task to defeat the English fleet so utterly that an easy way might be cleared for Parma to sail in, bringing his troops which would take the country.

The Spaniards suffered more acutely from the weather than our sailors. They were finding their splendid galleons unwieldy. Those who were captured said that the Spanish sailors were in terror of El Draque and only slightly less so of Juan Achines, by whom they meant John Hawkins, who like Drake had in his role of pirate of the high seas struck terror into the hearts of so many.

The battle was a hard one. My men had captured several of the Spanish ships and not one of ours was lost. We had the advantage in spite of our inferior armada. We were in home waters fighting for our own country. We could endure the adverse conditions as the Spaniards could not. My admirals were at liberty to act as they thought best suited to the occasion and to take full advantage of every opportunity which offered itself, Medina Sidonia was acting all the time on instructions from Philip. It was true my admirals did not always agree. It was hardly likely that adventurers like Drake and Hawkins would abide by certain formalities natural to a gentleman of Howard's upbringing. They clashed, and my bold Drake on one occasion disobeyed Howard's orders because he believed it would have been disastrous to have obeyed them.

Drake was proved to be right. He was my finest sailor. I can never think of those most fearful yet most glorious days without seeing Drake.

The greatest advantage throughout was fighting in our own waters while the Spaniards were far from home. When they ran out of supplies they had little hope of replacing them; it was different for us. I supposed this was why they planned to take first the Isle of Wight and thus establish a base from which they could supply their ships.

The Spaniards must have been in a sorry state. Parma had been unable to reach them for he had been blockaded by the Dutch. The Spanish sailors had lost their early euphoria. Where were the angels with the protective wings now?

It was decided to send fireships into the armada. It was not the first time this method had been used with success.

I heard of my captains' hurried council later. There was not time to send to Dover for the little ships they needed; the advantage would be lost by delay, so all the captains offered their ships for the purpose. Drake gave the *Thomas;* Hawkins offered one of his and others were soon provided for the purpose.

There was no moon that night, and there was a breeze blowing in the direction of the assembled armada while the tide was running toward them.

Conditions were ideal. Soon eight blazing ships were making their way straight for the Spaniards, sending out fire and setting them ablaze. The air was full of the sound of exploding ordnance as the fire reached the ships.

Complete demoralization throughout the Spanish armada ensued; they cut their cables and blundered about wildly; their riggings become entangled and they were blocking the way of escape for each other in the desperate attempt to escape from the fire ships. Sidonia fired off his gun trying to get the ships to assemble in some sort of order, but the call was ignored; every Spanish captain was intent on getting his ship out of reach of the fires. Thus the fireships had achieved in a few hours that certain victory for which my brave seamen had been fighting for days.

My men were ready to go in for the final attack when Howard, seeing one of the galleasses was in difficulties and realizing that it would be a rich prize, stopped to take it. It was an error because there were fighting men on the galleass who could give a good account of themselves. By pausing Howard had given Drake the opportunity to be the one who led my ships to victory. Howard's error was such as to rob him of a certain amount of the glory, for having captured the rich prize he left one of the small ships to guard it, but as it was nearer to Calais than England, the French boats came out to take it and although the English put up a good fight, artillery from the shore took part and forced my men to retire. So the entire enterprise had been a waste of time on Howard's part. I do not believe that Drake would have made such a mistake. He must have been laughing to himself as he swept down with all the squadrons on the limping Spanish armada.

The battle was not over immediately as it might have been if Howard had kept with the fleet instead of pausing; but the outcome was now sure.

It had seemed at one time that we should snatch not only victory but great prizes—enough to cover the cost of the campaign. But this was denied us. A squall arose. The weather had been our ally so far—and perhaps some would say still was, but it certainly robbed us of our prizes. Our seamen had to look to their own safety in such weather, and when the wind abated it was seen that many of the ships of the once proud Spanish armada were sinking or drifting along to the Flemish coast.

The wind ended the battle; and if we had lost the prizes we had hoped for, we had gained a glorious victory.

I HAD NOW COME to the saddest part of my life. Nothing could ever be the same for me again.

Naturally I wanted to reward the saviors of my country. I gave a pension to Howard and I made Essex a Knight of the Garter for he had played a part in the victory; but the one I wanted to reward most of all was Robert. He had not been at sea but he had been in charge of land defenses and he had worked indefatigably for our safety.

I wanted to make him Lord Lieutenant of England and Ireland, which would have given him more power than anyone in England under me. When I told him, it did me good to see his pleasure, although I was a little anxious about him for he did not look as well as usual. There was a certain pallor of his face, which was the more startling because of his natural high color.

I said: "You are not well."

He replied that he believed he had caught a fever when he was with the army near the salt marshes in Essex.

I gave him a very special remedy which had been given to me and I told him I had had painful headaches myself of late.

I said: "You must take care of yourself. That's a command, Robert."

He smiled at me with infinite love, and although I glowed with pleasure I kept that twinge of uneasiness which always assailed me when I thought he was not in good health. I scolded him lightly for neglecting himself and reminded him that that was the easiest way to earn my displeasure.

We were very close at that time. We always had been, but the defeat of the Spanish armada had brought home to us the intensity of our feelings and what we meant to each other.

I might have guessed there would be an outcry concerning the proposed new appointment for Robert.

Burghley was strongly against it and was supported by both Hatton and Walsingham. It was placing too much power in the hands of one man, said Burghley.

It was most unwise, declared Hatton.

"We shall have Leicester ruling us all," declared blunt Walsingham.

I realized, of course, that in my fondness for Robert I had perhaps gone too far and as the appointment had not yet been confirmed I decided it should be put aside for a while.

Robert was bitterly disappointed, but I did my best to console him.

"You must take good care of your health," I said. "Get well, Robin, and we will go into this matter then."

We decided that he should go to Buxton for the baths, which had done him good before, and he said farewell and went off to make preparations for the journey.

A few days after he left I received a letter from him. I read and re-read it and shall treasure it forever. Whenever I see that handwriting it brings him back to me so clearly.

"I most humbly beseech Your Majesty," he wrote, "to pardon your poor old servant . . ."

The two "o"s in *poor* were written to look like eyes—my name for him, which he had always loved to hear me use.

". . . to be thus bold in thus sending to know how my gracious lady doeth and what ease of her late pains she finds, being the chiefest thing in this world I do pray for, for her to have good health and long life.

"For my own poor case I continue still your medicine and find it amends much better than with any other thing that hath been given me. Thus hoping to find perfect cure at the bath, with the continuance of my wonted prayer for Your Majesty's most happy preservation, I humbly kiss your foot.

"From your old lodging at Rycott this Thursday morning, ready to take my journey.

"By Your Majesty's most faithful obedient servant,

"R. Leicester."

That letter was written on the twenty-ninth of August. By the fourth of September he was dead.

When they brought me the news I was stunned. I could not believe it. It was some hideous joke. Death! Not Robert! He had always been so alive. He was fifty-five years old—more or less my own age. Never to see him again! Never to hear his voice! Never to wonder what secrets he was hiding behind those enigmatic eyes!

There was no savor in life. There never would be again for Robert Dudley was dead.

I ordered everyone out of my apartment and shut myself in. I would have no intrusion on my grief. I lay on my bed and thought of everything . . . right from the time when we were children and had danced at my father's Court; I thought of those weeks when I had been in the Tower and he had been near; I thought of the day he had come to me and laid his gold at my feet, and how he had ridden into London with me at the time of my accession. So many memories. That was all I had left now.

I took his letter and read and read it again. I kissed it. It was wet with my tears. Then I wrote on it "His Last Letter" and put it in a jewel box. I would preserve it forever. Perhaps later I could draw comfort from it, but now it only brought home to me the magnitude of my loss.

Then I took out one by one the presents he had given me over the years. They had all meant something special to me because he had given them. There was the bracelet of gold adorned with rubies and diamonds. He had given me this in a purple velvet case embroidered with Venetian gold in the year 1572 when I had been fourteen years on the throne. The following year he had given me a collar of rubies and diamonds.

I put them both on and remembered the time he had brought them to me. I could see him with his handsome dark head bent as he fixed the collar about my throat.

Then there was the white feather fan with the two magnificent emeralds on one side of the handle and the inevitable rubies and diamonds on the other.

I brought them all out, his gifts over the years, love-tokens all of them.

And, I thought, there will never be another.

How ironical was life! God had given me this magnificent victory and had taken away the one I loved—shall I say better than anything else. No, that would not be quite true. I loved my country more than anything else, more than my own life or that of Robert. And I had just been given the finest example of God's grace when my seamen with the help of His winds had scattered the mighty so-called invincible armada along the inhospitable coasts of Scotland and Ireland and driven off the Spanish menace forever. But at the same time He had dealt me this most cruel and tragic blow.

He had taken Robert from me.

Time passed, but I did not notice. There were knocks at my door, but I ignored them. I could not bear to look on anyone at this time.

I do not know how long I kept them out. I don't know whether I should have eventually let them in.

Burghley spoke to me from outside, begging me to open the door. But I just sat in stony silence. I cared for nothing. I could think of nothing but: Robert is dead.

Vaguely I heard Burghley's voice outside the door.

"Your Majesty, for God's sake open the door. Are you ill? We beg you to let us in."

But still I sat there. I could only think of Robert, who had been so alive and now was dead.

There was a whispering outside my door. Then I heard the tremendous noise as the door burst open.

Burghley stood there. He hastened forward and seeing me cried: "Thank God. We feared for Your Majesty." He was on his knees. "Forgive me, Your Majesty. We were very much afraid. Your Majesty, you must rouse yourself. England needs you."

And as I looked at him—my dear tired old Spirit, who had been my good friend for so long—I knew that he was right.

I put out my hand. He took it and kissed it.

"You speak truth," I said. "I must about my business."

And then I began to live again.

CHERE WERE RUMORS about his death. They aroused my anger to such an extent that my grief was somewhat assuaged. Could it be true? There had been so many suspicions concerning the manner in which he had removed those who stood in his way, was it possible that he had met a fate which, many said, he had meted out to others?

Could it really have been that Robert had been murdered?

I should not believe it. It was idle gossip. Heaven knew, I had suffered enough from that—and so had Robert. But rumor persisted.

His wife, that she-wolf, Lettice Knollys, had taken a lover, it was said— her husband's young Master of Horse, Christopher Blount.

How dared she! She who had the most wonderful man in the country so to demean herself . . . and him . . . by taking a lover! I never hated her so much as I did at that time, for although I had hated her for taking him from me, I hated her more for turning to someone else who must be inferior—for how could anyone equal him?

It was said that Robert had discovered the liaison and had intended to take revenge on her. But she had maneuvered that he should drink the poisoned cup which he had prepared for her.

It could not be true. No one would ever be able to do that to him. I would not believe that he had died through poison. The doctors said it was a fever and I knew he had caught that in the Essex salt marshes. He had said so himself before he went back to her.

Yet I wanted to believe it. I wanted to hate her more than I had ever done before.

One of his servants declared he had seen the Countess give the Earl a goblet, after drinking the contents of which, the Earl had collapsed.

I believed she was capable of that and if she had taken a young lover . . . Oh, I had warned him that he would one day come to feel her poisoned fangs.

But the autopsy revealed no poison in his body and she was exonerated; but I should never be sure for I knew that the clever Dr Julio, like many Italians, had poisons which killed and left no trace.

I hated her because he had loved her enough to brave my wrath and marry her; but I would certainly hate her more if it were proved that she had hastened his death and robbed me of the one person I loved more than I ever could anyone else.

When his will was read it did not seem that he was aware of her infi-

delity, for he left her well provided for and there was no hint that he had a
rival for her affections.

How touched I was when I read what he had written:

*"And first of all, before and above all persons, it is my duty to remember my
most dear and gracious Sovereign, whose creature, under God, I have been,
and who hath been a most bountiful and princely mistress . . ."*

So he went on to praise me and to say that it had been his greatest joy
in life to serve me. He prayed to God to make me the oldest prince that ever
reigned over England. And he bequeathed to me a jewel with "three fair
emeralds with a large table diamond in the middle and a rope of pearls to
the number of six hundred." These gifts were to have been mine when he
entertained me at Wanstead . . . so he must have known that he was near
death.

After that he went on to write of his wife:

*"Next to Her Majesty, I will return to my dear wife, and set down for her
that which cannot be so well as I would wish it, but shall be as well as I am
able to make it, having always found her a faithful and very loving and obedient careful wife, and so do I trust this will of mine shall find her no less
mindful of me being gone, than I was always of her being alive . . ."*

He could have known nothing of her infidelity—if infidelity there
was—when he wrote that. He had left her Wanstead and Drayton Basset in
Staffordshire and two manors—Balsall and Long Itchington in Warwick-
shire. I was glad Kenilworth did not go to her. Strangely enough he
acknowledged paternity of Douglass Sheffield's son—that one who called
himself Robert Dudley—and he had left him well provided for. Although
Kenilworth had gone to Robert's brother, Ambrose, Earl of Warwick, on his
death it was to go to Robert's base-born son.

I was sure Lettice was grinding her teeth about that. The biggest prize—
splendid Kenilworth—was not for her.

I was glad. I could not have borne thinking of her there in that beautiful castle where I had spent such a memorable time with Robert.

So she was free now . . . free to marry her lover, which the brazen creature could not do immediately, but she did within a year of Leicester's death.
She was bold, that one. I admired her in a way—but I hated her more than
ever.

Robert proved to have been deeply in debt. His debts to the Crown
alone were over twenty-five thousand pounds. He had spent extravagantly
on gifts to me, and I was touched to discover that, apart from the upkeep of
his magnificent houses, that was his main expenditure. The houses had of

course cost him very dear; he had the richest curtains and tapestries I had seen outside royal palaces. In fact some of Leicester's rooms had been much grander than those of Greenwich or Hampton.

I had always rejoiced that he lived like a king even though I had denied him the satisfaction of being one.

Some of those houses had been passed on to Lettice Knollys. Well, she should pay his debts. I let it be known that I insisted that Lord Leicester's debts should be paid in full and the burden of those debts rested on the shoulders of that careful, loving and obedient wife.

She immediately declared that she had not the means to pay her late husband's debts to which I replied that she had valuable articles in those grand houses which were now hers and they could be sold . . . all those art treasures, all those fine carpets and hangings and four-poster beds. Their sale would meet the cost of Leicester's indebtedness.

How she must have raged! I imagined her at Wanstead among her newly acquired possessions. She had thought herself so clever to have married rich Leicester. Well, now she should discover that he owed his greatness to me, and if I said she should give up the articles she valued to pay what her husband owed, then she would do so.

I had scored a victory over the she-wolf, which brought me some satisfaction, though it did not ease the ache in my heart.

IF ONLY HE HAD been beside me how I would have reveled in those celebrations which were taking place all over the country in honor of the great victory over the Spanish armada.

The most important of them all was the thanksgiving at St Paul's when I rode in state through the city of London attended by members of my Privy Council, the bishops, judges and nobles of the land. I sat in a triumphal chariot shaped like a throne with a canopy over it in the form of a crown. Two white horses drew this and next to me rode my newly appointed Master of Horse, Robert Devereux, Earl of Essex.

It gave me some comfort to look at him. He was not Robert, of course, but there was an indefinable charm about him, and I had a special fondness for him. He lacked Robert's suave manners; very few of my men were as outspoken as Essex; he was the sort of man who would make no concessions in his conversation . . . even to his Queen. But he admired me. I knew that because I read it in his eyes, in his gestures; and being the young man he was his feelings must be sincere. With most of the others I should have known they were looking for advancement, but with Essex, he must admire me for he would not pretend to do so if he did not. In a way Essex was in love with me. It may seem absurd for a young man of his age to feel love for an old woman, but it was a special sort of love. It was not a physical emotion. That would have been abhorrent to me . . . but a kind of adoration. It might have been for my royalty or my strength of character; but there were times when he appeared to be dazzled by my person. I was always bejeweled with emeralds, rubies and diamonds and my gowns were decorated with scintillating aglets; my ruffs often sparkled with tiny diamonds; so I was a figure of splendid royalty. But Essex had a special kind of devotion to give me which was different from that I received elsewhere. All my beautiful men—Raleigh, Hatton, Heneage, Oxford, behaved as though they were in love with me. Some were—Hatton, I think. He had remained a bachelor all his life; not that he—unlike Robert—had hoped for marriage, but simply out of love for me. That was touching. Dear Hatton! Burghley, Walsingham . . . well, to them I was their beloved Queen and they served me devotedly. But with Essex it was different. There was an element of romance in his feelings for me—and that did more to soothe my pain at the loss of Robert than anything else could, and I must be grateful to him for that.

So it pleased me to see him riding beside me, looking extremely distinguished and handsome with that thick auburn hair and those big expressive dark eyes—that look of Lettice which irritated me a little. I was not sorry that the man I had taken such a fancy to was her son.

We passed through the gates of Temple Bar where I was received by the Lord Mayor and Aldermen, and after the ceremony of the keys the scepter was placed in my hands.

From the Temple to St Paul's the streets were hung with rich cloth and the people crowded out to cheer me. I entered the church under my canopy while the clergy sang the litany; and afterward I listened to the sermon which was given by the Bishop of Salisbury.

His text was: "Thou didst blow with the winds and they were scattered."

It was more than that, I thought. My gallant seamen did a great deal toward gaining that victory; and the winds which finally scattered the armada—*after* it was beaten—were responsible for our losing the prizes; the booty from those ships would have covered the cost of the enterprise.

After the service I returned through those decorated streets to the palace of the Bishop of London. The cheers thundered out and I knew that whatever tragedy had come to me, I still held the hearts of my people.

It was a time for rejoicing, and would have been the happiest time of my life if Robert had been beside me.

I was trying to stop thinking of him and I told myself that this victory was my great compensation. We had dispersed the menace of years. The Spaniards had been too crippled, too ignobly defeated, to come again to us.

My people revered me. They loved me. There could not have been a reigning monarch who was more beloved by the people.

I had another example of this a few days later when I was returning from the Council. It was December and dark and I came back to my palace lighted by torches.

A rumor had gone around telling the people that if they waited they would catch a glimpse of me. Thus, when I returned I found a crowd gathered at the gates.

A cheer went up as the people saw me and many of them cried: "God save Your Majesty."

I stopped my coach and called to them: "God bless you all, my good people."

Then the cry went up again from all assembled there. It was deafening. "God save Your Majesty."

I was deeply moved. I held up my hand and there was an immediate silence.

"Dear people," I said, "ye may have a greater prince, but ye shall never have a more loving one."

They were all about me. I smiled and waved my hand and they saw that I was as affected as they were. Some were in tears and I knew that they would have died for me.

My spirits were uplifted. My life had lost that which had made it joyous, but I had to go on. It was a fortunate ruler who after thirty years of rule could arouse such emotions.

I was amused that the Spaniards should attempt to tell their people that they had had a great victory. Philip must indeed be governing a country of fools. Did not the Spaniards know that they had lost their armada which they had been told was invincible?

A pamphlet which was being circulated throughout Europe came into my hands. It made us laugh. It was so ridiculous. It was supposed to have been written by an eyewitness of the great battle and was called *Relations and Advise come to His Majestie from the Happie Fleete whereoff is Generall the Duke of Medina in the Conquest of England.*

It explained how the English had been hopelessly defeated, fled or been captured, and the Duke of Medina Sidonia had El Draque as his prisoner.

We ceased to laugh because we feared that some people who were away might believe these lies.

Drake was furious; so was Raleigh; and one of them produced a counterattack in the shape of a pamphlet entitled *A Packe of Spanish Lyes, sent abroad to the world Now Ripped Up, Unfolded and by Just Examination, con-*

*demned as conteyning false, corrupt and detestable wares worthy to be damned
and burned.*

How I despised them! They had been overboastful before the conflict.
Surely it was tempting fate to call an armada invincible? They had come
with their instruments of torture to set up their vile Inquisition in our land
with their organization of pious persecution. They had been soundly beaten;
and now they sought to cover up their ignoble defeat by telling blatant lies
which they hoped the world would believe.

Where was the armada? Where were those braggarts who had set out to
conquer England? Many were at the bottom of the ocean, some faring not
too comfortably I imagined along the inhospitable coasts.

It is a pitiable nation which is boastful in planning and despicable in
defeat.

I ordered that this great victory should not be forgotten. I had two
medals struck. One showed the Spanish armada in flight and it was inscribed
Venit, Vidit, Fugit. Julius Caesar had said that he came and saw and conquered, so my medal said they came and saw and fled.

The other medal was inscribed *Dux Foemina Facti.* Well, there were
many men who doubted the ability of a woman to rule. In France they had
their foolish Salic law which prevented a woman's mounting the throne. It
was a mercy there was no such law in England. I wanted the whole world to
know that a woman was able to rule as well as a man—in some cases with
greater skill.

I did not mean to imply that I alone had driven off the Spaniards. I knew
our success had been due to our brilliant seamen and the planning of my
ministers. But I had been at the head of affairs. I was the figurehead. I was
the Queen for whom men fought; and I knew full well that a share of the
triumph was mine.

So the celebrations continued and all the time there was a dark shadow
over my life. He was gone. I should never see my sweet Robin again.

The Rise of Essex

LOOKING BACK, I WONDER WHY I LOVED ESSEX SO MUCH. IT must have been because I was looking for a substitute for Robert. It was a hopeless quest, because there could never be one to take his place, and in any case I was not the same young woman as that one of twenty-five who had fallen so deeply in love that I had almost been ready to share my throne with him.

Essex was handsome; his name was Robert; he was different from the other young men of my Court. His manner, which could be sullen, singled him out. Although why I should have been attracted by that, I cannot imagine. Perhaps somewhere in my mind was the niggling thought that he was *her* son and in winning him to my side I was taking him away from her.

Whatever it was I was more drawn to him than to any other—even dashing and often impudent Raleigh, who ran him rather close.

Essex never made concessions. I remembered him as a boy, not long after our first meeting at Chartley when he had been brought to Court and I offered to kiss him, for he had very handsome looks even then; he had quietly rejected the offer, which I had found amusing then, but which seemed to me now an indication of what was to come. I remember, too, that he wore his hat in my presence and it had to be snatched off his head for he would not remove it.

So perhaps I should have been prepared.

He was openly defiant. He presumed on my favors and there were many incidents when I almost felt I would send the young man from Court to teach him a lesson. If Robert had been there I should have done so. I should have had no need of him then; but talking with him, accepting his indifference to my crown, in some way helped me to forget that other Robert—and I needed to forget all the time.

Essex wanted his own way, but he was impulsive and there was nothing calculating about him; that was where he was so different from my other men. There had never been anyone quite like him. I knew it was unwise to indulge him too much, but whenever I saw that slightly stooping figure coming toward me, and when I looked up into the blazing admiration—which must be genuine for he would never pretend—my heart warmed toward him and I felt happier than I had believed I could possibly feel without Leicester.

A typical example of his behavior was when we were paying a visit to

Warwick's place at North Hall. Essex's sister, Penelope Rich, was staying there, and I did not care to receive her. For one thing she was Lettice's daughter, and if that were not enough to damn her in my eyes, she was conducting an adulterous intrigue with Charles Blount, who had become Lord Mountjoy on the death of his elder brother. Mountjoy was one of my favorite young men, being accomplished and handsome, and I deeply resented his indulging in this affair with Penelope Rich. If they had kept it secret, it would have been a different matter, but Penelope had openly left her husband and set up house with Mountjoy.

"Her mother's daughter" was my wry comment, when I heard of it.

And so I came to North Hall with my courtiers. We were met by Essex himself, who had come out to welcome us.

I soon learned the reason for his coming. He wanted to warn me that his sister was at North Hall and to beg me to receive her.

I should have welcomed him more warmly if I had thought he had come to greet me rather than to plead for his sister, so I coldly said that I would not receive his sister and that it would be better for her to remain in her apartments during my visit.

The color flamed into his face. He demanded to know why I received Mountjoy and banished his sister.

I replied that I had no intention of bandying words with him and turned away; but he remained beside me. I was unfair to his family, he said. I would not receive his mother at Court yet she had done nothing . . . officially . . . to displease me.

I could not say: She married Robert and she was not even faithful to him. So I signed to one of the others to take Essex's place beside me and he had no help for it but to fall back. He was really angry when, arriving at the house, I gave orders that Penelope Rich should stay in her apartments as long as I was at North Hall, as I had no wish to see her.

He was a hot-headed fool. He could never realize when it was wise to stop. Indeed that was his downfall. At supper he again tried to talk to me. Why should I not receive his sister? Was it not unfair to blame her? Had I not received Mountjoy? Surely I could not be prejudiced against my own sex?

"Your Majesty, I beg you to receive my sister . . . to please me."

I knew that many present were waiting on my words. They were beginning to say: She is as fond of Essex as she was of Leicester. But Robert would never have been so foolish as to pursue a matter such as this when I had clearly made my feelings known!

I said: "You are mistaken, my lord Essex, if you think you can persuade me to do something which I have determined not to. I shall not have it said that I received your sister to please you."

"No," he cried hotly. "You will not receive her because you wish to please that knave Raleigh." He was shouting. "You will always pleasure that pirate. You would disgrace both me and my sister because that country churl asks it."

"Be quiet, you young fool," I said. "I order you to say no more on this subject."

But he would not be quiet. He began to shout abuse of Raleigh, for the two of them were more jealous of each other than any two men I have ever known—and I had seen some jealousies at Court! I was alarmed for him—angry as he made me—for Raleigh was actually a member of this party. Quite clearly he was out of earshot at this moment, but I could picture those two fighting each other to the death of one of them.

I lost my temper too—which I did even more easily than I had in my youth. I said: "How dare you shout at me! How dare you criticize others in this way! Be silent! Or you will find there is no place for you at my Court. As for your sister, she is another such as your mother. It seems to me you are birds of a feather, and I should make sure that none of your breed enter my Court. I should send you away."

"Then do so," he cried. "I have no wish to serve a mistress who allows adventurers to fawn upon her. Raleigh wants me gone. Very well. I leave you to your favorites. I shall go away from here and take my sister with me."

No one had ever seen such a display of insolence before. If anyone else had attempted it, I should have ordered an immediate arrest.

But he looked so young, with the anger in his eyes, so I merely said: "I am weary of this foolish boy," and turned away.

He strode out of the hall.

The next morning I learned that he had left North Hall. He had sent his sister home with an escort and made his way to Sandwich, intending to embark for the Low Countries.

I immediately sent a party of guards to bring him back.

He was already on a ship which was about to sail so I caught him in time. When told that my orders were that he should return at once, he defiantly refused to do so; but the guards informed him that if he did not accompany them willingly, they would take him by force.

So he returned and in due course I sent for him.

He came to me—quite unabashed.

"You are a foolish boy," I said. "Never do that again or I shall send you to the Tower. I have been lenient with you and your tantrums, but you should take care that you do not try me too far."

He was sulky, but after a few days I forgave him, and he was back in favor again—as much as he had ever been.

He was one of those young men who created storms wherever he went. Sometime earlier he had quarreled bitterly with Mountjoy—who had been Charles Blount at that time. I had taken a fancy to Blount as soon as he appeared. Handsome, and with a great deal of charm, he was also clever, so he had all the qualifications needed to bring him into the group which I kept around me. I showed my pleasure in his company by presenting him with a golden chessman which he attached to the sleeve of his coat, so that the sign of my favor might be prominently displayed.

Essex had regarded himself as my very favorite young man at that time and he had been furiously jealous of the attention I bestowed on Blount, and being Essex he made no attempt to disguise his feelings.

In the hearing of several courtiers he commented: "Now, I perceive, every fool must wear a favor." This remark was reported to Blount without delay and that young man lost no time in challenging Essex to a duel.

I knew nothing of this or I should have stopped it, but it went ahead with the result that Blount disarmed Essex and wounded him—though only slightly.

I was furious. Although I liked to see my young men jealous, I was horrified at the prospect of some harm coming to them—so I reprimanded them both and sent them from the Court for a while.

"By God's death," I said, "it is fitting that someone should take Essex down and teach him better manners." The fact was that I was so relieved that no great harm had come to either; and with typical perversity, Essex expressed an admiration for Blount and from then on they became good friends. It was through this incident that Blount came to know Essex's family better, and in due course set up house with Penelope.

After the death of Robert I had found myself looking anxiously at my dear ministers and wondering morbidly who would be the next to leave me. I sometimes wondered whether I should ever find any to replace them. No one could take Robert's place, of course, but that was different. Robert was unique. But Burghley, Walsingham, Heneage, Hatton . . . men like that, who had served me well, were exceptional men. Each had his very special qualities and none appreciated more than I their rarity.

I was really worried about Walsingham. He must be sixty or near it and he had never been robust; he had worked every hour of the day and had never spared himself. The spy system he had created was the finest in Europe. We might never have beaten the Spanish armada if we had not been kept so well informed of its movements and of what was going on in the secret conclaves of diplomatic Spain. He had had his men in every conceivable place and they had been of inestimable value to us.

And now poor Walsingham was failing. All through the year he had been unwell, although he had continued to keep in close touch with his spies in every country in Europe.

So it was a very great blow to me when he died that April at his home in Seething Lane.

Another dear friend and able minister gone! This was the tragedy of growing old when one's friends went one by one like leaves falling from trees at the approach of winter.

One was left wondering: Who next?

He left a note in his will that he was to be buried without cost or ceremony because he was deeply in debt and had little to leave. He had spent his fortune lavishly on his spy organization, for he had wished to extend it beyond what the state was prepared to give. And thus he had little to leave to his own family.

They buried him late at night in Paul's church and, as he had wished, without ceremony.

I shut myself away to mourn. I wished that I had done more for him when he was alive. I should have questioned him about his financial position. It seemed churlish to have allowed him to spend his fortune on the welfare of the state. But that was how he would have it. There could never be a greater patriot.

I would keep an eye on his daughter Frances.

She was a good quiet girl and I was fond of her for her own sake as well as her father's. I had thought her an excellent wife for Philip Sidney, for she was a beautiful, gentle girl, and I was pleased that he should marry her and put that odious Penelope Rich out of his mind.

Frances Walsingham had a daughter by Sidney—she must have been about seven years old at this time—a pleasant child to whom I had acted as godmother. And when Philip had been wounded in battle, Frances, again pregnant, had gone out to nurse him. Unfortunately he had died and she, poor soul, had lost the child she was carrying and come near to death herself.

Since then she had lived quietly with her mother and I thought I should bring her to Court and perhaps find a husband for her. I owed that to Walsingham since his widow and daughter had very little money.

Not long after Frances had come to Court I noticed something about her which aroused my interest. At first I could not believe it. She was such a virtuous girl, and nothing had been said of any suitor for her hand. I should have been the first to know if any had honorable intentions toward her. Surely Frances was not the sort to indulge in immoral relations outside marriage. It was unthinkable. What would my poor Moor have had to say to that!

I decided I would watch her. It might be that she suffered from some minor ailment. Poor girl, she had gone through a good deal after the birth of that stillborn baby, and had been very ill. Perhaps it was the result of all the tragedy that I was seeing now.

But there came a time when I believed my suspicions to be correct.

I called her to me and said: "Frances, does anything ail you?"

"No, Your Majesty," she answered promptly.

I said: "Come here."

She came wonderingly and I prodded her in the stomach.

"I have for some time wondered," I said, "if you were carrying something which a virtuous widow would not be expected to."

Frances was so taken aback that she flushed scarlet.

"So," I cried, "I was right. You had better explain yourself, my lady."

Frances held her head high and looked defiant.

I slapped her face. I was so angry with her. I had misjudged her. I had thought her a good, quiet, virtuous widow and when any of those about me indulged in furtive love affairs I always felt enraged. Perhaps it was because of my own virgin state. I was not sure. I certainly did not wish it to be otherwise . . . and yet there was this anger at the indulgence of others.

I said impatiently: "Come, come. Who is the man?"

Frances astonished me then, for she held her head even higher and said: "My husband."

"Your husband!" Another of those secret marriages which I deplored! How dared they go behind my back and marry without my consent? If they wished to marry was I not the first to be told?

"Why was my permission not asked for this marriage?" I demanded.

Frances held her head still higher, her beautiful face showing a rare defiance as she replied: "I could not think that I was of sufficient importance to warrant informing Your Majesty."

"Not of sufficient importance! Did I not love your father! Did he not enjoy my highest regard? Have I not always looked to you for his sake? Not of sufficient importance indeed!"

I slapped her again. She took a few paces back and as I saw the red mark on her cheek where I had struck her, my anger increased.

I took her by the arm and shook her.

"Your father married you in secret to Philip Sidney. I berated him strongly for such an act and he made like excuse. Not important enough to warrant my attention! Did you know that I scolded him and told him he showed scant gratitude to me to tell me I thought him of no importance. Have I not looked to you since he died? I would have found a suitable marriage for you. Tell me now who is this man who has got you with child? I will not have this philandering at my Court."

She would not answer and I was beginning to feel uneasy.

I cried: "I grow impatient. His name! Come girl, do you want me to force you to talk?"

She fell to her knees and buried her face in my skirts. I was becoming quite sorry for her. She was really distressed, and the girl had had such a bad time with Sidney writing all those love poems to Penelope Rich while he was married to her, and then dying at Zutphen after her going out to nurse him and losing the child she was carrying. Yes, I was sorry for her. Perhaps she had been lonely. Well, I would make this knave marry her—if he were not already married—and the marriage should take place before the child was born.

"Are you going to tell me, Frances?" I said more gently.

She raised her agonized eyes to my face and nodded.

"Well?" I prompted.

She began to talk incoherently. "We met in the Netherlands . . . He was with the army . . . He was there with Philip . . . We have known each other well . . . We loved . . . We . . . married . . ."

"Who?" I demanded.

There was a pause of a second or two; then she said in a voice I could scarcely hear: "My lord Essex."

"Essex!" I thundered.

She rose to her feet and took a few paces away from me, and without asking permission she turned and ran as fast as she could from my presence.

Essex! I thought. My Essex! And he had philandered with this girl, Walsingham's daughter! No, he had married her. He had dared to do that without telling me . . . without asking my permission. Oh, the traitor! The deceiver! All the time he had been showing me how much he adored me, he had been making love with this girl . . . even marrying her!

I shouted: "Send for Essex."

He came sauntering in with that nonchalance which delighted me while it angered me.

He would have taken my hand and kissed it but I stood glowering at him.

"So, Master Husband," I said, "you are here."

Understanding dawned on him and what infuriated me was that he did not care. He knew that I had learned of his marriage and he was shrugging his shoulders. How different it had been with Leicester when I heard that he had married Lettice Knollys. He had made an excuse. I had refused him so many times, and he had been contrite and eager to make me understand that whoever came into his life, I was the first and always would be. With Essex there had been no suggestion of marriage with me. On the other hand he was my favorite young man and I had made it clear that I wanted to be aware of all the proposed marriages of my important courtiers.

He said rather carelessly: "So the news is out?"

"Your pregnant wife has told me."

"Well it could not remain a secret forever, could it?"

"And why must it be a secret?" I asked.

"Because I feared Your Majesty's disapproval."

"You were right to fear that."

"I thought you were fond of Frances. You are a godmother to Sidney's child. Her father was one of your most able statesmen and you always showed great appreciation of his services."

"To marry . . . without my consent . . . *you*!"

He replied coolly: "I adore Your Majesty. You are a divine being, apart from all others. I have loved you from my boyhood when I first saw you at Chartley. My great joy in life is to serve you . . ."

"And take steps behind my back?"

"I am a man who must live his own life and marry where I will."

"If there is one thing I hate most in my subjects it is deceit."

"No deceit was intended. Frances's father approved of the match."

"I've no doubt he did. He wanted his daughter well provided for."

"It seemed to us that his consent was enough."

"You are insolent," I cried. "You have enjoyed great favor at Court. I gave you that. I brought you to the position you now enjoy. You must not forget that I can cast you down as quickly as I brought you up."

"That is true," he said lightly, "and I must accept Your Majesty's decision as to my future."

"Why do this in secret?"

"I know Your Majesty's uncertain temper and I had naturally no desire to arouse it."

"You insolent dog!" I cried.

"That is not insolence, Your Majesty," he replied with a slight smile, "just honest frankness for which you have so often commended me. If I had come to you and asked permission, you would have refused it. Then I should have had to disobey you. Now I have merely displeased you."

I was so hurt, and angry with myself, for caring so much about this brash young man.

I said: "It is not the secrecy only which I find insupportable. I had plans for a grand marriage for you. I had been considering that . . . and now you go and tie yourself up with this girl . . ."

"Walsingham's daughter."

"Penniless!"

"I do not set great store by riches."

"Nor on royal favor either, it would seem. I believe you will be wanting to spend time with your wife . . . particularly in view of her condition. So, we shall not be seeing you at Court for some time, I gather."

It was dismissal. Banishment.

He bowed low and with great dignity retreated.

I WAS IN A mood of dejection for days. Essex's absence from Court reminded me of the old days when Leicester had not been there. What was it about them? Was it a certain magic in their personalities which made life seem flat without them?

Raleigh was much in evidence, and he was a charming young man, very interesting to talk to, as well as gallant in manner, behaving toward me as though he were a lover. That was soothing and helped to shut out from my mind the thought of Essex and Frances together. Perhaps I should cultivate Raleigh, let the beautiful young men squeeze Essex out. He had gone too far—not only by making this marriage but in his entire attitude toward me.

Poor Frances! I thought. If stories are true she will have a philanderer for a husband. She should not forget that Essex had the blood of that she-wolf in his veins.

I danced merrily with my young men. I did not ask for news of Essex; but I was sad and depressed. How life had changed! My dearest one gone. Walsingham gone. And poor old Hatton sick and ailing. Nothing would be the same again.

Hatton had been out of favor. It was a foolish matter over some money he owed the crown. I had always been insistent that debts should be paid. In fact when I played cards in the evening and won I never allowed anyone to default on payment. I had not realized that Hatton was financially pressed. These men of mine lived in such splendor and spent so lavishly that I imagined they were richer than they made out to be.

Hatton had pleaded an inability to meet the debt and I had insisted it be paid.

The effect of this had worsened his illness so that he was confined to his bed and I was horrified to learn that the doctors considered his condition to be grave.

I immediately went to Ely House where I found him in bed. They were trying to make him take a posset, and I was alarmed to see that his hands shook so much that he could not hold the dish.

As I entered this was taken away from him and he made an attempt to rise. I quickly forbade him to do this, and then I dismissed those in the bedchamber and sat down beside his bed.

I could have wept to see the ravages of pain on the face of my once so handsome dancing partner.

"Your Majesty does me great honor . . ." he began.

"Be silent," I commanded. "Talking takes too much effort for you. My dear old Mutton, here is a pretty pass. You must get well at once. I command you to do so. We miss you at Court."

He smiled and shook his head and an infinite sadness swept over me.

"My Eyes have gone. My Moor has left me. I must keep my old Bellwether."

"Your Majesty has made me very happy."

"Methinks we have made each other happy over the years," I said. "Now enough of this. What is this posset we have here?" I picked up the dish and sniffed it, recognizing it as a well known remedy and an efficacious one. "I know this well," I said. "Many times have I benefited from it. Eat it. It will give you strength."

He took the dish from me but his hands were shaking too much for him to lift the spoon to his mouth, so I took it and fed it to him.

"There," I said, as though talking to a child, "take every drop."

And he did so, smiling almost sheepishly.

"Your Majesty should not so humble herself."

"Humble myself!" I cried. "You are one of my men, and I love my men. They are to me the husband and the sons I never had."

I saw the tears on his cheeks. He was very moved.

I bent over him and kissed his brow, and I said to him: "You must obey your Queen, Chancellor, and she orders you to get well."

This was one of the occasions when Christopher Hatton did not obey me.

I felt his loss deeply . . . more than I had imagined possible. There were few of my own generation left now. New men were appearing on the horizon and I wondered whether I should get the same unswerving devotion from them as I had had from those who had brightened my youth. They were a different breed: Essex, Raleigh, Mountjoy . . . No, the days were passing. Life would never be quite so wonderful again.

Hatton's death was a loss to the country as well as a personal one. Because he had been so handsome and such a good dancer, people had been apt to underestimate him. He had been an excellent Vice Chamberlain before he had become Lord Chancellor and had organized celebrations and festivities with a masterly hand—which was another reason why he had not been taken seriously by some. But I knew that he had been an able politician and had seen as clearly as I did that one of the dangers in our country was that of religious conflict, which had brought civil war to others—as in the case of France. We wanted none of that in England. We had to take a stand between Puritans and Papists, and I did not know which sect I disliked most. Hatton had agreed with me that there must be no war over religion, which was a matter of an individual's conscience. In fact, he had been suspected of being a secret Catholic because of his leniency toward Catholics. This was not so. He felt as I did and we had been completely at one on this point.

Hatton had wanted to avoid excesses from both extremes, a view with which I heartily agreed. He had been a fine orator. True, he had liked rewards. Who does not? He had been very eager to acquire the London estate of the Bishop of Ely, and I had thought he should have it for he had need of a splendid home so that he could entertain visitors from abroad when necessary—and his Queen, of course. The lands were said to be some of the richest in England and comprised several acres of vineyard and arable land besides a house and chapel.

I had been delighted when this was passed to Hatton. He had been such a good servant and loyal courtier, and I had a specially fond feeling for him because he had remained unmarried. He had always said that he could love only one woman—even though it must be from a distance—his Queen. That seemed to me the ultimate gesture of love.

He had been a clever man and only had seemed less so because he had to stand beside greater statesmen like Burghley and Walsingham—and above all my incomparable Leicester.

So, another bitter loss.

I needed refreshing company, so I brought Essex back to Court.

I asked about the child which had now been born and was pleased that it was a boy and to be called Robert.

Essex and I were on the old terms. We played chess and cards together into the early hours of the morning. But I did not want to see the new Lady Essex. So Frances did not come to Court, but I believe lived nearby with her widowed mother, as she had before her marriage.

IT WAS GRATIFYING to me that although I was growing old my people did not love me less. I had lost a tooth or two; my skin was becoming lined, though it never lost its whiteness which I preserved most carefully; and my hair was growing scanty so that I had to resort to more false pieces and mostly wigs; but whenever I went out I was greeted with acclamations of joy and admiration. The people were uplifted by the defeat of the Spaniards; but other monarchs had been victorious in battle, yet none of them had ever had that firm hold on the people's affections which I had.

Never since the day of my accession had I failed to see the importance of this. I could be a virago in my private apartments—and often was. There was scarcely one of my ladies who had not had a blow or painful nip from me. I made no attempt to control my temper among them and if I was irritated I expressed my feelings forcefully. It was the same in the Council Chamber. My temper was quite uncontrolled. But on my progresses I never showed the slightest rancor toward my people. They could bring me absurd petitions; they could even criticize me to my face and I received all this with a degree of charming attention and tolerance. I was playing a part—that of the great benevolent monarch—and I knew that through it I kept my hold on my people's affections and I was determined never to lose that.

It was the reason for the firmness of the crown. My grandfather had suffered all his life as King from the fear of having come to the throne in circumstances which could be questioned; he must be looking over his shoulder all the time lest someone was preparing to snatch the crown from him. My father had had no fear of losing it. He saw himself as divine. He had a natural charm and an appearance of immense strength and he kept the approval of his people throughout his reign. He ruled through fear and great self-confidence which fostered an attitude of certainty that he would always do so. I held my people to me with love, and the bonds of love are the strongest in the world.

I tried always to act as my people would wish me to. We had persecuted the Catholics; we had hounded priests from their priest holes in the great Catholic houses and brought some of them to a barbarous death. I had allowed this because it was what the people wanted. They had an inherent fear of Catholicism, and it would linger I was sure. None of them could forget the terrible burnings at the stake during my sister's reign. People still talked in hushed whispers of Latimer, Ridley, Cranmer and Hooper. Certain seamen had been captured by the Spaniards and escaped to give accounts of the terrible tortures of the Inquisition. We wanted none of that in peaceful England. Pray God it would never come to that. So we must keep out the Catholics. I knew there were good Catholic gentlemen. They had supported us against the Spaniards in war. But the whole country was against that form of religion as practiced by Spaniards and upheld by the Pope.

On the other hand we had the Puritans—toward whom I felt a great abhorrence. They wanted to create what they called an English Sunday. This would ban fairs, hunting, rowing, cockfighting and bear-baiting—in fact any kind of sport. The Council would have passed that measure but I vetoed it. I could imagine what those people who had cheered me on my pilgrimages throughout the land would say to that. They worked hard, I said. They should have a little respite on Sundays and amuse themselves in whatsoever way they thought best. I was sure I was right as I was when someone tried to bring in an act which would mean the death penalty for committing adultery, blasphemy and holding heretical opinions.

No, no, no! I insisted. That would bring us close to what we had been fighting against. Why did men fight as they had against Spain? How was it a few men in inferior ships gained a great victory? Because they were fighting for freedom, was the answer.

No, I wanted no more religious bickering. I wanted my people to be free, happy and prosperous—and that meant to live good honest lives in peace. No wars! And freedom to worship as they thought best. As long as they obeyed the laws of Christ I could see no reason why they were not good Christians.

Let be, I wanted to cry all the time.

As an act of defiance against those who would close the theaters, I formed a band of players who would act for my delight. I called them the Queen's Men.

I looked forward always to my progresses through the country for I considered it of the utmost importance to show myself to my people. There was great rejoicing in the towns and villages through which I passed; and I must admit that there was little I enjoyed more than receiving homage and adulation.

I was so accustomed to displays of love and loyalty that it was a shock when I received evidence that I had dangerous enemies among the people.

One day when I was walking in the gardens at Hampton where a crowd had gathered to watch me pass, there was a sudden shout and I saw someone being hustled away by the Yeomen of the Guard. Another picked up a pistol which lay on the ground and hastened off after the group who were pushing their prisoner through the crowd.

There was a hushed silence and then someone in the crowd cried: "God save Your Majesty. Death to those who would harm you."

Then I guessed that this had been an attempt at assassination.

I made no show of haste to leave the place nor any fear because I had been in danger of losing my life, but paused to speak to some of the people who had thrust forward to see me. Some had petitions which I read carefully and promised they should have consideration, stressing that it would be the Council who decided, in case the decision should be adverse. Then the blame would not be laid on me!

As soon as I was back in the palace, I asked what the trouble in the gardens had been about.

It was disturbing to know that it had been an attempt on my life and I said I would personally question my would-be murderer.

To my amazement they brought in a woman. She looked at me defiantly as she stood there, a guard on either side of her. "Who are you?" I asked. "And do you admit to wanting to kill me?"

She replied: "My name is Margaret Lambrun, and I do."

"Well, at least you are honest," I said. "You are Scottish, are you?"

"Yes," she answered.

"So thought I. A murderous race, the Scots. They have given my ancestors and me a great deal of trouble. Why did you wish to kill me?"

"You killed my Queen and my husband," she said. "I wanted revenge for that."

"You refer to Queen Mary of Scotland who was found guilty of plotting against my realm and attempting to murder me."

The woman was silent.

"That is the truth, you know," I said softly.

"My husband was in her service. When she was executed he died of grief."

"He would have done better to have lived to look after his wife and prevent her from committing rash actions."

"He loved the Queen. He was heartbroken when she died."

Poor woman! That was the last thing she could have said to endear her to me. I had long been hearing of the fatal fascination of the Queen of Scots and I was exasperated that even after her death it was still effective.

"You were in possession of two pistols," I said. "Were you going to take two shots at me?"

"No. One was for you and then I should have turned the other on myself."

"Do you know what I am going to do with you, Margaret Lambrun?" I said.

"It matters not what you do with me," she replied. "My life is over."

"You are a youngish woman. There could be years before you. I say this: Forget that husband who died of a broken heart grieving for another woman. He is not worthy of your remembrance. I know men well. They are not worth dying for. You are an honest woman and have suffered much. I am going to give you a free pardon."

She stared at me in astonishment for a few seconds, then she fell to her knees continuing to look wonderingly at me.

"Methinks," I went on, "that you have heard evil tales of me. Perhaps through your husband's fascinating mistress. You foolish woman, do not again risk your life for the sake of a man. Get to your feet now and be gone from here." I called to the guards: "Take her away."

She hesitated. Then she said: "Would Your Majesty give me permission to speak?"

"Go on," I said.

"Those people out there . . . They believe that you are divine."

"It seems to me I must have some of the qualities you believed were in the sole possession of Mary of Scotland."

"Those people love you as she was never loved by the people."

"Well, my good woman, your eyes have been opened, and you have seen that I am not the monster who was to receive your fatal shot."

"You are a great queen," she said. "Those people will tear me apart because I tried to kill you."

"True enough," I agreed. "But you who are prepared to kill a queen cannot be afraid of a crowd of people."

It was a strange revelation. The fanatical young woman who had stood in the crowd and contemplated my death was gone, and in her place was a practical person who was beginning to think she might have some future after all.

I realized that my response to her attempt to kill me had bewildered her and yet at the same time it had made her see her future more clearly. She was not going to die. She was going to live, and life had become very precious to her. It must have been so for she was anxious to preserve it. "If Your Majesty would give me a safe passage to France, I would settle there and try to make a new life."

I smiled at her.

"It shall be," I said. Then turning to the guards I continued: "Take her away. See that she has safe conduct to the coast."

As she went she gave me a look of gratitude, amazement and something like admiration.

I smiled. In time, in her French haven, she might think as highly of the Queen of England as she had of the Queen of Scots.

FOR SOME TIME the Council had been trying to persuade me that we should carry our disagreements with Spain into Spanish territory. I had opposed this as I did any form of war, but at length I agreed that this particular action might be advantageous to us.

Since the year 1581 Don Antonio, the deposed King of Portugal, had been living in England in exile. Don Antonio was the bastard son of the previous King's brother, but because he was illegitimate, the Spaniards laid claim to the crown of Portugal on account of Philip's mother's being the late King's sister. He had sent Alva into Portugal to take it and this was speedily accomplished.

Don Antonio had had long talks with me. He was yearning to claim his crown. He told me how the Portuguese hated the Spaniards and that if he could only get back, the whole country would rise against Spain; and having been stripped of its power through the defeat of the armada, the Spaniards would suffer another humiliating defeat and Don Antonio would be back on the throne.

Drake came to discuss the problem and Drake's great aim in these enterprises was to bring back treasure. This I applauded. I wanted Spanish treasure to strengthen my exchequer; I wanted their gold and jewels to pay for my country's needs so that I did not have to resort to taxing my people.

Drake was the great pirate who knew how to bring treasure home. So I agreed and it was arranged that the expedition would be commanded at sea by Sir Francis Drake and on land by Sir John Norris.

I invested sixty thousand pounds in the enterprise; some of the generals put up about fifty thousand, and between the City of London and other ports throughout the country one hundred and forty-six ships were contributed to the scheme.

Essex wanted to join the expedition and I smiled fondly at his enthusiasm.

"I do not intend that you shall risk your life," I said. "Your place is at Court."

But he would not let the matter rest. He plagued me night and day. He wanted to go. He had need of the money. He would find treasure; but most of all he wanted to have a shot at the Spaniards.

"No," I insisted. "You shall not go." And I became angry with him and ordered him to drop the subject.

This he did and I thought he had come to his senses at last. I should have known better.

The expedition was ready and at Plymouth waiting to sail. It was then I heard what had happened.

Essex's brother-in-law, Lord Rich, came to me bringing a letter addressed to me in Essex's hand. Essex had sent him a key to the desk in which the letter had been placed and he had not sent the key until he was well on the way.

He had been determined to join the expedition, he wrote. Not only did he want to fight for England's glory, but he was in desperate need of money for he was deeply in debt. He owed at least twenty-three thousand pounds. I had been good to him and he would ask for no more. He was not of the nature of some (this was a dart directed at Raleigh who never failed to ask for what he wanted). He must go away. He must find fortune. And he trusted I would forgive him for going against my wishes.

Forgive him! I was furious with him. Never once in the whole of my time with Robert had he openly defied me. How dared this young upstart behave so!

I would show him that he could not go against my wishes.

Immediately I sent guards to bring him back, and his grandfather Sir Francis Knollys himself went to Plymouth.

I heard then that for days he had shut himself away making preparations. He had gone to the house of his brother-in-law Lord Rich to dine, to allay suspicions, for he feared he might have been watched. Outside his lordship's house was Essex's secretary and a groom waiting with horses ready to ride with all speed to Plymouth. They had ridden for ninety miles on the horses and then Essex had taken a post horse and sent his companions back to London with the horses and a letter to Lord Rich containing the key to the desk in which he had locked the letter to me so that it could be delivered after his departure.

Drake and Norris knew that I had forbidden him to go and I relied on them to send him back. But they did not see him, for Essex, guessing they would never let him board a ship, had made a secret arrangement with Captain Roger Williams who had agreed to take him. Thus Essex was able to board Williams's ship, the *Swiftsure,* and put out to sea.

So Essex had defied me again. I was so angry. I swore this should be the last time.

WAR NEVER PAYS. I could have told them that before the expedition set out; and I reminded them that I had only agreed to go on with their schemes because they had all worn me down with their importunings.

However if there was enough booty to come out of it I supposed I would consider it worthwhile.

I was worried constantly about Essex. He could be so foolhardy and I knew he was reckless. He would take such absurd risks and I wanted him back at Court. I was unwise, I knew, to set such store by him but I was missing Robert so much and I was desperately anxious to put someone else in his place. I needed that very special person in my life and I had no doubt that I had chosen unwisely in Essex.

Although I could never think of him as a possible lover as I had Robert, he did give me that very special brand of affection which I never quite sensed in the others; and because he was a young man who disdained to flatter and dissimulate, I knew it was genuine affection.

I sent urgent messages to Drake and Norris. Essex was to be sent back. But, of course, he was not with them and it was some time before the *Swift-sure* joined up with the rest of the fleet, and then there was not a ship available in which to send him home.

I wrote angrily to him:

"Essex,

"Your sudden and undutiful departure from our presence and your place of attendance, you may easily conceive how offensive it is, and ought to be, unto us. Our great favors bestowed on you without deserts, hath drawn you thus to neglect and forget your duty; for other constructions we cannot make of those your strange actions. Not meaning, therefore, to tolerate this your disordered part, we gave directions to some of our Privy Council to let you know our express pleasure for your immediate repair hither . . .

"We do, therefore, charge and command you forthwith upon receipt of these our letters, all excuses and delays set apart, to make your present and immediate repair unto us, to understand our further pleasure. Whereof see you fail not, as you will be loth to incur our indignation, and will answer for the contrary to your uttermost peril."

When he received such a letter written in my hand, he knew he dare not disobey, and he set sail for home.

The expedition was at an end. The Portuguese had not welcomed Don Antonio as he had believed they would. They did not like their Spanish masters, but they were too lethargic to bestir themselves sufficiently to make the change.

It would have been a disastrous affair but for Sir Francis Drake, who brought home enough booty to have made it just worthwhile.

I was prepared to upbraid Essex and banish him from Court until it pleased me to recall him, but when I saw him, looking a little pale from battle, and kneeling before me raising those fine dark eyes to my face, so full of loving admiration, I relented.

I was so pleased to have him back safely.

I said: "Never behave so again. If you did that could be the end of your hopes at Court."

That was all; and within a few days he was installed in his old place. And to prevent his going abroad again in search of fortune, I granted him a lease of the farm of sweet wines—which had been Robert's before he died and which would give him a large income that might settle outstanding debts and, I hoped, in future enable him to live within his income.

→>—<←

HE WAS RESTLESS. He was not suited to Court life. He lacked Robert's ambition as well as his tact; and he lacked Robert's shrewdness. Why had I thought there could ever be anyone to take Robert's place?

And yet he fascinated me. In a way, I thought of him as a son, loved none the less because he was wayward, and I was content only when he was near me. He could change my mood; he could make me feel young. He was in love with me in a way that most young men had been when I was a young woman. There was no question of a union of any sort between us, but it was love . . . of a rarefied kind. But I wanted that. It had to come naturally. It was not, as with such as Raleigh, for favor at Court. Essex did not seek favor; he was indifferent to honors. He supported lost causes. And he was honest. He could forget the respect due to me. Anger would flare up and he would not watch his words; but this was honest Essex; so that when he did show his affection for me I knew it was genuine.

He was something of a reformer. For instance, he told me frankly that I had been wrong in my treatment of Davison. He should not be in the Tower, he said. It was not due to him that Mary of Scotland had been executed. That specter still bothered me and I did not want to think of Davison. I could not bear to hear any speak his name—so no one ever did in my hearing. Essex knew this and yet he came to me and said that Davison should be released and given the post of Secretary of State which had become vacant on the death of Walsingham. He was such a reckless, foolhardy young man, I trembled for him. I discovered later that he had written to James of Scotland asking him to use his influence in the matter. Did he not realize that at any time his enemies could accuse him of being in communication with a foreign power, which could be made to look like treason?

I have to admit that he almost persuaded me. I did feel guilty about the treatment meted out to Davison. I should have liked to make amends; and the post of Secretary of State, which he was quite capable of holding, would have been a compensation for the injustice he had suffered.

I spoke to Burghley about this. He was against the idea. He did not think Davison could hold the post. He was efficient but not brilliant. I tried to argue in Davison's favor until I realized that Burghley wanted the post for his son Robert. And, of course, he was right. Robert Cecil—that little elf of a man, with his crooked back and slouching walk, had the same balanced outlook as his father. He had been coached by his father from the very earliest, and it was clear that if the post were given to anyone else, there would inevitably be trouble with Burghley.

So Davison did not get the post, but he was released from the Tower and went to live in his home in Stepney where he remained for many years.

Essex was still looking for adventure and when Henri Quatre of France asked me for help, he wanted to take a company of men over to fight for the King, who had come to the throne when Henri Trois had died. As a Huguenot he looked to England for help against the Catholic League which was determined to oust him on account of his religion. "It is necessary that we go to help," said Essex. "He shares our faith. He would be our friend if we helped him to hold his throne."

His eyes were shining with enthusiasm. He was somewhat naïve. Did he not know that kings were friends of other kings only when it was expedient to be so? But it was true that we did not want the Catholics to prevail in France. We had subdued Spain but France could be as great a menace. Essex threw himself onto his knees and begged to be allowed to take command of an expedition. His friends—and his mother, I believed—advised him against going abroad. He should stay behind and make his name at Court as all the most successful men had done. He should model himself on the lines of Leicester, Walsingham, Burghley . . . those who held first place in the Queen's regard. Perhaps they realized that he lacked the temperament of a great general. He was too rash, too impulsive, too careless of himself.

However he wearied me with his importunings and as it had been decided that we should aid Henri, I finally gave in and allowed Essex to command the expedition.

It was a sad day for me when he sailed from Dover with four thousand men.

He took with him Lettice's other boy, Walter Devereux, and I wondered how she felt at the prospect of two sons going to war.

I waited eagerly for news. I heard that Henri took a fancy to Essex and that they frolicked together. There was some fighting though, and in a skirmish outside Rouen young Walter Devereux was killed.

I was almost sorry for Lettice then, for I believe that she did love her children.

I heard that Essex recklessly exposed himself to danger and had come near to capture on two occasions. He was popular for he shared his men's hardships and then distributed honors on the battlefield, which he had no authority to do.

I made Burghley write to him in my name, disapproving and forbidding him to act in such a way. Moreover, he had no right to bestow honors. That was the Sovereign's prerogative.

I ordered so forcefully that he return home that at length he could make no excuses for not doing so.

He came back ebullient as ever, with no excuses for what he had done, and I was once more so delighted to see him that, after the first few reprimands, he was in favor again.

But all the time he wanted to return to France, so I let him go, giving him strict injunctions—as I once did to Robert—to take good care of himself.

Fortunately he was a young man who quickly tired of a project and after a while, when I told him I wished him to come back and relinquish the command to Roger Williams, who had shared his adventures on the *Swiftsure*, rather to my surprise, he eagerly obeyed the command.

I think he had taken the advice of his friends to seek his fortune at Court, where my undoubted affection for him would mean that he had a great chance of success.

I OFTEN THOUGHT of Christopher Hatton who had been so devoted to me that he had never married. I wished I had been kinder to him at the end. It must have been heartbreaking for him when I turned my back on his pleading to be allowed time to pay that silly debt. In the end I had gone to him and fed him with my own hands, but by then it was too late. Sometimes I wondered whether my harsh treatment of him had hastened his death. He had been a sensitive man and he had truly loved me.

Young men nowadays were less reverent; they were bold and inclined to be insolent—at least Essex was. He was quite unlike the men of my youth . . . Robert, Heneage, Hatton . . . They had been like romantic heroes. Nowadays it seemed that a young man's chief fancy was for himself.

I wished that I did not feel so deeply about Essex. Perhaps I should have done better to have fixed my affections on another. There was Raleigh, for instance. He was, some would say, more handsome than Essex, with his ruddy countryman's looks, his tall stature, his dashing manners and his wit. I even found that Devonshire burr in his voice attractive, though his jealous rivals sneered at him and called him the farmer's boy.

He had a commanding presence and a fine intelligence. I was very glad to have him near me. During those years when Essex had been behaving so recklessly I had encouraged Raleigh; and I was secretly amused to see the rivalry between him and Essex.

Raleigh was a born courtier as well as an adventurer. He had succeeded Christopher Hatton as Captain of the Guards; he had his knighthood and a fine residence in Durham House and had just acquired a ninety-nine-year lease of the Castle of Sherborne. He had founded a colony in North America which he had called Virginia in honor of me. I would never forget his coming home and telling me about his adventures. He had developed a curious habit which he had learned from the savages there and he explained this to me. It was a herb which was called Yppowoc. I had heard of it before when Sir John Hawkins first brought it into the country, but it was Raleigh who was responsible for calling the notice of the people of England to it. Apparently it had a soothing effect if put in a pipe and smoked. It was known as tobacco. Another product had come from Virginia. This I think was more useful than the smoking herb. It was the potato, which John Hawkins brought in about the same time as the tobacco, but it had not become popular until Drake brought it home in large quantities.

Raleigh had great hopes of that colony. It was my colony, he said, named in honor of me; and he let me know that he had spent forty thousand pounds of his own money in order to maintain it. He was heartbroken when it could not be kept going. Hakluyt, the geographer-writer, said it would require a prince's purse to have thoroughly followed it out.

It always pleased me when my men spent their own money in the service of the state. None did this quite to the same extent that Walsingham had done. It showed a genuine love of country which I applauded.

Raleigh was at heart an adventurer. I realized that he had too much talent in that direction to be kept at home. I sent him to Ireland—that hotbed of dissension—where he used his genius for organization as successfully as anyone could against such people who were determined never to conform to law and order and whose great mission in life was to create trouble.

He had done well; he had planted the potato there and the soil evidently suited it, so it provided food for thousands. He became the friend of the poet Edmund Spenser. I was interested in this young poet because Leicester had thought highly of him when Philip Sidney had introduced him to the young man's works. Robert had sought to help him, and had obtained for him the post of private secretary to Lord Grey de Wilton who had been appointed Lord Deputy of Ireland—which was why Edmund Spenser happened to find himself in that country.

Now Raleigh was back in England—more attractive than ever, full of plans, showing jealousy of Essex which amused me, for I told myself it was good for Essex, who seemed to think he had a right to monopolize my affections.

Raleigh was as obsessed by the Spaniards as Drake had been. He was constantly considering methods of attacking them and robbing them of their treasure. They had had intrepid explorers who had discovered new lands; they were good seamen; and men like Drake and Raleigh wanted to snatch the role of pioneers from Spain and make England the great exploring, empire-building nation; it was for us to rule the seas.

I clung to my conviction that war was folly and that even the victorious invariably suffered; but this war at sea was conducted by privateers whom a sovereign could disown if necessary; oh, yes, this gathering of treasures was quite another matter, far removed from open war. I knew in my heart that the conflict between Spain and England was not a brief struggle. It was a mighty struggle and it was not only for land, or even religion . . . not on our side at least; it was for supremacy at sea; it was to rule the óceans, to make them safe for England, to protect our shores and to make our country the greatest sea power in the world. Men like Drake and Raleigh understood this and their purpose shone like a beacon through all their actions. They wanted treasure; they wanted the glory of success in battle; but the prime object was that England should be in command of the high seas—and therein lay their greatness.

I had seen from the first that these men must be encouraged for on their bravery, their skill and their enterprise rested the might of England.

So I loved my adventurers and I was torn between a desire to have them with me at Court or to send them on those adventures which were fraught with danger.

So when Raleigh came to me with an idea for a new enterprise to go forth and bring back treasure for England, I agreed he must carry out his plan; but when the time came for departure, I decided that I could not spare Raleigh. He was too amusing, too brilliant an ornament at Court and I ordered that although the expedition should set sail, it should go without Raleigh. In his place Frobisher should go with Sir John Borough.

Raleigh was somewhat put out, but being Raleigh he did not make this obvious to me and pretended that to be near me was a complete compensation for having been denied the adventure.

I really was getting very fond of him. His manners were so much smoother than those of Essex; that was why his perfidy wounded me so deeply.

Nicholas Throckmorton's daughter, Elizabeth, was one of my maids of honor and she was an exceptionally pretty girl. I had promised myself that I owed it to her father to find a good husband for her, which I intended to do in due course.

I happened, however, to notice that she was becoming unusually absent-minded. This came to a head when she dropped some of the pins which held my hair-pieces in place. I told her she was clumsy and she murmured apologies; but she did not improve. I had noticed this look in young women before and I had my suspicions. It invariably meant one thing. The girl had a lover and if my intuition did not deceive me, their frolicking had gone beyond the bounds of respectability.

I decided to question her.

"You are very clumsy lately, Bessie," I said.

"I crave Your Majesty's pardon," she replied.

"There is a reason, I believe."

She flushed. Silly girl! She betrayed herself immediately.

"Well," I went on, "you had better tell me. It is wiser in these cases before matters go too far. How *far* have they gone with you, Bess Throckmorton?"

She stammered and flushed and I knew the worst.

"Who is the scoundrel?" I demanded.

She stood before me, eyes downcast, the picture of guilty confusion.

"You know I will not have immorality at my Court!" I shouted.

I gave her a slap at the side of her face which sent her reeling. "Come here," I said. "Closer." I took her by the shoulders and shook her. "Now . . . tell me. Who is it?"

She stammered: "Your Majesty must forgive me if . . . if . . ."

"If what?"

"If . . . I cannot tell you."

"You cannot tell me?" I caught her by the ear and she gave a squeal of pain as I nipped the lobe between my fingers. There were tears in her foolish eyes.

"Your Majesty," she began, "we love each other . . ."

"And you think that is an excuse for misbehaving? Who is it? You had better tell me, girl. How dare you stand there defying me!"

"Your Majesty, I did not mean . . ."

"Tell me," I commanded; and she knew then from the tone of my voice and my black looks that she could hold out against me no longer.

"It is Walter, Your Majesty."

"Raleigh!" I cried.

Anger was my first emotion. It was so like other occasions. Robert and Lettice Knollys; Essex and Frances Walsingham. These young men . . . they professed to care above all people for me and all the time they were philandering with my maids of honor.

"Get out of my sight, you slut," I said.

And she ran from the room.

Then I shouted to the guard: "Find Raleigh! Send him to me at once."

He came, his urbane charming self. I said: "So, Sir Adventurer, you have seduced one of the girls who has been put by her family into my care."

"Bess has been talking to you," he said.

"I prized it out of the little harlot. As for you, you sly snake, I do not want to see your false face for a very long time."

He began to protest. He had a way with words. He always had had, and it was one of the reasons why he had endeared himself to me. But I was hurt and angry. They meant nothing—these protestations of affection—except: What can I get by flattering the old woman?

My fury increased and I shouted: "Take him to the Tower."

That was what I had said when Robert had married Lettice, and dear old Sussex had persuaded me that I could not send him to the Tower merely because he had married.

There was nobody to speak for Raleigh. In any case there had been no marriage. This was a case of seduction.

Let him go to the Tower. I would forget all about him. There were many handsome young men ready to dance attendance. Why should I regret the loss of one?

So with Bess Throckmorton banished from Court and Raleigh in the Tower, Essex was supreme—the favorite with no serious rival.

CHE SCAY AC the Court of France had changed Essex. He had been greatly influenced by the King of France who was, by all accounts, a very impressive man. He had that rare quality—which he shared with me—of winning the hearts of the people so that they would follow him even in disaster. He was a simple man; he lived with his men in battle; he did not stand on ceremony; his attitude said: I am one of you. I suffer with you. I share your lot in battle. We are of a kind. I just happen, by accident of my birth, to be your leader.

That was the right approach. He knew, as I did, that it was the ordinary people who decided whether or not the crown was secure on the sovereign's head.

But he had one great weakness—and that was his fondness for women. He had a host of mistresses and was constantly looking for more. His love affairs obsessed him while they lasted, even though they were of short duration.

When Essex came back, he had lost a certain honesty; he was becoming more acquisitive. He was promiscuous and neglected poor Frances shamefully and there was a scandal about one or two of the ladies at Court. This was kept from me in detail and I decided not to probe. He courted me with more finesse than he had shown hitherto and although I believed that genuine affection was still there, he had hardened, become ambitious; in other words the Essex who had set out for his sojourn at the Court of France was not the same man who had come back from it.

The Cecils were his enemies. It said much for the abilities of Robert

Cecil that I was beginning to think of his father and himself as "the Cecils." Burghley had superintended his son's education well and had brought him up to think as he did and work in the same way. I was not displeased by this. I knew that sooner or later I had to lose my dear Spirit; and it was comforting to know that when he went I should have his son Robert to help me.

Raleigh was in the Tower and therefore posed no threat, but it appeared that Essex was forming a party, rival to the Cecils, and people were beginning to gather about him.

In spite of my fondness for Essex, I never lost sight of his weaknesses. It soon became clear to me that he was not stable enough to form a party in opposition to the Cecils, and he confined himself to doing everything he could to damage them in my eyes—an impossible task.

He had made the acquaintance of the Bacon boys—Anthony and Francis—nephews of Burghley. They were two clever young men, particularly Francis, I believed; but they had not learned the art of graciousness, and Francis irritated me by his interference in political matters. They were disgruntled, both of them, because they had hoped their uncle would find them places at Court. That I was sure he was prepared to do, but he was so intent on looking after his own son, that he made sure no one should be given a chance to outshine him.

Francis should have been given something useful to do, but he was too sure of himself, too definite in his views, and not inclined to modify them; which brought him my displeasure.

Then an event took place which filled me with horror. Henri Quatre changed his religion with the cynical comment that Paris was worth a Mass.

I had helped him. I had sent Essex over with men, arms and money in order to uphold the Protestant Faith, in order to make sure that we did not have a menacing Catholic state close to our shores. And now he had given way . . . abjured his faith for the sake of a crown!

I wrote off in a fit of disgust to the King of France without giving myself time to consider.

"Ah, what grief! My God, is it possible that any worldly consideration could render you regardless of divine displeasure . . ."

After I had sent that letter I regretted it because I remembered the days before my accession when I had feigned to accept the Catholic Faith in order to keep alive. What had Henri done? Realizing that the French, by their very nature, were Catholics—just as the English by theirs were Protestants—and would never accept a Huguenot king, with that nonchalant good sense of his he had said: Very well. If the only king you will accept is a Catholic king, then, as I am determined to be your King, I must become a Catholic.

And so he had.

We were of a kind really. How many times had I said that the method of worship was not important? It was Christianity itself which mattered. He had not changed his faith; he was merely accepting the Catholic form of worship. He was too clever, of course, to have done otherwise. I could imagine his guffaw of laughter when he received my letter, for he knew, as well as I did, that if England had demanded a Catholic monarch, then I should have been a Catholic and as England wanted a Protestant ruler—I was that.

I was alarmed. That was at the root of my indignation; but I took some comfort from the knowledge that Henri would not be as fanatical as Philip, and I was sure would have too much good sense to attempt to invade us.

Essex had been very interested in Walsingham's secret service, and he knew that it had been of the utmost benefit to us during our conflict with Spain. He imagined himself as another Walsingham, having spies all over Europe to report to him so that he would know immediately the country was menaced.

He was no Walsingham, of course; but no doubt Frances had talked to him often about her father and had inspired him with the wish to follow in his footsteps.

It was because of these activities that he came to me with an astonishing story concerning Dr Roderigo Lopez, whom I had made my chief physician. The doctor had come to England about the time of my accession and he soon began to impress the medical world with his skill. He had become house physician at St Bartholomew's Hospital, where he had made a name for himself not only by his skill in purging and bleeding but by introducing a very efficacious remedy for many ills. This was known as Arceus' apozema and Dr Lopez had talked to me about it. I was interested in such things and he found me a ready listener. I was quite fond of the man, so when Essex came to me and told me that he was a Spanish spy and was receiving orders from his masters in Spain to mix poisons with the medicines he prepared for me, I did not believe him.

I knew that Essex, in his endeavors to send his spies out round the world, as Walsingham had done, had tried to enlist the doctor in his service and had wanted him to return to Spain and worm his way into the King's household. This was not unlikely for he was famous for his skill. Thus he could become a spy for Essex.

I knew this because Dr Lopez himself had told me. I was most annoyed. This was another example of Essex's taking matters into his own hands.

I summoned Essex and berated him, telling him to look elsewhere for his spies and not try to rob me of one of the best doctors I had ever had.

At this time the Spanish nobleman Antonio Perez, who was being persecuted by Philip, had arrived in England and Lopez acted as an interpreter for him.

Essex had the notion that there were Spanish spies in the household of Perez and that they had come to England with orders to poison me; and he was looking for proof of this.

"The doctor has received a valuable jewel which is said to have come from the King of Spain," Essex told me.

I replied: "The doctor has many grateful patients—myself among them."

"I will show you," retorted Essex; and he was sullen and angry. I really wondered why I endured his overbearing temperament.

I sent for the doctor and was especially gracious to him. He was such a tender, gentle man, and I was not going to turn against him just because he was a Portuguese Jew.

Essex was not one to give way easily, nor was he afraid to act without authority.

He caused a member of the household of Antonio Perez to be arrested. This was a certain De Gama and Essex had the temerity to make the arrest when De Gama was visiting Lopez, so that the arrest was made at Lopez's house.

Essex was now certain that Lopez was involved and he acquired the Council's permission to make a search of the doctor's house. He was very crestfallen when this revealed nothing incriminating.

I was elated. I sent for Essex and told him he was a very rash young man and had no right to accuse people of crimes which he could not prove; and he had better not behave in such a way again.

"You are wrong!" he cried.

How dared he! No one told the Queen she was wrong.

"You presume too much," I shouted.

"I would presume in every possible way to protect your sacred person," he replied.

And with a bow he left me.

He was intolerable but the way in which he had delivered that last remark softened me toward him. He really was genuinely fond of me and refreshingly frank—such a change from the sycophants who surrounded me.

Essex was indefatigable in his attempts to prove the case against Lopez. Another of Perez's attendants was arrested and put to the torture, when he confessed that Lopez was involved in a plot to poison me.

There was nothing to be done but arrest Lopez and conduct him to the Tower. He was tried at Guildhall where Essex insisted on presiding over the court, and the case for the prosecution was conducted by Sir Edward Coke, the Solicitor-General.

"This doctor," declared Coke, "is a perjured and murdering villain, and a Jewish doctor worse than Judas himself."

Robert Cecil came to tell me the result of the trial.

"He is found guilty, Your Majesty," he said, "guilty of treason."

I was very saddened. "Who would believe, Little Elf, that one who appeared to serve me well should all the time have been planning my destruction?"

I was not completely sure that he was guilty. Essex had been so determined to prove him so ever since the doctor had refused to act as his spy. I have never trusted evidence which is wrung from a victim by torture. I deplored the use of it, but I knew it was necessary. Yet who could trust the information which came out of it?

I was very uneasy about Lopez. He was sentenced to death, and when they brought me his death warrant, I found it hard to put my signature to it—so I did what I had done in the case of Mary of Scotland; I delayed doing it.

Essex said Lopez was unsafe.

"What if there should be an attempt to rescue him? What if he escaped and went back to his masters in Spain? Think of the knowledge he would carry. Your Majesty must sign the death warrant."

"Essex," I said, "you must stop this habit of telling me what I must and must not do. No one tells the Queen how she must act."

"It seems that Essex does."

"Guard your tongue, my lord," I said. "It will be your undoing one of these days."

Then he repeated a phrase which he had used in one of his letters to me and which I read often.

"Your Majesty may turn from me, but I never will from you. While you give me leave to say I love you, my fortune is my affection, unmatchable. If ever you deny me that liberty you may end my life, but you will never shake my constancy, for it is not in your power, great Queen as you are, to make me love you less."

All my anger against him melted. He truly loved me. He would never pretend; he could not speak with such heartfelt devotion unless what he said was true.

I softened toward him. If he were brash, it was in my service. Why should I complain of that?

I took a ring from my finger then. It held a ruby in a cluster of diamonds. I had chosen it because the unusual setting made it unique.

Then I took his hand and slipped the ring on his little finger.

"This is a bond between us," I said. "If you are ever in trouble and need my help, send me this ring. I will remember this moment and how in it you assured me of your affection for me. Mine is in this ring. I shall always remember and come to your aid when I see it."

He took my hand and kissed it; and later that day I signed Lopez's death warrant.

He was taken to Tyburn on a hurdle and before he was hanged and quartered he made a speech to the watching crowd in which he said that he had never thought to harm me and that he loved me as he loved Jesus Christ.

Someone in the crowd shouted: "Jew! You never loved Jesus Christ."

And all the people there believed that in saying what he did he had admitted his guilt.

His death continued to worry me, because I still was not entirely convinced that he would ever have attempted to poison me. If it were really true that he would, then I knew nothing of human nature. I was sunk in depression as I always was after I had signed a death warrant for someone of whose guilt I was unsure.

I knew he had a wife, Sara, and five children. I gave orders that they were to retain his property, and later on his son was given a parsonage and a living.

The Traitor

RALEIGH WAS STILL IN THE TOWER AND I HAD NO DESIRE to release him. I was still very annoyed with him and he must be an example to them all. Essex was delighted. He had erred in the same way yet had not been treated so harshly and was now in higher favor than he had ever been. I was sure that rankled very much with Raleigh.

Robert Cecil did ask me if I thought he had been punished enough.

"It was not exactly a political sin, Your Majesty," he went on.

"I will not have immorality in my Court, little man," I said, "and that is an end of the matter."

Of course Raleigh had stood with the Cecils against Essex. He was an able man and I believed that they missed him. That might be but I was not in the mood to release him, though I heard rumors that he was pining away in the Tower.

"Because he misses his playmate Bessie Throckmorton?" I asked.

"He says it is because he is denied Your Majesty's presence."

"Fine words. Raleigh was always good at them."

He clearly had his friends who were anxious to help and they brought these accounts to me.

I had passed along the river in my barge, I was told, and through his barred window Raleigh had caught sight of me. He had been overcome with frustration. He said he knew how Tantalus had felt, and he had made a futile attempt to dash out of his prison and escape. He had, of course, been caught by his guards.

"They will doubtless keep a closer guard on him in future," was my comment.

It was not long after that when Robert Cecil mentioned that he had received a letter from Raleigh. "He mentions Your Majesty," said Cecil.

"Is that so?" I asked with indifference.

"In fact, Your Majesty," was the answer, "he talks and writes of nothing else."

"Perhaps he is a little more thoughtful of my wishes in prison than he was in prosperity."

"He is a man, Your Majesty," persisted Cecil," and men fall into these temptations."

Of course he was right. I had understood in the case of Robert and Essex. What infuriated me was that these men were telling me that they lived

only to serve me while they behaved shamefully in corners with my volup-
tuous maids of honor.

Seeing me softening a little Cecil said: "I should like permission to show
you his letter, Your Majesty."

I held out my hand.

"How can I live alone in prison while she is afar off—I, who was wont
to behold her, riding like Alexander, hunting like Diana, walking like
Venus—the gentle wind blowing her fair hair about her pure cheeks, like a
nymph. Sometimes sitting in the shade like a goddess, sometimes playing on
the lute like Orpheus. But once amiss, hath bereaved me of all. All those
times are past, the loves, the sighs, the sorrows, the desires, can they not
weigh down one frail misfortune?"

I liked what I read. Raleigh had always had a fluent pen and flowery
words at his disposal. I knew of course that the letter had been written for
my eyes to see. He had known his good friend Cecil was hoping to get him
released from the Tower in order to help to put a stop to Essex's increasing
rise to fortune. Raleigh had been his only serious rival. I saw through it all.
But I did like the tone of the letter, and to know how much he was longing
to come back to Court.

I handed the letter back to Cecil in silence.

"Would Your Majesty consider . . ." he began timidly.

"Yes, yes," I said. "I promise nothing, but I will consider."

But I let two months pass before I gave the order for his release. Even
then I would not receive him at Court.

I heard that he had married Bess Throckmorton.

"And about time too," I said.

They went down to Sherborne but I knew that he was longing to come
back to Court, and I supposed I would allow him to . . . in due course.

ESSEX WAS CONSTANTLY worrying me to receive his mother at Court.
I was set against it. I might in time forgive Frances Walsingham and Bessie
Throckmorton, but one I would never forgive was Lettice Knollys. Seeing
her would be too painful for me. I knew that she was very beautiful . . . even
now; she had a young husband whom she had married as soon as possible
after Robert's death, and there had been unpleasant rumors about her relationship with Christopher Blount before she married him. To me she would
always be the she-wolf.

But she was Essex's mother. That always seemed ironical to me. With
the two men whom I had most deeply loved, Lettice had been on the most
intimate terms—the wife of one; the mother of the other. I could forgive her
for the latter, but never for the former. Robert would always be supreme in

my life and much of the savor of it had gone with his death; and she had been his wife. He had married her in spite of the fact that he knew how I would feel about the marriage. He could have ruined his career at Court and that he had done for her sake. Perhaps he had been sure of my unswerving love for him. But he had taken a mighty risk . . . and for her . . . that worthless she-wolf, who, some said, had been trifling with Blount while Robert was yet alive—and even worse that she had hastened Robert's end.

Receive that she-wolf! Give her the satisfaction of coming to Court! At least I had been able to deny her that.

She had tried to live like a queen. She had tried to rival me . . . not only with him, but in outward show. Oh, the impudence of that woman! Receive her at Court! No, I said firmly. But Essex never knew when to stop.

I would silence him and he would be sullen. Sometimes he dared stay away from Court, pretending to be sick. I believed he used that method as Robert used it, and as I myself had in the days of danger. But I was never sure—as I had not been with Robert—and I would be very upset wondering if he really was ill.

One day, during one of these bouts of illness—he really did look rather pale lying in his bed—he told me that he was upset about his mother who was most unhappy because I had shut her out.

He looked so mournful that I wanted to please him so I said: "I shall be passing from my chamber to the Presence room the day after tomorrow. I shall have to see those who are in the Privy Gallery."

"Dearest Majesty." His smile was brilliant and I suffered a twinge of jealousy. He loved his mother. There was no doubt of that.

"And you will speak to her? Oh, if you did, that would mean so much. She would be able to come to Court again."

I said: "I have to speak to one or two as I pass through, you know."

He kissed my hand rapturously.

After I had left him, I scolded myself. See Lettice Knollys! I hated the woman. Every time I thought of her I saw her and Robert together. How much worse it would be actually to see her!

He had wrung that promise from me. Why had I given it? Because he looked so wan. Because I had wanted to please him. What had I said? I had not really promised that I would speak to her. I had merely stated that I would be passing through the gallery, which I often did. Some people were presented to me then . . . or caught my eye. Then naturally I would speak to them. But I had made no promise that I would speak to her.

The day came. I was in my chamber and my women were assisting at my dressing ceremony. All the time I was thinking: She will be out there. What will she be wearing? Something becoming. She had always known what suited her and she could look beautiful in the simplest of gowns. She would look young still. She *was* younger than I . . . but even she would be getting old.

Why should I see her?

"Is there a crowd in the gallery?" I asked.

One of my ladies replied that the usual crowd was gathered there.

I yawned. It was time for me to go. In a few moments I would be face to face with my enemy.

I had been forced to this. What right had Essex? I must not be so indulgent toward him. He gave himself airs. He had too high an opinion of his importance! He should be taught a few lessons.

"I do not think I will go to the Presence Chamber today," I said. "One of you must inform the people waiting in the gallery that I shall not be passing through today."

They were all surprised but they knew better than to hesitate.

My orders were carried out and the people in the Privy Gallery—Lettice Knollys among them—dispersed.

I laughed aloud. That would show Lettice that her son did not command me absolutely. And perhaps it would show her very clearly that I had no wish to see her again.

WHEN ESSEX HEARD what had happened he came storming to Court. He certainly looked pale and drawn, but he had arisen from his sick-bed to register his anger.

He really was a very rash young man and I marveled at myself for allowing him to act as he did. He would go too far one day.

He said: "You promised me . . . and you did not keep your promise."

"My Lord Essex," I retorted sharply, "pray remember to whom you are addressing this tirade."

"I am addressing it to one who has so little heed of me that she will not grant me the smallest favor."

"You ungrateful wretch! How many favors have you received at my hands?"

"I want this . . . for my mother. I want you to be gracious to her, to let her come to Court again. I asked you, and you promised me you would speak to her."

"I said that if I were passing through the gallery I might exchange a word with any who caught my eye, which is my usual practice. But I did not pass through the gallery."

"You did not because you knew that she was there."

"Be careful, Essex. And leave me at once. You offend me."

He strode away muttering that he had no desire to be where he was not wanted. I had given too much to that knave Raleigh, but this small thing he asked was denied him.

Let him go back to his bed. I made excuses for him. He was suffering from a fever. He was overwrought. But he was always overbearing, always rash, and spoke before he had given thought to what he was going to say.

I had news of him. He was very ill, it was said; and my conscience smote me. I went to see him and there was no doubt about his illness. He was not shamming this time. I had a terrible fear that I was going to lose him as I had lost Walsingham, Hatton and my dearest Robert.

I said rashly that I would receive his mother privately.

The effect on him was miraculous. Feverishly he kissed my hands. He said I was the kindest, most beautiful lady in the world and that he loved me as he never could love anyone else. He wished that he could die for me . . . this very moment. Nothing would give him greater pleasure.

I was touched and told him that the best way in which he could please me was to get well.

Then I began to think of meeting Lettice, and I found I was quite looking forward to the encounter. I wanted to see what the years had done to her. I was over sixty, so she must be in her fifties. Was she eight years younger than I? She had always been an outstandingly beautiful woman and she would know how to preserve her looks, I had no doubt. She seemed to have kept the devotion of that new husband of hers and he was twenty years younger than she was.

I considered what I should wear for the occasion. I wished to look my most regal so that Madame Lettice would not forget for a moment that she was in the presence of the Queen.

I chose a gown of white brocade with a red satin lining in the hanging sleeves which fell back to disclose my hands, and these less than any other part of me showed my age. They were still very white and supple, and I had always thought them my most outstanding beauty; and consequently everything was designed to bring them into prominence. They looked very beautiful adorned with jewels. My dress was ornamented with pearls set in gold filigree and the bodice was slashed with red velvet. My waist, which was as trim as it had been when I was a young girl, was encircled by a jeweled girdle, and my ruff scintillated with diamonds.

Thus I was ready to receive my enemy.

She knelt before me—graceful and still youthful—in blue, and wearing a hat with a curling feather. I saw that her hair was still plentiful and of that attractive color. She probably had some recipe for keeping it so. Trust her to discover the way to stay young. She doubtless had a good apothecary who could provide her with what she needed. And her eyes were large and darkly beautiful.

"You may rise, cousin," I said.

I stood up and we were close together. I put my hands on her shoulders and gave her a formal kiss. She flushed a little. I thought I caught a hint of triumph in her eyes.

I sat down and indicated a stool. She placed herself on it, gracefully gathering her skirts about her.

"It is long since I have seen you," I said.

"So long, Your Majesty," she answered.

"All those years since he died," I said. It was strange that while she was with me I could only think of Robert. "You have consoled yourself," I went on, almost angrily.

She bowed her head.

"You are like my aunt, Mary Boleyn. There must be men. Ah well, it is long ago, but sometimes to me it seems like yesterday. How did he die?"

"Peacefully. In his sleep."

"There were rumors about his death," I said, looking at her intently.

"There were always rumors about him."

"That is true. He was different from all others. Such a man. I never knew his like . . . nor ever shall. I mourn him still . . . after all these years."

She nodded in sympathy.

Then she said: "I want to thank Your Majesty for all you have done for my son. I trust he gives you satisfaction."

"Essex is a charming boy," I said. "But he is rash. You should impress on him the dangers of that."

"I know it well, Your Majesty, and it causes me great anxiety."

"You have a lively brood, Lettice. Methinks they take after their mother. Certainly not after poor Walter Devereux. He was a mild man . . . not suited to you at all, cousin. But you soon found that out, did you not? Still he gave you some pleasant children before he passed on. That was a tragedy but then . . . his usefulness was over, was it not?"

I looked at her sharply. Had Robert had a part in Devereux's death? Had she been party to it? She was a fascinating creature. I had to admit it. She had the sort of beauty which lasts as long as life. It was the contours of her face perhaps, perfectly molded, and of course, with youth, that flaming hair and those magnificent eyes she had been irresistible. One could not blame Robert. Perhaps I should have blamed myself. I could have had Robert at any time; but there was one question which would have haunted me all my life. Which was more attractive to Robert—myself or the crown? She had had no crown to offer him; he could lose a great deal by marrying her—yet he had done so.

I said: "I was sorry to hear of your son's death."

She looked sad and I thought: She does love her children.

She answered: "It was a great sorrow, but he wanted to go with his brother. He adored Robert. They all do."

"Essex has charm," I agreed. "He could do well for himself . . . but he must not be so reckless." Now I was conspiring with her; I was asking for her help for Essex. It showed how I worried about him—more than was wise and reasonable. I should say, Let him make his mistakes and pay for them. But I really loved that young man. "He speaks too freely," I went on. "He is so careless and I fear that he could fall into very serious trouble."

"I know it well," she answered, falling into the mood. We were cousins again as we had been when she had first come to Court and I had been attracted by her as I always was by beauty, no matter in which sex I found it. And the fact that there was a blood relationship between us had drawn me to her. "Oh Your Majesty," she went on, "I worry a great deal about him."

"He thinks much of you," I told her. "He is at least a devoted son. Warn him. Let him understand that he may go so far because of his charm and my affection for him . . . but he should watch that he does not take too many rash steps. There may come a time when even I cannot help him."

She rose then and kneeling, took my hand and kissed it. The face which she lifted to me was distorted a little by her anxiety; and if she became less beautiful in that moment, I liked her the better for it.

I said: "We will do our best for this wayward boy . . . both of us."

And for a moment we were close because of our love for him.

The moment passed and I said sharply: "You did not wait long after Leicester's death to take another to your bed."

"I was lonely, Your Majesty."

"And you were lonely before his death, eh?"

"He was so much at Court."

"It was his will," I reminded her. "I trust you find joy in this new husband."

"We have been married many years now."

"Oh yes, I remember. Leicester was scarcely cold when you took young Blount to husband. So you are happy in this third marriage? What a woman you are for marrying!"

"I am contented in my marriage," she said.

I went on: "And that girl of yours. She is another one to watch. Lady Rich is it . . . or Mountjoy?"

"Lady Rich," she said.

"Oh yes, Rich is the husband, Mountjoy the paramour . . . but I believe she is everywhere with Mountjoy and shares his house."

She was silent.

"And the other girl . . . rushing off and marrying Perrot. Yes indeed, Lettice, you have a lively brood."

"They have made me very happy," she replied quietly. "It is thus with children. We cannot expect to have the joys of parenthood without the accompanying anxieties."

There she stood—she had been wife to three men and was the mother of several children—Essex among them. And there was I . . . in my regal state with no husband or child. This was my life; that was hers. I could feel a fleeting envy, but I knew I would not have bartered my crown for any of her husbands—not even Robert—nor for any of the children—not even Essex.

I was tired of her. She depressed me. I brought the interview to an end.

"Essex persuaded me to receive you," I said, "and I gave in to him. So, Lettice, we have spoken to each other after all these years."

I held out my hand. It was the signal for her to take it, kiss it and depart.

ESSEX CAME TO ME glowing with pleasure.

"Your Majesty, my dearest Majesty, you have done this for me. How I adore you! My mother is so happy. It is the one thing she needed for her contentment."

"I received your mother to please you," I told him.

"How I thank you! From the bottom of my heart, I thank you."

All this excitement about receiving his mother! I was irritated. Moreover seeing Lettice again had depressed me considerably. She brought back too many memories of Robert and I had spent a most unhappy night recalling so much of the past, including that never-to-be-forgotten day when I had discovered that he had defied me . . . I might say abandoned me . . . to marry her.

The meeting may have gratified Lettice Knollys, but it certainly brought me no joy.

I had made up my mind that never again would I give way to Essex's whims. I would not see Lettice Knollys again. She would never be anything to me but the she-wolf who had spoilt the last years of my life with Robert.

"My mother says it was such a happy interview."

"I was unaware of that happiness," I said coldly. He should have realized it was dangerous to go on, but when had Essex ever been wise?

"She is looking forward to her next visit to Court."

"She may look forward for a long time. She will not have another visit to Court."

He looked at me in astonishment. "But you have received her! She has come back."

"My Lord Essex, your mother can only come to Court if I give her permission to do so."

"But you will, of course."

"I have decided not to."

"What?"

Really that young man was heading fast for trouble. He would have to learn to show some restraint.

I said coolly: "I did what you asked me to do. I have received your mother and there is an end to the matter. We have spoken and there is nothing more I have to say to her. And remember this: I have no wish to see her again."

He stared at me and the color suffused his face. He did not speak, which perhaps was fortunate, for if he had I was sure he would have said something which was unforgivable.

He turned and without asking leave to retire strode from my presence.

BURGHLEY CAME TO talk privately with me. He seemed a little concerned.

Poor Burghley! He was showing his age. His beard was quite white now and his once lithe and upright figure stooping. I always felt moved when I saw him; he had lost his youth and his health in my service and I used to say to myself: God forgive me if I ever forget what I owe this man.

He had had so many troubles and he had been such a good husband and father, too. He was fond of all children and nurtured his own with great care. He had looked after his grandchildren—those of the profligate Earl of Oxford who had married his daughter, a match which Burghley had never ceased to regret. He had cared assiduously for my welfare and had even provided me with his son Robert, my "Little Elf," so that when my dear old friend passed on there would be another as able—or almost as able—to step into his shoes.

When we were alone together I was always particularly affectionate with him. I wanted him to know how much I appreciated what he had done for me and for the country.

Of course he had put forward his son. What good father would not? He had kept Francis Bacon from office out of fear that he would displace the Elf. He never would. I wanted to make use of Robert Cecil's services because I recognized in him his father's particular qualities. Francis Bacon might be brilliant but that tutorial attitude of his would never have suited me.

It was a pity that Essex was in the opposing camp. I should have liked him to work with Burghley. But that was impossible. There could not have been two people less alike than Essex and either of the Cecils.

So when Burghley came to me I feared before he began to tell me that there was some fresh complaint against Essex.

"Pray sit down, my dear friend," I said. "I know it tires you to stand."

Gratefully he did so.

"First," I said, "tell me this: Have you been taking the possets I recommended?"

"Without fail, Your Majesty."

"Well, I trust they will do good work. My Spirit must take more care of himself. Why should he not rest more? He has that very able son of his to take over much of the work."

"It is a great pleasure to me that Your Majesty finds my son satisfactory."

"A clever little Elf. Yes, he pleases me, Master Cecil, and not only because of his good work. He is your son and that gives him special favor in my eyes."

Now the pleasantries were over, he came to business, and, as I had feared, it concerned Essex.

"Since the regrettable death of Walsingham we have sadly missed his excellent service," said Burghley, "but there are those among us who have tried to make sure that there are no secret plots which might put Your Majesty's life in danger . . ."

"Essex works well in that direction," I said.

"Ah, Essex, Your Majesty." He paused and I was full of foreboding. "I have made an alarming discovery and I have come here to tell you expressly of it. Essex is corresponding with the King of Scotland."

"That is impossible!" I cried.

"Alas, Your Majesty, I have evidence. I had discovered this was going on and have secured some of the correspondence."

"For what purpose was this?"

Burghley looked at me and lifted his shoulders.

"The correspondence started when Essex was trying to restore Davison and wanted the King of Scotland to join in the pleas for him since the trouble was about the execution of the King's mother. From that . . . the letters have continued."

"How did you discover this?"

"I planted a spy—one Thomas Fowler—at the Scottish Court. The letters have been copied and sent to me. It seems that the prime mover is Lady Rich. Her husband is with her in this."

"But she is with Mountjoy now."

"That is so, Your Majesty, but it seems the one thing Penelope Rich has in common with her husband, is a love of intrigue. They are all working for the aggrandizement of Essex. They have code names: Penelope Rich is Rialta, Lord Rich, Ricardo; Your Majesty is Venus and Essex the Weary Knight."

"It sounds like madness."

"Not such madness, Your Majesty. Essex is the Weary Knight because he is weary of his bondage to you. He looks for a change."

"He can have his change!" I cried. "He can go into exile at once. That is the change he will get."

"If I may advise . . ."

"Certainly, my friend."

"At this time the correspondence with the King of Scotland is not treasonable. It is clear to me that Penelope Rich—who is a schemer if ever there was one—is trying to ingratiate herself with James of Scotland, who some say would be the next in line to this throne. I think that is the reason for this correspondence."

"So they are waiting for my death, are they?"

"It would seem so."

"Traitors! Villains! By God's Precious Soul, they should all be in the Tower."

"They are disloyal to Your Majesty, but I beg you to restrain your anger. I want this correspondence to continue, for who knows when it might break into something of significance. If we let them remain in ignorance of our discovery, they will go on writing to each other, and if we are vigilant we can by this means discover whether they have some ulterior motive and are plotting and hoping for James's help. But we must not betray our knowledge of what is taking place. I am sure this is the way Walsingham would have worked."

"Oh my dear, dear Moor! How I wish he were with us now."

"Amen! But Your Majesty, you still have loyal servants here to work for you."

"My dear Spirit the chief of them."

"Then I have Your Majesty's permission to keep this matter dark? No indication shall be given to the conspirators—if conspirators they be—that we have made this discovery?"

"Yes, let it be so," I said.

"I have a letter here which was sent to Essex by Sir Francis Bacon in which he warns him of his treatment of you. I thought it would amuse you and let you know what these young men are thinking."

"The letter came to you through the same sources, I presume?"

"I have many men who are ever watchful of all that concerns Your Majesty."

I was in truth faintly amused by Francis Bacon's letter. He was telling Essex how he should treat me. Not too much blatant flattery, he advised; there were times, he wrote, when Essex appeared to be paying fine compliments rather than speaking sincerely. That should be changed. He should not slavishly imitate Hatton or Leicester, but as those two courtiers managed that sort of flattery very well, it would be advisable for Essex to study their methods.

Francis Bacon, I commented, was a young man who thought himself very clever. As for Essex . . . his behavior hurt me more than anything else.

I helped Burghley to his feet. His joints were very stiff.

I embraced him warmly.

"We are getting old, my friend," I said. "We notice it . . . and so do others."

MY FEELINGS FOR Essex were changing. I could not entirely abandon him, for he still had the power to charm me, and when he was with me, in spite of everything, I was still able to forget his faults. But there were times when I could not escape the thought that he was waiting for me to die. He wanted a new King—young James—and he and his sister were endeavoring to make sure of his favor when the change came.

It was perfidious of him. How could he pretend to love me! And how foolish I was, because I missed Leicester so much, to turn to this cruel young man.

He was philandering with one of my maids of honor, a Mistress Bridges. I pretended not to see what was going on, but it was really quite blatant. I heard that poor Frances was very unhappy on account of his infidelities. It had been a very sad day for her when she had married Essex.

He was his mother all over again. What could one expect from the cubs of the she-wolf!

I dismissed Mistress Bridges from Court for a few days—not because of her liaison with Essex, which I pretended to know nothing about, but because she had used the privy gallery to watch a tennis match, and the rule was that ladies should not use it unless they first asked for permission.

Essex knew that I was annoyed, for it was his game the girl had gone to see, and as I was very cool to him—and had been since Burghley's revelation—he retired from Court with the excuse that he had overexerted himself at the game and had a return of his fever.

Henri Quatre, having changed his religion, was fairly firm on the throne of France and, like myself, he was one who believed that peace brought prosperity. He was therefore trying to bring about a peace with Spain in which he wanted me to join.

Burghley was in favor of this, Essex against it. Burghley said that we needed peace and there was more to be gained from it than war. Essex made a fiery speech in which he extolled the bravery of the English, who had once defeated the Spaniards and would do so again.

Burghley did a strange thing then, which afterward people said was prophetic.

He took up a prayer book and turned the leaves. Then he placed the book in Essex's hands, indicating the words: "Men of blood shall not live out half their days."

We had other matters nearer home. Burghley stressed the fact that Ireland was giving trouble again, and it was really necessary to appoint a strong Lord Deputy and that we should give full consideration to this without delay.

We were at Greenwich and I called a meeting there.

Burghley was not well enough to attend but his son Robert Cecil was present. There was also Howard of Effingham who, much to Essex's chagrin, had now become the Earl of Nottingham, Essex himself and the Clerk of the Council.

I began by saying that I believed the best man to send to Ireland was Sir William Knollys, who had proved himself to be reliable, shrewd and honest.

Cecil said that he was in complete agreement and he believed that Sir William should be sent without delay.

It was then that Essex raised the objection. Knollys was not the man, he said. It was obvious to him that we should send Sir George Carew.

There was silence in the chamber. Robert Cecil looked taken aback, but I realized the motive behind Essex's outburst. I found that now I was always looking for motives behind his actions. Sir William Knollys was his uncle and he could rely on his support at Court, so naturally he did not want to lose him. It could be said that Knollys was of the Essex faction, whereas George Carew supported the Cecils. To lose Carew would be a blow to them; to lose Knollys would be equally inconvenient for Essex.

I had already agreed with Robert Cecil and the Admiral that Knollys was our best man, and Essex had had the temerity to ignore my views and express his own.

I said firmly: "Knollys should be informed at once that he should prepare to leave for Ireland."

"It is a mistake!" cried Essex. He was behaving like a petulant boy who has been denied a coveted plaything.

·   I was really angry with him. His follies were becoming intolerable. I thought of his philandering with the ladies of the Court and his reckless involvement with the King of Scotland. It was time he realized that he was not so sure of my favor that he could behave in such a manner. Robert, in spite of all that had been between us, had never been discourteous to me or raised his voice against me in public.

I saw his blazing eyes and the angry color in his face before he very deliberately turned his back on me.

There was a hushed silence in the chamber. I could not believe he had gone so far. This was something I would not endure. I strode toward him and boxed his ears.

"And now," I shouted, "go and be hanged."

That was not the end. He faced me, his fury evident. Then he put his hand on the hilt of his sword as though ready to draw it against me.

"I would not have taken such a blow from King Henry, your father," he cried. "It is an indignity which I never could—nor would—endure from anyone . . . No! Certainly not from a king in petticoats."

I was so taken aback that for a few seconds I did nothing, and just as I was about to call the guards, he dashed from the room.

NEVER HAD SUCH conduct been known. It was being discussed throughout the Court. This is the end of Essex, it was said.

Of course he should be in the Tower. He should suffer the traitor's death. But I was so shaken that I was uncertain how to act.

He is a foolish boy, I said to myself again and again.

He is a dangerous young man, said that wise part of me. Remember the letters to Scotland. What is the use of caring for him? He brings misery to all those who come into contact with him. Poor Frances Walsingham! I pity her. I can even be sorry for his mother.

I knew that his friends were trying to persuade him to attempt a reconciliation. If he had begged forgiveness, I supposed I should have granted it. I had to admit I missed him at Court. But the weeks passed and he remained in sullen retreat.

Then I ceased to think of him, for Robert Cecil came to tell me that his father was very weak indeed.

I went to his house in the Strand and I was shocked to see how ill the poor man was. He lay back in his bed, his eyes apologizing because of his inability to rise. I took his poor swollen hands in mine and kissed them.

I said: "My dear, dear friend, I did not know how ill you were until the Elf told me. Had I known I should have been here ere this."

"Your Majesty is so gracious to come to me."

"I shall come . . . and keep coming . . . until you are well again."

He shook his head and said: "I shall rise no more from this bed."

"I forbid you to say such things. You must get well. You have been beside me so many years. What should I do without you?"

He was overcome with emotion and so was I.

I rose from his bed and asked what food they were giving him. He could only take liquid food, I was told, and only a little of that. His hands were so swollen that he could scarcely lift a spoon to his lips.

I ordered them to make him a gruel which I knew was especially nourishing, and when it was ready I took it to him and fed my minister as though he were a child.

He said that his greatest grief in leaving this world was that he would no longer be able to serve me.

"No queen ever had a more faithful servant," I assured him. "I have scolded you sometimes, dear Spirit. I have raged against you, have I not? But I never ceased to love you. Nor have I ever been in doubt of your worth."

I sat in silence by his bed, staring into space. There could be no disguising the fact that he was near his end.

He said: "Robert will serve you well. I have brought him up with this object. He has a sharp and clever mind."

I nodded. Poor Burghley, he was such a good man and God had ill rewarded him in this life. He had loved his family and looked after them all; and in his care for my well-being he had brought forward his second son, Robert, knowing full well that his first-born, Thomas, who was something of a weakling, lacked the ability to follow in his father's footsteps. I knew I had another treasure in the Elf; but he was not his father. I should never know his like again.

I thought of how I should miss him, for, excellent minister that he was, he was also friend and confidant. We had shared so much—even ailments. He had suffered from his teeth and so had I. Many a pleasant half hour we had spent chatting about our pains. And when he—devoted family man that he was—had lost his daughter some years before, and his wife a year later, it was I who had tried to comfort him.

Life was cruel. His mother had died only a year before his daughter, so that there were three deaths in a row and all were people who were very near and dear to him. He had had trouble enough through his daughter's marriage with Oxford, and I knew full well how often he had wished that marriage had never taken place. But he had great comfort in his grandchildren. Such a good man, I mourned, and such sorrow!

The end was inevitable. I was going to lose another friend, perhaps the most able of them all. I felt lonely and bereft. They were all slipping away from me.

I visited him as frequently as I could while he lingered on, and if a day came when I could not go, I sent one of my ladies to inquire after him, and take affectionate messages and cordials from me.

I felt very very sad and could think of little else but Burghley during those days of waiting for the end.

Why did he have to die? Of course he was in his seventy-sixth year, and that was a goodly age. I remembered all he had done for his country and I doubted England had ever had a more faithful servant. It was so rare to find a man who was excellent in statesmanship and able to enjoy a felicitous family life at the same time. There was not a better husband and father in the land; his grandchildren loved him and his constant thought was for the welfare of his family. Thomas Cecil, the eldest son, must have been a bit of a trial to him because he was wild in his youth, and lacked that fine, keen brain which the younger son, Robert, had inherited. But Burghley with that great good sense, which went side by side with his tenderness toward his family, did not hesitate to bring along Robert, the slightly deformed little Elf whom he was now bequeathing to me. I should honor Robert—not only for his father's sake but for his own. It was typical of Burghley that he should have left me well provided for. We had such a lot in common; his love of music was another of these interests. I was going to be so desolate. I had named him aptly as my Spirit, and I should miss him sorely.

On the day he died his son Robert brought me a letter which his father had written to him. Burghley had been just strong enough to dictate it to his secretary, but he had signed it as well as his swollen hands would allow him "Your languishing Father, Burghley."

"I pray you diligently and effectually," the letter ran, "let Her Majesty understand how her singular kindness doth overcome my power to acquit it, who, though she will not be a mother, yet she sheweth herself, by feeding me with her own princely hand, as a careful norice; and if I may be weaned to feed myself, I shall be more ready to serve her on the earth; if not, I hope to be, in heaven, a servitor for her and God's church . . ."

He had added a postscript:

"Serve God by serving the Queen, for all other service is indeed bondage to the devil."

I lifted my eyes to Robert Cecil's face. They were filled with tears.

I said: "My grief is as great as yours."

HOW I MISSED Leicester at that time! The old days were gone forever.
Men were not as they had been. They were a disappointment to me. My
men were all leaving me—Hatton, Heneage, my dearest Leicester and now
Burghley.

I had Robert Cecil, but then he was not handsome, and I did enjoy having handsome people around me. Essex, it was true, was very attractive in
appearance, but so feckless and unreliable that he gave me more pain than
joy. He was still sulking in exile. Yet if he had been a little humble, a little
contrite, I could have pardoned him.

Henry Wriothesley, Earl of Southampton, was a good-looking man and
I would have favored him. He was clever and a lover of the arts. He had
become the patron of my favorite poet and playwright, William Shakespeare, and I applauded him for this; but he was reckless and arrogant, and
did little to win my favor.

I could have had a great interest in him for his chief passion in life was
literature; but he was such a wild young man—living among actors and writ-
ers of plays in odd corners of London. He was an adventurer of sorts but not
the like of Raleigh and Drake. He was a man who wanted to experience life
at all levels. He annoyed me because he must have known that I would be
interested in him, yet he snapped his fingers at the Court and preferred to
consort with his literary friends.

He had become a great friend of Essex; and that was one of the reasons
why I watched him with some anxiety. I felt sure that Southampton would
be a bad influence on Essex.

For one thing he was said to be fond of his own sex and I heard that he
had had many love affairs with men at the Court and outside it, which in
itself was enough to make me view his friendship with Essex in some dismay.

Some months previously he had made an unpleasant scene in my Presence Chamber. True, it was after I had gone to bed, but I frowned on such
conduct whenever it took place.

Southampton had been playing primero with Raleigh and another gentleman. On my departure the Squire of the Body, Ambrose Willoughby,
asked them to stop play, which was the custom after my retirement.

Southampton swaggeringly told him that he had no intention of stop-
ping play until he wished to, at which Willoughby retorted that he would
call the guard and forcibly stop the play. Raleigh, who had apparently been
winning, pocketed his gains and said he would leave. This infuriated
Southampton who shouted after Raleigh that he would remember this
against him. Raleigh, who never failed to take a financial advantage,
shrugged his shoulders and went off smiling; but Southampton then turned

to Willoughby whom he blamed for the whole matter. A fight ensued during which Willoughby got the better of Southampton and pulled out some of his hair.

When I was told of this next morning, I laughed aloud. I complimented Willoughby and made it clear to everyone that I was delighted because Southampton had been taught a lesson.

I suspected that Essex condoled with him. Let him! I thought. Essex was still in exile.

My dislike for Southampton did not diminish when I heard that he had challenged Lord Grey of Wilton to a duel.

Fortunately I heard of this in time and forbade it, sending messages to both Southampton and Wilton telling them that they should reserve their services for me, and not hazard their lives in private quarrels.

I would be glad to be rid of Southampton. I was growing to dislike him more and more. For one thing I found his friendships with other men distasteful. He was constantly with people like Francis Bacon; and they were all friends of Essex. Southampton was always in the center of some quarrel. If he was not challenging someone, he was urging others to do so. One of his friends, Sir Charles Danvers, picked a quarrel with a Hampshire nobleman named Long and killed him. Before Danvers could be brought to justice Southampton smuggled the murderer out of the country.

I was relieved when Southampton was given a minor post in an embassy in Paris. But while he was away I discovered that one of my ladies, Elizabeth Vernon, had become pregnant. This state of affairs always enraged me, and when I had slapped and pummeled the secret out of the girl, I was appalled to find that the man responsible was Southampton.

I sent her away in disgrace and shortly learned that, hearing of her plight, Southampton had hastened home from Paris and married her.

And all this without asking my permission! They were both sent for a spell in the Fleet Prison. They were not there long, but I did make it clear that Southampton's chances at Court were over.

I had at last decided that Essex should return to Court. I should have been very happy if he had given me an apology, and would most willingly have accepted it; but it seemed that was asking too much of his proud nature.

He did appear at Burghley's funeral. More than five hundred followed the hearse, and Essex, shrouded in a hooded black mourning cloak, was conspicuous among those who came to show their respect to the great statesman. I heard that he had seemed overcome with grief—some cynics suggested that it might be more for his own plight, than for the loss of the man in whose house he had once lived.

After the funeral he had gone to Wanstead House, there to live quietly as he was not received at Court.

If only he would have sent one little word to tell me he was sorry for his really outrageous behavior, I would readily have put it down to the indiscretion of youth. But he did nothing of the sort. He was too proud to admit himself in the wrong.

I thought then: What will become of Essex in the end? He has no greater enemy than himself.

News came that he was very ill at Wanstead. Some said he grieved because of his exclusion from Court. He was arrogant and foolish, but he was still Essex, the one to whom I had looked to soothe the hurt left by the loss of Leicester.

So I gave permission for him to return to Court, and I implied that that unprecedented scene in the chamber when I had boxed his ears, was forgotten.

But such scenes are never forgotten. I would remember that one for as long as I lived; and when he returned, pale and wan, but as arrogant as ever, I found myself longing for Leicester more than ever. It had become clear to me that there was no one who could take his place, and it was folly to pretend there ever could be.

Ireland was as usual in upheaval. We had not sent Sir William Knollys or anyone so far; but someone must go now. I wanted Lord Mountjoy to take the post. In spite of his irregular life with Penelope Rich he was an extremely able and reliable man, and I really believed he might have a chance of succeeding in this very difficult task.

Incredible as it might seem, Essex once more raised objections to this choice.

"No, Your Majesty," he said. "Mountjoy is not the man. He has no experience of war. He has only a small estate and therefore cannot supply many followers, and he is too interested in literature to make a good soldier."

I was so angry with him. He did not seem to understand that, although I had allowed him to return to Court, I now regarded him in a different light. I no longer had the same love for him. I was prepared to give it, it was true, because I needed to fill the gap left by Leicester, but I had made a discovery—that great affection comes about naturally and it cannot be forced. Much as I wanted that perfect relationship which had been between myself and Leicester, I now accepted the fact that I could never have it. It was the sort of thing which came once in a lifetime, if one was lucky. It could never happen to me again.

I looked at this brash young man. He was very handsome with that brand of interesting looks which appealed to me. I was sixty-six years of age. Was I going to inspire that romantic love I had had from Leicester? Never! It was over.

I turned on Essex and said: "My Lord Essex, you do not like my choice of a man for Ireland any more than you did before. I can see that you believe Mountjoy not to be worthy of the task. Well, perhaps there is one other who might be chosen."

I saw the satisfied smile play about his lips. I thought: Yes, Essex. You see me as a foolish, doting old woman. I am in some ways; but there is always my serious self looking on at my folly and never failing to make me aware of it.

"Yes," I continued. "You, my lord. I have decided to send you to Ireland."

HE WAS TAKEN ABACK. It was not what he wanted. He had planned to stay at Court and rule the country through me. To have forgiven him for that humiliating scene seemed to make it certain to him that he could behave as he liked and still come back to favor. I admit it seemed so. He was thinking he had more influence at Court than even Leicester had had.

When he realized he could not evade the appointment, I will say that he set about the adventure with enthusiasm.

He selected his followers with alacrity, and I was interested to see that his stepfather, Christopher Blount, was one he had chosen to go with him. I heard that there was a deep friendship between those two, and that Blount worshipped Essex—as I believe the whole family did. I wondered what the she-wolf thought about losing her husband and her son at one time.

I was interested to hear that Southampton was going with him. Oh well, I thought, that will rid us of that troublesome gentleman for a time.

It was a day in March when he set out for Ireland and when his caval-cade reached Islington there was a great storm and such a downpour of rain that the men had to take cover from it. People shook their heads over this and said it was a sign that the expedition would not be a success.

The prophecy was not far wrong.

Essex had no love for his task once the first enthusiasm had waned. He knew that to bring law and order to a people like the Irish was an impossi-bility. He made mistakes. He was unsuited to the mission. I wished that I had sent Mountjoy, who was a clever and steady young man, and who would not take an action without first giving serious thought to it.

Essex bestowed honors on those of whom he was fond. He had made his stepfather Marshal of the Army—a ridiculous appointment and one Blount could never have aspired to but for his relationship with Essex. My policy had always been to favor those whom I liked, but only if they were good enough to do the work. But I could not expect such wisdom from Essex.

He sent word to me that he was proposing to make Blount a member of the Council of Ireland. I promptly replied that there should be no such appointment.

As a result Christopher Blount returned to England. His health was not good, said Essex. Whether this was to be construed as petulance on his part or whether it was actually true, I did not know; and, as I had no intention of displaying the slightest interest in Lettice Knollys's husband, except to forbid him to take posts for which he was unsuited, I did not inquire.

Then came the most startling news. Essex had appointed the Earl of Southampton General of Horse, although he must have known that it was an appointment of which I would disapprove. How dared he give command to such a man—one to whom I had shown my dislike! The post should have gone to Lord Grey who was Southampton's superior in military skill in every possible way. Moreover when the appointment was made official, Grey would be serving under Southampton; and in addition to Grey's being the man of superior knowledge, he was also an enemy of Southampton, who had once intended to fight a duel with him—and would have done so if I had not stepped in.

What was Essex thinking of? He cared nothing for the cause. All he wanted to do was honor his friends—and one who was in disgrace at Court and had shown his defiance of me!

I wrote at once forbidding the appointment.

Essex's answer was that it had already been made and could not be rescinded. I heard too that Southampton, no doubt because he was robbed of the presence of Elizabeth Vernon, was becoming very friendly with the most handsome of the men. He shared a tent with a very good-looking young captain—one Piers Edmonds—and, said my informant, Southampton would hug him in his arms and play wantonly with him.

I was horrified. I sent orders to Essex that the command must be taken from Southampton without delay, and I did this in such authoritative terms that even Essex realized he must obey.

It was not surprising that affairs in Ireland were going badly.

VERY SOON IT became clear that the appointment of Essex had been a disaster.

He ignored my instructions, which were arrived at with the help of the Council. He would go his own way, which was the wrong one. He was defeated everywhere. His excuses were that there was sickness in the army before the battle commenced, or that the weather had been against him.

Why wasn't action taken when the army was in better state? I demanded. And why was the campaign started at the approach of winter? Why had not July or August been chosen? It seemed that none of the seasons of the year had been considered favorable. A messenger arrived to tell me that Essex had been parleying with Hugh O'Neill, Earl of Tyrone, after having come face to face with him at Ardee in Louth where Essex did not attack, his forces being so few in number compared with those of Tyrone. He should have known that it was Tyrone's custom to make agreements that he might break them when it suited him to do so. In any case, Essex had no right to make agreements without first receiving instructions from England.

That infuriated me. Essex was hopeless. There were some who were suggesting that he was serving the Irish better than the English, and that was tantamount to saying that he was a traitor.

It was Michaelmas time and I was at the Palace of Nonesuch. I had risen from my bed and was seated at my dressing table while my ladies were gathered about me ready to assist at my dressing.

I yawned for I was still sleepy. My hair, quite white now, hung about my face in disorder. I was sitting there in my bedgown when the door burst open and a man—muddied from a long ride, disheveled and his clothes awry—came bursting into the apartment. At first I thought he was an assassin—and then I recognized him.

"Essex!" I cried.

"Your Majesty!" He flung himself at my feet and kissed my hand fervently.

He had come from Ireland. He feared evil had been spoken of him. He had ridden through the night and had just arrived at Nonesuch Palace, and had been unable to wait longer before seeing his fair and beauteous Queen.

Fair and beauteous Queen! An old woman of sixty-five, her face pale and unadorned, her white straggly hair awry about her face!

He must be very frightened to talk so, I thought. This means great disaster in Ireland.

Then I was thinking how I must look. He had never before seen me in this state of undress—nor had any man, except one from my window and that was years ago when I had been younger. It was suddenly borne home to me that he must be as astonished to see me as I was to see him—though for different reasons.

My one thought was to get rid of him as quickly as possible. I could not bear that he should see me thus. How different I must look from that scintillating goddess in her jeweled gowns and ruffs and her magnificent curling red hair. He was trying not to look at me. Even he must spare a thought from his own affairs to realize how I was feeling.

I sat very still and spoke gently to him because it was the quickest way of getting rid of him. I would see him later, I said softly. He could tell me everything then.

After he went, I sat very still, trembling with the shock of what had happened. I took up a hand mirror and looked at myself. It was horrible. My face was drained of color. My hair straggled about my shoulders—gray and scanty. I looked what I was—a tired old woman.

How dared he come bursting in like that! Did he think he could behave as the whim took him and that I would forgive him?

I thought: Essex, you have gone too far this time. I will never forgive you for this.

I WAS ESPECIALLY careful with my toilette and when I was ready to go into the Presence Chamber I was sparkling with jewels. There was the faintest color in my cheeks, which gave a brightness to my eyes. Was it anger against this man who had dared see me in my natural state? No man had ever seen me like that before. I had thought none ever would. And he had dared! No, I would never forgive him for that. Always when I saw him I would see myself . . . old . . . unadorned . . . with nothing of beauty left to me.

He was there. His eyes alight with excitement. I thought: By God's Holy Son, he believes that he only has to smile on me and I am his slave. In his mind I am no queen for he stands above me.

You will never have to learn a harder lesson than you will learn now, my Lord Essex, I thought.

He knelt before me. I gave him my hand which he fervently kissed. He raised his eyes to look at me but my gaze was fixed over his head in the distance.

"My fairest Queen . . ." he began.

I said coolly: "You may rise, Essex."

"I came to you," he began breathlessly. "There is so much to tell you . . ."

I replied shortly: "You may tell it to the Council."

He was taken aback. I saw the deep color flood his face. He could not believe that I had spoken to him thus.

I turned to Robert Cecil and engaged him in conversation. Essex fell back, a sullen, angry expression on his face. All those present were watchful. They had expected me to give him a warm welcome, and that the erring young man would once more be forgiven his sins and be taken back into favor. But they did not know what he had seen that morning. I should never forget it, though. Every time I saw him, I should remember. And I did not want to be reminded.

HE WAS QUESTIONED by the Council and his answers brought to me. I said that I found them unsatisfactory and this was the general opinion.

It was decided that he should remain in confinement at York House. I traveled down to Richmond with the Court and tried not to think of Essex. I daresay I was sharper with my ladies than ever. I was never happy until I was fully dressed in all my finery, and yet I hesitated long over the gown I should wear. There were, I think, about two thousand of them to choose from. Then there was the wig to be selected from my collection of eighty.

Only when I was fully dressed and a shining sparkling vision looked back at me from the mirror could I feel a little happier.

But I did not want to think of Essex and I certainly did not want to see him.

When I heard that he was ill, I laughed. Was he not always ill when life turned against him? Oh I know Robert had been the same. How many times had I hurried to him to tend him when there was some disagreement between us? Yet I had never blamed him. How could I, when I myself had used the device often enough? I had always smiled indulgently at Robert's illnesses because they showed me he could not bear to be out of favor. He used to be really desperate when he was.

But Essex . . . now, if he were ill, then he deserved to be. He had been arrogant and too sure of himself. How dared he imagine he knew what was best for Ireland when he had gone there and made a bigger mess of it than any of his predecessors? But most of all how dared he come dashing into my bedchamber when I was unprepared to receive him!

Old Lady Walsingham came to me. I greeted her warmly. She had been a good wife to my dear Moor. She begged me to allow Essex to write to his wife who had just had a baby.

I said coolly: "He is under restraint. It is not permitted for those who are confined as he is to write letters. Moreover the Countess of Essex will surely not wish to hear from one who has treated her with such little regard. He is no more a faithful husband than a faithful subject."

Lady Walsingham wept, but I hardened my heart. He had treated poor Frances badly. I doubted he had bothered to write many letters to her when he was in Ireland.

Frances herself sent me a jewel in the hope that the bauble would soften my heart toward her husband. Foolish girl! I had jewels in plenty—and in any case nothing would soften my heart toward a young man who had seen me as he had. She should have more pride than to sue for him, considering the manner in which he had treated her, preferring the beds of his mistresses to hers and blatantly letting her know it. I sent the jewel back.

His sisters Penelope and Dorothy dressed themselves in black and came to plead for him. I did receive them, for I saw at once that they were greatly concerned for their brother. It was amazing what affection he had inspired.

I spoke to them gently and said that I understood their anxiety. Their brother was a most misguided young man. He had disobeyed my orders and his case was in the hands of the Council.

Penelope cried out that in my great mercy I could save him. I surveyed her coldly and said: "The Queen is not told by her subjects what she can and cannot do."

She was aghast. She thought she had done harm to her brother's cause, which she was trying so hard to plead, and I said more kindly: "You may go. His fate is in the hands of the Council. I understand your grief. You are bold because you are fond of him."

They went away heartened. They thought I had received them kindly and that was a good sign.

But I did not want to see him again because I knew that when I did, I would see myself in his eyes.

A rather disturbing matter arose at this time.

A certain John Hayward had written a book called *The History of Henri IV*. He had dedicated this book to Essex and had written a dedication in it in which he compared Essex with Bolingbroke. This had caused a ripple of excitement considering the position in which Essex now found himself. Cecil had been horrified at the book and others had found it to be distinctly subversive. Cecil thought there was in it an incitement to rebellion. As a result Hayward was put in the Tower.

Essex was brought before a court in York House and charged with making a dishonorable and dangerous treaty with the Earl of Tyrone, and also with contempt for the government. He had promoted the Earl of Southampton against the wishes of the Queen and Council and had distributed knighthoods when he had no authority to do so. It must have been galling to Essex to have the learned Counsel Francis Bacon taking part in the proceedings against him. It was not a trial, being entirely informal, and I believe that afterward Bacon tried to justify himself for speaking against the man who regarded him as a friend, by stating that in acting in this manner he was able to retain the Queen's confidence, which he hoped later to use in Essex's favor. However, the result of the tribunal was that Essex was dismissed from all the offices he held, and was to remain a prisoner in York House until further notice.

I could not forget him as I should have liked to. I had loved him, even though I knew his character to be too simple to give him any hope of fulfilling his high ambitions. He was too passionate and too candid; he was like a blundering but endearing schoolboy at his most charming; at his worst he was almost oafish. He was politically ignorant; he was vain in the extreme and there was no doubt that he had the power to fascinate the opposite sex. There had been many times when I had treated him as a lover—almost as I had Leicester; but he did not see it as a game I was playing. He had the myopia of the small mind which sees itself as a giant among pygmies. It was ridiculous for such a man to believe he could pit his wits against men such as Cecil. What a fool he had been. And because women liked him, he thought he could dominate me.

Meanwhile Mountjoy had been sent to Ireland and it was gratifying to find that he was beginning to make a success of that most difficult of tasks. I hoped Essex remembered that it had been my plan to send Mountjoy in the first place. How he must regret his opposition to that suggestion!

I did not want him to remain in confinement, and after three months he was released, but banned from any public posts and forbidden to appear at Court.

It must have been obvious, even to Essex, that his advancement at Court was over.

He was in a dire state; his health was failing; he had been cut off from the most influential men at Court, and he was in financial difficulties. One of the biggest sources of income for him had been the lease he had held on the sweet wines and which was a concession many longed for. I had given him a lease of ten years and that period was running out. If it were not renewed he would be poor indeed. He wrote to me begging me to renew it.

Why should I give this great concession to one who had flouted me? Moreover, I had heard that he was gathering together in his house a band of disgruntled men—those who had a grievance against the state and that meant against me; and much wild conversation took place there, which was occasionally brought to my ears.

So I refused to renew the lease on the sweet wines.

Perhaps it was not to be expected that he would sink into a life of obscurity. There would always be trouble wherever Essex was.

Tension was rising. Southampton, that man who displeased me so much, was visiting Essex House frequently. One day Southampton came face to face with Lord Grey near Durham House. The old enemies quickly picked a quarrel and during the fighting which broke out, one of Southampton's men lost a hand.

Such brawling was against the law and Grey was arrested since it was his man who had caused the damage.

Knowing Southampton's quarrelsome nature I agreed that Grey might not be to blame and he was released, much to the chagrin of Southampton—and of course of Essex.

I imagined Lettice's feelings at this time. How anxious she must have been for her son! She was clever enough to see that he was heading straight for disaster. One thing I was certain of: He should never come to Court again, though there were some who still believed that he would. They had seen my fondness for Leicester; they had marveled that after his marriage, which had so upset me at the time, I had received him back at Court and become as close to him as ever. They did not understand. With Leicester it had been a lasting love; with Essex it was a dream, a pretense, a ridiculous fantasy, which I had fabricated in the belief that I could catch at my youth again and be loved as Leicester had loved me.

Essex himself had brought real life into vivid existence when he had come face to face with an old woman.

The dream was over—and that could only mean the end of Essex, unless he was prepared to live quietly in some place far from Court. As if he ever would!

He was still writing pleading letters, still having bouts of illness; but although I sent him broth from time to time, I would not relent.

He had his enemies among the ladies of my Court—possibly those he had dallied with for a while and then deserted—and they did not hesitate to pass on gossip that was detrimental to him. I was shocked when I realized that his adoration of me had turned to vilification.

It was reported that he had said that now I was an old woman my mind was as distorted as my carcass.

And this was the man who, a short time before, had been extolling my beauty!

Clearly he knew that there was no chance of a reconciliation between us. If he had been wiser he would have known it from the time he strode into my bedchamber and confronted an old woman. But when had he ever been wise? When had he ever learned?

Desperate men were gathering at Essex House—men who had little hope of making their way in my Court. They were seeking a way to fame and fortune, and they knew that could not come to them through me. So they were looking elsewhere—some to the Infante of Spain for whom they could make out a remote claim; some to James of Scotland who was the next in line to the succession.

It seemed incredible that even Essex could be crazy enough to plan a revolution. But he had some to support him—all those failures who had not made their way at Court. Oh, the foolish boy! If ever anyone asked for self-destruction, it was Essex.

When his followers persuaded the players at the Globe to put on William Shakespeare's *Richard the Second,* I presumed it was to show the people how easy it was for one king to abdicate and to be replaced by another.

Raleigh—Essex's old enemy—came to me in a state of some excitement. He had rowed himself down the Thames and as he was passing Essex House, he had been shot at. He had been to visit Sir Fernando Gorges, a great friend of Drake's, who in spite of his name had come from a family who settled in England at the time of Henry I—a man who had served England well and had been governor of Plymouth—hence his friendship with Drake. Gorges told Drake that Essex had made an effort to enlist him in his enterprise.

"Your Majesty," said Raleigh, "the actions of Essex are now becoming dangerous. According to Gorges there are plots in progress, and Gorges does not like the sound of them. He says there will be bloodshed. And, as Your Majesty knows, Essex is capable of any wild act."

"I think," I said, "it is time some action was taken about the Essex House plotters."

I called the Council together and I chose four men to call on Essex. The Lord Keeper, Sir Thomas Egerton, was one of them and John Popham the Chief Justice another. They went with the dignity of the posts they held, and accompanying them was Essex's uncle, Sir William Knollys, who would naturally show some sympathy to his kinsman; the Earl of Worcester, who had at one time been a friend of Essex, was also of the party. I sent these men because I thought Essex would understand why I had chosen them; they were more likely to bring about a peaceful conclusion to the trouble than such as Sir Walter Raleigh.

But at the same time I ordered troops to be gathered together, ready to march on Essex House if need be.

Then I went about the ordinary business of the day.

Essex received the party of four and complained to them that his life was in danger and that he was only protecting himself, whereupon Egerton put on his hat, which proclaimed that he came in his official role, and made the usual statement.

"I command you all upon your allegiance to lay down your weapons and depart, which you all ought to do, thus being commanded, if you be good subjects and owe that duty to the Queen which you possess."

It was Essex's chance—not to come back into favor; he would never do that and he knew it—but to save his life.

But of course he would not help himself.

He pushed the councilors aside and left the house accompanied by two hundred armed men—among them his stepfather Christopher Blount.

I heard about it afterward—how he rode through the streets of London calling to the citizens to come and join him, really believing that James of Scotland would send an army to his aid. He was my enemy in truth, for the plot was to replace me, kill me if need be. It was galling to realize that this young man whom I had loved and tried to put into Robert's place could behave so.

Did he really believe that because he had enjoyed certain popularity with the Londoners he could turn them against *me*! I had been their beloved sovereign for more than forty years. They loved me. The Londoners were as shrewd as any people in this kingdom—or any other—and they knew that I had brought peace, prosperity and victory at sea which had made them secure. Did he really believe that they would overthrow me because a foolish boy was annoyed with me? Did he really believe *I* could be replaced by a princess from Spain or a young man from across the Border?

His little rebellion was soon quelled. Sir Christopher Blount was wounded and captured; and very soon Essex and Southampton, with others, were in the Tower.

HE COULD NOT be anything but guilty. He was a traitor who had plotted against the Crown, who had tried to raise men against the Sovereign and planned her assassination in order to put another in her place. It was blatant treachery and there was no other name for it. Therefore there could be no other course than to find Essex, with Southampton and Christopher Blount, guilty. They were sentenced to death and again it was my bitter duty to sign the death warrants.

I decided to spare Southampton's life for I was sure he had been drawn into the conspiracy by Essex, and eventually he was condemned to life imprisonment. Christopher Blount was to suffer the death penalty.

I knew there were some who believed I would not sign Essex's death warrant. They remembered how I had hated signing that of Mary of Scotland. They believed that I was weak where my affections were concerned; they considered how many times I had forgiven Leicester. It was true, I was faithful in my affections, and had I not forgiven him time and time again?

But there was a difference. I had not loved Essex as I had loved Leicester. My love for Robert had been as real as life itself; for Essex it was but a fantasy. I had tried to believe I was young again, capable of arousing love and desire, and when that brash young man had burst into my chamber so unceremoniously he had destroyed a dream and with it himself.

On a cold February day Essex walked out of his prison in the Tower to his execution.

He looked very handsome in a cloak of black velvet over a satin suit and wearing a black hat. He mounted the scaffold calmly and bravely, although he had been less so after his sentence and had accused all manner of people, including his own sister, of drawing him into intrigue; and he had heaped reproaches on Sir Francis Bacon, whom he had believed to be his friend and who had acted as one of the prosecution's lawyers.

"Oh God be merciful to me, the most wretched creature on Earth," he prayed.

He took off his hat and standing there beside the scaffold he addressed the assembly.

"My lords and you, my Christian brethren who are to be witnesses of this my just punishment, I confess to the glory of God that I am a most wretched sinner, and that my sins are more in number than the hairs of my head; that I have bestowed my youth in pride, lust, uncleanness, vainglory and divers other sins . . .

"Lord Jesus, forgive it us, and forgive it me, the most wretched of all . . . The Lord grant Her Majesty a prosperous reign and a long one, if it be His Will. Oh Lord, bless her and the nobles and ministers of the Church and State. And I beseech you and the world to have a charitable opinion of me for my intention upon Her Majesty, whose death upon my salvation and before God, I protest I never meant, nor violence to her person, yet I confess I have received an honorable trial and am justly condemned. And I desire all the world to forgive me, even as I do freely and from my heart forgive the world . . ."

When he had taken off his ruff and his gown, the executioner came forward and as was the custom asked his forgiveness.

"Thou art welcome," he replied. "I forgive thee. Thou art the minister of justice."

He took off his doublet and stood there in his scarlet waistcoat. Then he prayed for humility and patience.

Would to God he had cultivated those qualities in life. If he had done so, he would not have been standing where he was at that time.

He knelt on the straw and put his head on the block; and that was the end of my Lord Essex.

The End Draws Near

HE WAS DEAD, BUT I COULD NOT FORGET HIM. HIS HAND-
some face appeared in my dreams and when I awoke I remembered that I
should never see him again, and I was overcome with sadness.

They were all dying around me—all those whom I had loved and it
seemed that I was outliving them all. How much longer? I wondered sometimes. I was sixty-eight years old. Not many lived so long. Surely my time
must soon be at hand.

These thoughts occupied me very much in the quiet of the night, and I
used to think: "What will happen when I am gone? Who will take my place?
There must be no war. War is no good. England has known peace too long
to appreciate its blessings."

It would have to be *her* son. He was the natural heir. They had brought
him up in Scotland as a Protestant, so there would be no difficulty about
religion.

How strange! Mary Stuart's son, James the VI of Scotland and the first
of England. I wondered what he would be like. The son of one of the most
foolish of women and that oaf Darnley! If she had called me bastard—and
many would secretly say that I was—at least I had had a great king for a
father and a mother who must have been one of the most fascinating women
in England, to make a king break with Rome for her sake. That had turned
out well. It was better to be free of Rome; and the English, I was sure, would
in the future, thank God for Queen Elizabeth.

Another of my friends fell ill that year. I was very fond of the Countess
of Nottingham and immensely grateful for what her husband—Howard of
Effingham—had done for his country at the time of the war with Spain. I
visited her and as I sat with her it became clear to me that she had something
on her mind.

Her hands were hot and feverish, her eyes wild. I said to her: "You must
lie quietly. You need your breath, my dear."

But she could not rest and when she said: "There is something I must
tell you," I was not surprised.

Then it came out. She had a terrible secret and she could not rest without my forgiveness for she knew that she was about to die.

I said she must tell me what was troubling her and relieve her mind. It
was hard for me to believe that she had ever done me any harm.

She said: "It was the ring . . ."

I bent closer to her. "What ring?" I prompted.

"It . . . was to have been given to you. Sir Robert Carey sent a messenger with it . . . to give it to my sister when she was in attendance on you."

She hesitated again and I said: "Yes, yes, your sister, my dear Lady Scrope."

She closed her eyes. "He . . . he brought the ring to me . . . thinking I was my sister . . . and I took it . . . and when I showed it to my husband, he said I must not give it to you . . . because for the good of England he must die."

"Who? Who must die?"

"The Earl of Essex," she said.

Then I began to understand, and I felt myself go cold with fear of what was to come.

"The Earl told Sir Robert Carey that when you received . . . the ring . . . you would forgive him . . . you would save his life. He had . . . to get the ring to you."

"Oh, God's Holy Son," I murmured.

"Your Majesty, forgive me. My husband forbade me to bring the ring to you. He said Essex would always make trouble. He was preparing to bring revolution to the country . . . He was as dangerous as Mary Stuart had been in her time. More so . . . because the people liked him . . . and he was so reckless . . . he would attempt the wildest adventures . . ."

"So you kept the ring, and I did not know that he was sending to me for help."

She nodded her head. "I have left instructions that the ring be sent to Your Majesty when I am gone. But seeing you there . . . so kind to me . . . so good . . . I had to confess. It has been on my conscience . . . I could not die without telling Your Majesty and begging you to forgive me."

I sat there quite numb with emotion. I had always known that had he shown some spark of humility, if he had asked for forgiveness, I should never have signed that death warrant. I had prayed that he would make some sign, give me a way out. Once I had refused to sign it and then delayed for days. One sign from him would have made the difference. But I had believed he had continued in obstinate rebelliousness. And all the time . . . he had sent the ring. He had lain in the Tower waiting for a response from me—and none had come. He would have died believing that I had broken my promise to come to his aid if ever he should call me through the ring.

I should have hated the dying woman, but I could not. It was not her fault. Her husband had made her do it. And doubtless he was right. Of course he had been Essex's enemy, but then so were many others—Cecil more than any and with him men who were my good friends, and friends of the country therefore. My emotions would have betrayed me if I had seen the ring. Perhaps I should be grateful because it had been kept from me and I had been able to do what, in my heart, I knew was best for my country.

She lay there, her eyes appealing. All she wanted to bring her peace now was my forgiveness.

I took her hand and kissed it. I said: "It is all over now. He is dead . . . as we all soon shall be."

She was smiling contentedly.

The next day I heard she was dead. Another friend gone.

I HAD TO PUT him from my mind. I kept thinking how different it might have been. He would be alive today if I had received the ring and known that he was repentant. But what was the use? It was over. He had gone to join others whom I had loved.

Sometimes I felt very alone, although I was surrounded by my courtiers and rarely had a moment to myself.

But my health improved. There was so much to occupy me and I spent long hours with my Council. Affairs of state pressed heavily. Mountjoy was doing well in Ireland. The Spaniards were threatening again and rumor had it that they would go for our weakest point, which was Ireland. What loyalty could we rely on there! The Irish would be ready to sell themselves to Spain just to spite the English even though they knew that under the Spanish heel they would enjoy less freedom than they did at this time.

I was as popular as I had ever been. I had wondered whether I should lose a little of my people's affection after the death of Essex, for oddly enough, in spite of his many failings, the people had loved him and regarded him as a kind of romantic hero. They mourned him and there were ballads written about him. But they had lost none of their love for me. They were a realistic people and they would understand that I had had no alternative but to sign that death warrant.

I told the Parliament that though God had raised me high, what I regarded as the glory of my crown was that I reigned with the love of my people. "I do not so much rejoice that God hath made me a queen," I said, "as to be Queen of so thankful a people."

My dear, dear people! I had never once forgotten their importance to me—and they knew it.

Thus I could live in contentment—or as near to it as a lonely woman can be.

It was a good year. Mountjoy crushed Tyrone's forces and successfully put an end to the Irish rebellion. So the Spaniards gave up their plans of invasion. There had been some brilliant victories at sea which resulted in the

capture of several treasure ships; and when harvest time came we had a
higher yield than for many a year.

I was in better spirits than I had been for a long time, reveling in each
day and determined to make the most of it. I dressed with even greater care
and when I was wearing one of my splendid gowns, aglitter with gems, when
my luxuriant red curled wig was in place, my women assured me that I
looked like a girl—and I felt like one.

I took brisk walks; I danced three or four galliards without the least sign
of breathlessness. Sometimes, in the evenings when I would admit to a little
tiredness, I would watch the others dance and sit tapping my feet to the
music, having to restrain myself lest I get up and join them.

"You don't dance as high as I used to when I was your ages," I complained.

I was well all through that year of 1602. Peace and prosperity had settled on England. The days were satisfyingly full, and it was only at night
when I looked back sadly on the past and remembered all those who had
gone.

But as the winter progressed, I felt less healthy. I was becoming forgetful and could not remember the names of people I knew well. A weariness
would come to me and sometimes I felt an unpleasant dryness in my mouth
as though my body were on fire with fever.

I tried to plan the Christmas festivities, but a lassitude had come upon
me and I did not want to be bothered with them.

Sleep did not come easily now and I would lie awake thinking over the
past, and there were times when I could believe that I was back in those glorious days of my youth; I lived again through the time of my accession to
the throne, perhaps the greatest days of all of my life, when I had looked forward with such joy and confidence to what was to come.

I had never eaten heartily; now I found it hard to eat at all. My ladies
fussed over me and I was too tired to reprove them.

One night, when I was unable to sleep, I saw a strange light in my room,
and as my eyes grew accustomed to its brilliance, I saw a figure in the fire. It
was myself, exceedingly lean, and yet somehow radiant.

I thought: Leicester, Burghley, Hatton, Heneage, Essex . . . they have all
gone. Now it is my turn.

In the morning I spoke of the vision to one of my women. It might have
been Lady Scrope or Lady Southwell—I forgot such details almost as soon
as they had happened. I asked her if she had ever seen visions in the night,
and for a few seconds she could not hide her alarm and I saw the thoughts
in her eyes.

I said: "Bring me a mirror, for mirrors, unlike courtiers, do not lie."

So she brought it to me and I looked at my face—the face of an old woman who had lived for nearly seventy years . . . old, white . . . unadorned . . . tired and ready to go.

So the end is near. I was never more sure of anything. I can feel death all around me.

I shall write no more. This will be the last. So I sit, thinking of all that has gone, the dangers of my youth, the glory of my middle life, and the sadness of the end. Leicester, I thought, you should never have left me. You should have stayed to the end and we could have gone together.

Much has been said of me. There have been many rumors, and perhaps there always will be for kings and queens are remembered and spoken of long after their deaths. Their smallest acts are recorded and commented on and they are magnified or diminished, shown as good or bad, according to the views of the recorder. Of my life much will be written. But no one can take away the greatness of events and for those who love the truth it will be seen as a good reign.

And what will they say of me? I am not like other women. I did not seek to subjugate myself to men. I demanded their submission to me. I have been a good queen because I loved my people and my people returned my love. But men will say, Why did she not marry? There must be some reason why she refused us all. There was, but they will not believe it, because all people judge others by themselves. So many of them are so overwhelmed by the importance of the sexual act, that they cannot believe that it is of little importance to others. I had no desire to experience it. This they will never believe, but it is so. I enjoyed having men about me because I liked them as much as—if not more than—women. I wanted them to court me, to compliment me, to fall desperately in love with me. Did they not have to do that to win my favor?—except, of course, the brilliant ones whose minds I respected. I wanted perpetual courtship, for when the fortress is stormed and brought to surrender, the battle is lost. The relationship between men and women is a battle of the sexes with the final submission of the woman to the man. The act itself is the symbol of triumph of the strong over the weak. I was determined never to give any man that triumph. The victory must always be mine. I wanted continual masculine endeavor, not triumph. I wanted, during every moment of my life, to be in absolute control. All physical appetites were unimportant to me. I had to eat and drink for my health's sake, but I always did so sparingly. I did not want that momentary satisfaction which comes from the gratification of appetite in whatsoever form it is.

So I was always in control of my men unlike my poor Mary of Scotland, and consequently I had come to the end and could say with gratified resignation *Nunc Dimittis,* and pass on.

It has amused me to hear some say that I was, in fact, a man. Yes, that makes me laugh. I have been a good queen, a wise queen; I have brought my country into a far happier and more prosperous state than it was in at my accession. I have tried to be tolerant. I have failed in this on one or two occasions, but that was only because I feared it would be dangerous to be lenient. Therefore men say: "No woman could attain so much, so she must have been a man! Only a man could be so great and wise." So in spite of what I believe to be my excessive femininity they say: "She was secretly a man."

They hint that there was something strange about me, that I was malformed, that I could not have children and that was why I remained a virgin.

They are wrong, all of them . . . except Mary of Scotland's Ambassador Melville all those years ago. I shall never forget his words.

"I know your stately stomach. Ye think gin ye were married ye would be but *Queen* of England and now ye are King and Queen baith . . . ye may not suffer a commander."

He had the truth there. And I kept my determination to remain the commander of them all . . . and not even Robert could tempt me to share my crown with anyone.

My crown and my virginity . . . I was determined to keep them both, and I did.

I can feel the end coming nearer. I was born on the eve of the day which is celebrated as the nativity of the Virgin Mary. I wonder if I shall die on the festival of the annunciation. It would be appropriate for the Virgin Queen.

Now I lay down my pen, for the end is coming very near.

BIBLIOGRAPHY

Aubrey, William Hickman Smith *The National and Domestic History of England*
Beesley, E. S. *Queen Elizabeth*
Bevan, Bryan *The Great English Seamen of Elizabeth I*
Bigland, Eileen (edited by) *Henry VIII*
Black, J. S. *The Reign of Elizabeth*
Chamberlin, Frederick *The Private Character of Henry VIII*
Fraser, Antonia *Mary Queen of Scots*
Froude, J. A. *History of England*
Gorman, Herbert *The Scottish Queen*
Guizot, M., edited by Robert Black *The History of France*
Hackett, Francis *Henry the Eighth*
Harrison, G. B. *Life and Death of Robert Devereux Earl of Essex*
Hume, David *The History of England*
Hume, Martin *Two English Queens and Philip*
Hume, Martin *The Wives of Henry VIII*
Hume, Martin *The Courtships of Queen Elizabeth*
Jenkins, Elizabeth *Elizabeth the Great*
Jenkins, Elizabeth *Elizabeth and Leicester*
Johnson, Paul *Elizabeth I*
Luke, Mary M. *A Crown for Elizabeth*
Mattingley, Garrett *The Defeat of the Spanish Armada*
Mumby, F. A. *The Girlhood of Queen Elizabeth*
Neale, J. E. *Queen Elizabeth*
Prescott, William H. *History of the Reign of Philip the Second*
Rea, Lorna *The Spanish Armada*
Salzman, L. F. *England in Tudor Times*
Stephen, Sir Leslie and Lee, Sir Sydney *Dictionary of National Biography*
Strachey, Lytton *Elizabeth and Essex*
Strickland, Agnes *Lives of the Queens of England*
Wade, John *British History*
Waldman, Milton *Elizabeth and Leicester*
Waldman, Milton *Queen Elizabeth, Brief Lives*
Waldman, Milton *King, Queen, Jack*
Williams, Neville *Elizabeth, Queen of England*
Wright, Thomas *Elizabeth and Her Times*

ABOUT THE AUTHOR

JEAN PLAIDY is the pen name of the late English author E. A. Hibbert, who also wrote under the names Philippa Carr and Victoria Holt. Born in London in 1906, Hibbert began writing in 1947 and eventually published over two hundred novels under her three pseudonyms. The Jean Plaidy books—ninety in all—are works of historical fiction about the famous and infamous women of English and European history, from medieval times to the Victorian era. Hibbert died in 1993.

QUEEN OF THIS
REALM

JEAN PLAIDY

A READER'S
GUIDE

QUESTIONS FOR DISCUSSION

1 ✦ One of Elizabeth's earliest memories is of being used as a bargaining chip. She is three years old, and her mother—the doomed Anne Boleyn—waves her little hand at her father, who looks down from a palace window. The action is Anne's last-ditch attempt to placate Henry's wrath and appeal to his sense of family. It fails, and Anne is executed. What lesson does Elizabeth learn—or think she learns—from this macabre memory?

2 ✦ Elizabeth's stepmothers Katharine Howard and Katharine Parr fare very differently in the delicate position of wife to Henry VIII. What does Katharine Howard's demise teach Elizabeth about the male-female dynamic? What subtle gift distinguishes Katharine Parr, and eventually saves her life? Does Elizabeth share this gift?

3 ✦ Of her servants Kat and Parry, Elizabeth notes: "They were a pair of scandalmongers and I was often exasperated with them both. But they so obviously loved me, and I believe I was more important to them than anyone else; and for that reason I could never be annoyed with them for long." This leniency with anyone who adores her informs Elizabeth's later reign as Queen—especially in regard to handsome men. When, if ever, does this soft-heartedness spell disaster for Elizabeth? Does this character trait change as she ages?

4 ✦ As her brother Edward lies dying in Greenwich, young Elizabeth stays in Hatfield to await the outcome of the succession. "It is necessary to remain at a safe distance from great events, until one has decided what is the best way to act," she muses. This becomes her motto in many situations she faces as Queen, from signing death warrants to joining international wars. Does it serve her well?

5 ✦ When Elizabeth arrives at the Traitor's Gate in the Tower of London by orders of Queen Mary, her entrance is so dramatic, well-rehearsed, and sympathy-inducing that some of the guards burst into tears. Where else do you see Elizabeth shining in the limelight? Is she sincere, or is she a con-

summate actress? Does this dramatic flair ever undermine her ability to rule effectively?

6 ♦ At Mary's funeral, Dr White, Bishop of Winchester, refers to Mary as a "dead lion," and to Elizabeth as a "live dog," prompting Elizabeth's first public display of fury. She promptly sends White to the Tower. What pithy argument does Cecil make against executing White? What larger issue does Cecil gently reference with this argument?

7 ♦ "The sexual act was a symbol of domination on the part of the male, I had always thought, and I had no intention of being dominated for one moment even by the most attractive man I had ever known," insists Elizabeth. Or, as she more succinctly puts it: "When the fortress is stormed and brought to surrender, the battle is lost." Do you read Elizabeth's obsession with her own virginity as powerful or fearful? What spin does Plaidy put on this matter? Do you think Elizabeth's legacy would have been significantly different had she succumbed to her desire for Robert?

8 ♦ Elizabeth is haunted by her father's personal and political legacy. Where do you see her consciously avoiding his tactics? Where do you see her imitating them? Which of Henry's successful tricks of the trade does Elizabeth elevate to an art form?

9 ♦ What is the significance of *Father Parson's Green Coat*? What advice does Burghley offer Elizabeth in terms of dealing with it? What does he mean by the expression "A galled horse when he is touched will wince"?

10 ♦ "I was as good a statesman as any of my men," states Elizabeth, "but in addition I possessed a certain insight which was entirely feminine. It was not merely intuition—but that might have been part of it; it was an immense interest in people, which most men lack. They are too absorbed in themselves to bother much with other people's motives. Women want to know what is going on; they are insatiably curious. This gives my sex that extra knowledge of how people's minds work; it helps us to assess how they will act in certain circumstances." Do you buy this? If so, do you find any examples in modern-day statecraft?

11 ✦   What priceless and unusual gift does John Aylmer offer the Queen? Why does Plaidy include this anecdote in the narrative?

12 ✦   When Mary Queen of Scots is found guilty of treason, Elizabeth agonizes over the signing of her death warrant. She has always been simultaneously fascinated and infuriated by Mary. Why does she find this queen so compelling? What alternative plan does she suggest for Mary's punishment, and why does it go awry at the hands of William Davison?

13 ✦   While serving as commander of the English expedition to the Netherlands, Robert accepts an honor of sovereignty without consulting Elizabeth—a major faux pas. Furthermore, Elizabeth catches Lettice preparing to join Robert in the Netherlands amid great pomp and ceremony. After all these two have put her through, Elizabeth is primed to snap. Why is it politically shrewd for her to avoid publicly humiliating them for their rash actions? What price do they pay in private?

14 ✦   At Robert's death, what small "victory over the she-wolf" does Elizabeth achieve?

15 ✦   Essex is a vulgar, disrespectful, tantrum-throwing brat who is chronically unfaithful to his queen. Elizabeth's first impression of him reads: "He was very raw—and I saw at once that he had no political sense. He was the sort of man who spoke before he considered the effect his words might have—so he lacked the first quality of a courtier." When Elizabeth entrusts him with a political campaign in Ireland, she admits, "He ignored my instructions . . . He would go his own way, which was the wrong one. He was defeated everywhere." Yet despite all this, she tolerates him, even loves him. Explain why the event that finally ruins Essex in Elizabeth's eyes is a brief, innocuous meeting between the two in Elizabeth's chamber. What does she mean by "He destroyed a dream and with it himself"?

16 ✦   Why is Amy Robert's death riddled with scandal? Why does Elizabeth say, "The death of Robert's wife was the greatest lesson I was ever likely to learn and if I did not take advantage of that, I deserved to lose my crown"? Are you convinced of Robert's innocence?

LOYAL IN
LOVE

JEAN PLAIDY

Jean Plaidy's Queen's of England series
continues with the story of
Henrietta Maria, wife of Charles I

THE DOWAGER QUEEN

hen I sit here alone in my *château* of Colombes, which I inhabit by grace of my nephew that great and glorious ruler whom they call The Sun King, I often think back over my life—one which has had more than its fair share of sorrow, humiliation, intrigue and tragedy. I am old now and my word stands for little, but though no one listens to me, I am allowed my comforts, for after all they must remember that I am the aunt of one King and the mother of another; and Kings and Queens never forget the deference due to royalty, for if they did not show it to others a day may come when it is not shown to them. Royalty is sacred to royalty—though not always so, alas, with the people. When I think of the manner in which the people of England treated their King—the wickedness, the cruelty, the bitter, bitter humiliation—even now my anger rises to such heights that I fear I shall do myself an injury. I should be old enough to restrain my temper now; I should remind myself that I have my silent accusers who would say that if the King had not had the misfortune to marry me, he would be alive and on his throne at this moment.

That is all in the past . . . all dead and gone. It is a new world now. There is a king on the throne of England for the Monarchy has been restored. The people love him, I am told; and indeed I was aware of this when I paid a visit to England not long ago. My dearest Henriette—the best-loved of all my children—glows when she talks of him. She always loved him dearly. He is witty, they say; he loves pleasure but he is shrewd. He is his grandfather—the father I never knew—all over again. He has charm though he is ugly. He was born ugly—the ugliest baby I ever saw. I remember when they first put him into my arms, I could not believe that this little unprepossessing thing could possibly be the child of my handsome husband and myself—for in spite of my small stature and certain defects, I was regarded in those days— even by my enemies—as having a goodly share of physical charms.

Are the troubles over? Is this the end of the nightmare which over-shadowed England for all those years? Have people learned their les-son? With flowers and sweet music they welcomed Charles when he returned and there was rejoicing throughout London and the whole of England. They had done with the hideous Puritan rule. Forever? I wonder.

So royalty has come back into its own. But it is too late for me. I am here, grateful to be in my small but beautiful *château* during the sum-mer days, and in the winter, if I wish to go to Paris, my nephew has put the truly splendid Hôtel de la Balinière at my disposal.

He is kind to me—my glorious nephew. I think he has been a little in love with my sweet Henriette. And my son is kind, too. He always was—in that careless way which makes me think he would do any-thing for peace. I pray he will hold the crown. Louis respects him for all that he seems to devote himself to pleasure, and his great preoccupa-tion would appear to be with the next seduction.

He looked at me so wisely when I was last in England. I begged him then to come to the true Faith, and he took my face in his hands and kissed me, calling me "Mam" as he used to when he was a little boy. "When the time is ripe," he said enigmatically.

I never did understand Charles. I only know that he has this power to win people to him. He has grace for all his height, and charm which outshines his ugliness. If he could but get a child all would be well for England—as well as it could be, that is, unblessed by the true Faith as it is. And that may come. It has been my hope for so many years that it will.

Charles's wife, dear Catherine, is so docile and so much in love with him. How can she be when he parades his mistresses before her and refuses—though in that charming, lighthearted way of his—to give up his profligate way of life?

I tried to talk to him when I was there—though more of religious matters, I must admit, than the need to get an heir. Catherine must be at fault. God knows he has enough bastards scattered throughout his kingdom, and he distributes titles and lands among them with a free hand. One of his courtiers said that a time will come when almost every Englishman, even from the remote corners of the country, will claim to be descended from Royal Stuart. And he cannot get one legitimate heir!

Life is strange. And I am now near to the end of mine. I think often of my dear husband Charles—of his saintly goodness, his gentleness, his loving kindness, and most of all the love which grew between us, though we had many a disagreement in the beginning, and in those early days there must have been times when he wished he had never been persuaded into the marriage, for all the good it was said it would bring to our two countries.

I dream of him now . . . going to his death on that cold January day. They told me he had said: "Give me an extra shirt. It is cold and I could tremble from the wind, and those who have come to see me die would think I trembled in fear of death."

Nobly he went out to die. I see him in my dreams and I say to myself: "What did I do? If I had been a different woman, is it possible that this great tragedy, this murder, need never have happened?"

I want to go right back to the beginning. I want to think of everything that happened. And then I want to find the answer.

Could it have been different? Is it really possible that it need not have happened the way it did?

One cannot call the man who wielded the axe the murderer. But what of those cold-eyed men who passed the sentence?

I hate them. I hate them all.

But was I the one to blame?

THE EARLY DAYS

I was born into a troubled world and when I was only five months old my father was murdered. Fortunately for me at that time I was in my nursery and knew nothing of this deed which was said to have had such a disastrous effect not only on our family but on the whole of France.

Everything I knew of him was through hearsay; but I was one to keep my ears and eyes open, and for a long time after his death, he was talked of, so that by cautious questioning and alert observation, in time I began to learn a great deal about the father who had been taken from me.

He had been a great man—Henri of Navarre, the finest King the French had ever known—but of course the dead become sanctified, and those who are murdered—particularly those in high places—become martyrs. My own dear Charles . . . but that was a long way ahead in the future. I had much to endure before I was overwhelmed by the greatest tragedy of my life.

So my father died. There he was one day in good health—well, as near good health as a man of fifty can be who has lived a life of much indulgence—and the next a corpse brought home to the Louvre and laid on his bed in his closet there while the whole country mourned and the ministers guarded the palace and us children, particularly my brother Louis, who had then become King. And all the time I was sleeping peacefully in my cradle unaware of the action of a maniac which had robbed France of her King and me of my father.

There were seven of us in the nursery at that time. The eldest was Louis, the Dauphin, who was eight when I was born. After him came Elizabeth, who was a year younger than Louis. There was a gap of four years between Elizabeth and Christine and then the family increased with rapidity. There had been the little Duc d'Orléans who had died before there was time to give him a name, and after that Gaston and then myself, Henriette Marie.

My mother may have been unsatisfactory in the eyes of many but she certainly filled the nursery and that is said to be the first and most important duty of a queen. The people disliked her as much as they loved my father. For one thing she came from Tuscany, being the daughter of Francis the Second of that land; and the French had always hated foreigners. Moreover she was fat and not very handsome and was. of the Medici family. People remember that other Italian woman, wife of Henri Deux, toward whom they had shown more venom than to any other monarch, blaming her for all the misfortunes of France, including the Massacre of St. Bartholomew and the deaths by poison of many people. They had made a legend of her—the Italian poisoner. It was unfortunate that my mother should bear the name of Medici.

However, while my father had been there my mother was unimportant. She had had to accept his infidelities. He was a great lover of women. The Evergreen Gallant, the people called him, and right up to his death he was involved with women. The Duc de Sully—his very able minister and friend—had deplored this characteristic; but it was no use. Great King that he was he was first of all a lover and the pursuit of women was to him the most urgent necessity of his life. He could not exist without them. While this is doubtless a great weakness in a king, it is a foible which people indulgently shrug aside and indeed often applaud. "There is a *man,*" they say, with winks, nods and affectionate smiles.

Even at the time of his death he was involved in a romantic intrigue. I learned all about it from Mademoiselle de Montglat, who was the daughter of our governess and who, because she was so much older than I, had been set in charge of me by her mother. I called her Mamanglat as at first she was like a mother to me and later like an elder sister; and I was more fond of her than anyone I knew. Mamanglat became affectionately shortened to Mamie, and Mamie she remained to me forever.

We were all terrified of Madame de Montglat, who was always reminding us that she had the royal permission to whip us if we misbehaved, and as we were the Royal Children of France, higher standards had been set for us than for all other children.

Mamie was not a bit like her mother. Although in a way she was a governess, she was more like one of us. She was always ready to laugh, tell us the latest scandal and to help us out of those scrapes into which children fall and which would have brought down the wrath of Madame de Montglat on our heads if they had come to her knowledge.

It was from Mamie that I began to understand what was going on around me, what it meant to be a child in a royal nursery, the pitfalls to be avoided—the advantages and the disadvantages. It seemed to me that there were more of the latter and Mamie was inclined to agree with me.

"Your father loved you children," she told me. "He used to say you were all beautiful and he could not understand how two such as the Queen and himself could have begotten you. I used to have to peep out at you because my mother forbade me to appear before the King."

"Why?"

"Because I was young and not ill favored—good looking enough to catch his eyes, she thought."

Then Mamie would be overcome with laughter. "The King was like that," she finished.

Being very young and ignorant of the world I wanted to ask a great many questions, but did not always do so being afraid of exposing my ignorance.

"You were his favorite," said Mamie. "The baby—the child of his old age. He was proving, you see, that he could still get beautiful children—not that he need have worried. There was constantly some woman claiming that her child was his. Well, what was I saying? Oh . . . you were the favorite. He was always fond of little girls and weren't you named for him . . . well, as near as a girl could be. Henriette Marie. Henriette for him and Marie for your mother. Royal names both of them."

From Mamie I learned the gossip of the Court—past and present— much that was necessary for me to know and more besides. I heard from her that before he had married my mother, my father had been married to La Reine Margot, daughter of Catherine de Médicis—one of the most mischievous and fascinating women France had ever known. My father had hated Margot. He had never wanted to marry her and it was rather dramatically said that their marriage had been solemnized in blood, for during the celebrations the most terrible of all massacres had taken place—that which had occurred on the Eve of St. Bartholomew; and it was because so many Huguenots had been in Paris to attend the marriage of their leader's son to Catholic Margot that they had been conveniently situated for destruction.

I supposed something like that would haunt a bride and bridegroom forever. It was a mercy that my father escaped. But all his life— until the last fatal moment—he had had a knack of escaping. He had lived his life dangerously and joyously. Often careless of his royalty he had had an easy familiarity with his men. No wonder he had been popular. He had done a great deal for France too. He cared about the people; he had said he wanted every peasant to have a chicken in his pot on Sundays; moreover he had brought about a compromise between the Catholics and Huguenots and that had seemed an impossible task. He himself had paid lip service to the Catholics with his famous quip of Paris being worth a Mass when he had realized the city would never surrender to a Protestant.

He had been a wonderful man. When I was very young I used to weep tears of rage because he had been taken from me before I could know him.

He had been a good soldier, but it was said that he never let anything—not even the need to fight an enemy—stand in the way of his love affairs.

The object of his passion at the time of his death had been the daughter of the Constable de Montmorency. She was only sixteen years old but no sooner had my father set eyes on her than he declared she must be his "little friend."

Mamie loved to tell these stories. She had a certain histrionic talent, which she loved to display and which often made me helpless with laughter. She could never tell anything dramatic without acting it. I remember her explaining, dropping her voice to conspiratorial confidence.

"However . . . before presenting his daughter Charlotte to Court, the Constable de Montmorency had betrothed her to François de Bassompierre who was a very magnificent gentleman of the House of Cleves—handsome, witty, and as he was also a Gentleman of the King's Bedchamber, he was much sought after. Monsieur de Montmorency thought it an excellent match.

"But when the young lady came to Court and the King saw her, that was the end of her romance with François de Bassompierre."

How I loved to listen to her as she threw herself into the part she was playing for me!

"The King was determined that Bassompierre should not have her because he was a passionate young man and deeply in love with her and therefore could not be expected to become the kind of accommodating husband whom the King favored because they were always willing to stand aside when the need arose. One morning—so the story goes—when the King was about to rise from his bed, he sent for Bassompierre—remember he was a Gentleman of the Bedchamber. 'Kneel, Bassompierre,' said the King. Bassompierre was astonished for the King was never one to stand on ceremony, but if you wish to present some suggestion which may not be acceptable it is always best to reduce the person whom you intend to deprive or displease by stressing your own superiority."

I nodded. I could understand that.

"The King was full of guile. He knew men well and that meant he could usually wriggle satisfactorily out of awkward situations." Mamie had thrown herself upon my bed and assumed an air of royalty. " 'Bassompierre,' said the King, 'I have been thinking a good deal of you and I have come to the conclusion that it is time you were married.' " Mamie leaped from the bed and assumed a kneeling position beside it. " 'Sire,' said Bassompierre. 'I should be married now, but the Constable's gout has been troubling him of late and for this reason the ceremony has been postponed.' " She was back on the bed, royal again. " 'I have just the bride for you, Bassompierre. What think you of Madame d'Aumale? When you marry, the Duchy of Aumale shall come to you.' 'Sire,' said Bassompierre, 'have you a new law in France? Is a man then to have *two* wives?' " She was back on the bed. " 'Nay, nay, François. In Heaven's name, one is enough for a man to manage at a time. I will tell you all. I know of your commitment to Mademoiselle de Montmorency but the truth is that I myself have become madly enamored of her. If you married her I should begin to hate you . . . especially if she showed any affection for you. Now I am fond of you, Bassompierre, and I know you would be the last one to wish for a rift in our friendship. Therefore I cannot see you married to this girl. I shall give her to my nephew Condé. That will keep her near me . . . in the family . . . and she can comfort my old age. Condé likes hunting better than women. I shall make him an allowance as compensation. Then he can leave the delightful creature to me.' "

Mamie looked at me and raised her eyebrows. She was a little breathless jumping off and on the bed and having to play the two parts in the drama.

"Poor Bassompierre!" She was herself now, the wise storyteller. "He saw that it would be impossible to go against the King's wishes, and when he told Mademoiselle de Montmorency what was planned she cried: 'Jesus. The King has gone mad!' But very soon she grew accustomed to the idea and after a while she quite liked it. The whole Court was talking about the change in bridegrooms, and very quickly Mademoiselle de Montmorency became the Princesse de Condé.

"Now this led to other complications. The Queen accepted the fact that the King must have many mistresses but she hated there to be one who could influence him so much. She had never been crowned and a monarch always feels insecure until the crown has been placed on his— or her—head in solemn ceremony. So the Queen cried: 'I want to be crowned!' and because of the guilt he felt about Charlotte de Montmorency the King, who had brushed aside this matter of the Queen's coronation whenever it was raised, had to give way to save himself from violent recriminations. Then to make matters worse, the Prince de Condé became so enamored of his wife that he decided that he would no longer stand aside. She was after all *his* wife, and he secretly left the Court with the new Princesse and took her to Picardy, and since that might not be far enough he carried her on to Brussels.

"The King was desolate. He was mad with grief and threatened to follow her. Now a king cannot move far without everyone's knowing, and who would have believed that a king who had been on most excellent terms with so many women at the same time, should take such steps for one. People were saying that it was a secret move to go to war. So the King found himself in the center of a controversy. The Duc de Sully was worried and he told the King that his conduct over the Princesse de Condé was destroying his reputation . . . not his reputation for being a rake . . . that was unimportant and he already had that in any case. It was only when his amours intruded into statecraft that there was danger.

"The affair had made the Queen more restive than ever. She was demanding her coronation, and the King, feeling he owed her some recompense, at length agreed that it should take place.

"Now at this time the King had a strange presentiment. Kings' lives are always in danger so perhaps it is natural for them to have presentiments. Well, some time before, the King had been told that he would only survive a few days after the Queen's coronation, and it was for this reason that he had never wanted her to be crowned; and if it had not been for his guilt about the Princesse de Condé, he would never have agreed to it. However, now that she was to be crowned, the feeling of disaster grew and grew and he became so certain of his imminent death that he went to see the Duc de Sully about it, which shows how strongly he felt, for the Duc was not the man even a king would go to with a story like that.

"So the King went to the Arsenal where the country's weapons were stored and where the Duc de Sully had his apartments." She was acting again; the same role for the King, but Bassompierre had been replaced by the Duc de Sully. " 'I don't understand this, Monsieur le Duc, but I feel in my heart that the shadow of death is right over my head.' 'Why, Sire, you alarm me. How can this be? You are well. Nothing ails you.' The Duc de Sully had had a special chair made for the King to sit in when he visited him. It was low and very regal. The King sat in it, and looking very grave, he said: 'It has been prophesied that I shall die in Paris. The time is near. I can sense it.' "

"Did he really say that?" I asked. "Or are you making it up?"

"It is all true," Mamie assured me.

"Then he must have been a very clever man to see into the future."

"He *was* a very clever man, but this is apart from cleverness. It is the special gift of clairvoyance, and magicians and sorcerers had been saying that the King would meet his death in Paris, and if ever the Queen was crowned, then the blow would fall."

"Then why did he allow my mother to be crowned?"

"Because she would give him no rest until he did; he felt guilty about the Princesse de Condé; and he hated to deny a woman anything—even the Queen. He thought: Once I have given the Queen her coronation—which is what she wants more than anything—she will leave me to pursue my heart's desire."

"But if the prophecy was coming true how could he have his heart's desire with the Princesse de Condé?"

"I can tell you no more than what happened. In fact, the Duc de Sully was so impressed that he declared he would stop the preparation for the Queen's coronation as the thought of it so filled the King with foreboding. The King said: 'Yes, break if off . . . for I have been told that I shall die in a carriage, and where could it be more easily done than at such a ceremony?' The Duc de Sully gazed earnestly at the King. 'This explains much,' he said. 'I have often seen you cowering in

your carriage when you pass certain places, and yet I know that in battle, there is not a braver man in France.' "

"But they did not stop the coronation," I pointed out, "for my
mother *was* crowned Queen of France."

Mamie continued with her narrative. "When the Queen heard that
the coronation was to be canceled, she was furious." Mamie did not attempt to imitate my mother. She would not dare go as far as that. But
I could imagine my mother's rage.

"For three whole days the matter was disputed. There will be a
coronation. There will not be a coronation. And at last the King gave
way in face of the Queen's demands and the coronation was fixed for
the thirteenth of May at St. Denis."

"Thirteenth," I said with a shiver. "That is unlucky."

"Unlucky for some," agreed Mamie portentously. "So she was
crowned and it was arranged that on the sixteenth she should make her
entry into Paris. Now . . ."

She paused and I watched her with rounded eyes for I had heard
the story before and I knew that we were approaching the terrible
climax.

"Now . . . on Friday the fourteenth the King said he would go to
the Arsenal to see the Duc de Sully. He was not sure whether he wanted
to go or not. He hesitated. First he would go and then he thought he
would not . . . but in the end he made up his mind. It was just to be a
short visit after dinner. 'I shall soon be back,' he said. When he was
about to get into his carriage, Monsieur de Praslin, Captain of the
Guard, who always attended him even on the shortest journeys, came
forward. 'No need,' said the King. Mamie waved her hand imperiously.
'I don't want any attendance today. It is just to the Arsenal for a brief
visit.' Well, he got into the carriage and sat down with a few of his gentlemen. There were only six of them, not counting the Marquis de
Mirabeau and the equerry who sat in the front of the carriage.

"Now comes the dramatic part. As the King's carriage came into the
Rue de Ferronnerie close to that of St.-Honoré, a cart came into the
road, and because this blocked the way a little, the King's carriage had

to go near to an ironmonger's shop on the St. Innocent side. As the carriage slowed down, a man rushed forward and hoisted himself onto the wheel and thrust a knife at the King. It entered right here. . . ." She touched her left side. "It went between his ribs and severed an artery. The gentlemen in the carriage cried out in horror as the blood gushed forth. 'It is nothing,' said the King. Then he said that again so quietly that it could scarcely be heard. They took him with all speed to the Louvre. They laid him on his bed and sent for the doctors—but it was too late. To the sorrow of France, the King passed away."

I had heard the story many times and it never failed to move me to tears. I knew how the Duc de Sully had made everyone swear allegiance to my brother and how the entire country mourned, and that the mad monk Ravaillac was caught and torn apart by four wild horses to whom his body had been attached before they were sent off in different directions.

I knew that my mother had become Regent of France because my brother was only nine years old and too young to govern.

Had my father survived the assassination everything would have been different. As it was, I, a baby in her nursery, was to live my early years in a country torn by strife.

Read Jean Plaidy's
Queens of England series
in historical order:

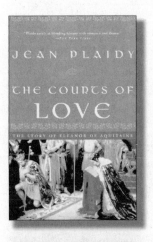

The Courts of Love
The Story of Eleanor of Aquitaine

AVAILABLE NOW FROM
THREE RIVERS PRESS

1

The Queen's Secret
The Story of Queen Katherine

AVAILABLE NOW FROM
THREE RIVERS PRESS

2

VISIT CROWNHISTORICAL.COM FOR INFORMATION
ON OUR NEWEST HISTORICAL FICTION.

The Reluctant Queen
The Story of Anne of York

AVAILABLE NOW FROM
THREE RIVERS PRESS

The Lady in the Tower
The Story of Anne Boleyn

AVAILABLE NOW FROM
THREE RIVERS PRESS

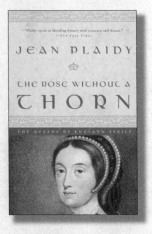

The Rose Without a Thorn
The Story of Katherine Howard

AVAILABLE NOW FROM
THREE RIVERS PRESS

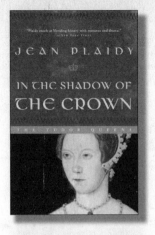

In the Shadow of the Crown
The Story of Mary Tudor

AVAILABLE NOW FROM
THREE RIVERS PRESS

Queen of This Realm
Memoir of Elizabeth I

AVAILABLE NOW FROM
THREE RIVERS PRESS

Loyal in Love
Henrietta Maria, Wife of Charles I

previously published as
Myself My Enemy
AVAILABLE NOW FROM
THREE RIVERS PRESS

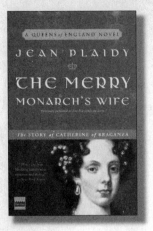

The Merry Monarch's Wife
The Story of Catherine
of Braganza

previously published as
The Pleasures of Love
AVAILABLE FROM
THREE RIVERS PRESS
IN SPRING '08

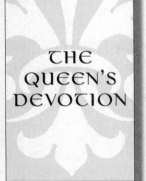

The Queen's Devotion
The Story of Queen Mary II

previously published as
William's Wife
AVAILABLE FROM
THREE RIVERS PRESS
IN SUMMER '08

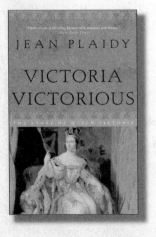

Victoria Victorious
Memoir of Queen Victoria
AVAILABLE NOW FROM
THREE RIVERS PRESS